Yella Gal

Queen of the Montclair

Linda M. White

ISBN #: 978-1-948390-09-5

Edited by: Stacey Allgeier

Cover Art by: Author

First Edition © 2018

Pen It! Publications, LLC

penitpublications@yahoo.com

www.penitpublications.com

YELLA GAL
Queen of the Montclair

by

Linda M. White

Dedication

To my loving husband Stuart who is my rock,
my wonderful son Hayden who never fails to
make me proud
and all my family and friends whose support
will forever be appreciated.

Part I

1897

Chapter 1

"Ugh! Why do I bother combin' my hair when it's just gonna frizz anyway?"

Birdie Fairfax looked at her scowling reflection in the mirror as she vainly tried to fight her unruly thick, coarse hair into a fashionable pompadour. A combination of St. Augustine's July humidity and her ethnic heritage made this a nearly impossible task.

Hortensia, Birdie's mother, stuck her head inside the door of her daughter's small, sparse bedroom. "Just put it up in a tight bun like I do. You're not going to a dinner party!" And like a flash, she was off to their tiny back garden with her daily basket of wet laundry to hang out to dry.

Birdie closed her eyes and sighed. She had no energy to deal with her mother this morning. Just ignore her, the seventeen-year-old told herself. The butterflies in her stomach had started gnawing away at her as soon as she arose that morning. Today was the day of her very first interview for a job she didn't even want.

It all started several weeks ago when Hortensia, who did laundry for several of the town's residents - mostly middle-class traders - knocked on the back-kitchen door of the home of Mrs. Della Compton.

"Hortensia!" Mrs. Compton bellowed as soon as she heard the laundress handing off the clean laundry bundle to her part-time cook Isobel. "Is that you? Come on in!"

Della Compton, a heavyset woman with an alabaster complexion which severely contrasted with her jet-black hair, had a loud and commandeering manner. Married to a humble, soft spoken accountant, Della had grand illusions of rubbing shoulders with the rich and powerful who populated the city's resorts. The thought never occurred to Mrs. Compton that the very people whose company she sought often did their best to avoid her.

"Yes ma'am," replied Hortensia as she made her way through the immaculate white washed kitchen that smelled of a freshly baked blueberry pie.

Mrs. Compton was doing needlework while sitting on a wing chair which, like a lot of her furnishings, she had inherited from an estate sale. If she could not afford the luxury of buying brand new household decor like the rich, she had no problems acquiring their cast offs. Even now, she sat in her second-hand chair like a regent on a throne.

"Hortensia dear. How old is your girl?"

"My Birdie is seventeen, ma'am," Hortensia haltingly replied, wondering why the other woman suddenly had an interest in her daughter.

"Well," said Mrs. Compton as she picked up a nearby fan and waved the black ringlets off her sweaty thick neck, "A friend of mine told me that the new hotel over on King Street needs servants. Just for the summer, and I immediately thought of your....uh....Biddie."

"Birdie, ma'am." Hortensia gently corrected her.

"Yes, of course, Birdie. My friend Iris is the head housekeeper there and she told me that they need extra kitchen help and chamber maids. They thought they wouldn't get their heaviest influx of guests until the winter, but this summer's boat race has taken our town by storm!"

The Independence Day Regatta had drawn boating enthusiasts from all over the United States and every hotel in St. Augustine was full, which was very unusual for this time of year, when visitors from the northern states found Florida's high temperatures too oppressive. The Montclair, which had only recently opened, now found itself understaffed and in sore need of temporary workers.

"I'll give your girl a glowing reference and have my friend Iris talk to her," Mrs. Compton firmly stated, never giving Hortensia a chance to respond. After all, she thought, she was doing them a great favor. Not only will this put a few coins in their pocket but Biddie...uh, Birdie...will be in the presence of the crème de la crème of high society. Best of all, helping the less fortunate would give Della Compton something to boast about to her friends and to the Ladies Aid Society at her church.

"Uh, yes ma'am. Thank you very much," Hortensia stammered as she wondered how her daughter would react to this act of charity. On the other hand, they could definitely use the extra income. Between her part-time cleaning job at the Eldridges and her laundry business, she was barely making ends meet. Besides, Mrs. Compton had her faults, but Hortensia believed that she was basically a good-hearted woman.

Later that afternoon, Hortensia broke the news to Birdie.

"What? A skivvy in a hotel? Ma! What were you thinkin'? I don't wanna work as a scrub girl! Why didn't you just say no? Or at least ask me first!" Birdie was red faced with fury. She had only just finished her second to last term of school a few weeks ago. Being fairly good with a needle and thread, she hoped to get a job as a dressmaker in town once she graduated at the end of the year.

"Oh, stop it Birdie! Why are you working yourself into a tizzy? It will only be for the summer. You'll earn a bit of money and then you can go back to school and your friends in the fall." Hortensia argued as she stirred the aromatic pot of conch chowder simmering on the stove.

Birdie sat at the rickety dining table in the kitchen with her head in her hands. She was so mad at that moment, she did not trust herself to say another word.

"Elbows off the table. You're a big girl and old enough to know better. What would people think if they could see you right now?" Hortensia carefully ladled the chowder into two mismatched bowls and set them down on the table.

What would people think? That is my mother's official motto, Birdie thought. She has always been worried about what everyone would think of them.

Birdie often bridled under her mother's odd dictates such as never walking through town without a companion or she might be mistaken for a harlot or always keeping her eyes downcast when out in public or people would think she was being insolent.

Birdie also couldn't comprehend why her mother left the Catholic church, where she was baptized and raised, for the strange, loud and judgmental Community Church congregation that met over in Jeremiah Bailey's house over on Fifth Street. The shouting and hell fire sermons did nothing to draw Birdie closer to a God that she now feared more than revered.

After several minutes of eating in total silence, Hortensia delicately asked, "So, if Mrs. Compton's friend agrees to see you, will you go?"

So NOW you ask me, Birdie angrily thought, but instead she muttered, "Yes, I'll go." Besides, she thought as she looked around their humble dwelling adorned with their meager possessions, we can use the extra money until I can get a proper job as a seamstress.

"Gracias a Dios!" Hortensia whispered and then said aloud, "I'll make sure your dark blue dress is cleaned and pressed."

Now Birdie continued studying the reflection in the mirror as she fixed her waist long, thick brown hair into something resembling a decent style.

The Afro Dominican blood of her mother coupled with the Anglo-Saxon roots of her father resulted in Bridie's golden complexion, stray freckles, light brown coarse hair and amber eyes.

Once when Birdie was five, Hortensia caught her vigorously scrubbing at her skin while taking her weekly bath.

"Mija, what are you doing?"

"Why am I so yellow?" Birdie had peevishly asked. "The white children call me a 'mulatto' and the coloreds call me 'yella gal'. Why can't I be white like daddy?"

Hortensia sighed and gave the youngster her usual response, "Because God made you special. Don't you ever forget that!"

"But I don't wanna be special! I wanna be white!" Birdie had wailed as her mother shook her head and muttered something in Spanish as she walked away.

After finally making her peace with her grooming efforts, Birdie slipped into the worn but clean dark blue poplin dress. The skirt had a very small bustle in the back, not like the larger ones worn by women ten years earlier. Birdie was very grateful for the simpler fashions of today. She often thought that women looked ridiculous back then with their skirts all bunched up high behind them looking for all the world like strutting peacocks.

The bodice had a high collar and gold buttons down the front. A waist length jacket with slightly puffy sleeves completed the ensemble.

"Ma!" she hollered, "Where are my shoes?"

Hortensia came back inside from hanging laundry, her clothespin bag still dangling from one hand while she carried Birdie's freshly polished shoes in the other.

"Well, you look very nice," she said as she kneeled down to help Birdie put on the unfashionable but sturdy black button up boots. While the young girl hated wearing them and longed for the trendy Cromwells and high heeled oxfords she had seen in Hartsfield's Dry Goods store, she knew her mother had put a lot of effort into making the boots look shiny and new. So instead, Birdie just replied, "Thank you, Ma."

Hortensia picked up the clothespin bag and started her litany of instructions. "Now mind how you go. Don't look anyone in the eye, especially the menfolk. And that reminds me - stay away from the construction site on Cuna. A young gal was compromised there last week."

Birdie was too busy thinking ahead to the interview to worry about the walk to the hotel. Her stomach was in knots and she was aware of her heart heavily banging inside her chest. It was bad enough having to prove herself worthy of a job she didn't even want, but to work in such an opulent place was intimidating. She automatically answered, "Yes, ma."

Hortensia continued, "And touch up your hair once you get there. It will no doubt be frizzy from this heat. I don't know why you won't use those new-fangled hot combs like some of the colored women use. And speak up when you talk to the lady - 'Yes ma'am. No ma'am,' Oh, and make sure to tell her that you have plenty of experience in laundry work."

Picking up her small reticule bag from her dresser and making sure her comb and handkerchief were inside, Bertie headed for the door. "I will, ma. See you later."

Once away from Hortensia's admonitions and into the bright morning sunshine, Birdie was able to breathe easier and her spirits picked up a little as she walked down the narrow path leading away from the Fairfax's tiny white clapboard house on Citrus Avenue.

Located on the edge of the colored part of town, the little bungalow's paint was peeling, and the roof needed repairing. Otherwise, Hortensia and Birdie kept it looking tidy. The vegetables, herbs, and flowers they planted produced bursts of color and a mixture of aromas.

Patrick Fairfax used to refer to the small abode as a doll house and when Birdie was young, he had his imaginative young daughter believing that the house was originally made for a rich little girl's dolls to live in. A wave of melancholy suddenly came over Birdie at the thought of her dear, deceased father. How she wished he were here today to give her one of his strong bearlike hugs and tell her that everything was going to be all right, but she quickly pushed away the sad thoughts and concentrated on her surroundings.

The street was already abuzz with the sounds of a typical morning in St. Augustine. The soft "clop, clop, clop" of the milkman's horse. The distant toot of a steam boat chugging its way up the Matanzas. The squeals and laughter of children at play. From a nearby kitchen came the sounds of dishes being washed along with the aroma of fresh coffee and bacon.

Birdie turned off Citrus Avenue and onto Lincoln Street. Ophelia Patterson, a large, plump Negro woman and mother to Birdie's best friend Ella, was sweeping off her front porch and shooing away two lazy grey tabby cats lounging on the steps.

"Mornin' Birdie! Where ya off to lookin' so pretty?" Sweet natured Ophelia had a smile so warm that one couldn't help but to grin back at her.

Birdie waved. "Mornin' Miss Patterson. I have a job interview at the Montclair today."

"Oh! Wait right there, child! I got somethin' for ya." Ophelia disappeared inside her front door and within seconds emerged with something in her hand. Birdie leaned on the rickety gate as Ophelia passed over a small furry object. It was a light brown rabbit's foot.

"This 'ere will bring ya plenty o' luck!" the older woman whispered as she pressed it into Birdie's hand.

"Oh..." replied a stunned and slightly repulsed Birdie. Remembering her manners, she said, "Thank you very much, Miss Patterson!" She tucked the rabbit's foot into her reticule, waved again and headed off.

The bell on the nearby Episcopal Church signaled that it was nine o'clock. Birdie sped up her gait in order to make her 9:15 appointment on time. The quickest way at this point was to cut through the alley behind Doheny's Saloon.

Hortensia would be horrified at the thought of her daughter going anywhere near one of the city's most notorious boozers. Fights, nightly occurrences, were often punctuated by gunshots. Drunkards and their "painted ladies" (as Hortensia called them) tumbled out of the front doors, verbally abusing passersby.

However, time was of the essence. Birdie cut through the narrow, pebbly path between Doheny's and the Moscovitz's tailor shop. The back door to Doheny's was wide open and several crates were neatly stacked outside. Colorful shards of brown and green glass from countless broken bottles provided a colorful mosaic quality to the rocks under Birdie's feet. The stench emanating from inside smelled of cheap cigars, whiskey and Gold Dutch Cleansing Powder.

Birdie soon emerged onto King Street, one of St. Augustine's busier thoroughfares. What seemed like an endless parade of horses, buggies and trolley cars raced by in both directions. There were definitely more folks in town than usual thanks to the Regatta.

A gay, carefree group of young men and women on bicycles rolled by singing "You'll Miss Lots of Fun When You're Married." Birdie looked at them forlornly and wished she could join them, but her immediate future involved hard back breaking work in the huge and imposing grey stone building which loomed before her across the street.

The Montclair Hotel was a four-story edifice with a terracotta tiled roof and wrought iron trimmings. Two round parapet towers stood on either side of the hotel's front facade, giving it a castle-like appearance. Newly planted queen palms lined both sides of the walkway leading up to the front entrance where a couple of young doormen wearing impressive dark green uniforms stood like sentries guarding their kingdom.

However, Birdie already knew that she was not to enter through the front of the resort and had to go around to the service entrance at the rear of the building. After looking both ways, she carefully stepped across King Street, making sure not to get any more dust on her freshly polished boots.

As she made her way towards the back of the property, Birdie noticed a few men tending to various areas of the garden. One of them, a boy not much older than herself, straightened up from where he was pruning a hibiscus hedge and caught Birdie's eye. He had flaming red hair that stood straight up, and a face dotted with pale freckles. Unlike the nicely turned out lads out front, his clothing was worn and patched. It hung loosely on his very thin frame and made him look like a living scarecrow. Birdie had never seen anyone like him before.

Despite years of her mother's warnings against looking at people in the eye, Birdie now found herself staring at this odd fellow in fascination. In turn, the young gardener gave her a toothy grin and raised his cap to her. "Mornin'!"

Birdie suddenly felt the blood rush to her cheeks and lowered her gaze as she quickened her steps. Before she knew it, she was at the service door. The door was shut and no one else was in sight. Birdie knocked at the door. When no one responded, she knocked again, a little harder. Still no answer. Unsure as to what to do next, Birdie felt a mounting panic in her stomach. Then she spotted a round brass button to the left of the door. Instinctively, she pressed it and was startled at the sound of ringing bells. Birdie had heard of doorbells but had never seen one with her own eyes.

The door was opened by a tall Negro girl wearing spectacles. She wore a blue and white striped dress covered by an apron and was carrying a copper bowl. "Yes?" she asked, arching her brows.

"Uh..." Birdie stammered. "Could you please tell me where I could find Miss Sutton. I am supposed to meet her this morning about a job."

"Come with me," the girl let Birdie in and motioned for her to follow. They went through a narrow corridor, passing a noisy kitchen that smelled of freshly baked bread. Maids and housemen scurried by, each one seemingly intent upon getting to wherever they were going as quickly as possible. At the end of the hallway near the servants' staircase, the kitchen maid stopped and softly knocked on a door which displayed a "Head Housekeeper" sign.

"Come in," came the response.

"A gal to see ya about a job, Miss Sutton," said the maid.

"Thank you, Tangie. Let her in."

Tangie nodded at Birdie before retreating back down the corridor. Birdie cautiously entered the office. Her steps seemed loud to her own ears as she stepped across the oak flooring. She halted just before she reached a worn but clean round tapestry rug. The office could only be described as controlled chaos. A heap of uniforms, aprons and caps filled one corner of the room. Crates of various cleaning products and soaps were neatly stacked along the back wall which was covered in a mauve colored wallpaper.

Iris Sutton herself was a wiry silver haired woman of about fifty. She wore a starched white blouse with a silver and turquoise brooch at the neck. The well-polished pointed toes of her shoes peeped out from under her tailored dove grey skirt. She was sitting at a roll top desk with a metal lock box and scores of small yellow envelopes in front of her. The desk had a dozen tiny cubbyholes along the top, each filled with odd slips of paper in a variety of colors. A large ring of about 50 large keys laid to one side.

Miss Sutton looked up at Birdie. "What's your name?"

"Birdie....I mean Brigid Fairfax, ma'am," Birdie replied, her eyes fixed on the designs in the carpet.

"Speak up, girl, and please do me the courtesy of looking directly at me when you address me," scolded Miss Sutton.

Birdie's head snapped up and she repeated, "Birdie Fairfax, ma'am!"

"Oh, that's right. Della Compton has certainly been singing your praises." Miss Sutton's thin lips seemed to purse at the mention of Mrs. Compton. "Her husband does the books for

Mr. Prescott. I've only met her a couple times." Birdie inwardly chuckled. So much for Miss Sutton being a "good friend" of Della Compton's! Iris Sutton continued, "Tiresome woman, but still, you seem to come highly recommended by her and we are in dire need of extra help at the moment. So, tell me something about yourself. What kind of work have you done before?"

"Well ma'am, I have helped my ma keep house all my life, so I know how to make beds, sew and cook, and I have also served at Mr. and Mrs. Eldridge's dinner parties. My ma works for them a couple days a week so when they have a fancy do coming up or need an extra pair of hands, I help out." Birdie then remembered Hortensia's final words from this morning. "Oh, and I've done laundry work, too."

"Hmm," Miss Sutton regarded Birdie with a squint, "since you seem to have a fairly adequate background in the basics, I suppose we can use you as a floater." Seeing Birdie's puzzled look, the older woman continued, "A floater is a member of staff who we place wherever needed. The assignment can, and often does, change on a regular basis. One day you can be making up beds and the next day you could be scrubbing pots in the kitchen. It pays five cents an hour and you'll make around $3.50 a week. You would be expected to arrive each morning at 5 o'clock and will often need to stay till 7 or 8 o'clock each night when dinner is served. Of course, you would have Sundays off. The job is only temporary until the majority of our guests depart at the end of the summer."

Giving Birdie a quick glance from head to toe, Miss Sutton continued. "You will need to wear your hair in a simple knot or bun. None of this fashionable nonsense, and I hope your shoes will be in better condition next time we meet." Birdie self-consciously hid the dusty tips of her boots back under her skirt. "So, Brigid, is this something that would suit you?"

"Yes ma'am," replied Birdie, who inwardly cringed at the thought of waking up at 4 o'clock each morning.

"Fine." Miss Sutton opened one of the many drawers in her desk and pulled out a form. "I will just need some basic information from you."

Chapter 2

"Mija, time to wake up," Hortensia softly shook Birdie's shoulder. "I'll get breakfast started."

Birdie sat up in her bed and for a brief moment had no idea what day it was. Then reality slowly crept in and she realized that today was her first day of work at the Montclair. Oh, what I would give for ten more minutes of sleep, she thought. Every fiber of her being longed to burrow back under her quilt. Instead she swung her legs over the side of the bed and tentatively placed her feet on the rickety wooden floor. Birdie knew that once her feet hit the floor, her day officially started.

Like a zombie, she trudged over to the small corner table and lit the lamp. With her bedroom now awash in a warm golden glow, she started her daily morning ritual of washing her hands and face in the basin atop the old walnut chest of drawers. Afterwards, she ran a brush through her hair, plaited it into a single thick braid and tightly coiled and pinned it to the back of her head.

Slipping on her robe and bed shoes, Birdie padded through the kitchen where Hortensia was making oatmeal and she headed for the outhouse. The night sky looked like black velvet studded with glittering diamonds. The entire world was deathly quiet, except for a lone cricket which serenaded Birdie as she eventually made her way back to the house.

"Do you want some cinnamon added?", asked Hortensia who with her high cheek bones and two long black braids hanging down her back looked like a red Indian. The bright peacock blue robe with the colorful silk embroidered flowers made her look even more exotic. The robe had been a gift from her husband shortly after they married.

"Yes. Thanks ma." replied Birdie as she returned to her room.

"Don't take too long. You don't want to be late on your first day," warned her mother.

Birdie slipped on her corset and laced it firmly. She hated wearing the constrictive device. She often joked that she preferred life in the B.C. era - Before Corsets!

After putting on her stockings and petticoats, Birdie slipped on the uniform that Miss Sutton issued to her after their meeting the day before. It was the same blue and white striped dress that Tangie had worn. Birdie's first assignment was going to be in the kitchen.

Because the sun had still not made its daily debut, Birdie found her way to the Montclair courtesy of the hotel's new electric street lamps which surrounded the property. The tall beacons with their eerie yellow glow scared Hortensia, who was mistrustful of anything electric. "Don't touch those light poles! You never know if you will get a shock!" she used to warn Birdie and Ella whenever they walked by there.

Hortensia was not alone in her apprehension. It was well known that Henry Flagler had to specially hire staff for his Ponce de Leon resort whose sole function was to switch on the rooms' electric lamps for guests too frightened to do it themselves.

At first, Birdie was cautious and gave the tall iron giants a wide birth whenever she passed them. That was until the day she and Ella encountered a group of white teenage boys while out for a stroll.

"Out of the way, nigras!" yelled the ringleader. "These streets are for whites only!"

As the girls were pushed off the sidewalk, Ella muttered an obscenity under her breath while Birdie had accidentally brushed up against a nearby lamp pole. She was so surprised that she didn't get an electric shock that the boys' hateful, discriminatory taunts did not register. Yet another of her mother's beliefs which became firmly entrenched within her own had been proven false.

Now Birdie chuckled inwardly at her groundless fear as she approached the hotel. While it was dwarfed by the massive resorts across the street, the building's vastness was still quite impressive. When she arrived at the service entrance, Birdie gave her boots a quick brush with her hands before confidently pushing the doorbell. The door opened and Tangie poked her head out. She looked Birdie up and down before saying, "Come on in. Miss Sutton told me that I'm to be trainin' ya today."

Tangie took Birdie over into the mudroom immediately to the left of the entryway. Wooden benches, coat hooks and rows of square shaped open storage compartments lined the walls. At the far end was a small wood burning space heater for the winter months. Near the doorway where the girls now stood was an umbrella stand as well as a scraper and rag for shoes.

Tangie pointed to the cubbyholes. "You can put yo' things up there, uh...Brid....Brigeet..." Birdie could see that she was wrestling with her given name, so she offered some help.

"Folks just call me Birdie."

Birdie placed her reticule bag in a nearby compartment before Tangie showed her to the kitchen, which was already buzzing with activity. The younger girl's eyes grew round as she took in the scene before her.

The kitchen was the largest she had ever seen. The bright white walls contrasted sharply with the two, mammoth-black cast iron stoves which had an array of bubbling pots atop them. Like the day before, the air was once again aromatic with the smell of baked goods as loaves of bread and trays of biscuits came out of the ovens.

Rows of dark cherry wood cupboards lined the walls over grey marble countertops. The floor was covered in small black and white tiles which made it look like the world's largest checkerboard. A doorway in the right rear of the kitchen led to the pantry and larder which housed an oversized icebox.

"You'll be workin' back here." Tangie indicated another smaller room off the left side of the main kitchen area. Unlike the kitchen, this room featured whitewashed brick walls and an oak floor. Two large stone sinks with water pumps were on the right side. Nearby was a rack where a dozen clean dish cloths were hanging. On the opposite wall was a shelf where all the hotel's everyday white china dishes were stored after they were cleaned and dried. On the back wall was another set of shelves which housed an array of pots and pans.

A Minorcan girl of about sixteen and a slightly older Negro girl both sauntered in and left a couple of mops and buckets in a corner. They looked at Birdie suspiciously as they each grabbed some cleaning rags before exiting.

Birdie remembered her father, who was once a footman on a small estate in England, describing a room like this as a "scullery." Back in his home country, it was where young female servants often started out. Not only did the job involve back breaking work from dawn til dusk, but scullery maids were also considered the lowest rung of the domestic service ladder and treated accordingly.

The only thing that kept Birdie's heart from sinking like lead was that this was only going to be a temporary job. Besides, Miss Sutton had told her she would be "floating" and helping out where needed. Unfortunately, this very issue rankled Tangie when she was notified by Miss Sutton the night before about Birdie's employment.

"We'll try the girl out in the kitchen first." Miss Sutton had informed Tangie and Rita, the head cook. "Let her start by scrubbing floors for a week. If she shows any promise, we'll let her help out in the main kitchen, and if she does well, I might talk to Mavis about trying her out upstairs should the need arise."

Tangie had inwardly seethed as she and Rita made their way back to the kitchen. I've been scrubbin' floors and polishin' silverware at this damned hotel since it opened, she had mutinously thought. Now this mulatto gal sails in here just to play kitchen maid for a couple of weeks before being sent upstairs to wait on the white folks. I'm not even allowed up there!

Tangie took a deep breath and centered herself before turning to the expectant girl beside her. "Put on one of them aprons hangin' behind the door and grab a couple of rags. You'll be helpin' Eva and Lizzie polish the brass rails outside. Once the sun starts risin' 'round six, come back in and get the china ready for breakfast."

"Yes ma'am," responded Birdie as she tied on her apron.

"You don't need to 'yes ma'am' me." Tangie rolled her eyes. "The only ‘ma'am' down here is Miss Sutton." And turning on her heel, she marched towards the pantry.

Birdie sighed as she picked up the rags and the tin of brass polish. Between Tangie's apparent coolness towards her and the laborious chores which lay ahead, this was going to be one of the longest days of her life, but Birdie quickly brushed the negativity aside and concentrated on the task at hand - tracking down Eva and Lizzie.

She made her way back through the kitchen, which now bustled with half a dozen kitchen maids preparing for the morning's breakfast service. Rita, the head cook, presided over the ruckus from one of the stoves, where she was checking on the status of the latest batch of buttermilk biscuits. She was a tall, angular woman who looked about 35. Her jet-black hair parted in the middle and pulled back under her cap, reddish bronze skin and flashing dark eyes made her look like a gypsy from a faraway land. All she needed was a colorful shawl, golden earbobs and a crystal ball to complete the look.

"Netta!" she shouted over her shoulder, "Check the icebox and see how much butter we have left! Mary, put a little more milk in that batter. Looks too lumpy". As she started to turn back towards the stove, Rita noticed Birdie timidly crossing through with the polishing items in her hands.

"You lookin' for them other two?" Rita asked. Birdie mutely nodded. Rita shot her a grin and pointed a thumb towards the back door. "They're just outside." Before Birdie could utter her thanks, Rita turned her attention back to Mary. "No! That's too much milk!"

Birdie found the colored girl just outside the back door rubbing the brass railings until they sparkled. The sky was beginning to lighten but it was still too dark to properly see what they were doing. The only source of light came from the electric lamp affixed to the wall just to the left of the doorway. Eva was nowhere to be seen.

The young woman looked up from her task and smiled when she saw Birdie. "You the new girl we been hearin' about? My name's Elizabeth but they call me Lizzie."

"I'm Birdie."

"Birdie?" Lizzie giggled. "That's a funny name! How old are you?"

"Seventeen," answered Birdie, who was a little annoyed by having her name laughed at. "But I will be eighteen soon." She added.

"I thought you looked kinda young. I'm nineteen," Lizzie proclaimed proudly as she straightened her spine. "I been workin' here two weeks." She then looked quizzically at Birdie for a moment and lowered her voice, "Say, are you colored or white?"

Birdie inwardly groaned. She had been answering this question all her life. With her light coloring she could easily, and often did, pass for white, but her amber eyes and kinky hair texture often gave away her true racial background.

"Both" she said, slightly amused at the puzzled look on the other girl's face. Taking the opportunity to change the subject, Birdie held up a rag and asked, "Where should I start?"

"Eva's up front so you can do the side doors by the rose garden." Lizzie replied, pointing Birdie in the right direction. "And when you hear the church bell, come back to the kitchen or Tangie'll be sore."

Birdie spent the next forty minutes polishing railings, lanterns and door trims. St. Augustine's humid conditions made the brass especially hard to restore to its original luster but with some sweat and a lot of effort, it was possible. Soon the cathedral bells tolled six o'clock and Birdie gathered up her cleaning supplies. The sky was now a lovely shade of peach, but Birdie had no time to admire it as she gathered up her cleaning supplies and hurried back to the kitchen.

By now more of the hotel staff had arrived and were milling about in the mudroom, dusting off shoes, putting away belongings, pinning on caps and touching up hair in the small mirror. The upstairs maids in their crisply starched pink dresses under white pinafore aprons chatted flirtatiously with the resplendently liveried doormen in dark green uniforms trimmed with shiny gold buttons.

Last to come in were the groundskeepers - a ragtag looking bunch compared to the rest. They were not issued uniforms like the other Montclair staff since they worked outside all day getting very grubby in the process. They were only allowed inside the hotel in the morning before their shift in order to get their daily instructions from the hotel's owner Johnathan Prescott Sr., who would meet them in Miss Sutton's office. The hotelier was very particular about his gardens.

Birdie spotted a familiar face. The flame haired young man who she saw the previous afternoon had just stepped inside. He wore faded but clean overalls and heavy work boots which he was now running over the shoe scraper. When he looked up and spotted Birdie once again staring at him, he smiled and raised his cap to her. "Hello again!" Birdie gave him a nod and an awkward smile before heading back to the scullery, where Tangie, Eva and Lizzie were stacking chinaware.

Within the next hour, they loaded up the dumbwaiter with stacks of plates, silverware and glasses, each time hoisting it up to the dining staff who set and later waited on the tables above. By the time Tangie and the girls had finished sending everything upstairs, Rita and her assistants had finished preparing most of the breakfast courses which lined the large chef's table. There were the buttermilk biscuits which Birdie had smelled baking when she first arrived, corn muffins, silver caddies lined up with golden triangles of toast, assorted pastries that looked to pretty to eat as well as mounds of bacon, sausages, tilapia, mullet, clam fritters, scrambled eggs and oatmeal which were keeping warm in large pans on the stoves. Like the place settings, the food would be delivered upstairs via the dumbwaiter.

Now Eva, Lizzie and Birdie readied themselves at the sink as Tangie brought in all the soiled pots and pans from the kitchen which involved a lot of water pumping, scrubbing, scouring and drying. By now Birdie's neck started to get stiff and her shoulders ached but she never uttered a sound. She did her best to keep pace with the others.

With the breakfast service now underway upstairs, the kitchen had gone from a busy hive of activity to complete silence. The kitchen maids cleaned up the cooking area while waiting for Rita to return from her daily meeting with Miss Sutton regarding the lunch and dinner menus.

The girls finished up cleaning the cookware and returned them to their proper places in the storage rack. Then it was time to scour the floors in the kitchen, the scullery and the mudroom. The girls divided up the rooms - Eva swept and mopped the mudroom, Birdie scrubbed down the scullery while Tangie and Lizzie shared the kitchen since it was a much larger space.

Once all three rooms were spic and span, the girls returned to the scullery where Tangie removed her spectacles, rubbed her eyes and breathed deeply. "Let's rest a spell before servin'."

"Serving?" asked Birdie as Lizzie and Eva went outside for a breath of fresh air.

"After the breakfast service," Tangie explained, "all the food that ain't been served gets sent back down here and we give it to the staff. Once they finish, any food left over goes to us and the men outside."

"Oh, I see," murmured Birdie, remembering her father's recollections of servant life back in England. It was standard practice for scullery maids to wait upon other servants at meal times.

"Go on and take a couple minutes." Tangie replied and grudgingly added, "You earned it."

Narrow like the mudroom but much longer, the staff dining room featured a vast oak table which ran most of the room's length and seated approximately forty people. It was an older, well-worn piece of furniture which had definitely come from another hotel or large estate house. A china closet, just inside the entry held the dishes, cutlery and glassware which were more utilitarian in style than the more ornate ware used for the guests upstairs. On a sideboard along the far wall were the trays of warmed over breakfast items.

After the four women set the table, Tangie stationed herself by the sideboard to portion out the food. Lizzie and Birdie would be serving while Eva poured tea and coffee. After a few minutes, the hotel staff started to saunter in. The first arrivals were Rita, Netta and Mary from the kitchen. Rita was fanning herself.

"You don't have to serve me today, Tangie darlin'. Just some tea'll do me." She looked at Birdie and smiled. "How you gettin' on, dear?"

"Fine. Thank you, ma'am." Birdie answered and grinned back. For some reason, Rita made her feel at ease. "Everyone's been mighty kind so far."

"Huh! Just wait til the rest of them come in," retorted Netta while Mary snickered.

"You two hush now!" hissed Rita just as the upstairs maids entered. There were about a dozen of them, mostly white, one Negro, and a few Minorcans. They were followed by three handsome colored housemen - two were short and wiry while the third one was tall and had a more muscular build. Lizzie quickly straightened up and shot him her biggest smile.

The elaborately dressed doormen arrived next, laughing heartily at some private joke between them. Then the upstairs dining staff filed in closely behind. As was customary, the final staff member to make her appearance was Iris Sutton. Everyone stood as she made her way to the head of the table. "Mornin' Miss Sutton." "Good morning, ma'am." "Mawnin Mizz Sutton." The housekeeper cordially returned each greeting before finally taking her seat. That was the cue for the rest of the staff to follow suit, and as was also the custom, Miss Sutton started off the meal by saying grace.

While all the heads were bowed in prayer, Birdie curiously looked at the scene before her and noticed the way everyone had positioned themselves. Miss Sutton was at the far end of the table, next to where Tangie was serving up the food. Seated near her were all the white servants such as the doormen, the dining staff and the white chambermaids. Then in the middle of the table where Rita sat were the Minorcans and Spaniards, and at the opposite end were the Negro staff - the housemen, Elmira, Netta and Mary.

Although segregation had been part of Birdie's life since birth, this was the first time she had seen it close up in this sort of setting. The way they were seated made them look like some sort of a human rainbow. With her mixture of white, Spanish and Negro blood, she wondered where she would sit if allowed.

After serving Miss Sutton first, Lizzie waited on one side of the table while Birdie did the other. She passed a plate over to one of the doorman, a slightly older gentleman, with greying temples and beard. "Say Iris," he queried as he nodded towards Birdie, "who is this lovely lass?"

"Behave yourself, Bert!" Miss Sutton laughed. Then, tapping on her teacup with her spoon, she brought the buzzing room to quick silence. Her next words made Birdie freeze in horror. "Attention ladies and gentlemen. I would like to introduce you to our newest member of staff who will be helping us out this summer. Her name is Brigid Fairfax. Say hello Brigid."

Birdie, who hated having attention drawn to her, felt her cheeks grow hot. "Uh...hello," she stammered as she looked at the floor. Why was Miss Sutton embarrassing her like this? There was an awkward second of silence before a couple of the maids giggled and the general chatter resumed.

A blond chambermaid looked up at Birdie in disdain as she was being served. "Brigid, eh?" she said to the brunette next to her. "Don't let that Irish name fool ya!" After she whispered something in the other girl's ear, they both erupted into a fit of giggles.

Meanwhile, Rita overheard a couple of the dining staff talking about the complaints that were received by guests over the quality of the biscuits. Unlike Birdie, the cook did not take the insult quietly.

"What are you talkin' about? Them biscuits were perfect and light as air when we sent 'em up. It ain't my fault if ya'll ain't servin' 'em properly. Ya gotta keep 'em covered! But you took the lid off, didn't ya?" she snapped.

Meanwhile, as Lizzie and Birdie served the colored staff, Birdie noticed Elmira, a coquettish maid, sitting next to Mose, the young man who Lizzie seemed to have eyes for. She was happily chirping away at the soft-spoken houseman, who politely responded to her barrage of questions.

"I just love a good ragtime band, don't you Mose?"

"Yeah, I reckon I do"

"I also love dancin'. What about you Mose?"

"Yeah, sometimes."

"I'd love to go out dancing some time."

"Is that so?" Mose answered non-committally.

Lizzie's face was impassive. The only giveaway to her rising temper was her mouth which had formed into a thin line. If she could get Elmira alone for just a minute, she would strangle her with her apron strings.

Luckily the staff meal was a very brief affair, lasting only twenty-five minutes. Soon the room emptied as quickly as it had filled.

It was almost 9:30 and the sun played peekaboo in a partly cloudy sky. The humidity was already getting unbearable. Only the inevitable afternoon thunderstorm will provide any kind of relief. Birdie's stomach rumbled. Although she had a small bowl of oatmeal around 4:30, all the morning chores had given her an immense appetite.

The girls filed through the vegetable garden behind the hotel and around to the groundskeeping shed. Beside it was a wooden table with two small benches on either side. Here they laid down plates. Tangie opened a basket and took out the silverware, eight tin cups and a large flask of coffee. Lizzie went over to the iron triangle that hung from the shed's porch and, picking up the metal rod that hung next to it, she loudly beat on all three sides of the triangle, creating quite a clamor. Within moments, four weary and hungry men appeared, including Birdie's freckle faced acquaintance, an older heavyset Negro and two Minorcans.

As everyone sat down, Tangie pointed and announced "This here's Birdie. She's startin' today." For Birdie's benefit, she made brief introductions. The colored man who was wiping his brow was Isaiah, the head groundskeeper who looked to be in his fifties. The two Minorcans who were conversing with Eva were Lito and Felipe, and the red-haired boy who Birdie had already encountered earlier that day was called Newt.

The food was cold by this point, but everyone heartily ate, not for pleasure but purely for the sake of refueling their bodies after a morning of hard work. The coffee, however, was still warm. It was the only luxury afforded to the group and they savored every drop. The meal was eaten in relative silence. Afterwards the Minorcans resumed their chatter while Isaiah showed Tangie the new patch he dug which would double the size of the herb garden.

Birdie put the dishes and cups back in the basket while Newt took a plug of chewing tobacco from his overall pocket and stuffed it in his cheek. Birdie inwardly grimaced. She hated seeing men chew and spit tobacco. The city streets were dotted with globs of the wretched brown goo and she always had to carefully mind where she stepped.

"So how are ya likin' it here so far?" Newt inquired as he watched her pack everything away.

"Oh, it's been fine I reckon," Birdie replied and then added softly, “Except for servin' the staff."

A look of disdain swept over Newt's freckled features. "Aw, don't let ‘em rile ya!”

Tangie and Isaiah soon reappeared. "Back to work!" the foreman called to the men, and to girls, "Thanks misses fo' the food."

Newt tipped his cap. "Nice chattin' with ya, Birdie." And he joined the others as they marched back over to the other side of the hotel property.

Birdie's entire body ached, and her feet felt like they were made of lead as she trudged back to her house. Although she only lived a mile away, as far as she was concerned, she might as well have been walking clear up to Jacksonville.

The sun had just set but the air was still heavy with mid-summer humidity and Birdie could feel herself perspiring through her uniform. She'll have to spot clean it as soon as she got home so she could wear it again tomorrow. Plus, her mother will no doubt have hundreds of questions about Birdie's day. Hopefully I can get to bed by ten o'clock, she thought to herself. That will give me at least six hours of sleep.

Chapter 3

After a week of ceaseless labor and extreme exhaustion, Birdie was glad when Sunday finally arrived. As she did every Sunday for as long as she can remember, she spent the morning sitting next to her best friend Ella Patterson in the back row of the chairs set up in Reverend Bailey's parlor as the rotund preacher expounded upon the virtues of gratitude. The congregation had recently raised enough to purchase the land across the street from the pastor's home and now were focused on converting the old barn that currently stood on the west side of the property into a sanctuary.

Despite the fact that both Birdie and Ella were now young women, they still couldn't help but stifle giggles whenever Jeremiah Bailey would punctuate each sentence with a prolonged "YES" when his preaching turned passionate. More often than not, Hortensia would turn around and give both girls a withering glance.

When the service was finally over, the girls headed back to the Fairfax home.

Once safely inside Birdie's room, Ella tore the hat off her head and threw it on the dresser. "Reverend Bailey say we gotta be thankful. Well I thank the Lawd that damned sermon's OVER!"

"Ella, you hush!" Birdie shut the bedroom door behind her, hoping that Hortensia did not hear that last remark. However, she couldn't help chuckling. "That man does loves the sound of his own voice, doesn't he?"

"You bet he does!" Ella replied as both girls sat on the bed. "And did you see the way he kept lookin' over at Widow Holmes? He's taken a shine to her. YES!"

"YES!" Birdie playfully repeated as she took her own hat off and placed it beside Ella's. "Ya know, I've sure missed ya!"

"I've missed ya too, Birdie. I thought we were gonna spend the summer together, but now you're workin' all the time and I only get to see ya on Sundays."

Ella and Birdie had been friends since they were both waist high. They first met when Birdie started going to the colored school on the south side of the city.

Although Birdie was half English and could have easily passed for white at the time, Hortensia did not want to take any chances. Patrick Fairfax was no longer around to help shield his daughter from the inevitable name calling and prejudice she would experience at the white school. Instead Hortensia enrolled Birdie in the small red brick Negro school which was located a few blocks away from their home. Unfortunately, the bigotry Birdie encountered there was just as cruel.

Half breed, mulatto, yella gal, hign yaller and quadroon were just a few of the unkind epithets that were routinely thrown at her. To the colored children and the teachers, Birdie with her light skin, amber eyes and long light brown kinky hair was like a creature from another world. "Look at them yella cat eyes" was a taunt Birdie often heard. The boys constantly pulled on her braids and the girls would exclude her from their playtime activities.

One day while walking home from school, Birdie was pushed to the ground by Virgie Samuels. As Birdie tried to stand up, Virgie pushed her down again, jumped on her back and tried to ride her like a horse. "Hey ya'll," she'd shouted to the amusement of the children who had formed a ring around them. "Look at my yella pony!" However, one child was not laughing - Ella Patterson. She slapped Virgie across the face which made the girl run home crying for her mother.

Short, stocky, and quick tempered, six-year-old Ella was a force to be reckoned with. The headstrong and boisterous child took pity on the shy light skinned little girl who was a head taller than herself despite their being the same age. Ella grew protective of Birdie over time and was not afraid to hit back at anyone who dared to bother her friend. Of course, this had caused Ella to receive countless whippings from their teacher Miss Bradley.

To Birdie, Ella was the sister she never had and always wanted. Ella always made sure that Birdie was included in any games the others were playing. Even though she was never totally accepted by the colored children as one of their own, they at least got used to her presence and over time became somewhat civil to her. Birdie and Hortensia were both grateful to Ella and had the girl over to their house regularly.

Hortensia would always make sure Ella had either a hot meal or at least a piece of pie or cobbler before she headed back to her own home. Last Christmas Birdie surprised Ella with an old shirtwaist which, thanks to her own needlework skills, was embroidered and made over to look like new. Ella basked in the attention she received at the Fairfax home as she came from a very large family of eleven children and often felt lost in the shuffle.

The past week of Birdie's employment at the Montclair was the girls' first time being apart for any significant length of time.

"Well," said Birdie, "we'll just have to make the best of our Sundays." She reached into the top drawer of her dresser and pulled out two worn copies of "The Delineator" magazine. Her mother periodically brought home old periodicals given to her by Della Compton. Once Hortensia was done looking through them, she would pass them on to her daughter. "Look what we got!" Birdie exclaimed with a wide grin.

Ella squealed with excitement. The girls loved leafing through the pages and reading the advertisements for tonics, soaps, washing powders, liniments, shoes, candies and other household goods. They especially loved the occasional colorful pages illustrating the latest designs in dresses and hats.

"Birdie! Dat dress'd look purty on ya!" Ella pointed to a picture of an auburn-haired woman wearing a lovely peacock blue tulip shaped skirt embellished with gold braid and a matching bodice with puffed sleeves. She carried an adorable aqua colored parasol with a feathery boa trim. Atop her head was perched a small flat straw hat with a matching peacock blue ribbon wrapped around the crown.

"Ooh, I like that one too. Here's one for you." Birdie turned to a page featuring an elegant blond woman in a formal lavender colored gown with a train and elbow length white gloves. A crystal tiara adorned her golden tresses.

Both girls sighed imagining themselves decked out in these creations. They often dreamed they had lots of money and were able to buy all the merchandise in the ads while dressed in the latest finery and living in the largest houses in town. Of course, their husbands would have to be very wealthy and come from the very best families.

Birdie interrupted their daydreaming. "That'll never happen to us, though. We're destined to be poor all our lives."

"You just hush now!" Ella vehemently replied. "If we can dream 'bout somethin', why can't we do it too? You ain't gonna be scrubbin' in that hotel all yo' life. You gonna be a world class dressmaker and will travel all over the world to them far off lands, and then you gonna make me the most beautiful dresses so I can catch myself a rich man. You just wait 'n see!"

Birdie quietly shook her head. As much as she loved Ella, she considered the other girl's aspirations to be mere childlike fantasies. Birdie prided herself on being a realist. Instead, she squeezed Ella's arm and softly said "Just make sure you remember me when you're rich, eh?" The two friends quietly giggled as they turned the page.

With Birdie working six days a week from dawn to dusk, her summer was flying by. For the first few weeks, each day was exactly the same - polishing brass work, scrubbing pots, pans and dishes, serving staff, scouring floors, peeling vegetables, more scrubbing. The only bright part of her day was the brief breakfast break with the other girls and the men from the garden.

In the beginning, Birdie was quiet and withdrawn. She was always uncomfortable around strangers, especially men, but she was soon drawn out of her shell and began to enjoy the company of the others.

Isaiah, being the oldest of the group, was a kind, almost fatherly figure who had a deep hearty laugh which was often heard when he spoke of the latest exploits of his children. He was also an excellent wood carver and would often whittle small animal shaped figurines for his young ones. Birdie would watch with fascination. One day he carved the most precious little bird out of a piece of basswood and presented it to her. "A lil bird fo' our Birdie."

Despite his short stature, Lito had a very big voice and would occasionally favor the group with one of the many folk songs of his ancestors. Although Birdie didn't understand one word, the beautifully exotic melodies carried her to faraway lands that she knew she'd never see outside of her imagination and books.

Felipe was the prankster of the bunch and would often teach Birdie new words in Catalan, but when she'd later repeated them to Eva, her eyes would widen as she'd whisper, "Ladies do not use those words, Birdie!"

Although his appearance and mannerisms tended to put Birdie off at times, she actually conversed the most with Newt Phillips. He would often ask Birdie questions about herself and she initially just gave him brief responses. She had always felt uncomfortable talking to white folks because she believed they were judging her or looking down on her. It took almost a week before Birdie started to realize that Newt had no such agenda and was just being friendly. So, she started to ask him questions too. Unsure at first as to what to talk about, she decided to keep it simple and inquired about the hotel's gardens.

Having worked on his family's land all his life before his employment at the Montclair, Newt Phillips was a font of information when it came to the area's vegetation. He told Birdie all about the different flowers that graced the property as well as what was currently in season in the vegetable garden. Sometimes after the meal was finished and they had a few minutes to spare, Newt would take Birdie for a short walk to point out various blooms, or sometimes they would take the scraps to a litter of cats which seemed to have made a permanent home by the gardening shed. Tangie would often suppress a smile when she saw the pair together. Even she slowly thawed her initial frostiness to Birdie. Although the girl was only going to be there for a short time, she worked just as hard as the rest of them and Tangie respected that.

Otherwise, life for Birdie was mainly one of constant labor which left her sweaty and aching each night. The only thing that kept her going (besides the extra money coming into the house to help out Hortensia) was the thought of returning to school in the fall for her final term and then finding a job as a dressmaker assistant. She also planned to set aside a small portion of her earnings to buy some fabric and make dresses for herself and her mother. Hortensia had been wearing the same dark green dress to church for the past few years and Birdie was resolved that she have something new.

However, two events happened that day which would eventually alter the course of Birdie's life - the first being a fight which erupted that morning between Lizzie and Elmira during the staff breakfast.

The day had started out normally until it was time for the staff to have their morning meal. As usual, Tangie was doling out the food while Birdie and Lizzie passed out the plates and Eva poured coffee.

Miss Sutton said the grace as she usually did before the assembled group broke off onto their separate conversations. Once again, Elmira sat next to Lizzie's Mose and coquettishly tried to engage him in conversation. Although Birdie could not hear what they were discussing, she did witness Elmira raise her hand and stroke Moses' lapel. Unfortunately, Lizzie saw it too.

"Git yo goddamn hands off 'im!" Lizzie shrieked as she hurried over and slapped Elmira hard across the face. Iris Sutton, who was talking to Hannah, immediately stopped mid-sentence. "What's going on down there?" she demanded.

Ignoring the head housekeeper, Elmira stood up, covering the reddened cheek that was just struck. "First of all," she said to Lizzie, "I was just brushin' some lint off 'is coat. And besides, he ain't yo man!" She pushed Lizzie so hard that she slammed up against the wall. Lizzie screamed and grabbed Elmira by the throat. Elmira punched and scratched at her in self-defense.

By now Miss Sutton had stood up and headed towards the fray. "Elmira! Elizabeth! Stop this at once! This is no way to behave!" Mose was attempting to pull Lizzie away from Elmira but was unsuccessful until Levi, another houseman, stood up and grabbed Elmira by the waist. Together the two men managed to pry the sparring women apart.

Lizzie was breathing hard and her hair was mussed. Elmira was in tears. Her right cheek was as red as an apple.

"I want the three of you in my office immediately!" shouted Miss Sutton. They all marched out and left the rest of the staff to finish their meal in relative silence. Although Birdie did catch Hannah telling Ruth, "That's exactly why they don't like the Negroes upstairs with the guests. You never know when they'll go off!" Birdie's blood boiled, and her heart raced. She was instantly tempted to follow Lizzie's lead and smack Hannah across the face but instead she steadied herself and mechanically started picking up the dirty plates as the staff took their leave.

Tangie was later asked to join Miss Sutton in her office, leaving Birdie and Eva to do the bulk of the cleanup themselves.

"What will happen to Lizzie?" Eva whispered as the girls stood side by side at the sink washing the plates.

"I don't know," Birdie replied, "Best we get on with things though!"

When Tangie eventually resurfaced, she gathered the girls together. Lizzie and Elmira were both fired and banned from the Montclair for good. And poor Mose also lost his job after being accused of giving Lizzie "false expectations" and inciting the incident. Birdie and Eva both gasped in disbelief.

Tangie delivered the last bit of information with a stern expression and tight jaw. "Birdie, you gonna be fillin' Elmira's spot fo da time bein'. Miss Sutton wanna see ya."

Birdie was stunned. At first, she thought she misheard what Tangie was saying but when Eva smiled and squeezed her arm, she knew it was real.

"Well, whatcha waitin' fo'? Go on!" Tangie shouted as Birdie took off her apron and hung it by the door. She quickly washed her hands and face and touched up her hair before she hurried down the corridor to Miss Sutton's office. Birdie knocked softly.

"Come in," answered Miss Sutton. Birdie stepped inside and carefully shut the door behind her.

"Ah, Brigid! Due to the unseemly display at breakfast, I have had to dispense with three employees this morning. Elmira Lawson's position as chambermaid is now vacant. I have been considering you as her replacement for the remainder of the time you are with us."

"Why, thank you ma'am," Birdie murmured and then added, "But what about the other girls who been here longer than me like Tangie and Eva?"

Iris Sutton shook her head as she cut Birdie off. "We want our maids to have a good grasp of the English language." The housekeeper chose her next words very carefully, "And it is also important that our room staff portray a certain image which positively reflects on the Montclair." Seeing Birdie's puzzled look, Miss Sutton lowered her voice as she continued, "You see, having Negro housemen is acceptable as they work in the common areas. However, we recently discovered that some of our guests are a tad uncomfortable having colored maids working in their rooms where their valuables are kept. Our guests might feel more comfortable around someone more like....uh...yourself."

Birdie was incredulous. It sounded to her like Elmira was going to be fired anyway. Her involvement in that morning's scuffle was a blessing in disguise for the hotel management who now had a more reasonable excuse to let her go, along with Lizzie and Mose. The only reason I was chosen to replace Elmira is because I can speak English and look whiter than anyone else working downstairs, she thought to herself. Poor Tangie and Eva would never see the rest of the hotel beyond the kitchen sink. No, I can't do this.

"I'm sorry Miss Sutton, but I don't wish to be a chambermaid. It wouldn't be fair to the other girls." Birdie said resolutely.

"Brigid, don't be foolish. This would be a step up for you. No more scrubbing pots and pans. No more polishing outdoor brass work. No more serving staff meals..." Miss Sutton's voice trailed off to let the last sentence sink in. She was fully aware that the girls disliked serving the others. Then, saving the best for last, she added, "I understand from Della Compton that you are quite accomplished with a needle. There will be plenty of opportunities to showcase your skills. We always have linens to mend and the occasional guest who needs something repaired or altered. It could even mean some extra money for you."

Birdie, who had been staring at her shoes, lifted her head at this last bit of information. She was now torn between her loyalty to the other girls and the chance to start on the road to becoming a dressmaker.

"I know you don't want to upset the others," Miss Sutton said kindly, "but they have been working here long enough to know their place in the scheme of things. Besides, you are only here on a temporary basis anyway. In a couple more months, this will all be behind you."

Well, she does have point, Birdie thought. I'll be gone soon anyway. Plus, I'll have some earnings to show for it.

"Okay Miss Sutton, I accept. And thank you."

"Wonderful! Go back downstairs and finish out the day. Then come back and see me before you go home so we can fit you properly for a chambermaid uniform."

After Birdie took her leave, Iris Sutton sat back in her chair and rubbed her temples. Thank goodness that mess was straightened out. Not only was she finally able to dismiss Elmira, but she got an immediate and suitable replacement. The mulatto girl will fit in better with the guests until she can hire a permanent white maid.

The second event that would ultimately affect Birdie's life occurred the moment she left Miss Sutton's office and accidentally ran into a young man who was coming up the corridor.

Birdie was horrified. The gentleman looked to be in his early twenties, had sandy colored hair, a well-trimmed beard and ice blue eyes that seemed to pierce her right through to her core. He wore a white linen suit and was carrying a straw summer hat. Although he had the bearing and posture of someone who came from wealth, he also had a friendly and easygoing air about him as he chuckled at the collision.

"Whoa there!" he said. "And where is someone so pretty going in such a hurry?"

"I'm so sorry sir!" Birdie replied shakily. She felt her entire body blushing. "I got to get back to the kitchen. My apologies." And with that, she fled.

The man knocked on Miss Sutton's door and let himself in before she could respond.

"Good morning Iris! Nice to see you again. I've been gone so long that I feel like a complete stranger around here."

Iris Sutton jumped out of her chair and greeted Johnathan Prescott Jr., son of the Montclair's owner and heir to the family's estate. He had not been expected back until the following week,

"Why hello Master Prescott. This is certainly a pleasant surprise. What can I do for you?"

Johnny Prescott looked back towards the door and replied, "First of all, you can tell me who that lovely girl was I just saw coming out of your office."

Chapter 4

Johnathan Prescott Senior winced as yet another knifelike pain shot through his abdomen. Reaching into the top drawer of his desk, he pulled out the bottle of Wells' Health Renewal Tonic that he always kept on hand for when his dyspepsia acted up. He took a swig of the vile concoction and grimaced as he resealed the bottle and put it back in its place.

This summer seemed to be the hottest one yet as he mopped the back of his thick neck with his handkerchief while going over the financial books that Cyril Compton, his chief accountant, presented to him the day before. While the Montclair's takings were adequate so far, the numbers were not as encouraging as Prescott had hoped.

Even though the Regatta had drawn thousands of visitors to St. Augustine, many of them preferred to stay at the larger resorts. Although the Montclair was a decent size and provided its guests with all the niceties that they expected, Prescott knew that he had to find that special niche in the tourism market which would make him stand out (and hopefully above) his competitor but finding that particular specialty was proving to be elusive thus far.

Getting up from behind the massive cherry wood desk, the portly, middle aged hotelier paced his office and ran his hand over his thinning hair as he often did when he had thinking to do. His son Johnny returned yesterday from New York.

"Johnny." Prescott sighed. Despite all the money that was spent on his son's education with the intent of him eventually joining his dad in running the Montclair, Johnny seemed more interested in expensive clothes, liquor and chasing women. Memories of the horrid Mabel Baxter affair still haunted him. After paying off the poor housemaid's family to quietly relocate, Johnny was sent up north until the child was born and placed in an orphanage as was agreed between

Prescott and the girl's father. Now the prodigal son has returned, if not wiser for the experience, then hopefully at least more cautious.

Standing before the large window overlooking the Montclair's gardens, Prescott fished a cigar out of his waistcoat pocket and lit it. Being a farmer at heart, Prescott enjoyed gazing at the well-kept grounds when he needed to calm his racing mind.

Having originally made his money as a citrus and cattle baron, he never intended to become a hotel magnate. That was his wife Lottie's notion. Lottie came from a wealthy family; her father having been the head of a large steel corporation in Pittsburgh. Accustomed to a luxurious lifestyle, Lottie was at first reluctant to marry Prescott until she learned just how profitable his business was. After moving to Florida and having two children, Lottie soon got bored with living in the South until Henry Flagler opened his first opulent hotel in St. Augustine. When she realized just how many rich northerners flocked to Florida in the winter, Lottie began a campaign to convince her husband to open his own resort. Not only would a hotel bring their family more wealth but also the high society which Lottie so desperately missed. She believed so ardently in her husband's ability to make a success of the hotel trade that he soon started to believe it himself at the time.

Prescott, however, often missed working the citrus groves. The sweet perfume of the orange blossoms, the picturesque even rows of trees laden with brightly colored fruit, and the wagonloads of the freshly picked produce going to market or the juicing plant. Unfortunately, all of this ended with the Great Freeze of 1894 which destroyed most of his crop.

The only thing Prescott loved more than the groves was his 600-acre cattle ranch. Sitting atop his chestnut stallion while he supervised his ranch hands rounding up the herds was one of his greatest pleasures. He sold both his ranch and what was left of the grove to help finance the Montclair (which was also partially financed by his father-in-law), Prescott yearned for the old days when most of his time was spent outdoors with very little human contact. Now he has to deal with demanding guests and a socially ambitious wife who was at times ornerier than any steer he ever had to contend with.

Prescott was still at the window admiring the Montclair's rose garden when he noticed the red headed Phillips kid leaning on his spade and dreamily staring at something in the distance. Goddammit, though Prescott. I pay that boy to work, not daydream! After that unpleasant mess with the three colored servants who they had to dismiss yesterday, the last thing he needed right now was a problematic staff.

Prescott firmly believed that the only way to make sure that things were done according to his wishes was to do it himself. This was the main reason why he refused to hire a general manager, choosing to oversee the hotel operations personally. This was also one of many points of contention with Lottie.

"It's bad enough we hired locals instead of recruiting experienced staff from up north," she had cried "But you NEED a general manager. You're the owner, for heaven's sake. Why do you insist on getting involved in all these trivial matters?"

Stubbing out his cigar, Prescott put on his coat. It was time to walk around and make sure everything was in order, but his first stop was the groundskeepers' shed where he was going to give that damned Phillips a verbal thrashing along with a lecture on productivity he'll never forget.

Yes, cattle were definitely easier to deal with.

Hortensia was proud to see her daughter wearing a chambermaid uniform. It meant she was able to work upstairs in the hotel and be part of a luxurious lifestyle that she might otherwise never know. Plus, she will have the opportunity to meet all kinds of important people who were pillars of society. On any given day Birdie could meet an Astor, a Vanderbilt, a foreign potentate or even the President of the United States! Besides, the pink uniform and long white pinafore apron suited her much better than the institutional looking ensemble she had to wear in the kitchen.

Although she wanted Birdie to finish out her final term of school, Hortensia was unsure about her daughter's dressmaking aspirations. She didn't think there would be enough business in a town like St. Augustine to provide Birdie with a steady income. Even she herself had to hold down several different jobs in order to make ends meet.

At least the Montclair could provide a reliable income. Hortensia secretly hoped that a permanent job would eventually open up for Birdie and even talked to Patrick about it.

Every evening after her prayers, Hortensia would have her nightly one-sided conversations with her long dead husband. This was a time for her to discuss her anxieties and concerns - which were usually about their daughter. Ever since her husband's untimely death, Hortensia made it a habit every evening to pretend that he was sitting next to her, so she could bear her soul to him and perhaps cry if the need arose. This was the only way she knew how to cope with her devastating loss, especially during those particularly difficult first couple of years.

Now that Birdie was a chambermaid, she didn't have to wake up so early and was able to get an extra hour of sleep. She also got home a little earlier, so Hortensia would be able to see more of her,

This morning Hortensia gave Birdie a hug as she was leaving. "I am so proud of you! Don't forget to do as you're told. Don't look anyone in the eye and stay tidy."

Birdie stifled an urge to roll her eyes. Instead, she hugged her mother and said, "Don't worry ma. Everything'll be fine. And if I can get finished in time, I'll run into Hartsfield's Dry Goods and get us that fabric we talked about for our new dresses."

Hortensia shook her head. "I wish you'd save that money for something more practical."

Birdie started to bristle. "Aw ma, let's not argue about this again. Why can't you just let me do somethin' nice for you for a change?"

Not wishing them to part for the day on bad terms, Hortensia just smiled and said, "Okay, querida. Bendicion."

Birdie felt strange as she approached the Montclair. Usually by this time she had already polished the outdoor brass fixtures while chatting amiably with Lizzie and Eva. No doubt Tangie had to help Eva polish brass this morning since they were now down to only the two of them. Birdie felt guilty and helpless. She did, however, try to help by suggesting her friend Ella as a possible candidate for one of the vacant positions. Miss Sutton said she would consider it.

With her stomach in knots, Birdie entered the back door along with a few others. As she stopped in the mudroom to place her reticule in one of the storage compartment, she noticed that Newt and Felipe were dusting off their boots before their daily appearance before Mr. Prescott. Both men were startled to see her in the new uniform.

"Well, what have we got here?" Newt asked good-naturedly. "Looks like someone's movin' up in the world."

Birdie didn't really want to go into the entire explanation, so she just said, "Something like that."

"You not eat with us now?" Felipe asked which made Birdie realize that she will no longer be able to sit outside and have her meals with the girls and the groundsmen. She was going to miss the camaraderie and easy conversations.

"No, I reckon not, Felipe," Birdie replied, adding, "I'll miss bein' with ya'll though."

Newt looked particularly crestfallen. Sitting next to Birdie every morning, even if it was only for twenty minutes, had soon become the high point of his day. Trying to hide his disappointment, he forced himself to sound cheerful. "Well, I 'spose we'll see ya around, any ways."

"I guess so." Birdie sighed. "Well, I better head upstairs." Newt wistfully watched her as she headed down the corridor and up the service staircase.

As Birdie ascended the service stairs, apprehension made her stomach churn and her heart race. She was always afraid of the unfamiliar. As she opened the door to the mezzanine, she walked into a new world.

The wooden floors were so shiny that Birdie was afraid to walk on them. The echo of her footsteps bounced off the ornately papered walls from which hung a variety of impressive paintings. The one she passed under now featured a precious little girl with blond curls wearing an adorable white dress with a frilly collar and carrying a doll which was similarly attired. Birdie marveled at how real the painting seemed and half expected the child to speak to her.

Birdie continued her way to the opposite end of the floor where she was to meet the head chambermaid by the housekeeping storage room. The mezzanine floor opened out onto the hotel's main lobby below. As Birdie peered down, her gait slowed as she took in the scene beneath her. It was as if a photo from a magazine had come to life.

The entry doors had large stained glass insert panels featuring a colorful motif of palm trees, exotic flowers and birds which paid homage to Prescott's love of the nature. The floor was covered with glossy grey marble tiles. A round Persian carpet with intricate designs of emerald green, gold and ruby red accented a lounging area of plush green velvet chairs and burgundy settees. Several finely dressed ladies and gentlemen were sitting and chatting amiably while sipping coffee from the white porcelain cups she had washed so often in the scullery.

The front desk fascinated Birdie the most. It was about twenty feet long and made of the same dark cherry wood that seemed to be ubiquitous throughout the resort. Emblazoned on the front of the mammoth desk was a large gold "M" in fancy typography. A small brass bell was placed in the center for guests to summon one of the clerks when necessary. On the wall behind the desk were rows of tiny open-ended mail boxes where room keys and guest messages were stored. There was a young man with slick down blond hair who was placing slips of paper in a few of the boxes.

Birdie was so enraptured with her surroundings that she forgot how nervous she was. She was drinking everything in with her eyes so that she can relate it all to Ella the next time they saw each other.

After remembering that it was time for work, Birdie tore herself away from the mezzanine's overlook and headed for the storage room and Miss Kinkade.

As a former chambermaid at the San Marco, Mavis Kinkade came to the Montclair with a lot of experience and was promptly hired as head chambermaid. She supervised a dozen girls and had the tactical skills of an Army general when it came to managing the domestic upkeep of the Montclair's 125 rooms.

A short, slim and chirpy woman in her mid-twenties, Mavis laughed easily, walked quickly and talked even faster.

“Come here...Birdie, is it?” Before Birdie could utter a response, Mavis continued, “I’ve got you assigned to the third floor with Ruth and Bessie. Most of our guestrooms are on the three topmost floors. Each floor has about 40 rooms including four large imperial suites on the fourth floor. Each of my girls will have ten rooms to clean and maintain during the day. I know it might not sound like much but believe you me, you can easily spend over an hour in each room. You'll be changing the linens and running them downstairs to the laundry, making the beds, thoroughly cleaning the bathrooms, sweeping and mopping the floors, taking away any refuse, beating carpets, and mending the odd piece of linen or a guest's article of clothing if they are not traveling with their own lady's maid or valet." As they reached the top of the staircase, Mavis looked over at Birdie and smiled. "Think you're up to it?"

"Yes ma'am," Birdie replied. "I've pretty much done all those things before. Except for the refuse part."

"That's all right," Mavis said kindly, "I'll be there to guide you for the first couple of days. As for refuse, just bring it out back to one of the groundskeepers. They burn it once a week."

The pair headed down the third floor's main corridor. Birdie had never seen so many doors so close together in her life, each one bearing a brass plaque with a number on it. The floor was identical to the one in the mezzanine but had long runner carpets running down the center. The multicolor floral-patterned rugs were an afterthought which resulted from complaints of noise in the hallways.

"Here we are", Mavis announced as they came to a small room. The door was open and two other maids were inside gathering up brooms, mops, buckets, and cloths among other things. Birdie recognized them both from the staff dining room, especially Ruth who usually sat next to the haughty blonde named Hannah. Ruth's impeccably neat and shiny dark brown hair made her fair skin look almost porcelain. She was quite tall and slender. Bessie, however, could not have been more different. She was short and plump with wisps of thin blonde hair falling from her cap. Both girls had stopped what they were doing and stared at Birdie – Bessie in friendly curiosity and Ruth with contempt.

"Girls," Mavis began, "This is Birdie. She'll be working up here with you for a few weeks. You're only here temporarily until you go back to school, right Birdie?"

"Yes Miss Kinkade," replied Birdie.

Bessie was relieved to see the new chambermaid. "I'm so glad you're here, Birdie! I was afraid they'd make us clean all of Elmira's rooms plus our own."

"We still might all need to assist Birdie until she gets used to things." Mavis said. Ruth rolled her eyes and sighed in frustration.

"I trust you BOTH will help out if needed." Mavis said sharply as she glared at Ruth.

"Yes ma'am," they both replied in unison.

"Good," Mavis looked down at her housekeeping notes. "Ruth, you have 301 through 310. Birdie, you take 311 through 320 and Bessie, you take the rest. Go on, you two. Birdie, stay with me."

When Ruth and Bessie disappeared down the hallway, Mavis looked Birdie in the eyes and said firmly, "There is one important thing you must always remember – you need to stay invisible when you are up here. Never talk to a guest unless they address you first, and never look them in the eye."

Birdie had been hearing this from her mother all her life. This will definitely not be a problem for her. "Yes ma'am."

"If you are cleaning a room and they enter, stop what you are doing and exit immediately. You can come back when they leave. This is why it takes a whole day to clean ten small rooms. There are just too many interruptions. If a guest is indisposed or just wants to stay in the room all day, only then are you allowed to speak to them to ask if they would like the room cleaned. Do you understand?" Birdie nodded. "Also, you are only to use the stairs. The elevator is strictly for guests." Birdie had already been warned about the elevator by Iris Sutton on her first day at the Montclair.

Mavis showed Birdie a list which was affixed to the back of the housekeeping closet door. "This is what needs to be done in each room. Everything you'll need will be in this room. The clean linens come back from the laundry every evening and will be here every morning." Mavis opened up a cabinet behind the door and grabbed one of the keys hanging inside which she handed to Birdie. "Here's your pass key. It will open any door on this floor. Guard it with your life during the day and return it to this cabinet when you leave in the evening. Before you use the key to open any door, always knock first and announce yourself as Housekeeping. Do you have any questions?"

Birdie shook her head. "No ma'am."

"I have to go upstairs now, but I'll be back soon to check on you." Before she turned to leave, Mavis added, "And Birdie, don't forget. STAY INVISIBLE."

Now alone, Birdie looked around the closet which boasted an impressive array of every cleaning product available on its shelves and rows of brooms, mops, sweepers and dusters along the walls. Birdie armed herself with the cleaning implements she was going to need and placed them all in a large bucket. Then she headed over to her first room.

Birdie knocked apprehensively on the door to 311. "Housekeeping!" she warbled. After a few moments, the door was abruptly opened by an older woman with greying ringlets and a pronounced overbite. Her dress was very well made but looked about twenty-five years out of date.

"Come back later," she barked and slammed the door.

Birdie's ire was stoked. How was she supposed to know when they go out? Shaking her head, she headed over to 312. After knocking a few times, Birdie tentatively inserted the key into the lock and let herself in. "Houskeeping," she repeated as she looked around. The room's occupants were thankfully out. Birdie breathed easier and went to work.

Johnny Prescott Jr. blinked several times as he stepped outside the Montclair and into the bright morning sunshine. It looked like it was going to be another scorching day, he thought as he dabbed at his temples with his pocket handkerchief. He still had the remains of a splitting headache thanks to last night's wild soiree at the Alcazar where the women were just as plentiful as the liquor.

Needing the perfect accent to set off his off-white day suit, he headed for the gardening shed.

"Anyone home?" he shouted as he entered. Newt Phillips was placing a hoe back up on the wall.

"Mornin' Mr. Prescott!" greeted Newt cheerfully. "What can I do fer ya?"

"I need something nice for my lapel. I'm going to be lunching with some old college friends who are coming to town today and I need to look dapper. Those who know me have come to expect it."

"You betcha!" Newt replied. "I got just the very thing. I'll be right back, sir."

During Newt's brief absence, Johnny looked around the gardening shed in disgust. Everything that wasn't covered in dust was caked in soil. Plus, the place smelled of manure. Taking his handkerchief back out of his pocket, Johnny kept it over his nose until he heard Newt return.

"Here ya go, sir," sad Newt as he proudly offered Johnny an impressive specimen of a gardenia.

"Ah, that will do nicely," replied Johnny as he broke off the extra length of stem and inserted the waxy white bloom in his lapel. He was getting ready to leave when he seemed to remember something. "Actually, why don't you fetch me a few more of these, my good man."

"Yessir." Newt went back and cut half a dozen fragrant gardenia blossoms and presented them to Johnny.

Watching Prescott, Jr. strolling back to the Montclair, Newt shook his head in amusement at this narcissistic man whose requests for flowers will soon become a daily ritual.

Birdie had just finished cleaning 312 when there was a sharp rap on the door which startled her.

"Housekeeping." To her great relief, it was Mavis. "There you are Birdie." As she did a quick glance around the room, she remarked, "You've done a good job in here. I'll check it more thoroughly when we get back. Right now, it is time for breakfast. Put your things back in the hall closet and join us downstairs as quick as you can." Mavis disappeared down the corridor as locked up the guest room and put her cleaning items away.

She walked at a quick pace down the hallway and was about to descend the stairs when she heard footsteps. This time she was certain that she would need to make herself invisible. However, she was out in the open and there was nowhere to duck behind. So instead she stood with her back against the wall, her hands clasped and her eyes looking downward. The next thing she saw was a pair of freshly polished men's shoes and crisp, cream colored pant legs which were sharply creased.

"Well, well," said a friendly male voice. "I see we meet again. At least this time there were no fatalities," he jokingly said as he alluded to yesterday's run-in.

Birdie couldn't help herself as she glanced up into Johnny Prescott's handsome tanned face and hypnotic blue eyes. "Sorry about that, sir." she gulped nervously. She could feel her heart pounding in her ears as she wondered why he hadn't taken the elevator as was his privilege.

"My goodness," said Johnny, "I don't think I've ever seen eyes like that before." He then leaned in so close that Birdie could smell the sweet perfume from the gardenia. "Are you real or some beautiful catlike creature who's come to entice me from another world?"

Birdie looked back down at her shoes as she stammered, "I...I'm sure I don't know what you mean, sir."

"What's your name?" Johnny had asked Iris Sutton for it yesterday, but she just dismissively mentioned that the girl was only a temporary employee.

"Brigid Fairfax, sir," Birdie said with as much formality as possible.

"Nice to meet you Brigid," said Johnny. "My name's Johnny. I hope to see more of you around here." He then continued to make his way up the stairs but quickly turned back as Birdie had started to descend.

"Oh, and Brigid?" he added. "Learn to take a compliment when a man gives you one, okay?" He flashed her a warm grin as he took his leave.

Birdie was not only shaken from her encounter on the stairs, but she was almost late for breakfast. She had barely made it into the staff dining room before Miss Sutton. Mavis flashed her a raised eyebrow. Rita, meanwhile, waved and motioned for Birdie to sit across from her.

The meal was every bit as uncomfortable as Birdie had feared. Miss Sutton had announced that Birdie had replaced Elmira which caused a few bemused looks from Hannah and Ruth.

Birdie had felt strange and out of place at that table, especially when she glanced over at the corner and saw Tangie and Eva trying to do everything by themselves.

Tangie came around and placed a plate in front of Birdie, who was the only one among the staff who said, "Thank you." But Tangie's face was stonily impassive as she moved on to the next plate.

On the other hand, when Eva came around serving coffee, she whispered, "Hi Birdie!"

She was glad when the wretched meal was over, so she could return to the third floor. She cringed when she remembered that she'd have to do it all again at dinner. For the moment, she decided to put that particular worry out of her mind as she turned her thoughts to the handsome man she just met who made her knees shake and her pulse quicken.

Charlotte "Lottie" Prescott was in a very foul mood as she threw her sister's letter down on the table where she and her husband had just finished their breakfast. The couple lived in the hotel's grand suite on the top floor which was maintained by their own private maids as opposed to the Montclair's staff. Her husband Johnathan was waiting for the hotel to become more established and start making a comfortable profit before undertaking the construction of the grand mansion which Lottie desperately desired.

Prescott, who was immersed in the St. Augustine Herald, was distracted by his wife's furious sighs. Taking a deep breath and steeling himself for whatever tirade was about to erupt, he folded the newspaper and asked, “Okay, what has Lavinia riled you up about now?"

Lottie, the youngest of five children, was always fiercely competitive with her sister Lavinia, who was a year older than her. Lavinia married Harold Grimsby, a wealthy shipping tycoon in New York and had four children. They lived in a twenty-two-room mansion in Long Island, and Lottie was green with envy. Lavinia's letters detailing her idyllic life up north only vexed her sister all the more.

"Seems that Percival and his new wife are expecting!' said Lottie indignantly. Percival was Lavinia's only son and the same age as Johnny.

"So that's what's stuck in your craw, eh?" Prescott muttered. "I will never understand this ridiculous competition you two have going on. One gets a large house, the other wants one too. One's daughter has a big, fancy wedding, the other one's daughter needs a bigger and fancier wedding." Prescott had paid a fortune for his daughter's wedding because Lavinia's girl had a lavish affair at a posh hotel in New York City.

"And now Lavinia's boy has settled down and married. Meanwhile your own son can't commit to one woman much less marry and start a family. Face it, you lost this time around, Lottie."

Sitting straight up and giving her husband a cold stare, Lottie said icily, "First of all, Johnny is OUR son, not just mine. Secondly, I am not in any kind of rivalry with Lavinia and I'm offended by your suggestion that I would be that shallow. I love my children no matter who they marry or what they accomplish."

"All right," countered Prescott. "Tell me. When is OUR son going to grow up and start taking some responsibility around here? He's only been back a day and he's already gone swanning off to carouse with those flighty friends of his. I need him around here to help me run this place and maybe share some of the business knowledge he supposedly picked up at that damned Yankee college you insisted on sending him to!" Feeling his usual stomach pains coming on, Prescott stopped his harangue and breathed deeply.

Lottie picked up Lavinia's letter as she stood up. "Well, I refuse to talk to you when you're like this. We'll discuss this later! I'm going downstairs to check on Myrtle and her mother. I still can't believe that after they traveled down all this way to see me, the best we could do for them is a third-floor room."

Before Prescott could remind his wife that all the top floor suites were already full, Lottie was gone.

After breakfast, Birdie managed to clean four more rooms including 311, which was finally vacant. When she knocked at 317, a frail voice quavered, "Come in." Birdie slowly opened the door and peered into the small room's parlor.

"Uh...Housekeeping," she said hesitantly.

"Come on in," said the voice which came from the bedroom. Birdie brought in her cleaning supplies and shut the door behind her. This is the first time she had to clean a room with someone in it. She remembered Mavis' instruction to stay invisible, so she went ahead and started to dust the front parlor. However, after a few minutes, the voice called out to her again, "Come in here, girl." Birdie nervously put down the dusting rag, approached the bedroom door and slowly pushed it open.

In the bed was a small, elderly woman wearing a lacy ivory night dress and frilly cap. Her advanced age was firmly etched into the lines on her face. However, the stark contrast between the large bed and her petite body made her seem more like a small child. She stared straight ahead and slightly cocked her head as if listening for something.

"Hello," her face lighted up with a smile. "I'm so sorry to trouble you but could you please pour me a glass of water. I am parched this morning."

She's blind, Birdie realized as she walked over to the nightstand where the water pitcher stood and filled up a glass. As she offered it to the woman, she softly said, "Here ya are, ma'am."

The woman reached out and grasped the glass with both hands. After taking her first sip, she asked, "What's your name?"

"My name's Brigid, ma'am," replied Birdie. Perhaps because the older woman had such a sweet demeanor that made Birdie instantly at ease around her, she added, "But most folks call me Birdie."

"Birdie!" exclaimed the old woman. "What a darling name. Mine is Olivia."

"It's nice to meet ya, Miss Olivia," said Birdie sincerely as she took the glass back after Olivia indicated she was finished.

"Now, Birdie, I know that you have a lot to do so I won't keep you standing here. You just go on with your cleaning. But is it okay if I talk to you while you work?"

Birdie's heart broke as she thought of this poor woman sitting alone in a hotel room in total darkness all day.

"Of course, Miss Olivia. I just need to finish up the front parlor first, but I'll keep the door open, so we can talk."

As Birdie swept the front room, Olivia told her about how she travelled from Pittsburgh to Florida by train with her daughter Myrtle, who was a lifelong friend of Charlotte Prescott, wife of the Montclair's owner. Charlotte had invited them to be guests of hers for the summer.

"That was mighty nice of Mrs. Prescott," remarked Birdie as she started to sweep and dust the bedroom.

"Yes, the whole family has been so incredibly hospitable to Myrtle and me. In fact, just this morning their son Johnny brought me these sweet gardenias. They smell divine!"

Johnny? Gardenias? Birdie's mind flashed back to the encounter she had on the stairs earlier that day with the attractive gentleman named Johnny who happened to be wearing a gardenia. Could this be the same man? Could she have actually been speaking with Johnathan Prescott, Jr.?

Remembering that she was supposed to be conversing with Miss Olivia, Birdie asked, "So what do ya think of Florida?"

"It is a bit too warm for me, I'm afraid, but Myrtle has promised me a trip to the seaside this afternoon, so I can get some fresh air and feel the ocean breeze. I have a dress ready over there. Do you think it will be comfortable enough for the beach?" Olivia vaguely pointed to the corner armoire. Next to the armoire was a chair, over which was draped a white lawn dress.

"Yes, I see it," said Birdie as she went over and picked it up. Although it seemed light enough to wear to the beach, Birdie noticed a tear near the hem. "This dress will be fine, Miss Olivia, but there is a little tear in the skirt's hem. I'd be happy to fix it for ya before your outing later."

"That would be lovely. Thank you, Birdie."

Birdie picked up the dress. "I'll be right back, Miss Olivia. There's a sewing box in the storage room. This won't take long."

As she left the bedroom and headed for the door, it opened before she could reach the knob. Two middle aged women entered. One was tall and rail thin. Her graying auburn hair was tightly wrapped in a bun behind her head. The other was short and stout. Her dark hair was hidden under an expensive hat and she carried a white ruffled parasol. Her face was a thundercloud.

"What are you doing with my mother's dress?" asked the first woman in total bewilderment. "I certainly hope you're not taking advantage of the fact that she's blind."

The second woman immediately started interrogating Birdie. "Who are you? What's your name? I've never seen you around here before! And what is the meaning of this?" she pointed at Olivia's dress.

Birdie tried to keep her composure and her voice steady as she replied, "My name's Brigid Fairfax, ma'am. I'm the new chambermaid. I was just goin' to fix this dress for Miss Olivia."

At that moment, Oliva called from the bedroom, "What's happening out there? Myrtle, is that you?"

Myrtle went to her mother, asking, "Are you okay, mama? We were just concerned when we saw this girl leaving with your dress."

"Birdie's just going to fix the hem for me, that's all. She has been delightful company. I hope I haven't gotten the poor thing into trouble," replied Olivia. Myrtle nodded in relief, satisfied with the explanation.

Meanwhile, Lottie Prescott glared at Birdie and, lowering her voice, said through clenched teeth, "Listen up, girl. You go ahead and hem that dress, but don't you ever catch me seeing you getting familiar with our guests again." Pointing at the cleaning supplies which were leaning up against the wall, she hissed, "Take your things and get out!"

"Yes ma'am," Birdie whispered as she made her retreat to the housekeeping closet where she shut the door, threw down the dress and burst into tears.

"What's troubling you, mama?" asked Myrtle as she gently guided her diminutive mother into the buggy. "If you're not feeling well enough to go to the beach, we can go back to the room."

"No, dear, it's nothing like that. I feel really bad about that poor child. I just know that I caused her trouble." Olivia had been unable to get the unfortunate incident out of her mind. "And God bless her, she still managed to mend my dress."

Myrtle, who felt remorseful of her initial misjudgment of the maid's motives, had inspected Birdie's needlework and was very impressed with the small, even stitches. "Don't worry, mama. Lottie was just in a bad humor today because she had another letter from Lavinia. I'll have a quiet word with her after dinner this evening. I might even have this girl...uh...Birdie ...mend my dark green dress. You remember, that one I was wearing on the train when I tore the sleeve on that door handle." Olivia nodded at the recollection.

"Don't fret, mama. We'll smooth things over," assured Myrtle.

Olivia sighed with relief as she sat back in her seat and smiled.

Birdie was exhausted, both physically and emotionally, by the end of the day. As Mavis had predicted, all three girls had to help Birdie clean her last room before they could all leave. Bessie took it matter-of-factly, but Ruth was clearly irritated. However, when she overheard Birdie recant her run in with Mrs. Prescott, she smiled in satisfaction. That girl won't last a week up here, Ruth thought smugly.

As Birdie trudged into the mudroom that evening to collect her belongings, she was shocked to see what else was among her things - a lovely gardenia flower!

As she walked home under the orangey purplish twilight sky, she took a deep sniff of the aromatic blossom and said to herself, "Even though Mrs. Prescott might not like me, at least her son seems to!"

For the rest of that week, Birdie found a different flower waiting for her each evening as she went to collect her belongings. Each one matched the buttonhole bloom which Johnny Prescott happened to be wearing that day

Chapter 5

That Sunday afternoon, Birdie and Ella took one of their after-church strolls by the sea wall. Ella was particularly excited because she was starting at the Montclair the next day as Lizzie's replacement.

"Thanks again for helpin' me get this job, Birdie. Miss Sutton says that if I do good, they might take me on perm'nent. My ma hopes that I can 'cause we sho can use the money."

Birdie's initial reaction to this piece of news was one of apprehension as the thought of going back to school without Ella was unthinkable. Ella protected and defended her against the taunts and jibes of the others for as long as she could remember. When she realized that she was being selfish, she just smiled and replied, "I'm pleased for ya, Ella." And she meant it.

They sat on the sea wall and dangled their feet over the bay while gazing out at the boats sailing by, most heading northward past the old Spanish fort. Several men were fishing further down the waterside. The Minorcans were using nets while others used simple bamboo fishing poles.

"Will I get to see ya durin' the day?" Ella was asking. Birdie hadn't the heart to tell her about the staff breakfast, so she just simply said, "Only at mealtimes," which was the truth as far as Birdie was concerned.

A few of the men who had been fishing were now leaving, each one hauling his day's catch in buckets or slung over his shoulder. Birdie was surprised to see that Newt Phillips was among them. He was casually chatting with Eddie Hartsfield from the General Store when he spotted Birdie sitting on the wall. He said something to Eddie as they parted ways before he headed over to the girls.

Birdie was embarrassed when she saw Newt approaching. He was unkempt as usual, barefooted, had a wad of tobacco in his cheek and wreaked of fish. Birdie wished at that moment that she were invisible. Ella, on the other hand, was looking at Newt with suspicion. Normally when a white man approached them in public, it was to sling racial slurs. But this particular white boy had a huge grin on his face.

"Howdy Birdie! What a nice surprise seein' ya here!" Newt exclaimed.

"Hi Newt," Birdie said flatly. The odor coming from the bucket he carried was overwhelming. She hoped he wouldn't stay for too long.

"Yer lookin' quite purty today," he said.

"Oh, we've just come from church," Birdie explained. Then she remembered her manners. "This is my friend Ella. Ella, this here's Newt. He works at the Montclair. Ella starts workin' there tomorrow."

Newt tore his eyes off Birdie long enough to nod at Ella and say, "How d'ya do?" Ella, whose mouth was still agape with bewilderment, just stared back.

Newt turned his attention back to Birdie. "We've sure missed ya since ya started workin' upstairs."

"Oh, we'll be seein' each other around. We ran into each other today, didn't we?" Birdie replied, trying to sound friendly.

"I reckon yer right," Newt admitted.

Birdie, wishing to put a swift end to the conversation, suddenly stood up and said, "Well, we'd better be going. My ma's waiting for us back at the house."

Ella knew that Hortensia was not waiting for them but was in fact visiting with Ophelia, but she realized that Birdie was trying to put an end to the conversation, so she said nothing and played along.

"I'll walk ya'll home if ya like." Newt offered.

Birdie was horrified at the thought. The last thing she needed was for her overly critical mother to see Newt.

"No, that's all right Newt. We don't have far to go." Birdie said a little too quickly.

"Well then, it was nice seein' ya. Bye Birdie."

"Bye Newt."

Jake Combes and Lonnie Stokes had just left their weekly poker game at Bill Duval's. For the third week in a row, Combes lost half of his weekly wages to Zeke Gilbert.

Spitting angrily on the sandy street, Combes grumbled, "Ain't no man on earth can have luck that damned good. I know fer a fact that varmint's cheatin'!"

Stokes was also outraged, but not about not about the poker game. Pulling the cigar stub out of his mouth, he replied, "Never mind that. What I wanna know is what the hell's that Phillips kid doin' over there talkin' to them two nigras in broad daylight."

As they walked back towards Birdie's house, Ella finally got her voice back and commenced with a litany of questions.

"Who's dat boy? Why's he makin' googly eyes at ya? What's he do at the Montclair? And why did ya lie 'bout havin' to go home? He seemed kinda decent. Ya know, I think he's the first white man who spoke to me on the street without callin' me names."

"Newt's a gardener at the Montclair. You'll be seen' him around. He wasn't makin' eyes at me, just bein' polite is all. And the reason I wanted to hurry home is...." Birdie's voice trailed off as she struggled with whether or not to divulge her delicious secret. Both girls stopped their stroll and Ella put her hands on her hips.

"Well?" she demanded.

Birdie leaned in closer and whispered, "Well, I didn't want to give Newt the wrong idea because I already got me an admirer."

Ella was shocked. "Who?"

Birdie proceeded to tell her best friend all about her couple of encounters with Johnny Prescott and all the lovely flowers he'd left her each day. She vividly described his stylish, handsome blonde looks and those eyes which were a shade of blue she couldn't describe. She only knew that they seemed to burn right through her and had been keeping her awake at night.

Ella, however, was doubtful. She raised her hand, indicating Birdie to stop speaking, and said, "Miss Birdie..." Birdie inwardly groaned. Whenever Ella called her "Miss Birdie", a lecture was not too far behind

Ella continued, "What makes ya think that a rich man like that...a rich WHITE man...would be seriously courtin' one o' his pappy's maids....a maid with Negro blood? I love ya like a sista, Birdie, but ya kiddin' yo'self."

Birdie's temper, a gift from her father's side of the family, reached epic proportions. Her face reddened as she cried, "You have no idea what you're talkin' about, Ella Patterson! I never said he was courtin' me. He's just a casual admirer, is all! And I don't see anythin' wrong with appreciatin' his attentions!"

Ella breathed deeply as she calmly tried to reason with Birdie. "I don't wanna rile ya. I just want you to be careful 'round him. You an' me heard stories all our lives 'bout white men havin' their way with colored women and gettin' away with it. Yet, if a colored man looks at a white woman the wrong way, he gets lynched."

Birdie was mulish. "I still don't see what all this got to do with me!"

Ella placed her hand on Birdie's arm as she gently warned, "Just be careful Birdie. You're courtin' trouble."

Tangie Foster tied on her apron and sighed. She had no idea how she was going to get through the day after only a couple hours of broken sleep last night. Her papa had been burning with fever again and Tangie took turns with her mother trying to cool him off with wet rags and keeping the younger children at bay. In his delirium, he would often mistake Tangie for Libby, her older sister who passed away two years ago from scarlet fever. Tangie had sent one of her younger brothers to fetch Doc Jennings, but he wasn't able to do much and just told the family to keep the old man comfortable and make sure he had plenty of fluids and rest.

As if life at home was not difficult enough, her days at work were almost too much to bare. It was bad enough losing Lizzie, but after Birdie got promoted and sent upstairs, she and Eva had to bear the brunt of responsibility. For the past week they often didn't get finished until just before midnight, only to have to turn around and return to the Montclair five hours later to start all over again.

At least there was hope on the horizon. The new girl, Ella Patterson, starts today. From what Tangie could gather, this Ella was a friend of Birdie's. That damned Birdie. The very thought of her made Tangie burn with fury. She was now earning more money for doing far less work upstairs. Meanwhile, because Mr. Prescott wanted to start cutting corners on the hotel's budget, he decided not to fill the second vacant spot in the scullery assuming that Tangie and others could cope with the workload.

She could hear the nearby church bells ringing and looked up at the kitchen clock. It was 5 a.m. A loud knock on the back door awoke Tangie from her ruminations. As she opened it, she came face to face with Ella who was decked out in a kitchen maid uniform and grinning from ear to ear.

"Mornin'," Ella said eagerly, "I'm 'sposed to be startin' today. You Tangie?"

Well, she's punctual. That's a good start, thought Tangie as she let the new girl in.

Johnny Prescott straightened both his tie and the yellow rosebud in his buttonhole as he approached the door to his father's office. Johnny had been dreading this inevitable meeting ever since he returned from New York last week. He rapped on the door which received the gruff response of "Come in!"

Johnny found the old man closing up the top drawer of his desk, so he knew that Prescott Senior was in a mood that was fiery enough to work up his dyspepsia. Johnny decided to take a peaceful, easygoing approach to whatever was about to be unleashed upon him.

"Good morning, Pop," he said with as much charm as he could muster.

But the old man was not to be placated so swiftly. "Sit down, boy," Prescott indicated one of the soft leather chairs which faced his desk. Once Johnny was seated, Prescott continued, "I have been wanting an audience with you ever since you returned but it seems like I have to make an appointment to see my own son these days. If you're not flitting off with your screwball friends, you're either drinking away our profits in the bar downstairs or sleeping it off until well into the afternoon!"

"I'm sorry Pop. I'll make more of an effort to see you from now on," promised Johnny.

"I was hoping after that Mabel business that you'd have learned from your mistakes and turned your life around." Johnny bristled at the mention of Mabel but remained silent while his father went on, "I thought you'd buck up and become an upstanding, responsible and industrious young man while you were away. Then when you returned, you would take your rightful place beside me and help run the Montclair. But that was until," Prescott held up a piece of paper and shook it, "I got this letter from someone named Alfred Quinn." Johnny dropped his head into his hands.

"Seems like you had some problems up north which explains why you came back so early. Would you mind telling me why this Quinn fellow insists that I owe him $500 or else he's got some interesting photos to share with the newspaper?"

With his head still in his hands, Johnny told his father the whole sordid tale of his gambling debts, the call girl and the photographer hired by Quinn, who reckoned that the only way he'd ever see his money again was to go after Johnathan Prescott, Sr. After all, as owner of North Florida's newest resort which is trying to build up a steady client base, he certainly can't afford any bad press right now.

"My God! You have got to be the most useless son a man could ever be cursed with. Are you out to ruin me? I can't afford to keep cleaning up your messes. When the hell are you going to straighten up and fly right? Get out of here! I don't want to see your face for the rest of the day!"

Johnny meekly rose and headed for the door. As he started to turn the knob, he glanced back at the old man, who was now standing and looking through a window over his beloved rose garden.

"I'm sorry Pop. I'll do everything I can to make this right." After getting nothing in reply except for cold stony silence, Johnny left.

With his father's admonishments still ringing in his ears, Johnny desperately needed a drink. Too impatient to wait for the elevator, he decided to take the stairs and head for the bar on the main floor. However, he soon realized that it was still early, and the bar wasn't open yet. He definitely needed something to perk his spirits, and then he spotted something even better than booze for his wounded ego. He saw Birdie knocking on room 319 and bringing her cleaning supplies straight in which most likely meant the room was empty.

Johnny walked down the hallway and knocked on the door. After a few moments, it slowly opened, and he was looking into those alluring golden eyes which had captivated him at first sight.

"Good morning," he said. When he got no immediate response other than a flabbergasted stare, Johnny asked, "What's wrong? Cat's got your tongue?"

"I'm sorry, sir. Good mornin'" Birdie stammered. When she heard the sharp knock on the door, she figured it was just Mavis or one of the other girls. The last person on earth she expected to see was Johnny Prescott. "What...uh....brings you here, sir?"

"Let's get something straightened out right now, Brigid," said Johnny as he stepped inside and shut the door behind him. "You can stop calling me 'sir'. My father is the one you work for. So, save the 'sirs' for him, not me. Just call me Johnny."

"Yes sir," said Birdie automatically.

"Uh," admonished Johnny, "Try that again."

"Oh...yes, Johnny." Being so familiar with her boss' son felt so unnatural to Birdie.

"That's much better," Johnny remarked as he sat down and made himself comfortable in the sitting room. "Mind if I keep you company? I seem to be at a loose end this morning."

Birdie remembered Mrs. Prescott's stern warning about getting too familiar with the guests. No doubt this also applied to her son as well. "I'm sorry Johnny. I would enjoy your company, but your mother might not approve."

Johnny waved his hand dismissively. "Oh, don't worry about my mother. She'll do anything for her son, and right now her son wants nothing more than to spend time with a beautiful woman named Brigid."

"I reckon that if I'm to call you Johnny, you may as well call me Birdie. That's what everyone else 'round here calls me. Except for Miss Sutton, of course."

"Ah, Iris Sutton." Johnny mused. Putting on his best high-pitched impression of the head housekeeper, he said, "Mind those corners, Brigid. Anything worth doing is worth doing well."

Birdie couldn't help but giggle. "Oh Johnny, you sounded just like her!"

"You know, I think she secretly fancies my old man," Johnny said conspiratorially as he settled his tall frame into a nearby wing chair.

Birdie gasped. "Oh no! You must be teasing!"

"No, honestly," replied Johnny. "I've seen the way she looks at him."

They casually conversed while Birdie cleaned. Johnny told Birdie about all the faraway places he had visited like Pittsburgh, New York, London and Paris, being careful to leave out the more sordid details.

Talking to this young pretty thing who was obviously attracted to him and hung on his every word soothed Johnny's deflated self-esteem after the browbeating he took earlier. When Birdie had finished the room, he felt strong enough to go back upstairs and get to work on restoring his relationship with his father.

"Thank you for brightening up what could have been a dreary day for me," Johnny said sincerely as he gazed deeply into Birdie's eyes. "I don't know what I would have done if it weren't for you." And, grasping Birdie by both shoulders, Johnny suddenly pulled her close to him and planted a kiss on her forehead. Then, his breath hot in her ear, he whispered, "I will DEFINITELY be seeing you again."

As he left the room, Birdie slowly exhaled. She could still feel Johnny's lips over her eyebrow and his close-cropped beard tickling her earlobe. It was almost time for the staff breakfast, so she hurriedly closed up the room and headed downstairs.

She was so giddy with happiness that she almost didn't notice that Ella was helping to serve breakfast this morning and only briefly acknowledged her with a nod. She'll talk more to Ella later and fill her in on what just happened.

After the staff breakfast was over, Ella quietly fumed as she stood at the sink between Eva and Tangie. They were up to their elbows in greasy soap suds as they cleaned the staff dinner plates. Birdie didn't say one word to her this morning and barely acknowledged her. Is she so high and mighty now that she no longer had time for lowly creatures like Ella and her colleagues in the kitchen? Ella attacked the plate she was scrubbing with extra vigor.

Tangie glanced over and observed Ella's bad mood. She had also noticed Birdie's aloofness at breakfast. So far Tangie was impressed with Ella who did as she was told and wasn't afraid of hard work, even if she did have a tendency to talk too much. Plus, Tangie and Eva could now go home at a decent hour thanks to Ella's speed. So Tangie was resolved to do whatever she could to befriend the girl.

Leaning over to Ella, she injected a sympathetic note into her voice. "I know how ya feel. Some folks 'round here think they're pretty high 'n mighty these days. Don't ya worry, Ella. Ya got me 'n Eva. We're yo' friends now."

Chapter 6

Birdie knocked on the door jamb of the groundskeeper's shed and shouted, "Hello? Anyone here?" She peered inside but didn't see Isaiah. Hearing footsteps approaching from behind her, Birdie turned around and saw Newt coming over, wearing his usual cheerful countenance. "Hiya Birdie! How are ya?"

After that morning's kiss from Johnny, Birdie felt higher than the puffy white clouds that dotted the bright blue midday sky above them. "I feel wonderful Newt!"

Newt had never seen Birdie looking so joyful. It made her even prettier than usual. Realizing that she must be there for a reason, he asked her, "What can I do fer ya, Birdie?"

"Actually, it was Isaiah who I need to see. I've got trash here that needs disposin'. When I went to dump my bin into the large can downstairs like I usually do, I saw it was gone. I thought maybe Isaiah had already started the burn."

"Naw," Newt replied. "Isaiah is talkin' with Mr. Prescott up front about puttin' in some new palms. I'm doin' the burnin' this mornin'. I was just fixin' to start. Wanna come?"

Birdie really didn't want to get behind on her rooms. As if reading her mind, Newt added, "Don't worry. It don't take long."

Birdie smiled and said resignedly, "Okay, let's go"

Newt took the trash bin from Birdie and carried it while they headed for the southernmost point of the Montclair's property on the other side of the arbor. They passed by Lito who was pruning a box hedge near the reflecting pool. He raised his hat to Birdie in salutation as she nodded politely in response.

Birdie gazed around the different areas of the grounds and said, "Ya'll do all kinds of things out here, don't ya?"

"Yep, "answered Newt, "I 'spose we do. We got the arbor to tend to, the vegetable garden, the maze, the reflectin' pool, the rose garden which Mr. Prescott is awful fond of plus all the land in front of the hotel."

Something just occurred to Birdie. "Don't ya have to help tend your own land at home, Newt? Or do your pa and brothers do that?"

Newt suddenly seemed far away as he replied, "I ain't got no brothers, just two little sisters, and my pa died last year. We have a tiny lil farm in the woods west of town. It's small enough fer my maw and I to manage by ourselves."

"But when do ya have time to take care of your place and work here as well?" Birdie asked.

"Well, I do what I can in the mornin' before work and finish up when I get home. Plus, maw does what she can durin' the day. On Sundays I catch up on what still needs doin'."

"My goodness," said Birdie, "It sounds like you're always workin'."

"I done it all my life so it ain't that bad," said Newt matter-of-factly. "When I saw ya on Sunday, that was my first time goin' into town for anythin' besides work in a long time."

When they finally reached the burn pile, Newt added the refuse which Birdie had brought down. "Stand back a lil, Birdie." Then he set the pile of yard trimmings, food trash, animal waste and room refuse afire, making sure that Birdie stayed upwind.

As they both quietly watched the smoke billow off the burning pyre of trash, Newt turned to Birdie and asked, "So how did ya come by the name o' Birdie anyway? Is it 'cause you sing like a bird?"

Birdie pealed with laughter. "No," she replied, "But I wish I did. Tell the truth, I named myself Birdie when I was a baby." Seeing Newt's bewildered look, she continued, "You see, my real name's Brigid, but when I was just learnin' to talk, I couldn't say Brigid and kept callin' myself Birdie. So, the name stuck ever since."

"I think Brigid is a fine name," said Newt as he picked up the refuse bin. "But truth be told, I like Birdie better."

As they sauntered back towards the Montclair, it was Birdie's turn to ask, "So how did you come to be called Newt?"

"My given name is Newton, but folks just shorten it to Newt, is all."

"Hmmmmm, Newton," Birdie sounded out the name thoughtfully. "I like it. It sounds like the name of one of those lawyers or bankers."

Newt chuckled. "Well I don't know 'bout that but I'm glad you approve. Besides, it's a heap better than my middle name."

"Ooh, what is it?" Birdie asked.

"Nah, I can't tell ya."

"Oh, please Newt. I really wanna know." Birdie pleaded, her curiosity now sincerely peaked.

"Aw gee Birdie. It's pretty dang awful."

"Come on, Newt. Now I'm dyin' to know so you gotta tell me."

"Well, I ain't sure...."

"How about I tell you my middle name first and then you can tell me yours. Mine is not very nice anyway."

"Okay," said Newt, "It's a deal."

"My middle name is Eugenie," revealed Birdie.

"Eugenie is a right purty name. There ain't nothin' wrong with it. You ain't playin' fair, Brigid," said Newt good-naturedly.

"Are you kiddin'? I hate my middle name." Birdie retorted. "Now we have a deal, Newton. It's time for you to confess your middle name. Let me hear it."

Newt stopped walking, put the container down on the ground and paused for a second before uttering, "Cuthbert."

Birdie gulped and tried her best to keep a straight face, but instead she collapsed in a fit of giggles. "Oh Newt, I am so sorry. I don't wanna hurt your feelin's, but that name is so funny! Cuthbert!"

"Aw Birdie. Promise me you won't tell no one," begged Newt.

Finally, having composed herself, Birdie replied, "Don't worry Newt. Your secret's safe with me."

"Whew! Thanks!" Newt handed the canister back to Birdie. "See ya later, Brigid."

Birdie playfully replied, "See ya Cuthbert!"

Newt stood and watched her walk away. Despite having deflated his own ego by revealing his detested middle name, it was more than worth it because it made her smile, which accentuated her beauty even more.

Fifty yards away stood Hannah who had been beating carpets when she had spotted the couple sharing a hearty laugh and Newt staring longingly at Birdie. A mischievous grin played on her lips.

Lottie made her way downstairs to the mezzanine searching for Mavis Kinkade, who she found leaving the housekeeper's storage room pushing a cart laden with boxes, cans and bottles of assorted cleaning products.

"Ah, Miss Kinkade, there you are. I need to have a word with you, if you please."

"Certainly, ma'am." Mavis, who dealt with Mrs. Prescott's critiques about her staff's performance on a daily basis, wondered who she was going to complain about today. Yesterday Lottie saw Bessie wipe her nose as she passed through the corridor and had given the girl a blistering lecture on decorum.

"I'd like to inquire about this new girl of yours. The mulatto girl with the light brown hair. I hear she's called Birdie or some such nonsense."

"You mean Brigid Fairfax, ma'am?" Mavis asked. Birdie had already told her about the confrontation she had with Mrs. Prescott last week, so she assumed that the woman was about to rehash the incident and remind Mavis to warn her girls about engaging the guests in conversation. However, Mavis was shocked to hear Lottie's next words.

"I understand the girl is very good with a needle. I saw the repairs she did to Olivia Davenport's dress. Small, evenly sized stitches which looked like they could have been done by machine. However, what has really impressed me was what she did for my friend Myrtle. She not only expertly repaired a torn sleeve but also did some quick alterations to the neckline which makes it look much more stylish. I need someone like that looking after my own wardrobe. Nothing against Violet, mind you, but this girl has much better sewing skills." Violet was Lottie's lady's maid.

"Yes, Mrs. Prescott," Mavis agreed. Then remembering an off-the-cuff remark which Birdie had made the other day, Mavis added, "She also hopes to become a seamstress someday."

Lottie looked pensive for a moment as if trying to make a difficult decision. "Starting tomorrow, I want the girl working for me. She can be a junior housemaid and will have also have the extra responsibility of my wardrobe until I can find a decent seamstress in this godforsaken town." Lottie Prescott had notoriously high standards which she expected from her personal staff. The fact that she was now demanding the services of one of the hotel's chambermaids, and a new one at that, was unprecedented.

However, Mavis had to compose her next words very carefully. "I'm sure Brigid will be flattered, Mrs. Prescott. However, the child does wish to return to school when the term starts next month."

Lottie seemed unconcerned. "Oh, we'll change her mind. This will be an excellent opportunity for the girl. After all, we're talking steady, year-round employment."

Later on that day, Birdie was summoned to the housekeeper's office and informed of Lottie Prescott's request to make her a permanent member of the family's private staff.

"Oh no, Miss Sutton, I'm sorry but I can't," replied Birdie, shaking her head for emphasis. "I was only meant to be here temporarily for the summer. You see, I only have one term of school left which I would like to complete. I'm so close to finishin'."

"I see," said Iris thoughtfully. She could certainly understand the girl's reluctance. Setting the school issue aside, Lottie Prescott could be a tyrant to work for. Her explosive temperament and snobbishness were well known amongst the staff. Iris believed Lottie's wish to recruit Brigid was yet another of her passing whims. Unfortunately, history had taught the housekeeper that what Mrs. Prescott wants, Mrs. Prescott must get or else everyone in her path will suffer her wrath - especially poor, dear Mr. Prescott.

"All right, Brigid. I know that your education is important to you, as it should be. So how about you go ahead and work for Mrs. Prescott during the short time you have left here at the Montclair. When the time is up, I'll give you the choice of staying on or going back to school. In the meantime, look at this as an opportunity to practice your needlework skills."

Birdie pondered the offer. Although she was a little fearful of Mrs. Prescott, the opportunity was a tough one to pass up. Plus, she'd be closer to Johnny! "Okay, Miss Sutton, I'll do it. When do I start up there?"

"Splendid!" Iris exclaimed. "Mrs. Prescott would like you to start tomorrow morning at 7." Birdie nodded that she understood as Miss Sutton continued, "Now Brigid, there are a few things you need to know before you start working for the Prescott family. First of all, you answer directly to Mrs. Prescott and no one else. Mr. Prescott might own the hotel and we all must obey his every directive when it comes to the Montclair, but it is Mrs. Prescott who runs their private household."

"Secondly, even though everyone who works at the Montclair must maintain discretion when it comes to the affairs of the clients, when you are working in the Prescott household, this rule is very strictly enforced. You must never divulge anything you might see or hear during your employment as the Prescott's personal housemaid. You must stay blind, deaf, and of course invisible. Do you understand, Brigid?"

"Yes ma'am," replied Birdie.

"And most important of all," warned Iris, "Never put yourself in a situation where you'll be alone with Master Prescott." Birdie snapped to attention at the mention of Johnny. "Master Prescott is an affable and charming man. But...em ...he can sometimes be inclined to overstep social boundaries."

"Uh...yes ma'am," replied Birdie as she wondered what Miss Sutton meant.

"Okay, as long as you accept the position and are agreeable to the rules, there is nothing left to do but find you a new uniform." Iris went over to one of the many clothing racks that lined her office and pulled out a formal looking black dress, a long white pinafore apron and a white cap. After instructing Birdie to report to Alma, the Prescott's head housemaid, she dismissed her and returned to her desk, rubbing her temples.

She felt somewhat guilty having to send that poor girl up to work for Lottie Prescott. Luckily Brigid will only have to withstand the woman for a few more weeks. Shame, the girl was a hard worker and could easily become a permanent employee if she so desired. Iris had never seen anyone move up the ranks so quickly. As long as she stays on the right side of Mrs. Prescott and avoids the young Master Prescott, she'll be all right.

My poor, dear Mr. Prescott! Running a hotel and putting up with such a family certainly can't be easy!

After receiving her new uniform from Miss Sutton, Birdie went to collect the rest of her things from the mudroom and found a small beautiful bouquet of yellow roses, identical to the one Johnny wore today. She smiled as she gently brushed the yellow rosebuds across her cheek. Is this what Miss Sutton meant by 'overstepping social boundaries'? If so, Birdie couldn't understand what was wrong with it.

As she walked outside and headed for home, she went mused over the day's events - a kiss and flowers from Johnny, a promotion courtesy of Johnny's mother and, best of all, learning that Newt's middle name was Cuthbert. She giggled aloud as she walked towards King Street.

Chapter 7

Hortensia was overjoyed when Birdie informed her about the promotion to the Prescott suite. This was more than she could have ever hoped for. Birdie working for none other than the owner of the hotel himself. Just wait until she saw Della Compton and give her the good news! After all, if it weren't for Della recommending Birdie in the first place, none of this would have been possible. She also couldn't wait to brag about it after church next Sunday during the altar guild meeting. She was so tired hearing Beulah Clark bragging about her daughter's upcoming wedding. Now Hortensia could boast that her own daughter was sought after by one of the richest families in town.

Only one thing still nagged at Hortensia and that was Birdie's insistence on returning to school. As far as her mother was concerned, there was really no need for that when she had an opportunity to become part of the Montclair staff. Certainly, an education was important but what more could she possibly learn? She already knew how to read, write and cipher. Wasn't that enough for any girl? This was a constant source of friction between them.

Just an hour before, Birdie had bristled when Hortensia had yet again raised the subject of leaving school and going to work.

"Ma, why can't I make you understand that I simply want to finish the education I started when I was six? Why go through 11 years of schoolin' only to quit just before I get my diploma? It doesn't make any sense!"

Hortensia had countered with, "But what more is there for them to teach you? You are just wasting time there when you could be out earning real money."

"But ma, I have plenty of time to earn money later. It's just one more term of school! Why are you makin' such a fuss?" Birdie had practically shouted.

"First of all, watch your tone, Birdie," scolded Hortensia. "And the one making a fuss here is you."

Birdie ended up retiring to her bedroom early. Hortensia was now in her own room changing into her night clothes. Before she got into bed, she knelt to say her evening prayers. This time she added, "And please Lord, I pray that Birdie changes her mind about school and decides to keep the job." She'll also be discussing the situation with Patrick afterwards.

When Birdie arrived at the Prescott suite, the first thing which struck her was the white, blue and gold color scheme which created an overall feeling of cold formality. The furniture was all French Provincial with polar blue velveteen upholstery. Large ornate glass chandeliers hung from the ceiling while expensive European rugs covered the floors. Like the lady of the household, the decor was well turned out but not very inviting.

Alma, on the other hand, was very warm and welcoming. An older, plump woman originally from Puerto Rico, she was pleased to have Birdie to talk to. Martine, the Prescott's part time cook, spent the short time she was there in the kitchen. Violet Holmes was as snooty as her mistress and Thomas, Prescott's coach driver, stayed downstairs in his own lodgings.

While the Prescotts were still in their rooms getting dressed, Alma took the opportunity to give Birdie a quick tour of the suite before starting the day's chores. The first stop was the kitchen, which was basically a much smaller version of the one downstairs right down to the black and white tile floor. However, unlike the cheerful noisy chaos of Rita's kitchen, this one was as quiet as a cathedral. A short thin woman was poaching eggs atop the shiny black iron stove. She greeted

Birdie with a thick French accent after being introduced by Alma. "Allo Brigid. Bienvenue!"

Just off the kitchen was the dining room which featured a massive white table covered with a gold damask cloth. It was set with glistening crystal glassware and white bone china with a beautiful pink and lavender floral motif. Birdie couldn't imagine putting food over something so lovely, but she supposed that rich people were so used to things like pretty china that they no longer noticed it after a while.

Before they returned to the front parlor, Alma showed Birdie where the housekeeping cupboard was. After they took out the cleansers, polishes and cloths they needed, they went to work in the parlor. Dusting was very important in this household full of lots of vases, lamps, figurines, and ceiling fixtures comprised of hundreds of individual teardrop shaped pieces of glass.

Noticing a door on the far side of the parlor, Birdie's curiosity was aroused. "Alma," she asked, "where does this door go to?"

"That leads to Master Johnny's rooms in the adjoining suite," Alma responded as she climbed a small stepladder to reach the parlor's chandelier. "He wakes up late, so we do those rooms last."

Still feeling where his lips had touched her a couple of days ago, Birdie's heart leapt. Johnny was just behind that door! Wait until he sees me working up here today, she thought as she happily started her polishing.

Footsteps sounded in the corridor which were soon revealed to be Mr. Prescott's. As he entered the living room, Alma quickly descended from the step ladder, bowed slightly and said, "Good morning, Mr. Prescott."

"Good morning, Alma," he replied before noticing Birdie standing in the corner.

Birdie copied Alma and bowed, "Good morning, Mr. Prescott."

The puzzled man just gave Birdie a curt nod before heading into the dining room.

Until then, Birdie had never seen Prescott close up. She only saw him from far away whenever she was outside, and he would be giving horticultural instructions to Isaiah, Newt and the others. Johnny definitely favored his father as far as looks go. Although the elder Prescott's hair was thin and greying, Birdie could see the strong resemblance.

Another set of footsteps announced the arrival of Mrs. Prescott, resplendent in a pretty mint green dress trimmed with ecru lace and accented with a topaz brooch. Her freshly coiffed hair sported a few ringlets at her greying temples.

Alma and Brigid both curtsied and greeted Mrs. Prescott in unison. Lottie's eyebrows arched when she saw Birdie.

"Ah, Brigid, is it? Welcome to our household. I trust that Alma has been showing you where things are."

"Yes ma'am," replied Birdie. Alma inwardly winced at what she knew was about to come next.

"First thing you must learn, Brigid, is that we stand on formality in this household. You are only to address me as Mrs. Prescott and not 'ma'am.' Is that clear?"

"Yes Mrs. Prescott," said Birdie, who despite feeling her cheeks burning with shame, maintained an emotionless expression.

"Very good. Alma, make sure that Brigid changes the linens in Johnny's room once he leaves for his tennis game later. I also left some mending for her with Violet, and please do something about these scuff marks by the front door. They're driving me mad." And with that, she was off to join her husband in the dining room.

Alma went back to the housekeeping closet to find something to remove the offending scuff marks. Birdie continued dusting the front parlor when she heard Mr. Prescott's voice from the dining room. "Would you mind telling me why the hell we have another maid? Exactly how many do we need up here?"

Remembering Mrs. Sutton's warning to stay blind, deaf and invisible, Birdie cowered as she ran her cloth over a porcelain figurine of a girl on a swing. It was awfully hard to stay deaf at the moment when the man who owned the hotel was obviously not pleased to see her in his own living quarters

"I'll thank you to keep your voice down, Johnathan! The servants do not need to hear our dirty laundry. As it happens, her name is Brigid and she was already working here at the Montclair. I figured that Alma could use some assistance."

"No," retorted Prescott, "I don't buy that. Alma is perfectly capable of looking after things herself. This place isn't that big, for Christ's sake! There's another reason you wanted this girl. Let me guess - Lavinia just took on another maid and now you have to have one, too?"

"How dare you accuse me of being so petty!" cried Lottie. "If you must know, Brigid possesses excellent needle skills. The alterations she did to that horrid dress of Myrtle's that made it look almost new was miraculous!"

"Oh, I see," replied Prescott, "You have been hounding me for weeks to hire a personal dressmaker for you and because I put my foot down and said 'no', you decided to get a little creative and recruit this poor girl under false pretenses, so you can take advantage of her sewing skills while only paying her a junior maid's wage so that I won't fuss about it. There's a word for that, Lottie, and it is 'exploitation.' And I won't have it."

Birdie's eyes widened as her fingers tightly gripped the dusting rag. At that moment, she wished more than anything for the floor to open up and swallow her, so desperate was she to escape.

Prescott wasn't finished with his harangue. "It's already bad enough that you have that Holmes woman back there who does nothing but dress and undress you like some member of the British royal family. This is America, Lottie, where we proudly do things ourselves! Why do you think I immediately fired that ridiculous valet you insisted I have? I can put on my own goddamned pants!"

"Please don't swear, Johnathan," scolded Lottie. "I'll have you know that Violet does more than dress me. She does my hair, keeps my jewels safe and is my confidante and constant companion. If it wasn't for her, I'd not dare set foot into this wretched town full of ruffians, drunkards and ne'er do wells."

"No ruffian, drunkard or ne'er do well would ever think of crossing swords with you, my dear," Prescott said gruffly. The sound of paper rustling signaled that he had once again ended the conversation by disappearing behind today's edition of the Herald.

"Well, I think I'll go downstairs and have breakfast with Myrtle and Olivia instead. They'll make for much nicer company!" cried Lottie.

The sound of her chair scraping back made Birdie jump. Hoping not to get caught in the parlor where she would obviously have overheard this discourse, Birdie hurried down the hall and found Alma on her hands and knees, trying to rub the scuff marks off the floor of the foyer.

"Uh...I'm all done with the dusting, Alma. What shall I be doin' next?" Birdie asked.

The sound of Mrs. Prescott's heeled shoes could be heard furiously clacking down the hallway. "Violet!" she bellowed. "Get me my wrap. I'm going downstairs to visit Myrtle!"

Alma, who was used to these daily shouting matches over the breakfast table, had long ago learned to tune them out. However, she could sense that Birdie was uncomfortable with the situation and softly said, "Why don't you go help Martine clean up in the kitchen until both of them leave. Then we can start on the dining room and bedrooms."

As the scullery maids and the grounds men sat down to their breakfast, Tangie filled them in on Birdie's new assignment on the top floor. Eva was shocked. "I can't believe it! But I am happy for Birdie."

Isaiah couldn't fathom it either. "I ain't never heard o' no one goin' from scrubbin' the kitchen all the way up to workin' directly fo' the boss so fast!" Although he'd only know Birdie a month, he felt an almost fatherly pride.

"Hmmph..." Tangie was skeptical. "We'll see how long Miss Too-Big-Fo'-Her-Britches lasts upstairs!"

"Now Tangie," admonished Isaiah, "ain't no need fo' dat kinda talk."

"You didn't see the way she carried on in the staff dinin' room yesterday. Didn't even nod or look at her friend Ella here!"

Newt had been as shocked as everyone else when he learned of Birdie's promotion to the Prescott suite. The only thing he felt was sadness that he'd probably see even less of her now as the Prescott staff tended to keep to themselves.

Noticing that Ella had remained silent during the discussion, he leaned over and asked, "What do you make o' all this?"

Ella looked at Newt. She'd only known him for a couple of days, but she sensed that he was a decent fellow. She even felt that she could trust him which was something she'd never thought she could say about a white man. She replied, "I don't like it, Newt. I got a bad feelin' in my gut. Not only is she changin', but she says that the young Mista Johnny had been sniffin' 'round her when she started upstairs, and now she's in his livin' quarters! No sir, I don't like it one bit!"

Newt said nothing. Lately he'd been hearing rumors about the real story behind Johnny's trip to New York. He gritted his teeth as he thought of the younger Prescott being near Birdie. The knuckles on his right hand went white as he tightly gripped his fork.

Johnny emerged from his room around 9:00, freshly shaven and looking resplendent in his new tennis outfit which consisted of a short sleeve white cotton shirt over white twill trousers. He set his tennis racket by his door as he headed to the dining room.

"Mmmm. Whatever's in that oven smells divine, Mademoiselle Martine!" he shouted as he sat at the table and grabbed a napkin. To his shock, it was Birdie who emerged from the kitchen and brought him his plate.

"Birdie! What are you doing here?" Johnny asked incredulously. "Don't tell me that you're the new maid my mother was talking about?"

"'Fraid so!" answered Birdie as she placed the warm plate on the table.

"I must say...:" remarked Johnny as he glanced up and down at Birdie, "the new uniform certainly suits you."

"Thank you, Johnny," said Birdie. "Now you eat up before that gets cold. I got some work to do."

As she started to leave the dining room, Johnny suddenly grabbed Birdie's hand and dragged her down into his lap. Before Birdie could react, he planted a swift kiss on her neck. "Welcome to the Prescott household, my sweet little Birdie," he murmured.

"Oh Johnny, don't! Alma or Violet might come in." Birdie whispered in reproach. Though she must admit, she felt both excited if not a bit fearful at his touch.

"Don't worry, my dear," Johnny said with mock arrogance. "No one here will bother you as long as I am around. You might work for my mother, but you are all mine.

It was 10:30 by the time Johnny had left for his tennis game and the Prescott's rooms were cleaned. Johnny's suite was next.

Birdie excitedly opened the door from the Prescott's parlor, eagerly waiting to see what his rooms looked like. She was actually a little disappointed to see that they really did not look much different from those in the rest of the hotel. The front parlor had the usual burgundy print wallpaper, the dark green settee with maroon wing chairs, and the small floral print Persian rug that she'd seen in other rooms. Other than a few expensive paintings and a couple of sculptures, she could have been standing in any other room in the Montclair.

Remembering Mrs. Prescott's instructions, Birdie entered the bedroom to change the linens. Just as the parlor, the bedroom differed little from the others at the Montclair. The only difference was that Johnny slept here. Feeling a bit wicked, Birdie sat on the bed. She sighed deeply as she imagined him sleeping on the very sheets she was now caressing and bringing up to her nose to breathe in his delicious aroma.

Waking herself up from her daydream, Birdie methodically stripped the bed and tossed the linens in the basket she had brought with her which already contained laundry from the other rooms. While the bed airs out, she'll make the trip out to the laundry wagon.

Due to several construction snags, the laundry room which was planned for downstairs was not as yet ready. So, an outside laundry service was contracted which came out to the Montclair daily to deliver clean linens and take away the soiled ones. The chambermaids had to carry their laundry baskets down to a long wagon which was parked on the west side of the property. Because it was kept out of sight of the guests, this meant a fairly long walk for the maids and their heavy loads.

"I'll be right back, Alma. I'm just taking the laundry downstairs." Birdie called out before leaving. As she slowly carried her basket down the backstairs she was pleased to see Mavis on the landing, holding the 3rd floor door open for Hannah and Ruth who were both carrying their own laundry baskets.

"Birdie!" cried Mavis. "How is it going up there? I was never got a chance to say congratulations."

"Thank you, Miss Kinkade. Things are going well so far," replied Birdie.

"That's good to hear. If you have any problems, don't hesitate to come and find me," Mavis said sincerely. She knew what a hard taskmaster Mrs. Prescott could be and wanted Birdie to know that she could count on her for support should the need arise.

"Thank you, Miss Kinkade. Much obliged," responded Birdie as she continued downstairs.

Hannah and Ruth exchanged looks of disgust as they followed her.

One by one, the three girls continued down the back stairs and out the hotel's side service door. It was a typical August afternoon - hot, sticky and damp - which made the dirty laundry smell even worse. Birdie couldn't wait to be rid of it.

As the maids walked by the reflecting pool and crossed through the arbor to get to the laundry wagon, they spotted Newt who was about five hundred yards away, digging an irrigation trench. When he spotted the trio, he politely tipped his torn straw hat to them. Birdie was about to wave back when Hannah smirked and remarked to Ruth, "Ugh! How would you like to wake up under THAT each morning?"

Ruth wrinkled up her nose. "Eww. That's not even funny, Hannah. He's got to be the ugliest thing on two legs."

Birdie silently burned as her jaw tightly clenched and her hands firmly clasped the handles of the basket. How dare they say something so vile about someone as kind, pleasant and hard working as Newt?

Hannah devilishly smiled as she sweetly said, "Well, I'm sure Birdie might disagree with you. Right Birdie? I saw you two together yesterday laughing like you hadn't a care in the world. You fancy him, don't you Birdie? You might think you're above us all now working up in the Prescott suite but we all know you really want to be Newt's wife and have a dozen ugly little red haired octaroon babies with him! Oh, can you even imagine what those poor little creatures would look like, Ruth?"

Birdie glared at Hannah as she retorted, "You better hush your mouth, Hannah! Newt's just a friend, is all." Although Birdie wouldn't be caught dead with someone like Newt, she felt disloyal by allowing this verbal attack to continue. Besides, her heart belonged to Johnny. She couldn't wait to see their shocked faces when they found out who her true admirer really was!

By now they were at the tail gate of the wagon and each girl emptied her basket into it. Birdie tossed hers in with more force than usual.

On their way back to the hotel, Ruth picked up where they had left off. "I don't blame you for being angry, Birdie," she said in mock sympathy. "If someone tried to link me together with Newt Phillips, I would kill myself first."

"I think Birdie would be a good match for him, and I'm sure Newt Phillips would like to bed something on two legs for a change." Hannah replied.

As both girls howled with laughter, Birdie's anger boiled into a blinding rage. At that moment they happened to be skirting around the reflecting pool, which had narrow walkways around it. Birdie steamed ahead and pushed past Hannah and Ruth, causing them to their balance and fall into the water.

Both girls screamed which caught the attention of Felipe and Newt.

Spitting out water, Hannah caught her breath and spluttered, "You half breed bitch!!"

Felipe grabbed Ruth by the arm and helped her out of the pool. "Much obliged," she said brusquely as she brushed him off.

However, when Newt waded into the pool to help Hannah, she screamed again and slapped at him.

"Don't touch me, you filthy dirt farmer!" spat Hannah, slowly pulling her soaked body out of the reflecting pool. As she stomped over to Birdie, who was standing with her arms crossed and glowering, Hannah hissed, "I swear I'll get you back for this!" Then she and Ruth both trudged back to the Montclair, wringing out their skirts.

Newt, who was stunned over the spectacle and still standing in the water, looked up at Birdie, stone-faced and breathing hard.

"You okay, Birdie? Whatcha do that fer?" As he climbed out of the pool and approached her, Birdie just shook her head and walked away.

As he and Felipe watched the women making their way back to the hotel, Newt took off his hat and ran his fingers through his sweaty hair.

"Felipe, as long as I live, I will never understand womenfolk." Felipe shook his head in commiseration.

Chapter 8

Over the next few weeks, Birdie slowly got acclimated to the routine and idiosyncrasies of life in the Prescott household. For instance, she learned that Mr. and Mrs. Prescott started almost every morning with an argument. The most recent quarrel began over chewing.

Mrs. Prescott started things off by remarking, “Must you do that?”

Johnathan Prescott looked up from the spinach and cheese omelet he was enjoying, his mouth still full of egg. After swallowing, he asked, “What in tarnation are you grousing about now?”

“Do you realize that you grunt whenever you chew? It’s really off-putting, Johnathan, not to mention gauche!” Lottie said disapprovingly.

“Oh, I am so sorry, dearest,“ Prescott mocked, “You see, I was just savoring this delectable meal which your French cook so expertly prepared for us. You really should try it sometime instead of cramming everything into your mouth and swallowing after only three bites. I’ve never seen anyone else eat like that. You’re like a damn crocodile!”

Lottie countered with, “Well that’s fine talk coming from a Cracker cowboy who’s more at home around manure than manners!”

Throwing his morning newspaper down on the table with vigor, Prescott stood up and left a parting shot as he exited the dining room. “If I seem more at home around manure, madam, it’s because I’ve had a lot of experience putting up with yours for all these years!”

Like Alma, Birdie became conditioned to take these verbal sparring matches in stride. In fact, some of Mr. Prescott’s insults were sometimes so funny that Birdie had to bite her tongue hard to keep from giggling.

She actually grew to like Mr. Prescott, as did the rest of the staff. He was a no-nonsense type of man who valued thrift, simplicity and common sense. He even stopped questioning Birdie's presence in the household and came to appreciate her excellent work ethic.

One evening as she was getting ready to depart, Mr. Prescott was in the front parlor quietly sipping an after-dinner glass of brandy while enjoying a tome from one of his favorite authors, Mark Twain, someone with whom he felt a deep kinship.

"Good night, Mister Prescott," said Birdie as she started for the door.

"Ah, Brigid, is it? Please come here."

Birdie was dumbfounded as she stepped into the parlor. Whatever could Mr. Prescott want with her? Was there something wrong? Had he noticed the mutual attraction between her and his son?

"Brigid, I know that most folks in this business, my wife included, usually only speak to their staff to dispatch orders or to point out what they did wrong. I am a staunch believer of pointing out to my staff what they are doing right. And you, Miss Fairfax, seem to be doing everything right. You complete all your tasks in a timely manner, you seem to be keeping my wife happy with your needlework and you have a pleasant demeanor. Although I initially questioned Mrs. Prescott about taking on another maid, this is one of the rare decisions of hers which I feel was justified. Thank you for your service, Miss Fairfax. I understand that you will only be with us for another couple of weeks, but if you ever wish to return to the Montclair, please rest assured that there will always be a job here for you."

Birdie was so touched that she felt tears stinging her eyes. Instead, she just said, "Thank you, Mr. Prescott. I appreciate that very much!"

"Good night, Brigid. It's getting dark so mind how you go and we'll see you tomorrow," the old gentleman said before turning his attention back to the copy of "Huckleberry Finn" which laid across his lap.

As for Mrs. Prescott, she was still demanding, fussy and unreasonable at times, but her sincere appreciation for Birdie's sewing talents made her negative traits bearable. She initially had Birdie repair small utilitarian items such as pillow cases and bedsheets. Once she was reassured of Birdie's expert stitch work, Lottie brought out an item that was near and dear to her. It was a thirty-year-old embroidered handkerchief that was once her mother's. The bird and floral design on it had somehow unraveled over the years. The bird and two of the flowers were half gone. Birdie took the handkerchief home and worked on it for a couple of nights. She restored the bird, the flowers and tightened up the rest of the original design so that it wouldn't undo itself again.

Lottie, who rarely displayed sincere emotion in front of her staff, cried like a little girl when Birdie presented her with the handkerchief. It transported her back to Pittsburgh, her youth and her beloved mother. "Thank you," was all Mrs. Prescott could trust herself to say.

After that, Lottie started assigning Birdie wardrobe related tasks. One day she brought Birdie to her changing room and brought out a lovely light blue silk ball gown. It must have been at least twenty or twenty-five years old.

"This gown is one I wore to a gubernatorial inauguration ball shortly after I married Mr. Prescott. He used to say it was his favorite out of all my dresses because it suited my complexion," Lottie said proudly. As she held the dress up in front of her, she seemed to be transported back to a happier, carefree time. She went on, "Our twenty-fifth wedding anniversary is coming up and I'd like to wear this again. However, as you can see, it is now woefully out of date. Do you think you can alter it so that it looks a bit more fashionable? The dress still actually fits me so at least you won't have to worry about having to let anything out."

Lottie handed the dress over to Birdie, who carefully studied it as she pulled out the voluminous skirt which was meant to be worn over a large hoop. Luckily there was so much extra fabric in the skirt that it could easily be taken out and used elsewhere on the dress. The sleeves and the neckline would definitely need to be altered. "It's going to need lots of work, Mrs. Prescott. When do you need it by?" asked Birdie.

"Not for a few weeks," replied Mrs. Prescott. "In fact, I'll cut down on your household chores so you can devote more time to the alteration, and I'll give you extra financial compensation. Is that reasonable?"

As she glanced at Mrs. Prescott's anxious face, Birdie felt a flash of sympathy for the poor woman who seemed so desperate to regain her husband's admiration. "Yes, Mrs. Prescott. I'll get started this afternoon."

For the next ten days, Birdie worked diligently on the blue silk, cutting down and reshaping the skirt to a more modern line with a bit of a train on the back. Puffy short sleeves replaced the longer originals. Birdie also squared the neckline and trimmed it with some of the cream-colored lace that she took from the old sleeves. The end result was a lovely, fashionable dress which looked stunning on Lottie Prescott when she tried it on, bringing on more tears. And best of all, it didn't cost Mr. Prescott a lot of money, other than the overtime owed to Birdie.

Johnny Prescott was becoming more and more forward with Birdie, particularly during the final week of her employ. The kisses on the hand and forehead which used to send Birdie into girlish ecstasy soon became full on kisses on the lips or wandering hands over bodice of Birdie's uniform.

One morning, as Birdie was in the process of stripping the linens from his bed, she felt a pair of arms slip around her waist which startled her as she believed she was the only one in the suite. Alma was bringing the laundry downstairs and Martine had gone out food shopping. Johnny was supposed to be sailing with a couple of friends down from Jacksonville.

"Hello, my sweet Birdie," his breath was hot in her ear. "Looks like it's just you and me. Whatever shall we do?" He turned her towards him and started kissing her on the lips as his hands cupped her buttocks.

"Johnny, no. We can't do this!" Birdie whispered fearfully. "Besides, what if Alma comes back?"

"It so happens," began Johnny as his hands moved from her buttocks up front to her breasts, "that I just now saw her talking to Mavis Kinkade in the hallway and it looks like they were heading downstairs."

"Johnny, please don't," begged Birdie. The hairs on the back of her neck were standing up as she perceived a great sense of danger lurking over her.

Johnny started to bite Birdie playfully on the neck and whispered, "Aw, come on, Birdie. You know how I feel about you and I know you feel the same. You've been wanting this from the moment we met." He pushed Birdie onto the mattress. As Johnny climbed on top of her, he reached under her skirt and slowly slid his hand up her thigh.

"No!" screamed Birdie, as she instinctively lifted up her knee and jabbed it hard into Johnny's groin causing him to curse and strike her across the face, breaking open her lip.

"You black whore! You tease me for weeks and now that we're finally alone, you decide to play the chaste virgin role. You're pretty damned lucky that I'm a gentleman and will forget this incident. Anyone else would've had their way with you regardless. Thank God you're leaving. Until then, stay the hell out of my way or you'll be sorry!" Getting up from the mattress, he straightened up his clothing and slammed the door on his way out.

Birdie, stupefied from the unexpected assault, was still laying on the mattress. Ella was right. Johnny was up to no good. Why didn't she listen! Wrapping her arms around herself, she silently wept.

Chapter 9

Later that afternoon, Hannah was just closing up the 4th floor housekeeping closet when she noticed Johnny Prescott, looking windblown and tanned, stumbling up the hallway. He had obviously been on one of his infamous alcoholic binges because he was now attempting to open one of the 4th floor guest rooms with the key to his own suite.

A sly smile crept over Hannah's face as an idea formed. Knowing that this particular room was unoccupied, she cheerfully said, "Hello Master Prescott. Are you having problems getting into your suite? Let me help."

Johnny Prescott looked at her blearily and mumbled something unintelligible as Hannah opened the door. "There you go, sir. You just get yourself into bed and I'll bring you a night cap."

"That's my good girl." slurred Johnny as he almost fell into the room.

"I'll be right back," cooed Hannah as she shut the door.

A few minutes later, the rest of her plan fell into place when Birdie, who was leaving for the day, came down the back stairs.

Hannah called, "Birdie! I was just on my way upstairs to look for you!"

Birdie frowned and wondered why Hannah of all people would be looking for her, especially as they'd been keeping their respective distance from each other since the reflecting pool incident. "Why? What's happened?" she asked.

"There's a woman in 425 who's very upset. She is supposed to be going to that fundraising ball over at the Ponce de Leon tonight but the lace on the neckline of the dress she plans to wear is torn. Apparently, Mrs. Prescott told her to ask you to fix it."

Birdie, whose lip was still swollen, silently groaned. It had really been a trying day and the last thing she needed was this unexpected crisis to make it longer. Oh well, if the lace just came off at the seam, it would probably be a quick repair job.

"You said she's in 425?" asked Birdie. Hannah nodded and suppressed a grin as Birdie headed for the door. She was getting ready to knock and announce "housekeeping" when Hannah interrupted her.

"The lady is in her dressing gown. She said that you were to go on in and head straight to the bedroom where she's waiting for you."

As Birdie went inside and shut the door, Hannah smiled. The thought of Birdie getting caught in a hotel room with Johnathan Prescott, Jr. would be grounds for immediate dismissal. Sure, she'll blame Hannah for luring her there but who's going to believe her?

"I told that bitch I'd get her back for what she did!" Hannah said softly as she hurried downstairs to search for Mavis.

Birdie pushed open the bedroom door.

"Housekeeping," she said. "Hello, ma'am. I'm here to fix your dress." As she peered into the room, she didn't see anyone until Johnny came out of the adjoining lavatory.

Each one was in a momentary state of shock at seeing the other. However, as Birdie made a move back to the door, Johnny was quicker and caught her by the wrist.

"So, you're here to fix a dress, eh?" he growled "I don't see any dresses in need of repair in here. Do you? But we can easily fix that!" And with a quick flourish, he tore open her bodice, exposing her corset. Birdie screamed as loud as she could before he clapped a hand over her mouth and pushed her onto the bed. Reaching into his pocket, he took out a handkerchief, wadded it up and stuffed it into Birdie's mouth.

Birdie tried to claw and scratch at him, but he quickly overpowered her. Restraining both of her hands with one of his, he used his free hand to rip open her corset and chemise, exposing her bare chest. Repulsed by his hands and his lips on her breasts, Birdie started to scream again but the gag in her mouth prevented her from making anything louder than a muffled moan.

Feeling his hand pulling down her drawers, Birdie panicked and kicked wildly but now his entire body was weighing her down and she was an open target. Soon she felt a sharp pain rip through her crotch and she howled in agony. Each thrust felt like another knife being sunk deep into her.

When he was through, Johnny stood, pulled up his pants and put his jacket back on. "Let this be a lesson to you. Don't ever tease a man, Birdie, or else you deserve what comes to you." Birdie waited until she heard him slam the front door shut before she moved.

Her hair had come loose and hung wildly over her shoulders. She had blood coming from her lip from where Johnny had hit her earlier that morning, and her face was splotched with red marks from the slapping. Every muscle in her body ached from the exertion of wrestling a man who outweighed her by a good sixty pounds.

She managed to put her undergarments and corset back on, but the bodice of her uniform was tattered, so she tightly wrapped her shawl around her upper body.

Just then she heard a knock at the front door and Mavis' voice. "Housekeeping!" Relieved that it wasn't Johnny, Birdie ran to the door, tore it open and flung herself into Mavis' arms sobbing hysterically.

"Birdie! What on earth happened? Hannah here tells me that she saw you and Master Prescott entering this room together. You know those are grounds for dismissal," Mavis said sternly.

Hannah, who had been standing behind Mavis, looked horrified at the state Birdie was in. She only meant for the situation to look compromising. She never thought that Master Prescott would actually attack Birdie.

Birdie looked at Hannah and shouted, "It was you! You tricked me! You knew he was in there!" She lunged at Hannah, but Mavis held her back.

"Let's take this inside, ladies. There's no sense in putting on a show for our guests out here," said Mavis as she ushered the two girls into the room. As she shut the door, she looked at Birdie and asked, "What happened?"

Birdie told Mavis how Hannah had duped her into entering the room on the pretext of fixing a dress for a fictitious guest only to come face to face with a drunken Johnathan Prescott Jr. She also told her how he had slapped her and sexually assaulted her.

Mavis was mortified. She turned with fury on Hannah. "Hannah Smith, as of this moment you are permanently dismissed. Please give me your pass key. You can return your uniform to Miss Sutton downstairs tomorrow."

Hannah burst into tears. "Miss Kinkade, I never meant for this to happen. Honest! I thought he was too drunk to do anything except pass out on the bed. I'm so sorry!"

"It's too late for excuses and apologies, Hannah. Even if nothing had happened between Master Prescott and Birdie, your original purpose of falsely accusing them of doing something unseemly is still grounds for your dismissal. Now please take your leave."

After Hannah left, Mavis put a protective arm around Birdie. She gently asked, "Did he....um...?"

Birdie wept. "Yes, I think he did."

"Okay," said Mavis, "First thing's first. Let's get you out of this room and do something about this torn uniform. We'll go downstairs and get you a new one, and then you can go home. We can send someone with you if you'd like."

"Can Ella come with me?" asked Birdie. "She works in the kitchen. Please, I need Ella." Birdie started to cry harder.

"Of course," replied Mavis soothingly as she took a lacy handkerchief from her pocket and dabbed Birdie's eyes. "Let's dry your tears and we'll go outside and through the back door to the kitchen. This way we won't have to parade you through the hotel. If you're ready, we'll go."

Newt listened impatiently to Mr. Prescott's instructions about the new irrigation methods he wanted them to start utilizing in the arbor and the vegetable garden. He, Isaiah and the other men had just locked away their gardening tools for the day when the portly hotelier made an unexpected late afternoon appearance. He'd been there for ten minutes already and showed his captive audience no signs of an end to his discourse.

It was almost quitting time and Newt had not seen Birdie all day. In fact, he barely saw her at all over the past couple of weeks - only a quick glimpse of her now and again running laundry downstairs or airing out rugs. Ella had mentioned that this was Birdie's last week, and Newt hoped to see her at least once more before she was gone for good.

As Prescott droned on about water sources, Newt's attention shifted to some faraway movement behind the old man's left shoulder. Two women had emerged from the side service door of the hotel. One had her arm protectively around the other, who looked like she was crying. Why, that was Birdie! What was wrong, Newt wondered. Were those other two gals riling her up again? He wished with all his might that Prescott would stop talking and let them go so that he could rush over and see what was wrong, and put his own arm around her.

Tangie, Ella and Eva were surprised to see Miss Sutton rush into in the scullery as they were sorting the china and silverware for the evening's dinner service. Although she occasionally visited Rita in the kitchen, she never made her way to their little room in the corner.

The head housekeeper addressed Ella in a serious and urgent tone. "Miss Patterson, will you please escort Miss Fairfax home this evening? She has met with an unfortunate incident and needs your company. You may have the rest of today off and you will be compensated for it. You will find Miss Fairfax waiting for you in the mudroom. Good evening, Miss Patterson."

"Yes ma'am. Good evenin', Miss Sutton." Ella took off her apron and swiftly departed, curious as to what could be wrong.

Iris Sutton turned to Tangie and Eva. "I'm sure you both can cope without Miss Patterson for one evening."

"Yes ma'am," they both said in unison.

"Good. I'll see you at the staff dinner later, then." Iris headed back to her office, leaving behind the two perplexed kitchen maids. Tangie in particular was peeved.

"Once again, we have to work late because of Miss High-n-Mighty," she grumbled as she opened the silverware chest and started sorting out the utensils.

As soon as Ella saw Birdie and her injuries, she knew that Johnathan Prescott, Jr. was behind it.

"He did somethin', didn't he?" Ella asked.

"Oh Ella, you were right about Johnny. Everything you said!" Birdie started to weep.

"Let's get away from here first. We'll take a walk by the shore and you'll tell me everything. Okay?" Birdie nodded in agreement as both girls set forth towards the bay.

Upon returning to Miss Sutton's office, both Iris and Mavis sat down, trying to make sense of what happened that afternoon and how they were to go forth.

"It's an awful business, Iris. What do we do now?" asked Mavis. "In reality, Master Prescott committed a crime. Are we to get the Sheriff involved?"

Iris pinched the bridge of her nose. "On one hand I agree with you, Mavis. Especially given the fact that this is not the first transgression of this kind committed by Master Prescott. That is why I specifically warned Miss Fairfax to take measures not to be alone with that young man. Did she happen to tell you if he...uh...?"

"Yes, he did," answered Mavis, "which begs another question. What happens if there should be a child involved later on?"

Iris shuddered. "On the other hand, if word gets out about any of this, the repercussions would be devastating. The Prescotts would be ruined both socially and financially, the hotel would go under leaving all of us unemployed and, worst of all, it could prove fatal to Mr. Prescott who is not in the best of health as it is."

"I suppose you're right, Iris," admitted Mavis. "All we can do now is to be practical. Birdie was going to leave at the end of the week anyway, so we'll just tell Mrs. Prescott that a family emergency necessitated her leaving a few days earlier."

"Yes," said Iris. "And we'll need to take measures to keep this nasty business quiet. Besides you, myself and Miss Patterson, who else knows right now?"

"Only Hannah Smith, who as you are aware, instigated the whole mess and was terminated on the spot. She seemed pretty shaken up and even repentant about what happened. So, I don't think she'll be an issue. She's too ashamed of herself right now."

Iris seemed placated. "That's fine then. I don't believe Miss. Patterson will be keen to spread the word about her friend's traumatic experience. So hopefully that should take care of the gossip."

"But what about Master Prescott? As you said previously, word has it that this isn't the first time he's been involved in something like this. What's to be done about him?" asked Mavis.

"Hmmmmm, what indeed?" echoed Iris.

By the time Mr. Prescott finally released the groundskeepers to go home that afternoon, Birdie had long since departed so Newt never did get to find out what was wrong. The next day, he resolved that he was going to find a way to speak to her at some point come hell or high water.

There was no sign of Birdie that morning either so by the time Ella and the other women came out with breakfast, Newt was getting pretty anxious.

Taking Ella aside, Newt asked, "What was wrong with Birdie yesterday? I was talkin' to Mr. Prescott and saw her outta the corner o' my eye. She looked like she was cryin'."

Ella looked at Newt for a moment as she decided whether or not she should betray her friend's secret trauma. She was always devoted to Birdie and took care not to betray any trust that her friend had instilled in her. However, she'd also grown fond of Newt over the past few weeks. He was a decent man who obviously adored Birdie. Ella noticed it the first day she met him at the sea wall. He never took his eyes off her friend the entire time. Ella wished that the blinders would come off Birdie's eyes, so she could see it too.

"Please Ella," implored Newt," I know somethin's wrong. Please tell me. Maybe I can help her."

Ella's eyes narrowed. "I think maybe you can help, Newt. Someone has hurt our girl real bad and needs to be taught a good lesson." Ella then proceeded to tell Newt the entire story which Birdie had revealed the day before during their walk on the beach.

Chapter 10

Johnny awoke with a dull headache after a long night of drinking and dancing at the Ponce de Leon. He and his friend Nash Barton had picked up a couple of willing young ladies who entertained them well into the early morning hours. Johnny looked over at the clock and saw that it was 10 am. At least his parents would be gone by now. He thought he heard Iris Sutton and his mother in the parlor a little while ago. Iris had said something about Birdie being called away and not coming back to the Montclair. Of course, his mother did not take the news very well and started shouting something about "ungrateful servants."

Oh well, at least he didn't have Birdie to contend with any more. Johnny slowly raised himself from his bed. His back felt like it was on fire. As he shuffled over to the full-length mirror in the corner of the room, Johnny turned around, lifted up his pajama top and twisted slightly to one side to get a better look at all the red scratch marks which lacerated his back.

Unlike his father who flew into a rage at the drop of a hat, particularly when drunk, Newt Phillips had always prided himself on being a fair, easy going sort who fought only in self-defense or when necessary. Today it was of the absolute necessity.

His blood had been boiling since Ella revealed to him the details of Birdie's attack. He had heard of blind fury before but never understood it until now. Although he went through the motions of his daily chores out on the grounds, he couldn't see or think of anything else other than killing Johnny Prescott with his bare hands. Every stab with the spade was a knife into that cad's heart. Every furrow Newt dug was Johnny's grave.

The opportunity finally presented itself shortly after 11:00 when Johnny made his regular morning appearance at the groundskeeper shed to ask for whatever was blooming that day. Isaiah, who was repairing a trellis in the vegetable garden saw him first and started to proceed towards the shack. However, Newt, who had also seen young Master Prescott approaching, ran towards Isaiah and, feigning a cheerful eagerness, said, "Don't worry yerself, Isaiah. I'll take care of it!" Isaiah nodded and went back to his task while Newt marched over to the groundskeeper shed with an unblinking eye on Johnny who was making his way inside.

Newt quietly crossed the threshold and shut the door behind him. Johnny looked up, puzzled by the closed door. "Ah, Phillips! What have you got for me today?"

"Here's what I got for ya!" Johnny roared as he drew his fist back and punched Johnny Prescott square in the nose.

"What the hell...." Johnny managed to splutter before Newt hauled off and threw a second punch, this one landing on Johnny's left jaw.

By now the junior Prescott was in full self-defense mode and start to strike back at Newt, once in his right eye and another just under his ribcage. At one point the two men were locked in a hold and after pushing each other back and forth, they both rolled onto the table which broke under their combined weight. Johnny, who was a bit heavier than Newt, managed to get atop him. "What the hell's wrong with you? Have you lost your damned mind?" he asked as he fought for breath.

"Ya know what ya did, ya sonofabitch! Ya hurt Birdie." Newt hollered as he used every last ounce of his strength to throw Prescott off of him. As his opponent fell backwards, Newt jumped on him and started pummeling Johnny across the face. "Enjoy beatin' up ladies, do ya? Time fer a bit o' yer own medicine!"

"That colored bitch was no lady," spat Johnny. "She was always making eyes at me, teasing me. Hell, the only reason she took that job in my family's suite was just to get into my bedroom"

Newt wrapped his hands around's Johnny's throat. "Yer lyin'."

Johnny maliciously grinned and replied, "Believe me - that girl's legs spread easier than butter on hot toast."

"No! Yer lyin and now yer gonna die, ya bastard!!!" Newt tightened his grip on Johnny, who frantically tried to throw him off.

The front door of the shed flung open and Isaiah's heavyset frame filled the doorway. As he took in the scene of the broken table and Newt strangling Prescott, who was starting to turn maroon, Isaiah went into action.

"Newt, no!" he shouted as he tried to pull him away from Johnny. "He ain't worth you goin' to jail. Let 'im go, Newt."

Newt turned to Isaiah with red rimmed eyes and cried, "Ya don't understand. He raped Birdie."

Isaiah momentarily closed his eyes and shook his head. "Lawd have mercy." Then to Newt he repeated, "Let 'im go, Newt. You ain't gonna be helpin' Birdie at all behind bars."

Newt started to loosen his grip on Johnny's collar but still didn't let go. "Yer right Isaiah, killin' him might not help but at least this might." Turning to Johnny, he said menacingly, "Listen up, you sonofabitch. Yer gonna leave town tonight and not come back, ya hear? Several of us know what ya did to Birdie and word spreads purty fast 'round here."

"Who's going to believe the tittle tattle of a bunch of colored and white trash servants?" asked Prescott as he rubbed his neck.

Newt grabbed Johnny by both lapels and growled, "I'll tell ya who! Yer ole man! He's down here with us every day. If you'd have been o' more help to 'im, you'd have known that. Plus, yer pa is already sickly and under a lot of stress. News of yer latest victim might just kill 'im,"

"Are you trying to blackmail, you piece of white trash?" hissed Johnny.

"Oh, no sir. I ain't askin' fer nothin' fer myself. I just want ya to leave town and never come back so's Birdie can feel safe again." Newt explained as Johnny stood up and dusted the soil off his trousers and jacket.

"Do you really think you can oust me from my family's hotel?" asked Johnny mockingly.

"Naw, I have a feelin' that yer ole man will eventually cotton on to what happened, and he'll do it 'imself. Fer now I'll be obliged if ya just stay away from both me and Birdie."

Johnny stood nose to nose with Newt as he hatefully murmured, "I'd rather burn in hell than lay eyes on either one of you two wastes of human lives ever again." Pushing past Isaiah, he stormed out of the shack.

Nursing a glass of brandy as he sat in his favorite wing chair in the parlor, Johnathan Prescott Sr. shook his head as he tried to make sense of the day's occurrences. First the Fairfax girl didn't show up this morning which produced a hysterical tirade from Lottie. Iris Sutton appeared later on and explained that the girl had some family matters to tend to, but his wife was not so easily mollified.

What a damned shame, thought Prescott who had started to grow fond of the girl as did his wife, who had been talking endlessly about a dress that Brigid had fixed up for her which somehow saved him hundreds of dollars for a new one. This made Prescott appreciate the girl all the more.

Then his son appeared at lunch with a bruised and cut up face causing his mother to scream and almost faint. Johnny's explanation about a punch up between himself and some well-heeled swain over a girl he had been dancing with didn't ring true with Prescot.

Now he is talking about going on some fool trip with Nash Barton up to New Orleans to look into the possibility of running one of the casinos up there. This caused a heated argument between father and son as well as hysterics from Lottie.

"What the hell do you mean you're leaving?" Prescott had bellowed when Johnny had revealed his plans. "You only just got back here last month. Why did I even bother sending you to college if you won't be helping me run THIS place?"

"But Pop, I'll be learning a whole new side of the resort trade and will bring that knowledge back here with me." Johnny tried to reason.

"All you will bring back with you are more goddamned gambling debts!" shouted Prescott.

Lottie, who was sobbing into a lace handkerchief, scolded, "Johnathan! Please don't shout and curse. Our son is leaving us again and my nerves are already fraught."

Johnny raised his own voice as he shouted, "That's all right, mother. I'm used to being on the receiving end of his sharp tongue. I'll never be good enough to carry the precious name of Johnathan Prescott, will I? What was that you called me not too long ago? Oh yes, 'the most useless son a man could ever be cursed with'. Well I would think you'd be glad to see me go!" And with that, Johnny stormed out of the suite and had been gone ever since. Lottie was so distraught over the whole situation that she immediately took to her bed, with Violet waiting in attendance.

Prescott heard a door close and footsteps next door in Johnny's room. Now that he had returned, Prescott decided that perhaps it was time to bury the hatchet before the boy left for New Orleans. Although he butted heads a lot with his namesake, he certainly didn't want any bad blood between himself and his son before he departed.

Prescott strode over to the mahogany liquor cabinet and grabbed the crystal brandy decanter along with a couple of glasses. They might as well toast his new venture. Heck, he had no meetings scheduled tomorrow morning, so he could even take Johnny to the train station himself.

Knocking quietly on the door, Prescott entered his son's room. The small front parlor area was empty, but the bedroom door was open. There stood Johnny who was in the middle of changing his shirt - all the scratch marks on his back visible.

Prescott stood still for a second in horror. Realizing that Johnny had not seen him, he quietly shut the door and retreated back into his own suite. Suddenly everything about the day made perfect sense - the girl's sudden disappearance, the bruises on his son's face, those scratches on his back and his sudden desire to leave town!

Setting down the decanter and glasses, Prescott did something he hadn't done in years. He wept.

He must have attacked that Fairfax girl some time yesterday after she left the family's suite. She put up a heck of a fight judging by those marks on his back. Then earlier today someone came to defend her honor and somehow scared him enough to where he felt compelled to flee town.

Not believing this has happened yet again, Prescott sat there for a long time before he dried his eyes and stood up. With his mind firmly made up, he trudged back towards his changing room. As he passed through the bedroom, Lottie sat up in the large four poster bed and asked, "Are you retiring for the night, Johnathan?"

Prescott ignored her as he headed back to his closet. Opening the safe door which was located on the far wall behind the tailcoat he wore on special occasions, Prescott pulled out five thousand dollars. It was all the private cash he had on hand, but it should be enough. Tucking it into his pockets, he again purposefully strode through the bedchamber.

This time, Lottie said peevishly, "I just asked you a question! Why don't you answer me?"

Prescott again ignored her as he squared his shoulders, held his head high and marched through the front parlor, stopping at Johnny's door. After knocking sharply, a couple of times to make sure he was heard, he pushed it open. Johnny, who was on his way to see Nash and a couple of mutual friends, was fully dressed in an elegant evening suit. He looked surprised to see his father after the fallout they had earlier.

"Hello Pop," he said cautiously. "And to what do I owe this pleasure?"

Prescott took the bills from his pockets and threw them on the small table that stood nearby. Clearing his throat, he said, "There should be enough there to set you up nicely. Don't ever come back to St. Augustine again while I'm still alive."

Johnny stared wordlessly as his father turned and walked out.

1898

Chapter 11

Three seagulls sailed past the roof of the front porch as they raced each other towards the sea. The cool spring breeze, the salty smell of the surf and the hypnotic sounds of the crashing waves lulled Birdie into a relaxed state of semi-sleep as she slowly rocked her chair. The dress she was working on fell into her lap as she nodded off. As usual, the baby growing inside her chose that very moment to start kicking. Birdie slowly rubbed her protruding stomach as she tried to soothe the little creature back to sleep.

As always, her dreams took her back to St. Augustine. Back to that terrible day six months ago when she was finally forced to tell her mother that she was pregnant, and the resounding slap Hortensia had given her in response.

"Who was it?" Hortensia had demanded furiously. Birdie then told her about how Johnny Prescott had accosted her in one of the hotel rooms at the Montclair.

"Why didn't you ever say anything about this to me?" Hortensia cried. Then she stopped for a second as if something had just occurred to her. "Wait. Did this happen that day you came home early with Ella saying that you got into a fight with one of the maids and was told not to go back?" Birdie had just nodded.

"Why all the lies, Birdie? The truth always comes out in the end," scolded Hortensia.

"Because I didn't want to worry you, ma, and I never imagined that I would get pregnant with it being...you know....my first time and all."

"That's ridiculous, Birdie!" replied Hortensia. Clutching her head with both hands, she cried, "Oh, what will people think?"

That was when Birdie lost her temper. "That's why you're so upset, isn't it, ma? It's not about me or what I'm about to go through. It's all about what folks in that church of yours are gonna think!"

Hortensia raised her hand as though she was about to hit Birdie a second time. Instead she lowered it and said through gritted teeth, "Don't you ever talk to me like that again, and don't ever think I don't care about you. Of course, I care about you and part of caring about you is worrying about what others are going to do when they find out about your condition. Of course, you'll have to leave school before you start showing."

"Ma, no! I only just started back last month." Birdie cried.

"No, it's out of the question. I also think it's best if you stay with your Uncle Epifonio and Aunt Josefina up in Fernandina Beach until after you have the baby. We'll just say that Aunt Josefina is sick, and you are up there helping them out until she gets better. Then you'll come home afterwards like nothing ever happened."

"But what about the baby? "asked Birdie.

"What about the baby? It will be sent to an orphanage. You certainly can't bring it back here." Hortensia shouted.

Hortensia's words have haunted Birdie ever since she left St. Augustine on a northbound train shortly afterwards. She knew that she couldn't bring the baby back with her. However, the thought of having to give up a child that would be growing inside her for the next nine months saddened her.

She had spoken about it with Ella before she left. Dear Ella had been a pillar of strength for Birdie throughout the entire ordeal by giving her practical advice, lending an ear or shoulder when Birdie needed to cry, and helping to keep up the subterfuge of why Birdie was leaving town.

As Birdie wondered about how she'd deal with giving up her unborn child, Ella replied, "Miss Birdie. You half white and the baby's daddy was white. So yo' child will most likely be white. What kinda life will a white child have livin' with you in the po' colored section of town and bein' looked down on by other white folks? But if you let the orphanage take the baby, it might get adopted by some rich white folks who can't have one o' their own, and the child can grow up in a big house, have lotsa nice things and go to a good school. What ma wouldn't want the best fo' their child?"

Birdie had to admit that the orphanage sounded like a much better prospect, but as each day passed, the attachment Birdie had to the baby grew stronger. Even now as she napped on her uncle's porch by the beach, she cradled her swollen stomach in her arms.

As he pushed the wheelbarrow of yard waste across the back lawn, Newt looked up at the distant clouds which signaled an afternoon shower. He was hustling this morning to get the trash burned before the rain came. Mr. Prescott, who had become exceedingly short tempered and withdrawn since his son left, had noticed that the outdoor trash receptacle was overflowing with debris and was outraged.

“Why the hell hasn’t this damned thing been emptied?” he’d shouted to Newt, who was the only groundskeeper who happened to be nearby at the time. “Get this shit burned immediately before it starts to stink!”

Newt dumped the contents of the wheelbarrow onto the garbage pile and set it aflame. As he stood back and watched the plumes of smoke drift upward, his mind drifted back to the previous summer when he and Birdie stood on this very spot, watching the same ribbons of smoke trail skyward and her laughing at his middle name. The memory made him smile even though his heart was broken.

Birdie had been gone for months now. Did she ever think of him? Did she even remember him? Newt shook his head. Don't be a fool, he told himself. She's got a lot of things to deal with at the moment.

Newt still remembered the day he last saw her, even though she was far away and didn't see him. It was a Thursday afternoon, about two months after she'd left the Montclair. Newt had just finished work for the day and was on his way home. As he walked past Cedar Street, he saw a couple of women walking into Doctor Jennings' office. One of them was Birdie! She looked very pale and was being guided by a dark-complexioned woman who Newt assumed was her mother.

Worried that Birdie was sick, Newt purposefully came into work early the next day to talk to Ella, who was outside polishing the brass railings on the east side entrance of the hotel. She was surprised to see him at the Montclair before sunrise.

"Mornin' Newt!" she cheerfully greeted him. "Why you here so early?"

"Ella," his tone was serious, "I saw Birdie going into Doc Jennings's office yesterday. She looked white as a ghost. What's wrong? She ain't seriously ill, is she? I've been mighty worried 'bout her."

Ella stopped polishing the rail she was working on and put down her rag. She had taken great care to keep Birdie's business from everyone else, but when she glanced at Newt, she could see even in the semi-darkness that his face was full of concern and his eyes were anxious. This boy had been in love with her friend for quite some time now and Ella was determined that he know the truth.

"Newt," she said gravely, "Birdie's with child."

Feeling like he was just punched in the stomach, Newt exhaled and sat on the lowest step where the railing ended. Ella seated herself next to him and continued.

"It's Johnny Prescott's. Birdie says the only time she ever laid wi' him was that one time when he beat her and forced himself on her. When she started noticin'...well, you know....she had to tell her ma. They went to see the doc yesterday to make sure. When I went over to visit Birdie last night, she said she was expectin'. So now her ma's makin' plans to send her away to stay with her kinfolk fo' a while."

Newt slumped over and buried his face in his hands. He reckoned that when he beat up Johnny Prescott and scared him into leaving, that would have been the end of things. He'd even hoped that he might see Birdie around town. Now who knows when, or if, he'd see her again.

"Do you know when she's leavin' and where's she headin'?" he asked mournfully.

Ella's own heart ached just looking at him as he tried to take it all in. "I ain't sure when she's leavin' but I do know she's goin' to her uncle's house. I don't remember where he lives but it's somewhere north o' Jacksonville."

"Will she be comin' back, d'ya think?" asked Newt.

"Oh, she'll come back to us," said Ella resolutely. "You'll see! She'll be back befo' we know it!"

Her words had resonated with Newt over the past several months and the hope they conveyed were what had been keeping him going each day. Watching the last embers slowly burn out, Newt picked up the empty wheelbarrow and headed back to the groundskeepers shed.

The clock over the fireplace seemed especially loud as it ticked away each passing second. It was dinner time and Hortensia sat listlessly at the dining room table, looking down at her plate of fried fish and boiled potatoes with indifference. Her appetite had greatly diminished over the past six months which left her looking severely gaunt. Sleep had also eluded her and left two dark hollows in her eye sockets.

Della Compton had taken notice of Hortensia's physical decline and had made mention of it earlier that morning when

Hortensia had gone over to perform her usual half day of housekeeping for the Comptons.

"Hortensia, are you ill?" Della had asked pointedly. "You look like death warmed over. Have you been to the doctor?"

"No, ma'am," Hortensia replied. "I'm not sick. Just a bit tired, that's all."

"Ah, that's right. Your girl had to go help out your sister-in-law, didn't she?" asked Della.

"Yes ma'am," fibbed Hortensia. "With Birdie gone, I have had to do both her chores and my own, and, of course, I'm still worried about my sister-in-law Josefina."

"Poor thing," purred Della sympathetically. "When does Biddie get back?"

"Birdie, ma'am," corrected Hortensia. "I'm not sure when she will be back. Hopefully not too much longer."

"What a shame that she had to leave the Montclair. I heard she was doing quite well there. My Cyril said that none other than Mr. Prescott Sr. himself was quite impressed with your girl. You must be proud." Della clucked.

Hortensia shuddered at the mention of the Montclair. She hated that hotel and she hated herself even more for urging Birdie to work there in the first place. The guilt ate away at her every day, especially now with Birdie gone and the house empty.

Until now, Hortensia had never lived alone a day in her life. She never realized this until she put Birdie on that northbound train to Fernandina and had to return to a vacant house full of bittersweet memories. Her eyes welled up as she recalled the happy times in the front parlor when Patrick would get on his hands and knees, pretending to be Birdie's stallion, which made the three-year-old scream with glee. "Watch out for that table," Hortensia would always warn them as she smiled at their antics.

Birdie. Thinking of her daughter always brought forth tears. Like her daughter, Hortensia often thought back to that day her daughter nervously approached her and broke the news of her pregnancy. Although her initial reaction was one of rage which made her physically lash out, Hortensia had regretted her reaction ever since. She wished Birdie were here now, so she could comfort her and reassure her that everything will be okay.

There was one thing, however, which Hortensia will never regret and that was insisting that Birdie go away to have this baby and immediately hand it over to the Sisters of St. Mary's. Her brother Epifonio had written her about them shortly after Hortensia had alerted them of Birdie's predicament. The convent was located in southernmost Georgia, just north of the Florida state line and not too far from Fernandina Beach. Epifonio had been in touch with them and made all the necessary arrangements.

Although her daughter believed that Hortensia was ashamed of Birdie having a baby out of wedlock, nothing could have been further from the truth. Hortensia feared for Birdie's future. Being biracial has made it hard enough for her to find a husband but bearing an illegitimate child will make it impossible. Sending Birdie away to have the baby and hand it over to the nuns seemed the only logical thing to do. It would give both her and the poor innocent little creature a chance for a fresh start.

How she desperately wished that Patrick were here now with her instead of lying six feet underground in the public cemetery outside town. Although she always felt him close by in spirit and talked to him every night about the day's events, she needed to feel his supportive arms around her during times like this when she felt so small, lonely and afraid.

A knock brought Hortensia back to the present. She put her dinner plate back in the oven to keep warm and went to open the front door. Ophelia was standing on the porch holding a small plate covered with a napkin. "Evenin', Hortensia. How ya doin'?"

"Oh, I'm all right - considering. Come in," Hortensia offered as she stepped aside to let Ophelia pass through.

Living only a few houses down from the Fairfaxes, the Pattersons had kept a tight watch on Hortensia over the past several months. Ella often stopped by to see if there was any news of Birdie or to ask Hortensia if she needed anything picked up from town. Ophelia's husband Cletus or one of her older sons would come over if any household emergencies needed attention, such as last week's stopped up sink..

But it was Ophelia herself who came by to check on Hortensia almost every evening since Birdie left. She would usually bring something with her to knit or mend while they sat and chatted. Other times, like today, she'd bring something to eat.

"With it bein' strawberry season and all, I figured I'd fix us a strawberry pie!" Ophelia removed the napkin from the plate which revealed two small slices with golden crusts and a deep red filling. "My man and my young 'uns tore into it so quickly, I barely got these pieces outta the house for ourselves!"

"Thank you, Ophelia. It looks delicious." Hortensia smiled as she set about making coffee and retrieved two forks from a drawer. She'd much rather have the pie with Ophelia than her own bland dinner which she'd probably have for breakfast the next day.

As both women sat at the table, Ophelia asked, "Have ya got any news from Birdie?"

"I got a letter from her today," Hortensia replied. "She told me about Epifonio's new horse that they named Amigo, the progress she's made on the dress she'd been working on, and..." Hortensia sighed, "how excited she was to feel the baby kicking. Oh Ophelia, what if she is already getting too attached to this baby? What is going to happen when the time comes to give the baby up?"

Ophelia stroked Hortensia's arm. "Of course, Birdie's gonna be a lil excited to feel that baby movin' 'round inside her. It's becomin' mo' real to her now. Remember how that felt?"

Hortensia nodded. "I remember it full well. That's the problem. I know how she feels now and it's only going to make it worst later on."

"You might not think so but yo' Birdie is made o' strong stuff," remarked Ophelia. "I remember my Ella tellin' me how much name callin' and hittin' that po' lil gal suffered in school but she still went every day, and if it weren't fo' this pregnancy she'd be there now, finishin' it out. Yo' gal might be a lil shy sometimes, but she got a quiet strength that'll get 'er through."

Hortensia's brow anxiously furrowed as she replied, "I pray to the Lord you're right, Ophelia."

Birdie changed into the nicest dress she'd brought with her. Tonight, they were expecting her Aunt Esmeralda, who as the oldest sibling, was the honorary matriarch of the Gomez clan. She was coming up from Titusville with her husband Enrico. Birdie had never met her Aunt Esmeralda as she had only just arrived in the US a few years ago from the Dominican Republic. From what Hortensia had said, her oldest sister was a very staunch supporter of the old ways of life they had on the island. English was rarely used in their household and all of her five children were brought up speaking only Spanish.

When Patrick was still alive, only English was spoken during Birdie's childhood. After he had passed away, Hortensia continued to raise Birdie speaking only English so that she could more easily assimilate into society, especially amongst the whites. Birdie's knowledge of Spanish was limited to a few basic words and phrases.

She was therefore nervous of meeting her Aunt Esmeralda, especially given her plight. She heard a knock at the door downstairs followed by the excited sounds of greetings. Rubbing her stomach, she said aloud to her unborn child, "Don't worry. We'll get through this together!"

As she shyly descended the steps and approached the crowd in the front parlor, Birdie glanced at the middle-aged woman who was chattering away to Epifonio. She looks just like ma, thought Birdie. Her hair is a little grayer and she's a bit shorter, but otherwise she could be ma's twin!

Aunt Esmeralda caught sight of Birdie and approached her with a smile and outstretched arms. She then said something in Spanish which Birdie couldn't understand. Birdie stepped forward and dutifully gave her aunt a polite hug. "Pleased to meet you, Aunt Esmeralda."

Noticing his sister's puzzled look, Epifonio said, "Ella no habla español, Esmeralda."

"Que?" asked the woman incredulously followed by something else that Birdie couldn't comprehend

Epifonio translated. "Your aunt is shocked that your mother never taught you to speak Spanish. She said that your gringo father is to blame for that."

Birdie silently burned as she sat down in a corner. How dare she say such things about my parents and call me father a gringo. I supposed that makes me half-gringo, she thought ruefully.

As Aunt Josie and Luisa passed around drinks, Enrico came over and gave Birdie a hug. He was a tall, quiet man who wore spectacles. Sensing that his wife had somehow offended Birdie, he tried his best to smooth things over despite his very limited command of the English language.

"I sorry for what Esmeralda say. She no mean to make you feel bad," he said anxiously.

"Gracias, Tio," replied Birdie who cast Enrico a very grateful smile. He squeezed her hand before leaving to join the others. For the rest of the evening, Birdie sat listening to everyone gabbing away in another language while she tried her best to follow along and smile.

Even within her own family, she still felt as much of an outsider as she did amongst the whites and the Negroes back home.

Birdie's ears perked up when she heard Esmeralda mention Hortensia and Patrick.

"What's she saying about my parents?" Birdie asked Aunt Josie who was sitting closest to her.

"She's just reminiscing about how they got together," replied Aunt Josie. "You must already know that story."

"No, actually ma never really talks much about how she and pa met. Please tell me what she's saying, Aunt Josie," pleaded Birdie.

"Okay, just a minute," said Aunt Josie as she held her index finger up to Birdie. She said something to Esmeralda and then added, "I just asked her to tell us the whole story and that I'll be translating for you. Okay, she's starting now...."

Hortensia was eighteen when she first met Patrick Fairfax. A bookish, shy girl who was the best student at the local grammar school, Hortensia's favorite subject was English, and she was fairly fluent when she met the tall, fair skinned young man with the wavy light brown hair and the elegant sounding British accent.

They met at the dock one day where Hortensia's father Xavier Gomez, a black Dominican whose mother came from Africa, worked on a fishing boat. Hortensia had gone down to bring Xavier his lunch when she spotted Patrick trying to communicate with one of the deckhands. She went over and offered to translate for him. He was trying to find out where he could find work and a place to stay.

Patrick Fairfax, who was instantly smitten with Hortensia, told her about how he had left his job at a large estate house in England where he worked as a footman to set sail to the New World and hopefully a new life. All he had on him was his life savings which wasn't very much and a small duffel bag of his belongings.

Hortensia, who was also quickly taken with the foreigner, promised that she would ask around on his behalf about a job, but in the meantime, she took him back to her home where she introduced him to her mother Gloria, who provided him with a hot meal and some suggestions on where he could stay in town.

Eventually Patrick settled into a rented room and found a job unloading incoming cargo ships. He spent any free time he had with Hortensia and soon they fell in love. Patrick went to Xavier to ask for Hortensia's hand in marriage but was refused. The older man knew that his daughter was opening herself up to social disapproval and prejudice if she were to marry a white man. He had similar problems when he married Gloria, who was a light skinned Spaniard. He didn't want his daughter to have to endure the same racial intolerance that he had to overcome.

One night, Patrick and Hortensia decided to board a U.S. bound ship to Florida. There they would get married and start a new life together. Unfortunately, when they landed in Jacksonville, they discovered that they couldn't legally marry in the South. By this time, Hortensia was pregnant with Birdie so, pretending that they are already married, Patrick used the money he brought with him from England along with his earnings in the Dominican Republic as a deposit on the small bungalow on Citrus Avenue in St. Augustine. Birdie was born a few months later.

For several years, the little family existed on Patrick's earnings from odd jobs he did around town – carpentry, orange picking, masonry, and even laying down railroad tracks. He was often the subject of taunts by local Klansmen. One day when he was out on the docks with Hortensia and little Birdie watching the boats pass by, a man ordered "that nigger and her mulatto pickaninny" off the pier as it was for whites only. Patrick made Hortensia take Birdie home before he punched the man in the jaw, breaking a few of his teeth. A full-blown fight ensued. The sheriff was called out to break up the fight and throw Patrick in jail for assault. The sheriff also took the opportunity to officially charge Patrick with breaking Florida's anti-miscegenation law which carried a stiff jail time penalty. After languishing in jail for six months, Patrick contracted tuberculosis from the cramped conditions and died.

"What?" cried Birdie. "Ma never told me any of this! They were never married? I don't believe it! And my poor pa died in jail? Ma had told me that he was away working on the railroad and had an accident. Oh, my poor pa!" Birdie collapsed into tears.

Esmeralda jumped up from her chair and went over to hug Birdie. She cooed some words in Spanish and kept saying, "pobrecita," over and over again.

Uncle Epifonio told Birdie, "Your aunt apologizes for upsetting you. She thought you had already known how your pa died."

"No, I didn't," said Birdie as she dabbed at her eyes. "Poor pa. Thrown in jail like a common criminal!" Esmeralda handed her a handkerchief as Birdie turned to her and said "Gracias, tia." Esmeralda kissed her on the cheek and gave her another squeeze. She said something to Aunt Josie, who stood up and held out her hand to Birdie.

"Your Aunt Esmeralda says you've had a shock and should go upstairs and lay down, and I agree with her. Come on, my dear."

Birdie bid everyone good night and followed Aunt Josie upstairs. As her aunt helped her out of her dress and into her nightgown, Birdie asked, "Did you know about any of this?"

"Well, I knew that your mother and father were never really married. And I do remember hearing that your father had died in jail, but I never knew why he was there in the first place until tonight. The one thing I recall from that time was the great fuss that his folks in England made about getting his body transported back over there for burial in their home town, but your ma was adamant that he stayed here in St. Augustine and she won out in the end."

After Josefina had left, Birdie laid in bed and thought about the story she had just heard. Her parents were never married so that made her a bastard child. No wonder her mother had been so upset with her when she learned about the pregnancy and reacted the way she did. It must have been a painful reminder of what she herself had gone through, but unlike Birdie who was raped by a scalawag, Hortensia had Patrick who stayed by her side and loved her until the day he died.

"Oh Pa, I miss you more than ever now," sobbed Birdie.

Chapter 12

The relentless heat and humidity made the stray wisps of hair hanging down from Birdie's bun cling to the back of her neck as she waddled from the porch down to the end of the street and across to the beach where she took off her shoes and cooled her feet off in the surf. It was only May 29th, but Fernandina Beach was already experiencing July temperatures.

Birdie caressed her abdomen as she gazed out across the sea. She often wondered where she would end up if she were to hop on a boat and sail it straight across. Ireland? Spain? Or perhaps some exotic African port? Maybe one day she'll get to see what was on the other side of the Atlantic.

She felt exhausted. Between the baby's movement and severe back pain which had her on all fours at one point, she had very little sleep the night before. The sound of the incoming waves was soothing and hypnotic as they rolled in toward her. She wished she could drag her bed outside and sleep right where she was standing. The image that it conjured in her mind made her smile.

Suddenly, her smile faded as she felt a warm liquid running down her leg. She wasn't urinating but yet, her drawers were soaked. Horrified, she remembered that her Aunt Josie had warned her about her waters breaking when it was time for the baby's arrival. Not wanting to bend over, Birdie didn't bother putting her shoes back on. Instead she walked as fast as her legs could carry her back to Epifonio's house.

The walk back seemed to be twice as long as it took her to get the beach. When she got to the end of the street and could see the house in the distance, a sharp pain tore through her pelvis and she screamed. The sound brought one of Uncle Ep's neighbors, Blanca, out onto her porch. When the old woman saw Birdie doubled over in pain and clutching her stomach, she ran over to her.

"Here, child. Take my hand. Looks like the baby's coming," said Blanca softly. "Just breathe, my dear. Everything will be all right."

When they arrived at the front of Epifonio's house, Blanca shouted, "Josefina! Luisa! Come quickly! Birdie's in labor!"

Aunt Josie appeared in the doorway holding a dishrag. When she saw Blanca leading a panting and crying Birdie, she ran toward them.

"Birdie! Is it time?" she asked. All Birdie could do was nod and grimace as another contraction overtook her.

"Fernando!" shouted Josefina. "Fernando! Get out here now!!"

As Josefina and Esmeralda helped Birdie up the final step, Fernando appeared followed closely by his wife Luisa. He was about to ask what all the shouting was about but when he saw the state of his cousin, he immediately knew what was happening.

"Ah, there you are. Fernando, run over to 9th Street and get Tola. Tell her that Birdie's time has come. And hurry."

Fernando sprinted off the porch and down the street. The women helped Birdie upstairs to her room and laid her on the bed.

About fifteen minutes later, Tola appeared in the bedroom doorway and took over. "Hola Birdie. How are we doing?" she asked.

"Her pains are about ten minutes apart," replied Josefina. "She had some back pains last night and was telling me that she had some cramping this morning."

"Okay, we still have some time," said Tola as she opened the large tapestry bag she brought with her. "Luisa, please boil these for me." Birdie heard the sound of metal objects clinking together.

After a couple of hours, she was in so much pain and so tired that she couldn't see straight any more. She felt as if she'd run for miles, far enough to reach the mysterious African port she'd imagined was on the other side of the ocean.

"Don't push yet," was all she kept hearing both Tola and Josefina tell her, but she so much wanted to push the baby out so that she'd be free of the pain. "Not yet, Birdie."

She eventually blacked out but heard Tola's insistent voice in her ear saying, "Okay Birdie. It's time. I need you to push."

"I can't," Birdie feebly whispered.

"Yes, you can! You need to push!" said Aunt Josie firmly. "Come on Birdie. I know you can do this. Push!"

Gathering up every bit of strength left in her body, Birdie pushed with all her might.

"Good girl!" said Tola. "Take a breath and then I need you to push again. Ready? Push!"

Birdie moaned and shook her head. Again, Aunt Josie shouted "Birdie, you have to push! You can do this! PUSH!"

Taking a deep breath, Birdie bared down and pushed with all her might.

"Okay, now we have the baby's head and shoulders out. One more push Birdie and it'll be all over. You're doing good! One more push!" encouraged Aunt Josie.

Birdie pushed one final time and fell back into peaceful blackness.

Epifonio had been out fishing with his youngest son Dionisio that afternoon and was surprised to see Tola leaving his house when they returned.

"Hola, Doña Tola," said Epifonio. "Am I safe in assuming that there is a new lodger in my house?"

Tola laughed. "Yes, a lovely baby girl. Both she and Birdie are doing fine. They just need some rest. I'll be back tonight to check on them," the old woman said as she slowly descended the steps, her tapestry bag in her hand.

Epifonio and Dionisio found Josefina out on the back porch laundering several bloody rags and sheets. She looked exhausted and red faced from the heat. Wiping the sweat off her forehead, she raised her eyebrows when she saw her husband.

"I saw Tola leaving," said Epifonio. "She said all went well."

"Yes," said Josefina. "You know what we need to do now. We promised Hortensia."

Epifonio sighed as he went back into the house. He retrieved a pen, the ink bottle and a sheet of paper from Josefina's writing desk and wrote a short note. As he let it dry, he called for Dionisio.

When his son appeared in the doorway of the parlor, Epifonio told him, "I need you to go into town and take this note down to the telegraph office and have this message sent to the Sisters of St. Mary's Convent in Georgia."

"Sure thing, Pa," replied Dionisio before swiftly departing.

Epifonio thoughtfully watched him go, dreading the eventual fallout from the message about to be wired to St. Mary's. He slowly climbed the stairs and knocked on the door to Birdie's room. Luisa quietly opened it and let him inside. Birdie was still asleep. Her face looked paler than usual and she had dark circles around her eyes.

"How's she doing?" whispered Epifonio.

"She's been asleep ever since the baby came," answered Luisa. "But she did really well, and the baby is adorable. She's over there in the basket."

Epifonio walked over to the large straw laundry basket in the corner where, snuggled in a blanket, was a tiny little girl with sandy colored curls and an alabaster complexion. She looked like one of those china baby dolls he'd seen in the general store. Her little eyes were tightly shut and fringed with gold lashes. With her lower lip pushed out, she reminded Epifonio of Birdie as a child but much lighter.

As he lightly touched the baby's tiny fist with his index finger, she tightly clasped onto it. Epifonio teared up as he looked at the little creature. He wished that he and Josie could have taken her in and raised her as their own, but they were getting on in years. Plus, his sister was very adamant about putting the baby up for adoption.

Luisa walked over and placed an arm around him. “I feel the same way, Epifonio. I wish Fernando and I could take her too. Our little Isabella would love a baby sister.”

Not trusting himself to speak, Epifonio just nodded and gave her a squeeze before going to Birdie’s bedside. As he kissed her on the forehead, she stirred and opened her eyes.

“Well, hello there, mi sobrina,” murmured Epifonio. “I go out fishing for a few hours and come back to find a brand-new baby in the house! How are you, my dear?”

Birdie blinked several times before she was able to keep her eyes open. Her mouth felt so dry. “I’m okay, Uncle Ep. Just sore, is all. Where’s my baby?”

Luisa stepped up with a glass of water. “Here Birdie, drink this. You must be thirsty. The baby girl is fine. She’s just having a nap.”

Birdie took a few sips which quenched her parched throat. “A girl? Can I please see her?”

Luisa looked questioningly at Epifonio who nodded at her. He reckoned Birdie was going to have to see the baby at some point. They certainly weren’t going to hide the child from her until the nuns arrived. After Luisa placed the infant in Birdie’s arms, she and Epifonio left the room, quietly closing the door behind them.

Birdie’s first reaction to seeing her daughter for the first time was one of wonder at how fair she looked. She marveled at the baby’s porcelain-like skin and golden hair. And those curls! She’d never seen such a lovely head of hair on a newborn. As she inspected the tiny hands, she noticed that the right one had a dark brown marking on it. It looked like a crescent moon or the letter C. This small area of discoloration seemed to be the only part of the child which attested to its maternal birth line. Otherwise she looked pure Caucasian.

Just then the baby yawned and briefly opened her eyes. They looked to be a greenish amber color, and it was in that brief moment of eye contact that Birdie felt an instant connection with her child. No, she thought, I can't give you up, my little darling. You're a part of me, and I'll always be a part of you.

Looking at the birthmark on the little girl's hand, Birdie thought it looked more like a C than a moon. That was when she decided to call the baby Clara.

Chapter 13

Josefina found Luisa hanging up laundry on the clothesline behind the house. The ocean breeze made the assorted shirts, dresses, chemises and sheets billow like sails.

"Luisa, I'm getting worried about Birdie," said Josefina anxiously. "It's been a week, and she's getting too attached to this baby. I just knew this would happen! She's even given her a name."

"Well of course she's going to become attached, Josie," said Luisa who was sympathetic of Birdie's plight. "Especially as she's been breastfeeding the child. You remember how that is. It creates a special bond between a mother and her baby."

Josie sighed. "I certainly understand how she might feel but it still doesn't change the fact that there are nuns on their way here to take the little one away. Epifonio just went downtown to meet their train." Josie's voice cracked as she dabbed her red rimmed eyes with the corner of her apron. "My heart is already breaking for that poor girl upstairs!"

Luisa closed her eyes and tried to keep her own composure. She couldn't imagine having to give up Isabella, especially so soon after the birth. "Does she know that the sisters are coming today?"

Josie shook her head and, still crying, replied, "She only knows that they've been summoned. I was going to tell her this morning, but when I found her singing to the baby, I didn't have the heart." She looked up to the sky and prayed, "Dear Lord, please give our Birdie the guidance she needs to make the right decision and the strength to deal with the aftermath."

Meanwhile, up in her room, Birdie was standing over Clara's basket, watching her nap. She loved how the little girl's lower lip would stick out as she slept. She wondered what kind of personality her daughter would have when she grew up. Would she be a cheerful girl who laughed a lot? Would she be very studious and bookish? Would she like to do boyish things like climb trees and play with insects or would she prefer more feminine pursuits like needlework and dolls?

Birdie sighed as she realized that she'll never know the answer. The nuns were coming any day now so her time with Clara was short. All she could do was to hope that the baby was placed with a loving family and will have the best life possible.

She stared at Clara for a long time, remembering every little detail of her face, her little hands, her toes, the birthmark, every curl on her head. She wasn't an artist by any means, but she mentally etched a portrait of the baby in her mind so that she'll never forget what she looked like. She wanted to always be able to close her eyes and see Clara, just as she looked now.

The sounds of voices, a wagon and horses were heard in the street. Birdie walked over to the window and saw Epifonio helping one of two nuns out of the wagon as Josie and Luisa were coming around from the back of the house. Oh no! They're here, she thought. God, I didn't think it would be today. Clara's leaving me today!

Even though Birdie knew for the past eight months that this moment would come, panic still set in. In her head, she knew that putting Clara up for adoption was the best option for her to get a decent start in life, but her heart was telling her to take the infant, sneak out the back door and run away.

And that is exactly what Birdie impulsively decided to do at that moment. To hell with what her mother wanted! Clara was hers and no one was going to take her away from her. Besides, once Hortensia saw her own granddaughter, she'll fall in love with her, too.

Birdie peeked out the window and saw that Epifonio, Josie and Luisa were still out front speaking to the nuns. Picking up the baby and her reticule that contained just enough money for a return fare to St. Augustine, Birdie quietly stepped out of the room and tiptoed down the stairs. Seeing no one else about, Birdie stealthily dashed into the kitchen and out the back door.

She hadn't been outside for a week and the sun was almost blinding. She also hadn't walked any long distances for a while, either. Still healing from the birth, she had to take slow, small steps.

Hiding behind the hedge that bordered her Uncle Epifonio's property, she waited until the street was clear before making her escape up the road and headed in the direction of town.

As she purposely took the back streets to town to avoid her Uncle spotting her, Birdie's eyes darted from left to right as she crossed over 10th Street. Every time she heard horse hooves or the squeaky wheels of a wagon, she ducked behind the nearest tree, hedge or fence. Still healing from childbirth, she found that gravity was pulling her uterus straight downward, making her insides feel like they were made of lead. So, every step she took required twice as much effort as usual. Sweating profusely and with her heart hammering from panic, she cradled Clara against her chest as she continued to make her way towards the town.

Her conscience was also heavy with guilt. She felt bad about leaving Uncle Ep's house the way she did after he and his family had taken her in and been so welcoming. She didn't know how she was going to explain all of this to Hortensia when she got back to St. Augustine. All she knew was that Clara was hers and she did not want to give her up. She thought about moving to another town and pretending she was a widow. At least that would be more socially acceptable than having a child out of wedlock.

Birdie's head was spinning. She hadn't walked this far in months. She just needed to sit for a moment and get her head together. She desperately wished that Ella were here. She would know what to do.

Clara yawned and rubbed her eyes with her little fist. Birdie kissed her on top of her head. "Don't worry my darling. We'll be in St. Augustine soon."

I hope there is a southbound train going out this afternoon, Birdie thought. I'd hate to have to wait around the station any longer than I need to. What if the next one doesn't leave until tomorrow? Where will we stay the night? Well, that's just a chance I'll need to take!

Her dizziness was getting worse and she desperately needed to rest. There was a nice patch of grass between a couple of houses near the end of 3rd Avenue. Here Birdie sat with her back against a pine tree with Clara clutched to her chest. A couple of women walking by carrying baskets looked at Birdie and Clara quizzically.

I just need a short break, thought Birdie as she closed her eyes. We'll have a little nap and then continue on our way.

About fifteen minutes later, a small group of people surrounded Birdie. A man asked, "Does anyone know who she is?"

"I've never seen her around here before," replied a woman.

"I tried to rouse her, but she won't wake up. I think she fainted," said another.

"Someone get the baby away from her and call the doctor!" shouted the first man.

Just then, Epifonio's wagon came up the street. He had seen the group surrounding someone laying on the ground and his worst fears were realized when he got closer and found Birdie unconscious with Clara clinging to her mother and crying incessantly.

Epifonio jumped down from the driver's seat and ran up, pushing a few of the people out of his way. "That's my niece! Stand back and give her air."

Taking Clara into his arms, he went back to the wagon and made a small nest of blankets in the bed. Then he returned, picked up Birdie, and laid her in the bed next to the infant. After closing the tail gate, he slowly drove back to the house.

The curious onlookers watched them drive off. “Those poor creatures,” said one of the women shaking her head. “I think they both need our prayers.”

“That woman needs a doctor,” observed one of the men.

Sisters Thomasina and Mary Margaret quietly sat by Birdie’s bedside and softly prayed over their rosaries. Afterwards, they sat in silence. They had just arrived by train that morning from the convent located just above the state line in Georgia. Unaccustomed to railroad travel, both sisters were relieved to be back on steady ground.

Sister Thomasina, the older of the pair, looked at the unconscious young woman and slightly shook her head in sympathy. She had seen too many of these cases over the years. In most cases, the mixed-race babies were nearly impossible to place into adoptive homes and were instead sent to orphanages throughout the state. However, in this instance, the little girl looked to be an ideal prospect for a young couple living nearby who were desperate for a child.

Mary Margaret, meanwhile, was worried for Birdie. She knew from personal experience the pain and heartbreak of having to give up a child. It was the reason she entered the convent three years ago. She’s not much older than I was, the young nun thought as she gazed down at Birdie, whose eyelids were starting to flutter as she slow regained consciousness.

“I think she’s waking up, Sister,” Mary Margaret whispered to Thomasina.

Birdie groaned as she opened her eyes. Her head felt fuzzy and she saw two nuns sitting next to her. Was this a dream? After her mind cleared and she recognized her surroundings, Birdie panicked. She never made it to town! Birdie shot up and attempted to get out of the bed.

"No!" she shouted. "Don't take my baby! Please! Don't take her away from me!"

Sister Thomasina placed a gentle hand on Birdie's shoulder. "Calm down, my dear. No one is taking anyone right now. Our top priority is making sure that you are all right."

"Where's Clara?" asked Birdie suspiciously.

"She's downstairs with your aunt.," replied Sister Mary Margaret. "Don't worry Birdie. She's doing fine."

"I need to see her," said Birdie.

"You can see her if you want to. But first we'd just like to talk to you," said Sister Thomasina.

Birdie laid back into the bed and drew the coverlet up to her chin. She wished with all her heart that the nuns would go away and leave her and Clara alone.

"Where were you going with Clara earlier, Birdie?" asked Sister Thomasina.

"I was taking her back home to St. Augustine," replied Birdie defiantly. "After all, she is MY baby, isn't she?"

"Yes, she is," replied the nun. "But it was our understanding that you were planning on putting the baby into our care."

"That was my mother's idea, not mine!" snapped Birdie.

"Oh, I see," said Sister Mary Margaret. "And why does your mother want you to give up the baby?"

Birdie thought back to that horrendous day when she had to reveal her pregnancy to Hortensia and shuddered. "Because I ain't married."

"Do you know who the father is?" asked Sister Thomasina softly.

Tears formed in Birdie's eyes. "Yes," she whispered.

"If you were to return to St. Augustine, would there be any chance of you and he getting married?"

Birdie was sobbing now. "No! He never wants to see me again. I was...uh...I mean...he, uh..."

Sister Thomasina had seen more than her share of situations like this before. The baby was obviously the by-product of a non-consensual union. Instead, she changed the course of her questioning. “So, if you were to return to St. Augustine with the baby, where do you intend to live?”

“At home with my mother, of course,” replied Birdie impatiently.

“I understand that your father is deceased,” said Sister Mary Margaret.

“Yes, what about it?” asked Birdie insolently.

“How are you and your mother getting by, if you don’t mind us asking,” inquired Sister Mary Margaret

“My mother works. She takes in laundry and cleans for a few folks in town,” answered Birdie.

“What about you?” asked Sister Thomasina. “How do you contribute to your household?”

“Well, I was working at the Montclair hotel over the summer, but it was just a temporary job. I had planned to go back to school so I could graduate,” replied Birdie. “I had wanted to become a dressmaker afterwards.”

“That sounds grand,” said Sister Mary Margaret. “But if you were to bring home the baby, will you still be able to follow your dream?”

“Well, not right away,” said Birdie. “I’d have to stay home and take care of her until she’s old enough to go to school.”

“What kind of school would you be sending her to?” asked Sister Thomasina pointedly. “Your daughter is very fair complexioned and will no doubt pass for white. Would you be sending her to a white school in St. Augustine? Would they allow her to enroll given your own ethnicity?”

Having just been a mother for a week, Birdie hadn’t had time to consider this. Sister Thomasina continued, “Or would you be sending her to a colored school? She might feel out of place there.”

Birdie didn’t have an answer. She’d hate for her daughter to feel as out of place at the colored school as she did. If it weren’t for Ella, she didn’t think she’d have survived it. Then again, she couldn’t very well enroll her in the white school either. Not in St. Augustine, anyway, where folks knew her.

"Birdie," said Mary Margaret gently, "We know of a nice married white couple in Georgia who are unable to have children of their own and who could give your daughter a very loving home."

Birdie shook her head emphatically. "No! She's mine."

"They have a beautiful estate just outside of St. Mary's where she would never lack for anything, and she would be sent to the best of schools. I understand that the gentleman raises horses, so she'd probably grow up to be an excellent rider."

Birdie shut her eyes tightly and willed herself not to cry any more. She considered what Mary Margaret just told her. Imagine! Clara growing up on an estate as the daughter of a rich couple. She'd have lots of toys and horses, and she'd be very well educated.

The only thing Birdie could offer the child was her love. Otherwise, she'd be doomed to a life of always being an outcast and scraping by in the little house on Citrus Avenue. At that moment, Birdie realized that she needed to do what was right for the child and put her own feelings aside.

A large tear escaped from her left eye and slid down her cheek. "Can I see her one more time before you take her away?"

"Of course, you can," said Sister Thomasina. "Take as long as you need."

Birdie slowly got up from the bed and, followed by the nuns, made the longest walk of her life down the stairs and into the parlor where Aunt Josie was holding the baby. Epifonio was staring listlessly out the window. Everyone else went to Blanca's house, no doubt to escape the drama which was about to unfold.

Sister Mary Margaret nodded wordlessly to Aunt Josie, signaling that everything was settled. Aunt Josie stood up and gave Clara to Birdie.

Birdie stared intensely at Clara's face one last time and kissed her forehead. "Oh Clara. I'm so sorry." The tears now started to freely flow. "I wanted so much to keep you but that would have been selfish. You deserve a better life than I had, and you have a good chance of that with the man and woman that the sisters found for you. Please know that I love you very much and that is the only reason why I'm givin' you up. I'll never forget you and you'll be in my heart every day for the rest of my life."

Aunt Josie clung onto Epifonio and quietly wept into his arm. He fished a handkerchief from his pocket to wipe his own eyes before offering it to his wife.

Birdie kissed the baby one last time on her cheek before handing her over to Sister Thomasina. "Goodbye Clara. I love you."

Not wanting to see her baby being taken away, Birdie retreated up the stairs to her room and slammed the door shut. She cried for the rest of the day until her head ached.

Chapter 14

Hortensia paced the "coloreds only" side of the train station platform impatiently and for the hundredth time that morning, glanced up at the clock behind the ticket window. Birdie's train was due in at 8:40AM – only five minutes from now!

It had been almost a year since Hortensia had last seen her daughter on that overcast October day when Birdie departed for Fernandina Beach. She had been frightened about the impending birth, apprehensive over staying so far away from home and angry about having to leave school.

At first, mother and daughter had exchanged letters on a weekly basis. During that period, Hortensia was easily able to keep abreast of what was happening in Fernandina Beach. Then after the baby was born, the letters from Birdie stopped coming. Eventually Josefina took over the correspondence, enlightening Hortensia as to the chain of events which occurred after the birth.

Hortensia was horrified to hear of Birdie's attempted escape with the baby after all that Epifonio and Josefina had done for them. She immediately wrote back and apologized for her daughter's behavior, but Josefina later replied that there was nothing to apologize for. Birdie was understandably not in her right mind and everyone in the family sympathized with her.

The far-away sound of a train whistle brought Hortensia back to the present. Her daughter would be there within minutes! Josefina's warning in her last letter that Birdie was not her normal self had been bothering Hortensia for the last couple of days. She hoped and prayed that time, along with some rest and loving care, will be all that would be needed to help Birdie get on with her life. She was too old now to return to school but perhaps she could get a job somewhere – as long as it wasn't at that hotel.

As the train pulled into the station and made a complete stop, Hortensia's attention turned toward the windows on the last car which was where Birdie would be sitting. Once all the white travelers disembarked, the door to the last car opened and all the colored passengers filed out. Hortensia's eyes narrowed as she looked for signs of her daughter. When she eventually spotted her, she almost cried out in shock.

That bone thin, pale faced girl with the dark rings under her eyes could not be her Birdie! She looked like a shell of the vivacious woman that she once was. Her dress hung loosely on her which made her resemble a rag doll. The clutch bag she carried with all her possessions seemed to weigh her down.

As she caught sight of her mother, Birdie managed a feeble smile.

"Birdie!" cried Hortensia as she ran towards her and enveloped her daughter in her arms. Kissing her on the cheek, she murmured, "My goodness, you are so skinny! I need to fatten you up again."

"Hello ma," said Birdie weakly. "Had you been waitin' long?"

"I was so excited to see you that I got here an hour ago!" said Hortensia. "Here, let me take that bag for you. You look so tired, mija."

Birdie started to protest that she could carry it, but Hortensia took it from her with little effort as her daughter was so weak.

As they started the long walk back to their house, Hortensia said, "Birdie, I know you are in a lot of pain right now, but with the Lord's help, this too shall pass. You did the best thing you could possibly do for that child. She will now have a chance for a better life with parents who can properly take care of her and bring her up as a fine young woman. I am very proud of you, mija. You did the right thing. Now it's time for you to put this all behind you and get on with the rest of your life."

All the anger and bitterness which Birdie had been harboring over the past year had just reached its boiling point.

"How can you be so cold, ma?" cried Birdie. "You expect me to give up my child and then forget she even existed?"

As a few curious heads turned their way, Hortensia whispered, "Hush Birdie. You're causing a scene."

"I don't care if they can hear me clear over in Jacksonville!" Birdie spiritedly responded. "That little girl was your own flesh and blood! How can you even begin to think that I would get over it and just carry on like nothing happened? But that's you all over, ain't it? At the end of the day, it's always about appearances and what people will think, and you call yourself a Christian! Ha!"

"That's enough out of you, Brigid!" Hortensia ordered through clenched teeth. "You're not yourself. Let's just get you home so you can rest."

They walked the rest of the way in complete silence, with Birdie keeping twenty paces in front of her mother the entire way. Hortensia sadly looked at the back of Birdie's head which slightly bobbed with each angry step she took. If only she knew how I long to see that baby myself, thought Hortensia. She constantly wondered if the little girl resembled Birdie or even Patrick. All Josie had written her was that the babe had a halo of tiny golden-brown curls and very fair skin with a birthmark on one of her little hands. And even though it had been planned for months, Hortensia's heart still broke once she got the letter advising her that the sisters had come and retrieved the infant. As much as she would love to be a grandmother, her first priority was her own daughter. She needed to make sure that Birdie's reputation remained untarnished so as not to ruin any future opportunities for matrimony.

“You go ahead and hate me for as long as you need to, mija, but in years to come, you'll understand," Hortensia whispered under her breath.

Newt's lower back was in excruciating pain as he headed for home after a long day of planting rows of queen palms in the front of the hotel. Prescott had them brought up from Miami on a freight train. Mrs. Prescott felt that the original palms on the property were too short and sparse. The new tall elegant giants gave the Montclair a more-stately look. Newt, Isaiah and Felipe had spent the last couple of days digging and making sure the palms stood straight in perfect rows.

After a full day of hard labor at the Montclair, Newt still faced a few more hours of work on his family's farm. Ever since his father 's death, Newt had to become the man of his household as well as a wage earner to help provide for his mother and two younger sisters. Today was one of those days when he felt like a man four times his age.

As he trudged down King Street, heading west for home, Newt saw a female come out of Hartsfield's general store. As Newt's tired eyes came into focus, his heart leapt for joy when he realized that the woman was Birdie. After a year of her absence, it was all Newt could do not to run up and wrap his arms around her. Especially now as she looked painfully thin, sad and lifeless, her eyes fixed to the sidewalk in front of her as she carried a large straw basket over her arm. She moved slowly, almost like an elderly woman who had suffered a great loss and had given up all hope.

As Birdie got closer, Newt called out to her. She raised her eyes and, upon recognizing Newt, gave him a small smile. "Hello Newt," she greeted him softly. "It's so nice to see a friendly face. Hope you been keepin' well."

Her brave attempt at maintaining amiable chatter while she was obviously so despondent made his desire to hold her even stronger.

"Why Birdie! Yer a sight fer sore eyes. I sure missed ya! We all have," he said cheerfully. "When did ya get back?

"Yesterday mornin'," replied Birdie. "I haven't even seen Ella yet. In fact, besides my ma, you're the only one I've spoken to."

Newt felt selfishly pleased that he was the first one to see Birdie. He wanted to have her alone to himself even if it was just for a little while. "Where ya headed now?"

"I'm goin' back home now. I just had to stop by the store for a few things."

"Please, let me walk ya home," offered Newt.

"But you just finished your shift at the Montclair, didn't you? And I remember you told me that you work your family's farm at night. Oh Newt, I'll be okay. I appreciate your kindness, but you should just go on home." said Birdie.

"Now Birdie," responded Newt, "I haven't seen ya in over a year. Please let me spend at least a little time with ya."

Birdie smiled. "You've always been so kind to me. To be honest, I'd be grateful for your company."

"Then it's settled. Lemma carry that fer ya," Newt pointed at the basket.

"Thank you," said Birdie as she passed it over to him. "Now, tell me all about what's been going on here while I was gone and don't leave anything out."

"Well, let's see," started Newt, "Isaiah just found out he's gonna be a grandpappy. His oldest son and his missus are expectin'." As soon as he finished saying it, Newt could have kicked himself. Birdie probably didn't want to hear about other folks having babies right now. But again, he was not supposed to know about her pregnancy. Keeping up this subterfuge was all too complicated as far as he was concerned.

But surprisingly, Birdie's face lit up at the news. "Oh Newt, I am so happy for Isaiah. He'll make a wonderful granddaddy. I'll have to knit a little something for the baby."

Newt glanced sideways at Birdie in sheer wonder. Changing the subject, he remarked, "Oh, we had some English royalty stayin' at the Montclair last month. Some Duke. I don't remember 'is name. Mr. and Mrs. Prescott were raisin' quite a fuss, and Tangie says that poor Miss Rita was workin' up until almost midnight the whole week they was here, preparin' all them fancy dishes."

Oh heck, Newt thought, maybe I shouldn't have mentioned the Prescotts!

But Birdie just laughed and said, "Oh my! I can just imagine all the chaos that must have caused, especially for Miss Kinkade. She no doubt had to tend to their room personally."

"I heard they brought their own folks to clean and wait on 'em."

"Oh, well I suppose with them bein' royalty and all, they'd feel better havin' their own maids around them and their things," reasoned Birdie.

Newt filled Birdie in on a few other happenings like the Fourth of July parade, the fireworks and the large alligator which was found crawling down Hypolita Street until Earl Rogers and a few other men managed to trap it.

As they crossed over St. George Street, Newt remembered Birdie's cover story and asked, "How's yer aunt doin'?"

Birdie was silent for a moment before she replied, "She's doin' well, thanks."

"That was kind o' you to go up and help 'er out," Newt said, trying to be helpful in keeping up her charade.

For some reason that Birdie couldn't explain, she found herself unable to lie to Newt any longer. His innocent and trusting face was full of concern for her and she hadn't the heart to tell him anything but the truth. As they reached Bay Street, Birdie cleared her throat and said, "Uh, Newt. Would it be okay if we walked down by the sea wall for a bit? I've been staying near the ocean over the past year and I kinda miss being by the water."

"Sure," replied Newt, "Anythin' you want."

It was quiet down by the bay except for a couple of men fishing off the wharf. A soft breeze came in off the water and felt refreshingly cool. Strands of Birdie's hair whipped into her eyes as they walked along in silence. Newt longed to reach over and tuck the disobedient curly tresses behind her ear. Any excuse just to touch her.

"So, has anyone at the Montclair mentioned me since I left?" Birdie asked.

"I ain't sure 'bout anyone else but I been askin' Ella 'bout ya purty regular," Newt answered.

Birdie grinned and responded, "Oh, I thought maybe folks might have been talkin' about why I left."

"Just that you were goin' back to school," said Newt. "Then we heard yer aunt got sick and ya had to go to north and help out the family."

Tears started to well up in Birdie's eyes. She had been putting on false fronts, pretending all was well and denying her own feelings for so long. She needed to tell someone the truth - her truth - before she lost her mind.

"Oh Newt, none of that is true," Birdie whimpered. "None of it!"

As they stepped off the sea wall, Newt put an arm around Birdie as he gently guided her towards a rotting overturned canoe that had been abandoned in a clump of palmettos. They both sat down on its underside. Newt drew Birdie close to him and let her sob on his shoulder.

"Ain't no one around, Birdie. You cry as much as ya need to," he said soothingly.

Birdie burrowed into his chest and wept. Even though Newt was wiry, she could feel through his shirt the muscles he'd developed over years of hard physical labor. He smelled of sweat, soil and tobacco which, strangely enough, comforted her. They were masculine smells which made her feel safer than she had in a long time.

Still holding him, she said, "That day I left the Montclair, I was attacked. It was Johnny Prescott. I went into this room thinkin' a guest needed somethin' and he was there. And he...he..." Birdie started to cry again. Newt clenched his jaw tightly as he stayed silent. He already knew the story but didn't want Birdie to feel like Ella betrayed her. Plus, it was important for Birdie to tell him herself.

"My clothes were tore up and I was beat up pretty bad. Miss Sutton and Miss Kinkade knew what happened and they sent me home. I never told my ma. I didn't want her to worry, ya see. I just told her that I quit a few days earlier, so I can start studyin' for school. Everything seemed to be all right for a couple months until..." Birdie's voice broke off. Newt knew what was coming next. "I was gonna have a baby. Then I had to tell my ma what happened. She was so mad at me. She told me not to go back to school and that I had to leave St. Augustine before I started...ya know...showin'."

Birdie stopped to wipe her nose and her eyes. Newt laid his cheek against the top of her hair as she continued, "Ma sent me to my uncle's house in Fernandina Beach. I had the baby there in May. Oh Newt, she was so tiny and so beautiful. She had green sparkling eyes and golden hair, and she had this curious moon shaped mark on her hand. It looked like a C, so I called her Clara." Then Birdie's shoulders started to shake as she broke down again. "But a week later, the nuns came. I tried to run away with my baby but didn't get far. They said they had a rich couple in Georgia who would were lookin' for a baby and that she'd have a better life with them. So, I gave her to them." Birdie sobbed even louder. Once she was able to speak again, she continued, "And now that I'm back home, my ma expects me to just get over it all and carry on as if Clara had never been born. I had no one else to talk to about this until now." Newt put both of his arms around Birdie as she clung tightly to him and released all the anguish she had been feeling for months.

"I'm sorry, Newt," said Birdie, wiping her eyes. "I hope you don't think too badly of me puttin' myself in such a compromisin' position with Johnny. I never meant to, ya know. I always thought he was a gentleman."

"Birdie, what are you apologizin' fer? You were the one who got done wrong. Don't ya ever feel sorry 'bout that. The only thing I feel is hatred fer that goddamned Johnny Prescott! And sad fer what ya been through." Newt said sincerely as he gently patted her back.

Birdie, who was still holding onto Newt, now felt as if a great weight had been removed from her and she could finally breathe again. She was suddenly aware of a few other feelings she was having - mostly gratitude for Newt's non-judgmental compassion and his kind heart. But she was also enjoying being so close to him, feeling his hands on her back, his lips in her hair, his hard biceps under his shirt. Before she realized what she was doing, she lifted her face from his chest and sought his lips with her own.

Despite being caught off guard, Newt kissed her tenderly at first, reveling in how sweet she tasted. In response, Birdie wrapped her arms around his neck and pressed her bosom tightly against him, releasing every desire Newt had long held for her. He grunted as his tongue slid into her eager mouth. He couldn't believe this was actually happening and hoped it wasn't a dream.

Suddenly Birdie froze in alarm. What was she doing? Had she lost her mind? She was behaving like those wanton women who hung around Doheney's. Johnny had been absolutely right about her. She was a tease who deserved all the misfortune that had befallen her. "Oh God" she cried as she pulled away from him, "I'm so sorry, Newt! I shouldn't have... I'm sorry!" Red faced with shame, Birdie stood, picked up her basket and raced up the embankment, disappearing across the road.

Newt, who was still breathing hard and unable to move, forlornly watched her retreat as he damned himself to hell and back for going too far and scaring her off.

25-year-old Alonzo Reginald Stokes considered himself a fairly reasonable man and upstanding citizen. He worked hard on his small citrus grove on the north end of town which had been started by his grandfather and which he hoped to one day pass on to his own children when he eventually settled down, married and started a family. Although he was a frequent patron at Doheney's, he never drank to excess and always left the saloon with all his senses intact. He was even a member of the Sheriff's volunteer posse and went to church on Sunday as often as he could.

The only thing that riled Lonnie Stokes to the point of murderous fury was the thought of mixing races. He firmly believed that the good Lord had created people in different colors and separated them into different parts of the world for a reason. Therefore, mankind had no right to intermingle and create half-breed babies. As much as Stokes hated Injuns and Negroes, he despised half-breeds, quadroons and octaroons even more - like the one Newt Phillips had just paraded down the sea wall.

He and Grover Morrison were hauling in a pretty good catch of redfish off the rickety pier on the bay when Stokes caught sight of the couple. Phillips was carrying her basket and gaping at her with a sickening, love-struck look on his simple, in-bred face. Stokes spat and cursed.

Grover, who'd been preoccupied with taking an unusually large redfish off his line, asked. "What's eatin' ya, Lon?"

Stokes jutted his chin out towards the couple slowly walking down the promenade, "This is the second time I've seen that dumb ass Phillips makin' goo-goo eyes at that quadroon. As a member of the Sheriff's posse, I think it's my public duty the next time I see him to make sure he's upholdin' the law in case he has any foolish notions about the gal."

Florida, along with the rest of the South and other parts of the US, had laws banning mixed-race marriages. Each couple faced fines and prison sentences as did anyone who performed interracial marriage ceremonies.

Grover shrugged his shoulders and said, “Who cares. Isn’t the law mainly to keep black men away from white women?”

“No, my friend. The law also prohibits any white person from coupling with anyone of Negro descent.”

Of course, Stokes was fervently against race mixing for other reasons besides Florida law. He still recoiled at the memory of that night almost 20 years ago when he awoke to the sound of his mother screaming and throwing things in the front parlor. Six-year-old Lonnie and his two younger brothers silently crept out of bed and cracked open their bedroom door to see their mother hitting their father with both fists. "Get that nigger and your bastard child outta my house!" Lonnie's eyes were drawn to the young Negro woman cowering behind his father. She was holding a baby with skin the color of caramel and eyes as green as those of Lonnie's dad.

The boy had quietly shut the door and shooed his siblings back to bed. Despite his youth, Lonnie knew what was happening in the next room and correctly assumed he wouldn't see his father again. Sure enough, the following morning his mother explained to the boys that their father had set sail for the Caribbean and would not return.

"Yeah, Grover. Next time I see that boy, we're gonna have a serious chat."

“You did WHAT?” exclaimed Ella a few days later after Birdie had related her encounter with Newt. Both girls had just left church and were walking a few yards behind Hortensia and Ophelia, whose head turned sharply.

“Ella Patterson. Don’t you be shoutin’ on the Lawd’s day,” scolded Mrs. Patterson. “You a young lady now. Start actin’ like one.”

“Shhhh,” whispered Birdie. “I don’t need everybody knowin’ my business, Ella. Yes, we walked along the sea wall. I told him my troubles, and then I kissed him. I don’t know why I did it. It just happened, is all.”

"I can tell ya exactly why, Birdie Fairfax!" Ella cried as she tried her best to keep her voice down. "It's 'cause you love that man as much as he's loved you. The whole time you was gone, he was always askin' after ya and wishin' you'd come back. The only difference between the pair o' ya'll is that Newt knows that he's in love. You ain't got the good sense to know that ya love 'im too!"

"Listen to me, Ella," retorted Birdie, "I do not love Newt Phillips. He's just a dear friend who has always been very nice to me, but that is as far as it goes. I have no romantic notions about him. The only reason I kissed him was because I had just bared my soul to him and started feelin' all sortsa things I never felt before. I was just confused."

"Let me ask ya this, then," said Ella stubbornly, "What made ya bare yo' soul to him in the first place?"

Birdie walked a few paces in silence as she pondered the question. "I'm not sure. I guess because I always feel comfortable with him and that we could talk about anything. He always seems to understand me, even if I don't understand myself sometimes."

"And why do ya think that is?' queried Ella as she arched her eyebrows and pursed her lips.

Birdie shrugged her shoulders obstinately. She refused to admit something that she herself was starting to suspect, but Ella was more than willing to once again point out the obvious.

"It's because ya'll love each other, Miss Birdie, and no amount of pretendin' that ya don't is gonna change things."

Birdie closed her eyes in frustration and took a deep breath as they continued their way to the Fairfax house in silence.

Chapter 15

Ronnie Simms jauntily sprang down King Street on his way to the Montclair. He had an interview for a houseman job and given his previous experience at the Cordova hotel, he reckoned the job was already his and that the interview was just a mere formality. Now that his school days were finally behind him, Ronnie was trying to learn every aspect of the resort business. He had dreams of one day opening a hotel of his own.

His father was a porter at the town's railroad station. His stories of negro travelers getting off the train only to discover that there was virtually nowhere for them to stay (other than a few boarding houses) inspired Ronnie to one day open up his own inn for coloreds.

As Ronnie's mind was on his future endeavors, he failed to see the horse manure that was directly in his path until after he stepped in it. "Ugh!" he muttered as he strode up the path leading to the back door of the Montclair. As he scraped the manure off his shoes on the back steps, he rang the bell.

Ella opened the door and, seeing Ronnie standing there, glared at him questioningly and asked, "What can I do for ya?"

Ronnie shot her his most charming smile and began, "Hello. I'm here to see Miss Iris Sutton for..."

Ella wrinkled up her nose and cried, "What's that smell?" She sniffed the air around Ronnie and as she glanced down at the steps, she saw the brown tracks of manure. "What the hell is that? Is that horse shit? I just scrubbed these damned stairs!"

A wave of embarrassment washed over Ronnie but after swiftly regaining his composure, he once again grinned at Ella and said, "I'm so sorry. I didn't mean to cause ya any trouble. I'm here to see a Miss Iris Sutton for the houseman position."

"Well, ya can't go to her office with them shoes lookin' and smellin' like that," said Ella. "Ya better come on into the mudroom and clean 'em off."

Ronnie stepped inside and dutifully followed Ella into the mudroom where he ran his shoes through the scraper and dusted them off with a rag.

"Thank you, sista!" said Ronnie.

"I ain't yo' sista," retorted Ella. "Follow me."

Ronnie, already captivated with the short and sassy kitchen maid, cheerfully accompanied her down the hallway to Miss Sutton's office.

Johnathan Prescott made one of his rare trips downstairs to his Head Housekeeper's office. The aroma of the evening's meal being prepared wafted down the passageway from the kitchen. As he approached Iris Sutton's office, her door opened up and a young, well dressed colored man emerged. When he saw that Prescott was on his way into the office, he held the door open for him, bowed his head and politely said, "Good afternoon, sir." Prescott nodded as he entered and shut the door behind him.

"Who was that cheery looking fellow, Iris?" asked Prescott.

Miss Sutton, shocked to see the hotel owner downstairs in her office, instantly rose up to greet him. "Why Mr. Prescott! What a pleasant surprise. That was Mr. Ronald Simms. He's just been hired on as a houseman. He comes from the Cordova with an excellent written reference.

"Ah, very good. Very good," muttered Prescott who obviously had something else on his mind.

"Is there anything I can do for you sir?" asked Iris.

Prescott seated himself in one of the chairs opposite Iris' desk. "We need to discuss Brigid Fairfax."

"Miss Fairfax?" Iris was guarded as she wondered how much of the situation was known to Mr. Prescott. "She left our employ about a year ago."

"Quite abruptly, as I recall," said Prescott.

"Well..." started Iris, "From what I remember, she was eager to return to school."

"Iris," replied Prescott, "I'm a straight shooter so let's get right to the point. I know that my son was responsible for the circumstances under which Miss Fairfax left us. I also heard that she left town abruptly two months later and recently returned, which leads me to believe that she's since given birth to a child – my grandchild."

Miss Sutton opened her mouth as if about to reply but quickly closed it again. Mr. Prescott was very sharp and perceptive. He was also very direct, which she found refreshing. So, she decided to be straight forward with him as well.

"Yes, sir," she finally replied. "As far as your son's involvement is concerned, you have surmised the situation correctly." Although Iris was not 100 percent sure that Birdie had indeed left town because she was in the family way, all the clues certainly seemed to add up.

"You know my son's past predilection for maidservants. I already had one grandchild out there somewhere and now I'm sure there's another one, and just as I did for Miss Baxter, I wish to make financial amends to Miss Fairfax. Of course, that can never make up for the physical and emotional distress she endured but it is the least I can do."

"That's very commendable of you, sir," said Iris. "How do you intend to compensate Miss Fairfax?"

"I'd like to offer her a job," said Prescott. "I remember I once told her that if she ever wanted to return, there would always be a position waiting for her, and I intend to make good on that promise."

Iris, who was doubtful that Birdie would want to come back, had to choose her next words carefully. "Mr. Prescott, don't you think that Miss Fairfax would find being here at the Montclair a bit too upsetting given what had happened? She'll no doubt have terrible memories of the...um...incident every time she had to work on that particular floor or clean that particular room. Perhaps a monetary reimbursement would be more in keeping given the circumstances."

Prescott looked thoughtful. "You bring up a good point that I hadn't considered, Iris. I could indeed give her money, but how far would that get her? No doubt speculation and gossip over her year long absence will spread all over town. She might have problems finding a decent job. I think I would be doing her a lot more good by offering her a fresh start right here. It doesn't have to be as a chambermaid. We could put her back in the kitchen."

"I don't know if she'd accept, sir," Iris said doubtfully.

"Well, find a way to sweeten it up," said Prescott. "Go over and see her today and present my offer. Let me know how it goes." As he stood up to leave, he winced as the familiar stabbing pains in his stomach started their daily attack.

"I will, sir," responded Iris as she watched him leave. That poor dear man, she thought. Between his nagging harridan of a wife, his wayward scoundrel son and the running of this floundering hotel, he's got so much on his plate. And yet he still worries about the likes of Brigid Fairfax.

Hortensia was sweeping leaves off her front porch when a black lavish horse drawn carriage stopped in front of her gate. As she wondered who it could possibly be, the extravagantly liveried driver jumped down and opened the carriage's door. A plain but well-dressed middle aged woman with grey hair stepped down and briskly marched up the path towards the porch.

"Good afternoon," she greeted Hortensia. "My name is Iris Sutton. I'm the head housekeeper at the Montclair."

The Montclair! Hortensia froze with the broom still in her hand. She was hoping she'd never hear the name of that cursed place again. Forcing a smile on her face, she replied, "Hello. I'm Hortensia Fairfax. What can I do for you?"

"I'd like to speak to Brigid, if I may," said Miss Sutton.

"Well, she's been resting," said Hortensia unsurely. "I don't know if she's up for company, but I'll check on her. Please come in, Miss Sutton."

Iris followed Hortensia inside. The house was very tiny but neat as a pin and very cozy. A half-made dress was draped over a chair in the parlor. It was made of light blue fabric with a white lace inset on the front bodice.

"This looks like it's going to be lovely," remarked Iris. "Is this your work, Mrs. Fairfax?"

"Oh no, my Birdie did that," said Hortensia proudly. "She is a much better seamstress than I am. I'll be back in a moment, Miss Sutton."

Iris took a closer look at Birdie's handiwork and was very impressed with the pleating that was done down the front. The young woman definitely had talent.

A few moments later, Birdie entered the room followed closely by her mother. She looked a bit tired and sickly, Iris noticed. She wondered if Birdie was physically capable of working in the Montclair's kitchen, but she had Mr. Prescott's orders to follow so she pressed on.

"Hello Brigid. It's so nice to see you again after all this time," said Iris sincerely.

"Hello Miss Sutton. I'm pleased to see you too. What brings you here today?"

"Actually, Mr. Prescott is the reason I am here. He has asked me to see you and offer you a job at the Montclair."

Birdie's eyes widened, and Hortensia gasped. Iris continued, "He was so impressed with your work ethic, as we all were, and when he heard you were back in town, he wanted you to know that you still had a job awaiting you at the hotel."

Birdie politely replied, "Thank you so much, Miss Sutton. Mr. Prescott's faith in me is much appreciated, but I'm not sure I want to go back."

Hortensia chimed in, "And I definitely don't want her going back there. I think it's disgraceful that Mr. Prescott would even think that my daughter would go back to the very place where she was brutally attacked!"

Iris was afraid that this would be their reaction, so she tried a different tactic. "I completely agree with you, Mrs. Fairfax, and I even told Mr. Prescott that Brigid would not feel comfortable returning given what happened. However, he still feels responsible for Brigid's plight and would like to atone for what happened by making sure your daughter has a stable, permanent job."

"That's nice of him but I don't want her anywhere near that hotel," said Hortensia.

"Again, I understand your feelings, Mrs. Fairfax," replied Miss Sutton. "However, what if we were to put her back in the kitchen? She'd stay downstairs and would never come near the rooms."

"You mean going back to the first job I had with Tangie and Eva in the scullery?" asked Birdie. She didn't fancy scrubbing floors again.

"Actually no," replied Iris, "I was thinking more along the lines of a cook's assistant."

"You mean working with Rita?" Birdie asked. She liked Rita and the thought of learning to cook under her tutelage was indeed enticing.

"Well, I don't know," said Hortensia.

Iris then dealt her final card. "I understand that Ella Patterson is a good friend of Brigid's. You can rest assured that Miss Patterson, who also works in our kitchen, will always be nearby. And I'm sure you know, Mrs. Fairfax, that Miss Patterson is a force not to be reckoned with."

Hortensia laughed and nodded at the last bit. "Yes, she is." Looking thoughtful for a moment, she said, "If Birdie wishes to go back to working in the Montclair's kitchen, it is fine by me."

Iris turned to Birdie, "And what do you say, Brigid? Will you come back?"

Birdie paused thoughtfully for a moment before replying, "Yes, Miss Sutton. When would you like me to start?"

Iris Sutton responded, "As you only returned home, I'll let you have the rest of this week off. You can start next Monday."

"Thank you, Miss Sutton, and please thank Mr. Prescott for me as well," said Birdie.

Chapter 16

Newt walked to work the following Monday morning with butterflies in his stomach. Ever since Ella took him aside last week and told him that Birdie was returning to the Montclair today as a cooking assistant, he felt a strange combination of happiness and anxiety. The thought of once again seeing her every day filled him with sheer joy. The past year without her presence made the days seem extra-long.

Unfortunately, their encounter at the sea wall last week was now a source of tension and embarrassment. Newt still kicked himself for his overeager response to Birdie's kiss and making her feel like she'd done something wrong. He couldn't help himself, though. When the woman he loved had wrapped her arms around him and kissed him so passionately, he reacted the way any other red-blooded man would. However, the fact still remained that things were probably going to feel strange between them.

As he approached the Montclair, he saw several hotel employees converging on the back entrance. As he got closer, he finally saw her. Birdie was back in the blue and white uniform of the kitchen with a white cap on her head. How she managed to still look beautiful in that drab looking ensemble was a mystery. He saw a couple of the others coming up to greet her.

Although he wanted more than anything to be part of that happy group reunion and feel her in his arms once again, Newt hung back and waited until they had all gone inside before he approached the back door.

When she saw Birdie step into the kitchen, Rita put down the bowl of hotcake batter she was stirring and went over to give the girl a tight hug.

"You got no idea how glad I am to see ya!" Rita said sincerely. "I was so happy when Iris Sutton told me that you were comin' back and workin' for me. Mary had run off and gotten married two weeks ago, so it's just been me and Netta keepin' things goin' here. So, we're grateful to have ya here with us. And even if Mary hadn't have left, I'd still be just as happy to see ya!"

Birdie was overcome with emotion. "Thank you, Rita. Oh, I'm sorry. Mrs. Alvares."

"Oh, spare me that 'Mrs. Alvares' nonsense. You call me Rita, ya hear? I know Miss Sutton stands on formality, but I don't," said Rita.

Just then Ella came out of the scullery and squealed when she saw Birdie. "Girl, it's so good to see you here again! You're a sight for sore eyes to a few of us 'round here," she said as she pointed her head in the direction of the back door. Newt had just entered and nodded towards the group of women before quickly disappearing to get his daily orders from Prescott. Birdie shyly nodded back before looking down at her shoes. This strange exchange did not go unnoticed by Rita and Ella, who shot knowing glances at each other.

"Ella! Get back in here and count out that silverware!" roared Tangie as she charged into the kitchen. When she spotted Birdie in the middle of the trio, she brusquely said, "I heard you was comin' to work here again. Welcome back, I 'spose." Turning to Ella, she ordered, "Back to the kitchen and don't ever run outta there again without askin'."

"Sorry Tangie," said Ella through gritted teeth. "Won't happen again."

Birdie could tell that Ella was about to lose her temper, so she whispered, "We'll talk later. Go on."

As Tangie and Ella retreated to the back room, Rita said in a hushed tone, "That's the first time I ever heard Tangie raise her voice to Ella. I think she's jealous of the friendship between you two."

"Oh dear," said Birdie. "I'm back five minutes and I'm already causing trouble!"

"No, don't be silly," said Rita dismissively. "That's Tangie's problem, not yours. You've done nothin' wrong! Now, let's go to the pantry and the icebox to gather all the ingredients we're gonna need today!"

As Birdie dutifully followed Rita, she felt uneasy about the potentially uncomfortable situation with Tangie.

"Listen here. Just 'cause yo' friend is back don't mean you can swan in and outta here whenever you want," Tangie warned Ella. "You don't see Eva here runnin' off whenever it suits her." Eva, who had been quietly stacking up plates, watched the other two women with trepidation.

"It was only this one time 'cause it's Birdie's first day back," retorted Ella. "You talk like I've been doin' it all the time."

"I'm gettin' mighty tired of your attitude and sassin'. You keep this up and I'll be havin' a word with Miss Sutton 'bout you!" Tangie shouted.

Ella decided that it was best to stay quiet at that point, so she bit her tongue. For someone who had always accused Birdie of acting "high and mighty," Miss Tangie was doing plenty of that herself.

Picking up a stack of plates to load into the dumbwaiter, Eva breathed a thankful sigh of relief that this latest clash didn't escalate any further.

Ella began to count out the pieces of silverware for the morning's breakfast when she noticed that a couple of spoons were missing. "Hey Tangie," she called over her shoulder, "Did'ya know we're missin' some silverware?"

Tangie testily replied, "You just didn't count 'em right. Do it again!"

At the staff breakfast later that morning, Birdie sat between Rita and Netta. Despite being away for over a year, she still was uncomfortable being served by people she considered her friends, especially Ella. Rita must have noticed her discomfort and whispered, "I know this isn't your favorite part of the day. Just look at it as a chance to talk to some of the folks you usually don’t get to see."

Just then Iris Sutton entered, and everyone respectfully stood. Once she sat down, the others did likewise. After she said the blessing, she looked across the table and announced, "I'd like to introduce a couple of new members of our staff but first I would like to welcome back Miss Brigid Fairfax. So good to see you back with us, Miss Fairfax."

Birdie blushed and softly uttered, "Thank you, Miss Sutton."

Tangie, who was heaping pancakes onto the plates, tightened her jaw.

Iris carried on with her introductions. "I would also like to welcome two of the newest additions to our housemen staff, Mr. Arthur Dickson who comes to us from the Alcazar Hotel and Mr. Ronald Simms, formerly of the Cordova."

The two young men both nodded courteously at the housekeeper. "Thank you, ma'am."

As everyone broke off into their separate conversations, the usual buzz descended upon the room. Ronnie and Arthur chatted with Birdie and Rita, describing the resorts where they were previously employed.

"Not only do they have a pool inside, “Arthur was saying, "but when they have these fancy parties, they drain it and decorate it with lotsa furniture, carpets, plants and statues. When you're standin' in the middle of it, you'd never think it was a pool!"

“Oh! I bet it looked so beautiful!” gushed Rita.

"Speakin' of beautiful things, here she is now!" Ronnie proclaimed flirtatiously as Ella came over and set his plate before him.

"Hmmph, watch out for this one, Birdie. He looks like one of them smooth talkin’ types to me." said Ella. Turning to Ronnie, she remarked, "I see ya got the job then. Good thing I made you clean that shit off yo' shoes."

“Ella!” said Birdie sternly as Arthur burst into laughter. Birdie glanced up the table to see if Miss Sutton had overheard. Luckily she was holding court with the doormen and front desk staff.

“No, no,” said Ronnie with good humor, “she’s right. I accidentally stepped in somethin’ outside the day of my interview and your friend – Ella, is it? – saved me from a potentially embarrassin’ situation.”

Birdie ended up enjoying the meal more than she anticipated. Rita was right. It was a nice opportunity to talk to other folks she normally wouldn’t see within the course of her working day.

After breakfast, Birdie headed back to the kitchen with Rita and Netta. They had to start preparing several varieties of finger sandwiches for the afternoon tea – ham salad, anchovy spread, smoked salmon, sardines and egg salad. Birdie was charged with the tomato and cottage cheese sandwiches. As there weren’t enough tomatoes in the larder, Rita sent her out to the vegetable garden to pick some more.

The cool autumn air felt refreshing as she stepped outside and raised her face into the mid-morning sunshine. So far her day had been a pretty enjoyable one, and working with Rita was proving to be very educational.

With a small basket under her arm, Birdie headed towards the tomato vines. She heard the sound of voices and looked towards the gardeners’ shed to see the kitchen maids chatting amiably with the groundskeepers over their breakfast. Birdie missed the camaraderie she had with them back in her earlier days at the Montclair. She especially longed for the days when she and Newt would have their easygoing chats and short walks in the garden after their meal.

Ella caught sight of Birdie watching them and waved her over. "Birdie! Come on over here and talk to us!" Tangie stood behind everyone with her arms crossed while Eva got up from the table and ran over to Birdie.

"Now I can say hello!" she said as she embraced Birdie. "We all missed you."

"I missed ya'll too, Eva. I always asked after you in my letters to Ella," said Birdie.

As they approached the table, Isaiah stood up and warmly took Birdie by the hand. "How you doin', child?"

"Oh, I'm fine Isaiah. I hear you're about to become a grandfather. When's the baby due?"

Isaiah smiled proudly, "Any day now. I been prayin' that it's a boy, but tell ya the truth, I'll be just as happy with a lil gal."

Lito and Felipe both came over and welcomed Birdie back. Newt, meanwhile, concentrated on the food on his plate. This didn't go unnoticed by neither Ella nor Tangie.

Birdie also noticed but pretended not to. Instead she cheerfully said, "Well, Rita sent me out to pick a few tomatoes, so I better get back to it. Bye ya'll."

As Newt watched her walk away, Ella sat down and quietly upbraided him. "Newt Phillips! Over the past year, you have done nothin' but ask me when that gal was comin' back. Now she's back and you sit there pretendin' she ain't even't here. What the hell's wrong with ya?"

A small smile played on Tangie's lips as she remarked, "Oh, come on, Ella. It ain't all Newt's fault. Birdie wasn't exactly talkin' to him, either. Ain't she got a tongue in her head? After all, she was talkin' a mile a minute at breakfast this mornin' to them two fine lookin' new housemen."

Newt threw down his fork, got up from the table and stormed off to the arbor where he'd been working all morning. The other men, puzzled at Newt's behavior, said their thanks to the women before returning to the garden.

Ella slammed her hand had on the table and turned on Tangie. "You damned bitch! You did that on purpose. You know how Newt feels about Birdie. And for your information, Birdie was NOT flirtin' with them fellas this morning. I don't care that I work under ya. You ever do anythin' like that again and I'll kick your ass. Understand?"

Putting her face inches from Ella's, Tangie hissed, "Don't you EVER talk to me like that again or you'll be the one who's sorry!" She turned on her heel and stormed back to the hotel while Eva quietly cleared the table.

Lottie Prescott knocked sharply on her husband's office door before letting herself in. Her husband was going over the books with Cyril Compton and Frank Turner. Judging by the tense looking countenances all three gentlemen, Lottie guessed that profits were still not as high as they had hoped. Each day her dream of their family mansion finally coming to fruition was getting further and further away.

Upon seeing Mrs. Prescott, Cyril and Frank immediately stood up out of politeness. Her husband, who had been absent-mindedly chewing on the end of his cigar, looked up from the books and, visibly irritated by Lottie's intrusion, muttered, "And to what do we owe the pleasure of your company, my dear?"

"I would like to know why Miss Fairfax is working downstairs in the Montclair's kitchen!" demanded Lottie.

"Uh, gentlemen, let's reconvene after lunch," suggested Prescott. Sensing that another argument was about to ensue between the couple, Cyril and Frank courteously took their leave.

Once they were alone, Lottie said, "Martine went downstairs to the hotel kitchen this morning to borrow some garlic and she told me that she saw Miss Fairfax, in a kitchen uniform, helping out Mrs. Alvares. She said she even spoke to the girl and was told that she was now a cook's assistant. Care to explain how that came about and – more importantly – why she isn't working in our own suite?"

Prescott leaned back in his leather chair and pinched the bridge of his nose as he replied, "It's all quite simple, darling. I had heard that Miss Fairfax had returned to St. Augustine after a year's absence. I remembered that she was a commendable servant during her tenure with us and, assuming that she might be in need of employment, I sent Iris over to offer her a position at the Montclair."

Lottie suspiciously narrowed her eyes as she asked, "Except for when you recruited Donald Speer to manage the front desk, I've never known you to take such a vested interest in offering a job to anyone. Why her? And again, why is she in the kitchen and not working directly for me like before?"

Taking a thoughtful puff on his cigar, Prescott exhaled and replied, "As I said, she performed her duties impeccably while she was here last year and now that she is done with her schooling, I reckoned she would be seeking employment. When I sent Iris over, the girl expressed a desire to work in the kitchen. Since Rita Alvares had recently lost one of her assistants to matrimony, I offered Miss Fairfax the vacant post and she accepted. Simple as that."

"But I don't understand why she would want to work down there in the hotel kitchen when she can work for us upstairs for a lot more money. It doesn't make any sense," insisted Mrs. Prescott.

By this point, her husband's patience had reached its limits. He was still reeling from the bad news that his bookkeeper had brought to his attention that morning and now his wife was interrogating him about a cook's assistant who was working downstairs and doing no one any harm.

"Dammit Lottie, just let it lie!" he shouted. "Who's in charge of this hotel? Me or you? If you want to run this place, let me know because you are more than welcome to it! If not, then get the hell out of here and let me get back to work!"

"Good heavens, Johnathan. You don't have to bite my head off. I was just asking a question! I won't stand here and take any more of your abuse!" Lottie slammed the door after her, rattling the pictures which hung on the wall.

Prescott sat back in his chair and closed his eyes. The last thing he needed in his life right now was Lottie finding out the truth about their son and Miss Fairfax.

Meanwhile, as Lottie Prescott ascended in the elevator on her way back to the family's suite, her mind started to reel. Why on earth was her Johnathan so interested in the welfare of that young girl and why on earth was she working for lower wages in the kitchen? None of it made any sense to her. Then a terrifying thought popped into her head.

Could Miss Fairfax be her husband's lover? The more she pondered upon it, the more plausible it seemed. Of course, he wouldn't want her working in their suite and instead had her installed in the furthest part of the hotel – the kitchen. That way she'd still be close enough for him to see her but not right under Lottie's nose.

No wonder he became so enraged when I started asking questions, Lottie thought as her imagination continued to spin out of control. Well, I'll be keeping a close eye on them both! Especially the girl. If she thinks she's going to get her hands on any of the family's fortune, she'll regret the day she ever set foot in the Montclair.

As Newt furiously swung his axe at the fallen pine tree, Tangie's words still rang in his ears. So what if Birdie wanted to talk to a couple of "fine lookin' housemen?" I've got no claim on her, he bitterly thought to himself. What right do I have to be upset? Each new thought brought with it another hard whack of the axe.

Isaiah, who was working on the maze nearby, watched Newt take out his frustrations. Realizing that the boy needed to calm down or else he might injure himself, he decided it was time for action.

"Hey Newt!," he called. "Come help me trim these hedges. Mr. Prescott is takin' some guests through here later and wants everythin' lookin' 'first class', as he says."

Newt threw down his axe and marched over to Isaiah. He picked up a pair of clippers that were on the ground and started trimming the stray twigs and leaves which protruded from the curving and winding greenery. Isaiah was silently pruning the opposite side of the same hedge. They worked quietly beside each other for a while before the older man spoke up.

"Ya know, Newt," he started, "You mustn't let anythin' Tangie says rile ya so. She got some kinda grudge against Birdie and is always tryin' to stir up trouble. Don't take it to heart, son."

Newt stopped clipping and was silent for a few moments before he spoke. "It ain't just what Tangie said. Somethin' happened between me and Birdie a week ago that's made us afraid to talk to each other. I don't like feelin' like this. I wish things could go back to how they use to be."

Isaiah pondered Newt's predicament for a few seconds and then replied, "Seems to me like the only way you gonna get through this is to talk to Birdie yo'self. Maybe tell her how you really feel instead of keepin' it inside and tearin' yo'self up over it."

"I wish I could, Isaiah," said Newt defeatedly, "but Birdie has been through so much this past year. I don't wanna put any more pressure on her."

"Somethin' tells me that Birdie sets a greater store by you than you give her credit for. Just talk to the gal, Newt," urged Isaiah. Both men continued their chore in complete silence. Isaiah concentrated on getting the task done by Mr. Prescott's deadline while Newt was lost in his thoughts.

Chapter 17

As week after week went by, Birdie started to feel like she'd never left the Montclair. With Netta's assistance, she learned where everything in the larder was stored and reckoned she could walk in there blindfolded and find any ingredient that was needed. As she watched Rita deal with the different tradesmen who appeared at the back door on a regular basis, Birdie learned how much ice, milk, butter and eggs needed to be ordered each week.

One day, while Rita was outside talking with the ice man and Netta was picking green peppers in the garden, Birdie was alone in the kitchen dicing onions. She was shocked when she looked up at the sound of approaching high heeled footsteps and saw Lottie Prescott enter the kitchen. Birdie straightened up and stood to attention.

"Good morning, Mrs. Prescott! What can I do for you?"

"Well, if it isn't Brigid Fairfax," cried Lottie in false surprise. "Fancy seeing you down here! How long have you been back with us?"

"Oh, about five weeks now," replied Birdie.

"Well, it is nice to see you again," said Lottie. As she carefully scrutinized Birdie's reaction to her question, she continued. "We certainly missed you when you left us. I heard you had left town for a bit. A pleasure trip, I presume?"

Birdie paused for a second before responding, "Well, uh, it wasn't exactly a pleasure trip, I'm afraid."

I bet it wasn't, thought Lottie.

"I went up to Fernandina Beach to help out my Aunt Josie's family while she was taken ill," explained Birdie.

"Oh, and what was ailing your aunt? Nothing serious, I hope," said Lottie sweetly.

Birdie mentally fumbled for an answer. Other folks who have heard her cover story had never asked for details. They just took it on face value.

Clearing her throat, Birdie responded with the safest explanation she could think of. "Uh, my aunt was experiencing some female trouble, Mrs. Prescott. This laid her up for a while and I was needed to perform the usual household tasks in her house while she recuperated." There! That should satisfy the nosey woman, thought Birdie. Any time "female trouble" was mentioned, there was never any need for further explanations.

Lottie looked a bit flustered as she replied, "Oh, I see. Well, I suppose she is better now since you are back in St. Augustine."

"Yes, ma'am," said Birdie who was starting to get a bit uncomfortable with all these questions about the past year. "Uh, is there anything I can do for you, Mrs. Prescott?"

Lottie again looked like she was caught off guard. "Oh, right! Um...yes. I came down here to see Rita about her family's recipe for her famous Sauce Espagnole. I had it at a recent staff dinner and thought I'd pass the recipe to Martine."

"Rita's with the ice delivery man right now. I'll go get her," offered Birdie.

"No!" cried Lottie. Then, in a calmer voice, added, "No need to bother her now, my dear. I'll be seeing her later anyway, so I'll ask her about it then. I best be going. Once again, it was a pleasure to see you. Good afternoon, Miss Fairfax."

"Good afternoon, Mrs. Prescott," replied Birdie.

Lottie marched down the corridor, past Iris Sutton's office and up the service staircase to the main floor. Miss. Fairfax was obviously lying about her trip out of town. It's time to do a little more digging and uncover the truth.

Rita came back inside and looked over Birdie's handiwork. "Your knife skills are improving. In another week, you'll be cutting better than me."

"Thanks, Rita," said Birdie. "I would have done more, but Mrs. Prescott came down here looking for you just now."

"What?" Rita was astonished. "I don't think Mrs. Prescott has ever come down here since the hotel opened! What in the world does she need to see me about, I wonder."

"She said she wanted your recipe for Sauce Espagnole," said Birdie.

"Sauce Espagnole?" repeated Rita. "Are you sure that's what she said."

"As sure as you're standin' there," assured Birdie. "Why?"

"Because I've never made Sauce Espagnole in my life."

The late November sky was blanketed with clouds that blocked out the sun. The air, chilly and crisp, was invigorating as Birdie set off, with a basket on her arm, to the citrus trees which skirted the arbor. Rita needed lemons for the tartlets she was making.

The shrill sounds of laughter and children's voices coming from the nearby Catholic school made Birdie smile as she thought of Clara. One day her daughter will be going to a nice school like that and will be laughing and screaming in delight, too.

Although her heart was still broken from having to give her up, now Birdie was able to think of Clara without crying. She'll always miss her baby but the fact that her daughter was placed with a well-to-do couple in a nice home gave her comfort. She will be able to imagine Clara doing all sorts of things that wealthy children do.

Birdie was so enmeshed in her thoughts that she didn't notice Newt working nearby. He was on his hands and knees scrubbing the stonework that bordered the reflecting pool. Isaiah had told him to drop what he was doing and to make sure the reflecting pool was in top condition because Mrs. Prescott was showing some out of town guests around the gardens later that day. Because his back was to her, Newt hadn't noticed Birdie strolling up towards the orchard.

The branches of the lemon trees were abundant with the bright yellow fruit. As Birdie reached up to pick the first lemon, she noticed some movement in the grass off to her right. Her eyes widened in horror as she discovered that it was a brightly colored red, yellow and black snake. Birdie dropped the lemon and her basket as she screamed and started to run.

Newt, hearing the scream, stood up and saw Birdie running back towards the hotel. "Birdie!" he shouted, "What's wrong?"

Birdie stopped and turned around. Shaking from a combination of fright and the chilly air, she said through chattering teeth, "A snake...over by the lemon trees..."

"Wait here," said Newt as he ran back to where he had been working and grabbed a shovel. He walked over to the lemon trees and looked down at the ground. After a few moments, he grinned and beckoned to her, "Come on over, Birdie. It's okay."

Birdie slowly crept over to Newt and stood beside him. The snake was about ten feet away, but Birdie still felt that was too close. She started to tremble again. She had a lifelong fear of snakes and even lizards. Just the thought of them filled her with trepidation.

Pointing to the snake, Newt said, "Ya don't have to be scared of this one, Birdie. Ya see how the black marks separate the yellow and red ones?" When Birdie nodded, he continued, "Well, that means he is just a regular old scarlet king snake which ain't poisonous. Now if he had red and yellow rings that touched each other, then he'd be a coral snake, which IS dangerous."

Seeing that she was still shaking and backing away, Newt came over and took her hand. Suddenly, the uncomfortable misunderstanding that had hung between them quickly disappeared. "I'm so glad you were here," said Birdie softly. "I'm scared to death of snakes, whether they're deadly or not!"

"I'm glad I was here too!" said Newt as he looked down at Birdie. They both broke into laughter, thankful that the awkwardness between them was now gone. As Newt continued to hold her hand, he was pleased to see that she didn't seem to be in any hurry to let go, either.

"Rita needs me to fill this basket with lemons, but I don't wanna get near those trees again!" Birdie shivered as she thought about going back there.

"I'll make ya a deal," said Newt good-naturedly. "If ya hold the basket fer me, I'll pick the lemons myself. Don't worry. You can stand back a ways if you like."

"I'll stand next to you," said Birdie resolutely. "I know nothing bad will ever happen to me if you're around." She smiled sincerely at him, not knowing that her words had just touched Newt's heart.

Birdie, holding out the basket as Newt dropped the fruit into it, kept a sharp lookout for the snake the entire time. Luckily it seemed to have slithered away.

"Would you mind if I walked ya back to the kitchen?" asked Newt.

"I'd like that very much, thank you," replied Birdie bashfully.

"I sure missed talkin' to ya like this," said Newt. "I'm awful sorry if I scared ya off that day at the bay."

Birdie stopped and turned to him. "Oh no, Newt. You don't need to apologize for anything. I was so ashamed and upset with myself for being so forward!"

"Tell ya the truth, I didn't mind that part," said Newt conspiratorially. Once again, they both shared a laugh.

"Oh, Newton Cuthbert, you say the most scandalous things," teased Birdie.

"I was hopin' that after a year away, you would've forgotten about my damned middle name," joked Newt.

"Never!" declared Birdie jovially. "I love it and think it's the best name in the whole world." It felt so good to be able to talk to him again, Birdie thought, as they both slowed their gait to prolong their walk back to the hotel.

Newt casually asked the question that had haunted him for weeks. “So, I hear they’ve hired on some new housemen. Have you met ‘em yet?”

“Oh, you mean Ronnie and Arthur?” asked Birdie. “Yeah, they’re nice fellas. They’ve worked at some of the swankier resorts here in town so I’m always askin’ them questions. Actually, I think Ronnie is sweet on Ella! Can you believe it? I think she likes him too, but she sure won’t make it easy on him! That’s a shame because he has lotsa plans for the future and would make her a good husband. He tells me that he wants to open a hotel for colored folks here in St. Augustine! It would be nice for folks like us to have a place to stay when we’re travelin’.”

Newt started intently at Birdie. “Ya know, I tend to forget that the world looks on ya as ‘colored’ cause when I look at ya, I don't see no colored, no white or no Spaniard gal in front o' me. I just see Birdie."

Birdie regarded Newt in silence for a moment. It was rare that anyone ever saw her as anything but a mysterious racial enigma. With sincerity, she said, "That is the nicest thing anyone has ever said to me."

Chapter 18

Johnathan Prescott removed his spectacles and rubbed his eyes. He'd spent the past hour going over reservations and that day's check-ins with Donald Speer. Although the hotel had plenty of guests for the winter, occupancy was not as high as he'd hoped. The Alcazar, the Cordova and Henry Flagler's behemoth resort a couple of blocks away were killing the fledgling Montclair. Prescott still hoped to find a special niche or service which the other hotels were not providing that the Montclair could offer.

A couple of soft raps on the door summoned him back to the present moment. It must be Miss Fairfax who he had just sent for.

"Come in," he said aloud.

The door slowly opened and Birdie carefully stepped inside. She nervously cleared her throat as she asked, "You wanted to see me, sir?"

"Yes, sit down, Miss Fairfax!" Prescott replied cheerfully. "I gather all is going well for you downstairs since you've returned?"

"Oh yes, sir!," Birdie emphatically responded. "Rita has been ever so patient and has taught me a lot."

"Good to hear," said Prescott. "I bet you're wondering why I've asked you up here."

"Well, yes to tell the truth," replied Birdie cautiously. She was hoping that it wasn't to tell her that her services were no longer required.

As if he was reading her thoughts, Prescott said assuringly. "No need to worry, Miss Fairfax. I am hoping that you will be leaving this office with a big smile on your face in a few minutes as I am about to present you with a gift."

"A gift, sir?" asked Birdie incredulously. She was so busy imagining every possible disastrous scenario in her mind as to why she was asked upstairs that she never even considered that it could have been for a more positive reason.

"You see, we have been doing so well since we opened earlier this year that I decided to give my staff a bonus for Christmas as a way of thanking you all for helping make the Montclair one of St. Augustine's top hotels. So, here you are, Miss Fairfax." Prescott handed her a small yellow envelope.

"Why, thank you, sir!" said Birdie, who was astonished at this unexpected windfall. "That is very kind and generous of you."

"Not at all," blustered Prescott. "It's the least I could do," he said sincerely. "I only ask one thing of you."

"Certainly, sir," replied Birdie.

"Please don't tell anyone else about the bonus," said Prescott. "You see, no one is expecting it so I want each and every staff member to be genuinely surprised when they receive theirs. You wouldn't want to ruin it for them now, would you?"

"Oh no, sir. Don't worry. I won't say a word," promised Birdie.

"Good girl," said Prescott. "Well, I won't keep you any longer. Good afternoon, Miss Fairfax."

"Good afternoon, Mr. Prescott," answered Birdie with a wide smile. "And thank you again!" She exited the office, closing the door softly behind her. Feeling his dyspepsia acting up, Prescott opened up the top drawer of his desk and took out his bottle of health tonic and a spoon. As much as he hated lying, he felt like he had no other choice where Miss. Fairfax was concerned. He couldn't help but to feel responsible for his son's actions and even though the child had obviously been put up for adoption, he still had a compulsion to look after Birdie financially even if it was under false pretenses.

Meanwhile, as Birdie was leaving Prescott's office, Lottie Prescott and two women were emerging from the elevator. Although they were deep in conversation, Lottie managed to spot Birdie out of the corner of her eye. She had a huge smile on her face and was tucking what looked like a pay envelope into the pocket of her apron. What the hell was going on? Was Johnathan actually paying his concubine for her services? A look of anger mixed with repulsion crossed her face.

Margaret Wallace, one of her friends who was down from New York for the holidays, noticed Lottie's countenance and asked, "Are you feeling okay, dearie? You don't look well."

Gathering her wits about her, Lottie plastered on a smile and with all the gaiety she could muster, she brightly responded, "Oh, I just have a small headache, but it's nothing that a nice hot pot of tea can't cure. I am so looking forward to our walk around the gardens so we can catch up!"

As soon as Birdie noticed that Mrs. Prescott and her companions were nearby, she immediately followed the Montclair's rule of staying invisible as she stepped into a small alcove to let the ladies pass by.

However, as the group overtook her, Lottie Prescott pointedly stared at Birdie and coldly said, "Good afternoon, Miss Fairfax." This threw the younger woman into a brief turmoil as she debated on whether or not she was supposed to say respond. She decided it was probably best to just nod and stay quiet while they continued their way down the corridor

Birdie reflected on Mrs. Prescott's strange behavior over the past several weeks. Although she was still civil towards Birdie whenever she saw her, Lottie's attitude towards her had become progressively icy. And there was that odd visit she had made to the kitchen to ask Rita for a recipe for a dish which the cook claims she'd never made.

Birdie inwardly shrugged as she headed towards the servant's staircase and descended down to the kitchen. At least she's no longer working directly for Lottie Prescott and rarely had to see her. Plus, the bonus she just received more than made up for the woman's weird conduct. Birdie happily hummed as she patted her apron pocket.

Christmas Eve was a very festive and merry time at the Montclair. Isaiah, Felipe, Lito and Newt all helped to lift a 25-foot Fraser fir tree from the delivery wagon and carry it into the hotel where it was erected in the main lobby and decorated by contingent of housemen and chambermaids perched on tall ladders and the nearby staircase. Branches of holly were brought in from the garden and adorned all the fireplace mantels and the registration desk.

Downstairs that morning, the kitchen was a hive of activity where Rita, Birdie and Netta had worked furiously over the past week in preparation for today. They baked hundreds of cookies and cakes which were stored in the larder. There were buckets of oysters ready to be served on the half shell as well as baked into stuffing for the roast turkeys and geese. A variety of vegetables were skillfully cut and arranged into crudité trays. Birdie even learned from Netta how to make cranberry jelly, which was a specialty of hers. Boxes of bonbons and sugared almonds were stacked on the pantry shelves alongside the plum puddings.

Since Christmas Eve was on a Saturday this year and most of the staff would be off on Sunday except for a few key personnel, Mr. Prescott authorized a Christmas party for his all of his employees in the staff dining room which was to take place after the upstairs dinner was over and, best of all, the food was to be as fresh and hot as what was going to be served to the guests. No leftovers were to be served to them today!

Because all the employees, including all the wait staff, scullery maids and groundskeepers were invited, an extra table and chairs had to be brought in by Ronnie, Arthur and another houseman named Peter Bledsoe. Lito brought in some extra holly boughs for the staff dining room along with the sprig of mistletoe that Ronnie had asked for.

As Ella and Eva artfully created wreaths and strings out of the holly and placed them throughout the dining room, Ronnie chased after Ella with the mistletoe hoping to steal a kiss from her. Ella laughed as she outran him. "Get away from me, fool!"

"Okay, how about you then Eva?" asked Ronnie as he held up the mistletoe and puckered his lips. Eva also giggled as she tried to elude him.

"Ya'll don't know what you're missin'!" cried Ronnie in mock outrage. Spotting Birdie in the kitchen helping Netta shuck the oysters, he said, "Now there is a woman with good taste." Holding the mistletoe back up, he said, "What about it, Birdie?"

Birdie chuckled and said, "Sorry Ronnie, I don't have time for romance. I gotta finish openin' these oysters without cuttin' any of my fingers off."

At that moment Tangie came out from the back room carrying a stack of dishes. Ronnie tried once more. "Tangie?"

Tangie blew past him and muttered, "Get out my way, jackass."

Ronnie, Ella, Netta and Birdie all looked at each other and stifled their laughter. Rita turned from the stove where she was putting together the stuffing for the turkey and joked, "You might as well give up, Ronnie. Seems like you have no admirers here."

"Oh, I ain't givin' in just yet," said Ronnie. He grabbed a stool from the kitchen and walked over to the nearby mudroom where he climbed up, produced a tack from his pocket and hung the mistletoe over the entry.

As he returned the stool, he winked and vowed to Birdie, "You just wait 'n see. I'll get Miss Ella under there yet before the night is over!" Birdie smiled sympathetically at him as she reached for another bucket of oysters.

Once the dinner was finally served upstairs later that afternoon and the kitchen was cleaned, Rita and her assistants were finished with their chores. They took off their aprons, washed their hands and checked themselves in the mudroom's mirror. Then they peeked into the staff dining room which had undergone a festive transformation thanks to Tangie and her girls. Both tables were covered with red cloths, and fine white china and crystal goblets which were normally used upstairs for everyday dinner services. Tall silver candlesticks holding slim white tapers were festooned with the holly.

To make the gathering feel more like a family dinner, the food platters were placed up and down the table for everyone to pass around because tonight Tangie, Ella and Eva would be sitting with the rest of the Montclair personnel instead of serving them.

Eventually the maids, waiters, housemen, desk clerks, doormen, and groundskeepers made their way to the dining room. Although it was a bit more cramped than usual, everyone was in a jolly and convivial mood. Birdie was sitting in her usual place near Rita and Netta. When she saw Isaiah, Newt and the others hesitantly enter the unfamiliar room, she asked Rita if she could join them. Rita smiled and said, "Of course you can!"

Birdie's familiar and friendly face made the men feel a little more at ease. After she greeted them, she showed them to the second table where they all sat together with Birdie between Isaiah and Newt.

As they looked around the room in all its finery, Isaiah asked, "Lawd, is this how ya'll eat every day?"

Newt added jokingly, "No wonder they don't let us in. We'd only lower the tone!"

Birdie, who never thought it was fair that the men should be forced to stay outside, tried to brush it off by saying, "No, it doesn't look this nice all the time. It's just for tonight."

"Oh, have you heard Isaiah's news, Birdie?" asked Newt.

"No," replied Birdie as she turned to Isaiah. "What's happened?"

"I'm finally a grandpappy!" said the garden foreman proudly. After Birdie squealed in glee, he went on, "My daughter-in-law had a boy. He's a big 'un with a loud set o' lungs on 'im! My son named him Isaiah Jefferson."

Birdie patted Isaiah's hand and exclaimed, "I'm so happy for you! How lovely of them to name him after you. I've been working on some booties and a receiving blanket. I'll definitely bring them in on Monday. Congratulations Isaiah." The new grandfather beamed with pride.

Ella, Tangie and Eva came in and slid into the seats across from Birdie. Ronnie and Arthur came over and joined them, introducing themselves to the gardeners.

Just then, Iris Sutton entered and silence fell over the room as everyone stood up and sat back down once she took her usual place at the top of the main table.

As Iris scanned the crowded room, she said, "It is very heartwarming to see everyone here all together for once. Even though most of us have our own families to return to this evening, I feel truly thankful that we were blessed with this opportunity to get together with our Montclair family to celebrate the birth of our Lord. Please bow your heads."

When Iris finished praying and the assembled mass said, "Amen," she made it a point to announce, "Before we eat, please note that the bottles of wine in the middle of each table were sent down by Mr. Johnathan Prescott, our employer, with his compliments for a job well done. Please fill your glasses so we can make a toast."

Ronnie and Arthur took charge of filling everyone's glasses at their table. Once the entire room had a filled glass in front of them, Iris Sutton raised hers. "To Mr. Prescott for his generosity and to all of you for your loyalty, diligence and hard work. May you all have a Merry Christmas."

"Cheers." "Merry Christmas." "Here here." The clinking of glasses echoed throughout the room.

Birdie had never drunk wine before and found it a little too sour for her liking. But not wanting to look ungrateful for Mr. Prescott's kind gesture, she dutifully took another sip.

Newt couldn't help grinning as he watched Birdie trying her best to conceal her distaste of her drink. He leaned over and whispered in her ear, "It's all right. I ain't that partial to it myself."

Birdie looked over at him and tried to stifle a giggle as she whispered back, “Oh no! I wasn’t that obvious, was I?”

They both chuckled which caught Ella’s attention. She was happy to see Birdie enjoying herself, especially with Newt. Teasingly she asked them, “What are ya’ll whispering and laughin’ about over there?”

“Aw, leave ‘em alone, woman,” said Ronnie. “Come sit over here by me and I’ll whisper somethin’ in yo’ ear, too.” Ella rolled her eyes at him and laughed.

Arthur, who was trying to make conversation with Tangie, asked “What do ya think of the wine? This is pretty good stuff. We used to serve it at the Alcazar.”

Tangie shook her head. “I think it’s the least Mista Prescott coulda done fo’ us. ‘Specially those of us who were here since the hotel opened. I hear that the kitchen maids over at the some of the other hotels got money bonuses.”

“Yeah,” said Arthur. “Mista Speer at the front desk was sayin’ that no one at the Montclair was gettin’ any bonuses this year.”

Birdie sharply glanced over at Arthur as she tried to take in what he just said. If it was true, why on earth did Mr. Prescott see fit to give HER a bonus? She had only just returned a few months ago, and even before that, she’d only worked there a couple of months before she left. With horror, she wondered if he was aware of what happened between her and Johnny.

Noticing that she became suddenly quiet, Newt softly asked, “Anything wrong, Birdie?”

Coming out of her reverie, Birdie decided not to let this mysterious act of Mr. Prescott’s ruin her evening. She was surrounded by good friends and sitting next to a man who cared about her so much that he was able to detect even the subtlest change in her mood. Looking up at him with sincere affection, she said, “Nothing at all. It’s just nice to be here with all of you. I wish it was like this all year and not just for Christmas.” She picked up a bowl that was sitting in front of her and asked, "Can I tempt you with some of this delicious oyster stuffing? I helped shuck 'em, you know!"

The rest of the evening went by too quickly. Everyone looked relaxed and seemed to enjoy themselves. Even Tangie laughed at the stories that Ronnie and Arthur were telling about some of the unusual guests they had run across at their former hotels. Eva managed to coax Lito into "Silent Night". Their entire table was riveted by his clear baritone. Soon the whole room had quieted down to listen and when he finished, the humble gardener was awarded with loud applause and cheers.

Soon afterwards, people started to take their leave and the scullery maids cleaned up the dining room and took the dishes to the back room to be washed. While the other three gardeners departed, Newt hung back as he wanted to spend a little more time with Birdie, who was helping bring the uneaten food back to the kitchen. Since there wasn't much left, Birdie urged Rita and Netta to go on home, assuring them that she could handle things by herself.

Rita noticed that Newt was still hovering nearby and sensed that both of them wanted to be alone, so she gave Birdie a wink and said aloud, "Come on, Netta. Let's get goin' before Birdie changes her mind!"

As she left, Rita patted Newt on the arm and said, "Merry Christmas, dear. And please make sure Birdie gets home safely."

"Yes ma'am," said Newt. "Good night."

As Birdie wrapped up the leftovers, Newt came over and joined her at the kitchen table. With the sounds of dishes clinking in the other room, they talked easily as he watched her work.

"So, what will you be doin' for Christmas tomorrow?" asked Birdie.

"Oh, not much. I got my sisters and maw some gifts from the general store, and maw will no doubt be cookin' somethin' good fer dinner. I'll probably catch up on some sleep. I don't get to do that too often." Birdie felt a rush of sympathy for this hardworking man who considered sleep a luxury.

"And what about you, Birdie? How will you be celebratin'?"

"Seems like my day won't be much different from yours. I got a present for my ma and she'll be cookin' something for us too. Except I won't be sleepin'. I got some baby booties and a blanket to finish up for Isaiah's new grandbaby!" Newt loved how Birdie was always so thoughtful that she'd actually spend her Christmas knitting things for a baby despite recently having to give up her own.

Just then, Ronnie Simms nimbly ran down the hallway towards the mudroom. Putting his finger to his lips in a shushing gesture, he hid behind the corner. Newt looked puzzled but Birdie, guessing what was about to happen, just laughed.

Shortly afterwards, Tangie, Eva and Ella emerged from the scullery. Ella was pleasantly surprised to see Newt was still there talking to Birdie. Knowing that they would be alone once she and her companions left, she said "I guess we should get goin'. I'll see ya tomorrow, Birdie. Merry Christmas, Newt."

"Good night Ella," Birdie and Newt said in unison. "Merry Christmas, ladies," Newt said to Tangie and Eva.

"Merry Christmas!" they replied as the trio entered the mudroom. Suddenly there was a scream as Ronnie jumped out and kissed Tangie by accident. She slapped him hard across the face and shouted, "What the hell d'ya think you're doin'!"

Birdie, Newt and the others stood transfixed by the scene. Ronnie was mortified. "Oh Lawd, Tangie! I never meant to kiss ya. I was waitin' for Ella to come in!"

Tangie grabbed her things from the storage cupboard and flounced out the door. As soon as she left, everyone except Ronnie doubled over with laughter.

"I don't know what's so damned funny. I coulda been killed by that barracuda!" he exclaimed which made them laugh even harder.

"Come on, Ella," said Newt. "I think the man deserves somethin' for what he just been through!"

Ella deeply sighed. "Oh, all right." Then she reached up, took Ronnie's face with both of her hands and planted a tender kiss on his lips. Eva, Birdie and Newt all cheered, whistled and clapped.

As Ella let go and went to collect her things, Ronnie turned and asked her, "See, that wasn't so bad, was it?"

Pushing past him, Ella haughtily replied, "Don't be eatin' any onions next time."

As he followed her out the door, Ronnie shouted, "Wait! You mean there WILL be a next time?"

Eva, still laughing, waved goodbye at Birdie and Newt before she closed the door behind her.

Birdie shook her head as she finished wiping up the kitchen table. "Poor Ronnie had been planning to get Ella under that mistletoe all day only to plant his lips on Tangie! I'm glad Ella finally gave him a break."

"Me too. Ya know, lately when we've been outside eatin' in the mornin's, she spends half the time talkin' about that feller."

"I always suspected she fancied him," confided Birdie. "But she sure does her best to hide it."

As she took off her apron, Birdie sighed. "There ya go again," remarked Newt. "Ya ga a faraway look in yer eye like there's somethin' on yer mind, just like in the dinin' room earlier."

Birdie smiled. "It's funny how you always seem to know what's going on in my head, sometimes before I do. Actually, I was just thinkin' about my baby. I wonder how she's doin' tonight and what kind of Christmas she's gonna have."

Newt took her hand and said, "I'm awful sorry, Birdie. I didn't mean to pry into somethin' so personal and painful to ya."

"No, I'm actually grateful that you gave me a chance to talk about her," said Birdie. "I can't do that at home with my ma."

"Well, I think the lil gal is going to have a wonderful Christmas and that is all thanks to you fer givin' her to them rich folks so she can live like a lil princess."

Birdie clasped his hand with both of hers and said, "Thank you, Newt. What you just said makes me feel so much better and will give me the strength I need to get through Christmas."

Changing the subject to something more light-hearted, she said, "Oh, before I forget – I have something for you!" Going back into the larder, she brought out two paper wrapped bundles. "I set aside some cookies, turkey and cranberry jelly for you and your family."

Newt was touched as he accepted the parcels. "Thank you very much, Birdie. I'm sure we're all gonna enjoy these, and as it so happens, I brought you somethin' too." He went over to the mudroom and picked something up from the corner.

As he turned around, Newt presented her with large potted holly plant. The bright red berries and white flowers were a beautiful contrast against the shiny dark green pointed leaves.

Birdie murmured, "Oh Newt! They're absolutely beautiful. Thank you." She admiringly fingered the wax-like foliage while Newt lovingly gazed at her.

Suddenly realizing the time, Birdie remarked, "I 'spose we better go before the doorman comes by to lock up."

Newt helped Birdie on with her coat and picked up his packages as well as her plant. As they walked out the back door and down the steps, Newt stopped and turned to Birdie.

"I know yer goin' through a lot right now and we're just meant to be friends, and I'm all right with that. But I want ya to know that I've been in love with ya since the first time I laid eyes on ya. I wanna be a better man every time I'm around ya. Heck, I even gave up chewin' 'cause I suspected that ya weren't partial to it. Truth be told, I'm willin' to wait as long as it takes to make ya my wife."

Birdie felt shy having never heard anyone declare their love for her before. "Please know I'm awfully fond of ya too, Newt. You know me so well and you're the only one I know that I can be myself around." She sadly added, "But we both know there's a law against us bein' together."

"To the devil with the law!" cried Newt. "I'd rather rot in jail for the rest o' my life for tryin' to be with ya than to never have ya at all."

Birdie shivered from a combination of cold and sudden fear. "Oh, please don't say that, Newt! I couldn't bear the thought of anything happenin' to ya. Let's just stay good friends for the time bein'." Remembering the story of her pa dying in jail because of his relationship with her mother, Birdie broke into tears. "Oh, please Newt! Let's just be friends. I don't want to lose ya. Please!"

Newt put everything down and took Birdie into his arms. "Don't worry. I ain't goin' anywhere. If we just gotta be friends, then friends we'll be, but I got a burnin' desire right now to do somethin'." After a quick look around to make sure no one was nearby, he took from his pocket the sprig of mistletoe he had taken down from the mudroom. Holding it over Birdie's head, he bent down and gave her a lingering kiss on her lips as she wrapped her arms around his neck, drawing him closer to her.

Remembering that they had just promised to remain friends, they both quickly withdrew from each other. Newt sighed heavily while Birdie timidly glanced down at her shoes.

"Come on, let me walk you home!" Newt said cheerfully, trying to restore an air of normality between them. "Ya know, this has been one of the best Christmas Eves ever."

"Funny, I was just thinking the same thing," replied Birdie.

Chapter 19

Lottie Prescott glanced in her mirror to check her hair and admire her jewels one last time before her guests arrived. She was sporting the diamond necklace that her husband had given her as an early Christmas present. It was perfectly set off by her burgundy evening dress.

She checked the clock. It was almost 8:30. Where in the world was Johnathan? It was unlike him to be late for a dinner party, especially on Christmas Eve. Most of the staff were gone so it couldn't be anything work-related which was delaying him.

Suddenly the image of Brigid Fairfax coming out of his office carrying a money envelope took shape in her mind. Perhaps she is the reason why Johnathan was so late this evening, thought Lottie. Maybe he wanted one quick tryst before the girl went home for the holiday weekend. The thought of her husband with a girl less than half his age repulsed and infuriated her.

A sharp knock at the front door awoke Lottie from her feverish thoughts. She quickly pulled on her satin evening gloves as she heard Alma open the door. The loud, high pitched voices of Margaret Wallace and Fanny Bridges against the lower tones of their husbands could be heard all the way in her room.

As Lottie emerged, she held her arms aloft and gaily cried, "Welcome, my dears and Merry Christmas! Please follow me into the front parlor and make yourselves comfortable. Unfortunately, Johnathan has been delayed. I hope your ride around town was an enjoyable one."

Margaret replied, "Yes, it was indeed. I love the winter weather down here. Just a bit of a chill but not unpleasantly cold. We actually just came back from Anastasia Island. I see that there is an alligator farm over there. We must go back and visit it next week."

"I'm glad you're enjoying your stay," said Lottie as she opened the door to the liquor cabinet. "Can I tempt any of you with a drink while we wait for Johnathan? I'm sure he'll be here at any moment."

"A brandy would be divine," said Fanny. "Lottie, we saw the most curious thing out in back of the hotel just now as we drove up in the carriage. There seemed to be a couple kissing just outside your back-service entrance."

"Although I might be able to tolerate a quick peck on the cheek in public," said Margaret haughtily, "This couple was going above and beyond the limits of respectability. The man was kissing the woman with vigor and she was practically wrapping herself around him."

Lottie was aghast. "Were you able to see what they looked like?"

Fanny replied, "The woman was definitely a maid of some sort as she had a uniform on. I couldn't see if she was colored or white."

Margaret continued, "As for the man, we couldn't quite make him out as they were in semi-darkness. In any event, it certainly doesn't reflect well on the Montclair, I must say."

Goddamn bastard, thought Lottie. He's downstairs groping his mistress while I'm up here putting on a masquerade and entertaining our friends all by myself! Tonight's the night I'm going to tear him limb from limb. Just wait until this dinner is over!

"Good evening, Mista Prescott," greeted Arthur Dickson respectfully as he passed his boss in the top floor corridor as he was leaving for the day.

"And a Merry Christmas to you, young man," replied Prescott. He quickened his pace as he made a beeline for the suite. He was expected for dinner a half hour ago. Lottie will no doubt want his head on a platter next to the Christmas centerpiece which adorned their dining room table.

He had just left bar downstairs where he'd been entertaining J.R. Rivers, the general manager of the Alcazar Hotel. Prescott was hoping to get Rivers liquored up enough to spill some rumored plans that Flagler supposedly had for the resort. Still looking for an edge on his competition, Prescott took advantage of every opportunity which came his way.

When he had seen Rivers in the downstairs lounge having a quick drink with some friends, he introduced himself and bought another round for the entire bar using the excuse of being in the holiday spirit. But alas, after an hour, his efforts were fruitless. Either Rivers was being very tight lipped or Flagler actually had no immediate plans in the works.

Now all he had left to do this evening was smooth his wife's feathers which will definitely be ruffled. Perhaps he'll just give Lottie her other Christmas gift early. The shiny bauble that was shipped from New York and wrapped in the golden paper will surely put a smile on her face.

Despite the delay, the rest of the dinner went smoothly. Prescott was jocular and in good spirits and his wife was a most charming and vivacious hostess. Once the guests left with promises to get together next week for New Year's Eve, Lottie released both Alma and Martine to go home, wishing them both a Merry Christmas. She then sent her personal maid Violet downstairs to the lounge to have a drink and listen to the band that was performing a special holiday concert that evening.

As soon as Violet had shut the door behind her, Lottie turned on Prescott and struck him hard across the face. The glass of brandy he was holding shattered on the marble flooring.

"What the hell was that for!" he shouted as he touched his reddened cheek. "Have you gone insane?"

"You know what that was for!" screamed Lottie.

"Well, why don't you tell me because I have no idea what's gotten you all unhinged!" Prescott yelled as he brushed off some of the brandy that had spilled onto his jacket sleeve.

"Okay, if you're going to insist on this charade of ignorance, I'll tell you in two words – Brigid Fairfax!" Lottie shrieked.

"Brigid Fairfax?" Prescott was stumped. "What about her?"

"Oh please, Johnathan. You've been caught. You can stop playing the innocent role now," said Lottie.

Realizing that in order to get any sense out of his wife, he was going to have to calm her down first, Prescott took a deep breath and steadied his voice. "Lottie, please. Let's sit down and see if we can straighten this out."

Lottie sat as she was directed but was still irate. "There's nothing to straighten out. I know that you and Miss Fairfax are having an affair!"

"What the……" Jonathan spluttered. "What are you talking about? I'm not having any affair, especially with Miss Fairfax! Why, I'm old enough to be her father! Now how the hell did you come to that crazy conclusion?"

"What else was I supposed to think?" asked Lottie. "First you hire her back without telling me. Then you don't even place her back with us but instead have her working in the kitchen, and when I asked you about it, you got all cagey and angry. So, you obviously wanted her back but not working for me. Then a few days ago, I saw her leaving your office tucking a money envelope into her apron pocket. And the last straw was when Margaret and Fannie told me that they saw a maid kissing a man just outside the back-kitchen door earlier this evening. Because you were late for dinner, I assumed that the mystery man was you and the maid was Miss Fairfax."

Prescott, who had been gaping open-mouthed at his wife's explanation for her suspicions, was incredulous. "Let's get one thing perfectly clear, I am not having an affair with anyone, let alone Miss Fairfax. I don't know who Margaret and Fannie saw kissing outside the hotel but I am certainly going to have a word with Iris Sutton about it on Monday! I will not have the Montclair's reputation smudged just because a couple of my workers can't comport themselves properly!"

But Lottie still had unanswered questions. "Then why all the secrecy surrounding her re-instatement here at the hotel and what was the reason for giving her money when she wasn't owed any just yet? The employees don't get paid until next week."

Prescott sighed as he stood up and walked over to the front parlor's small wet bar. After pouring brandy into a couple of glasses, he returned to the settee and handed a glass to Lottie. It was time for him to tell her the truth. Taking her other hand in his, he said, "Charlotte, there is something you need to know about Miss Fairfax."

"What is it, Johnathan?" asked Lottie anxiously. Her nerves were already in pieces and she felt like she couldn't handle any more distressing news.

"First take a sip of that brandy," ordered Prescott, "And then take a deep breath." After Lottie did as she was told, Johnathan continued, "You were right. Miss Fairfax did have a close relationship with Johnathan Prescott, but alas it was not me."

Lottie frowned, making the small horizontal line between her eyes and the ones on her forehead more prominent than usual. "Do you mean Johnny?"

Prescott nodded. "Yes, our son."

Lottie exhaled and suddenly took on a superior air. "Well, no wonder poor Johnny left so abruptly. That vixen was trying to get her hooks into him and he had the good sense to get away from her! But why on earth did you have to hire her back and give her that money?"

Prescott shook his head. "You don't understand, Lottie. Johnny was NOT the pursued, he was the pursuer."

"What?" Lottie was astonished. Shaking her head, she said, "No, that's preposterous. Why would our handsome, well-educated son, who could have any well-bred woman he wanted, opt to chase after a mulatto maid? I'm sorry, Johnathan, but I don't believe any of this. She's obviously lying."

"I saw the scratches all over his back the day before he left, Lottie," replied Prescott. "I also talked to Iris who confirmed the entire story."

"No, no.... not my boy.... not again!" Lottie started to cry. "Not again!"

"He was drunk and attacked her in one of the guest rooms. The girl's uniform was in tatters by the time Mavis Kinkade found her and took her downstairs to Iris."

"Oh my God, Johnathan," cried Lottie. "Why? Why did he do it again after what happened last time?"

"It's got to be the drink," answered Prescott. "It changes him something fierce. That probably also explains the gambling debts he brought back with him."

Lottie continued to sob as Prescott put a comforting arm around her. After a few minutes when the weeping subsided, she asked, "Why is she back here, Johnathan? I would think that this would be the last place she'd want to work."

"Well, there's more to the story, Lottie," Prescott replied. "You see, shortly after Miss Fairfax left, she was apparently sent out of town a couple of months later and stayed away for almost a year."

"Oh Lord, you don't mean..." began Lottie.

Prescott nodded. "I'm afraid so, my dear. Going by the events, the time frame, as well as some gossip that was overheard downstairs, it seems that we have another grandchild out there somewhere. When I learned that Miss Fairfax was back in town, I felt remorse over our son's actions and thought it was my Christian duty to try to make things right for her, at least financially. So, I sent Iris over to Miss Fairfax's home and offer her employment at the Montclair in the kitchen as Rita's assistant. That way she would be earning almost the same as she was as a chambermaid but would remain in the kitchen – as far away from our suite as possible."

"Oh! I see now..." thought Lottie aloud. "And the money you gave her?"

"Well, again I felt compelled to do something for her with this being Christmas and all. I gave her a small amount of money and called it a bonus, but I asked her not to say a word to anyone."

"Oh, the poor dear. I've been so beastly to her," said Lottie. "Well, I'll just have to make up for it somehow."

"Now Lottie, you have to promise me not to say anything about this to her," said Johnathan firmly. "She is never to discover that we are aware of the situation. As far as Miss Fairfax is concerned, we know nothing about the attack or the baby. She just thinks I hired her back and gave her that bogus bonus because I am impressed with her work ethic. So we need to keep quiet about this, okay?"

Lottie nodded. "I promise, dear. I won't say a word, but can I at least be nice to her?"

Prescott thought for a second and said, "There's no need for you to change a habit of a lifetime or else she'll really get suspicious."

"Oh Johnathan. You make me sound like an outright dragon!" wailed Lottie.

Prescott winked at her and they both laughed together for the first time in what seemed like ages. He put down his brandy glass and said, "I'll be right back with your gift. I think you'll like this one. And best of all, it's something your sister Lavinia doesn't have."

Lottie smiled at her husband as he retreated down the hall. She headed for the kitchen to get a cloth and a broom to clean up the broken glass and puddle in the parlor.

“What a lovely holly plant,” said Hortensia as she inspected it closely. “Who gave it to you?”

“One of the gardeners,” said Birdie dismissively. She had never mentioned anything else about Newt to her mother because she knew that Hortensia would disapprove of Newt on two counts, the first being that he was a poor backwoods farmer and the other being that he was white. Her mother had always told her to find herself a nice colored man or Spaniard, reckoning from her experience with Patrick that loving a white man only leads to heartache.

Before Hortensia could ask any more questions, Birdie went to her room to change out of her uniform. “I’ll be right back, ma.”

As she slipped out of the dress, she felt the envelope that Mr. Prescott had given her still in the pocket. Birdie pulled it out and frowned at it as she sat back onto her bed. She still wondered why she was the only Montclair employee who received a Christmas bonus. Because Hortensia was still edgy about Birdie going back to work at the Montclair, she was afraid to show the money to her mother and explain the strange circumstances under which she received it. So for the time being, Birdie decided to store it in a small jewelry box.

As she held the pewter box, Birdie looked around her room for a place to hide it. Then she remembered a loose floorboard under her bed. She kneeled down, lifted up the wooden slat and gingerly placed the box in the small opening below. Once the slat was put back into place, Birdie decided to just leave the money in there until she could figure out what to do with it.

On the following Monday morning, Iris Sutton called the entire staff into the downstairs dining room where they had all converged for the Christmas party just a couple of days beforehand. Unfortunately, this time the occasion was not a pleasant one.

"It has come to our attention that some hotel guests spotted a couple of our employees kissing outside the back door this past Saturday evening. Because it was nightfall and the lamps were dim, the identities of those involved are not known."

Birdie froze with fear. Someone had seen her with Newt! She surreptitiously looked over to where he stood at the other end of the room next to Lito. He quickly glanced at her before staring down at the floor.

Iris continued, "Let me make this perfectly clear. While we encourage our staff to be friendly and respect one another, any romantic or lewd behavior between employees, especially on hotels grounds, will not be tolerated and will be cause for immediate dismissal! Inappropriate behavior is a direct reflection on the Montclair and we must not do anything to tarnish its image, particularly as this is still a relatively new resort. Does everyone understand?"

There was a general chorus of "Yes, ma'am."

"That is all. You're dismissed," said Iris and she headed back to her office.

Both Birdie and Newt left the room, not daring to look at each other. Even though they weren't identified, they both felt exposed.

1899

Chapter 20

As January rolled on in all its icy glory, the new year had indeed started off with a bang at the Montclair. Ever since the "mystery couple" had been seen kissing behind the hotel, Iris Sutton had issued strict edicts again romantic relationships between male and female members of staff. Public displays of affection were completely off-limits.

To further complicate matters, Ella and Ronnie became the center of controversy when Tangie requested a meeting with Iris Sutton one morning shortly after New Year's Day. Having had Ella in her cross-hairs for a while since their last disagreement regarding Birdie, Tangie finally had the upper hand as she sat in front of the head housekeeper's desk.

"What can I do for you, Miss Foster?" asked Iris, who was deeply curious as to the reason for the visit. Tangela, a taciturn woman who kept to herself, had never initiated a meeting with her before.

"Well, ma'am," Tangie began. "I do believe that one of the housemen is havin' inappropriate relations with one o' my gals. In fact, I think they might be them folks that were seen kissin' back there on Christmas Eve."

Iris Sutton's brows arched as she took in what was just said. "And who are the staff members in question?"

Sighing deeply, Tangie replied, "Ronnie Simms and Ella Patterson, ma'am."

"I must say, these accusations are shocking," said Iris. "Mr. Simms in particular has been an exceptional employee. Why don't you start at the beginning and tell me what's happened?"

Tangie then relayed to the housekeeper the events on Christmas Eve involving the mistletoe and how Ronnie was chasing Ella around the kitchen with it, trying to kiss her and every other female in sight. "And then, when I was in the mudroom gettin' my things so I could leave, he jumped out and caught me right on the lips! I screamed 'cause he about frightened the life outta me. Everyone else was laughin'." She wiped a few tears from her eyes as Iris Sutton promised to take care of the matter.

Later that day both Ella and Ronnie were verbally reprimanded. Ronnie protested that although he was guilty of bringing the mistletoe into the kitchen, he and Ella were not the couple seen outside that night. Iris told them that because they both were currently in such good standing at the Montclair, she would let the issue lie for now. However, the couple was warned that if any further rules were broken, their employment would be terminated immediately.

Birdie was heartbroken and felt guilty about what had happened. She spoke to Newt about it at length one day a few weeks later while she was gathering rosemary and sage from the garden.

"Oh Newt, it's all our fault that Ella and Ronnie got into trouble," she wailed. "It's not fair that they're getting' blamed for kissin' out here when it was really us. Maybe we should say somethin' to Miss Sutton."

"Well, I'm the one who started the kissin' so it's actually MY fault," Newt corrected her. His jaw tightened as he added, "Ole Tangie really started somethin'. If Miss Sutton finds out, we can BOTH git fired."

"Now Ella and Ronnie can't even be seen together when they're here," said Birdie. "I feel awful for them. Isn't there anythin' we can do?"

"I believe that if folks really love each other, they'll find a way to be together no matter what," Newt said as he looked longingly at Birdie. "But that don't mean we can't give 'em a little help along the way!"

That was when Newt suggested a Sunday afternoon drive over to Anastasia Island for the four of them. Birdie enthusiastically supported the idea and offered to bring a picnic lunch. The thought of being able to do something to help bring her friends together without being scrutinized and punished brought Birdie some relief. As for Newt, he was overjoyed at the thought of being with Birdie for an entire afternoon.

As Ophelia and Hortensia walked home from church the following Sunday morning, they compared notes on their daughters' behavior over the past couple of weeks.

"I don't know what's going on with my Birdie," said Hortensia. "She's been so secretive lately. I'm glad she's finally getting back to her old self. She's got color in her cheeks again and she's put a bit of weight back on. I even caught her singing yesterday. But she doesn't talk to me anymore. Not since she got back from Fernandina. Oh, she's polite enough, I suppose. Even though we still live under the same room, I have no idea what's going on in her life."

"Yer lucky, Hortensia," said Ophelia, "At least your gal is happy. My Ella, on the other hand, has been as angry as a nest o' hornets lately. Anythin' we say to her just sets her off. I think somethin' happened at that hotel."

Hortensia shivered. "I still can't believe I let Birdie go back there after what happened to her. It's only because your Ella is there to protect her that I even considered it. Don't worry, Ophelia. If anyone can handle themselves against anything, your Ella can, and hopefully this picnic that Birdie is taking her on today will put a smile back on her face."

"I hope you're right, sister."

Birdie and Ella were walking about fifty yards behind their mothers. The sermon today seemed interminable to them both but for different reasons. Birdie was anxiously awaiting the fun that awaited them later and Ella was just in bad humor.

She scowled as she kicked at a small stone on the road. "I don't care what Pastor says about forgiveness. I will never forgive that snake-in-the-grass Tangie Foster. Every time I look at her, I just wanna snatch her bald headed!"

"Aw Ella, don't ruin the rest of your day by thinkin' about Tangie," said Birdie. "Just forget her. I have a special afternoon planned for us. We'll go back to my house and grab the picnic basket I packed earlier this morning and we'll have lunch by the sea wall. Then we can stroll by the plaza and hear the band play later. Doesn't that sound nice?"

Ella tried to appear cheerful even if it was only for Birdie's sake. All she really wanted to do was go home and crawl into bed. Instead, she said, "Yes, it sounds like fun."

After they went by Birdie's house to pick up the basket and drop off their bibles, the girls headed over to the sea wall. For some reason unknown to Ella, Birdie suddenly stopped and glanced around as if she was looking for someone.

"Why are we stoppin' here?" asked Ella. "We ain't gonna open that basket and have our lunch in the middle of the road, are we?"

"Uh, no, of course not," said Birdie, who was furiously trying to think of an excuse. "I think I might have forgotten somethin' but for the life of me, I can't remember what it was."

"Are you feelin' well, Birdie?" Ella shot a puzzled look at her friend. "'Cause you ain't makin' no sense."

At that moment, Birdie caught sight of Newt and Ronnie rounding the corner and she breathed a sigh of relief. When Ella spotted them, she was both shocked and confused.

"What's goin' on here?" she demanded.

As the wagon came to a stop beside them, Ronnie stood up and politely tipped his hat. "Good afternoon ladies. Goin' our way?"

"And just where the hell are ya goin'?' asked Ella.

Birdie quickly explained, "Ella, this is a surprise we've been keepin' from you for the past few days. I felt bad that you and Ronnie haven't been able to see each other. So, Newt kindly helped me plan today's trip out to the island."

"They saw how much you were missin' me and thought you needed a good dose of Ronald Simms to perk ya right up!" said Ronnie jovially.

"Hush now and help me into that wagon," Ella playfully barked.

"Ya hear that, Newt?" asked Ronnie. "Now THAT'S how a woman in love talks to her man."

Newt laughed and Birdie giggled as he reached down, took the basket from her and helped her up onto the driver's seat beside him. Ronnie helped Ella onto the back bench.

"Everyone on board?" Newt asked.

"Yes, captain!" replied Ronnie. "Full steam ahead!"

And with that, Newt picked up the reins and clicked his tongue to get the two large Cracker horses moving. The wagon wheels turned and slowly picked up speed as the merry group headed for the bridge to Anastasia Island.

As he winked and smiled at her, Newt quietly reached for Birdie's hand. Observing this affectionate gesture from the back seat, Ronnie and Ella slid closer together. Ronnie put an arm around Ella as she laid her head on his shoulder.

As the wagon made its way down the long wooden bridge that stretched over the Mantanzas, Ronnie started to croon, "When You Were Sweet Sixteen." The others took up the chorus:

I love you as I never lov'd before,
Since first I met you on the village green.
Come to me, or my dream of love is o'er.
I love you as I lov'd you
When you were sweet, when you were sweet sixteen

As they made their way past the lighthouse and the alligator farm, Ella began to sing her favorite song, "A Hot Time in the Old Town Tonight."

Come along get you ready, wear your bran, bran new gown,
For dere's gwine to be a meeting in that good, good old town,
Where you knowed ev'ry body, and they all knowed you,
And you've got a rabbit's foot to keep away the hoodoo;

Where you hear that the preaching does begin,
Bend down low for to drive away your sin
And when you gets religion, you want to shout and sing
There'll be a hot time in the old town tonight!

Then everyone joined in heartily for the refrain:

When you hear dem a bells go ding, ling,
All join 'round and sweetly you must sing
And when the verse am through, in the chorus all join in,
There'll be a hot time in the old town tonight.

The strong salty smell of the sea air signaled that they were almost at their destination. Soon the terrain started to turn sandy as the Atlantic Ocean finally came into view. The cool February temperatures made the water too cold to swim in so the beach was practically deserted save for the occasional strolling couple or shell seeker.

Because Negros were not allowed on the beach, Newt parked the wagon across the street in a patch of grass and smooth broken shells. The rhythmic waves of the ocean were hypnotizing to eye and ear. A pelican with a fish still wriggling in its beak flew overhead. Although the air was chilly, the bright sun in the clear blue sky kept everyone warm enough.

Once they found the perfect spot to settle upon, Ella and Birdie laid down the blanket which flapped in the breeze and set the picnic basket upon it. When they had all seated themselves, Ella looked around her.

"Ain't this lovely?" she exclaimed. "Ya know, this is my first time out here by the beach."

"I've only been out here a couple o' times myself," said Ronnie. Nodding at the shoreline across the road, he added, "Great spot for fishin' from what I've seen."

"Yes it is," agreed Newt. "Now and again I'll come over here with Eddie Hartsfield or one of the Seeger boys and we'll go out on the water 'n see what we can haul."

Birdie opened up the basket and pulled out the dishes which were on top.

"So, what did ya bring us, Birdie?" asked Ronnie. "Ya got two hungry men here. My man Newt here's been up since 4:30 this mornin' doin' chores and I'm always a bottomless pit."

Birdie cast a sympathetic look at Newt who must have been exhausted before she turned her attention back to Ronnie and answered, "I packed us some fried chicken, potato salad, strawberries, gingersnaps and lemonade."

"Birdie makes the best fried chicken," said Ella and looking directly at Newt, she teasingly added, "She'd make a perfect wife for someone someday."

Newt just smiled and looked over at Birdie, who felt her cheeks turning red as she purposely focused on emptying the basket.

Ronnie broke the tension by saying, "All right now. Stop embarrassin' our friends here. Serve it up, Birdie. The line forms behind me!"

After they all had their fill, Ronnie sat back and patted his full stomach. To Birdie, he said, "My compliments to our charming hostess." Then he turned to Ella and remarked, "I hope you been takin' notes, Ella. I might end up havin' Birdie here be my cook and right-hand woman when I open my hotel unless you can show me that you're at least as good if not better."

"Ha!" replied Ella. "Is that yo' way of askin' for an invitation to dinner?"

"Mmmmmm...maybe," answered Ronnie. "Just remember, I like my chicken crispy, my cornbread pipin' hot and my apple pie served with vanilla ice cream on top."

Newt and Birdie laughed. Newt said, "Better stay on yer toes, Ella. This is a man who knows what he wants."

"What he wants is a smack," said Ella.

"Ah, ya say that but ya got love in them eyes," Ronnie cooed.

Ella stood up and said, "Come and take me fo' a walk. We'll leave Newt and Birdie alone fo' a while."

Birdie, who was packing away the leftovers, started to protest. "Oh Ella, please don't feel like you gotta leave. We love your company."

Ronnie said, "No, my lady here is right. Besides, I got some wooin' to do myself." Taking Ella by the hand, they casually strolled southward on the sandy road which ran parallel to the shore.

When Birdie had finished packing up, Newt took the basket and placed it to the side before sliding closer to Birdie and putting an arm around her.

"Ella's right ya know," he said. "You'll make...someone...a good wife someday. Thank you fer the food. I think yer the best cook in the state. Maybe Ronnie should go ahead and hire ya."

Birdie looked up at him and softly answered, "I think I'd rather just cook for loved ones."

They both looked out at the sea. After a few minutes, Newt said, "Sometimes when I'm out there fishin', I like to imagine what's over on the other side."

Looking up sharply at him, Birdie exclaimed, "That's funny! The day that Clara was born, I was wadin' in the ocean earlier that mornin' and was wonderin' the same thing! Do ya ever think that maybe one day you'll be on the other side and thinkin' about the folks back here?"

Newt looked thoughtful for a moment and replied "Naw, I doubt it. I have no yearnin' to go nowhere. Everythin' I could ever want is right here." He ran his fingers gently up and down her spine which made her curl up closer to him. "I'm happy enough just guessin' what it's like over there. And how 'bout you? Got any inklin's to sail away?"

"I used to. My pa came over from England and for a while I was wantin' to go back and see where he came from. I really don't think about it anymore."

"If ya don't mind me askin', how old were ya when your paw passed?" asked Newt.

"I was five," Birdie replied. "Truth be told, I don't have very many memories of him 'cause I was so young. The only times I remember were when we'd be playin' around or he'd be tellin' me stories. My ma doesn't like to talk about him much. She was never the same again after he died."

"Well, at least ya got some good memories of your paw to comfort ya," said Newt soothingly. "Mine passed two years ago from drinkin'. He spent more time at Doheny's and the other saloons in town than he did at home."

"Don't ya have any fond recollections of him?" asked Birdie.

"Yeah, a couple I 'spose," replied Newt with a faraway look in his eyes. "I remember him teachin' me to fish and takin' us into town fer the parades where he'd pick up my two little sisters so they could see over the crowd. I was the oldest and an only child for many years before my sisters came along. So I got to spend the most time with him. When he passed, I was eighteen and old enough to take on the farm myself. Of course, by then he'd been drinkin' pretty hard and I'd already been pretty much runnin' it myself."

"Sounds like you're a year older than me," observed Birdie. "I turn 19 in March."

"I'll be 20 in May," said Newt. "Looks like we'll be the same age fer a couple of months anyway."

"So, if you were already takin' care of your family's farm, what made ya start workin' at the Montclair?" asked Birdie.

A shadow crossed Newt's face as he replied, "My paw left behind a few debts, most of them from gamblin'. When he died, his debtors came after us for what they were owed. So, I had no choice but to go out and find work. Luckily the Montclair was openin' around that time. Best thing I ever did. Not only have I paid off most of paw's debts, but not too long after I started there, I...," he began to stammer. "I...uh...saw ya for the first time."

Birdie instantly felt an overwhelming affection for Newt. The man had been working so hard almost every day for the past couple of years. Remembering that he'd been up since 4:30 that morning, Birdie gently coaxed him to stretch out and lay his head on her lap. She ran her fingers through his bright ginger colored hair and slid them across his biceps and down over his forearms which were well toned.

With a stomach full of delicious food, the soothing sound of the ocean waves and the love of his life stroking his brow, Newt fell into the deepest and most relaxing slumber he had in years.

Birdie fondly gazed at him for the longest time until she felt her own eyelids grow heavy. Sliding down next to Newt, she tucked herself into his chest as he sleepily wrapped a protective arm around her. Eventually the rolling tide and the cries of the seagulls lulled her to sleep.

An hour and a half later, Ronnie and Ella returned hand in hand. They'd walked all the way down to the public park where a brass band was performing. Ella was cheerfully humming a few of the tunes as they made their way back.

"Am I hearing the sounds of a woman enjoyin' her day off or a woman in love?" asked Ronnie.

"Well," replied Ella, "maybe a little of both." They stopped as they shared a long kiss. The only sounds came from the seagulls overhead and the crashing waves across the road.

"I'm glad you're havin' a good time 'cause when you become my wife, we're gonna have lotsa Sunday afternoons just like this," said Ronnie.

Ella looked at him in wonder. "I ain't never met anyone in my life who was so sure of everythin'. You never say the word 'if'. It's always 'when'. Have ya always been so sure 'bout things?"

"Lemme tell ya somethin', Ella," said Ronnie seriously. "The only way we're ever gonna get anywhere in life is to believe that we're gonna get there. Like the Good Book says, 'For as a man thinketh, so is he.' I learned a long time ago that we can't just hope or wish for things. We have to believe that we already have them and before ya know it, it's true!"

"Does it really work?" asked Ella doubtfully.

"How do ya think I got my first job at the Cordova when there were thirty other fellas goin' for it?" Ronnie asked. Then grinning at Ella, he added, "And how do ya think I won yo' heart? Especially after that first impression I made? I just kept believin' that you were already mine and now ya are."

"Well, don't be too sure o' that!" said Ella with spirit.

"Just tell me when and where the weddin' is and I'll be there," said Ronnie jovially. Suddenly, he squinted as he focused on something in the distance. "Uh, Ella. What are Newt and Birdie doin' over there?"

Ella scrunched up her eyes and replied, "Oh my Lawd. They're layin' down. Oh Ronnie, we can't go over there right now. They might be...doin' somethin'."

Ronnie, still squinting, shook his head. "Naw. They ain't movin' or thrustin' or anythin'."

"Don't be vulgar!" Ella shot back in disgust. "It looks like they're...sleepin'!"

"Sleepin'!" exclaimed Ronnie. "Naw, not Newt. I can't see him wastin' an afternoon takin' a nap with a fine gal like Birdie around."

When they got close up to the dozing couple on the blanket, Ella murmured, "I'll be darned. They're both asleep!" Newt still had his arms around Birdie. "Aw! Don't they look sweet, Ronnie?"

"I 'spose we better wake 'em. The sun'll be settin' soon and it's already startin' to get cold."

Ella kneeled down and gently shook each of them by the shoulder while Ronnie said impishly, "Wake up, you two! Not even married yet and already sleepin' together. Ooh, Miss Birdie! Wait'll I tell your pastor!"

"Hush now!" whispered Ella who knew how embarrassed Birdie got when it came to Newt.

They both sat up groggily. Birdie rubbed her eyes while Newt stretched. When they were aware of Ella and Ronnie standing over them, they both turned beet red.

"How long have we been asleep?" asked Birdie.

Newt looked up to see where the sun was in the sky. "Looks like it's been a while."

"We done walked all the way down to the pier and back," said Ronnie.

Birdie and Newt stood up and stretched some more while Ella took the blanket downwind to shake the sand out of it. After she folded it, she shouted to Ronnie. "Pick up that basket and help me take these things to the wagon."

As they walked away, Birdie and Newt looked at each other and smiled.

"Did you sleep well?" asked Birdie.

"Honest to God, Birdie, that was the best sleep I had since I don't know when," answered Newt emphatically.

Birdie was pleased. "I'm so glad to hear that. You certainly deserved it."

"I must confess though," said Newt. "I love wakin' up next to ya. A man could definitely get used to it!"

Birdie blushed as she thought about how nice it felt to fall asleep next to him. She wasn't sure how to respond and was relieved when Ella interrupted their conversation.

"Wagon's all packed up!"

The foursome rode back to town in relaxed silence as each one basked in the afterglow of the delightful afternoon they'd spent together. By the time they reached the end of the bridge, the sun was rapidly dropping on the horizon. They passed a boisterous party of merry and somewhat inebriated men and women who had gathered at the sea wall. The wagon then turned towards the colored section of town.

"Shit!" said Lonnie Stokes as he threw his cigar stub on the ground. Most of the others were too busy singing and passing around the whiskey bottle to notice his bad temper.

"What's wrong, Lon. Run outta hooch?" asked Jake Combes.

"Nah. It's that damned Phillips kid. Not only is he squirin' that quadroon around town again but he's also got two other niggers with him. Time to have that long overdue chat. Let's go. There's only one road outta town that leads to his place. We'll wait there."

Ophelia and Hortensia had just finished their bible reading and were enjoying a cup of tea in Ophelia's parlor when they heard the sound of wagon wheels come to a stop in front of the Pattersons' house. Ophelia walked over to her front window and peeped through the muslin curtains.

"Why, it's our girls," she gasped. "And they got two fellas with 'em!"

Hortensia rushed over to the window and looked over Ophelia's shoulder. "Who are those men? Birdie said that they were going on a picnic but she never mentioned any menfolk going with them."

Ophelia watched as Ronnie stepped down and, taking Ella by the waist, lifted her down off the wagon. After saying something to her, he kissed her on the cheek. "Isn't my gal's beau handsome!" exclaimed Ophelia. "And look how her eyes are shinin'! I ain't never seen her this happy!"

But Hortensia wasn't paying attention to Ella. She couldn't take her eyes off the young man who took her own daughter by the hand and helped her down. She'd never seen skin that freckled or hair that orange before. He looked like one of those white trash backwoods types who frequented the city's saloons and threw racial slurs at her whenever she had to go into town. To make matters worse, her daughter was gazing up at him with loving eyes.

"Looks like your Birdie's also smitten, Hortensia!" observed Ophelia.

That's exactly what I'm afraid of, thought Hortensia. Memories of herself and Patrick quickly flashed through her mind – the family disapproval, the shunning, the discrimination, the verbal and physical attacks. Oh Lord, I need to put an end to this before it goes any further, she resolved.

As Ronnie and Newt pulled away from the Pattersons' house, the sky was turning a fiery red with the setting sun. The town's streets were almost empty save for a few carriages that could be heard over on the main road.

Ronnie turned to Newt and asked him the question that had been foremost in his mind since they left the beach.

"So, tell me, Newt, what the hell were ya'll doin' nappin' back there? I could think of plenty o' other things ya'll coulda been doin' while we left ya alone."

Newt laughed and said, "Yeah, I coulda thought of a few other things myself, but it was Birdie's idea. And ya know what? It was the best thing anyone ever did fer me. I feel like a million dollars!"

"Birdie's a great gal," said Ronnie. "You could do a lot worse, my friend. Do ya have any intentions of makin' her yo' wife?"

"I'd love nothin' else," replied Newt, "but she's scared about the law comin' down on us. I don't worry about that 'cause I'd move up north in a minute just to be able to legally make her mine, but she's not ready yet. And I'm willin' to wait."

Ronnie nodded and said, "That's the spirit. Don't let anyone, even the law, keep ya from what ya want. Or who ya want."

Just then the wagon was abruptly intercepted by two men on horseback.

"Whoa!" shouted Newt as he sharply pulled back on the reigns to stop his team. "What the hell are ya'll doin'?" he shouted at the two mounted men.

Stokes dismounted and walked over to Newt, who instantly recognized him as a frequent patron of Doheney's during those nights when he had to go drag his intoxicated father home. "Oh, it's you Stokes. What do ya want?"

"Just a short chat, Phillips," replied Stokes. Looking over at Ronnie, Stokes added, "In private, if ya please."

Newt handed the reigns to Ronnie before he jumped down. "Okay, ya got my attention. Say yer piece so I can git goin'."

"I've been meanin' to speak to ya for a while now," began Stokes. "That mixed breed gal you been sparkin' with around here – ya know that if ya'll are havin' any kinda relations, you're breakin' the law."

Newt was instantly indignant as he shouted, “Don’t ya ever call her a ‘mixed breed’ or any other name again, ya hear me! And what we do is none o’ yer goddamned business!”

Ronnie looked over at the two men who were about to square off and fidgeted in his seat. He had seen situations like this too many times in his life and was not about to see it happen to Newt. As if reading his mind, Jake Combes drew his pistol and aimed it at Ronnie. “Not one move, nigger, or I’ll blow yer head clean off yer shoulders.”

Newt looked over at Combes and shouted, “Let ‘im be! He ain’t done nothin’.”

“I see yer friendly with the niggers as well as the quadroon these days,” said Stokes. “Let me explain somethin’ to ya, Phillips. There’s a reason that the Good Lord made the races live in separate parts of the world and that’s because he wanted to keep them pure. We can’t have folks like you out there muddyin’ things up.”

“One more word and I swear I’ll punch ya right in the mouth!” threatened Newt.

“Look Phillips, I don’t want any trouble with ya today. I’m just here to give ya a warning, is all. Stop squirin’ yer nigra all over town and we’ll leave ya alone.”

Newt drew back his fist and punched Stokes square in the mouth. As he reeled from the blow, Lonnie jumped on Newt, knocking him backwards onto the road and slugging him several times in the ribs and across his jaw.

“I always thought you were a bit dim, Phillips, but never this stupid. Then again, what else can we expect from someone who had a no-good drunkard for a father. Consider this a warning. And if you continue to flagrantly break the law, I can either run ya into jail or turn your gal over to another institution I belong to which specializes in lynchin’s.” He kicked Newt in the ribs with the sharp toe of his gator skin boots before withdrawing back to his mount.

Newt, battered and bloodied, attempted to stand up and continue the skirmish but Ronnie shouted, “No, Newt. He ain’t worth it.”

“Shut the hell up, coon,” shouted Stokes, “Or you’ll get worse!”

Once Stokes and Combes rode away, Ronnie jumped down from the wagon and ran over to where Newt lay in the middle of the street. Taking a handkerchief from his pocket, he wiped the blood off Newt’s left eye which was already starting to swell up. His lip was split open and his ribs felt like knives stabbing him each time he inhaled.

After helping Newt into the wagon, Ronnie asked, “Can ya talk, Newt?”

“Yeah,” replied Newt in a hoarse whisper.

“All right, you direct me to where ya live and I’ll get ya home.”

“Ronnie,” said Newt, “Please don’t tell Birdie ‘bout this.”

“I won’t,” said Ronnie. “I promise.” Although he was a lifelong devotee of optimistic thinking, Ronnie feared for the couple who were now walking targets of the Klan.

Birdie was already inside the house and washing the picnic dishes when Hortensia came back from the Pattersons. Not sure how to go about broaching the subject, Hortensia decided that in this instance the direct approach was probably the best choice. Placing her bible on the fireplace mantle, she took off her shawl and joined Birdie in the kitchen.

“Hi ma,” said Birdie as she wiped the last dish dry and stored it back in the cupboard.

“So how did the picnic go?” ask Hortensia.

“Fine,” said Birdie. “Ella is in much better spirits now.”

“Yes, I saw that for myself when you two were dropped off in front of Ophelia’s house,” said Hortensia sternly. The tone of her voice warned Birdie to steel herself for whatever was coming next.

"First of all, Birdie, why didn't you tell me that you were going out with a couple of men?"

"Ma, I am almost 19 years old and I wish you'd stop treatin' me like a child. And besides, they're just friends of ours from the hotel," Birdie replied testily.

"Well you certainly weren't acting like you were just friends!" said Hortensia angrily. "Both of those men brazenly laid hands on you girls right there in the middle of the street. Ophelia might think it's sweet but I was outraged."

"Of course, you are!" snapped Birdie. "Let me guess! You're worried about what other folks are gonna think."

"Don't be fresh, Birdie," ordered Hortensia. "I just don't think it's proper for two young ladies to be traipsing off to God-knows-where with two men who Ophelia and I don't know. Anything could have happened to you!"

"Ma!" cried Birdie. "You're gettin' carried away now. I told ya that we know these men from work and they're good friends of ours. They'd never hurt us. We only went over the bridge to Anastasia Island and had a picnic by the beach."

"Anastasia Island?" Hortensia asked incredulously. "Why did you feel the need to have your outing way out there if there wasn't anything improper going on?"

Oh God, she's starting to sound like Miss Sutton, thought Birdie.

"Birdie, who was that red-haired man?" asked Hortensia.

"His name is Newt and he's a gardener at the Montclair," answered Birdie.

"Newt? What kind of name is that?" asked Hortensia with a look of distaste.

"It's a perfectly good name," retorted Birdie. "He is also a dear friend to me and Ella."

"No, he is not just a friend," said Hortensia. "Not the way you were looking at each other."

"And what if we're not just friends?" asked Birdie. "What if he was courting me? What's wrong with that?"

"I'll tell you what's wrong with that," answered Hortensia. "He looks like a poor Cracker. I always wanted better than that for you, Birdie. I've always told you to find an ambitious and well-spoken colored boy. I'd hate for you to wind up as white trash like this Newt looks to be."

Birdie turned on her mother and fiercely said through clenched teeth, "Don't you ever call him white trash again."

"And don't you ever speak to me like that again!" shouted Hortensia.

"Or what are you gonna do, ma? Hit me? Send me back to Uncle Ep's?" cried Birdie. "Now I might have let you push me around when I fell pregnant with Clara but that was only because she had a chance for a better life. But now we are talking about MY life and I ain't lettin' you push me around no more. He loves me, ma, and wants to marry me. But I haven't given him an answer yet because I know what really happened to pa and I don't want the same thing happenin' to Newt."

Hortensia gasped. "What do you mean?"

"When I was staying up in Fernandina last year, Aunt Esmeralda came over one night and told me the whole story of how you and pa met, how you were never really married and how pa was thrown in jail for bein' with ya. He never died while workin' on the railroad, like you told me, ma. My poor pa died in jail like a common criminal, didn't he?"

Wobbling as if she just received a physical blow, Hortensia weakly sat down in one of the dining table chairs. "She shouldn't have told you that! How dare she!"

"Why?" asked Birdie. "It's the truth, ain't it? Or are you once again afraid of what someone will think of you?"

Hortensia was ready to strike her daughter but instead steadied her voice and said, "Birdie, I'd like you to leave the room right now or else I can't be responsible for what I'm about to do."

Birdie threw down the dishrag she'd been holding and stormed off to her room, slamming the door behind her.

Hortensia took a deep breath and slowly exhaled. Large tears started to stream down her cheeks. She was furious with Esmeralda for telling Birdie about Patrick's death and bringing the painful past back to life. More than anything else, she was fearful of her daughter's apparent affection for this Newt character.

Chapter 21

The next morning, Birdie woke up earlier than usual to avoid running into Hortensia. They had barely spoken the previous evening other than to ask for the salt at the kitchen table or to say, "God bless you" if the other sneezed. Birdie felt that what Hortensia had said about Newt was unforgiveable while Hortensia found Birdie's insubordination towards her to be spiraling out control. She felt like her back was against the wall. If she disapproved of her daughter's relationship with that seemingly penniless, odd looking gardener, the girl might just abscond with the young man. So, the two women remained in a stalemate.

When Birdie arrived at the Montclair, the only other living soul downstairs was Tangie, who was not at all pleased to see her when she peeked into the scullery to look for Ella.

Tangie, who appeared to be in the middle of sorting silverware, look startled and shouted, "What the hell are ya doin' here? Stay outta my way!"

Birdie reared back as if bitten by a snake. Then her own temper started to surface as she replied, "For goodness sake, Tangie. I was just sayin' hello. No need to bite head off!"

She went to the larder and started pulling the ingredients for that day's breakfast and began to mix together the biscuit dough exactly the way Rita had taught her.

Outside, Ella was coming down the street and getting ready to step onto the path leading to the hotel's back door when she heard footsteps running up behind her and Ronnie calling, "Ella! Wait up! I gotta talk to ya!"

Ella frowned. "Ronald Simms! What's so damned important that you're gonna risk us bein' seen talkin' to each other?"

Ronnie was not his usual jovial self. "Shut up and listen to me, woman!" Ella immediately knew something was wrong because it was unlike Ronnie not to greet her with a grin and some sort of flirtatious comment.

Looking furtively around, he pulled Ella behind a tall hedge and whispered, “The Klan got to Newt last night and beat him up pretty bad!”

“Oh, my Lawd! Why?” cried Ella.

“Shush! He don’t want Birdie to find out. The only reason I’m tellin’ ya is because he’s got lotsa black and blue marks all over his face and his eye is so swollen up he can barely open it. So ya gotta try to keep Birdie away from him for a few days until he starts to look a bit better. He don’t want her to know what happened.”

“But why did they beat on ‘im, Ronnie?” asked Ella.

“Lonnie Stokes and one of his friends saw us comin’ back from the island yesterday and he was awful sore ‘bout Newt bein’ so friendly with Birdie. He started talkin’ bad ‘bout her and Newt just had enough and started to wail on ‘im. But Stokes ended up beain’ the hell outta Newt and left him layin’ on the ground. I wanted to jump down and help but his friend had a gun pointed at me the whole time!”

Ella shrieked again. “What? Oh Lawd, Ronnie. You coulda been killed!” She threw herself at him and wrapped her arms around his neck. “I don’t care anymore if anyone sees us! From now on, I ain’t goin’ one day without seein’ ya, even if it means getting up at three in the morning. Ya mean too much to me for me to lose ya now!”

Ronnie kissed Ella lightly on the lips. It was nice to hear her finally admit that she had feelings for him.

“By the way, Stokes wasn’t that crazy about Newt being out with the two of us either so you and I should also make sure we ain’t seen with ‘im in public,” advised Ronnie.

Ella looked disappointed. “That’s just awful. I had a lotta fun with ‘em yesterday and was lookin’ forward to more rides together.”

"Me, too" said Ronnie. "But for now, we all gotta lay low if we wanna save Newt from any more beatin's or worse. And that includes Birdie."

"So, I'm supposed to keep Birdie away from Newt and not tell her why?" asked Ella. Shaking her head, she muttered, "You might as well tell me to part the Red Sea."

When Rita and Netta came in a little while later, they were shocked to see that Birdie had everything already in place. Rita was very pleased to see Birdie so ambitious while Netta laughed and said, "Looks like I'll have to start gettin' up early too before Birdie starts makin' me look bad."

"Oh, I didn't mean to show anyone up," cried Birdie in alarm. "I just needed to get out of the house and decided to come in a bit earlier than usual today."

"Relax, Birdie," said Rita soothingly. "Netta was just kiddin'."

Netta nodded and reassuringly replied, "Yeah Birdie. I was just jokin' 'round. Thanks for gettin' everythin' out for us. Ya made my mornin' much easier!"

"I'm sorry," said Birdie. "I just ain't myself today."

"That's all right, my girl. It's all forgotten," cooed Rita as she patted Birdie on the shoulder. "Now let's get started on the hotcakes."

As the other employees started to file in, Birdie kept looking up, hoping to catch sight of Newt. He filled her thoughts all throughout the previous night. She wanted so much to throw her arms around him and shield him from her mother's derogatory comments and snap judgements.

Lito and Felipe had entered and tipped their hats to her as they carried on down the hallway to get their daily instructions. A few minutes later, Isaiah came in and, as he was running his boots over the scraper in the mudroom, Birdie wiped the flour off her hands and went over to talk to him.

"Hi Isaiah," she greeted him brightly. "Have ya seen Newt today?"

Isaiah hesitated for a second before he smiled and replied, "Mornin' Birdie. I got Newt workin' on the new rock garden fo' Mrs. Prescott up front so he'll be pretty busy fo' the next few days."

"Oh," responded Birdie in a small voice as she tried to hide her dashed hopes. Attempting to sound cheerful, she added, "Well, give him my regards."

Isaiah tipped his hat and hurried toward Iris Sutton's office, figuring out how he was going to explain Newt's absence to Mr. Prescott much less try to keep it from Birdie. The boy showed up that morning looking like he'd been run over by a team of horses and walking like an old man. When Newt told him about his encounter with the Klan, Isaiah knew that he couldn't risk having Newt present himself to Mr. Prescott. The hotelier would assume that Newt had been in some sort of bar fight and would possibly fire him on the spot. Mr. Prescott set a great store about his male staffers staying sober in public and avoiding fisticuffs, so the telling the boss the truth was certainly out of the question.

All throughout the morning, Birdie kept a watchful eye out for Newt, occasionally peeking through the rear kitchen window. She so desperately needed to talk to him but there was no sign of him anywhere. As she wasn't allowed up front, she had no other choice but to wait until the scullery maids and groundskeepers gathered for their breakfast outside.

However, when the time finally came and Birdie stepped into the vegetable garden to have a look, there were only the three other gardeners eating with Tangie, Ella and Eva. Birdie was puzzled. Where was Newt?

After they returned inside, Birdie accosted Ella and asked, "Ella, have you seen Newt today? Why wasn't he eatin' with the rest of ya'll?"

A fleeting look of uncertainty flitted across Ella's face before Tangie spoke up. "Ella! Get back there and finish those dishes! If you don't mind, Rita, please tell your assistant to stop botherin' my staff with her personal problems."

Rita, who was busily preparing a conch chowder, looked up and admonished, "Birdie. Keep your attention on your work, dear. Come chop up this celery for me, please."

Tangie flounced out of the room behind Ella while Birdie miserably started to cut up the celery. Folks were sure acting strange today, she thought. First Tangie had shouted at her when she first arrived, then Isaiah looked a little uneasy when she asked about Newt. Even Ella wasn't her usual self, and for some reason Newt skipped his daily meal, which he never missed.

Ella silently fumed as she put away the mop after cleaning out the scullery. The way Tangie hollered at her and told on Birdie to Rita rankled her to the core. She looked forward to the day that Ronnie opened his hotel for real and not just in his mind. On that day, Ella planned on taking off her apron, throwing it down in front of Tangie and telling her, "Kiss my ass. I quit," before shoving her head in a sink full of dirty water.

Ella had pulled Isaiah aside earlier that day and confessed that she knew what really happened. Isaiah told her about the rock garden excuse he had to use for both Birdie and Prescott. Poor Birdie. All she wanted to do was talk to Newt but for her sake, they were forced to play along with the charade until he was a little more presentable. Luckily the others were all clueless as to what happened and were therefore unable to let anything slip.

The next couple of days were anxious ones for Birdie as she kept vigilant for any signs of Newt. On Wednesday Iris Sutton appeared in the kitchen and motioned for Birdie to drop the canapés she was working on and follow the housekeeper to her office.

As Birdie followed Iris through the door, she was shocked to find Lottie Prescott seated in front of Miss Sutton's desk. She motioned for Birdie to sit beside her as Iris took her own seat.

"Hello Brigid," said Mrs. Prescott cheerfully. Taken aback by Lottie's sudden friendliness, Birdie proceeded with caution as she sat down.

"Good morning, Mrs. Prescott," responded Birdie respectfully.

"Brigid," began Lottie. "I was wondering if you'd like to start sewing for me again."

As Birdie inwardly cringed at the thought of going back to work in the Prescott suite, Lottie quickly assured her, "You'll still be working down in the kitchen, of course. This would be a project you'd be doing for me on the side, and you will be compensated for it quite handsomely."

The proposition intrigued Birdie. "What exactly would I be working on, Mrs. Prescott?"

"Well, Iris here was telling me that you do lovely pleat work and I'd love for you to make me a white cotton blouse for the summer," said Lottie.

Iris jumped in, "When I went to your house a few months ago, I took note of a piece of needlework you'd been working on at the time. It looked like a very professional job. Strong, even stitches and excellent precision."

Birdie jogged her memory to try to recollect what she had been working on around that time. It must have been Ophelia's light blue Sunday dress.

"Yes, Mrs. Prescott. I'd be happy to take on the job," Birdie replied. "If you could have your ladies' maid take your measurements for me and send them down to me, I'll get started."

"Splendid!" Lottie opened her purse and took out a crisp five-dollar bill. "Here you are, Brigid. This should get you all the materials you'll need. And when you are finished, I'll pay you for your labor."

Birdie's mouth dropped open before she remembered herself. Five whole dollars just for the materials? My goodness, that's what I make in a week, she marveled to herself.

"Thank you, Mrs. Prescott. I'll have it to you as soon as I can," said Birdie.

"Take your time, Brigid," said Lottie who was pleased to have her seamstress back under her commission.

"Thank you, Brigid," said Miss Sutton. "You may return to the kitchen now."

"Yes ma'am," said Birdie as she stood up and placed the money in her apron pocket.

"Have you seen my new rock garden, Iris?" asked Lottie.

Birdie's ears pricked up as she headed for the door.

"Yes, our groundskeepers did a wonderful job. It's very pleasing to the eye," remarked Iris.

"Actually, Johnathan tells me that it was all done by the young Phillips boy, and can you believe that he managed to get it all done in one day? God bless him," said Lottie.

As Birdie was shutting the door behind her, Mrs. Prescott's words rang in her ears. "He did it all in one day." If Newt did all that work on Monday, then why hadn't she seen him since? Where was he?

Newt sat on an overturned wheelbarrow as he watched the long plumes of smoke rise up from the burning pile of trash he'd just set aflame. Since he passed out from pain while lugging stones for Mrs. Prescott's small rock garden, Isaiah had him doing less rigorous chores over the past few days like pruning, weeding and burning garbage. He was grateful to Felipe and Lito for stepping in and finishing up the rock garden in one day.

He reckoned soon the bruising would be healed enough so he could face Birdie, who he missed something awful. The evenings, when his desire for her would reach its painful peak, were the worst. Adding to his misery were the injuries he suffered courtesy of Lonnie Stokes. Every time he took a deep breath, a knife ripped through his ribcage. He was able to speak properly again as his lip started to heal, and his eye was no longer swollen like a grapefruit and was now a dark shade of purple.

His mother cried in terror when she first laid eyes on him Sunday night. Newt was able to mollify her with a story about a bar brawl which got out of hand and that the other party in question looked much worse than he did.

Every time he thought of Stokes, Newt burned. He hated him and all others like him who, like a cancer, rapidly spread their narrow-mindedly evil ideas everywhere they went. The fact that Stokes seemed to particularly be pinning his prejudice on Birdie made Newt want to kill him all the more.

He sharply turned when he heard the sounds of footsteps and twigs breaking in the grass behind him. The sudden movement almost made him groan in agony until he saw that the intruder was Birdie. He slowly stood as she approached.

"There you are, Newt! Where've you been for the past three days? I just knew I'd find ya here when I saw the smoke in the sky!" Birdie stopped talking and gasped as she got up close enough to notice Newt's bruises and abrasions. "Good Lord, what happened to ya?"

Newt immediately recited the excuse he'd concocted for Birdie since Sunday night. "Oh, I tried to shoe one of the horses after we got back from the beach and got kicked mighty hard. I was too ashamed fer you to see me like this."

As much as he hated lying to the woman he loved, Newt felt that it was more than justified in this situation and was compelled to shield Birdie from the brutality of Stokes and others like him - even if it meant misleading her.

"How could you even think that? You know I wouldn't be bothered by it one bit." Birdie ran her fingertips ever so softly over his eye and his lip. "I ain't hurtin' you, am I?"

"Heck no," replied Newt sincerely. Looking around to make sure no one was watching them, he took Birdie's hands in his and kissed them. "I hated not seein' ya. These past three days have been pure hell fer me."

"And me," agreed Birdie. Before Newt was able to react, she gave him a quick hug around his waist which elicited a pained groan as he shrunk back.

Birdie was baffled. "Oh my, I DID hurt you! I'm so sorry. Let me take a look...."

"No!" cried Newt, much firmer than he intended to. The stunned look on her face made him feel bad about his reaction, so he quickly added, "We've already been seen kissin' out here once. No sense givin' anyone the wrong idea."

"Sorry. I guess I better get back," said Birdie. "Nice seein' ya again and I hope you heal up soon. Bye."

As she scurried back to the hotel, Newt called after her, "Birdie, wait!" But she didn't turn back and continued on her course back to the kitchen. Newt smacked his forehead hard in frustration. I'm such a jackass, he scolded himself.

Tears burned at Birdie's eyes as she headed for the hotel. Not only were things at home tense with her mother, but everyone at the Montclair has been behaving so oddly this week. Even Newt, the one person who she felt that she could turn to, was acting the most bizarre of all. She just couldn't figure any of it out.

One thing was for certain. Newt's injuries definitely were not from a simple kick from a disgruntled horse.

That Sunday afternoon, Birdie was helping Ella into the maroon dress she had just finished altering for her. Both the color and the cut were very flattering on Ella's short, stout frame. Ella regarded herself in the floor length mirror in the bedroom that she shared with two of her sisters.

"Birdie, I declare you never cease to amaze me! Somehow you managed to take this old dress of Mrs. Compton's and turn it into somethin' stylish that looks like it was made just fo' me!"

Whenever Della Compton had a clothing drive for the poor, she would often give Hortensia some of the cast-offs which Birdie would promptly make over for her mother, Ella or herself. Birdie took great pains to revamp the dresses so that they not only looked more stylish but so different from their previous incarnations so as not to be recognized by their original owners.

"Thank you, my sister!" said Ella as she gave Birdie a hug. "I wish I had half yo' talent with the needle!"

"No need to thank me, Ella. You know I'd do anything for ya," said Birdie. Grinning, she added, "Will you be wearin' this when you meet up with Ronnie later on?"

Ella smiled coyly and said, "I just might."

Every morning over the past week, Ronnie would meet Ella at the plaza which was the halfway point between his house and hers. From there they would walk to the Montclair together. Then he would spend the next hour before his shift talking to Ella while she polished the brass work outside, taking great care not to be seen by Tangie or anyone else. Luckily he was able to do this under the cloak of darkness as the sun didn't rise for another hour. This week they made arrangements to go to the social that was being held at Ella's church.

"Well, you look so beautiful, you'll leave him speechless!" declared Birdie.

"Are you kiddin'," said Ella, "that man has never been speechless in his life. I believe he came out of the womb already talkin' up a storm!"

"Oh, you know what I meant," said Birdie with a laugh. "You joke about him a lot but you ain't foolin' me, Ella Patterson. I know how much he really means to you."

"I reckon yo' right," said Ella. "I just don't wanna give him a head more swollen that what he got now."

"Oh Ella, you are something!" giggled Birdie. "I hope that soon the four of us can go back to the beach again. That was a lot of fun, wasn't it?"

Ella was hesitant. After a moment, she haltingly replied, "Well Birdie, I think now that Ronnie and I are courtin', maybe we should spend our free time alone so that we can get to know each other better. I hope ya understand. It's nothin' against ya'll." It was the hardest thing she ever had to say to her lifelong friend. But if it meant saving the four of them from a run-in with Stokes and his gang, then she had no choice but to do what was necessary to keep everyone safe.

"Oh. All right," murmured Birdie as she closed up her sewing basket that was on the floor behind them. "Well, you and Ronnie have a wonderful afternoon. I want to hear all about it tomorrow!" Feeling more alone than ever, she quietly left and headed home.

Ella sat down on her bed feeling both frustrated and helpless. Birdie was obviously hurt but her hands were tied. "Dammit!" she said aloud.

Chapter 22

For the next couple of months, Birdie decided to focus on the only stable area in her life – her job. Both Rita Alvares and Lottie Prescott were islands of normality in a world where all her friends and even her own mother were acting out of character. So, Birdie started to show an increased interest in the more complex dishes which Rita produced for the evening meals. When she wasn't learning how to prepare gourmet dishes with exotic names, she spent every spare moment working on Mrs. Prescott's blouse, which actually helped her break the ice with Hortensia.

One night Hortensia saw Birdie staying up late to trim one of the sleeves with a thin lilac satin ribbon. She curiously watched as her daughter expertly wove the ribbon through a layer of open weave lace.

"That's pretty," said Hortensia. "Is it for yourself?"

"No, it's for Mrs. Prescott," replied Birdie as she started to loosely draw the ends together and tie them in a bow which she tacked into place with a few stitches. This would form the top of the leg-o-mutton sleeve.

"Mrs. Prescott!" exclaimed Hortensia in awe. "She actually asked you to work on this for you?" When Birdie nodded in the affirmative, her mother cautiously asked, "But you're not going up to her suite, are you?" Even though she was pleased that Birdie was being noticed for her God given skills, she was still uncomfortable with her proximity to anyone related to Johnny Prescott.

"No, ma," answered Birdie. "Her personal maid Violet gave me her measurements and I do everything here. Once I'm done, I'll send it upstairs to Violet who'll have her try it on. She'll let me know if any alterations are needed."

Hortensia breathed a bit easier. To Birdie's surprise, her mother hugged her and said, "I'm so proud of you, mija. I've always believed that your sewing skills which the Good Lord blessed you with will take you far."

"Thanks ma," said Birdie sincerely.

And hopefully they'll take her far away from that red-haired dirt farmer, thought Hortensia.

Newt distractedly pushed the grits around his breakfast plate. He hadn't had much of an appetite lately. Ever since he inadvertently shouted at Birdie, he'd felt awful. What was worse was that an opportunity to see her alone had not presented itself. He only saw her as he passed through the kitchen each morning before his shift or when she was picking vegetables in the garden while he was over at the table eating with the others. Each time he saw her, she was very friendly and talkative enough. But he sorely missed their times alone.

Ella, who'd noticed Newt's moodiness, detached herself from a conversation she was having with Eva and Lito and slipped over to the end of the table where he sat alone. "I'd offer ya a penny fo' yo' thoughts but I already know who you're thinkin' 'bout."

"Why the hell did I have to holler at her?" Newt asked.

"Fo' cryin' out loud, stop beatin' yo'self up about it," said Ella impatiently. Then, in a more sympathetic tone, she added, "You didn't do it on purpose. You just didn't want her seein' yo' cuts 'n bruises, is all. Anyone would've done the same. Besides, she still comes over and talks to ya whenever she sees ya out here."

"But that's only 'cause there's other folk around," muttered Newt.

"Look Mr. Newt," said Ella seriously, "I know how ya feel. Do ya think it was easy fo' me havin' to tell Birdie that me and Ronnie wanted to be alone on Sundays? I sat and cried for the longest time afterwards. It took Ronnie a whole lotta convincin' for me to go to that church social with him afterwards."

"Well, I reckon you do know how I feel," said Newt, "but it don't make it no easier."

"This'll all come out all right in the end," assured Ella. "For now, all we need to do is show her how much we care 'bout her."

Their conversation was brought to a swift end when Tangie announced that it was time to return to the kitchen. Newt chewed on what Ella had told him as he picked up his machete and headed back up front to continue trimming the thick fronds from the palms lining the main walkway.

Johnathan Prescott Sr. was gazing through the north window on the front side of the Montclair and stared at the new rock garden below. As soon as Lottie had read to him a portion of her sister Lavinia's latest missive describing a rock garden that she just had installed, Prescott immediately commissioned one for the front of the Montclair for his wife. Young Phillips did a fine job, he thought. But I'll be hanged if I can figure out how the heck he did it all in a day by himself.

A sharp knock at his office door brought Prescott out of his musings. "Come in," he directed as Iris Sutton entered. "Ah, good morning, Iris. Have a seat," he said as he motioned toward a chair in front of his desk.

As he sat down into his soft black leather chair, Prescott asked, "Things running smoothly today?"

"Yes, sir," replied Iris. "Other than the back order on the laundry equipment and the missing pieces of silverware that we had previous spoken about, everything is fine at the moment."

"Well, there's nothing we can do about the first issue and as for the second, we'll keep an eye on that. I'm sure it's just a matter of someone miscounting," said Prescott. As he took a cigar from the box of Cubans on his desk, he asked, "How is Miss Fairfax coming along downstairs?"

"From all accounts, she is excelling in the kitchen under Mrs. Alvares' tutelage," reported Iris. "She's even cooked one of tonight's main courses all by herself."

Prescott lit the cigar and sat back in his chair. Taking a thoughtful puff, he said, "I know that Lottie was absolutely delighted with the blouse that Miss Fairfax had made for her. She couldn't wait to show it off to her friends at the ladies salon yesterday. Apparently, they were quite impressed and want some made up for themselves."

Iris nodded and said, "I am not surprised, Mr. Prescott. I have been well aware of Miss Fairfax's aptitude at dressmaking for a while now."

Prescott took another puff and as he slowly exhaled, he asked, "Iris, what do you think about us capitalizing on Miss Fairfax's talents?"

Intrigued, Iris asked, "In what respect, sir?"

"Well, perhaps we could offer her dressmaking services as an extra little perk for our regular female guests. Just our more influential visitors, mind you. We certainly couldn't do this for all our female guests without overwhelming Miss Fairfax," said Prescott. "Your thoughts?"

"I think Miss Fairfax definitely has the aptitude and skill required. However, I'd still need to talk to her to see if she is willing to do so," began Iris. "As you are no doubt already aware, sir, there are the logistical matters that will need to be dealt with."

"Yes, yes, of course," said Prescott.

"First and foremost," began Iris, "I am aware that the girl primarily works by hand. A sewing machine would obviously be needed in order for her to keep up with orders. I'm not sure she's ever operated one before."

"Oh, I'm sure our budget can accommodate a sewing machine and even the cost of someone to show her how to operate it. Plus, she'll no doubt need some sort of workspace," added Prescott. "We certainly don't expect her to continue doing this at home. I know we have a limited number of small empty rooms left in the building. It would have to be somewhere that is accessible to our guests but not too close to the main lobby. I suppose it would also need a window so that she'll have extra light during the day."

An idea suddenly occurred to Iris. "Sir, what about the extra storage room just off the smaller ballroom on the mezzanine?" Prescott looked puzzled so Iris continued, "It faces the south side of the hotel and has a nice sized window for light."

"Oh yes," said Prescott. "I know the very one you're speaking of. That's an excellent idea, Iris. Let's bring Miss Fairfax up here and present her with our offer."

Similar to one in Miss Sutton's office, Prescott had a speaking tube cabinet installed in the wall behind his desk. He opened the cupboard door and pulled out one of tubes. After blowing into it and activating the whistle down at the front desk, Mr. Speer answered.

"Speer," said Prescott loudly into the tube, "Get one of your housemen down to the kitchen to get Brigid Fairfax. I need to see her in my office immediately."

Birdie was in the garden looking for a few decent sized eggplants. As much as Birdie loved Rita's stuffed eggplant which was on that evening's menu, Birdie was much more fascinated with the pretty flowers which bloomed just before the fruit developed. Looking like bright purple five-point stars with vivid yellow centers, they captivated her just as much as the finest blooms in the rose garden. As she gingerly touched the delicate blossoms, she was startled by Newt's voice behind her. "They're right pretty, ain't they?"

“Why, yes,” she said as she tried to compose herself both from the shock of his stealthy approach as well as the excitement she felt from being alone with him for the first time in what felt like ages.

“They look like they just fell outta the night sky,” said Newt.

“Yes! They sure do,” agreed Birdie as she picked up the basket that held the four eggplants she had already plucked.

“If ya like these, let me show ya somethin’ even better!” Newt led her around the back of the vegetable garden where rows of broccoli grew in varying stages. In the corner was a taller, bushy plant comprised of what looked like several bouquets of tiny buttery yellow flowers. Birdie gasped in delight.

“Oh, how pretty!”

“Smell ‘em,” said Newt.

“What?”

“Go on, smell ‘em,” repeated Newt with a smile.

Birdie looked at him with a suspicious smile for a moment before walking over and inhaling the little floral blooms. The scent was very familiar and shocking. Standing up again with wide eyes, Birdie cried, “Oh my! These smell just like Rita’s broccoli salad!”

Newt laughed. “That’s what happens when broccoli is left on the stem too long and over ripens. Ya end up with a beautiful bunch o’ flowers that smell good enough to eat!”

“Well if that don’t beat all,” said Birdie wondrously.

Realizing just how much he’d missed these private conversations, Newt fought off the urge to grab her and pull her up close to him. Instead, he quickly took the opportunity to say what he’d been wanting to say to her for a while.

“Birdie, I’m so sorry for shoutin’ at ya. I didn’t mean nothin’ by it. It was just my pain talkin’. That mule must have kicked some of my sense outta me, too,” said Newt.

“I thought it was a horse that kicked ya,” replied Birdie.

"Oh, right," said Newt as he mentally berated himself for slipping. "Ya see, I had the sense kicked right outta me!"

Birdie noticed that his usually placid eyes looked clouded. "It doesn't matter to me what – or who - kicked ya, Newt. I'm just glad you're okay." She squeezed his hand as she placed her basket over her arm.

Before they could say any more, Ronnie Simms' voice called out, "Birdie! Hey Birdie! You out here?"

"Back here," shouted Birdie. As Ronnie followed the sound of her voice, he was pleasantly surprised to find her and Newt together in the garden. "Birdie, Mista Prescott wants you upstairs in his office NOW!"

"Whatever for?" asked Birdie in astonishment.

"I have no idea, but ya better get up there," replied Ronnie.

Birdie looked apprehensively at Newt, who stared back at her with concern. Neither had any idea why the hotelier wanted to see her and hoped she wasn't in any kind of trouble.

"I'll be out here if you need me," said Newt reassuringly. Birdie nervously smiled back before leaving with Ronnie.

Newt felt uneasy. He didn't know what was bothering him more - Birdie being called up to Prescott's office or the fact that she obviously didn't believe his cover story about his injuries.

Rita almost dropped her pastry bag onto the lemon cake she was laboriously decorating when Birdie came into the kitchen excitedly shrieking.

"Rita! Netta! You'll never guess what just happened!"

"Good God, Birdie! You just about made my heart stop beatin'," exclaimed Rita. "What's gotten into ya?"

The faces of the three scullery maids appeared in the doorway upon hearing the commotion.

"Mr. Prescott has given me a chance to be a dressmaker right here at the Montclair!" announced Birdie.

Ella screamed with glee and ran over to give Birdie a hug as the two women jumped around like two young school girls. Eva and Netta also gave Birdie hugs and words of congratulations. Rita waited for the others to calm down before she came forward and warmly embraced the Montclair's new seamstress.

"I'll miss ya, my dear, but I am so happy for you!" she said with emotion.

"No, Rita," replied Birdie with the widest of grins. "That's the best part of all! When I told Mr. Prescott and Miss Sutton that I really liked workin' with ya, they said that I could still work down here in the mornin's and then go upstairs and do the dressmakin' in the afternoons. So ya won't be losin' me after all!"

Now it was Rita's turn to shout with joy. "You're right! That was the best thing I've heard all day!"

As the women gathered around Birdie and heard about the new sewing machine and studio, Tangie quietly returned to the scullery where she grabbed the nearest bone china teacup and violently threw it against the wall where it shattered into countless pieces.

The following Monday afternoon, Johnathan Prescott had given Birdie permission to start clearing out the small storage space that would become her sewing room. He also allowed Ronnie Simms to assist her, primarily to help with the heavy lifting as there were stacks of crates, folding chairs and tables which needed to be moved to the main storage room on the other end of the mezzanine.

Ronnie frowned as he picked up a crystal and silver pickle castor, "Why on earth do folks need somethin' this fancy fo' pickles? Tell me. There are so many fancy gewgaws on the tables in the dinin' room here that there ain't hardly no room fo' the food!"

Birdie, who was storing her sewing accessories in the cupboard behind the desk, couldn't help but to agree as she often thought the same thing. "You're right, Ronnie. I don't know how folks can remember which fork they're supposed to be usin'."

"When I open my hotel, my dinin' room ain't gonna have all these flashy whatnots. Each o' my guests will have one fork, one spoon and a knife and that's all. Our tables'll be loaded down with the best food you'll find in the South."

"Cooked by Ella, who'll no doubt be your wife by then," said Birdie with a smirk.

"No doubt about it!" replied Ronnie confidently. "Speakin' of wives, when are you gonna put my man Newt outta his misery and run away with him up North. I saw ya'll out there in the garden lookin' pretty cozy together when I came to get ya last week."

Birdie felt her face grow hot as it often did when someone mentioned Newt to her. Ever since she returned from Fernandina last autumn, they have both shuffled back and forth in a dance between friendship and repressed passion.

"Oh Ronnie, you devil. Newt and I were only talkin, is all," she replied, more to convince herself than him.

Remembering how Newt stood up for Birdie against Stokes and the beating he got because of it, Ronnie said, "Your lips might be saying you and Newt are 'just good friends', Miss. Birdie. But I can hear that heart o' Newt's declarin' his love for ya loud 'n clear!"

Before Birdie could reply, their discussion was interrupted as Arthur entered carrying a delivery crate.

"Hey Birdie. Miss Sutton told me that this here box is 'sposed to go to you."

"Oh, thanks Arthur!" replied Birdie excitedly. "I think I know what this is!"

Producing a small flat screwdriver from his pocket, Arthur pried open the top of the crate for Birdie. The inside was packed with crumbled paper. Birdie rummaged through it and pulled out a highly varnished wooden case that had a rounded top and an ornately carved handle. The sides of the case were adorned with gold trim. As Birdie lifted off the lid, she squealed with glee as she caught her first glimpse of her new sewing machine.

It was a Singer hand crank model made of a shiny black metal with decorative gold trim. The word "Singer" was stamped on top in beautiful gold and red lettering.

Arthur whistled in appreciation. "That's one fine lookin' machine, Birdie. You ever work one o' these before?"

"To be honest, Arthur, no," replied Birdie. "I've only ever sewn by hand, but Mr. Prescott says they can get someone in to show me how to use it."

"My mama got one o' these," said Ronnie. "She sews up dresses fo' all the womenfolk in our family. I'm sure I can get her over here to show ya how it works."

"Oh, could you, Ronnie?" asked Birdie. "I'll ask Miss. Sutton about it. I'd much rather we pay your mama for her time than some stranger. I'll even prepare a nice lunch for her myself!"

"I'm sure she'd be happy to help, especially if she'll get to taste yo' famous chicken!" said Ronnie with a grin.

"And she can meet Ella, too." said Birdie.

"Oh...yeah," said Ronnie, whose smile suddenly clouded. "She'll get to meet Ella, too!"

Betty Simms was a tall, intimidating, no nonsense woman. Her powerful voice made her a natural for the role as soloist in her church choir. Having successfully raised seven children who were well educated, confident and ambitious, she didn't suffer fools easily.

Before marrying Lincoln Simms, Betty was a teacher at the Negro primary school and took pains to make sure that all her pupils, as well as her own children, spoke English properly. No one dared say "ain't", "ya", or "dat" when Betty was around. Ronnie was constantly being upbraided by his mother for having what she called a "lazy tongue."

She also taught her children to always walk straight with their held high and to look others in the eye when talking to them, even the white folks. Should the whites accuse them of being insolent, they should always speak respectfully and not be impertinent.

Having already been warned by Ronnie about his imperious mother, Birdie nervously took pains to speak and behave her very best around the older woman. But she needn't have worried as Mrs. Simms took an immediately liking to her, especially when she saw how quickly Birdie had grasped the operating fundamentals of the machine.

"Now keep an even speed on the crank, Birdie," instructed Betty as she sat behind her pupil and watched her take her second try on a piece on scrap fabric. "Good. Very good. I'm certain that you'll be an expert on this Singer by the time I leave today."

Birdie turned in her chair and beamed. "Thank you so much, Mrs. Simms. I could never have learned how to use this without you. Until the machine came last week, I had visions of me sewing by hand day and night trying to keep up with the orders. It seems like all of Mrs. Prescott's friends want something new to wear for the summer."

Betty stood up and walked around the small work room. There were three dresses in different stages of creation hanging on a metal railing. Looking closely at the intricate needlework on the sleeve of a pastel yellow dress, she remarked, "This is the work of a truly gifted seamstress. It was very prudent of Mr. Prescott to elevate you to this position."

"Coming from you, that's high praise indeed," said Birdie. "I hear you're an accomplished dressmaker yourself."

"Oh, I make clothes for my girls and myself. Sometimes for some of the sisters at church, but nothing of this caliber," Betty replied as she inspected a dusty rose-colored evening dress. "I can't believe you did this complex neckline by hand!"

"Yes ma'am," replied Birdie. "I like workin' on necklines best. I think they define the dress. Don't you?"

Oh no, thought Birdie. I said 'workin'' instead of working. She tensed up as she anticipated an upbraiding on her grammar. However, Mrs. Simms seemed to be thinking about something else.

"Um, yes. Yes. I absolutely agree," Betty responded. After a couple of moments, she added, "I hear that you are an excellent cook as well."

"Oh, I don't know about being an excellent cook," Birdie humbly replied, "but I've always helped my ma at home. Plus, I've been learning new recipes from Rita, our head cook here at the hotel. I work for her in the mornings before coming up here after lunch."

"Well, my Ronnie told me that you make the best chicken and gingersnaps around," said Betty.

"That's awfully kind of him to say. I've actually fixed you a nice lunch for later," said Birdie.

"I'm looking forward to it," said Betty sincerely. With a quizzical look, she added, "Someone as lovely and talented as yourself must certainly have a beau. Are you being courted?"

Birdie turned pink as she shyly replied, "Well, not really."

There was a quick, sharp knock at the door. Ronnie poked his head inside. "Just checkin' to see how you ladies were comin' along,"

"Ronald, it is 'checking' and 'coming' – not 'checkin'' and 'comin',” admonished Betty. Turning to Birdie, she said, "Go on, my dear. Try a few more rows of stitches. I'll be right back. I just need a quick word with my son."

As Birdie cranked the machine once again, Betty stepped outside and shut the door behind her.

"Is everything all right, mama?" asked Ronnie.

"Oh, yes," whispered Betty emphatically. "Birdie is doing very well. She's a fast learner. Say Ronald, is Birdie colored or white?"

Ronnie looked puzzled at the unexpected question. "She's a little of both. Plus, her mama's Dominican, I think. Why are you askin'...asking?"

"No reason. I was just curious," replied his mother. "She's a pretty young thing, isn't she? She sews like a professional dressmaker and she cooks too. She'll make someone a nice wife one day."

Ronnie knew where this was going and decided that he needed to put an end to the insinuations right then and there. "Mama, Birdie's already spoken for."

"Well, I just asked her if she had an understanding with anyone and she denied it," remarked Betty.

"It's a bit complicated, mama," said Ronnie. "One of our gardeners here has had his eye on Birdie since the first time he saw her. Birdie just doesn't realize that she feels the same way yet. Plus, there are...um...other reasons why they ain't together."

"Oh, that's preposterous," said Betty. "She shouldn't be tied down to a gardener when she could be married to a fine, upstanding man as yourself who has a bright future ahead of him!"

"Mama! I ain't got no romantic notions about Birdie. She's just a friend," argued Ronnie. "Besides, I've done told you about Ella many times. She's the one I've got my sights on."

"Oh yes, the dishwasher," his mother said flatly. "Ronald, why are you wasting your time with some two-bit common girl when you could have someone like Birdie?"

"Ella's no two-bit common gal, mama," retorted Ronnie. "You ain't even met her yet and you already got your mind made up about her! Give her a chance, ma. She's dyin' to meet ya."

"All right, I'll meet her," said Betty. "But you better watch your tone and your language with me, boy. Do you realize that you've said 'ain't' to me three times in the past couple of minutes?

"Here you go, Mrs. Simms," said Birdie as she set the lunch tray down in front of Betty, who was now seated at the cutting table in Birdie's work room. "I've made you some of my fried chicken, French cut green beans, potatoes au gratin, and fresh biscuits with gravy. Ella is bringing up the dessert which she made herself last night. She's a wonderful cook in her own right, ma'am."

"I'm sure she is," said Ruth dismissively. "But for now, I'm looking forward to indulging in this feast you've just set in front of me. Won't you join me, Birdie?"

"Oh, thank you ma'am but unfortunately I can't," replied Birdie. "Miss. Sutton has strict rules about when staff can dine. Besides, I'd like to practice rethreading the machine while you have your lunch, if that's okay. I'd like to see if I can do it on my own."

"That's highly commendable of you, dear. Go right ahead and pretend I'm not here," said Betty as she took her first bite of the chicken. "Oh, my Ronnie wasn't lying. This is indeed the best chicken I've ever tasted."

Birdie smiled as she unthreaded the machine. "Thank you, Mrs. Simms." She slowly worked the thread back onto the machine as Betty savored the rest of the meal. A few minutes later, Ella and Ronnie arrived. Ronnie looked like extremely nervous while Ella had a huge grin on her face as she carried a covered dish in front of her.

"Mama," began Ronnie. "This here is Ella Patterson. Ella, this is my mother, Mrs. Elizabeth Simms."

"Please to meet ya, ma'am," said Ella who punctuated the sentence with a movement resembling a curtsy.

"Good afternoon, Miss Patterson. It's a pleasure to finally meet you," replied Betty.

"I made ya this peach cobbler fo' yo' dessert," said Ella as she uncovered the plate which was loaded down with a golden flaky pastry over the bright, fleshy fruit.

Betty visibly cringed at Ella's poor grammar. Her reaction was not lost on her son, who inwardly groaned.

"Tell me, Miss Patterson," said Betty, "Are your parents Reverend Lawrence and Betty Patterson of the Methodist church on Vine Street?"

"No ma'am," answered Ella. "My folks are Cletus and Ophelia Patterson of Citrus Avenue. My daddy's a sharecropper and my mama takes in washin'. We live a few doors down from Birdie."

"Oh, I see," said Betty. "Is that why you're here working as a dishwasher? To help your family out?"

Birdie and Ron both looked at each other worriedly as they wondered what turn this conversation was going to take.

"Yes ma'am," said Ella. "I reckoned I was old enough to start helpin' my folks out so I quit school and took the job here." Defensively, she added, "It's honest work after all."

"Of course, it is," remarked Betty condescendingly. "And where do you see yourself in the future?"

"Hopefully married to a rich man!" joked Ella. But Mrs. Simms was not laughing – or even smiling.

"Uh, mama," interceded Ronnie, "why don't you try Ella's peach cobbler? It's one of her best dishes."

"I'd be delighted to," said Betty as she dug in with a fork and took a bite. After chewing for a few seconds, she asked, "Birdie, could you please get me a glass of water?"

Birdie quickly rose and hurried to the pitcher of water and glasses that were set up on a nearby table. She poured the glass and brought it back to Betty, who downed half the glass before setting it on the tray. Ella and Ronnie looked on in horror.

"Miss Patterson," began Betty, "how much cinnamon did you put in this cobbler?"

"About two teaspoons, ma'am," replied Ella.

"That accounts for the strange taste, my dear," said Betty. "A good cobbler only needs about a quarter of a teaspoonful of cinnamon, my dear. The fruit should always be the star of the dish – not the spices."

Birdie's heart wrenched for Ella, who piteously looked like she was about to cry.

"Oh, I...um...I'm sorry, Mrs. Simms," she stammered. With a forced chuckle, she promised, "I'll make sure to work on that recipe."

"That would be a good idea," said Betty. "But thank you for your efforts. It is very much appreciated and it was a pleasure meeting you, but I'm afraid I must get back to Birdie now. Good afternoon, Miss Patterson. I'll see you at home later, Ronald."

Chapter 23

Hartsfield's General Store was a mainstay in town since the late 1870's and prided itself on selling "a little bit of everything." The small shop was chock full of all sorts of dry goods, groceries and sundries. Although there were several other such stores in the city, Birdie and Hortensia preferred Hartsfield's not only because they had the best fabric and houseware selection, but both Edward Hartsfield Sr and his son Eddie were always pleasant to deal with compared to other merchants in town.

Birdie patiently stood in the corner of the shop until all the white customers had been waited upon. On days such as this when Hortensia had to work a special function at one of her client's homes, Birdie would do the shopping after work. Looking at the hastily scrawled list, Birdie tried her best to decipher whether her mother wanted "coffee" or "toffee."

As he finished waiting on the elderly woman in front of her, Eddie Hartsfield smiled and said, "Hey there, Birdie! How ya doin'?"

Eddie had been a casual acquaintance of Birdie's for years, mainly through their dealings at the store. He was also a good friend and fishing companion of Newt's. Because of this, Eddie was well aware of the affection his pal had for Birdie. Being more liberal minded than most, Eddie treated Birdie, her mother and any other person of color who entered his shop with just as much respect as he did his white clientele.

"I'm doin' well, Eddie. How about you?" asked Birdie.

"Oh, I can't complain," replied Eddie. The front door bell jingled as a man came in. Eddie nodded politely at him as he continued, "but I must confess that I ain't seen much of my fishin' buddy Newt lately. You wouldn't happen to know why, would ya Birdie?" he asked teasingly.

"Aw, you just hush now Eddie," rebuked Birdie jokingly. Handing him the note, she said, "Here are a few things we need. I think that last word is coffee because I don't know why my ma would want a half pound of toffee!"

Eddie chuckled as he gathered her order together. When he had finished and handed the wrapped parcels to her, he asked, "Will this be goin' on your account?"

"Yes, Eddie. And thank you," said Birdie. As she turned to leave, she took care to politely give way to the man behind her and as she always did when face with a white stranger, she automatically looked at the floor as she passed him. To her shock, he went over and opened the door for her.

She curiously glanced up at him as she passed by. He appeared to be in his mid to late twenties and sported a thick, long mustache which was waxed on the ends. He looked like he just came out of the barber shop because his hair was wet, slicked back and smelled of Macassar oil. She couldn't recall ever seeing him before.

"Thank you, sir," said Birdie as she was again kept her eyes downcast and left the store.

The man returned to the counter and left a nickel to pay for his newspaper and package of tobacco. "Here ya go, Eddie."

"Thanks, Lon," replied Eddie as he rang up the sale and dropped the coin in the register.

Lonnie Stokes exited the store and, seeing Birdie walking southward down St. George Street, quickened his pace until he caught up with her.

"Hello again," he said. "So...you're Birdie."

Alarm bells started to ring loudly in Birdie's head. Who was this strange, well-groomed man and what did he want with her? She thought about running back to the store for safety but what the stranger said next made her stop in her tracks.

"Seen anythin' of Newt Phillips lately?"

Birdie suspiciously asked, "How do ya know Newt?

"Oh, I've known him and that family o' his for a long time, especially that good for nothin' pappy," said Stokes. "They're a pretty harmless, inbred lot, but young Newt's gettin' to be a cause for some concern 'round here."

Birdie looked puzzled. "What do ya mean?"

Stokes suddenly grabbed Birdie's wrist and pushed her into a nearby alley. As he slammed her against a wall which made her writhe in pain, he leaned so close to her that she could feel his hot breath burn her right cheek as his hate filled green eyes drilled a hole right through her.

"I'll tell ya what I mean. For the past couple o' years I've been watchin' that jackass Phillips squirin' ya about town in full daylight without a care in the world. Watchin' him slobberin' over a quadroon like yourself makes me sick to my stomach. Races were meant to be pure and mixed breeds like you are yet another abomination to everythin' that is good and decent," spat Stokes. "The last straw was when I saw him drivin' ya right through town last month, along with two other nigras. I caught up with him later and gave him a beatin' he'll never forget while his nigger friend had no choice but to sit by and watch."

Birdie's eyes widened with terror as she took in what Stokes told her. Suddenly things were starting to make sense - Newt's injuries as well as his avoidance of her. He must not have wanted her to know the full extent of how badly he'd been hurt. Ella would have learned what happened from Ronnie, who witnessed the whole thing, and cooked up that excuse of them wanting to spend time alone. They were obviously protecting Newt from further run-ins with this dangerous man.

Stokes continued, "I sure as hell hope that Phillips has had the common sense to steer clear of ya because if I see ya'll together again, I'll beat 'im to death next time."

Birdie cried in terror but the street was vacant. "Please sir, don't hurt him. I promise I'll never go near him again. I'm beggin' ya - please don't do anythin' to him." She started to weep.

"Awright. Awright! Quit your damned bawlin'. Just stay clear o' him and there won't be any trouble, ya hear?"

Birdie nodded mutely and wiped the tears from her eyes. Stokes released her wrist and before leaving, he hissed, "I'll be keepin' an eye on ya so don't try anythin' funny." With that, he took his leave.

Rubbing her sore wrist, Birdie watched him stroll down St. George and disappear into Doheney's.

As she started to cry again, Birdie asked herself, why do I always end up losing the ones I care about most? First Pa, then Clara and now Newt! She walked home through a misty haze of tears.

Once Birdie got to the house, she locked the door behind her and peered through the front window to make sure that the man hadn't followed her. She wondered if he was a Klansman and shuddered at the thought. Even though she'd contended with prejudice and racism all her life, she'd never personally dealt with anyone in the Klan before.

Birdie's thoughts immediately turned to her father. She wondered how many times he had been threatened and beaten before eventually winding up in jail and dying there. Her mother's warnings about the perils of falling in love with white men were coming to pass.

Taking refuge in her bedroom and locking the door, Birdie curled up on top of her bed and jumped at every noise she heard from the outside - a cat howling, a dog barking, children screaming, a loud thud from a construction site several blocks away. Every sound she heard filled her imagination with images of the dangerous green-eyed man coming back for her. After a couple of hours in this state, her nerves were in shreds.

Just after dusk fell, she heard a sharp knock at the door. Birdie quickly sat up in the darkness. Oh my God! It's him, she panicked. What should I do? Again, there was a loud thumping on the door. Birdie slowly stood and looked for something to use as a weapon. She picked up an old, bronze candlestick as she slowly opened her bedroom door and tiptoed out into the parlor.

After a few more loud rappings, she raised the candlestick over her head in self-defense. Then she heard her mother's voice from outside, "Birdie! Are you in there? Unlock this door!"

Dropping the candlestick and breathing a heavy sigh of relief, Birdie ran over to the door and unlocked it to find her mother on the front porch looking indignant and carrying a couple of baskets, one atop the other.

Pushing her way past Birdie, Hortensia stepped into the parlor and exclaimed, "Why did you lock the door? My hands are full and I couldn't reach my own key. And why is it so dark in here? What have you been up to, Birdie?"

Fighting the urge to run over to her mother and cry her heart out, Birdie paused and said, "I'm sorry, ma. Today was a very busy day at the hotel and I was so tired when I came home that I laid down to take a nap and only just now woke up."

Hortensia lit the lamp on the kitchen table and replied, "I'm not surprised. They've been running you ragged over there. I wish they'd just get you out of that kitchen and make you a proper full-time seamstress. It would be much more respectable, and you wouldn't be coming home so worn out."

Not being in a proper mental state to substantiate her reasons for wanting to work in the Montclair's kitchen, Birdie only nodded and lowered her head. Hortensia softened as she saw what she perceived was exhaustion.

"Mija, why don't you go to bed and I'll bring you a hot cup of tea. I also have some food from the Nelson's party that they let me bring home. I'll put a little on a plate for you. Go on to your room and relax."

Birdie went to her room, undressed and got into bed. However, it would be a long time before she would be able to relax again.

For the next two days, Newt didn't see any sign of Birdie. She was not in the kitchen when he walked by in the mornings.

He also didn't see her picking vegetables from the garden, tending to the stray cats or tossing out the refuse. He even asked Ella if anything was wrong.

"She's been a bit quiet lately, but I ain't noticed anythin' else," Ella had said with a shrug.

Reckoning that maybe her new job upstairs was keeping her busier and out of the kitchen, Newt decided to wait for her one evening after work.

As Birdie came into the mudroom to collect her belongings, she was startled to find Newt sitting on one of the benches. Birdie looked around to make sure no one else was within hearing distance. Even though Rita and Netta had left, Tangie and the others were still in the scullery scrubbing the dinner dishes.

"Newt, what are you doin' here?" she asked. "You're usually long gone by now."

"I'm sorry, Birdie," he replied, "I just ain't seen ya for a couple days and wanted to make sure everythin' was all right."

Birdie had been dreading this conversation ever since her harrowing encounter with that man in town the other day. She mentally rehearsed the scene many times but, in the end, decided that the best way to handle things was to be direct.

"I need to talk to ya, but not in here," she whispered.

Flashing Birdie a grin, he said, "Don't worry. I promise I'll keep my hands to myself."

But Birdie was not smiling as she asked, "Can we talk in the groundskeeper's shed? I don't want us to be seen together."

Realizing that something was indeed wrong, Newt said, "Uh...yeah. Let's go."

With a heavy heart, Birdie followed him outside and over towards the wooden shack. As the sun was starting to set and darkness was setting in, Newt opened the door and lit an oil lamp which sat on the worktable.

"What's goin' on with ya, Birdie?" he asked anxiously.

"Newt, I know where ya got them bruises from a couple o'months ago," she stated matter-of-factly. "And I also know WHY ya got them. It was because o' me, wasn't it?"

"No, Birdie," Newt said quickly. "I already done told ya, it was one o' my horses...."

"Newt, if ya really love me like ya say, then please start tellin' me the truth," urged Birdie. "I know for a fact that ya got into a fight with a man who didn't like seein' us together. I also know that Ronnie was there when it happened."

Newt sighed heavily, realizing it was time to stop the charade. "So, Ronnie told ya?"

"No," said Birdie. "And Ella didn't tell me either. It doesn't matter how I know."

"Wait a minute," said Newt as a horrible realization came over him, "Stokes got to ya, didn't he? I swear, if he laid one finger on ya, I'll tear him apart with my bare hands!"

"I have no idea who this Stokes is," said Birdie truthfully. "I just know that your life is in danger..." she started to cry, "as long as you and I are together. And I can't let that happen."

Knowing what she was about to say next, Newt vehemently shook his head and said, "No, Birdie! I won't let anythin' happen."

Birdie also shook her head and said, "Nothin' ain't gonna happen because I ain't gonna give 'em any reason to hurt ya. I'm sorry Newt but we can't be seein' each other anymore."

"Birdie, please don't do this!" Newt pleaded. "I'm beggin' ya!"

Taking his hand in hers, Birdie looked up at his eyes which were starting to redden and said, "I'm sorry, Newt but I don't want to take any chances on anythin' happenin' to ya. I care for ya too much. I don't want to do this, ya know, but I ain't got no other choice."

A thought suddenly occurred to Newt and, grabbing Birdie by the shoulders, he cried, "But we DO have a choice, Birdie. Run away with me! We'll go up north. I don't have enough money saved up yet for the train fare but we can make our own way in my wagon. We'll leave tonight!"

Birdie hugged Newt tightly as she considered his offer. Knowing that she had enough money for the fare in the jewelry box hidden under her floorboards, she couldn't help but to remember Stokes' parting words to her about not doing anything foolish. For all she knew, he could be watching them at that very moment.

With a heart like lead, she pulled away from him and said, "No, Newt. I won't be running off with ya. It's too dangerous. Plus, I don't wanna leave my ma alone without any explanation. From now on, we just work in the same hotel, that's all. Good night."

With that, she left the shed. Newt, still in shock at what had just transpired, distractedly sank onto a bench by the worktable, bereft and heartbroken.

As Ronnie walked Ella to work a couple of days later, their first topic of conversation was Newt's foul temper as of late. His usual friendly and easy-going demeanor was replaced by sullen silence and occasional angry outbursts at the slightest provocation. The dark rings that were starting to form around his eyes attested to the sleepless nights he had been spending in his barn, thinking of Birdie as he downed shots of whiskey just so he could temporarily forget her and maybe get at least a couple hours of slumber.

"Do ya think he had a fight with Birdie?" Ronnie asked Ella.

"Of course he did," replied Ella. "Who else does he care about that much? When I asked him at breakfast yesterday if he'd seen her, he just got up and left. Didn't say a word to me."

"What's Birdie got to say 'bout it?" asked Ronnie

"I wish I knew," replied Ella. "I ain't seen much of her in the last two days. They been really busy in the kitchen preparin' them fancy petit four cakes and such for them ladies' gatherin's they doin'. Then Birdie goes upstairs later on to sew and I don't see her again til the next day. But wait til Sunday! I'm gonna get the truth outta her if it kills me!"

"I got no doubt about that!" exclaimed Ronnie. "Once ya get yo' mind set on somethin', ya always make it happen!

"That reminds me, Ronnie," began Ella, "there is somethin' else I'd like to make happen. I want another chance to make a good showin' for your mama."

Ronnie raised his eyebrows in surprise and asked, "You sure you wanna do that again?" He remembered how upset Ella had been over the cobbler incident and how she had sobbed on his shoulder afterwards.

"Yes, please do this for me, Ronnie," pleaded Ella. "Things'll work out better this time, I swear."

"And just how are ya gonna manage that?" asked Ronnie.

"Well, our church is havin' a picnic potluck next Sunday and I'm invitin' you and your mama to join us. I'll be bringin' a dish with me that I just know she's gonna love! You just wait 'n see!"

As she did ever Wednesday afternoon, Lottie Prescott held court at the weekly ladies' tea and luncheon in the hotel's main dining room. She sat at the head table with all her closest friends surrounding her. Acquaintances were seated in the middle of the room while everyone else occupied the tables on the far side. The acoustics of the dining room were so clear that Lottie could often hear what was being said on the opposite side of the room which often made for more juicy gossip to share later on. At the moment, an accomplished lady pianist, Ethel Strawbridge, performed a few Beethoven sonatas as well as a few pieces by Chopin in the background while the ladies sipped Darjeeling tea and dined on colorful macarons, petit fours, tartlets and scones.

"Lottie, that dress is divine!" gushed Eleanor Montague, who had come down from Youngstown, Ohio with her recently widowed sister Harriet Wagner. The two siblings couldn't look less alike. Eleanor was short, plump and her once golden hair was fading with age. Harriet, on the other hand, was tall, willowy and had a head of dark chestnut brown hair with a white streak that went down the middle. Their temperaments were also polar opposites with Eleanor being soft spoken while Harriet was more forceful when dealing with people.

"Why thank you, Eleanor," said Lottie as she basked in the compliment as well as the attention she was getting from the other ladies in the room. Ever since Birdie started creating pieces for her wardrobe, she has been the object of praise and admiration for her fashion sense. After years of living in this godforsaken state that was devoid of culture, good cuisine and fashion, Lottie was pleased to see it was once again alive and well in her own hotel, thanks to Johnathan's idea to cater to the female guests.

"Is that another one of your girl's creations?" asked Eleanor.

"Yes, indeed," replied Lottie. "Actually, I should take you over to her work room so you can see what she's dreamed up for a friend of mine!"

"I'd like to see that, actually," said Harriet.

Lottie motioned for a waiter and asked him to summon Iris Sutton. When the head housekeeper appeared five minutes later, Mrs. Prescott asked. "Iris, is Brigid in her workroom right now?"

"Yes, Mrs. Prescott," answered Iris. "She's been there for the past hour. Shall I summon her for you?"

"No need," replied Lottie. "I just wanted to show my friends here her latest creation."

"I'll go now and let her know you're on your way," offered Iris.

“Thank you, Miss Sutton,” said Lottie dismissively as she turned her attention back to the other two women.

“Shall we go, ladies? We’ll be back in time for Mrs. Strawbridge’s finale. I hear it’s going to be Mozart’s piano concerto number 22 and is not to be missed.”

Birdie was down on the floor of her workroom putting the final touches to the hem of the ivory ball gown with the pink satin drape across the hips and the long ivory lace train in the back. As always when there was no one around, her thoughts would turn to Newt. Every night that week her mind was haunted by the crushing look of defeat on his face when she last left him.

Birdie remembered the poems they used to read in school about love and how wonderful it made people feel. Now she wondered why she felt so much pain instead. Maybe I don't deserve love or a happy ending like the women in those storybooks, she thought. Even the love they spoke of in church seemed to elude her. To Birdie, God had become some distant figure who had no time for her. Where was He when Pa, Clara and now Newt were wrenched from her life?

A loud tap brought Birdie back to the present. Iris Sutton poked her head in and, seeing Birdie kneeling on the floor with the dress's hem in her hand, she said, "Brigid, I just wanted to let you know that Mrs. Prescott will be bringing two of her friends by to see you in a couple of minutes. I believe she wants to show off your work."

Birdie immediately stood up and smoothed her dress. "Thank you, Miss Sutton. I'll be ready."

Iris looked at the evening gown on the dressmaker's form and at the five other completed dresses which hung on a rack across the back of the room. "I am impressed at how much you have gotten done, Brigid. Have you caught up on the orders?"

"Yes ma'am. That sewin' machine's really saved me so much time!"

"Splendid!" Iris replied with a smile and added, "Keep up the good work," as she quietly closed the door behind her.

Thankful for the distraction of Mrs. Prescott's visit, Birdie quickly picked up the scissors, lace scraps and the sewing basket off the floor.

A few minutes later, Lottie and her companions burst into the room.

"Good afternoon, Brigid."

"Good afternoon, Mrs. Prescott," replied Birdie nervously.

"Ladies, this is Miss Fairfax, who is responsible for the attire I am presently wearing as well as this beautiful gown she has made for my friend Aurora Harrell's daughter, Estelle." Turning to Birdie, she asked, "Have you finished it, dear?"

"Yes, Mrs. Prescott," replied Birdie. "It is ready to be packed and shipped."

"Very good," said Lottie. "Now if you come this way, ladies, I'll show you what else Miss. Fairfax has produced."

For the next ten minutes, Lottie showed Eleanor and Harriet each of the dresses hanging on the rack which were met with a chorus of "oohs" and "aahs." Birdie stepped in when necessary to answer any questions related to the construction of each garment. By the time Lottie and her company left, Birdie had orders for two more dresses - a lavender evening gown for Mrs. Montague and a black day dress for Mrs. Wagner.

Her spirits were buoyed by the women's praise and the additional orders. I might not be lucky in love, she thought, but my work has never failed me in the past. Birdie realized that once again this is what would help her cope with the pain in her heart. She needed to plunge herself further into her food and fashion creations.

It was late April and the temperatures in St. Augustine were already starting to climb. Many of the Montclair's guests had long since returned back north. However, this year there seemed to be more guests who wanted to extend their stays with many actually remaining through the summertime.

Prescott sighed heavily as he picked up his cigar and strode to the window overlooking the rose garden which usually gave him solace when he was troubled. He was really taking a risk on this plan to stay open all summer with a smaller staff. It was no trouble back in '97 when the Regatta was in town which drew record numbers of guests for that time of year. But now he was relying on custom from the locals to frequent the new skating rink and moving picture theater which he was having built on the first floor near the rear of the property. Will these new ventures help keep the Montclair afloat?

Glancing down at the garden, he spotted Newt Phillips busily cutting the dead fronds off one of the queen palms. Prescott initially thought the young gardener was a shiftless daydreamer but over the past couple of years, he had grown to like the young man who showed a lot of promise and, at times, initiative.

Prescott then noticed movement underneath his window and glancing further down, saw that Birdie had come out of the side entrance and was carrying a basket of kitchen waste which she tossed into the trash receptacle. When Prescott glanced back at Newt, he was surprised to see that he had stopped his labor to gaze longingly at Birdie, who didn't see him.

"Well, well, well," he said softly aloud, "it looks like Phillips has been struck by cupid's bow and fallen for our own Miss Fairfax." Even though he discouraged relationships between his male and female employees, Prescott was nonetheless amused with Newt's apparent fondness for Birdie.

Why not, he thought. Every good man needs a good woman behind him. Like my Lottie, who, despite being a downright pain in the backside, can be a divine source of inspiration at times.

"Eva, have you seen that silver bread platter with the roses on it?" Ella asked as she opened another cupboard and searched each shelf.

"No, I no see it," Eva replied.

Tangie, who was counting out the silverware needed for the afternoon's luncheon, said impatiently, "For land's sakes, Ella, just use a different platter!"

"But Mista Hayes in the dinin' room says that every Wednesday when they use the rose pattern plates, they like to use the rose pattern silver platters, too," argued Ella.

"I don't care what Mista Turner told you. I'm tellin' ya to use a different damn plate!" snapped Tangie.

"All right, ya don't have to holler!" shouted Ella as she opened the cupboard again and pulled out another platter. "It ain't my fault that things are disappearin' into thin air 'round here!"

Chapter 24

Springtime came and went as Birdie grew more morose each day. Other than an occasional greeting or a nod in passing, she had not spoken to Newt since she broke things off with him months ago. She awoke on the final day of May with a heavy heart. She slowly got up and made herself ready for the day ahead. As she plodded into the kitchen, Hortensia turned from where was pouring a cup a coffee by the stove and asked, "Would you like some?"

"No thanks," said Birdie lifelessly.

"What's been the matter with you lately, Birdie?" asked Hortensia. "You've been walking around for months looking so glum, and for the past week, you've been especially prickly. You're a lovely girl. You need to smile more."

"And what exactly do I have to smile about?" snapped Birdie.

"Well, you have a steady job that appears to be a year-round one now," said Hortensia, "Your dressmaking is finally being recognized and rewarded. You have a nice house and a loving mother who looks after you. And you no longer seem to have that horrid looking gardener sniffing around after you so now you can finally find someone more suitable."

Her mother's barbs this early in the morning were tough enough to bear on their own, but the added insult against Newt was too much. Birdie rose up so fast from her chair that it tilted over backwards and crashed to the floor, startling Hortensia.

"A 'loving mother', huh? That a laugh," Birdie hissed with venom. Before Hortensia could come to her senses and respond, Birdie grabbed her reticule and as she was leaving, hissed "By the way, today is your granddaughter's first birthday!" She slammed the door behind her.

"I don't know what's wrong with Birdie this mornin'," Ella was saying to Eva and Newt over breakfast. "She's been quieter than usual all this week and today, when I said 'Good mornin' to her, she just said 'Ain't nothin' good 'bout it' back to me. I have no idea what could be eatin' her."

"Oh, I know what's stuck in her craw," cooed Tangie who had been lurking nearby. "She's just mad that she'll be workin' part-time fo' me this summer while you and Eva are gone. Miss High-n-Mighty gotta wash dishes again, just like she did when she first started workin' here."

"You hush yo' mouth, Tangie Foster!" Ella cried, "First of all, Birdie ain't workin' fo' you. She's just helpin' out with dishes at lunchtime, that's all. So, don't be getting' all puffed up about it 'cause it don't mean a thing."

Newt ignored the bickering women and looked pensive. Hadn't it been a year that Birdie's child was born? No wonder she was so upset. He was surprised that Ella hadn't figured it out but he'll talk to her later. An idea had just come to him. He pushed back his plate and rose from the table.

Ella stopped arguing with Tangie and asked, "Where you goin', Newt?"

"Thanks for the vittles, ladies," he replied. "I'll see ya'll later."

One of Johnathan Prescott's plans for revitalizing the Montclair was the addition of a women's finery shop featuring ladies' hats, gloves, parasols and other assorted trippery in addition to some men's items. However, the main draw would be the large glass display window which would feature one of Birdie's custom-made gowns.

"Oh, that is going to be absolutely breathtaking, Brigid," exclaimed Miss Sutton as she clapped her hands in glee. Birdie had never seen the housekeeper look so pleased. She was glad that her preliminary sketches of the evening gown had elicited such a positive reaction. "And I can't believe that you managed to stay under the budget."

"Yes, ma'am," replied Birdie, "I've been forced to be frugal most of my life so it comes easily to me, I suppose."

"Well, this dress is certainly going to look anything but inexpensive. This fabric is absolutely exquisite. Where did you get it?" She gently picked up and inspected the shiny grey fabric which had a bit of a silver shimmer to it.

"Mr. Moscovitz, the Jewish tailor over on Cuna Street, had this bolt of fabric that he said was of no use to him because it's too lightweight to hold up as a man's suit. But as soon as I touched it, I knew it would be perfect for a ball gown!"

"Splendid," said Iris. "Now Brigid, I hope you don't find your new schedule too taxing. It's just that with your skills in both the kitchen as well as up here, you are a valuable member of our summer work force. However, if you find it to be problematic, please do not hesitate to come see me."

Birdie was touched by Miss Sutton's concern. Straightening her spine and lifting her chin, she said, "There won't be any problems, Miss. Sutton. I can handle it all."

Iris smiled warmly at the young woman and said, "My, you have certainly grown up a lot over the past couple of years, Brigid. You are so much more confident than the shy girl who came to my office two years ago and couldn't keep her eyes off the floor."

Birdie was pleasantly surprised by the observation. "Why, thank you for your kind words, ma'am."

"It's the truth, my child," said Iris as she affectionately patted Birdie on the shoulder. "Well, the sun will be setting soon so don't tarry too long or else you'll be walking home in the dark."

"Yes, ma'am," said Birdie.

"Good night then, Brigid. I'll see you tomorrow."

"Good night, ma'am," replied Birdie.

After Miss Sutton had left, Birdie put away her drawings and folded up the cloth. She rubbed her shoulders and neck, both of which had been tensed up all day. It was a rough one that started out badly but she got through it. Thankfully there were enough dress orders as well as chores to keep Birdie busy over the summer and keep her mind off her troubles.

Birdie shut off the electric light of her workroom and headed downstairs. The kitchen was empty and clean. The only sounds were those of Ella, Eva and Tangie in the kitchen cleaning up the last of the dinner service plates. Birdie made a mental note to apologize to Ella tomorrow for her brusqueness earlier.

She grabbed her reticule from the mudroom and stepped outside where setting sun was turning the sky a bright fiery orange. As she left through the back door, she was shocked to see Newt sitting on the bottom step.

"Newt! Why are you still here?" she asked. "Shouldn't you have gone home a couple of hours ago?"

"I was but I had to bring somethin' back with me," he answered. "Wanna see what it is?"

"Sure." Birdie was mystified as to why Newt, who lived a good two miles away, would go all the way home and back. She could barely walk the six blocks to her own home after a day of work.

Newt stood and smiled. "Come on, then." He led her across the lawn and into the groundskeeper shed. Inside, a lantern filled the small room with a warm golden glow. Birdie hesitated inside the doorway.

"It's okay, Birdie. I ain't gonna do anythin' ungentlemanly to ya, as hard as that'll be fer me." Birdie laughed as she stepped inside and shut the door.

Newt reached down, picked up a small crate that was on the floor and placed it on the bench. He motioned for Birdie to come over and sit beside him. When she did, he reached into the crate, which was lined with a piece of an old horse blanket, and pulled out a tiny white kitten, placing it in Birdie's hands.

"Oh, my goodness!" Birdie whispered excitedly. "What a beautiful kitten. It's so tiny. Is there another litter under the shed?"

"No, my sister Susie found a litter of kittens near our place and had been hand feedin' 'em for the past few weeks because the mama cat ain't nowhere to be found. We reckon she might've been killed."

"Oh, how sad," said Birdie as she lovingly stroked the tiny feline between its miniature ears. "But why did you go all the way home and bring her back here?"

Newt gently took the kitten out of Birdie's hands and placed it back in the crate, which he moved to the table behind them. Then he held Birdie by both hands and said, "I think I know what's been grievin' ya lately, Birdie."

Birdie stayed silent and just looked down at his hands that were enveloping her own.

"It's your child, isn't it? I reckon she was born about a year ago and that's what's been makin' ya look so sad lately."

Birdie felt her body start to shake and tremor as all the emotions she'd repressed over the past two weeks began to overwhelm her. Newt pulled her close to him and said, "It's okay to cry. God knows ya got every right to."

The floodgates opened and Birdie started to sob as images of her newborn baby in her arms, which had haunted her all day, once again emerged. Now Clara was in someone else's arms. Someone else had woken her up this morning and said, "Happy Birthday, my darling little girl." Someone else had given her a present and laughed as she tore at the wrappings.

"Oh Newt, I still miss her somethin' terrible," Birdie cried piteously on Newt's shoulder.

"Of course, you miss her," said Newt. "She's a part o' ya. No matter who raises her, it won't matter because she will ALWAYS be a part o' ya and nothin's ever gonna change that. So, it's only natural that yer gonna miss 'er on the day ya bore her into the world, and it's all right to be sad and even cry about it, too. And don't ever let anyone tell ya otherwise."

Birdie wept for a few more minutes before she opened up her reticule and, blinded by her tears, fumbled around for her handkerchief. Seeing her distress, Newt took out her handkerchief for her and unfolding it, carefully blotted her face.

She gazed into his quiet blue eyes which had a calming effect upon her. How was it that this man was able to figure out what was wrong and yet her mother as well as her best friend merely went on as if today was any other day?

Birdie remembered another time last October when Newt had comforted her when she'd told him all about the rape and Clara's birth. He had been kind and understanding then as well. She also recollected her spontaneous kiss and the terrible awkwardness that had occurred as a result. Well, this time there will be no shame or guilt.

Reaching up and bringing his head down level to her own, she kissed him softly on the lips and said, "You know me better than anyone I've ever known. Thank you."

Newt resisted the urge to gather her up in his arms and return her kiss tenfold. She was still in too vulnerable a state. Instead he brought her attention back to the young feline.

"Now yer probably wonderin' why in tarnation did I bring ya this lil kitten," he said as he reached over back into the crate and lifted out the small creature. When Birdie nodded in response, he continued, "Well, I know yer a sweet, gentle woman with a lot of love to give. But because of the Klan watchin' us, ya don't feel safe givin' yer love to me. And because yer lil girl got taken away, ya can't give yer love to her neither. And with yer pa long gone, I know ya miss him, too."

"Yes, every word you're sayin' is the God's honest truth," whispered Birdie.

"Yer a beautiful woman inside and out, Birdie Fairfax, and a woman like you with a heart full o' so much love needs somethin' to pour it out on. So, I'd like to give ya this lil kitten, who could really use it right now. She's had a rough start in life with her mama gone and will probably wind up dead herself from larger critters, a trolley car or someone's shotgun."

"Oh! I'll never let anythin' bad happen to her," promised Birdie, who reached over and took the kitten from Newt. Holding it to her heart, she kissed it softly on the head. "Is she really mine?"

"You bet. She's all yers," responded Newt with a wink.

"Will you help me name her?" asked Birdie.

"Well, she's sweet and white. How 'bout Sugar?" suggested Newt.

"I love it! "exclaimed Birdie. Bringing the cat to eye level, she lovingly cooed, "Your name is Sugar from now on!" The kitten mewed in response. As she gently placed it back in the crate, Birdie turned to Newt.

"Please don't ever forget what I'm about to say," she said as she placed her arms around Newt's neck. "I could never love anyone else as much as I love you right now." Pulling him close to her, she kissed him with more passion this time and he gladly reciprocated.

"Aw Birdie, you already know how much I love ya," whispered Newt. "And ya know what else? It's good to see ya smile again!"

Stroking his cheek, Birdie replied, "It's always easy for me to smile when you're around." She went to pick up her reticule bag and the small crate as they prepared to leave. Newt blew out the lantern and shut the shed door behind them. By now the sun had set and darkness fell.

"I'll take ya home, Birdie," he offered.

"No!" she cried, "No, please. It's too dangerous. I'll be fine, I promise. I only have to go a short way. It's you who should be careful. You live much further."

"That's all right. At least I brought the wagon and don't need to walk," answered Newt amiably. Then in a more serious tone, he added, "Well, if ya ain't gonna let me take ya home, then I'm gonna watch from a distance and make sure ya get there all right."

Birdie thought about it for a moment and then nodded. "That's all right, then. But from a distance. And make sure no one sees ya."

With that, she waved and set off. As he had said he would, Newt watched her walk down the street from the hotel until she had to make a right turn. He got into his wagon and slowly followed, making sure to keep a few blocks distance between them. He caught sight of her again as she entered the Lincolnville district where she lived. She walked another two blocks before she turned onto her own street. By then Newt felt better that she was amongst her neighbors and turned his horses toward home.

Hortensia had been feeling terrible all day after Birdie's outburst that morning. How could she be so unfeeling and unsympathetic as to forget her own granddaughter's birthday? She was a fool to believe that Birdie would be able to get over the child within a year's time. She'd been looking forward to Birdie coming home so she could apologize to her before serving her favorite dinner – chicken gumbo.

However, when Birdie returned that evening carrying a kitten, Hortensia's original intentions of apologizing were immediately overshadowed by her dismay at the prospect of having a pet in the house.

"What is that?" she asked when she saw the tiny ball of white fur inside the little wooden box.

"It's a kitten, ma," replied Birdie as she set her reticule down and picked Sugar up out of her box. "Isn't she adorable?"

"Yes, but why is she here?" asked Hortensia.

"Because she's mine," said Birdie matter-of-factly. "And don't worry, ma. I know how you feel about animals in the house. I'll keep her in my room and put a small box of sand in the corner for her to relieve herself. I'll clean it out every day."

"But Birdie, why the interest in keeping animals all of the sudden? You never mentioned wanting a cat before."

Knowing full well how her mother felt about Newt, Birdie didn't dare mention where the kitten had come from. So instead she told a half truth. "She's a stray, ma, and might not survive out there otherwise. I miss my baby terribly and I so desperately need something to shower my love upon. Plus, Sugar here needs me." She cuddled the cat up against her cheek.

"Sugar?" asked Hortensia. Shaking her head, she knew she was beat. Birdie definitely needed a distraction from the painful memories of her child. "All right. But make sure Sugar stays in your room until she is house broken."

"Thanks ma," said Birdie. "And I'm sorry about this morning."

"No, Birdie," said her mother. "I'm the one who should apologize for not remembering the anniversary of the baby's birth. I should have known that it would be painful for you."

Birdie blinked back tears as her mother gave her a hug and patted Sugar on the head. "Now you put the cat in your room, wash your hands and come to the table. I've made you something special!"

Early the next day before the sun rose, Ella woke up, got dressed and waited on the step. It felt strange not heading over to the hotel this morning. She felt the same way last summer when the hotel had closed down. Now she heard that it was going to stay open all year but with only a few staff working. She was happy for Birdie and Ronnie being retained but, if she had to tell the truth, she was also jealous that she was among those temporarily laid off. She was also concerned about Birdie working for Tangie again which was one of the reasons she got up early this morning to try to catch her friend as she headed for work. The other reason was at the forefront of her mind as soon as she saw Birdie come out of her house.

Ella bounded off her porch and through her front gate. "Mornin' Birdie!"

Birdie was surprised but very happy to see her best friend. "Why Ella! What are you doin' up so early today? If I were you, I'd be catchin' up on my sleep!"

Ella laughed as she walked beside Birdie, "Oh, there'll be plenty o' time for that, but today I wanted to make sure I saw ya so I can apologize. Birdie, I am so sorry for not rememberin' yo' child's birthday yesterday. It must have been tough on ya. I'm so glad that at least Newt remembered. He's the one that reminded me."

Birdie smiled and sighed at Newt's thoughtfulness. "Yes, that was so kind of him."

"He also told me what he was fixin' to do when he left to go home. Did he come back to see ya before ya left?" asked Ella.

Birdie reddened and nodded. Ella continued, "He told me the idea he had about the lil kitten and I 'bout cried. Did ya take it home?"

"Yes, I did," replied Birdie.

"Oh Birdie, I am so glad to hear that. Ya know, that man loves ya to pieces. Please promise me that you'll always love him back," said Ella earnestly.

"I will. And I told him as much yesterday, I'll have ya know," said Birdie.

"Good," said Ella with a sigh of relief. "Ya'll have been through so many ups and downs. It's time ya'll get together and find a way to make it work."

"That's the problem, Ella," said Birdie. "You and I both know full well that the only way Newt and I will ever be able to properly get together will involve us movin' far away. And that'll take some time. Plus, I don't dare be seen with him outside the Montclair as I'm afraid of that Stokes character watchin' us and waitin' to beat on him again, and this time he might kill 'im!"

Birdie shuddered as the thought of Stokes still frightened her to the core. Once she realized that he was the same man who had accosted her in town, she took great pains to keep a very safe distance from him. "And after the hotel management came down on us earlier this year about relations between men and women on staff, we can't be even seen together inside the hotel. It's almost like God don't want us together, either."

"Naw, don't even think that Miss Birdie," said Ella. "God ain't the one tearin' ya'll apart. He's the one who keeps putting ya back together. He's the one who whispers in Newt's ear and gives him all these ideas, like the one about that lil kitten."

Birdie walked in thoughtful silence as she considered Ella's words. As they got closer to the hotel, they spotted Ronnie waiting at the next block.

"Aha!" teased Birdie. "So that's why you were up so early today, and here I thought you were wantin' to see ME."

"Oh, hush now," said Ella. "I did need to see ya, but Ronnie and I have a plan worked out to see each other every mornin' and afternoon this summer. And the hotel management can't say a dang thing because I ain't an employee right now!"

Birdie laughed at Ella's logic as the girls joined Ronnie and walked the rest of the way to the Montclair in friendly camaraderie.

Wasting no time, Birdie got right to work on the display gown. The silvery grey fabric felt like water in her hands and was very easy to cut. It was going to drape very nicely, thought Birdie. By the time she had to go downstairs and help prepare lunch, she had already stitched up a good portion of the skirt.

After helping Rita and Netta peel vegetables, shuck scores of oysters and prepare croquettes using leftover ham and mashed potatoes from the previous day's dinner, Birdie had some free time before she had to go in the scullery and help with the dishes. She collected the kitchen debris and headed outside for the trash receptacle. She hoped to see Newt but he didn't appear to be anywhere out back. After emptying the basket, Birdie caught sight of Isaiah and Felipe on the west side of the property leaning on the shovels and looking at something in the distance.

Birdie, curious as to what was captivating them, walked over. "Good mornin' gentlemen! What are ya'll lookin' at?"

Felipe smiled and tipped his hat to Birdie while Isaiah replied, "Mornin' Birdie. We're just watchin' them unloadin' over there." He pointed towards a large delivery wagon where Newt and Lito were helping the two deliverymen unload hundreds of highly varnished narrow wood planks.

"What are those for?" Birdie asked him.

"All I know is that Miss Sutton asked me to provide two of our younger, stronger men to help unload that wagon. Then I heard Mista Speer, who was standin' nearby and not lookin' too pleased, say somethin' about it being the flo' to skate on."

"A floor to skate on?" asked Birdie in wonder. "Like a skatin' rink? They're puttin' one in here?" There was already a rink on the northwest side of town. She wondered why Mr. Prescott would want one at the Montclair.

By the time, Birdie went back to the kitchen, the luncheon dishes were starting to arrive from the main dining room. Birdie went into action and started to gather the dishes which were coming down the dumbwaiter and carried them back to the sink where Tangie was already scrubbing the first set.

"You're late," she remarked curtly.

"I'm sorry, Tangie. I was only outside to toss away the garbage. I didn't realize that the dining room dishes would start coming down so quickly." responded Birdie.

"Well, tomorrow you might wanna stay closer to the kitchen instead of traipsin' 'round outside after yo' beau," muttered Tangie.

Birdie's temper flared. "I'll have you know that I was not doing any such thing! I told Rita that I was going to the trash bin!"

"Well ain't that convenient for ya. Where else are ya gonna see him?" taunted Tangie.

"I was nowhere's near him! If ya don't believe me, ask Isaiah. He saw me out there just now!" cried Birdie.

"Listen, I ain't gonna stand here arguin' with ya all day. Just shut yo' mouth and git to work!" shouted Tangie.

"Who do you think you're talkin' to?" yelled Birdie.

"Oh, I'll tell ya who I'm talkin' to," hollered Tangie. "I'm talkin' to a high toned high yaller who thinks she's better than anyone down here just 'cause she can sew and work upstairs fo' part o' the day. You ain't nothin' but another nigger to them white folks up there and don't you ever forget it!"

Suddenly a sound of a throat clearing was heard behind them and to their horror, they discovered Iris Sutton's angry face in the doorway with Rita looking anxiously over her shoulder.

"Ladies! I could hear you clear down the corridor from my office! What is all this screaming about?"

Tangie made sure to plead her case first. "I'm sorry for the ruckus, Miss Sutton. But Miss Fairfax was late gettin' to the scullery and when I pointed it out to her, she started hollerin' at me."

Iris turned to Birdie and, with raised eyebrows, asked, "Is this true, Brigid?"

"No, not entirely ma'am," replied Birdie. "I was taking out the kitchen waste to be disposed of and saw Isaiah...I mean Mr Johnson nearby and asked him a question about what was going on out front. By the time I got back, the dishes were already starting to come down from the dinin' room and Tangie...I mean Miss Foster...accused me of socializin'."

At this point, Rita interrupted. "Iris, if it helps any, I did allow Birdie to take the yard waste outside once we were finished cooking lunch."

"I see," said Iris. "Thank you, Mrs. Alvares." Addressing the two younger women, she sternly advised, "Miss Fairfax, please see that you are prompt in the future. And Miss Foster, we are a respectable hotel and therefore frown upon our staff, especially those in supervisory positions, raising their voices and shouting like fishwives. Now I want you both to comport yourselves like adults from here on out. There will be no noise coming from this room other than the sounds of dishes, pots and pans being washed. Am I understood?"

"Yes ma'am," both women said in sullen unison.

"Good, then I hope this will be the last time I have to come down here," said Iris as she turned and left.

Tangie and Birdie glared at each other before sticking their hands in the warm soapy water and scrubbing the remainder the dirty dishes in hostile silence.

Hiram Meriwether waited impatiently as he checked his pocket watch once more. That gal will be late to her own funeral, he silently groused to himself. However, she's always managed to come through with the best pieces of silverware for him, which was why he tolerated her constant tardiness.

Sliding open the small window of his luxurious coach, he shouted up to his driver, "Once more around the block, James."

"Yessir," said his long-time Negro driver as he took up the reins and set the horses in motion once again.

Hiram sat back in the plush seat upholstered in gold velvet. The last thing he needed was to attract attention. His personal motto was, "If you're always on the move, you'll be that much harder to catch."

He never considered himself a criminal. He was merely a purveyor of fine goods. Where those goods came from, he made it a practice to never know nor care. He made a very good living at acquiring the very best treasures he could find, pay as little as possible for them and then sell them on for a tidy profit. Over the years, he'd amassed what came to a small fortune and kept his wife in the finest silks and jewels and his children in the very best schools. His sizeable donations to charity made him an upstanding member of both his church and community.

Once again, the coach came to a stop at the usual meeting point on Ribera Street just outside Lincolnville. Hiram opened one of the windows and peeked out. The sun had just set and darkness was closing in. In the distance, he could make out the silhouette of a female hurrying up the road toward the carriage. Hiram quietly cursed and whispered, "How many times have I told her not to run up to the carriage!" Almost as if the woman heard him, she slowed down to a walk when she was within a block of the coach. Hiram breathed easier and sat back.

Within moments there was a knock. Hiram opened the carriage door and let her in.

"You're late," he chastised.

"Sorry Mista Meriwether," replied Tangie. "I'm mainly workin' the scullery all by myself for the summer now so I'll be finishin' later than usual."

"So, what have you brought me?" asked Hiram.

Tangie reached into her deep apron pocket and produced a set of silver salt and pepper shakers, a gravy boat and bud vase. Hiram inspected the pieces carefully. He might have a taker for these, but they weren't as nice as that silver tray with the rose etching she brought him last time. That fetched him a tidy sum.

"Say, can you get your hands on any crystal?"

Chapter 25

Birdie was almost finished with the skirt of the display dress when she realized that she was going to need more black velvet ribbon for the trimming. That meant a quick visit with Miss Sutton and a trip into town.

She went down to see the housekeeper who granted both her request to go into town and the necessary funds. As she opened the cash box and counted out the coins, Iris remarked, "I trust things will go smoother in the kitchen today, Miss. Fairfax."

"Oh yes, ma'am," replied Birdie earnestly. "I am sorry that things got outta hand yesterday. I certainly didn't mean for them to. I for one will keep quiet today and just do those dishes and not say a word."

Iris knew that Birdie was not one to make trouble. "That's fine, Brigid, and remember what I told you a couple days ago. If things get to be too difficult for you, please come and see me before they escalate again."

"Yes, Miss Sutton, I will," promised Birdie.

"Fine. Now you best be going and don't be too long." Iris said with a smile.

As Birdie strode through the kitchen on her way out, she stopped and told Rita, who was cutting up a chicken, "I'm just goin' into town for some sewing notions. I'll be back in time to help out with lunch!"

Rita waved and said, "All right. See ya soon."

Tangie, who happened to be passing through from the scullery at that moment, said, "It must be nice to be able to come and go as ya please. You just make sure you're on time today when them plates start comin' back here!"

By then Birdie had gone through the door and shut it behind her. It took some effort, but she resisted the urge to talk back. She could still hear Tangie ranting to Rita as she made her way down the path to the side street.

As his shop was on her way to the general store, Birdie went to see Mr. Moscovitz first just in case he had what she was looking for and could get her a better deal. However, he said he didn't often have any ribbon on hand so Birdie continued to Hartsfield's. Today the shop was empty. Eddie Hartsfield was stacking boxes of Carter's Little Liver Pills on the counter by the cash register.

"Hiya Birdie," he said when he saw her. "Can you believe it? Instead of ordering 2 crates of these pills, I ordered 12! My pa about killed me. Say, you don't have any headaches, constipation, dyspepsia or biliousness, do ya?"

Birdie laughed, "No, sorry Eddie. It's only a need for black velvet ribbon that brings me here today."

"Oh, all right," he said with mock disappointment. Walking over to the shelves which held an assortment of fabric bolts and sewing notions, he reached up and pulled down a spool of thin black velvet ribbon. "How's this?" he asked.

"Hmmm. Do ya have anything wider?" inquired Birdie.

"Well, let's see," Eddie said as he rummaged through a few more spools. He brought down another which held a slightly wider ribbon. "What about this?"

"Perfect!" exclaimed Birdie. I'll take whatever's left on there."

As Eddie measured up what was on the spool, he remarked, "I ain't seen much of Newt these days. Have you been keepin' him busy on Sundays?" he asked coyly.

Birdie nervously gulped and replied, "No, I only see him around the Montclair now and then."

"Oh, I'm sorry," said Eddie. "I thought he was courtin' ya."

Birdie looked around to make sure no one else was in the shop. Feigning a nonchalant gaiety, she laughed, "Oh, we're just good friends, is all."

“Okay, then,” replied a bewildered Eddie as he handed over the small white parcel. “That will be forty-nine cents for the ribbon, Birdie."

"Thanks, Eddie," said Birdie, who desperately wished to put a quick end to the transaction before he made any more mention of Newt. "Oh, could you please give me a receipt for the Montclair?"

"Sure thing," he replied as he hastily filled in a form from his receipt book, tore it out and handed it over. "Nice seein' ya and say 'hey' to Newt for me if ya see ‘im."

Birdie waved as she made a swift escape. Thank goodness no one else had entered the store. She quickly hurried down the street and as she made a right turn onto King, she ran straight into Lonnie Stokes who had been glancing at the front page of the Herald.

Stokes was about to tip his hat and say, "Excuse me, ma'am" until he glanced up and recognized Birdie. His demeanor immediately darkened. "Oh, it's you. Watch where you're goin', nigra. I certainly been watchin' out for you. Looks like you're bein' a good lil quadroon, keepin' away from that jackass Phillips and the rest of the white boys. That's a good gal. Make sure it stays that way." Sneering at her, he brushed by Birdie, almost knocking her over in the process.

Birdie was certain her knees were about to buckle, but she somehow managed to make it back to the Montclair. She didn’t feel safe until she stepped into the kitchen and saw Rita’s friendly face.

“You got back quick!” she said. “We’re still preppin’ the vegetables.” Noticing Birdie’s sudden pallor, Rita asked, “Are you all right, honey? You look like you just seen a ghost!”

Using every bit of courage and strength she had in her, Birdie smiled and said, “Why I’m all right, Rita. I’ll just take this ribbon upstairs and I’ll be back in two shakes of a lamb’s tail to help you with lunch!”

Birdie shakily climbed the stairs, went into her workroom and shut the door behind her. Going to the corner and hiding behind a rack of finished dresses, she leaned against the wall and slowly slid to the floor as her knees buckled under her.

Tangie arrived much earlier than usual one morning. Even though Miss Sutton and any of the other staff had not yet arrived, she still tiptoed up down the corridor and up the service stairs like a cat. She looked carefully around her, and seeing no one around, she stealthily moved towards the main dining room, which was still dark as the sun had not yet risen.

Creeping toward the back of the dining room and making sure not to run into any tables or chairs, Tangie found the storage room where all the crystal ware was kept along with the special occasion porcelain in a locked glass paneled hutch. Afraid that it might get broken during its trip down the dumbwaiter or while in the hands of the scullery maids, the crystal and porcelain was washed and kept under lock and key by Mr. Hayes, the dining room manager and maitre'd. Tangie could see the prismatic sparkle of the crystal reflecting the electric light outside the window.

Tangie wondered how she was going to get her hands on the crystal and how she was going to sneak it out of the hotel. She sighed heavily as she yet again regretted getting into this whole business.

Ever since her father's death and her mother's subsequent nervous breakdown, Tangie became the head of her family. Two of her brothers were helping out by picking citrus and doing odd jobs around town, but their small wages as well as what Tangie was earning at the Montclair was barely enough to keep a roof over their heads and food on the table.

One day when she was bemoaning her desperate situation to their neighbor Kelvin Barnes, who had recently been released from jail for petty larceny, he told her about a man he knew who bought expensive things that people would bring him and sell them up in Jacksonville and over in Tallahassee. That was the beginning of Tangie's association with Hiram Meriwether.

Having always been a strictly religious woman at heart, Tangie initially had a hard time taking things from the Montclair. But when she went home at the end of every day and watched her mother and siblings devour the few bits of food she was able to take back with her each evening, Tangie reckoned that it was no longer stealing but a matter of survival.

That was why she had nothing but disdain for people like Birdie Fairfax for whom things seemed to come easy. Despite the fact that Tangie had started at the Montclair when it first opened, Birdie was now earning almost three times as much as she was and that has not been sitting too well with Tangie lately.

She softly closed the door of the storage room. As she tiptoed back down the servant's staircase, her mind was busily trying to solve the dilemma of the crystal ware.

Birdie's recent encounter with Stokes had renewed the terror in her heart over Newt's safety. But she kept it all well hidden from him in fear that he would try to retaliate and get killed in the process. She didn't even dare to tell Ella.

Her only source of consolation these days was Sugar, who had grown much stronger over the past month. Birdie made her toys from fabric scraps and yarn which gave the small kitten something to pounce on and carry around the room. Sugar was an endless source of amusement during the day and a comforting presence at night when Birdie would hold her close and stroke her between the ears until they both fell asleep.

In addition to the cat, there was also a lot of activity going on at the Montclair which helped Birdie take her mind off her troubles.

She had finished the silver evening dress and delivered it to Miss Sutton well before her two-week deadline. The housekeeper was awed and called both Mavis Kinkade and Rita to have a look at it.

As the three women admired the gown, Rita said, "I bet this'll look even lovelier on a real woman instead of this dress form. Birdie, go try it on!"

"Yes, go on Birdie!" urged Mavis.

"Oh, no," laughed Birdie. "I ain't one of them fashion models." She looked uncertainly at Miss Sutton who smiled indulgingly.

"Go on, Brigid. I imagine it won't do any harm to see how it looks on you. Help her out, Mrs. Alvares."

Birdie took the dress off the form and, followed by Rita, disappeared behind the rack of uniforms which hung across the back of the office. A couple of minutes later, Rita emerged with a big smile on her face followed by Birdie.

The dress fitted her perfectly. The silver bodice featured puffy black velvet sleeves which ended just above the elbows. The low-cut neckline which skimmed the top of her bosom was trimmed with black velvet ribbon and bows. The bottom of the silver tulip shaped shirt was also adorned with three rows of the black velvet ribbon.

The three women collectively gasped. Mavis murmured, "Birdie, you look like a beautiful gift wrapped in silver with velvet bows."

Iris looked on approvingly. She held up her index finger as an idea suddenly came to her. Going to the speaking tube cabinet, she called down to the houseman's station.

"Mr. Simms. Is Mr. Prescott still over there?" After placing her ear to the tube to hear the response, she again spoke into it, "Splendid! Please tell him I'm on my way over to show him something."

Taking Birdie by the hand, she said, "Come with me, Brigid. You too, ladies." The three women looked at each other in bewilderment as they wondered where Iris was taking them but dutifully followed her up the service stairs. They traversed the almost empty lobby to where the new shop was being installed. Standing in front of the store window was Mr. Prescott who was speaking to a carpenter about the shelving that was being constructed. Behind the two men, Isaiah and Newt were helping a deliveryman unload crates of merchandise which had just arrived. When the men saw the group of women appear, they all stopped what they were doing.

"Good morning, Mr. Prescott," began Iris. "I am sorry to interrupt but I thought you might wish to see this. Miss Fairfax?"

Birdie, who had been standing behind Rita and Mavis, nervously stepped out in front of them. Always hating to be the center of attention, she took a deep breath and steadied herself. She looked up and was surprised to see not only the hotelier but also Newt and Isaiah, which made her even more self-conscious.

"Well, I'll be. Look at Miss Birdie! "exclaimed Isaiah softly. "Ain't she a vision!"

Newt stood rooted to the floor as if hypnotized. Birdie looked like she just stepped out of a storybook. Even though he could tell she was nervous because she kept her eyes downcast, she was still prettier than any of the women in the paintings that surrounded them in the lobby. As always, he had an overwhelming urge to sweep her up into is arms and taste her sweet, full lips.

Iris went on, "This is the dress that Brigid has made for your window display. As you can see, it's an exquisite design, very well made and definitely eye catching."

The deliveryman whistled appreciatively and remarked, "You can say that again, lady!"

Mr. Prescott whirled around and told him sternly, "That's enough out of you."

Turning back to Birdie, he smiled and said, "Well done, Miss Fairfax. Very nice indeed! It is just the thing we'll need in this window. My only fear is that Mrs. Prescott will see it and want to buy it. We'll soon need to reserve the entire 4th floor just for her clothing. Again, a job well done, Miss Fairfax. You look like the belle of the ball."

"Thank you, sir," murmured Birdie.

"Well, we'll let you get back to your task. Thank you for humoring us, Mr. Prescott," said Iris.

"No, it is I who should thank you. Now I'm even more ambitious to get this store opened," replied Prescott with a chuckle.

As the men resumed their chores and the women descended the service stairs back to the housekeeper's office, Rita leaned over and whispered to Mavis, "Did you see Newt Phillips? He couldn't take his eyes off her!"

Chapter 26

The blistering August heat coupled with record high humidity seemed to make everyone at the Montclair move at a slower pace than usual. The electric fans in the kitchen didn't do much to cool it down and instead only moved the hot air around.

Birdie glanced out the kitchen window as she stirred yet another pitcher of iced tea for the ladies' luncheon. She had made almost a dozen pitchers, most of which were keeping cool in the ice box until it was time for them to be sent upstairs.

Catching sight of Isaiah who sweated profusely as he lifted a heavy load of gravel on his back and carried it out to the front of the hotel, Birdie had an idea. She set aside an extra pitcher and counted out four glass tumblers.

"All the iced tea is made, Rita," she said to the cook who was piping the filling into dozens of deviled eggs. "Did you need me to do anything else for ya?"

"No, my dear. Netta just finished the salads and I'm about done with these eggs. Everything else is ready. Go ahead and take a break. Lunch ain't even started yet so you got plenty of time."

"Thanks, Rita," said Birdie. "I'm just gonna take this pitcher out to the men. I'll be right back."

Taking care not to be seen by any guests, she headed out the back door and walked around to the front of the hotel where she found Isaiah and Felipe, who were resurfacing the garden paths near the entrance. They were both grateful for the break from their toil as well as the cold beverages.

"You sure are a life saver, Birdie! Thank you very much," said Isaiah.

"You're quite welcome," Birdie replied. "Where are Lito and Newt?"

"Lito's over in the arbor and Newt's choppin' a tree down over on the south side," answered Isaiah.

Birdie headed over to the arbor where she found Lito squatting down and looking intently at something in the reflecting pool. Birdie treaded carefully over to Lito who smiled when he saw her and pointed at a baby alligator which had crawled into the water. Gator sightings were common in the area. Occasionally, a large adult gator would make its way into the town, causing panic until it either moved on or was caught.

"What are ya gonna do with it, Lito?" asked Birdie.

"I take it to the canal," replied Lito, referring to the canal which ran across the western side of town.

"Do you think its mama is nearby?" asked Birdie uncertainly. She still had to find Newt and she didn't care to cross paths with a large female gator searching for her baby.

Lito shrugged and smiled. "I don't know. Don't worry. Gators are afraid of us," he replied as he tried to reassure Birdie.

"I hope you're right," said Birdie as she poured out a glass for Lito, who gulped it down eagerly.

Birdie headed out towards the rear of the property to find Newt. As she followed the chopping sounds of the axe, she kept her eyes peeled for any signs of an alligator. Every twig that cracked set her nerves on edge.

About two hundred yards away, Newt wiped the sweat from his brow before it trickled into his eyes. Stripped to the waist as he systematically cut down a diseased sycamore tree, the August sun relentlessly scorched his naked back. The humidity which heralded the approaching afternoon rainstorm made the air feel thick and heavy. As he continued to rhythmically swing his axe in a heat induced trance, Newt didn't hear or see Birdie as she walked up.

Having never seen Newt shirtless before, Birdie was mesmerized by the sight of his bare chest and arms. Although he was not overtly muscular like the strong men that she'd seen in the traveling circuses, his upper body was very well toned and defined from years of farming and physical labor.

Stepping back behind the trunk of an elm, Birdie quietly watched Newt as he continued working. Every time the axe made contact with the trunk, the muscles on his arms bulged and his abdomen tightened. She longed to reach out and touch him, wondering how the curly ginger hair on his chest would feel under her fingertips.

Leaning her head up against the elm's trunk, Birdie closed her eyes and imagined herself in Newt's arms with her face nuzzled up against his bare torso as she ran her hands up and down his sturdy back. A sudden loud cracking noise forced her eyes back open as a long branch from the sycamore fell to the ground a mere two feet in front of her, causing her to scream. Both the pitcher and tumbler she was carrying fell the ground.

Newt snapped his head around and shouted "Birdie!" as he dashed towards her and grabbed her by the shoulders. "Are you okay? What are ya doin' out here? I had no idea you were over there."

Too embarrassed to tell Newt that she'd been standing and gaping at him for the past few minutes, Birdie replied, "It's all right, just startled is all. I'd brought ya some iced tea but..." she looked over at the now empty glass pitcher and added, "I reckon it's all gone now. I'm sorry. I can go back and get ya some more."

"Aw, forget about that,'" said Newt dismissively. "I just wanna make sure ya weren't hurt. I'd never forgive myself if anything had happened to ya." Grabbing her firmly by the shoulders, he gently chided her. "Next time I'm cuttin' something down, please let me know when yer there, so I'll be more careful. Promise me, Birdie."

Birdie was too transfixed to speak so she just nodded. They both glanced into each other's eyes for what felt an eternity to Birdie. She immediately came back to her senses and stammered, "I...um...I....I better get back to the kitchen now. Tangie must be lookin' for me and I don't want any more problems with her. Once again, I'm sorry, Newt." She gently pulled herself out of his grasp. Smiling self-consciously, she said, "I'll see ya later."

New stared after her in bewilderment as he picked up the pitcher and glass that she left behind. "Birdie!" he shouted. "You forgot the......" But she had already scurried a good distance away and didn't look back.

Mr. Lawrence Conrad, a reporter from the St. Augustine Herald, was in attendance at the Montclair Fashion Emporium's grand opening along with his photographer Elmer Richards. Used to covering larger stories involving politics and crime, Conrad balked when his editor handed him this cream puff assignment.

He had done his homework on Johnathan Prescott and learned that the former cattle ranch and grove owner was in over his head with the Montclair and reckoned that these latest undertakings at the hotel reeked of desperation to keep up with Flagler's resorts. He also heard rumors of Prescott's son's sudden departure amid whispered allegations of rape. It was Conrad's wish to uncover the identity of the victim, so he could talk to her and blow the lid off the Prescott family's phony façade. It would be the biggest story of the year! In the meantime, Conrad accepted the assignment figuring that at least it would at least help him get his foot into the door of the hotel.

So, he politely interviewed Prescott, talked to Edward Jason, the store's new clerk, and had Elmer take photos of both the store and of Prescott and his wife. As he was getting ready to leave, he saw the silver dress in the window and noticed the attention it was getting from Lottie Prescott's female friends, who had gathered for the occasion. Thinking it might be worth including in the article, he asked Edward, "Mr. Jason, this dress is drawing a small crowd. Where did it come from?"

"It was actually made by one of the women who works in our kitchen," Edward replied. "It's quite extraordinary, isn't it?"

"She works in the kitchen?" asked Conrad incredulously. "Can you give me her name? I'll make sure to include it in the article."

"I can do better than that, sir," replied Edward. "She's standing just over there." He pointed to the group of Montclair staff who were standing in the mezzanine and peering down onto the store and the goings-on.

Birdie was standing with Rita, Iris, Ronnie and Hayes, watching the grand opening unfold and witnessing all the attention that the silver dress was receiving. She noticed that Edward Jason, the nice young man from the shop, was pointing their way and beckoning.

"Who's Jason pointing at?" asked Frank.

"I'll go down and see what's the matter," said Iris as she made her way towards the stairs.

"Uh, Birdie," began Ronnie. "I think he's wantin' YOU."

"What?" exclaimed Birdie. "You're crazy, Ronnie. Why on earth would they want me down there?"

"He's lookin' right at ya," said Ronnie.

Iris arrived downstairs and spoke briefly to Edward, Prescott and Mr. Conrad. She turned around, pointed specifically to Birdie and mouthed, "Come down, Brigid."

Birdie's heart started to hammer. What on earth could they want me for, she wondered. Her legs felt like jelly as she slowly walked down the stairs and towards the Emporium.

"Mr. Lawrence Conrad," began Prescott. "This is Brigid Fairfax, our in-house seamstress. Miss Fairfax, Mr. Conrad only wants to ask you a couple of questions. No need to be nervous," he added kindly.

"Miss Fairfax, I was told by Mr. Jason that you made this very exquisite dress that is in the window. He also tells me that you work in the kitchen. Is that true?"

"Yes sir," replied Birdie.

"But how on earth are you able to fulfill your duties in the kitchen while creating these exquisite gowns? Do you have anyone helping you?" asked Conrad.

"No sir," answered Birdie. "I only work in the kitchen until lunchtime, then I go upstairs to my workroom for the rest of the day."

"Interesting," said Conrad. "And you're able to keep up with the orders you get? How do you manage that?"

"Yes sir," said Birdie. "It's hard to explain how I do it. I mainly make the dresses in stages and get somethin' like an assembly line goin'. It makes it all go much faster."

It sounded to Lawrence Conrad that Prescott was fully taking advantage of this poor girl by making her slave away in both the kitchen as well as her sweatshop. A smile spread across his lips as inspiration struck.

"Miss. Fairfax, would you care to stand in front of the window by your delightful creation, so we can take a photograph?" asked Conrad.

"Oh, sir! I look a fright! I just couldn't," cried Birdie who looked to Iris Sutton and Johnathan Prescott for support. Other than a portrait she took as a child and another with Hortensia several years ago, she was a novice at posing for photographs.

"You look fine, Brigid," said Iris.

Prescott concurred. "Go on, Miss Fairfax. You will represent the Montclair very well."

Smoothing her hair and her skirts, Birdie stepped uncertainly over to the window. Elmer took a few moments to set up his camera and pose Birdie before he took a couple of photos.

Meanwhile, Lottie Prescott stood by the wayside, fuming in silence. It should be her being photographed in front of that window. After all, it was she who gave her husband the idea to open the store in the first place!

The next morning when Birdie met Newt at the kitchen entrance, she excitedly related to him all the events of the previous day.

"Aw, I ain't surprised that yer dress got lots of attention," said Newt. "It sure looked nice on ya the other day. But again, I was staring more at you than the dress."

Birdie gave his hand a surreptitious squeeze before they headed inside, where they found Iris, Rita, and Netta standing at the cook's table looking intently at something. Upon closer inspection, Birdie discovered that it was the daily edition of the Herald.

Looking up, Rita exclaimed, "There she is! The Queen of the Montclair herself!"

Iris picked up the newspaper and brought it over to Birdie and Newt. "I thought you'd want to see this, Brigid."

Birdie looked at the newspaper and saw her own face staring back at her. It was a strange feeling. "Oh, my goodness! I can't believe it. I never thought I'd be in the newspaper." She looked at Newt in astonishment.

Forgetting himself for a moment, Newt replied, "You look beautiful as always. I'll have to make sure to get me a copy!"

Iris smiled and said, "You may keep this, Brigid. We have others. And congratulations."

She left Birdie, Newt and the rest to look at the paper as she made her way back to the office. There was one thing about the article that bothered Iris. Although he didn't outwardly say it, Lawrence Conrad seemed to have portrayed Birdie as a poor soul who was being taken advantage of by Johnathan Prescott. She sensed that the reporter had some sort of agenda and hoped that this would be the last they'd ever see of him.

Sunday afternoon's dark, ominous sky and thick air signaled that the usual afternoon summer storm was approaching. The high temperatures had made the morning's church service almost unbearable. Not wishing to spend any time over a hot stove, Hortensia decided to fix a cold dinner for herself and Birdie. As she started to collect a couple of tomatoes and a head of lettuce for the salad, there was a knock at the door.

Birdie's voice came from her room. "That's probably for me, ma. I'll get it!"

Curious as to who was visiting her daughter, Hortensia slowly placed the head of lettuce on the counter and peeked through the kitchen doorway as Birdie, still in her Sunday dress, passed by on her way to the front door. As she opened it, Hortensia slowly stepped up behind her to get a peek at who was on the porch.

A tall, handsome young black man in a very nice suit was smiling and saying, "Good afternoon, Birdie!" He looked to be carrying a jacket over his arm.

"Hello Arthur!" greeted Birdie. "Come on in!"

Arthur stepped inside and nodded politely to Hortensia. Noticing her mother standing there, Birdie said, "Oh, Arthur, this is my mother. Ma, this is Arthur Dickson. He's a houseman at the Montclair."

Hortensia smiled warmly and said, "It's so nice to meet you, Arthur. To what do we owe this pleasure?"

"The pleasure's all mine, ma'am," replied Arthur. "Birdie's offered to mend this jacket fo' me. I don't know how but I somehow managed to lose not one, but two buttons! My ma doesn't have any that match so I reckoned I'd come see the best seamstress I know!"

"I'll take that from ya, Arthur," offered Birdie as Arthur handed her the jacket. After a quick inspection, she added, "I'll replace all the buttons so that they'll look alike. I've got a spare set of brass ones that'll go nicely with this dark green material."

Hortensia took a quick liking to the young man. "We were just getting ready to sit down to dinner. Won't you please join us, Arthur? It's only vegetable soup and a salad but we have plenty!"

Smiling gratefully, Arthur replied, "As much as I'd love to, ma'am, I'm expected back at my house. Ya see, my aunt and uncle are visitin' from Jacksonville so the whole family is gettin' together fo' dinner. Perhaps another time?"

"Of course," said Hortensia with a wide grin. "You are welcome here any time!"

Birdie looked at her mother quizzically for a second before saying, "I'll have this done for you by tomorrow, Arthur. I'll bring it to work with me."

"Thanks Birdie," said Arthur. "And let me know how much I owe ya." Turning to Hortensia, he said, "It was nice meetin' ya, ma'am."

"Likewise," said Hortensia.

As he and Birdie headed back to the front door, Arthur said, "I'll see ya tomorrow, Birdie. And again, thanks!"

"You're welcome, Arthur. See ya," replied Birdie as she opened the door for him and watched him walk down the garden path to the street.

Closing the door, Birdie turned to Hortensia who was still beaming. She'd never seen her mother invite someone she'd just met to dinner before and was puzzled.

"Arthur's very nice, isn't he?" remarked Hortensia.

"Yes, he is," said Birdie cautiously.

"And very handsome, too," said Hortensia. "I assume he is unmarried. Do you know if he is courting anyone?"

Birdie's suspicions were suddenly confirmed. "Ma, me and Arthur are just friends. That is all. Please don't start gettin' any ideas about us!"

"But Birdie, he is a very eligible young man with a good job. A far cry better than that white Cracker gardener I saw ya with earlier this year. Mija, you need to think about your future. And I feel that someone like Arthur would be better suited for you."

Birdie was stung by the insult to Newt and replied, "Ma! I like Arthur and yes, he is handsome and has a steady job, but I have no romantic notions about him. Once again, we're just friends."

Taking Arthur's jacket with her, she retreated to her room and shut the door. Hortensia returned to the kitchen, picked up her best knife and slowly started to slice the tomatoes.

They might be just friends for now, she thought, but that should only make it easier for the seeds of romance to eventually blossom.

Chapter 27

Once the last of the luncheon dishes that had come down from the dining room were scrubbed, rinsed and dried, Birdie left the kitchen and went upstairs to her workroom. As usual, she took a couple of small sandwiches with her instead of eating with the others in the staff dining room.

An ivory lace dress hung on the wire form which stood in the center of the room. Birdie was working on the sleeves, which were giving her some trouble. Unhappy with how they were looking, she stood and stared at the dress as she took a bite from one of the egg salad finger sandwiches, hoping that a sudden flash of inspiration would hit her. Instead, a bolt of lightning streaked across the grey sky in her window.

Staring outside, Birdie saw that it was starting to rain. Even though it was only a quarter to three, the outdoor landscape grew darker by the minute. The wind soon started to pick up speed, blowing the raindrops sideways.

I hope Newt and the other men are downstairs in the kitchen, she thought. No one should be out in this weather. Luckily Ma is over at Ophelia's this afternoon baking pies for their upcoming ladies' society fundraiser and Sugar should be safely tucked up in my room. I'd just feel better about them both if I were home right now, but it looks like I won't be going anywhere for a while.

Just then the overhead light went out, leaving her in semi-darkness. She could hear faint shouts and exclamations from downstairs. Carefully groping her way to a shelf on the wall, she brought down an oil lamp and a box of matches. Once she lit the lamp, she carefully made her way out of her workroom and headed for the kitchen.

As she got to the service stairs, Birdie encountered Ronnie who was running back up after getting a key from Iris Sutton.

"Hey Birdie," he said breathlessly. "Looks like me and Arthur are gonna be on candle and lamp duty." With that he was gone.

When Birdie finally arrived downstairs, she saw Rita, Netta and Tangie lighting lamps and candles and placing them around the kitchen. Birdie put down her own lamp and helped them.

"What'll we be doin' 'bout dinner, then?" Netta was asking Rita.

"Luckily, we got gas stoves, so we can still cook," Rita responded, "We might be able to get away with a simple supper tonight. Iris is gonna check with Mr. Prescott and will let us know. For now, she just wants us to keep count of the staff in our area and make sure everyone's inside."

"Anyone seen the gardeners?" asked Birdie.

"We've been so busy rootin' 'round in the dark fo' candles and lamps, we done forgot about 'em," said Tangie.

"Oh my God," cried Birdie. "Don't tell me they're still out there!"

Rita, who was stirring a pot of oyster stew that was simmering on the stove, turned to Birdie and said soothingly, "Don't fret, child. They're grown men and won't be hurt by a bit of rain and wind."

"Maybe they're up front," suggested Netta. "Miss Sutton said she'd be goin' 'round the hotel and makin' sure we're all here."

"I hope so," whispered Birdie, anxiously praying they were safe.

Noticing Birdie's apprehension, Rita decided that the best course of action was to keep the girl preoccupied. "Birdie, would you do me a favor? Could you go to the larder and bring me that large tin of oyster crackers?"

"Yes, Rita," said Birdie dutifully as she took one of the lamps and headed to the pantry. Placing the lamp on top of the large storage bin that held potatoes, she searched the shelves for the crackers.

"Where are those things? I just saw them two days ago," she said aloud.

After shifting a few boxes and canisters around for a few minutes with no luck, she realized that the oyster crackers must be on one of the higher shelves. Birdie grabbed the step stool and just as she was about to climb up onto it, a series of loud, desperate knocks on the outside delivery door startled her. She quickly unlocked the door and opened it. The raindrops which blew in pelted her face like tiny needles.

Isaiah and Lito tumbled inside. Both were drenched and breathing heavily. Isaiah appeared to be holding up Lito, who was limping. Birdie quickly pushed the door shut and locked it.

"Oh Lord! I can't believe you've been out there all this time. What happened to ya, Lito?" Birdie asked as she scrambled for the clean kitchen rags that were stacked in the corner and proceeded to help the men dry off.

"We cannot see out there," said Lito. "I step in hole and twist my foot."

"Rita!" Birdie shouted, "Come quickly and bring some large towels with ya!" Turning to Isaiah, she asked the question that was burning on her lips. "Where are Newt and Felipe?"

Isaiah, who was mopping off his face with one of the towels, shrugged. "I wish I knew, Birdie. Me and Lito were only over there in the vegetable garden and it took us a long time to find our way back. Newt and Felipe were workin' way out in the arbor before the storm started. God knows where they are now." Seeing Birdie's frightened expression, he gently added, "Maybe they're in the groundskeepin' shed."

Rita ran into the pantry with an armful of kitchen towels. "Oh, my goodness! Ya'll look like two wet cats. Come on into the mudroom with me and dry off by the fire."

As the men followed Rita, Birdie grasped the canister of oyster crackers to her chest as worry started to consume her. Where were Newt and Felipe?

In the kitchen, Nettie poured two cups of steaming hot coffee and brought them over to the two soaking wet men who were drying off in the mudroom. Rita had brought out a couple of larger towels from the storage cupboard and was wrapping each of them up.

"Where do ya reckon them others got off to?" asked Rita. "There's a young gal in the next room who's lookin' mighty jittery. Do ya think there's a chance they're in the front lobby?"

Isaiah savored the delicious hot java before swallowing. "Maybe. But if Newt was in this hotel, he would've made his way back here to Birdie by now."

Rita sighed, "I thought as much but was afraid to say it."

"But like I told her, maybe they managed to get to the gardener's shack," Isaiah said as he tried to sound hopeful.

Birdie appeared in the doorway and asked "Do ya really think they're in there?"

"Stands a chance," replied Isaiah.

Birdie walked over to the window between the back entrance door and the kitchen, squinting hard as she desperately tried to see outside. On a clear day, the groundskeeper's shack was visible from the kitchen even though it was a good distance from the hotel, but with the rain and darkness, it was virtually invisible.

The sound of heels clicking up the corridor signaled the approach of Iris Sutton. Because the staff was accustomed to the sound, they all immediately stopped what they were doing and congregated in the kitchen, where she was undoubtedly heading.

Iris seemed to look relieved when she saw Isaiah and Lito. "I'm glad to see you, Mr. Johnson and Mr. Santiago. I got a bit worried when I didn't see any of you out front. Where are Mr. Phillips and Mr. Delrey?"

Birdie interrupted before Isaiah could reply. "You mean Newt and Felipe weren't up front?"

"Why no, Miss Fairfax. I was hoping all four men would be back here," answered Iris.

Swallowing a sob, Birdie ran to the larder. Iris looked after her questioningly. Rita explained, "Birdie and Newt Phillips are good friends. She's just concerned about him and Felipe, is all."

"Oh, I see," said Iris with a nod. She suspected there was more than friendship between Brigid Fairfax and Newton Phillips but as long as there was no illicit behavior on hotel property, she was willing to turn a blind eye to it as long as no one else brought it up before her.

"Rita," continued Iris, "I need to notify Mr. Prescott that two of our gardeners are missing. When I return, we'll go over tonight's menu and arrangements for overnight staff accommodations just in case the storm doesn't let up."

Lottie jumped every time she heard a thunderclap. Out of all the many things she despised about Florida, she hated the summer storms the most. She saw her fair share of bad weather back in Pittsburgh but nothing as savagely intense as the tropical monsoons that relentlessly pelted the Florida peninsula.

Her personal maid Violet was even more of a nervous wreck but did her best to keep her trembling hands under control as she methodically brushed out Lottie's hair. Several lit candles and an oil lamp illuminated Mrs. Prescott's dressing room as the rain and winds pounded steadily on the curtained windows.

"Oh, I do hope the electricity comes back on soon," said Lottie. "I feel like we're inside some dark, gloomy haunted house! It's bad enough that we can't go over to the Ponce de Leon to dine with the Daltons but now we are sitting here with nothing to do but jump out of our skins!" The sound of the front door opening and shutting made Lottie stop her tirade.

"Johnathan? Is that you?" she called hopefully.

"Who the hell else would it be?" came the response.

"Bring me my silk wrap, Violet," Lottie softly instructed the maid. After she covered herself and slid her feet into her peacock blue Turkish slippers, she picked up a candle and headed to the front room. As she passed down the hallway, the smell of roast quail which emanated from the small gas oven in the kitchen lent an appetite inducing aroma to the air.

When she arrived in the parlor, Prescott was in the middle of pouring himself a small glass of brandy. Turning to his wife, he raised an eyebrow and asked, "Care for some?"

"No thank you," said Lottie. "When will the electricity be back on?"

"Tomorrow at the earliest," said Prescott as he peeked out of the front parlor window. "It's looking pretty dark across the street, too, so I'm guessing that Flagler's power is also out."

"Oh, I detest these storms!" exclaimed Lottie.

"This isn't an ordinary rain shower, my pet," replied Prescott as he continued to stare out into the squall. "This is an honest to goodness cyclone. It looks like several of my trees out there have already been blown down."

"What?" Lottie was alarmed. "Do you think anything will happen to the hotel?"

"You've got nothing to worry about there," said Johnathan confidently. "This building is made of solid concrete and is completely windproof. By tomorrow the storm will have blown through and the electricity will hopefully be restored. Everything will be all right. You'll see."

Feeling slightly reassured, Lottie was about to sit on the settee but a knock on the front door made her stop short and head to the entryway. As she opened the door, the tight lipped serious countenance of Iris Sutton was lit by the small hand lantern she carried.

"Good evening, Mrs. Prescott," said the head housekeeper tonelessly. "Is Mr. Prescott available?"

Lottie always found Iris Sutton's intrusions annoying, especially when her husband was meant to be off duty and enjoying a bit of quiet time. She hesitated before saying, "Is it important, Iris? He only just came in a few moments ago."

Iris fixed Lottie with a steely eyed glance and responded, "I'm afraid my business is urgent, Mrs. Prescott."

Before Lottie could respond, her husband called out from the front room, "Who's there, Lottie?"

"It's Iris Sutton, dear," Lottie replied.

"Let her in, for God's sake," bellowed Prescott.

Lottie stepped aside and beckoned for Iris to enter. The housekeeper smugly brushed by her and entered the front parlor where she found Prescott standing by the window staring out at the raging storm.

"What's the status, Iris?" asked Prescott, who had become an expert at reading her face over the past couple of years and knew as soon as she walked in that something was wrong.

"Two of our gardeners are missing."

"Which ones?"

"Newton Phillips and Felipe Delrey."

"Where are Isaiah and the other Minorcan?"

"In the kitchen getting dried off. They only just came inside."

Prescott set his drink down. "Any of them hurt?"

"I only saw them for a minute. Mr. Johnson looked okay but I believe Mr. Santiago has injured his foot."

Taking Iris by the elbow, Prescott said, "Let's go."

Lottie, who was standing in the corner, cried, "Johnathan! Where are you going? You can't leave me up here in this dark mausoleum!"

Prescott lost his temper. "My God, woman! I've got a hotel with no power, guests who need attention, staff who will need beds for the night and most important of all - two men somewhere out there who might be in danger. Did you think I had intended to stay? I only came back for a drink to steady myself."

Duly chastened, Lottie sighed and said, "Of course not, dear. Let me know of there is anything you need me to do."

Prescott looked at her and softened. With her anxious eyes and hair hanging loose down her back, she reminded him of the young girl he first met many years ago. "Just save me some of that quail!" He gave Lottie a wink and she grinned in return. Iris inwardly grimaced.

Iris returned to the kitchen and gathered everyone together.

“Mr. Prescott has put the Montclair under lockdown. Because of the dangerous conditions outside, no one is permitted to leave the premises until the storm has passed. Therefore, you will all be staying the night here at the hotel. Ladies, once the dinner service is over and the staff has eaten, go upstairs and get your room assignments from Mavis. We’re opening up some of the second-floor rooms for our employees. Mr. Johnson and Mr. Santiago, you may go upstairs now if you wish. Dinner will be served in the staff dining room at 7:00.”

Turning to Rita, Iris handed her a hastily scribbled note. “Here is the menu for this evening’s dinner. As you’ll see, it will be an abbreviated version of what we usually serve on Thursday evenings. We’re certain that our guests will understand given the circumstances.”

Rita looked at the menu and nodded. “This is fine. Half of the food’s already prepared anyway.”

Birdie, who had been distractedly chopping vegetables with Netta and Tangic, asked, “Miss Sutton? Any word yet on the missing men?”

“Not yet, Brigid,” replied Iris gently. “But Mr. Prescott is aware of the situation.”

Even though there was only a fraction of the usual number of guests staying at the Montclair that summer, the housemen and maids were busier than usual. The guests were not only inconvenienced by the power outage, but some were bored after being forced to stay indoors all day while others were just frightened and needed reassurance that the building was strong enough to withstand the high winds.

After running more candles and lanterns to the second floor which was being opened for the staff, Ronnie paused on his way downstairs to catch his breath. He heard urgent footsteps hurrying down from the top floor and when he looked up, he saw the grim face of Johnathan Prescott. He had a raincoat over one arm and was carrying a small leather case in the other.

"Ah, Simms. I could use your help," he began. "How good is your eyesight?"

"Very good, sir," replied Ronnie.

"Splendid! Come downstairs with me. We'll grab an extra overcoat out of the cloakroom and head for the tower."

Even though it had only been a couple of hours since the storm started, it felt like an eternity to Birdie as she continued to slice up the ham which had come out of the oven. She tried her best to focus on her tasks and keep her fears at bay. Birdie attempted to artfully arrange the meat slices on the platter like Rita had showed her. The kitchen was illuminated with dozens of candles which, while lending the room a comforting warm glow, made ordinary tasks more challenging due to the decreased lighting.

It was times like this that Birdie wished she had the religious faith of her mother. Hortensia would know exactly how to pray and what comforting verses to look up in her well-worn bible. The only prayer that kept going through her mind was “Please God, let Newt be okay and bring him and Felipe back safely.”

She kept glancing over to the window, hoping to see some sort of human life outside in the swirling dark grey tempest but visibility was zero. Birdie fervently hoped that they were at least taking cover in the gardener’s shack but according to Isaiah, they were way out in the arbor and nowhere near it.

A sudden loud crash made all the women in the kitchen jump and scream at the same. Birdie froze with fright, tightly clutching the meat fork she’d been holding.

“Oh Lawd!” exclaimed Netta as the plate she was carrying smashed to the floor.

“What was that?” asked Tangie in a small, frightened voice.

Rita peeked out the kitchen window and said, “I can’t see a damned thing out there but I’m willin’ to bet it was a tree fallin’ down.” Looking back at the frightened women, Rita resolved to stay strong and calm. “Now ladies, no need to be afraid. By tomorrow, all this will be over. I’ve lived through my fair share of storms and managed to survive them all.”

The others returned to their chores while Birdie slowly put down the meat fork and wiped the tears from her eyes. If the winds out there now strong enough to blow down trees, anyone still out there was in grave danger indeed.

"See anything, sir?" shouted Ronnie.

"No one yet," replied Prescott. "But it looks like we just lost one of our oaks back there." Despite the swirling torrent, he was still able to make out the form of the uprooted tree in his binoculars.

Standing at the top of one of the Montclair's two towers, the men had a roof which protected them from most of the downpour. However, the sides were open which still exposed them to the ferocious elements.

In addition to the binoculars, they had also brought up a large, emergency gas lantern with a reflective backing which made the light exponentially brighter and larger than that of an average lamp. Ronnie had never seen anything quite like it before.

"Aim it towards the front grounds again in case they wandered over that way," yelled Prescott, hoping the bright beacon would help guide the missing men back to the building.

Ronnie continued keeping his eyes peeled as he scanned the grounds. His thoughts, as they'd been doing all that afternoon, returned to Ella and his family. He hoped that everyone was safely inside. Having heard too many stories of houses being destroyed and folks getting killed, Ronnie was understandably concerned when he learned that two friends were still out there somewhere.

As he glanced towards the west, Ronnie thought he saw something move. Thinking it might be a tree branch or a piece of debris, he stayed still and kept his eye on the same spot for a few moments. Suddenly he saw movement once again which seemed to be travelling of its own accord and not just something being blown about,

"Sir! Over there!" Ronnie pointed. "I think I see someone'!"

Prescott raced over and aimed the binoculars in the general direction where Ronnie was pointing. He couldn't see anything but swirling grayness.

"Here!" he cried as he handed the binoculars to Ronnie, "See if you can spot them better with these."

Ronnie grabbed the binoculars. Not seeing anything at first, he moved the lenses slightly to the right and then he spotted two dark human figures. Because they were still very far away, he wasn't able to see if they were indeed Newt and Felipe.

"I see two folks over there!" Ronnie shouted. Handing the binoculars back to Prescott.

Prescott finally spotted the pair. "By Jove! There they are. Looks like they spotted us!" shouted Prescott. After a couple more minutes, the figures got larger and were now identifiable. "Yes! They're our missing men, all right!"

Ronnie was now able to see them a bit more clearly with the naked eye. He also noticed that one of them looked seriously injured. "I think one of them's hurt, sir!"

Prescott took another look through the binoculars. "You're right. Looks like it's Phillips."

Without asking permission, Ronnie immediately ran back inside and down the stairs, taking them two at a time. When he got to the bottom, he tried to push the outside door open, but the winds were trying to push it shut. With as much strength as he could muster, Ronnie pressed his entire weight against the door and managed to crack it open. He wedged himself through the opening and once outside, pointed himself in the direction of where he saw the men approaching.

For every three steps he took, Ronnie was blown a step back. The raindrops felt like needles against his face. There was so much water going into his mouth and nose that he had to occasionally look backwards so that he could breathe. Calling out to Felipe and Newt was impossible.

Soon he was able to detect their shadows a few yards ahead of him. Waving his arms so they could spot him, Ronnie ran as best as he could into the prevailing winds until he was finally face to face with Felipe, who was practically dragging an unconscious Newt. Ronnie grabbed Newt's other arm and together the trio made their way back into the hotel.

Chapter 28

After the last of the food had been sent upstairs to the main dining room, Rita said, "Take a break, ladies. You both did a fine job gettin' everything out so quickly even though you've been worried sick. Lord knows, so have I. Take fifteen minutes and then we'll start fixin' the staff's meal." She and Netta helped themselves to a couple cups of hot tea.

Birdie closed her eyes and rubbed her temples, hoping it would help alleviate the headache she felt coming on. Having neither an appetite nor interest in the staff dinner, Birdie intended to ask Rita if she could be excused from it. Maybe she could get a head start on the cleanup while the others ate so that they all would be able to get their assigned rooms earlier.

She walked over to the window for what seemed the hundredth time that day and peered out. It was almost pitch black outside now so all she could see was her own reflection from the lamplight.

The sound of running footsteps made Birdie sharply turn from the window and the others stop their quiet chatter. Ronnie burst into the kitchen and seeing Birdie, grabbed her by the arm and cried, "We found 'em! They're back!"

Birdie cried with joy and hugged Ronnie around the neck as she excitedly jumped up and down. "Thank God! They're safe at last!"

"Praise the Lawd!" exclaimed Netta while Rita and Tangie smiled with relief.

Noticing Ronnie's grave expression, Birdie stopped jumping. "What's happened, Ronnie?"

Taking a deep breath, Ronnie said, "Newt's hurt awfully bad, Birdie. When I found 'em out there, Felipe had been draggin' 'im around for a while tryin' to find the hotel. Newt was struck by a fallin' tree. He's out cold and might have a broken bone or two."

"Where is he?" asked Birdie.

"Mista Prescott had him put into one o' them grand rooms up on the top floor. One of the guests is a doctor and is seein' to him now."

Birdie turned to the head cook and started to ask, "Rita, may I..."

Rita smiled warmly at her and said, "Go to him, child. He needs you more than we do."

"So how bad is he, Tom?" asked Prescott.

Dr. Thomas Winthrop, an old friend of Prescott's from his ranching days, finished wrapping the final bandage around Newt's chest.

"This young man's very lucky. If that branch had pierced him a couple of inches further to the left, he'd have been a goner. The leg doesn't appear broken, but it was deeply lacerated and needed stitching as did that gash on his head. I've done all I can with what little medical supplies I've brought with me. He'll need looking after until he can be moved to his home."

"That shouldn't be a problem," said Prescott. "Thanks again, Tom. I owe you one."

"Not at all. Was glad to help," replied the humble doctor. "I'll look in on him tomorrow morning."

As Dr. Winthrop closed up his leather medical bag and followed Prescott out to the suite's small front room, there was a knock at the front door. Prescott opened it and was surprised to see a very anxious looking Brigid Fairfax standing next to Ronald Simms. Her red rimmed eyes betrayed the fact that she'd been crying. Remembering how much Phillips seemed fond of the young woman, Prescott was surprised to discover that she apparently felt the same.

"Well, hello Miss Fairfax," said Prescott. "I'm assuming you're here to inquire about Philips."

"Yes sir," replied Birdie. "And if it is possible, may I see him?"

"Of course, come on in," answered Prescott. "You too, Simms. Dr. Winthrop here just patched him up and was leaving."

"He'll be fine," reassured the doctor. "He just needs some rest. I'll be by again tomorrow." With that, he slipped out the door and was gone.

"How's Felipe doing?" asked Birdie.

"Other than a few scrapes and bruises, he's all right," answered Prescott. "In fact, if it weren't for him, Phillips might not have made it. Delrey's a hero in my book as is Simms here, who ran out into the storm and brought these men back inside. I'm going to make sure you both are rewarded come pay time." he said to Ronnie.

"Aw sir, I didn't do anythin' that any other man wouldn't have done in the same spot," Ronnie protested.

"Nonsense," argued Prescott. "You showed quick thinking and true courage. There might be a promotion in this for you, but we'll talk about that later. Go on downstairs, get yourself something to eat and then see Miss Kinkade for your room assignment. I had a word with her to place you in one of the empty suites up here near Mr. Phillips and Mr. Delrey."

Ronnie's eyes widened incredulously. "Oh yes sir! Thank you, Mista Prescott." Before shutting the front door behind him, he added, "See ya later, Birdie."

Prescott turned to Birdie and guided her towards the bedchamber. As soon as she saw Newt's pale face peeking out from the coverlet, she started to weep uncontrollably, mostly from relief.

"There, there Miss. Fairfax," murmured Prescott consolingly. "He only looks worse for wear because of exhaustion. He'll heal up and be good as new before you know it."

Mortified that she had let her guard down in front of Johnathan Prescott of all people, Birdie replied, "I'm sorry for carryin' on so, Mr. Prescott. Newt is a dear friend and I'd been worryin' somethin' awful all afternoon."

Prescott softly chuckled and shook his head. "Miss Fairfax, you can stop all this 'dear friend' nonsense. I might sit up here in my so-called ivory tower all day, but I know pretty much all that goes on under my roof. I'm well aware how Phillips here feels about you and I now see that his affection is reciprocated. Don't worry about the 'inappropriate behavior' rule. That's just meant to discourage openly wanton recklessness that might rankle our guests or, worst, disrupt operations here at the hotel. That obviously isn't the case here."

Birdie visibly relaxed and stopped wringing her hands. "Thank you, sir. You've always been so kind to me."

Prescott shrugged and gruffly replied, "It's not a matter of kindness. I just call them as I see them."

Birdie stepped over to the bedside to get her first close look at Newt. His head was wrapped up to cover the sutures on his forehead just below his hairline. She also noticed that a larger bandage was wrapped around his chest. She slipped her hand into one of his and grabbed onto it for dear life.

Feeling like an intruder witnessing such an intimate scenario, Prescott awkwardly cleared his throat and announced, "Well, now that everyone is safely inside, I think I will return to my suite and what's left of a cold quail supper."

Birdie quickly stood and said, "Thank you, Mr. Prescott, for all you've done for Newt...and Felipe. No matter what you might say, I think you're the kindest man I ever met."

"Then do me the favor of never letting that get out to the others," said the tired hotelier with a twinkle in his eye. "I have a reputation to protect." Both he and Birdie chuckled as she walked him over to the front door.

"One last thing, Miss Fairfax. The doctor asked that someone watch over Phillips tonight. Just in case of fever or some such thing. I'm pretty certain I know how you will respond, but I'll ask anyway. Would you care to stay with him here tonight?"

"Of course I will, sir," replied Birdie. "I would have done so regardless. I mean...with your permission of course."

Prescott just smiled and continued, "I reckoned as much. Now if something happens overnight and he needs medical attention, Simms will be next door in 405. Send him for Dr. Winthrop. He knows which room the doc's in. For now, I'll give you both some privacy and will bid you a good night."

"Good night, sir," replied Birdie. After Prescott had gone, she quickly returned to the bedchamber and pulled a chair up to Newt's bedside. She picked up his hand and lovingly stroked his cheek as she silently thanked God for bringing him back to her.

“Ain’t that just typical!” cried Tangie as she angrily slammed Ronnie’s dinner plate on the table in front of him.

The rest of the staff had just finished their meals and were leaving when Ronnie came downstairs after being excused by Prescott. Rita, Netta and Tangie were also sitting down to eat. Ronnie had just told the women about rescue of the two men, Newt’s condition and how Birdie would be spending the rest of the evening upstairs.

“What’s got you madder than a wet hen?” asked Rita.

“I’ll tell ya what’s got me angry and what should have everyone else around here angry too,” Tangie shouted. “It’s the fact that there’s one set of rules for Birdie and another set for the rest of us.”

“What are you talkin’ about? No one’s givin’ Birdie any special treatment,” Rita replied testily.

“You do it yourself all the time. She constantly gets out of doin’ work down here in the mornin’s ‘cause you lettin’ her chase Newt Phillips around. ‘Go to him, Birdie. He needs you.’

Didn't Miss Sutton herself asked us to report any goin's on between the menfolk and womenfolk around here?" said Tangie as she glared at Ronnie.

Ronnie shot her a dark glance and muttered, "Yeah, Ella and I both remember that well, and you're lucky she didn't kick yo' ass like she was wantin' too."

"But Miss Sutton read you both the riot act, didn't she?" asked Tangie. "Do ya think she'll say one word to Birdie about spendin' a night in a room with Newt? Of course not!"

Rita stood and held up her hands as she tried to curtail Tangie's tirade. "All right, I'm puttin' an end to this nonsense. First of all, Birdie's upstairs takin' care of Newt, who's too hurt to do anythin' with her right now even if he wanted to. And if it looks like I've been encouragin' her affections for Newt, I ain't ashamed to say that I am. They're both nice young folks and deserve a shot at love. And I'll remind you that Birdie does plenty of work around here – both downstairs and upstairs. She's done everythin' that's ever been asked of her without any sass or attitude, unlike yourself. Yes, she's moved up quickly but that's because she's worked hard and she has talent. Not because anyone is giving her special treatment."

"Bullshit!" hissed Tangie. "Ya'll go on kissin' that yella quadroon's ass. Just don't expect me to!" She slammed the teapot on the table as she stormed out of the dining room and headed back to the scullery, where she could be heard slamming the dirty pots and pans into the sink.

Netta shook her head as she picked up the teapot, poured it into three cups and handed them around. "I'll never understand that gal if I live to be a hundred. She's always so angry."

"Especially when it comes to Birdie," remarked Rita.

"It's jealousy, ladies," commented Ronnie as he took a bite out of a ham sandwich, "Plain, simple jealousy. She's got a rough life and resents anyone who she thinks got it better off than her."

"Well, as far as I'm concerned, that young couple upstairs doesn't have it easy and you both know it. A white man with a mixed gal ain't gonna go down well in these parts. What kinda life are they gonna have down here?" She paused thoughtfully before adding, "I guess that's why I like to help them when I can, and right now, that's just what I'm gonna do." She got up from the table and purposefully returned to the kitchen.

Netta and Ronnie gave each other a puzzled look as they continued finishing their meal.

Birdie laid her hand across Newt's cheek to check his temperature. It was slightly warm, so she brought a small basin of water and wash cloth from the lavatory next door. Wetting the cloth, she lightly dabbed his face. As she placed it back in the basin, she caught a glance of the clock on the nightstand. Was it really only 8:15? She thought it was much later. The day had been a very long and tiring one.

There was a small tap at the front entry. Thinking it might be the doctor or Mr. Prescott, Birdie hurried into the front room and opened the door. She was glad to see Rita standing in the darkened hallway holding a small lamp in one hand and a plate in the other. A white dressing gown was slung over her arm.

"Hi Birdie," she whispered. "How's your patient?"

"He's still asleep," Birdie replied. "Come on in, Rita."

Rita entered as Birdie quietly shut the door. "I figured you might be hungry, so I brought you a sandwich. There's one for Newt, too. And here's a dressin' gown so you can get comfortable."

Birdie gratefully took both the plate and the dressing gown from the cook. "Thank you, Rita. I don't know what I'd do without ya."

"You'd be just fine and you know it."

"Come on back, Rita," said Birdie as she guided her to the bedchamber.

"My, these suites sure are grand, ain't they?" said Rita as she looked around the bedroom in wonder. "I bet Newt'll be surprised when he wakes up and finds himself in here! I know I'd think I'd died and gone to heaven." Looking closely at Newt, she said, "Oh, look at him. He seems so peaceful, doesn't he? If it wasn't for the bandages, you'd think he was just restin'."

"Yeah, I thought the same," said Birdie as she yawned.

Rita looked over at the younger woman and noticed the dark circles forming under her eyes. "Birdie, I want you to do something for me while I'm here."

"Sure, what's that?" asked Birdie.

"First I want you to eat that sandwich because I know for a fact that you've been in a state of panic all day and you must be starvin' by now. Then, I want you to go wash your face, let your hair down and change into this dressing gown. You need to relax and take care of yourself so that you have the strength to look after Newt. Go ahead. I'll sit here with him in the meantime."

Birdie was hesitant to leave Newt's side but knew that Rita was right. She reluctantly agreed and went into the front parlor where she sat on the settee and picked up the plate. As she took a deep breath and exhaled, she felt more relaxed than she had all day. Because she was finally at ease, her hunger quickly returned.

As she devoured the sandwich, Birdie took in the surroundings. The wallpaper was a deep burgundy color with a gold fleur de lis overlay. Over this hung assorted paintings featuring lakes, meadows and bowls of fruit. The Persian carpet under Birdie's feet were dotted with exotic looking flora of golds, ruby reds and deep greens. The sofa she was sitting on as well as the chairs were upholstered in emerald green plush velvet.

Birdie still couldn't believe that she'd be spending the night in one of these rooms which she used to clean as a chambermaid only a couple of years ago. The memory of Johnny Prescott Jr. suddenly came to mind and she shuddered.

She rose and went back to the bedchamber where Rita was dabbing Newt with the cloth.

"Does he feel feverish?" asked Birdie.

"No, just makin' sure he stays cooled off. He's starting to move a little, though. I have a feelin' he might be wakin' up soon," Rita said softly.

"Oh, I hope so," said Birdie. Taking the dressing gown with her, she went to the adjoining changing room and changed out of her uniform and corset. She looked at her face in the mirror. No wonder Rita told her to wash up. I look like I'm ninety, Birdie said to herself.

She unwrapped the rose soap that was by the basin and washed her face and hands. The floral scent helped perk her up. She removed the pins from the tight bun in the back of her head which released the braid that now hung like a rope down her back. As she again peered at the mirror, her reflection regained its youthful appearance.

When she exited the bathroom, Rita looked up and nodded appreciatively. "That's much better. You look a lot more relaxed now."

"I feel a lot better," said Birdie as she hung her uniform up in the armoire. "Thank you so much, Rita. I really needed this."

"Well, I'll leave you to your nursing duties. There is a nice, comfortable bed downstairs with my name on it! Don't worry about comin' down to the kitchen for work tomorrow mornin'. As far as I'm concerned, Mr. Prescott has you assigned up here to take care of Newt until he says otherwise."

Birdie walked over to Rita and give her a big hug. "You're just as kind of Mr. Prescott is. Thanks again, Rita. And good night."

"Good night, child. I'll see myself out." Rita softly closed the bedchamber door behind her.

Birdie softly padded over to the bed and glanced at Newt, who stirred a little but continued his deep slumber. She kissed him lightly on the top of his head and walked over to the bureau, where she slowly undid her braid and released her hair which fell down to the center of her back. It was going to be a long night, so she figured she might as well be as comfortable as possible. Reckoning that she'll need to put the two chairs in the bedroom together to create a makeshift bed, Birdie went to the armoire to fetch the spare blanket she'd seen in there earlier. As she opened the door, she heard a feeble groan. Closing the door, Birdie looked over at Newt was beginning to stir.

"Newt," she whispered as she hurried over to the bedside and clasped his hand. "Newt, can you hear me?"

"Birdie?" Newt murmured hoarsely as his eyes opened and he was able to focus on her. His powder blue eyes looked confused as they took in her loose hair and the dressing gown. She looked absolutely angelic. Was he dreaming?

"Yes, Newt," Birdie was saying, "I'm here. I'm right here and not going anywhere. How are you feelin'?"

Newt winced in pain and croaked, "My head and my chest feel like they got knives stabbin' 'em. What happened?" The last thing he remembered was pruning trees in the arbor. Why was he hurting so badly and where was he?

"You and Felipe got caught outside in that bad storm. It's still goin' on but it's quieted down some. Felipe said a cyclone came through and started blowin' down some of the trees out there. One of them fell on ya and cut your head and poked a hole in your chest. Your leg got pierced too. Felipe dragged you out from under the tree and tried to get you both back to the hotel, but he couldn't see anythin'. That's when Mr. Prescott and Ronnie went up in the tower and spotted ya'll. Ronnie ran out into the storm and brought ya back inside. They saved your life, Newt."

As he started to recall the horrific events of the afternoon, Newt slowly nodded. "Oh yeah, it's startin' to come back to me now. Where are we, Birdie?"

"Mr. Prescott put you up in this suite until you're better. He said I could stay here and take care of you. A doctor that's stayin' here is the one who stitched you up. He's comin' back tomorrow."

Newt tried to make sense of it all as he looked around the luxurious suite. He'd never slept in a real bed before, and best of all, Birdie was here. He clutched her hand and brought it to his lips, gently kissing it. "I'm just happy yer with me."

"Can I get ya anything?" asked Birdie anxiously. "Would ya like some water? Or are ya hungry? Rita brought up a sandwich earlier."

"I'll just take the water fer now," said Newt as he tried to sit up. A strange looked crossed his face as he lifted up the sheets and peered underneath. "Hey. I'm naked as a jay bird. What happened to my clothes?" Looking saucily at Birdie, he teased, "Was it you who undressed me? Please say yes!"

Birdie, who was pouring water into a glass, almost spilled it when she heard the question.

"Newt Phillips! What a thing to say!" she exclaimed. "By the time I arrived, you were already in bed. The doctor, Mr. Prescott and Ronnie had all been up here before me. I'm guessin' it was Ronnie who put ya to bed."

"Damn," said Newt. "Just my luck I suppose. I almost lose my life. I'm stripped naked by a man. And now I'm layin' here in my birthday suit with the woman I love but I'm hurtin' too much to do anythin' with her."

Birdie giggled as she handed him the glass of water and watched him gulp it down. If he was already making jokes, he was going to be okay.

As she took the empty glass, Birdie looked at him lovingly. "You have no idea how worried I've been about ya today. There were times when I wasn't sure I'd see ya again."

Newt clasped her hand. "You'll never get rid o' me that easily." Turning to the window and listening to the rain pounding against it, he asked, "How long have I been up here?"

"I'd say about two and a half hours. Luckily Ronnie spotted ya'll before it got dark," said Birdie.

"Yeah, I owe him and Felipe a debt I'll never be able to repay," remarked Newt thoughtfully. As another gust of wind rattled the pane, a shadow crept across his face. "Just listen to that. Hope my ma and the girls are okay. The bridge over the creek's gotta be flooded over by now. That's the only way out to my place."

Birdie patted his hand and asked, "Have ya got any neighbors nearby who can check on them?"

"The nearest ones would be the Turners but they're still about a couple miles away," replied Newt.

"I can understand you bein' worried about your ma. I've been thinkin' about mine, too," said Birdie. "Ya know, I wouldn't be surprised if Sugar's burrowed into my bed by now!"

"So, I'm not the only one gettin' to sleep in a grand bed tonight, eh?" joked Newt as he looked around the room. "Say, what kinda folks stay in a room like this anyway?

"Well, they're usually close friends of the Prescotts. Lawyers, entertainers, important businessmen, and even some politicians might've stayed in here and slept in that very bed," replied Birdie.

Newt's eyes widened as he patted the quilt. "How 'bout that? Wait'll I tell ma that I got to sleep in such a fancy room and in the same bed as rich folks like that! Me, a lowly gardener. I'll never forget this as long as I live. And how lucky am I to get you as my personal nursemaid. Do I have Mr. Prescott to thank for that?"

Birdie grinned, "I reckon so."

Newt reached out and gently stroked Birdie's hair, wrapping a curly tendril around his index finger. "I love yer hair when it's loose like this." Seeing her blush in response, he continued, "So where were ya plannin' on sleeping tonight?"

"I was just goin' to push those chairs together over there," answered Birdie. "In fact, when you came to, I was fetching the spare blanket from the armoire."

"Please, I need ya here next to me," said Newt as he slightly lifted the coverlet and patted the mattress beside him.

Birdie's eyes widened as she stammered, "But you're.... um.... you're not wearin'...."

"I know," said Newt. "But my head's throbbin' and I got burning pains in my leg and my chest. I couldn't do anythin' to ya no matter how much I want to. I just want to hold ya, like we did that day on the beach, remember? "

Birdie nodded. Her desire to be close to Newt far outweighed her shyness about lying next to a naked man. She nervously slipped out of the dressing gown and, clothed only in her chemise and bloomers, she reddened as Newt hungrily eyed her from head to toe. Birdie quickly turned out the lamp and cautiously climbed into the bed.

At first, she kept her arms at her sides for fear of accidentally touching the wounds and causing him pain, but Newt managed to roll onto his side towards her and wrapped his arms around her, drawing her up against him.

Newt quietly grunted and whispered, “Mmm, you feel so good. I wish I wasn’t in so much damned pain.”

As he cupped her face with his hand and kissed her gently on the lips, Birdie couldn’t help but wonder what it would be like to be his wife and able to sleep together every night. But for now, she nuzzled up against him and slowly stroked his back until he eventually fell asleep. Shortly afterward, the steady sound of the raindrops drumming on the terra cotta tiles above lulled Birdie into a peaceful slumber.

All that remained of the storm the following morning was a light misty drizzle and an overcast sky. The city’s streets were littered with palm fronds, weather vanes, crates, broken signs, wooden roof tiles, and assorted debris. Towering oaks which once stood tall and proud were now strewn across lawns like wounded soldiers.

Ella carefully picked up her skirt as she trudged through the muddy, puddle ridden streets between her house and Ronnie's. Luckily, all the neighboring homes came through the storm unscathed. Hortensia, who had stayed the night at the Patterson's house, went back home earlier that morning and was relieved to see that she only lost a tree. Ella saw Arthur Dickson leaving the Fairfax's porch earlier that morning and assumed that Birdie must have sent him over to check on her mother. That was when Ella decided to take it upon herself to visit Ronnie's family for him as he was obviously busy over at the Montclair.

As she passed the house on the corner of Citrus Avenue and Central, she saw Mr. Jordan and his two older boys picking up the oak that had fallen across their front doorway, blocking the entrance to their house. A couple of streets away, a group of men were trying to lift an overturned delivery wagon. Everywhere else, Ella saw women and children picking up litter or looking for belongings which had blown off their porches.

When Ella arrived at the Simms' house, she was shocked at the devastation. The front porch had completely collapsed, and half of the roof was gone. Ella ran to the back door and knocked at it furiously.

"Mr. and Mrs. Simms! Are you there?" she shouted. She knocked again until she heard footsteps approaching.

"Who is it?" asked the frightened voice of Betty Simms.

"It's me, Ella Patterson. Are you all right, Mrs. Simms?"

The door creaked open. "Oh, it's you Ella. Please come in," Betty remarked with another-worldly look in her bloodshot eyes. "I'm afraid Ronnie isn't here. Can I get you a lemonade?" Her normally well-coiffed hair was mussed, and the bodice of her dress was not buttoned correctly.

This woman's not in her right mind, Ella observed silently. Aloud, she said, "Since Ronnie's stuck over at the Montclair and can't get to ya yet, I thought I'd come over and see if ya needed anythin'. Where's Mr. Simms?"

"He went with Lionel and Dexter to town for supplies and a tarpaulin for the roof to keep the rain out. I stayed behind in case Beulah comes home," said Mrs. Simms.

Beaulah? Who was Beaulah? Ella wracked her brain. Ronnie's sisters were both married and had left home. Suddenly she remembered that Beulah was the family's poodle she'd heard so much about.

"When was the last time you saw Beaulah?" asked Ella.

Mrs. Simms lower lip trembled as she started to weep. "I had let her out back yesterday after breakfast. When the rain started, I called for her but she never came. I reckoned that she must have gotten into one of the neighbor's yards but before I could head out and properly look for her, the storm grew worse and the winds started blowing. I haven't seen my Beaulah since."

The older woman collapsed into sobs as Ella lightly patted her back. The shock of the state of her house coupled with the disappearance of her beloved pooch had overwhelmed her. Ella put an arm around Betty's shoulders and gently guided her to a chair at the kitchen table. "You sit right down, Mrs. Simms, and let me take care of ya." Betty dutifully sat and looked straight ahead as if in a trance while Ella rifled through the cupboards. Finding a kettle and a tea tin, she set about fixing a soothing warm beverage for Betty while she made amiable chit chat and helped the older woman re-button her bodice.

Once the pot had boiled and she poured the hot water into a pretty daisy patterned china cup, Ella dunked the tea infuser and watched as the water turned a deep mahogany color. After adding a little sugar from the canister, she set the cup in front of Betty.

"Now you just relax and drink this and try not to worry," said Ella soothingly. "Your menfolk will have this place lookin' like new in no time, and I'm gonna go out and search for Beaulah. She couldn't have gotten too far."

"Thank you, Ella," said Betty as she took a sip from her cup. "That's awfully nice of you."

"That's what neighbors are for," said Ella. "Besides, Ronnie means the world to me. So, if ya'll got problems, then they're my problems, too!"

Overcome by Ella's kindness, Betty once again started to sob as Ella embraced her and soothingly murmured words of encouragement. They were interrupted a few minutes later by Ronnie's shouts from the outside as he bounded up the back steps. "Mama! Daddy!" He tore open the door and found his mother crying in Ella's arms. He ran over to the women and hugged them both.

"Arthur just told me about the house. He was in the neighborhood earlier today checkin' on his own place. He saw Daddy and the boys up on the roof pushing that elm down off it. If I'd only known, I'd have been here sooner! I'm so sorry, mama."

"It ain't yo' fault, Ronnie," said Ella. "That tree would've fallen if you'd been here or not. No use frettin' 'bout it now."

Ronnie kissed Ella on the forehead and whispered, "Thanks for comin', Ella. I love you!"

Ella smiled and said, "I know. I love you, too." Standing up and taking charge of the situation, she added, "Your daddy and brothers are in town gettin' some things for the house. Take care of yo' mama here and make sure she finishes that tea. Then find a place where she can take a nap. I'll go over to the Montclair and let 'em know about yo' house. They'll just have to make do without ya for the rest of today. After that, I'm gonna go search for Beaulah. Tell me what she looks like."

"Beaulah! Come here girl!" After searching for the lost little dog all afternoon, Ella's voice was hoarse. She traipsed through all of Lincolnville and beyond. She crawled through underbrush, scoured neighbors' yards, looked behind woodbins and outhouses and even checked the roads for carcasses but to no avail.

As she sighed deeply, Ella was convinced that the search was futile and that Mrs. Simms was going to have to eventually accept the fact that Beaulah was gone. She wondered if there were any more stray kittens under the groundskeepers' shed at the Montclair. Maybe Betty would be open to raising a cat.

As she turned back onto Central, she was pleasantly surprised to see Birdie walking home. Ella waved and called out, "Hey Birdie! Wait up!" Birdie waved back and stopped to allow Ella to catch up to her.

"Hey Ella, I haven't seen ya in a few days. Did ya'll make it through the storm all right?"

"Oh yeah, nothin' of ours got blown away or knocked down. Yo' ma stayed with us last night."

Birdie nodded. "Yes, I'm glad she was with ya'll. What about the rest of the neighbors?"

"Most of our street was lucky. But Ronnie's house....oh Birdie...you should see it!" Ella went on to describe her visit with Ruth earlier that day.

"Poor Ronnie. No wonder I didn't see him this afternoon," said Birdie. "I just reckoned that he was busy downstairs. The power has been off at the Montclair and the guests have kept everyone busy."

Birdie then proceeded to tell Ella about the goings on at the hotel, the heroic actions of Felipe and Ronnie, and how she stayed with Newt throughout the night.

Ella said coyly, "So let me get this straight, Mr. Prescott - the owner of the Montclair - allowed you and Newt to sleep in the same room? I thought they were all fired up 'bout not wantin' any relations between the menfolk and womenfolk. So...what did ya'll get up to?" She smiled devilishly at Birdie as both women turned onto Citrus Avenue.

"No, Ella, it wasn't like that at all," Birdie protested. "Mr. Prescott only let me stay up there because Newt was unconscious and needed lookin' after. Other than a couple of kisses, we didn't do anythin'. He COULDN'T do anythin'."

"Well, I am sorry to hear that," retorted Ella.

"Ella! You talk as scandalous as Newt does sometimes!" cried Birdie reprovingly.

They amiably chattered on and headed to Birdie's house. As they approached the front gate, they could hear the insistent yapping of a small dog.

"Is that the Nelson's dog?" asked Birdie. "He usually howls, not barks."

"It sounds like it's coming from 'round back," remarked Ella.

Birdie frowned as she headed towards the rear of the house with Ella close behind her. The pine tree that used to stand at the south side of the property had blown across the back yard, knocking down the clothes line in the process. The two young women carefully stepped over the branches as they crossed the yard. There was no dog in sight yet they could still hear it yapping nearby.

Birdie rounded the northeastern corner where her bedroom window was and there they found a small poodle with a dirty, matted coat jumping up and down under Birdie's window. Inside the glass pane, Sugar was hissing at the animated canine.

"Aw, the little fella is just tryin' to get at Sugar," said Birdie.

Ella, however, was clapping her hands and, like the dog, jumping up and down. As Birdie stared in bewilderment, Ella said, "That ain't no fella. Come here, Beulah! Come here, girl."

Hearing her name, the poodle stopped barking and obediently trotted over to Ella.

"Whose dog is that?" asked Birdie.

"She belongs to a woman whose day is about to get a lot better," replied Ella as she stroked Beulah behind the ears.

By the end of the week, Newt had been sent home to recuperate, the electricity had been restored to the Montclair, and much of the debris and damaged trees had been removed. Mr. Patterson and a couple of neighbors lifted the tree that fell across Hortensia's back yard and chopped it up into small logs for firewood.

When Birdie came home from work on Saturday evening, she could smell the intoxicating aroma of a freshly baked cake as soon as she approached the front porch. Once inside, she was surprised to see her mother busily cutting up and seasoning a chicken.

"What's all this about, ma?" asked Birdie. "Is that your famous chocolate cake I smell?"

"Yes, it is," replied Hortensia. "As it so happens, we are having a friend of yours around to dinner tomorrow afternoon."

Birdie, who had been on her way to her room to change out of her uniform, stopped short and turned back towards her mother. Her brow furrowed as she asked, "A friend of mine? Do you mean Ella?"

"No, not Ella," answered Hortensia mysteriously. "It's a young man."

"Who is it, Ma?" asked Birdie suspiciously.

"Well, I was in town earlier today and I ran into that nice Arthur Dickson. I told him that I was so thankful for his coming to check on me after the storm and insisted that he come to dinner tomorrow after church," said Hortensia with a self-satisfied grin.

"Why, Ma?" asked Birdie. "Isn't that a bit too much? After all, it was I who sent him over to check on you."

"Birdie!" admonished Hortensia. "I thought I raised you with manners. Whether or not you'd sent him, he still had to go out of his way to get here. The least we could do is show him that we are grateful."

"I know that, Ma!" cried Birdie. "But isn't dinner a bit much? Wouldn't a simple pie have been enough?"

"Don't be silly, Birdie," scolded Hortensia. "I didn't think you'd mind Arthur joining us for dinner. After all, you are friends, aren't you?"

"Yes, of course we're friends and I don't mind him comin' to dinner. This is just a surprise, is all."

"Go change and when you come back, you can help me by using some of those kitchen skills you learned at that fancy hotel of yours," Hortensia said teasingly.

Birdie sighed as she resolutely shook her head. “All right, Ma. I'll be right back.”

Hortensia stared at her daughter as she headed down the short hallway to her bedroom. She planned to feign her arthritis flaring up so that Birdie would prepare most of the meal. This way her daughter's domestic skills would be showcased in front of this very eligible suitor.

"Would you care for some more greens, Arthur?" asked Hortensia as she once more offered him the bowl of collards.

"No thank you, ma'am," answered Arthur as he finished swallowing a mouthful of chicken. "I've had two helpin's already. I'm liable to bust if I have any more. You’re a mighty fine cook, ma'am."

Hortensia was quick to respond, "Oh, but it was Birdie who prepared most of this meal. All the compliments should go to her."

Birdie looked up from her plate and stared over at her mother. Just what was she up to? I hope she's not match making again, she thought. Aloud, she replied, "Well, we both did our parts."

Arthur grinned at Birdie as he continued to address Hortensia. "I reckon Birdie's a very good cook in her own right just goin' by all them fancy dishes she helps Rita with at the Montclair. And all them dresses she's been makin' for the store window have been gettin' lotsa attention. When I'm down by the front desk, I hear the ladies talk all the time about the beautiful gown they saw and how they want one like it."

Hortensia swelled with pride hearing about the impression her daughter's talents were making on the upper class. As Arthur finished his plate, she said, "I hope you saved room for dessert. I made you one my special chocolate cakes. Why don't you and Birdie go sit in the front parlor and I'll bring it through with some tea. Just leave those plates, Birdie. I'll take care of them."

Birdie again shot a withering glance at Hortensia as she stood up and said, "Well, if you insist, ma. Come on, Arthur."

As Hortensia gathered up the dinner plates and took them into the kitchen, Birdie and Arthur retreated to the front parlor where Birdie sat in the wing chair while Arthur perched on the settee. Birdie smiled at him and shook her head.

"I apologize for my mother's behavior," she said. "I've never seen her take on so with one of my friends before."

Arthur grinned knowingly and replied, "It looks to me like she's got her heart set on us courtin'."

Birdie nodded sympathetically. "I'm afraid so. I hope this isn't causing you any embarrassment."

"Don't worry, Birdie," replied Arthur. "I know that you're spoken for and I respect that. Hasn't your ma met Newt yet?"

Birdie whispered, "No. She's only seen him from far away and took a quick dislike to him. My ma doesn't want me gettin' romantically involved with any white men. She and my pa, who was white, went through a whole lot of sufferin' and she doesn't want the same for me, I reckon."

"I can understand that," Arthur responded. After a few pensive moments, he continued. "Ya know, Birdie, I like Newt and I really hope the two of you can get together one day and make a go of it. But please know that if things were different, I'd be more than happy to court ya. You're pretty, a top cook and ya got a heart of gold."

Birdie reached over and grabbed his hand in platonic affection. "Thank you, Arthur. You're a wonderful man and I can understand why my ma is so taken with the thought of you as a potential son-in-law."

Hortensia entered the room carrying the desserts just as Birdie and Arthur had clasped hands and, misunderstanding the gesture, she gleefully said, "Oh my! Sorry to disturb you young folks. I'll just leave you with the cake while I go and finish making the coffee."

As Hortensia quickly scurried from the room, Birdie and Arthur looked at each other and burst into laughter.

Chapter 29

Iris Sutton was somber as she faced the crowd. Fredrick Hayes, equally glum, stood next to her.

The first week of September heralded the beginning of the new tourist season and the return of the entire Montclair staff. The ballroom that morning was a cacophony of shouts, greetings and laughter as everyone gathered for a mandatory meeting. Birdie, particularly pleased to see Newt back, flashed him a smile from across the room.

Clearing her throat, Iris began, "Good morning. It's nice to have you all back after the summer break. I am pleased to announce that our reservations for the upcoming winter season have increased from last year and we will be booked to capacity. Therefore, it is of the utmost importance that each and every one of you do your very best to help make the Montclair the perfect home away from home for our clientele."

There were a few nods of understanding from the audience as Iris continued. "Unfortunately, that is not the sole reason for this brief meeting this morning." She stared back at Hayes before adding, "Last night we had a theft here at the hotel. Someone broke into the dining room's storage closet and made off with several expensive pieces of crystal and silver."

There were assorted gasps and exclamations from around the room, followed by a low buzz of whispers. Iris raised her hand in a signal for silence.

"Mr. Hayes, have you determined what exactly was taken?"

Frank stepped forward and replied, "So far, we're missing several crystal goblets, a rare Austrian crystal wine decanter, silver salt and pepper shakers, and a couple of condiment dishes."

"Thank you, Mr. Hayes," said Iris. Addressing the room at large, she added, "The matter is currently under investigation, so I cannot discuss any details. However, we urge all of you to stay vigilant. If you see anything or anyone suspicious, please report it to your superiors."

As they later left the ballroom, Birdie asked Newt and Isaiah, "Who on earth would be bold enough to steal all that glass and silver from the dinin' room? It's not like jewelry or money that's small enough to stash away. Some of those pieces are pretty large and would make an awful ruckus."

Newt shook his head and asked, "Do ya reckon it's one of the guests?"

Birdie shrugged. "Maybe. Your guess is as good as mine."

"Times like this make me glad I work outdoors," exclaimed Isaiah.

"Very nice," crooned Hiram Meriwether as he eyeballed the crystal pieces which Tangie carefully produced from an old tapestry bag. Each piece was wrapped in a handkerchief.

Hiram seemed particularly taken with the decanter, knowing it was worth a lot more than what he was going to offer. Clearing his throat, he casually remarked, "A very good haul. I'll give you ten dollars for the lot."

Tangie raised her eyebrows as she remembered Mr. Hayes describing the decanter as "rare" in yesterday's meeting. "Ten dollars? You gotta be jokin'. I know fo' a fact that the decanter's worth mo' than that by itself."

Damn! This gal knows what she's got, thought Meriwether.

Feverishly thinking about how high he can go without shrinking his own profit margin, he countered, "All right. Fifteen dollars."

Tangie knew she had the upper hand and firmly countered with, "Twenty-five dollars or I'll find somewhere else to take my business. I know for a fact that you ain't the only wheeler dealer in town!"

Hiram leaned back in his seat and gave Tangie a cold, hard stare. He didn't care for most of the pieces, but he absolutely had to have that decanter as he already had a buyer in mind. He decided to take the risk.

"Twenty dollars. That's my final offer. Take it or leave it," he said dismissively with a wave of his hand.

Tangie as thoughtful for a moment before she replied, "You got a deal."

Hortensia held up a bolt of dark blue calico decorated with sprigs of white flowers. She was sorely in need of a new everyday work dress and thought the fabric would be more than suitable.

“What about this, Birdie?”

Birdie, who was admiring a gold colored satin, looked up and nodded. “Yes, that’ll look good on ya, ma.”

As usual when Hartsfield’s received a new shipment of fabric and notions, Birdie and Hortensia were among the first customers to come in and get first pick of the new goods.

The elder Hartsfield, Eddie’s father Adam, was working the counter. No white customers were in the shop, so the Fairfax women had his complete attention. As good natured and courteous as his son, Mr. Hartsfield made polite conversation with the women as he measured out the length of calico for Hortensia and the satin for Birdie.

“Is Eddie out fishin’ today?” asked Birdie.

“You bet he is. He and Newt Phillips went out shrimping early this morning,” replied Hartsfield.

The mention of Newt made Birdie smile inwardly while Hortensia’s jaw tightened.

“Anything else today, ladies?” asked the merchant.

“Yes, I have a list here of a few things we need,” said Hortensia as she handed it over.

While Hartsfield set about gathering the various items for Hortensia, the bell on the front door jingled. As the women turned, they smiled as they recognized Arthur.

“Good afternoon, Mrs. Fairfax. Birdie.” Arthur grinned and politely nodded to them both.

“Arthur! So good to see you. How are you and your family keeping?” asked Hortensia.

“Just fine, thanks,” said Arthur. “My ma just sent me down to get her a can of lard.”

“Well, we’re just finishing up here. I hope you’ll be able to walk at least part of the way home with us,” said Hortensia. Birdie looked over at her mother incredulously. She almost sounded like she was flirting!

“Why of course I will. I’d like nothin’ more,” replied Arthur.

Newt and Eddie headed towards the town’s main street carrying a large bucket of shrimp between them. The evening’s haul had been a very successful one and they were each looking forward to cooking them up for dinner.

As they approached the mercantile, Newt was taken aback to see Birdie, her mother and Arthur Dickson exiting the store. Birdie’s mother was chattering away happily to Arthur who carried her basket while Birdie, smiling politely, walked on his other side. Together they looked like a very contented family unit.

A wave of sadness overtook Newt. He knew he would never be able to be part of such a scenario. Although Birdie had never spoken on the subject, he was fairly sure that her ma would disapprove of him. And his own mother would be even more dead set against his relationship with Birdie.

At that moment, as he and Eddie passed Doheny’s, the front door flew open and a drunken Lonnie Stokes stumbled into the street in front of them.

Newt and Eddie stopped short to avoid colliding with Stokes. The water in the shrimp bucket they carried sloshed against its sides. Newt looked disgustedly down at Stokes who was feebly trying to stand. The last time they had been face to face was during their fist fight earlier in the year. Since then, they had only laid eyes on each other a few times in passing.

Lonnie Stokes shot a hateful glare up at Newt as he rose on two unsteady feet and slurred, "What the hell you gawpin' at, Phillips?"

"Nuthin' but a two-bit drunk," sneered Newt.

Stokes chuckled. "Well, ain't that a switch comin' from the son of a man who was face down on this here same street almost every night when he was alive."

Before Newt was able to respond to the slight towards his father, Eddie said, "Easy now, Newt. Don't let 'im rile ya."

As Stokes bent down to pick up his hat which was still lying in the middle of the sandy road, he caught sight of Birdie, Hortensia and Arthur who were now a good distance away.

Stokes laughed again and remarked, "Well, well! Look what we got here. Seems like your quadroon found herself a proper nigger to squire her about town."

In mock sympathy, Stokes continued, "That's too bad for ya, boy. But ya see, that nigra at least got the common sense to stick with her own kind."

By this point, Newt had enough. He dropped his end of the shrimp bucket, ran up to Stokes and punched him square in the jaw, knocking the drunken man unconscious and lying flat on his back in the middle of St. George Street.

Eddie walked up and joined Newt who was breathing hard with anger as he looked down at Stokes. "Leave him be, Newt. He'll wake up later on and won't remember any of this." Clapping his friend on the shoulder, Eddie went back to retrieve the shrimp bucket.

Stokes might forget this, but I sure as hell won't, Newt thought as he looked once again at the tiny figures of Birdie, Hortensia and Arthur as they disappeared around the corner.

"A New Year's Eve ball for the entire staff?" asked Lottie incredulously. "Have you taken leave of your senses again, Johnathan?"

Prescott leaned back in his favorite wing chair and took a deep sip of his after-dinner brandy. The evening's roast beef meal, although a delectable treat for his taste buds, now sat in his stomach like lead. The impending argument with his wife will no doubt result in another bout of dyspepsia.

"And why, pray tell, is it such a bad idea? Our staff has worked very hard this past year, especially those who stayed on during the summer. Hell, one of our men almost lost his life during that storm. The least we can do to show our appreciation for all their hard labor is to throw them a party so they can relax and ring in the new century."

Lottie closed her eyes and sighed deeply before responding. "I don't begrudge our staff a New Year's Eve party. Of course, they all deserve a bit of fun, but who is going to be serving our guests in the main ballroom that night. After all, we will be hosting our own gala, or have you forgotten?"

Prescott shrugged as he fished a cigar from the breast pocket of his jacket. "We"ll bring in some temporary help for the evening. There are plenty folks here in town who would be willing to earn some extra money."

Lottie's eyes widened as she dropped the handkerchief she was embroidering. "Do you mean to tell me that you are actually considering having inexperienced locals serving our guests during the biggest celebration of the year? You really have lost your mind!"

Prescott was silent for a moment as he lit his cigar, took a deep, thoughtful puff and raised his face upwards as he exhaled. "Well, if giving our staff a night off while providing jobs, albeit temporary ones, to the townspeople is considered a mark of insanity, go ahead and have me committed!"

"I still ain't sure about this color, Birdie," said Ella who frowned with uncertainty as she held up the basque of the claret colored dress she was trimming with brass buttons.

"I declare, Ella. I told you again and again that it really suits your complexion. Trust me on this," urged Birdie. With a devilish grin, she added, "Ronnie won't be able to take his eyes off ya!"

The two women sat on Ella's front porch as they put the final touches on their evening dresses. The hunger-inducing aroma of the Pattersons' Sunday dinner wafted through the open windows. The air was getting chillier as the sunset approached, coloring the sky a vivid peach hue. The street, which had earlier teemed with boisterous children, was now empty and still, except for the occasional bark of a dog or sound of a distant wagon.

Ella, mollified by her friend's reassurance, chuckled and added, "If he knows what's good for him, he won't be eyeballin' anyone else but me!"

Birdie laughed softly as she completed the final stitch on the low neckline of her gold satin gown. As she held it up to assess her work, Ella glanced over at the dress and remarked, "Once Newt sees you in that dress, he'll be tongue tied!"

Remembering his reaction when Miss Sutton brought her downstairs to model the silver dress for Mr. Prescott, Birdie blushed. As she carefully folded up the gown, she sighed deeply.

Noticing the subtle change in mood, Ella gently asked, "Is somethin' wrong?"

Birdie's frowned as she packed away her needle, thread and ribbon in the small wicker sewing basket. "Honestly, Ella, I'm startin' to wonder if makin' this dress was a waste of time."

"What do ya mean?" Ella cried. "It's fo' the New Year's ball. We're all goin'. Me and Ronnie. And you and Newt. Right?"

Birdie shrugged as she looked down at the wooden slats of the porch's floor, muttering, "I ain't sure. He ain't asked me yet."

Ella was dumbstruck for a moment before she was able to utter, "What? I don't believe it! The ball is only a week away! Of course he'll ask ya. Maybe he just forgot."

Birdie looked uncertain but replied, "Yeah. Maybe." As she watched Ella fold up her own gown, Birdie asked, "Have you noticed anythin' different about Newt lately?"

Ella once again frowned and shook her head. "Nope. He been the same Newt he always is. What do ya mean, Birdie?"

"Well, he just seems so distant these days," said Birdie. "I mean, he's still nice and kind to me as usual, but he always looks like there is somethin' weighin' heavily on his mind."

"Have ya'll been quarrellin'?" asked Ella as she closed the lid on her own sewing basket.

"No, not at all," responded Birdie, "That's what's been puzzlin' me. We've been talkin' every day but he just don't seem himself. And even though everyone else at the Montclair has talked about nothin' but this ball, he hasn't said a word to me about it. I guess it's my own fault. All year long I've been keepin' him at arm's length so that he won't get into any more scuffles because of me, and now here I am expectin' him to take me to the biggest party of the year."

Ella's heart swelled in sympathy as she looked at Birdie's sad and anxious face. Gently squeezing her friend's hand, Ella murmured, "Aw Birdie. Stop lettin' yo' imagination run away with ya. This party's markin' the beginnin' of a new century. Who else would Newt rather be with to see it in than with you?"

Birdie nodded. "Yeah, you're right. No sense me workin' myself into a tizzy."

Ella smiled. "That's my girl! I'll see ya tomorrow, and I wanna see a smile on that face because ya straightened things out with Newt."

Unfortunately, Birdie never got a chance to speak to Newt the next morning. She found Isaiah cleaning off his work boots before making the trip down the hallway to get his daily instructions.

"Mornin' Isaiah," said Birdie. "Have you seen Newt?"

Isaiah momentarily stopped, his left boot still atop the shoe scraper, and smiled up at Birdie.

"Mawnin' Birdie. Nope, I ain't seen Newt just yet. That's cause he and Felipe are already workin'. They been at it since six o'clock."

"Six o'clock?" Birdie repeated.

Noticing her puzzled expression, Isaiah explained, "Last night befo' we left, Mista Prescott told us that he needed Newt and Felipe fo' a special project that Missus Prescott wants doin' fo' that fancy New Year's ball. Somethin' 'bout transformin' the main ballroom into a 'tropical paradise' with ponds, islands, trees and flowers. I reckon we won't be seein' much of them two until it's all done. Missus Prescott'll be havin' 'em workin' from mornin' til late at night."

"You there!" Newt bristled as Lottie Prescott's domineering tone reverberated across the half empty ballroom from where she stood flanked by a small group of her friends and Monsieur Lefevre, a short, portly French maitre'd who she had flown in from New York to help plan the New Year's gala, much to the consternation of her own dining room manager Frederick Hayes.

Newt had only ever seen Mrs. Prescott on a couple of occasions before he was informed late yesterday that he and Felipe were going to be under her direct supervision on this ballroom project. Little did he realize just how bossy and demanding she was. Her inclination to refer to Newt as "you there" particularly tested his patience.

Forcing himself to be polite, Newt slowly turned from the artificial pond which he and Felipe were framing with ferns and courteously replied, "Yes ma'am!" How the hell did Birdie put up with this damned woman?

"Mr. LeFevre and I both agree that be pond should be more kidney shaped instead of circular. More natural looking," said Mrs. Prescott as the Frenchman nodded in agreement.

Looking puzzled, Newt scratched his head and asked, "Kidney shaped, ma'am?"

Lottie Prescott rolled her eyes impatiently as a tall, grey haired woman on her left shook her head. Whipping a small notepad and pencil from the breast pocket of his jacket, the Frenchman quickly scribbled down something and showed it to Mrs. Prescott, who nodded in approval. LeFevre then walked over to Newt and showed him the rough sketch he'd doodled of a kidney shaped pond. "Like zees," he said in his thick Gallic accent.

They've gotta be joking, thought Newt mutinously. Why the hell didn't they think of this before Felipe and I finished the framework? Aloud he merely said, "I see, ma'am. We'll get it done fer ya."

"Splendid," replied Lottie. "I want this place transformed into a lush outdoor tropical oasis with palms, colorful flowers and exotic birds. We only have a couple of weeks left so we need to get moving." Lottie clapped her hands a couple of times to punctuate her directive before departing, her small entourage at her heels.

Newt's face burned as he turned his attention back to the pond. "Why don't they just have their stinkin' party outdoors instead of tryin' to bring everythin' inside? I'll never understand rich folks."

Felipe muttered something in his native tongue which seemed to echo Newt's discontent.

Towards the end of the staff lunch later that afternoon, Ella made sure to establish eye contact with Ronnie and discretely cocked her head towards the doorway, indicating that she needed to talk to him afterwards. Ronnie, who by now was used to reading Ella's looks and moods, immediately received and understood the non-verbal cue. He casually hung back, pretending to finish his cup of coffee, as the rest of the staff filed out of the dining room.

Ella slowly stacked the dirty plates as she waited for Tangie and Eva to take the rest of the food back to the kitchen. Once they left, Ella swiftly dashed to the doorway to make sure that Iris Sutton was nowhere to be seen before rushing back to Ronnie's side.

"So, ya got me all to yourself. Whatcha wanna do?" Ronnie asked jovially with a wink.

"Hush!" whispered Ella. "We ain't got time fo' foolishness. I need you to talk to Newt and find out if he's goin' to the ball."

Ronnie shrugged and asked, "Ain't he takin' Birdie?"

"Birdie says he ain't asked her. She says he's been actin' kinda strange lately and she's afraid he's goin' off her."

"Aw shucks. You and me both know that ain't true," Ronnie replied with a wave of his hand.

"Just talk to him," hissed Ella. Just then she caught sight of Arthur Dickson trotting by as he headed out the back door on an errand. An idea started to take shape. "Tell Newt that Birdie's goin' to that dance whether he takes her or not. I'm gonna see to that."

"What are ya up to, woman?" asked Ronnie suspiciously.

"Never you mind. Just do as I say. Go on now!" Ella scolded as she shooed Ronnie out of the dining room. A sly smile spread across her face as she picked up the stack of plates and headed towards the scullery.

For Newt and Felipe, the following week flew by in a haze of endless labor and extreme exhaustion. Because they started before sunrise and went home well after sunset, they had little contact with anyone else at the Montclair except Mrs. Prescott, who was a constant annoying presence in the ballroom, and Tangie, who was instructed to bring them their meals.

Aside from having to work on his own farm in the evenings after a full day of intense labor, the worst part for Newt was not being able to see Birdie. This only escalated his uncertainty about the friendliness he noticed between her and Arthur.

Remembering the kiss they shared after last year's Christmas party, Newt was hoping to at least be able to see her at this year's holiday gathering. However, it was not meant to be as Lottie Prescott had ordered that he and Felipe skip the party so they could finish up in the ballroom, which was near completion.

The New Year's staff ball weighed heavily on Newt's mind. Even though he knew that Birdie was waiting to be asked, he was ashamed to admit that he had neither the dancing skills nor the suitable clothing. Having been a poor farmer all his life, Newt wore overalls seven days a week, even on the rare occasions when he stepped into a church.

Recalling how Birdie subtly cringed when he used to chew tobacco, Newt hated the thought of becoming a source of embarrassment for her in a social setting. Maybe she would have a better time if she went with Arthur, who was always well groomed and up on the latest dance crazes.

Newt was lost in his gloomy thoughts as he and Felipe put the finishing touches on the small floral festooned "islands" which dotted the room. It was Ronnie's cheerful voice coming from the main entrance that brought Newt out of his reverie.

"Hey Newt! Where ya at?"

"In the back, Ronnie. Left corner'" Newt shouted.

Ronnie whistled appreciatively at lush greenery, vibrant flora and colorful caged macaws as he made his way towards Newt.

"Ya'll did a fine job!" he hollered. "If I didn't know any better, I'd swear I accidentally wandered outside."

Newt grinned as Ronnie finally emerged, carrying a crate of small fuschia bougainvillea plants.

"They just dropped off a wagonload of these out back for ya. I hear they came up on the freight train from Miami."

Newt nodded as he took the crate from Ronnie. "Yep. No expense is bein' spared accordin' to Mrs. Prescott." Taking a bandana from his pocket and wiping the dirt from his hands and face, he added, "Thanks Ronnie. Felipe and I can bring the rest up."

Seizing the opportunity to talk to Newt, Ronnie replied, "I don't mind helpin' ya'll out for a spell, seein' that you're under the gun. At least until Mr. Speer calls me back downstairs."

Newt smiled as he stuffed the bandana back into his pocket. "Much obliged, Ronnie." Glancing over his shoulder, he shouted, "Felipe, we got more plants out back."

"Okay!" Felipe yelled back from the opposite corner of the ballroom.

As Ronnie and Newt headed to the front of the ballroom, Ronnie began, "Uh Newt, you takin' Birdie to the party?"

Newt's jaw visibly tensed for a fraction of a second before he answered. "We haven't really discussed it."

Ronnie feigned surprise as he responded "Is that so? Accordin' to Ella, Birdie is goin' to the dance. I just figured she was goin' with you but I guess I got it wrong."

Newt sighed heavily. Arthur must have already asked her. He decided to use the most obvious excuse available to him. "Truth be told, I'm mighty tired. Felipe and I have been workin' ourselves to the bone fer the past couple o' weeks and all I wanna do is sleep fer a couple of days straight. Plus, I got my own land that needs tendin'. I ain't got time fer parties."

"Newt, we're talkin' 'bout ringin' in a whole new century. This is a once in a lifetime opportunity! Ya got plenty o' time for sleepin' and tendin' yo' farm afterwards. Come on, man. Do yourself a favor and go to the dance. Free food. Free booze. A live band. What have ya got to lose?"

Giving Newt a friendly pat on the back, Ronnie headed for the service stairs while Newt paused in the doorway of the ballroom. Maybe Ronnie was right. After putting up with the likes of Lottie Prescott and her fancy Frenchman all week, Newt reckoned he was owed something in return even if it was only a night of food and drink.

As darkness fell on New Year's Eve, Birdie's bedroom was a hive of activity. Ella had come over to help Birdie get dressed while Hortensia bustled in and out, making sure both girls had everything they needed. Tickled pink that her daughter was being escorted by Arthur, her job for the evening was to entertain him and Ronnie in the front parlor while the girls finished getting ready.

"Honestly, Ella. I don't know why I let you talk me into going to this dance. Although it's nice of Arthur to take me, I just don't feel right goin'," Birdie said peevishly. The gold evening gown she had made for herself was very flattering on her and set off her skin tone perfectly.

Ella, who was already dressed in her new claret gown, watched Birdie glowering in the mirror as she unsuccessfully tried to fight her thick coarse tresses into something resembling a Gibson Girl.

"Oh, I HATE my hair." Birdie whined, "I wish it was straight, shiny and bouncy just like those ladies in the magazines."

Ella shook her head. She had heard this complaint countless times over the years. She also knew that Birdie's sour demeanor had more to do with not seeing Newt than with her hair. So, she decided to distract her friend by offering some practical advice.

"Miss Birdie," she started, "have you ever considered workin' with yo hair instead of against it?"

Birdie turned away from her mirror and with a furrowed brow, asked "What do ya mean?"

"You ain't never gonna have that straight, fine, silky hair that the white ladies do so there ain't no sense in tryin' to look like 'em. Yo hair is thick and curly. What you gotta do is fine yo' own style usin' what the Good Lawd gave ya."

Birdie gazed pensively at her friend and sighed. "I reckon you might be right. But what can I do with this?" She grabbed a handful of her frizzed up locks.

Ella got up and gently picked up one of Birdie's tresses and an idea immediately came to her. "Leave it to me. I gotta run home real quick and get something. I'll be right back." And with that, she was gone.

Newt felt self-conscious as he approached the Montclair. Dressed in an ill-fitting old suit which had belonged to his late father, he was unaccustomed to the discomfort of collar stays. And because Jeb Phillips was considerably shorter than his son, the jacket sleeves as well as the trouser legs were a couple of inches too short. Newt hoped that the ballroom will be dark enough so as not to be noticed. He planned to hang by the bar, get his fill of drinks and dinner before quietly retreating back home.

The lights of the Montclair shone like bright jewels against the black velvety sky. The side streets were lined with the luxurious coaches of the hotel's guests, who swept in through the front entrance dressed in their finest. The cool evening breeze carried with it the scents of lemon verbena, rosewater, tobacco and hair oil.

Newt headed for the back entrance, where some of the staff was already arriving for their own celebration in pairs and groups. He relaxed a little when he noticed a few of the other men were also without female companions. At least he wouldn't be the only stag there.

As he entered the back door and headed down the corridor to the service stairs, Newt wished that Isaiah were there. But the old gardener had said that he and his wife were too old and preferred to see in the twentieth century from the comfort of their home, choosing to leave the boisterous revelry to the "young folk."

The staff ball was being held in the smaller, auxiliary ballroom on the second floor near the dining room. Although not as ornate as the main ballroom, it was nevertheless festive with vibrant red poinsettia plants, candles and ivory damask tablecloths. Up in front, just off the dance floor was a makeshift stage where a six-piece Negro ragtime band was warming up. Several couples sat at tables sipping punch and nibbling on canapes. To Newt's delight, the main chandelier was dimmed so his suit wouldn't be too noticeable.

Hortensia's heart swelled with pride as she watched her lovely daughter set off with Arthur, Ella and Ronnie. When Hortensia first saw Birdie's choice of the gold colored fabric for her evening dress, she had misgivings. Thinking that the yellowish hue would make Birdie's own skin tone look washed out, she tried to steer her towards an emerald colored satin. However, the dress perfectly complimented Birdie's complexion and made it glow.

And thanks to Ella's knack with the curling tongs, Birdie's hair was coiffed into an upswept mass of corkscrew tendrils, a few of which hung down the back of her neck. It looked much more natural and flattering on her than the usual trendy styles which she tried in vain to copy.

Hortensia had never seen her daughter look more beautiful. Best of all, she was being squired to the ball by none other than Arthur Dickson who was looking rather dapper himself in a formal black evening suit and matching top hat. What a nice-looking pair they made as they strolled down the street a few paces behind Ronnie and Ella.

Hortensia turned from the front parlor window and happily padded over to the kitchen to make herself a cup of tea. She softly hummed "The Wedding March" as she set the kettle on the stove.

Chapter 30

The band had started just started with an up-tempo number when Birdie and her friends arrived. Ronnie started snapping his fingers and tapping his toes.

"Ooh, that band is swingin'. Come on, Ella. Let's show 'em how it's done!" With that, he grabbed her by the hand and headed for the dance floor which was filling up quickly.

Arthur grinned at Birdie and gallantly offered her his arm. "Shall we?" Birdie nodded and let Arthur lead her towards the front of the room.

Although her new shoes were pinching her feet, Birdie was determined to enjoy herself and managed to keep up with Arthur as he expertly guided her across the floor. The first song ended and was immediately followed by two more lively tunes. By the end of the third song, Birdie's feet were throbbing and she politely asked Arthur if they could sit.

As they headed back to their table, Birdie spotted a group of men standing in the corner, deep in conversation. She recognized a couple of the others and Lito, but she could not place the stranger who had his back to her. Must be one of the new men in the dining room, she thought. As Birdie was taking her seat, the man turned around to peruse the room and stopped when his glance caught Birdie's. She couldn't believe it. It was Newt Phillips!

This was the first time she saw him without his usual overalls and straw gardening hat. He looked freshly scrubbed and shaven. His hair was washed and slicked back. Although his light grey jacket looked a bit small on his frame, it fitted him better than anything Birdie had ever seen him in. Why, he looks quite dashing, Birdie marveled.

Arthur broke into her thoughts. "Shall I get you some punch, Birdie?"

"Yes, thanks Arthur," she replied absently as she kept her gaze on Newt.

Newt had to consciously keep his jaw from dropping as his eyes took in the lovely vision across the room. Although he had always admired Birdie and thought her beautiful, tonight she was absolutely stunning. The gold dress perfectly molded to her body and showed off her slender figure, and the way her hair hung in ringlets down in the back made Newt want to run his fingers through it. He kept his hands clasped behind his back to hide the frayed cuffs of his father's old jacket.

Lito and Travis Mackey, one of the newer housemen, continued their discourse completely unaware of Newt's reverie.

"Damn! I never knew Birdie was such a looker!" Travis was saying.

"Yes," agreed Lito. Nudging Newt, he asked him in broken English, "What you think, Newt?" Getting no response, Lito looked over and saw that the gardener was still transfixed. Lito grinned and winked at Travis as he silently pointed to Newt.

Now aware of what was going on, Travis lowered his voice and, sidling up to Newt, asked, "Why don't cha pick yer tongue up off the floor and go stick it down her throat? Unless you can think of somethin' better to stick in there."

Turning brick red in the face, Newt turned a menacing look toward Travis and quietly growled, "Why don't ya shut the hell up before I kick yer ass!" With that, he pushed through the crowd and headed for the bar.

"What'll ya have?" barked the balding, red faced barman who normally worked downstairs and was not used to serving hotel staff, Negroes and white trash like the flame haired gardener who was now standing in front of him.

"Whiskey," growled Newt who was still burning from Travis Mackey's lewd remark.

At the other end of the bar stood Arthur, who was about to bring a glass of punch back to Birdie until he spotted Newt, looking morose and knocking back a shot of whiskey. Ronnie had spoken to Arthur earlier that evening about Birdie and Newt. Noticing that Birdie was looking wistfully at Newt,

Arthur decided to take matters into his own hands. Picking up the glass of punch, he headed towards the other side of the bar.

"Hey Newt!"

Newt turned around and was surprised to see Arthur approaching. He thought the houseman would have been back on the dance floor with Birdie.

"Howdy Arthur," Newt replied, trying his best to sound cheerful. "Lotsa folks turned out tonight."

"Yeah," said Arthur measuredly. "There are lotsa pretty wallflowers over there and I intend to dance with every single one of 'em!"

Newt looked confused. "But aren't ya here with Birdie?"

Arthur smiled. "Yeah. I walked her in and danced to a few songs with her, but you and I both know who she'd rather be with."

Newt stared into his empty glass. "I ain't much of a dancer."

"It won't make no difference to Birdie. She'll just be happy to be near ya. I thought you were sweet on her yourself. What's goin' on, Newt?"

"Well, from what I've seen, I reckoned her ma would rather have you as a son-in-law. It would make Birdie's life a lot easier," a despondent tone had crept into Newt's voice.

"Son-in-law?" Arthur repeated. "Listen here, Newt. I ain't sure what ya saw and I don't care how much her ma likes me. I ain't ready to settle down just yet. Don't get me wrong. Birdie is a fine gal and will make some man a good wife someday, but she and I are just friends, nothin' more. I ain't got no claim on her. Besides, it's you that she really loves, and ya feel the same, don't ya?"

Newt looked pensive as Arthur slid the glass of punch towards him. "Now take this here glass over to Birdie. She's mighty thirsty after all that dancin'." Lowering his voice, he added helpfully, "Wait til the band starts a slow number. It'll be easier to follow along. Just shift yo' weight from one foot to the other." Patting Newt on the back, Arthur straightened his bowtie as he headed towards a table of giggling laundry maids.

Newt took the glass and started the long walk across the room to where Birdie was sitting. Her attention was turned toward her shoes, which she was surreptitiously trying to slip off without anyone noticing so she didn't see Newt approaching until she heard his voice above her, making her head snap up.

"Evenin', Birdie." Newt set the glass on the table.

Smiling up at him, Birdie replied, "Evenin', Newt."

As the band started a slow waltz, Newt asked, "Care to dance?"

Although her feet were in severe pain, Birdie wanted nothing more than to be in Newt's arms so she crammed her shoes back on and answered, "I'd love to!"

Taking her by the hand, Newt led Birdie out to the dance floor where he awkwardly held her close and tried his best not to step on her feet. His hands were sweaty while Birdie's were ice cold. She felt nervous for some reason but wasn't sure why.

With his lips close to her ear, he softly said, "You look mighty nice tonight but I 'spect you done heard that lotsa times already."

"You look very dapper yourself, Newt." Birdie replied. "You know, I didn't even recognize you at first." As soon as the words were out of her mouth, Birdie inwardly winced. She hoped it didn't sound like an insult because she certainly did not mean it that way.

To her relief, Newt chuckled and said, "Honest? Well, maybe if they held more o' these dances for us, I'd bathe more often!"

Birdie's shoulders shook as she tried to suppress an oncoming fit of giggles. When she felt that Newt was doing the same, she started to laugh aloud as he joined her. They were starting to get strange stares off the other couples but it didn't matter. The ice was broken and it was the first time Birdie felt at ease the entire evening.

Newt was also more relaxed as he led the loveliest lady in the room around the dance floor, praying that the song would never end. Both he and Birdie were disappointed when the number eventually finished and a fast-paced Dixieland number started.

"Can I tell you a secret, Newt?" Birdie asked conspiratorially.

Puzzled but intrigued, Newt said, "Sure Birdie. You can tell me anythin'."

"My feet are killin' me!" she confessed.

Newt grinned and countered, "Guess I better confess somethin' too. This daggum collar's chokin' me." Birdie smiled sympathetically as Newt thought for a moment. "Well, if it's not too cold out, would ya like to sit in the rose garden fer a spell?"

"The rose garden sounds heavenly! Let's go!" Birdie eagerly replied.

Newt protectively guided Birdie through the festive throng as they headed towards the cloakroom to get her wrap. Ella, who was dancing with Ronnie, caught sight of the pair departing together and smiled. It's about damned time, she thought to herself.

Once out on the mezzanine, Birdie started to head for the back stairs leading to the kitchen, but Newt put his hand on her arm and stopped her.

"No," he said. "I won't have ya leavin' out the back like some poor servant. I just won't have it! Tonight, I am takin' you out the front door! Besides," he added, "it is a much shorter walk to the rose garden that way."

"Newt Phillips, you've lost your mind!" Birdie exclaimed. "We aren't allowed up front. What if someone notices us?"

"Other than them havin' some money, them folks down there ain't all that different from us. We all eat, we all sleep and we all bleed red." Birdie stared wondrously at Newt. She had never heard him speak like this before, but everything he just said was no different to what she felt inside most of her life. She smiled at Newt which emboldened him even more. Taking her arm in his, the couple made their way down the elegant staircase which led into the front lobby.

It took every ounce of Birdie's energy not to scrunch her shoulders and look down at the floor. Even though her nerves jangled, she stared straight ahead and keeping her chin held high while using Newt's elbow to steady herself.

Newt firmly grasped Birdie's arm as they slowly descended the main staircase into the lobby. It was hard for him to believe that only an hour ago he was ashamed to be seen in his faded suit and now here he was flagrantly flaunting hotel rules by walking through the Montclair's reception area and forcing Birdie to do likewise. His sudden decision to buck social conventions had more to do with the woman on his arm than the shot of whiskey he downed earlier. Regardless, Newt didn't care about any possible repercussions and was prepared to take the blame if the need arose. Birdie was just as elegant as any of the women who were nibbling caviar and sipping champagne in the main ballroom. Why the hell shoudn't she be able to walk through the front of the hotel like they do?

As they reached the first floor, Newt could feel Birdie tremoring, so he gave her hand a reassuring squeeze. As they held their heads high and casually headed for the front door, they couldn't help but glance in awe at the opulence around them.

An older colored gentleman in a tuxedo was seated at the grand piano near the lounge, softly playing instrumental pieces, which provided a melodious backdrop to the elegant gathering. Several small groups of guests dotted the lobby, the more inebriated ones talking loudly and laughing at their own jokes.

A few men in a small cloud of cigar smoke were exiting the ballroom. Birdie was mortified to see that the gentleman on the far right was none other than Jonathan Prescott, Sr. himself. She quickly looked up at Newt, who apparently had also seen the hotelier, but his face remained impassive.

Prescott spotted the couple and slightly raised his eyebrows. He said something to his three companions and, leaving them to their discourse, he made a beeline for the young couple. Birdie felt her heart drop into her stomach. Even Newt's hands started to feel clammy.

"Good evening, Phillips," he said casually to Newt. Nodding at Birdie, he added, "Miss Fairfax."

"Good evening, Mr. Prescott," they replied in unison.

"Are you enjoying the staff ball? I hope the entertainment and refreshments have been to your liking," said Prescott.

"Oh sir, the ball is wonderful and we're having the best time. Thank you so much," Birdie responded earnestly.

Newt added, "It's just that we needed a little air and I was escortin' Miss. Fairfax outside. I didn't want her to have to walk too far so I reckoned the shortest route was through here. I'm awful sorry if we're trespassin'. It was all my idea."

Prescott's eyes twinkled as he puffed on the stogie. He liked both of these young folks and was pleased to see them together after watching Newt pine after Birdie.

"Nonsense, Phillips," he said. "I'll let the rule relax just for tonight." Noticing their relief, he continued, "In fact, before you head outside, why don't you go into the ballroom first and show Miss. Fairfax your handiwork? You boys did a fine job on the greenery and pond in there. It's been a big hit with my guests. You should hear what they're saying! There will certainly be a little something extra in your next pay packet."

"Thank you, sir," said Newt.

"Won't your guests mind seeing us in there?" asked Birdie uncertainly.

Prescott waved a dismissive hand. "Balderdash! Most of them are too tipsy to notice much of anything now anyway, and if someone says something to you, tell them you are personal guests of mine." Pulling a business card from his inside breast pocket, Prescott handed it to Newt. Noticing a waiter nearby with a tray of filled champagne glasses, he called him over,

Taking two glasses off the tray, Prescott handed one each to Newt and Birdie. "There you go. Now you really look like you belong in there. Go on, Phillips. Enjoy yourselves. And Happy New Year."

"Yes sir," said Newt. "Happy New Year, sir."

Birdie smiled gratefully at her employer and added, "Thank you, Mr. Prescott. We'll only have a quick look and then we'll leave. Happy New Year."

Prescott watched as Newt again took Birdie by the hand and together they took a faltering step inside the ballroom. Once he was satisfied that the couple was not being challenged by anyone, he rejoined his friends who were now seated in the lounge and enjoying glasses of scotch.

Both Birdie and Newt were so transfixed by their surroundings that for a moment they forgot their nervousness. Newt couldn't believe his luck. He not only had the woman he loved on his arm, but he was able to get her into the poshest party in town.

As for Birdie, she was awestruck at Newt and Felipe's indoor landscaping. The small "islands" which dotted the room were ablaze with vivid red hibiscus flowers, the fuschia bougainvilleas, and bright yellow mandevillas - most of which were brought up from South Florida.

"Oh my," she exclaimed softly, "I can't believe you and Felipe did all this by yourselves in just a couple of weeks! It looks like the Garden of Eden in here!"

Newt chuckled at the biblical reference and replied, "Yep, with Mrs. Prescott on our backs day and night, Felipe and I were darn set on gettin' this done as soon as we could!"

Birdie was serious, however. "I'm so proud of you, Newt. Look at how everyone is admiring your hard work." She pointed to a group of middle aged couples who were marveling at the pond. "I just want to shout at the top of my lungs that all of this is down to you!"

"Aw shucks, Birdie," said Newt bashfully. "I was just doin' what I was told to do. Besides, Felipe worked as hard as I did."

"I know," said Birdie. "And I wish he were here tonight, too. Why didn't he come?"

"His missus is expectin' another young 'un any day now,'" answered Newt.

"Well, since Felipe ain't here tonight to share the credit, I'm just gonna have to keep on singin' your praises," said Birdie spiritedly. Raising her champagne glass to Newt, she toasted, "To the best gardener in St. Augustine!"

Raising his own glass, Newt countered with, "And to the prettiest and best dressed woman here tonight!!" They clinked their glasses and took a sip of the champagne.

Neither of them liking the taste, they both made sour faces and broke into stifled laughter.

"I know this stuff is expensive, but I just can't bring myself to swallow another mouthful," confessed Newt.

"But I'd hate to be wasteful," said Birdie. "Should we try to finish 'em?"

Taking Birdie's glass, Newt placed it next to his own on a nearby table. "Trust me. No one's gonna let that go to waste. Let's head on outside to the rose garden."

Birdie slid her arm into Newt's as they strolled back towards the entrance. Little did she know that she was being watched by a very angry pair of eyes.

Newt was right about Birdie being the best dressed woman in the ballroom. In fact, several women also noticed Birdie and were fascinated with her gown. Even though Birdie was only in the ballroom for a few minutes, she unwittingly caused a stir amongst the more fashion minded women. Soon conversations turned to the mystery woman in the gold dress. The gossip eventually reached the ear of Lottie Prescott, who was curious to see the dress with her own eyes.

"Ooh, there she is," exclaimed Eaulalie Glossop, who was seated next to Lottie. "What an exquisite gown. My Catriona would look darling in something like that!"

Lottie looked to where Eaulalie was pointing and all the blood drained from her face. What on earth was Miss Fairfax doing in here? And who is that with her? Oh no! He's that gardener!

By now the couple had exited the ballroom. However, Lottie was on the warpath. Putting on a false smile, she trilled, "Excuse me, my dear. I need to find Jonathan and remind him about something. I'll be right back."

Knowing that her husband was no doubt smoking and drinking with those old ranching friends of his, Lottie headed for the lounge where Jonathan was holding court. All four men, who were enjoying a ribald joke just told, cut their laughter short when they saw Mrs. Prescott approaching.

"Ah, Lottie dear," Prescott said with a bit of a slur. "What brings you out here away from your party?"

Lottie smiled for the benefit of her husband's companions as she replied, "Just a small matter that needs your immediate attention, my dear." To the others, she sweetly asked, "You gentlemen don't mind if I borrow Johnathan for a moment, do you?"

"No, of course not!"

"Go right ahead, ma'am."

Taking her husband by the arm, Lottie discretely guided him towards a vacant sitting room across from the Emporium. After she switched on a lamp and quietly shut the door, Lottie turned a thundercloud face to her husband and hissed, "Can you explain to me why I just saw our seamstress and the gardener walking around the ballroom like they owned the place?"

Prescott decided not to relate where he first encountered Newt and Birdie that evening because it would anger his wife even more and possibly result in a demand for the dismissal of both. So, he told a half-truth instead. "I just so happened to come across them earlier and invited them inside the ballroom for a quick look at Phillips' labors. I thought the lad would benefit from seeing the delight it has brought to all our friends."

"Be that as it may, the fact remains that you allowed servants into a ball reserved for guests. Those people have their own gathering upstairs, remember? The party you insisted upon - against my wishes I might add! What's the point of throwing a ball for the servants if you're just going to let them mingle among our guests?"

"First of all, I prefer to call our employees 'staff', not 'servants'," said Prescott. "And secondly, I should remind you that one of those 'servants' bore your grandchild!"

"How many times are you going to bring that up?" cried Lottie. "Do you have any idea what it's like for me? I was sitting there having a nice chat with my friends when suddenly people, started talking about a woman in a lovely gold dress. When the girl in question is finally pointed out to me, I discover that she is our seamstress. On the arm of a gardener! Now people want to know who she is. What on earth am I supposed to tell them? It's bad enough that we had to hire local ruffians to serve tonight because our staff is at a ball. Now I've got this issue to contend with. I'll be a laughing stock!"

Feeling contrite, Prescott replied, "I'm sorry, Lottie. I honestly thought that with all the plants and dim lights, no one would have noticed Phillips and Miss Fairfax, especially with all the booze flowing in there. I had no idea that Miss\ Fairfax would garner so much attention. They were only having a drink and a short walk-through. They wouldn't have spoken to anyone. Leave the matter to me. I'll think up a reasonable excuse for their appearance."

Lottie, who had been weeping, wiped her eyes. "Well, I suppose I should look on the bright side."

"Oh? What's that, my dear?" asked Prescott.

"It looks like Miss Fairfax will be getting more dress orders after tonight."

Prescott chuckled as he ushered his wife out of the sitting room.

Once they were finally outside in the rose garden, Birdie exhaled and exclaimed, "I can't believe we just did that! Did you ever in your wildest dreams think we'd be rubbin' shoulders with all those rich folks tonight?"

"Nope," answered Newt. "I was only plannin' to stay a short spell and then head home. Until Arthur spoke to me, that is."

Birdie blushed and asked, "Will I need Arthur to escort me home tonight?"

Newt grinned. "Mr. Dickson and I came to an understandin' and his services for this evenin' are no longer required."

They both laughed until Birdie remembered the problems Newt previously had when he was seen with her. She quickly sobered and asked, "But Newt, maybe Arthur should walk me home. I don't want any trouble between you and those awful Klansmen."

"Aw, they ain't gonna be botherin' us," assured Newt. "They'll be passed out in the gutter after midnight, and those who are still standin' won't be able to see straight any way. They'll be celebratin' the new century like everyone else. So stop worryin' and let's start enjoyin' ourselves!"

"All right, then,'" said Birdie. "I'm gonna start celebratin' by gettin' comfortable and takin' off these shoes!" Newt gently averted his eyes as Birdie sat on a nearby stone bench and raised her skirt to slip off her shoes and stockings. The cold pebbles and grass of the garden path soothed her aching feet.

"I think I'll join ya," declared Newt as he removed his collar and rubbed his newly freed neck. "Ah! I can breathe again."

Feeling comfortable and relaxed, Birdie tilted her head back and inhaled deeply. "Ya know, when we first saw Mr. Prescott back there, I was so frightened. I really thought we were done for."

"I'm sorry if ya got scared, Birdie," said Newt, "but I ain't sorry fer walkin' ya through that lobby. I meant what I said. Yer the finest lookin' gal here tonight. In fact, ya look just like a queen and I wanted to show ya off to the world."

Birdie erupted in giggles. "Me? A queen? I declare I don't know what's gotten into you tonight, Newt Phillips!"

But Newt wasn't laughing. "I'm dead serious, Birdie. You look like you walked right outta one of them storybooks." Newt paused as a thought struck him. Snapping his fingers, he added, "Wait right here. I'll be right back,"

Watching him disappear up the garden path, Birdie softly chuckled and shook her head.

"No peekin' now!" Newt called back.

Off in the distance, the Episcopal church bell tolled ten o'clock. The temperature had dropped since she had arrived at the hotel earlier that evening. Birdie wrapped her shawl tightly around her shoulders.

After few minutes, Newt returned up the walkway with his hands hiding something behind his back and looking quite pleased with himself.

"What are you up to now,? You look like the cat that ate the canary!"

"Now ya just close them pretty eyes, missy!" Birdie did as she was told while Newt placed a makeshift crown of orange blossoms, jasmine, swamp sunflower and cross ivy on top of her ringlets.

"Okay, you can open 'em now. All hail the Queen of the Montclair!"

Birdie lifted her hands to her head and gingerly fingered the garland she was now sporting. The sweet floral aromas hung heavily in the late-night air.

"What on earth...." Birdie was speechless. No one had ever made such a fuss over her before, so she wasn't quite sure how to feel. A wave of shyness suddenly crept over her.

To ward it off, she stood up and, doing her best impression of an elegant, well-bred lady, she playfully said in a haughty voice, "Bow before your queen!"

Getting into the spirit of Birdie's pantomime, Newt got down on one knee as Birdie took her hand and tapped Newt once on each shoulder. “I dub thee Sir Newton, brave defender of the Empire!"

Newt bowed his head and melodramatically replied, "Thank you, yer majesty. It'll always be an honor to defend you and yer Empire."

"Now rise, Sir Newton, and escort me as we take a royal stroll of my kingdom."

"Yer wish is my command, yer majesty." Newt offered Birdie his arm as they walked through the rose garden's path in companionable silence.

As they passed under one of the outdoor lanterns, Newt gazed at Birdie. The angle of the lamplight combined with that of the half-moon overhead created a luminous curly halo around Birdie's head. At a loss for words to describe the radiant beauty in front of him, Newt stopped short and took one of Birdie's hands in his. It was soft but calloused - a hand of a woman not afraid of hard work. Birdie caught her breath as Newt carefully raised her hand to his lips and planted a soft kiss in the middle of her palm. Then, one by one, he slowly kissed each fingertip.

As Birdie gazed into Newt's eyes and saw true love staring back at her, she knew right then and there what she wanted. Just as she was about to speak, however, a loud crashing noise coming from the direction of the back entrance startled them both.

"Careful or you'll blow us all to kingdom come!" a man's voice shouted amid whoops of laughter.

Ronnie, Arthur and a couple other men were carrying large wooden crates and heading towards the east side of the hotel. Ronnie noticed the couple in the garden and shouted, "Hey ya'll. They're servin' dinner up there now. Better go get ya some before it's all gone."

"Thanks," said Newt. "Whatcha got there?"

"Fireworks," answered Arthur. "We'll be settin' 'em off at midnight over the bay. The band's comin', too. You won't wanna miss this! See ya down there!"

"See ya, fellers," replied Newt. Turning to Birdie, he asked, "Would ya like to go back up and get somethin' to eat?"

Birdie, who was still spellbound by Newt's earlier romantic gesture, softly whispered, "I'm not really hungry right now." Remembering her manners, she swiftly added, "But if you would like to eat, I'll be happy to join ya."

"Naw, I ain't hungry, either," admitted Newt.

A few seconds of awkward silence passed between them before Birdie eventually found her voice.

"Newt, do you mind if we don't go see the fireworks?"

"Why no, I don't mind at all," said Newt. Then, with concern, he asked, "Are ya feeling all right, Birdie? Is it gettin' too cold out here fer ya? Would ya like my coat?"

Touched by his offer, Birdie replied, "No, thank you. I'm fine. It's just that I don't feel much like bein' around lotsa folks right now." As she looked down shyly at her hands, she said softly, "Actually, I'd rather see in the new century alone...with you."

Newt's pulse quickened. Despite his wanting to show Birdie off to the world earlier that evening, the thought of being alone with her was even more enticing.

Taking her hand in his, Newt whispered, "It goes without sayin' that I feel the same."

Once again, Birdie felt just as resolute as she did before Ronnie and his companions had interrupted them a few minutes ago. An idea came to her as she glanced up at Newt. "Come with me!"

Birdie went back to her belongings on the stone bench, slid her shoes back on and picked up her reticule, stuffing her stockings inside it. Carefully removing the floral crown from her head and hanging it over her arm, she led Newt through the kitchen and down the corridor to the service stairs. Wondering if Birdie had changed her mind and was heading back to the staff party, Newt was surprised when they got to the top of the stairs and Birdie walked past the auxiliary ballroom. The aroma of the roast beef dinner being served hung in the mezzanine. The room was buzzing with lively chatter and laughter. Relieved that most of the staff was still at dinner and no one saw them, Birdie made a quick left into a narrow corridor and stopped in front of a door.

Unfamiliar with this portion of the hotel, Newt asked, "Where are we?"

Birdie opened the door and switched on the electric light. "My workroom."

The tiny room was crammed with bolts of fabric, spools of ribbons and lace, boxes upon boxes of buttons, and threads of every color imaginable. The sewing machine in the back corner was barely visible behind a large rack of dresses in various stages of completion. A cutting table took up the opposite corner. The moon was visible through the narrow window overlooking the rear of the hotel.

Newt whistled softly. "So this is where you work yer magic makin' all those fancy dresses for them rich womenfolk downstairs." Picking up a sleeve of a plum colored dress, he added, "You sure are a marvel, Birdie!"

Birdie set the inside latch on the door. "Actually, I didn't bring ya up here to brag on my sewin'," she began. Newt watched with curiosity as she grabbed an oil lamp from under the cutting table. "This is where I thought we'd see in 1900."

Birdie lit the small lantern and placed it on the table. Then she reached behind the rack of dresses and produced a couple of old bed quilts which were beyond repair. Newt curiously watched as she folded them into a large square bundle and placed them in an empty corner.

As Birdie turned off the overhead light, the room was plunged into darkness, with only the golden glow of the lamp and the moon outside providing any light.

Taking Newt's hand, Birdie continued, "A while back, you mentioned marriage and said you would wait til I was ready. Well, tonight I'm finally sure. I'm ready. If ya still want me, that is."

Newt blinked and swallowed hard as he took in what he just heard. "Oh Birdie! Of course, I still want ya. Do ya mean it? Yer ready to be my wife?"

Birdie nodded as she slightly tightened her grip on Newt's hands. "Yes, I want to live the rest of my life with ya. Before I met ya, I never felt comfortable around anyone, except Ella and my ma. It's hard havin' white, black and Spaniard blood in my veins and not bein' accepted by any of them."

Birdie fought back the tears which were starting to sting her eyes as she continued, "But you're different, Newt. You've always made me feel like a regular human bein', not some mixed up oddball. When we're together, I not only feel accepted and safe, but I feel like anythin's possible."

"Tell ya the truth, I always felt the same 'round you," remarked Newt. Seeing the look of surprise on Birdie's face, he added, "I ain't got much and I sure ain't much to look at either, but when I'm around ya, I feel like the luckiest man alive."

"You're also the kindest and bravest man alive as far as I'm concerned," said Birdie. "And now I want to spend the rest of my life givin' ya all the things you deserve - all my love and devotion, a nice home, and...and children." As she shyly peered down at the quilts in the floor, Birdie whispered, "Marriage ain't the only thing I'm ready for tonight."

Newt was rendered temporarily speechless. He stroked Birdie's cheek, cupped her chin and raising her mouth to his, hungrily devoured her eager lips. Feeling her respond in kind as he pressed himself up against her, Newt's long simmering carnal desires for Birdie were unleashed.

"Ya got no idea how long I've waited fer this," Newt rasped as he ran his fingers through her curls. "Are ya sure, Birdie?"

"I've never been so sure about anythin' in my whole life," murmured Birdie. "And Newt, when we...uh...lay together and you're ready to.......ya know.....ya don't have to pull it out."

Newt's usually serene pale blue eyes rounded in shock. "Ya mean want ya want me to..."

Birdie nodded. "Yeah, plant your seed, Newt. I want a baby with ya. I want lotsa babies. You'd be a such a good father."

Now it was Newt's turn to fight back the tears. "I might not be the richest man in this hotel tonight but no one here's happier than me right now."

Birdie lovingly kissed him on the cheek before disappearing behind the dress rack where she started to disrobe. Taking a cue from her, Newt's hands shook with excitement as he began removing his own clothing.

As he waited for his fiancée to emerge, Newt's thoughts turned to the future, when he'd come home to his beloved Birdie after the end of a long hard day. But before he'd have a chance to wrap her in his arms, he'd first be overrun by a group of giggling children. He hoped the girls will be curly headed and sweet tempered like their ma. As for the boys, he would teach them how to ride a horse and take them fishing. He'd make sure to give them the stable, loving childhood he never had.

Birdie bashfully poked her head out from behind the rack but was too nervous to look directly at Newt. Instead, she looked down at her bare feet and stammered, "Are....uh....are ya ready?"

Newt could feel his heart pounding as he managed to utter a soft monosyllabic "Yep."

Birdie took a couple of faltering steps forward. She'd released her hair and it was now a frizzy cascade of curls which hung off her shoulders. Her breasts were small but well-rounded with dark brown nipples. Her hands were tightly clasped together in front of her crotch. She was visibly shaking and looked for all the world like a frightened fawn. Newt noticed her trembling and as much as he wanted to draw her into his arms and comfort her, he stood paralyzed.

Although Birdie's head was still tilted downward, her curiosity at seeing a naked man got the better of her. As her eyes glanced upward, she sharply exhaled as she caught sight of Newt's large, fully erect penis which was surrounded by a thick patch of flame colored hair. She wondered if this was going to be as painful an experience as the one she had with Johnny Prescott.

They stood before each other in the soft glow of the lamplight for what seemed like an eternity but was actually only a few moments. Newt reached out, took Birdie by the hand and guided her over the quilts where he gently laid her on her back.

Shouts and peals laughter could be heard in the hallway as the staff finished their meals and started to make their way out and over to the bayside for the midnight festivities. The band had also relocated to the sea wall where they were warming up before their next set.

But Newt and Birdie were in a world of their own. As he laid on his side and softly traced Birdie's facial features with his index finger, Newt leaned over and once again tasted her full, slightly parted lips. Birdie, who was beginning to relax, reached out and gently stroked Newt's face.

As he gazed down into the captivating amber eyes which seemed to sparkle in the lamplight, Newt whispered, "I wish ya could see how beautiful ya are." Laying back on his side, his right hand started its slow, deliberate exploration of Birdie's body.

Her earlier fears and apprehension had all but vanished as Birdie succumbed to the sensual delights of Newt's touch. Moaning, writhing and arching her back, she never dreamt she'd enjoy being with a man after what she endured a couple of years ago.

Birdie had an overwhelming urge to give Newt as much physical pleasure as she was receiving so she reached out and stroked his chest. His fair, freckled skin was sparsely covered with a fine layer of curly, ginger hair. Her fingertips traced the scars from the injury he received during the storm a few months ago.

As her eager fingertips nimbly made their way down Newt's torso, he lustfully grunted as she grazed his hardened manhood.

Mistaking his reaction for pain, Birdie naively asked, “I’m sorry. Did I hurt ya?”

Newt huskily replied, "No. Please....don't stop."

Birdie continued the gentle stroking until Newt didn't think he could hold out any more. He climbed atop Birdie and straddled her.

"Are ya ready fer me?" he drawled.

"Yeah."

"I promise I'll go easy at first. Just let me know if it hurts."

"All right."

Knowing that Birdie's previous sexual encounter had been a violent and painful one, Newt proceeded slowly and carefully. He tenderly kissed her neck as he started to make penetration, causing Birdie to softly groan.

"You all right, Birdie?"

"Yeah. Please keep goin'." Birdie started to thrust her hips. Taking this as a cue to go deeper, Newt followed through and plunged in all the way. Being inside her felt exactly as Newt had always imagined. He bit his lip hard in an effort not to release himself too soon. Despite not having much more sexual experience than Birdie, he intended to make this last as long as he could.

Their bodies quickly fell into a syncopated rhythm as Birdie wrapped her legs around Newt and clasped her ankles together behind his back. For the next hour, they were as one. Soon they heard the cheering from down by the bay and the thundering of the fireworks. Shortly afterward, Birdie shuddered as her entire body went into an orgasmic frenzy just as Newt finally climaxed.

As Newt rolled off her and laid by her side, still panting, Birdie whispered, "Happy New Year."

Taking her into his arms, Newt replied, "Welcome to the twentieth century, my darlin'."

Just as Newt had figured, the streets were virtually empty as he walked Birdie home. The party down at the bay was still in full swing and Doheny's had a few stragglers slumped over the bar, too inebriated to risk movement.

No longer in their own private sanctuary of Birdie's workroom and back out into the cold world, the newly engaged lovers started to make plans. The possibility that they may have just conceived a child was a matter not to be taken lightly. First and foremost, they will need to flee to the north to get married right away.

"Mr. Prescott mentioned a bonus in my next pay packet," said Newt. "That'll help pay for our train fair."

Remembering her own stash under the floorboard in her bedroom, Birdie replied, "And I have some more I'd been saving. We could use part of it to live on until we get settled, but I also want to leave some for my ma."

The repercussions of their impending marriage on their respective families was yet another significant issue that weighed heavily on their minds. Both of their mothers were widows and in Newt's case, there were also two young children still at home.

"Yep, I can't leave either 'til I can get one of my ma's kinfolk from Palatka to come take over the farm and chores for me. I reckon that should only take a couple weeks or so."

Birdie, who had been thinking about her own familial challenges that lay ahead, replied, "I won't lie to ya, Newt. My ma ain't gonna be happy about this at all. She still has her heart set on havin' Arthur as a son-in-law."

Remembering how chummy Birdie's mother looked with Arthur that day in town, Newt just nodded and ruefully muttered, "Oh yeah, I 'spect so."

"Well, no matter, I'm gonna tell her that we're gettin' married and that's all there is to it," said Birdie stoutly. Patting her stomach, she went on, "Besides, once I tell her that I might be with child, she'll have no choice. But once we get settled and the baby is born, we can send for her. When she sees her grandchild for the first time, the nice home we've made for ourselves and how much you love me, she'll love you too. I just know she will. In the meantime, I'll send for one of my cousins to come stay with her for a spell."

Newt smiled at his bride-to-be's innocently positive outlook. "I reckon we both have some telegrams to send tomorrow. We'll go together to the telegraph office after work. Did you want me to be with ya when ya tell yer ma?"

Birdie wrapped an arm around Newt's waist and held him close as they continued walking side by side towards Lincolnville. "That's mighty kind of ya, Newt, but I think I better talk to her myself first."

Uneasy about Birdie having to face her mother's possible wrath alone, Newt replied, "Well all right. But if ya need me, let me know."

"That's why I love ya so much," said Birdie. "You're always lookin' after me. I can't wait to look after YOU for a change."

Newt stopped them in their tracks as he turned towards Birdie and held both her hands. "We now have the rest of our lives to look after one another." He leaned down and planted a soft kiss on her lips which Birdie hungrily returned. Newt ran both his hands down her back and cupped her rear end, pressing her close to him.

"Aw Birdie," he murmured into her ear as he started to kiss her neck, "Yer makin' my loins ache again."

Looking up at him with an impish smile, Birdie replied, "Do I need to start leavin' my bedroom window open for ya?"

"I 'spect so. At least til we can leave town and I can finally make ya mine." As he moved his hand across Birdie's abdomen, Newt whispered, "Do ya think we made a baby tonight?"

"I hope so," Birdie sincerely replied. "But even if we didn't, we'll just have to keep on tryin'."

Newt chuckled, "That's somethin' I really look forward to!"

The pair were passing an old abandoned bungalow which was only a couple blocks away from the Fairfax house. They headed for the side of the house where they resumed their passionate embrace. Newt continued kissing Birdie's neck and slowly made his way down to her bosom. Feeling his warm breath on her breasts and his growing erection jabbing her hips, Birdie tilted her head back and softly groaned.

Bong! Bong!

The unexpected tolling of a nearby church bell shattered the blissful silence and startled them both.

"It's already two o'clock. I'm sorry Newt but I better get home," said Birdie. "I've never been out this late before. Ma's probably worried sick."

Newt, still panting and trying to regain his composure, simply nodded and leaned back against the side of the house.

"No sense gettin' her upset before I have to sit her down and tell her about our engagement," Birdie added as she picked up the reticule, wrap and floral crown which she had dropped. Once she placed the wreath back on her head, the pair continued towards Birdie's house.

Now able to speak, Newt grinned and cheekily remarked, "I wouldn't worry too much 'bout that, Birdie. Yer maw still thinks yer out with Arthur, her future son-in-law who can't do nothin' wrong in her eyes."

Birdie laughed and shook her head. "You're awful, Newt Phillips. But I still love ya."

As they approached the front gate, Newt replied, "And I love ya, too, Mrs. Birdie Phillips."

Birdie smiled thoughtfully. "Mmm. I like how that sounds."

"Ya know somethin'? I kinda like it myself," said Newt playfully as he gave her a final chaste kiss on the forehead. "I reckon I got just enough time to get home, have a catnap and get dressed fer work."

Birdie replied, "Me, too! See ya in a few hours."

"See ya."

Birdie watched as Newt continued his way up Citrus Avenue. Before making the northward turn towards King Street which would take him out of town, Newt turned around and waved. After waving back, Birdie tiptoed up the porch steps and into the house.

Hortensia, who had evidently been waiting up for Birdie, had fallen asleep in her rocker with her bible in her lap. Birdie leaned down and gently patted her mother's hand.

"Ma," she said softly. "I'm home now so you can go on to bed."

Hortensia opened her eyes and blinked a few times before she whispered, "Birdie. What time is it? You'll need to get up for work soon."

"I know, ma," replied Birdie as she gently helped Hortensia out of the chair. "I'll have a short nap and will be just fine. You need some rest yourself."

"How was the dance? Did you and Arthur have a nice time?"

"Yes, we did, ma," said Birdie. Well, it IS the truth, she told herself. We both had a good time. We just spent it with different people.

Hortensia looked up at Birdie for the first time and noticed the floral wreath. "What's that on your head? Did Arthur get it for you?"

"I'll tell ya all about the dance tomorrow, ma," said Birdie as she ushered Hortensia to her bedroom. "Right now, we both need our sleep."

"All right, mija. Good night," said Hortensia. Birdie kissed her on the cheek before going to her own room. As she shut the door and leaned up against it, she caressed her stomach as she recalled the events of the evening and her wonderful secret. 1900 was going to be an unforgettable year.

Other eyes were also on Newt as he turned off Citrus. In fact, they had been silently watching the couple ever since they were spotted walking away from the Montclair together.

Jake Combes asked, "So whatcha wanna do?"

Lonnie Stokes took a puff on his cigar and slowly exhaled. "Go get the others. Leave Phillips to me."

1900

Chapter 31

Newt whistled as he made his way through town and headed west towards the homestead. It seemed like just yesterday when he had seen Birdie for the first time. After over two years of loving her from a distance, she was finally his! What a way to start the new century! 1900 was going to be his best year yet. He knew he wouldn't be getting any sleep that night and would be counting the hours until he could see her again. Completely lost in his thoughts, Newt never heard Lonnie Stokes tailing him.

Jumping him from behind, Stokes knocked Newt to the ground and proceeded to pummel him.

"Ya goddamned nigra lover! I been watchin' ya. Looks like ya ain't been heedin' my warnin's so now yer gonna pay!"

Having recovered from the element of surprise, Newt was now on the offensive. Grabbing Stokes by the neck, Newt managed to crawl out from underneath him. Now it was his turn to do the battering.

"Ya better leave 'er alone or I swear I'll kill ya and anyone else who messes with 'er."

Stokes was able to sharply jab his knee just under Newt's ribcage, which made him momentarily lose his breath. Stokes grabbed Newt by his jacket and threw him up against a nearby oak tree trunk where he continued his assault, accentuating each sentence with a punch.

"What's wrong Phillips? Ain't white women good enough fer ya? We need to keep the white race pure 'n stop pollutin' it with nigger, spic and Jew blood. There's already too many mulattos and quadroons like 'er walkin' 'round. Soon they'll be takin' over. Why the hell would ya wanna make more?"

Newt knocked Stokes back to the ground and hit him square in the eye socket and then broke his nose with a follow-up jab. "I don't care if I swing fer it. I'll kill ya Stokes if any o' ya'll lay a hand on 'er!"

Stokes' fumbling hand picked up a nearby stone and slammed it into Newt's temple causing him to crumble to the ground as blood spurted from the fresh wound.

Stokes rose up and extracted his sidearm from under his coat. He stumbled over to where Newt was laying and kicked him in the ribs to see if he was still alive. When Newt groaned, Stokes kneeled down next to him and shoved the barrel of his pistol into Newt's neck as he hissed, "Now here's how it's gonna be. I don't believe in killin' white folks unless they're robbin' from me, but I won't think twice 'bout killin' a nigger or a mongrel. So, ya got ten minutes to leave town or we'll string up yer lil quadroon and her half breed ma from this here tree!" Stokes patted the oak's trunk.

The sounds of a wagon and men laughing could be heard approaching.

"Just to show ya we ain't totally heartless, we'll let ya have a couple minutes with yer maw before we personally escort ya outta town. And don't try anythin' funny or we'll burn yer house down. And ya don't wanna have yer maw and her young 'uns livin' outside in the wild, do ya?"

Newt was half conscious but the threats to Birdie as well as his own family came through loud and clear. He tried to rally and sit up but was too weak from the blood he was losing.

The wagon stopped a few feet away from them and Combes jumped down.

"Good God, Lon. Didya kill 'im?" he asked.

"Naw! He's just a lil tired is all. We're gonna take him over to see his maw one last time and then we're gonna have ourselves a farewell party. Ain't we, boy?" he said to Newt. Stokes ordered Combes and the other men to get Newt into the wagon before they continued on to the Phillips' homestead.

As the wagon made its way over the bumpy trail, Newt tried to open his eyes but one was covered with blood from the gash in his temple and the other one was starting to swell. Combes and Stokes rode up front while two men with shotguns kept watch over him in the wagon bed. Newt squinted as he tried to focus on their faces. One of the men looked like Ken Dalton from the blacksmith shop. Although he couldn't be sure, Newt thought the other man looked a lot like Yancey Mayes the postal clerk.

Birdie! Newt struggled to sit up. He needed to get to her and keep her safe from these murderous animals.

"Settle down, lover boy," muttered Dalton as he pointed his shotgun barrel at Newt.

Feeling weak as a kitten, Newt quietly wept as he thought of never seeing Birdie again. It was only an hour ago that they were wrapped in each other's arms on the floor of Birdie's workroom, still flushed from lovemaking. He finally had the woman he cherished within his grasp only to have her yanked cruelly away from him. He wished that Stokes had just shot him dead instead. It would have been a lot less painful. But again, perhaps this was the Klansman's twisted idea of revenge.

"Well now! Looks like the boys have been busy!" Stokes shouted.

The smell of burning wood met Newt's nostrils. As he raised himself up to look over the side of the wagon, he saw that the stable had been set ablaze. The family's cow, calf and two horses were tethered to the rickety fence well away from the flames.

His mother was standing on their front porch in her nightgown shouting obscenities while his two young sisters cowered and sobbed behind her. The words "nigger lover" had been whitewashed down the side of the house.

Newt's bloodthirsty rage had returned. "No! Leave 'em alone!" He pushed himself up and over the side of the wagon, falling onto the sandy ground. Stokes jumped down from the front seat and picked Newt up by the collar.

"Now don't try to be no hero," he warned. "Just go and say yer farewells to yer maw."

Emelia Phillips screamed in terror when she saw her battered, bruised and bloodied son stumble out of the darkness. She ran to him and threw her arms around him.

"Newt! What did they do to ya? And why are they burnin' down our stable?" Emelia untied the headscarf she was wearing and used it to dab the blood off Newt's face.

Stokes came forward and replied, "It's simple, Mizz. Phillips. We're just teachin' yer son here that he shouldn't be messin' 'round with nigra women."

Emilia turned on her son. "What the hell have you done, Newton Phillips?"

Again, Stokes spoke up. "Seems like he's taken quite a shine to a quadroon named Birdie who works at the Montclair. I saw 'em with my own eyes pawin' and grindin' on each other right out in the open."

Emilia Phillips could barely breathe. Her son was caught in the clutches of some colored girl by these hooligans who were notorious local Klansmen. Scared to death that her son would be hung for this, she got on her knees.

"Please mista. Don't kill ma boy. I lost my husband to drink a few years back and Newt's the only man left on the place!"

Stokes removed his hat in a condescending manner and mockingly responded, "Don't worry, my dear lady. I have no intent to kill yer son, though ya must pardon me for havin' to rough 'im up a bit to teach 'im a lesson. But we made a deal. He's gonna leave town or else we'll string up the girl."

Emilia Phillips shouted, "I don't give a damned 'bout the girl. Let ma boy stay!"

Newt spoke up. "No maw! I can't. Not if they're gonna hurt Birdie. I love 'er and plan to make her my wife."

"What the hell has gotten into ya, boy? Yer gonna just let me and your sisters starve to death with no man on the place? Yer ruining all our lives on account of some two-bit whore!" Emilia was indignant.

Newt bristled at his mother's remark about Birdie. Instead, he hugged her and said, "Don't worry ma! I'll head out to Uncle Ernie's over in Palatka and have 'im send over Ralph to help ya out. I'll find me a job and once I get settled, I'll send fer ya."

Emilia cried piteously on Newt's shoulder. When she noticed he was wearing his father's jacket, she sobbed even harder. Now she felt like she was losing them both. "Take care, child!" she whispered as she kissed him on the cheek.

Newt knelt down and hugged his sisters, who he prayed he would see again before they were full grown women. He kissed each of them on the forehead and said, "Ya'll be good and take care o' maw for me."

Stokes was getting impatient. "Okay, let's go." Turning to Emilia, he tipped his hat to her. "Evenin', ma'am." Emilia spit in his general direction.

As the men walked behind Newt with their shotguns and pistols drawn, Emilia's blood boiled. She didn't know who she hated more at that moment - Lonnie Stokes for all the destruction he's caused, Newt for being so foolish, or that goddamn colored gal.

The wagon stopped on the southbound road leading out of town. Stokes jumped down as Dalton and Mayes pushed Newt out of the tail gate.

Once again, Stokes shoved his pistol under Newt's chin and growled, "Now don't forget our deal, boy. Ya stay outta town for good and yer nigra gal gets to live and yer maw keeps 'er house. But if ya set one foot back in St. Augustine, all bets are off! And don't think 'bout sendin' messages to yer lil mulatto gal or yer buddy Hartsfield, 'cause we'll be keepin' a sharp eye on 'em both."

"I mean it, Stokes. Don't touch Birdie or her ma! Or yer a dead man!" shouted Newt.

For the second time that night, Stokes removed his hat and mockingly retorted, "You have my word, sir, as a gentleman."

"Go to hell, you son-of-a-bitch!"

Stokes chuckled as he climbed back into the wagon. "You got some walkin' to do, boy, so ya better get movin'." He picked up the reins and shouted, "Gidd'up!"

As they pulled away and headed back towards town, Yancey Mayes was puzzled. "I don't understand, Lon. Why the hell didn't we just kill 'im?"

Stokes maliciously grinned. "Don't worry none, Yancey. He'll end up doin' it himself soon enough.

Newt shouted every obscenity he could think of at the retreating wagon. Even though the bleeding was starting to subside, his head felt like it was being split in two by a hatchet. He also couldn't take a breath without a searing pain ripping into his side. Stokes must have busted a rib.

Newt's thoughts turned to Birdie as he limped along the dark, lonely road with only the crickets and the moon for company. As he remembered how breathtaking she looked under the moonlight earlier that evening, a crushing wave of sadness swept over him. The reality of never seeing her again was now sinking in.

Newt fell on his knees and like a baying wolf, cried out to the sky in a spine-chilling primal howl, "BIRDIE!!!!!!"

Birdie lay in her bed, feverishly tossing and turning. She could still feel Newt's hands caressing her. She looked over at the floral crown lying on her dresser and remembered how he had sweetly kissed her palm and fingertips. Smiling, she tucked that hand up under her cheek and eventually drifted off to sleep.

Too excited to see Newt, Birdie rose earlier than usual that morning. Even Hortensia was still in bed by the time Birdie was dressed and out the door.

As she approached the hotel's back entrance, she saw Rita and Ella confronting a thin, middle aged woman with unkempt strawberry blond hair, a dirty apron and old black work boots. The woman's face was contorted with rage. Birdie slowed down her gait, wondering if it was safe to approach as the stranger appeared ready to brawl.

As Rita spotted Birdie getting ready to come up the path, she surreptitiously shook her head as if warning Birdie to stay away. The woman noticed Rita's non-verbal cue and turned around. As her eyes met Birdie's, she scowled.

"This gotta be her!" the woman shouted. Her eyes narrowed as she asked, "You Birdie?"

Although Birdie was frightened, she automatically nodded causing the woman to rush up and slap her so hard across the face that she fell backwards into a hedge. Rita and Ella both came running. Isaiah, who had just left the grounds keeping shed and saw the ruckus, dropped the shovel and rake he was carrying and hurried over.

Ella's face was a thundercloud and her fists were balled up and ready for a fight. "Don't you dare lay a hand on Birdie, ya white trash! She ain't never done nothin' bad to nobody!"

As Rita and Isaiah helped a stunned Birdie out of the hedge, the woman whirled around on Ella. "I ain't takin' any sass off you, nigra. And for yer information, she DID do my family wrong! It's because of this quadroon hussy that the Klan ran my boy outta town last night and set fire on my property!"

Birdie was shocked. This crazed woman was Newt's mother! But what was this about him being run out of town?

"What'd they do to Newt?" Birdie asked.

"I just tole ya, stupid bitch. They forced him to leave town and never come back, 'cause they saw ya'll together - tonguing and gropin' each other. Just like the slut you are. The Klan don't take kindly to our white boys getting mixed up with you coloreds. They just 'bout beat his brains out and tole him to leave and not come back or they'd hang ya. My fool son decided to play hero and leave to save yer worthless nigra hide! I wish to God that he'd stayed and let ya DIE instead!"

Emilia Phillips howled as she jumped on Birdie, scratching at her like a wildcat and trying to rip out her hair. Birdie screamed and tried her best to wrestle Newt's mother off her. Ella was about to pummel Emilia, but Isaiah pushed her aside, stooped down and scooped Emilia Phillips off Birdie. Rita immediately ran to Birdie's aid and helped her up again.

"Put me down ya black fool!" shouted Emilia. "Don't cha see she lost me my only son? I ain't finished with her yet!!"

"Like hell you ain't!" screamed Ella. "You keep beatin' on her and you'll have me to tend to!"

Isaiah set Emilia back down and admonished her, "You done said yer piece and beat up on the gal. You just git now befo' we get the law on ya."

Emilia laughed at Isaiah. "The law! Ha! Lots o' them are friends o' the Klan an' won't be in such a hurry to help ya." As she turned to leave, Emilia glared at Birdie, whose clothes were disheveled and face tearstained. "You mind yo'self, gal. I ain't done with ya!" After spitting at Birdie, Emilia took her leave.

Rita now took charge of the situation. She needed to get everyone out of the way before the rest of the staff arrived. She certainly didn't need Iris Sutton finding out what happened.

She patted Ella on the arm and said, "Thank you Ella. Ya did good. Now run inside, wash your face and fix your hair before Tangie notices you're runnin' late with your chores."

Ella gave Birdie a quick hug before heading back to the kitchen.

"Isaiah, help me get Birdie into the groundskeepers shed. I'll clean her up there."

Each of them took Birdie by an elbow and gently guided her to the wooden shack. There was a work table and bench along one wall and this was where they sat Birdie.

"I'll be right back. I'm just gonna dash into the kitchen and make sure that Netta has everything under control. Birdie's had a bad shock, so I'll bring her back some cookin' brandy for her nerves." Rita left the shack in a flash of colorful petticoats.

Up to this point, Birdie had been in a trance. Everything was unreal - the attack by Emilia Phillips, the racial slurs, the cuts and bruises now on her body. It was as if Birdie was looking at someone else's life through someone else's eyes. She didn't feel anything at that moment. Only two words kept repeating themselves over and over in her head. Newt's gone.

Despite her stupor, Birdie tried to take in her surroundings and realized that she was in the gardener's shed. She remembered the last time she was alone in there with Newt. It was when he had presented her with Sugar to help her with cope with her grief over missing her baby. Her Clara. The memory brought fresh tears to her eyes.

Isaiah saw Birdie crying and sat down on the bench next to her. Although he prided himself on being a peaceful man, his blood was boiling. He had seen too much over the years when it came to the Klan. He had known too many people who had friends and family members lynched for crimes which would usually merit a slap on the wrist for Caucasians. Isaiah was enraged that they should target two of the nicest and most harmless young folks he ever met.

Isaiah put his arm around Birdie's shoulder and drew her in close like he did with his own children when they were hurt. Birdie bawled inconsolably. "I love him so much, Isaiah. We were gonna go up North and get married."

"Aw Birdie, please don't take on so. You'll make yo'self sick."

"But Newt's gone! And I'll never see him again." Birdie wept so furiously that her head was beginning to hurt.

The older man looked up at the bare wooden ceiling rafters thoughtfully as he decided to enlighten Birdie on a few things which Newt had asked him to never share with her.

"Birdie, I truly believe that there ain't nothin' in this whole world that'll keep that boy away from ya. Not even the Klan."

"But he thinks he's protectin' me by stayin' away," whimpered Birdie.

"Did ya know that the first time that boy ever set eyes on ya, he was smitten? Every time you went out to the garden to get somethin' or was outside scrubbin', he'd stop what he was doin' and just stare at ya. One time, Mista Prescott came outside and hollered at po' ole Newt somethin' fierce 'bout daydreamin' on the job. Gave that boy a tongue lashin' he never forgot!"

Birdie had stopped weeping and listened quietly as Isaiah continued.

"Then when Mista Prescott Junior came back from New York wearin' all dem fine, expensive city clothes, he'd come outside and get Newt to find him the best flower in the garden to put in his lapel. That's when the boy got the notion to pick a few extra flowers and place them with yo' thangs in the mudroom every day after that."

Johnny never gave me those flowers, Birdie thought. It was Newt the whole time. It was so obvious. God, why was I such a damned fool not to see it?

"And when Newt found out what Mista Prescott Junior did to ya, he just 'bout beat the life outta that man. If I hadn't o' come by, I do believe he woulda killed 'im." Birdie gasped. This was all new information to her.

Hearing about Newt's unbeknownst acts of love made Birdie remember all those earlier times when she was embarrassed and sometimes repulsed by his him. This made her hate herself all the more. She started to cry again.

"Now Birdie," Isaiah said softly, "I ain't tellin' ya these things to make ya feel worse. I tole ya all this to make ya see how much the boy truly loved ya. And if he loves ya that much, I do believe he will do everythin' in his power to get ya back. Birdie," he said sternly as he gingerly grabbed her wrist, "don't ya ever give up hope."

The combination of Isaiah's soothing deep voice and these last words gave her a bit of comfort.

Just then Rita returned with the bottle of brandy, a glass, a wet cloth and Birdie's reticule.

"Thanks for lookin' after her Isaiah. Now how are we gonna explain Newt's absence? Miss Sutton and Mr. Prescott will wanna know, and if they find out the truth, Birdie here might lose her job."

"I'll just tell 'em that Newt had family business to tend to outta town and will be gone fo' a spell."

Gone for a spell, Birdie repeated silently. I hope Isaiah is right. I can't cope with losing Newt. I just can't. I'll die if I never get the chance to hold him again and tell him how much I love him.

Chapter 32

Birdie's hopes of being pregnant with Newt's child were dashed when her cycle began a few weeks later. This latest setback was too much for her to bear. She was torn apart inside and unable to talk to anyone about her heartache other than Rita, Isaiah and Ella.

Even worse, Birdie's vivid imagination evolved into a paranoia that the Klan was watching her every move and ready to hang her at any moment. As she only felt safe at home and at the Montclair, Birdie eventually stopped going into town during her free time. Walking to and from the hotel, especially in the dark, was pure terror. Each snap of a twig or rustling of leaves sent her pulse racing.

Hortensia was getting more and more worried about Birdie's lack of appetite and sickly pallor. She called for Doc Jennings to come examine Birdie but, not finding anything physically out of order, he merely diagnosed her as anemic and prescribed her a vile tasting tonic which was said to work wonders.

The sleepless nights at home became a living hell as Birdie's mind raced with thoughts of Newt. Where was he? Was he even still alive or did he eventually succumb to the injuries she heard he had received? Would she ever see him again or would he in time forget all about her and find someone else to love? Someone he could be seen with and not fear social disapproval?

Daytime was not much better, especially when she was at work. She couldn't bear being in the gardens any more. Every time Birdie would have to walk by them, she expected to see Newt wave at her before resuming his digging, pruning or hauling. He had carefully worked every inch of these grounds which were vivid reminders of all the encounters they had there. Thinking of their last night together in the rose garden where he made her the crown of flowers and sensually kissed her hand always brought on bitter tears.

But as difficult as the garden was for her, having to spend every afternoon in her workroom was even worse. Birdie couldn't bring herself to look at the quilts which they had laid upon, so she added them to the trash pile for burning.

Birdie still kept the crown on her dresser. The flowers had long since dried up and the leaves turned brown. One day, Hortensia was about to discard it when Birdie flew into a rage. "Leave it alone! Don't touch it! Don't ever touch it!"

Hortensia flinched at her daughter's angry outburst and at that point she was certain that Birdie's problem was not just anemia. She wondered if maybe it had anything to do with Arthur. Birdie hadn't mentioned him since New Year's Eve. Perhaps they had a quarrel. Suddenly a thought occurred to Hortensia. Could Birdie be pregnant again? Dear Lord, I hope not, she thought as she crossed herself. Besides, the doctor surely would have discovered it during his examination.

Hortensia was perplexed but resolved not to push the issue until Birdie was ready to talk. All she could do for now is to make sure her daughter was eating and getting enough rest.

Birdie wished she could share her burden with her mother but if Hortensia discovered that she and Birdie had barely escaped a Klan lynching because of Birdie's indiscretion with Newt, she would go apoplectic. Hortensia was by nature very neurotic and anxious, so the least little thing could send her over the edge. No, she must never find out. It was only because of the masquerade she put on for her mother's sake that Birdie was able to survive those first few months after Newt's departure.

At least she had Rita to confide in. The cook had become a second mother figure to Birdie and whenever they had the rare quiet moment in the kitchen, they would go to the pantry where they would sit among the tinned goods, cheeses, and cured meats while Rita let Birdie cry on her shoulder. Rita wouldn't say much because she knew that Birdie was in a state of grief and needed to cry when the mood struck her. She would often just rub the girl's back until the sobs subsided.

Because of Birdie's aversion to the garden, she didn't see much of Isaiah these days. Every so often she would encounter him in the mudroom in the morning before he reported to Mr. Prescott. He would often pat her on consolingly on the arm and ask, "How you doin', chile?" One day he presented her with a worn blue kerchief that was torn in one corner.

"I was cleanin' out de shed yesterday and found this ole kerchief o' Newt's and thought you might wanna have it to hold it fer 'im til ya see 'im again."

Birdie's eyes watered. She didn't know which warmed her heart more - having something of Newt's or Isaiah's certainty that they would eventually be reunited. "Thank you, Isaiah," she choked.

Of course, her greatest source of strength was Ella, who had been her protector and sister if not in blood but in spirit as long as Birdie could remember. Despite Ella's long hours of labor in the scullery, she always took time to give Birdie a quick hug or squeeze in her arm whenever she would pass her in the kitchen.

She still came over to Birdie's house on Sundays like she'd been doing for years. Even though Birdie's growing agoraphobia put a halt to their weekly walks through the town, Ella didn't mind. She regaled Birdie with the latest tittle tattle as they sat on Birdie's front porch.

One Sunday evening as Ella was leaving, Hortensia took Ella aside.

"I'm worried sick about Birdie. Please, Ella, I know something is going on. Tell me what's wrong with my girl," Hortensia pleaded.

Ella was in a quandary. Although she dearly loved Mrs. Fairfax as much as her own mother, she had also promised Birdie that she would never say a word about the whole business with Newt and the Klan. She did something she thought she would never do. She boldly lied to the kind woman who had welcomed her into home and treated her like a daughter for most of her life.

"Aw, Mizz Fairfax, no need t' worry," Ella said as she gave the older woman a wide grin of false confidence. "Birdie's just missin' the baby is all."

"But I thought she'd gotten over the birth by now," Hortensia said doubtfully.

"Well, even though she ain't got the baby with her, she still birthed it and feels connected to it. That'll never go away. If you had to give up Birdie after she was born, wouldn't you also be feelin' low now and then?"

"I guess so," Hortensia replied with uncertainty. "I've just never seen her like this."

"This is just a spell, is all. She'll be her ole self soon. I'll help see t' that!" Ella said earnestly. She gave Hortensia a hug as she left.

I hope I was convincin' enough 'cause I can't go on lyin' like this, thought Ella. She wished she could confide in Ronnie but, like the rest of the Montclair staff, he thought that Newt left town to help kinfolk. Not wishing to betray her best friend's trust, Ella resolved to remain silent for the time being.

As Newt had promised his mother, he sent Ralph Clayton over from Palatka, who took up the caretaking duties of his Aunt Emilia's place. A few years older than Newt and a bit of a hell raiser when he was on the booze, even Ralph was horrified at the sorry state of his cousin when Newt showed up at their farm one night looking like he's been mauled by a bear.

After Newt told the family about the blood-chilling encounter with Stokes and company, it was decided that Ralph would be sent out to St. Augustine as soon as possible. Meanwhile, Newt looked for work. He talked a lot about a girl named Birdie and how he wanted to eventually get her out of St. Augustine so they could head north and get married.

Ralph scrubbed off the racial slur that the Klan had scrawled onto the house. He also rebuilt the stable, replanted the crops which had gone to seed and tended to the animals. Within a few months, the property looked better than ever. Emilia was well pleased and asked Ralph to move in permanently. Having him around helped her cope with the losing Newt and made her feel safe for the first time since that terrible night.

Ralph hadn't planned on settling in St. Augustine and was unsure as to whether he was keen on the idea. He had a thriving moonshine business that he hated to give up. When he discussed his reluctance with Emilia, she cunningly pointed out that there were several large ranches nearby with ranch hands who would be more than happy to give him custom instead of having to drive into town for their libations. "Lotsa thirsty menfolk 'round these parts," she said. "We'll have a field full o' corn in the fall. You'd make some purty good money, especially durin' the cattle drives."

That was enough to convince Ralph. He went into town the next day to send a wire to his pa. He was going to need his still dismantled and carefully transported to his Aunt Emilia's.

Over the next few weeks, Ella tried patiently to convince Birdie to expand her horizons beyond those of the house and the Montclair. At first, they just ventured over to Ella's house where Birdie visited with Ophelia and watched the younger children play. How she wished to be that young again and have no real worries or troubles.

The next weekend, Ella suggested a slightly longer stroll by the sea wall on the bay. She'd forgotten that this spot held bittersweet memories for Birdie as that was where she and

Newt had shared their first kiss after she returned from Fernandina Beach, but Birdie bit her lip and went on the walk, averting her eyes.

Clueless to Birdie's thoughts, Ella smiled and said, "You doin' good. And there ain't no Klan out here t'mess with ya. And if they do, they'll have t' go through me first."

Birdie squeezed Ella's hand. She knew this wasn't mere empty talk. If anyone was brave enough to take a stand against the Klan, it was Ella.

Emilia Phillips made one of her rare appearances in town one Sunday to deliver eggs to Joe Hardy who ran the bakery on Cuna Street. He lived in a small apartment above his business. After Emilia finished her transaction with Joe, she headed back down the steps. Before she reached the bottom, she caught sight of that wretched quadroon walking with the loudmouth nigra from the hotel.

Emilia felt her blood pressure rise as she thought of how her son was almost beaten to death and then banished from the city. According to what she's heard through letters from Ernie, her fool son was STILL in love with this slut. It was time to put an end to this.

Emilia squared her shoulders and marched down the remainder of the steps. By then, the girls had spotted her. Birdie's eyes grew round in fright while Ella's jaw tightened as she mentally braced herself for either a verbal or physical assault.

Emilia immediately went on the offensive. "How dare ya walk 'round this town shamelessly, ya nigra slut! Yer the reason my life's been destroyed. I wish to the great Lawd above that they had gone ahead and strung you up instead."

Birdie felt her heart racing as her hands turned to ice. She also started to feel dizzy. I need to get home, she kept telling herself.

Ella, aware that Birdie was in distress, jumped in. "Shut yo' mouth and go 'way, white trash! We don't want no trouble."

Emilia angrily replied, "No one's talkin' to ya, nigra. Besides, one good thing done come outta all this." A dangerous smile spread across her thin chapped lips as she uttered with glee, "Ya see, my Newt done foun' himself a good woman, a good WHITE woman, over there in Palatka and got himself married last week! I got a letter from my brother yesterday with the good news! So, you can forget 'bout any designs you may o' had on ma boy."

Birdie grabbed the wall of the house she was standing next to. She felt woozy and couldn't breathe. Suddenly the world turned black and she crumbled to the ground.

Ella screamed for help as Emilia returned to her wagon feeling vindicated and very pleased with herself. There was only one thing left to do and then her son would finally be free from the clutches of that damned bitch.

"Birdie! Please wake up!" Ella cried as she patted Birdie's cheek. "Somebody help us!" she screamed. With it being Sunday, the town was virtually empty. "Oh Birdie. Please open yo' eyes."

It was then that Eddie Hartsfield happened to come strolling around the corner. He had been fishing off the bridge over the bay and the long string of snook hanging over his shoulder attested to a very successful catch. When he caught site of Ella's distress and Birdie laying in a heap in the ground, he came running over.

"What happened?" he asked as he patted Birdie's hand.

Ella paused for a split second before answering, "She been feelin' poorly lately. I 'spect she overdid it by walkin' too much in dis heat."

Eddie nodded. He had seen plenty of women faint or even gone insane from the oppressive Florida heat. It's no wonder given all the silly undergarments and layers of clothing that they wear. Now the Indians, they have the right idea.

"Here, take these," Eddie gave the string of fish and fishing rod to Ella. He then picked up Birdie who, given her loss of appetite, was extremely lightweight. "Let's get 'er home."

When Hortensia saw her unconscious daughter being carried up the garden path by Eddie, she screamed.

"Mija! What happened to her?" she demanded as Eddie brought Birdie into the house and gently placed her on the settee.

"To be honest, Mizz Fairfax, Birdie ain't been takin' her 'nemia medicine lately. While we were walkin' in town, she started to feel dizzy and fainted by the bakery." Ella felt bad that her story will no doubt result in Birdie being forced to drink more of the horrible tonic.

"I think she's comin' around," said Eddie as Birdie started to moan. Hortensia knelt by her side, weeping and kissing her daughter on the forehead while both Eddie and Ella took their leave.

As they reached the garden gate, Ella decided to speak up. "Say....uh...ain't ya a good friend o' Newt's?"

"Sure," replied Eddie. "I've known him for years. Shame he had to leave town so quickly."

"Yeah," said Ella slowly. "Have you heard anythin' 'bout him takin' a wife recently?"

Eddie's eyes rounded in shock. "Why no! He was always sweet on your friend Birdie. Hey, is that why she fainted? Who said Newt got married?"

"Oh, it's just somethin' that's been goin' 'round town," Ella replied.

After they parted ways, Eddie decided to pay Newt's ma a visit.

Ralph pulled a rag from his overalls and mopped his sweaty brow. Despite it being late in the day, the heat was still relentless. After being stooped over for the past hour patching up the chicken coop, it felt good to stand and stretch out his lower back. In the distance, he heard the unmistakable sounds of an approaching horse.

Ralph peered down the dirt road and recognized the rider as Newt's friend Eddie from the store.

Raising his hand in greeting, Ralph called out, "Howdy Eddie!"

"Hey there, Ralph," replied Eddie amiably as he dismounted, carrying a paper wrapped parcel under one arm.

"Whatcha got there?" asked Ralph.

"Ever since my fishin' buddy Newt left, I've been catchin' his share as well as my own. I thought I'd spread the wealth around!"

Ralph chuckled, "That's mighty neighborly of ya, Eddie."

"Oh, not at all. Newt was like a brother to me," replied Eddie. "Least I can do while he's gone is check on ya'll now and again. Looks like you settled in very well, Ralph."

"You bet," said Ralph. "Lotsa folks been mighty kind to us since Newt left."

At that moment Emilia, who appeared in the doorway to toss out a tub of dirty dishwater, spotted Eddie talking to Ralph and overheard him say, "I just heard the good news about Newt."

Dammit! Those two nigras didn't waste any time runnin' their mouths, Emilia thought. The last thing I need is the Hartsfield boy sniffing around here. Before Ralph, who was looking completely confused, could utter a word, Emilia cheerfully called out, "Eddie Hartsfield! How good to see ya! Come on over here!"

Eddie tipped his hat as he walked up the front porch steps. "Good afternoon, Mrs. Phillips. Here's some snook for ya - freshly caught!"

Emilia clapped her hands in artificial glee. "Why, how kind of ya! Thank ya so much."

"My pleasure, ma'am," said Eddie. "I was just sayin' to Ralph here that congratulations seem to be in order..."

"Oh, yes," said Emilia, who quickly added, "Ralph, could ya go get me some logs from the woodpile?"

"Uh...sure thing, Aunt Em," replied a puzzled Ralph as he headed towards the woodshed behind the house.

Emilia turned her attention back to Eddie. "Yeah, I got the good news a few days ago in a letter from my brother. Newt met himself a nice gal and they got hitched right away. You could've knocked me over with a feather!"

Eddie was astonished. "I must say, ma'am, I'm pretty surprised. It just seems so unlike Newt."

"Well, I reckon she's a very special kinda gal if she was able to steal my son's heart as quick as she did," cooed Emilia.

"That's great to hear. I can't wait to meet her," said Eddie.

"Oh, I don't believe Newt will be returnin' to St. Augustine. His wife Katie - that's her name - wants to stay near her hometown," replied Emilia.

"Whereabout's is that? Maybe I'll pay 'em a visit," remarked Eddie.

Emilia felt the panic rise as she watched her lies start to spin out of control. But she managed to maintain her composure as she responded, "Ya know, I can't fer the life o' me remember the name o' that town. It was some Injun soundin' name. It's way down south o' here – near Orlando I believe."

"Oh well, just let me know once you find out where it is. I reckon I better be heading back before it gets dark," said Eddie.

"Well thanks for stoppin' by, Eddie, and thanks again fer the fish!"

As she watched Eddie and the horse retreat back towards town, Emilia sighed deeply with relief. That was too damned close. From this point onwards, they're going to need to keep to themselves.

Chapter 33

Emilia was overcome when she saw her dear brother Ernie drive up one morning in a rickety wagon which held the components of Ralph's still. She hadn't seen him since her husband Jeb's funeral a few years ago so they had some catching up to do. Plus, she was desperate for news of her son who she hadn't seen in over six months. After patiently waiting for Ernie and Ralph to unload and set up the contraption, she invited Ernie inside for some fried corn mush and a chat.

"How's ma Newt doin', Ernie?" she anxiously inquired.

"Well, he's purty damn good in the fields but he don't know shit 'bout moonshinin'." Ernie chuckled.

"Aw come on, Ernie! This ain't no joke. I ain't seen 'im for so long. Please tell me how he's doin!" Emilia begged.

"I'm sorry, 'Melia." Ernie said contritely, "Yo' boy is doin' fine. He's lookin' better nowadays from when he first come to us. Them Klansmen sho' did a number on 'im, didn't they?"

Emilia didn't want to talk about Stokes so instead she changed her line of inquiry, "Does he ever ask after us?" Ernie and Emilia had exchanged a couple of letters over the past several months. In her correspondence, Emilia would include messages meant for Newt, but he couldn't write back fearing that his communication might cause further reprisals from the Klan.

"From time to time he'll ask me 'bout the news you write t' me, but the one person he misses and talks 'bout the most is this Birdie. It's been Birdie this and Birdie that ever since he come to ma house. Yo' son is stubborn like you. Once he gits a notion, he won't let go. And now he's got it into his thick head that he's gonna have the gal smuggled outta town so she can join him and git married. In fact..." Ernie reached into his coat pocket and pulled out a folded up piece of paper. "He asked me to make sure this note gits to 'er.

Dammit to hell, thought Emilia. The boy is still smitten, and now he was risking his uncle's life. It was time to put the final part of her plan into play.

Artfully arranging her facial features to look genuinely concerned, Emilia sighed. "Oh Ernie. I'm afraid I got bad news fer ma poor boy. Truth is that Birdie Fairfax done run off and married some Negro servant in that hotel she worked at. Happened a few months back or so I hear. Of course," Emilia lowered her voice "the word 'round town is that she done got herself pregnant and had to git married."

Ernie scratched his head. "Ya don't say! Newt sure set a great store by this Birdie. This news'll just about kill 'im."

Emelia shook her head. "Don't fergit, Ernie. You say ma boy's stubborn like me. Well, he's strong like me, too. He'll git over the gal 'cause he's survivor like his maw! As soon as he gits that quadroon off his mind, he'll settle down into a good job, get himself a nice place and marry a good white woman. You just see!"

Ernie was uncertain. "I 'spose yer right but I ain't too sure." Lifting up the note, he asked, "And what am I 'sposed to do 'bout this?"

"I'll take care of that fer ya," replied Emilia as she took the slip of paper from her brother's hand.

Later than evening, long after Ralph, Ernie and the girls had turned in, Emilia tiptoed over to the fireplace. She took the note bearing Newt's childlike scrawl from her apron pocket. Not bothering to read what it said, she tossed it into the blaze and watched the flames swallow up the paper, which curled up and slowly turned into ash.

"This is fer yer own good, boy."

Birdie was a walking shell of a woman for the next few weeks. It was as if she had left her body and was watching everything from a distance. She felt like she was trapped in a cold, grey world while everyone else lived, loved and laughed in full color.

Newt was married. The more she had said it to herself, the more unreal it sounded. At first Birdie refused to believe it but then as it slowly started to register, an overpowering combination of anger and sadness washed over her. How could he marry someone else so soon? Was he just trifling with Birdie all this time until he could get his hands on a white woman? Was everything he ever said to her just one big lie?

Early the next morning before work she took the dried up floral crown and blue kerchief with her. She strolled towards the sea wall and tossed the crown into the bay. She sat on the wall for a few minutes and watched as the wreath slowly drifted over the ripples which were tinted orange by the rising sun.

Later on that day, she went to see Isaiah who was planting tomatoes in the vegetable garden.

"Howdy Birdie. Looks like we 'bout to git some rain. These tomatoes'll be thankful fo' it."

Birdie didn't respond. She pulled Newt's kerchief from her apron pocket and handed it to Isaiah. "Here, take this Isaiah. I don't want it no more. Use it as a cleanin' rag or somethin'."

Isaiah slowly stood up and cocked his head quizzically at Birdie. "What's wrong, child?"

Without emotion, Birdie replied, "Newt got married. I won't be seein' him again." Isaiah watched her as she retreated to the kitchen.

Looking down at the kerchief balled up in his hand, he shook his head. No, something about this didn't feel right. That boy loved Birdie too much. Something was definitely wrong.

Once inside, Birdie straightened her spine and fixed her hair in the mudroom's mirror. For the first time she noticed the extreme contrast between her pallid yellow skin and the dark bluish circles under her eyes. Her rapid weight loss left her with sunken cheeks and a very sharp angled face, making her look much older than her almost 20 years.

No! No more of this self-pity, Birdie resolved to herself. It was time to move on. There was nothing left to grieve for. Her days of being a crying, sickly weakling were now over. She did it once before after Clara was taken from her, and she will do it again.

Newt sat motionless on the front porch as he was serenaded by the frogs, crickets and cicadas. The moon and stars were hidden by a thick, low lying cloud cover so he stared out into virtual nothingness. The darkness only enhanced his mood as his Uncle Ernie's words still rang in his mind. Birdie was married and with child. The “Negro servant” was no doubt Arthur Dickson.

The woman he cherished above his own life has taken up with Arthur and is having his baby. But is the baby even Arthur’s? There’s a chance she could be carryin’ my child, Newt thought. All the beating he took from Stokes and being forced from his home was for nothing. Birdie was lost to him now.

For a moment, Newt entertained the thought of returning to St. Augustine. What the hell? Birdie would be safe now that she married a Negro. But the thought of seeing her married to another man and watching them raising a child – possibly his own – would be much worse to bear than anything Stokes and his men could do.

Newt scowled as he rose from the wooden rocker he had been sitting on. Feeling his way to the stable, he saddled up Ranger, his uncle’s favorite horse. Then he went around to the back of the house and reached under the porch where Ralph had stored numerous bottles of moonshine before he had left for St. Augustine. Once Newt had one in his grasp, he pulled it out and headed back to the stable. He tucked the bottle under his arm as he climbed up onto the saddle.

Turning south onto the dusty road which led out of town, he and Ranger disappeared into the night.

Ralph Phillips mopped his brow to keep the sweat out of his eyes as he drove into town. He disliked going into the city. The trolley cars crammed with Yankee tourists spooked his horses. The buildings and houses were too close together, and the law was too close by for Ralph's comfort. His still had been making him a tidy profit. Rafferty's men have been drinking him dry. If it wasn't for Emilia, he would be back at the house bottling up his latest batch right now.

His aunt flew into a rage a few days ago when she received his pa's letter with the news that Newt had flown the coop without nary a word to anyone. Ralph thought his cousin was a damned fool getting so worked up over some half breed. His aunt Emilia said the gal was married and pregnant anyway. Why the hell didn't Newt just come back home? Now that the girl was out of the picture, surely the Klan won't be bothering him. Ralph sighed and shrugged. None of it made any sense to him.

He turned onto King Street and looked for the Montclair Hotel. His aunt had sent him over to collect any pay that was still owed to Newt. She had reckoned that if he was going to leave the family high and dry, they were due at least a little compensation.

Once Ralph located the resort, he parked the rig on a side street and made his way around the back. A large black man with grizzled greying hair was lifting large bags of fertilizer from the back of an extended hauling wagon and carrying them over to a vegetable garden on the other side of the building. Thinking that the Negro might be able point him in the right direction, Ralph approached him as he was returning back to the wagon.

"Hey!"

Isaiah stopped when he heard the shout and looked over. Upon seeing the red headed, freckle faced stranger, he thought for a split second that Newt had returned, but this man was shorter, stockier and a bit older.

"What can I do fo' ya?"

"I need to see someone about some wages that are owed to my cousin." replied Ralph.

"And who would yer cousin be?" asked Isaiah, although he believed he already knew.

"Newt....I mean Newton Phillips. Ya prob'ly know 'im. He was a gardener here."

"I sho did!" said Isaiah, "He was one o' the best workers we had." Isaiah paused as he decided to pry a little. "I hear tell he got hisself married."

Ralph looked baffled. "Huh? I dunno who tole ya that. Newt ain't married."

Isaiah nodded in silence while inside he leapt for joy. He knew it couldn't be true! He couldn't wait to see Birdie and tell her the good news.

Ralph was growing impatient and wanted to get this business done as soon as possible so he could get back. "Say, you couldn't tell me who I need to talk to, could ya?"

Isaiah pointed towards the building. "Go 'round to the back do' and ask fo' Miss Sutton."

For the rest of the morning, Isaiah would glance towards the kitchen door every now and then hoping to catch sight of Birdie or even her friend Ella, so intent was he on restoring some hope to that young lady's life.

Looking up, he noticed that the dark grey clouds were already moving in. It is a common joke among the locals that you never needed a watch in Florida because if it was raining, it was three o'clock, and it seemed like today was going to be no different. With Newt gone, Isaiah was now doing the work of two men until they can get a replacement, so he needed to get moving.

He stepped up the pace as he hauled the manure sacks over to various points of the garden. When he dropped a bag over by the jasmine trellis, Isaiah felt the first knifelike pain rip through his chest. Leaning one hand on the trellis for support, he tried to catch his breath but couldn't. He felt like a mule had just kicked him in the middle of his ribs. His arms were starting to go numb and the world started to spin.

Isaiah tried to call out to Lito who was digging a trench over by the arbor but he couldn't get the words out. He fell to his knees and gasped one last time before his lifeless body hit the grass.

PART II

1915

Chapter 34

Ella's grip on the rolling pin tightened as she felt yet another sharp jab under her ribcage. Turning from the floured kitchen counter where she had been busily preparing a pie crust, she lovingly placed a hand on her protruding belly.

Her three boys had never kicked and moved around this much. This child is definitely a girl and most likely a dancer, Ella thought to herself with a silent chuckle.

Although Ronnie was proud of his sons, Ella knew that deep down he fervently hoped this next baby will be the girl he had been wanting for a long time.

The father-to-be stuck his head inside the kitchen doorway. "Ella, the Hathaways are checkin' out...." Noticing his wife's discomfort, Ronnie hurried to her side and anxiously asked, "You all right? Is it time? Do I need to go fo' yo' ma or Birdie?"

Ella grinned as she shook her head. "Now you know it ain't time yet. We still got another month and a half to go. Besides, Birdie would be at work right now. Baby's just kickin', is all." Standing tall, smoothing her hair and straightening her apron, she added, "Now let's go see the Hathaways off."

Just over the bridge from downtown and south on Anastasia Island, the Simms Guest House for Colored Travelers provided accommodations for Negro visitors who were prohibited from staying at the city's main resorts.

Ronnie had found the large, dilapidated two story house shortly after he and Ella had married. Because it needed a lot of work and was located in a remote corner of the island, they were able to secure it at a decent price.

Over the following year, Ronnie and his brothers worked on the building's repairs while Ella, Ophelia, Birdie and Hortensia helped clean the interior and sew up curtains, pillows, bedding and various other linens.

When he wasn't working on his own guest house, Ronnie worked at the Montclair on a temporary basis for a few months. Ella raised their three boys while setting up the guest rooms as well as their own family quarters in the expansive house.

When the Simms realized that they were not going to have enough money to finish furnishing the last two of the six bedrooms, Birdie saved the day by offering them much of the money that Prescott had inexplicably given her all those years ago under the guise of a Christmas bonus.

Ella was shocked to see so much cash rolled up in Birdie's hand. When she asked where it came from, Birdie was evasive and insisted that Ella not look a gift horse in the mouth. Ronnie thanked Birdie and made a point of telling her that the money was a loan and that it would be paid back with interest. Again, Birdie was insistent that it was a gift and not to be paid back.

In the end, the Simms decided to make Birdie a silent partner in their new venture and that she was to receive a small portion of future profits, and as their business grew over the years, they kept their promise. Birdie, in return, would create decorative items for the inn such as throw pillows, quilts, table cloths, napkins, and formal aprons.

Aaron and Ethel Hathaway, a middle-aged couple from Detroit, were waiting in the front parlor. Their worn black leather travel trunk was on the front porch and ready to be loaded into Ronnie's wagon.

"We just wanted to thank you for your hospitality and settle up our bill," said Mr. Hathaway. A dentist by trade, he and his wife started coming down to Florida over the past few years. They had heard and read about St. Augustine but because they had no family in the area, they had nowhere to stay until the Simms opened up their inn. Now they were able to come down each year for a few weeks and take in the tropical weather and witness the splendor of Flagler's resorts themselves, even if it was only from the outside.

"Yes, everything was lovely as always," said Mrs. Sybil Hathaway in her usual breathless manner. She was a short, wiry woman who had a weak disposition and was diagnosed with bad lungs. She loved Florida's warm climate.

"Well, Ella and I are mighty sorry to see ya'll leave," replied Ronnie sincerely. He liked the Hathaways. They had money but didn't put on any airs about it. "But we hope you'll be comin' back to stay with us next year."

"Oh, no question about that!" exclaimed Mr. Hathaway before he proceeded to pay his bill. As the men conducted their business, Ella handed a basket of fried chicken and fresh biscuits to Mrs. Hathaway to take on the train as the dining car would be for white passengers only.

Once Ronnie left with the Hathaways for the train station, Ella headed back to the kitchen to finish her pies. She sighed with contentment as she picked up the finished round crust from the counter and placed it over the sliced apples, sugar and cinnamon that covered the bottom crust in the pan. As she started to flute the edges, Ella felt a stabbing pain in her lower abdomen which made her grab the edge of the counter and bite her lip hard to prevent a scream from escaping. She didn't want to scare her children or the other guests.

That was when she felt the familiar trickle run down her leg. Her waters had just broken, and Ronnie would not be back for another hour or so. Ella took a deep breath and tried her best not to panic.

She straightened up and walked over to the door. Keeping her voice as calm and steady as she could, she called out to her oldest son, "Lawrence! Where you at, boy? Oh, there you are. I need you to run next door and tell Miss Wilson to come on over right away."

Twelve-year-old Lawrence Simms, who was coming in from the back porch, looked quizzically at his mother. Before he could utter a word, Ella cut him off. "Now don't waste my time by asking any questions, boy. Go on and get Miss Wilson. Now!"

Lawrence who vividly recalled the events surrounding the births of his two younger brothers, knew that the look in his mother's eyes and the tone in her voice meant that he better move fast.

"Yes, ma!" he shouted as he ran past her and out the front door, taking the porch steps two at a time.

Ella slowly made her way upstairs to her bedroom, mentally noting where the other guests were. The Parkers were in town visiting cousins for the day, the Nelsons were out for a stroll and Mr. Lee had been out fishing since sunrise. As she reclined on the bed, Ella rubbed her belly and softly whispered, "Okay my gal, if you gotta come today, do it quickly before the guests come back. I don't want them hearin' me hollerin' and cursin' all afternoon."

Mavis Kinkade quietly swore as the soft lead in her pencil broke for the third time as she entered the weekly figures into her accounts book. Slamming the pencil down on her desk, she took a deep, steadying breath as she rubbed her eyes in frustration. Ever since she was a young girl in primary school, she hated figures. She hated them with a passion. But unfortunately, she had to make her peace with the mathematical part of her new position.

How on earth did Iris do it, she asked herself repeatedly. In addition to all the other myriad tasks that were a head housekeeper's responsibility, the paperwork and regular reports for Mr. Prescott were not only tedious but extremely time consuming.

Although she was always on friendly terms with Iris Sutton, Mavis had never fully appreciated the other's role in the daily running of the Montclair until the older woman's recent retirement. When Johnathan Prescott had offered Mavis the position, her initial reaction was a delirious enthusiasm. Being a head housekeeper was a position of prestige and, more importantly, it meant a raise in pay, but within 24 hours, the reality of the situation dampened Mavis's eager spirit. Then fear and doubt began to creep in.

Her mind overflowed with negative thoughts. The hotel is so big. How am I going to keep track of everything and everybody? What if I'm not up to it? Perhaps Mr. Prescott overestimated my abilities. I've never supervised more than a dozen maids, but now I'm over the kitchen, dining room and laundry too? And while the housemen answer to the front desk and the groundskeepers get their orders directly from Mr. Prescott, I'll have to occasionally give them instructions as well. I'm not used to working with men. Oh, I'm going to tell Mr. Prescott that I can't do it!

Mavis had worked herself up to the point where she was going to turn down the promotion the very next day. However, a brief unexpected meeting with Johnathan Prescott early that morning changed everything.

That was when she learned that due to a drop in dressmaking and tailoring sales, the Montclair was going to suspend those services. Because of her experience both in the kitchen and as a maid, Birdie was going to be Mavis's assistant. The news both comforted and thrilled the new housekeeper. Birdie had been at the Montclair for well over 15 years now and knew it from the inside out. Come to think of it, so do I, she realized.

Although it had only occurred a month ago, it seemed much longer. The last several days had been busy ones. Both Mavis and Birdie were there from morning til night. Sometimes they even left long after the scullery maids had gone home.

A soft knock at the door woke Mavis from her reverie. She looked at the mantel clock and grinned. She knew who it was.

"Come in, Miss Fairfax," she called out.

Birdie hesitantly opened the door. "Good morning, Miss Kinkade." Although she was now in her early thirties with a slightly softer figure and a couple of grey hairs on her head, Birdie still didn't look much different than when she first started all those years ago. Now instead of a kitchen uniform or her dressmaker's apron, she wore a regular white blouse and long grey skirt.

"Oh Birdie! How many times do I need to tell you that you don't have to knock on this door every time you come in? You share this office too, you know," Mavis cheerfully scolded.

Birdie smiled. "I'm sorry, Mavis. It's just a habit with me, is all. I always knock on closed doors. That's the way I was raised and that's the way I'll probably always be."

Mavis chuckled and shook her head as she watched her assistant sit down at the small table in the corner which served as her desk. While the women addressed each other publicly as Miss Kinkade and Miss Fairfax, the head housekeeper insisted on informality behind closed doors.

For the hundredth time, she wondered why Birdie never married and started a family of her own. She was an attractive woman who could cook, sew and no doubt keep a very nice home. Yet, Mavis never saw Birdie in the company of any men. Of course, there was that unfortunate business with Master Prescott, but surely by now she would have found someone and settled down. The only man Birdie ever seemed sweet on was that red headed gardener who worked here all those years ago but left suddenly. Some sort of family issue.

"Guess who I saw in town yesterday," Birdie was saying. "Marvin Foster, one of Tangie's brothers."

"Did you speak to him?" asked Mavis.

"Yes. I asked about Tangie, of course. He said that she was released a few years ago," said Birdie. "She's keeping to herself these days and taking in laundry when she can."

"It's odd that we haven't seen her around town lately," remarked Mavis. "But I guess she's wise to keep her head down after all that happened. She'll never be able to work anywhere else again."

In 1902, Hiram Merriweather was arrested for dealing in stolen goods after he was caught inadvertently selling a ruby necklace back to its original owner. After being offered the opportunity of a shorter sentence in exchange for the names of his suppliers, Merriweather sang like a bird which resulted in several dozen more arrests including Tangie Foster's.

Birdie could still remember the scene vividly when Deputy Lou Fuller dragged her from the scullery, screaming like a banshee, as the rest of the kitchen staff stood around helplessly witnessing the spectacle. "What the hell ya lookin' at, ya yella ass bitch!" were Tangie's last words to Birdie before the deputy forced her out the back door.

Soon afterwards, Eva was promoted and was now over the scullery. In the meantime, Lawrence Conrad had gotten wind of the story which immediately made its way into the Herald with the headline, "Thievery Runs Riot at the Montclair." The Prescotts were understandably upset.

"Oh Mavis," said Birdie as she looked at the grandfather clock which ticked loudly against the front wall, "Don't forget that you need to meet with Mrs. Prescott in the dining room in twenty minutes about those new table runners for Christmas."

"Ugh," sighed Mavis. "I almost forgot about that. Christmas! I know it's still a couple months away but it will be here before we know it!"

Birdie remained silent. Christmas always brought thoughts of her daughter to mind. Clara would be a young woman of sixteen by now. She might even be married. For all Birdie knew, she herself could even be a grandmother by now.

Mavis interrupted her ruminations. "I better get upstairs. Those two new girls I hired yesterday afternoon start today. I told them to stop by this morning for a quick inspection before they go upstairs and report to Cora. Would you mind handling that for me? And Rita will be dropping off tomorrow's order for the dairyman."

Birdie smiled and replied, "Don't worry Mavis. I'll take care of it all."

After Mavis left, Birdie commenced with the tedious task of inspecting the dining linens. Although the laundry maids were responsible for watching out for such things when they did the washing, more often than not tears and holes would be later discovered. Although it was far from Birdie's favorite responsibility, she nevertheless made sure to carefully inspect each tablecloth, runner and napkin as she was keen to make a good impression in her new position. She eventually became so engrossed in her work that she barely heard the knock at the office door.

“Come in,” Birdie called as she straightened up from the stack of linens and smoothed her hair.

The door opened and a short, slender Negro girl of about sixteen entered. She looked wide eyed and a bit frightened. Birdie remembered her own discomfort when she came to the Montclair for the first time. Wanting to put the girl at immediate ease, Birdie smiled warmly and said, “Good morning. Are you one of our new scullery maids?”

“Yes’m,” replied the girl. “My name’s Henrietta Caldwell.”

“Welcome to the Montclair, Henrietta. My name is...,” before Birdie could finish, the second maid entered through the still open door. She was white, tall, a few years older than Henrietta and had bright red hair. Birdie was momentarily dumbstruck. Although she had never laid eyes on the younger woman before, there was something very familiar about her.

Quickly regaining her composure, Birdie said, “Good morning. Are you our new chambermaid?”

The girl looked at Birdie curiously as she nodded.

“And what’s your name?”

“Maisie,” the girl said with an almost suspicious air. A faint band of freckles ran across the bridge of her nose and she had a distinctly prominent chin that gave her a permanent look of stubbornness. “Maisie Phillips.”

It couldn't be, thought Birdie. Phillips is a fairly common name around these parts but that hair. And she possessed the same light blue eyes fringed with long pale lashes. Birdie felt like she was once again staring into Newt's eyes.

Taking a deep breath, Birdie knew she had to keep a tight grip on herself and remain professionally aloof despite the memories that were flooding her heart and feelings that were now coursing through her veins.

"As I was just saying to Henrietta here, welcome to the Montclair. My name is Miss Fairfax. I am the assistant to our head housekeeper, Miss Kinkade, who you've already met. She's asked me to look you over before sending you to your assigned areas this morning."

Henrietta stood up straight and clasped her hands behind her back while Maisie, who made sure to stay several feet away from her colleague, continued to stare at Birdie.

Starting with Henrietta, Birdie looked the young girl over. Her hair was neatly tied back into the requisite tight bun behind her head. Her kitchen uniform seemed to fit adequately except for the apron's bow that sagged below Henrietta's spine.

"Here, let me help you with that," said Birdie as she re-tied the bow. "It takes some getting used to. Let me see your hands." The young girl's hands were clean and calloused. She obviously was used to hard work.

"Very good," said Birdie as she turned her attention towards Maisie. She felt a nervous pang in the pit of her stomach. She was not used to inspecting staff, especially the white staff. She steeled herself as she went about her task. Maisie's uniform looked fine and her hands were clean, though just as calloused as Henrietta's. The only thing Birdie could find out of place were several wisps of unruly ginger tresses. "That's fine, Maisie. You just need to tuck in a few of these curls." Birdie noticed that the young maid slightly flinched as Birdie's fingers touched her hair.

Birdie pronounced both maids ready to start their duties. She gave Maisie instructions on where to find Cora Cogburn, the head maid, on the second floor before dismissing them.

It wasn't until she sat back down at her table that Birdie realized her legs had been trembling. Not only did Maisie have her brother's eyes, but she also had the same thin, colorless lips as her mother Emilia.

The stubborn wine stain in the carpet of room 304 was just not coming out no matter how hard Maisie scrubbed. Her knuckles were a bright red, in sharp contrast to the paper white freckled skin on her hands. Rich people are such slobs, she thought spitefully. You'd think with all the breedin' they supposedly have, they'd take better care of things.

It was bad enough that she was forced to go out and find a job since that "good fer nuthin'" cousin of hers was gone for longer periods of time these days, hawking his homemade libations. He offered to send for one of his brothers, but Emilia's pride wouldn't let him. She said she and her daughter could look after things til he returned.

However, this time he'd been gone for a couple of months. Maisie and Emilia did what they could in the fields, but with Emilia getting older and frail, their efforts unfortunately made little impact. With no money coming in yet from Ralph, Emilia sent a letter to her brother Ernie. But he had come down with a bad case of ague while his two youngest sons were working on a railroad construction project in Gainesville. It was soon decided that Maisie needed to go out and earn some sort of income until Ralph returned.

At first, she unsuccessfully tried a couple of the saloons in town, offering her services as a washer woman. The bartender at the second saloon suggested that she try the resorts instead. Although she felt uncomfortable being around the well-to-do, or "hoity toities" as she called them, Maisie decided that she'd apply at the Montclair. After all, Newt had managed to get a job there. Maybe she'd have good luck as well.

As it happened, the hotel was in desperate need of chamber maids. Although she was after a job in the laundry, Maisie reckoned that being a chamber maid would most likely be a step up and bring in a little more money. So, whitewashing her background and with a couple of fabricated references, she managed to get hired on. Maisie took extra care not to mention her brother, whose banishment from town was a stain on her family's honor.

All seemed to be going well until she met Miss Fairfax. There was no doubt in Maisie's mind that this was the same mulatto slut responsible for Newt's run-in with the Klan. She remembered hearing that name in whispered conversations between her ma and her uncle when she was a child.

Despite the questions she and her sister Susie (who had long ago run off with an itinerant salesman) used to constantly ask, Emilia never spoke of Newt or why he was forced to leave. All she said was that he had gotten married and then disappeared to parts unknown. Since then, Emilia, the girls and their cousin Ralph stayed in the woods and rarely ventured into town. Maisie had never laid eyes on Birdie until she met her in the office a few weeks ago. It took all her resolve not to scratch the assistant housekeeper's eyes out.

So not only was she forced to go back to work, but she was now working for the same woman responsible for the situation she and her mother were in. If it wasn't for her, Newt could have kept the farm and looked after their ma. And, like Susie, she could have been married and raising her own family.

Maisie viciously spat at the stain and, putting her whole body into it, savagely scrubbed. However, she didn't see the carpet but Birdie's clueless face instead.

"Goddamn nigra whore!" she hissed under her breath.

Over the past several years, more automobiles were starting to appear on St. Augustine's streets. Branded "stink wagons" by some, the newfangled loud contraptions which belched out noxious fumes on innocent passersby and frightened horses were avidly sought after by the well-to-do, and Lottie Prescott was no exception.

Her husband, however, initially wanted no part of what he considered a mere fad. A born horseman to the core, he preferred the comfort and familiarity of his own team and luxurious carriage. And on the very rare occasion he had some free time, he would take his trusted mount, Chief, on short jaunts down the dusty trails just south of town. He relished those all too brief rides which revitalized his soul.

But, as often happened, Johnathan Prescott eventually acquiesced to his spouse's wishes, partly because he loved his wife and wanted her to be happy, but mainly because he wanted peace and quiet. He had one of Ford's Model T's ordered and delivered to him on a southbound train.

Lottie's latest campaign was to commission a new riding costume designed and made for herself. Automobile riders were exposed to a lot of dust as well as the elements, so protecting one's clothing and (especially for women) hair was of the utmost importance. But when she suggested to her husband that he needed a new riding costume as well, Prescott firmly put his foot down.

"If you feel you need this new get up, so be it, but I'll be hanged if you are going to make me wear such folderall," he exclaimed.

So one afternoon the following week, Mavis came back from a staff meeting and appeared in the kitchen pantry where Birdie was going over a delivery order with Rita.

"Miss Fairfax, may I have a word with you, please?"

As the pair headed to the housekeeper's office, Mavis said,

"Mrs. Prescott needs to see you upstairs as soon as you can get up there." Looking over at Birdie and seeing a fleeting look of alarm cross her features, the housekeeper smiled and added, "Don't worry. She only wants to talk to you about a riding outfit she would like you to make her. She's just going to tell you what she has in mind and then you'll take her measurements. That's all."

Birdie breathed a little easier. "Well, it will be good to get back into the sewing room again."

Mavis smiled. "I knew you'd feel that way."

As the women returned to their office, Mavis sat at her desk while Birdie searched for her measuring tape and notebook in the sewing basket that she kept in the corner cabinet.

The head housekeeper closed her eyes and rubbed her temples as she chuckled ruefully. "It never fails, Birdie. Every time I go upstairs for one of those meetings, I'm handed a new catastrophe. This week it's the laundry. Apparently the new soap powder they're using is causing some of our guests to break out in hives."

Birdie shook her head as Mavis continued, "Plus I still need to get with Cora and see how those two new maids are working out." She sighed as she added, "But first, there's that unpleasant mix-up with the dairyman that I still need to sort out. When you get back from seeing Mrs. Prescott, could you please sort through last year's receipts and pull out every transaction we've had with Mr. O'Connell?"

"Sure, Mavis. I'll be as quick as I can," Birdie promised as she made her exit.

The aroma of grilled onions and sautéed liver permeated the hallway. Birdie salivated as she took a deep breath. She hoped whatever Rita and her girls were cooking would end up on the staff dining table later that day.

As she crossed the marbled floor of the mezzanine, Birdie glanced over the railing that overlooked the main lobby below. Vernon Bradley, a small wiry bald man with a relentlessly cheerful disposition, was checking in a young well-heeled couple. Honeymooners, Birdie wryly thought as she continued toward the back stairs to the upper floors.

When she was about two thirds of the way down the second-floor corridor of guest rooms, Birdie spotted Maisie Phillips coming down from the back stairs and heading towards room 220. She was carrying a set of mauve colored sheets that were trimmed with a lovely embroidered floral and hummingbird motif. Birdie immediately knew she had to intervene.

"Miss Phillips," she called out to the maid. "May I see you for a moment?"

Maisie looked wordlessly at Birdie as she casually sauntered over. No "Yes, ma'am" or "Yes, Miss Fairfax" which were usually uttered by the other staff members Birdie dealt with. Just stone-cold silence. Birdie, regardless, kept her tone friendly and helpful.

"Miss Phillips, those sheets you are about to take into room 220 actually belong on the top floor. I'm sure you haven't been familiarized with that portion of the hotel just yet." Birdie momentarily paused as Maisie continued to stare hard at her. Trying to be more helpful, Birdie added, "When I was a maid, it took me a while to remember which sheets were used on which floor. You see, the one's you're holding are used for the Prescotts' important guests and close friends. For the lower floors, we use the white cotton linens with the leafy patterns. We keep those on the lower shelves. Lower shelves for the lower floors. That should help you remember."

Maisie mutely nodded in response. Birdie sensed that this was a good time to depart so she nodded in return and continued her way up to the Prescott suite.

When she arrived at the top floor, Birdie found Cora coming out of 412 carrying a broken lamp shade that needed replacing.

"Hello Miss Fairfax," greeted the head chambermaid. "Is there something Miss Kinkade needs?"

"Oh no," replied Birdie. "Mrs. Prescott has sent for me."

Cora looked relieved. "I was afraid it might have had something to do with Miss Phillips."

Birdie was puzzled. "Miss Phillips?" she repeated.

"Yes, I know she's only been here a week but I'm afraid she's just not cut out to be a chambermaid," said Cora. "She's too slow and pays no attention to detail in her cleaning. It's come to the point where I have to come behind her and re-do most of her rooms! I've got enough to tend to without shouldering her workload as well." Lowering her voice to a whisper, she added, "I've already gotten a couple of complaints from guests on her assigned floor. I'll need to talk to Mrs. Kinkade before she gets wind of this from someone else!"

A sickly pang struck Birdie's stomach. Although Maisie had been nothing but taciturn and borderline impudent with her, Birdie couldn't help but feel sorry for the woman who obviously needed this job badly.

Birdie was about to plead on Maisie's behalf when a guest exited 414 at that moment, putting an end to their conversation. It was always a strict rule at the Montclair that chamber staff never be seen conversing to each other in front of paying guests.

With a heavy heart, Birdie sighed mournfully as she continued towards the Prescott suite.

Chapter 35

Horst Metzger finished placing the final batch of pumpernickel loaves in the oven. They had to be delivered to the Montclair by 9AM. Checking his watch, the young baker saw that he had time for a short break until the bread was done.

As he often did when he took the handkerchief from his pocket to mop his sweaty brow, Horst once again asked himself why, out of all the places to settle down in America, did he and Frieda choose the hot, sticky climate of Florida. It was the worst place for a bakery – the humidity wreaked havoc on his more delicate pastries and there was no respite from the heat that emanated from his oven because often the temperature outside felt just as hot!

The sound of his new bride's cough from upstairs made Horst immediately contrite. He had known Frieda since they were in the same primary school back in Hamburg. She was always a small, frail, sickly child who caught colds easily. A bad case of pneumonia a few years ago which had almost claimed her life left her with weakened lungs. The doctors always gave her the same prescription – rest, good food and plenty of sunshine.

So soon after they married last year, the Metzgers decided to depart for the United States. They had heard of Florida from itinerant merchants and sailors who had patronized their small bakery. It had sounded like an exotic, tropical place that boasted the warmest weather in the country. The decision was soon made and the business was put up for sale. Using the proceeds, the Metzgers boarded a Jacksonville bound steamer.

The sound of Frieda's footsteps on the stairs brought Horst back from his reverie. Despite her painfully thin frame and pale complexion, she possessed an inner strength and serenity which was very evident in how she carried herself. Her rosy cheeks, small pointed chin, blue-green eyes and hair that was so fair it almost looked white gave her an endearing, pixie-like quality.

Frieda beamed as she saw her husband taking a much-needed rest. She was always concerned that Horst worked too hard. With a steaming cup of coffee in one hand and that day's newspaper folded and tucked up under her other arm, Frieda slowly descended from their living quarters upstairs. The delicious smell of freshly baked bread and pastries never failed to cheer her up each morning. However, her happiness was often short-lived owing to the increasing shortage of customers.

Frieda handed the cup to her husband as she joined him behind the counter. Peering anxiously at the door, she asked, "Has anyone been in this morning?"

"Of course!" replied Horst, sounding more optimistic than he felt. "I've already sold several custard strudels and a few loaves of rye. And I have this order to take to the Montclair." Sensing Frieda's anxiety, Horst put down his cup and gave his wife a hug. "Don't worry, mein liebling. All is well!!"

A smile of gratitude spread across Frieda's features as she beamed up at her husband. She was well aware of the state of their business but chose to keep silent. Her husband's attempts to quell her fears and shield her from harsh reality made her love him all the more.

"Take a break, Horst," she urged as she handed over the newspaper. "You've been down here since 4:30 this morning working on that hotel order."

Horst waved dismissively. "Ach! I feel fine. Trust me, liebling, all this will be worth it if....

"...we get the Montclair's regular business," finished Frieda, who had heard this last line dozens of times since Horst had met with the hotel's head cook last week. Although the Montclair made all their own cakes and biscuits, they did not have the resources to make the some of the specialty breads and European pastries which the Metzger's bakery offered.

Horst teasingly swatted his wife on the back of her skirt with the folded-up newspaper which caused Frieda to playfully squeal like the schoolgirl he remembered. As she ascended back upstairs, Horst took a sip of coffee as he unfolded the Herald and scanned the front page.

The war in Europe waged on. The Battle of Loos continued in France with thousands of casualties. Meanwhile, the Germans executed a British nurse for helping Allied soldiers escape from Belgium.

Horst sighed as he set the paper down and glanced around the empty bakery. Despite the neutral stance the United States has officially taken, German immigrants were already starting to notice a change in their social standing which ranged from mild wariness to outright discrimination and even violence. Some German families went so far as to change their surnames to ones sounding more Anglican in nature in the hopes of better blending in.

Although the Metzgers had not personally experienced any discriminatory behavior by their fellow townspeople as of yet, there was no doubt that business had indeed dropped off substantially over the past couple of months. At first, Horst believed the decrease in custom was purely due to the local economy. However, after recently strolling by Joe Hardy's bakery over on St. George Street and noticing the long line in front of the counter, his worst suspicions were confirmed.

That was when Horst struck upon the idea of turning to the town's largest consumers of baked goods - the hotels. If he could get the regular custom of at least one of these behemoths, the bakery would not only have a steady income but could also boast about being the official bakery of one of St. Augustine's prestigious resorts.

Unfortunately, the town's largest hotels already had experienced European pastry chefs in their employ. However, the cook and head housekeeper at the Montclair seemed receptive to the concept of outsourcing their baked goods. They gave Horst a trial order and, depending on the outcome, might possibly continue on a weekly basis.

Peering inside one of the ovens to check on the progress of the pumpernickel, Horst silently prayed that this order will be the beginning of a profitable partnership. His livelihood depended upon it.

Maisie angrily stormed past the kitchen and into the mudroom where she blindly collected her belongings. Stone faced, she re-emerged into the corridor, yanked open the back door and slammed it shut behind her, rattling the kitchen's southern window panes. A bewildered Rita and her assistants stopped their dinner preparations and gaped wordlessly at each other.

Each step that Maisie took further fueled her inner rage as Mavis Kinkade's words still rang in her ears. "I'm sorry but your services are no longer required."

Although Maisie had hated working in town as a maid, she needed the income. Her ma, who was now getting up in years, has become increasingly stubborn and unreasonable.

Despite Maisie's pleas, Emilia refused to write to their Palatka relations for help insisting that she was not going to be anyone's charity case, not even her brother's. In the meantime, she and Maisie would work their own meager strip of land between them until Ralph decided to return.

It had taken the death of their oldest and strongest workhorse to get Emilia to finally relent to Maisie's insistence on looking for a job in town. Up until then, Emilia had managed to keep herself and Maisie from venturing into the city. Stokes and his men had wreaked havoc upon her family and Emilia never wished to set eyes up any of them again, and that went double for that damned quadroon at the hotel who started all the trouble in the first place.

Maisie clenched her jaw as she continued to head towards the hotel's side street that lead out to the main road. Although her mother had been unpleased to hear that Maisie had found work at the Montclair and was in daily contact with Birdie Fairfax, she was going to be even more livid now that the job was gone.

Birdie Fairfax. Maisie seethed with ire as new thoughts thundered through her mind. It was all her fault. I should've known she'd go tell tales on me to that Kinkade woman after she saw me with those damned sheets yesterday. Who the hell does she think she is? Uppity, yellow eyed nigra pretendin' to be a white person.

As she rounded the eastern portion of the hotel by the rose garden, Maisie spotted her prey. Birdie was talking to Hattie, one of the chambermaids, who had a small rolled up carpet over her shoulder which had been brought outside to air.

Maisie felt something akin to a pop inside her head and before she was fully aware of what she was doing, she had knocked Birdie to the ground and was on top of her, trying to choke her. Hattie had dropped the rug and was screaming at the top of her lungs.

Felipe and Simon, a tall, young Negro hired years ago to replace Newt, were in the process of cutting down a rotten palm in front of the hotel. They heard the commotion and came running at full speed around the corner. The surreal scenario of Birdie, purple faced, trying to claw at a wild-eyed Maisie whose red hair had come undone and surrounded her face like a lion's mane caused both men to break into a sprint towards the melee and separate the pair.

"Get her out of here!" shouted Felipe to Simon, who had grabbed Maisie by the waist.

"Git yer goddamned hands off me!" shouted Maisie as she ripped herself from Simon's grip. "I'll git the law on ya fer that. And you," she said to Birdie, who was still on the ground in Felipe's arms trying to catch her breath, "I'll kill ya if I ever see ya again!"

With that, Maisie stormed off towards King Street.

Hattie, who was kneeling next to Birdie and had taken one of her hands into her own, asked softly, "Are you all right, Miss. Fairfax? You're bleedin' awful bad."

Birdie, who still struggled to breathe and find her voice, nodded weakly. She winced as she reached up to feel the open gash on her forehead.

"Help me get her inside, Felipe," said Hattie as she and the head gardener slowly lifted Birdie to her feet. "Simon, pick up that rug for me and just set it inside the door. I'll tend to it later."

As the group slowly headed back inside, a sharp pain stabbed through Birdie's head and she felt as though her skull was about to split open. Memories of the assault by Emilia Phillips on New Year's Day, 1900 immediately came to mind. Like mother, like daughter.

Chapter 36

Dr. Winston Stokes inhaled deeply as he walked up the path leading to the Fairfax house. The sweet, tangy aroma of the citrus blossoms from a nearby grove perfumed the air. A new arrival to St. Augustine, Dr. Stokes was quickly becoming a fixture in Lincolnville which was sorely in need of a physician since the death of old Doc Jennings last spring. Not only was there a steady stream of patients in his office each day, but numerous emergencies which necessitated house calls.

A houseman from the Montclair had come by his office earlier that afternoon and informed him of a woman who had suffered some sort of head injury at the hotel and had a suspected concussion. The doctor's knock at the recently whitewashed front door was answered by an anxious looking Hortensia.

"Good afternoon, ma'am. I'm Dr. Stokes," Winston said. Having spent his entire youth and a portion of his adulthood in Jamaica, his English had a slightly Caribbean lilt to it.

Hortensia looked curiously at the doctor for a second before she remembered her manners and replied, "Thank you for coming. It's my daughter, Birdie...I mean Brigid. She was knocked over by a horse that got frightened by one of those new motor cars. I don't know why folks insist on driving those contraptions! They'll never catch on."

Before Hortensia could continue her tirade, Winston asked, "Where is the patient?"

"This way, doctor," replied Hortensia as she led him towards Birdie's room.

"The doctor's here, mija," Hortensia called from the doorway as she motioned for Winston to enter.

As he looked over to the patient who was sitting up in her bed and sewing what appeared to be a tiny dress, Winston stopped short. He had expected to find a teenage girl or a young woman in her twenties. However, this woman was older – around his own age. She also had the most striking amber colored eyes he'd ever seen.

Recovering his composure, Winston greeted Birdie, who looked at him as quizzically as her mother had. Although he had a fair complexion, crystal-like green eyes and chestnut brown hair, he also possessed distinctly Negroid facial features. He was a quite handsome figure. While he spoke with a slightly exotic, almost musical, accent, his vocabulary was that of a man obviously well-educated.

"Hello Miss Fairfax. I hear you suffered an injury today. What happened?"

Birdie looked over at Hortensia for a split second before relaying the story of how she had been on her way to see the butcher in town about an order for the Montclair when a nearby automobile suddenly backfired, which scared the horse she had been passing. The mare kicked Birdie in the head with her rear hooves.

"May I take a look?" asked Winston as he proceeded to examine Birdie's bruises. He gently probed the black and blue marks on her cheeks and temples. If she had been kicked by a horse, she would have suffered far worse if she wasn't instantly killed. He noticed several scratch marks behind her neck as well as fresh scabs just inside her hairline. Something was not adding up here. This woman was physically assaulted by a creature of the two-legged variety.

Looking from Birdie to Hortensia, Winston smiled and cheerily said, "What this patient could use right now is a good cup of tea. And, quite frankly, so could I."

"Oh yes, doctor," said Hortensia eagerly. "And I'll get you some peach cobbler too!"

After she departed, Winston turned to Birdie and softly said, "Now that your mother's gone, tell me what really happened to you."

Birdie glanced up sharply at the doctor who stared back in silence. His eyes were not the usually clinical ones of a physician but instead were filled with sincere concern.

Over the years, Birdie had kept a lot of things from Hortensia for fear of her mother's health. She knew the older woman had a highly strung disposition and that any bad news would send her into a spiral of hysterics. She'd never told her mother about what happened with Newt, the Klan threats, or how Emilia Phillips had attacked her. She now hoped to keep Maisie's assault a secret as well.

"Please doctor," she whimpered in a small voice. "Don't tell my ma. I don't want her to worry."

"Anything you tell me will be held in strict confidentiality," assured Winston. "You don't even need to tell me who did this to you if you don't want to. But as your doctor, I must know if you are in any further danger."

"No," replied Birdie. "I don't think we'll be crossin' paths again."

"Good," Winston resumed his examination as he checked each of Birdie's eyes. There didn't seem to be any signs of concussion. "Other than the scratches and that laceration on your head, you seem to be all right." With a smile, he added "But, to be on the safe side, I do think you should take it easy for a couple of days until that cut heals. I'll send a note to the Montclair."

Birdie started to protest. She still had to finish Mrs. Prescott's driving costume and help Mavis with the kitchen requisitions.

Winston immediately cut her off. "Now I don't want to hear another word about it. The hotel isn't going to crumble to the ground just because you aren't there for two days, is it?"

The absurdity of this last line made Birdie laugh despite herself. "I guess not."

Winston couldn't help but chuckle also. The woman was even lovelier when she smiled. "I'll return in two days to check on you and make sure you're well enough to go back to work."

Birdie nodded and replied, “Yes. Thank you, doctor. I’m sorry. I didn’t catch your name.”

“Stokes. Winston Stokes.”

A shiver ran down Birdie’s spine as Winston picked up his bag, nodded courteously at her and left the room to join Hortensia in the parlor.

"You see, Mr. Prescott, in light of the circumstances, I thought it prudent that Miss Fairfax be sent home immediately and seen to by a physician. I just received a note from him advising that Brigid was ordered two days of bed rest."

Mavis stood stiffly in the front parlor of the Prescott suite as the hotelier and his wife sat, dumbfounded, on the newly upholstered davenport next to the large window which overlooked the town's growing skyline of resorts, bank buildings and church steeples. She always felt ill at ease whenever she had to visit the Prescotts, mainly due to the Lottie's pomposity.

Johnathan Prescott removed the cigar from between his teeth. "Of course, of course. Let Miss Fairfax know that she can return to her job whenever she is ready and that we will cover the doctor's expenses." Lottie shot her husband a sharp glance which was ignored as he carried on. "Do I need to get the Sheriff involved?"

Mavis shook her head. "Miss Fairfax doesn't wish to pursue the matter any further."

"So, tell me again who this maid was and why on earth did she attack Miss Fairfax?"

"Her name is Maisie Phillips, sir. The gardeners told me she is related to Newt Phillips who used to work here and abruptly left back in 1900. As for her motive for the attack on Miss Fairfax, I'm afraid I haven't the vaguest notion."

"Oh yes, I remember Phillips," said Prescott pensively as he puffed on the fat Cuban stogie. Red headed kid who was a bit of a daydreamer but a good man and a hard worker. His sudden disappearance had raised a few eyebrows at the time. Rumors abounded that the Klan had hustled him out of town.

Lottie interrupted his thoughts. "And to think, this all happened in broad daylight right next to the hotel! Are you sure there weren't any guests around to witness this barbaric scene, Miss Kinkade?"

Mavis tightened her jaw. It was no surprise to her that Lottie Prescott was more concerned with appearances than the welfare of a longtime member of staff. "Yes, ma'am. Both gardeners and the chambermaid stated that there were no guests in the area at the time."

Sensing the annoyance his head housekeeper was feeling towards his wife, Prescott intervened. "Thank you for bringing this matter to my attention. Do pass our best wishes onto Miss Fairfax for a full recovery. I know you're quite busy and we'll not keep you up here any longer."

"But..." Lottie began.

"Thank you, Mr. Prescott. Good day, sir," replied Mavis as she swiftly made for the door and departed.

"Johnathan!" exclaimed Lottie, "Why did you rush her out of here so quickly. I didn't get a chance to ask if Miss Fairfax was well enough to do a little sewing on my riding outfit while she recuperated."

As he shot his wife an incredulous glare, all Prescott could manage to utter was, "Damnation" as he retired to his private study.

Stokes. Winston Stokes. Birdie spent a restless night turning the doctor's name over and over in her mind. No, I'm just being silly, she told herself countless times. There certainly couldn't be any connection between the kindly mulatto doctor and the bloodthirsty Klansman who filled her with terror.

Stokes was a common name, after all. It stands to reason that in a town as large as St. Augustine, there would be more than one family with that particular surname.

But those eyes. She was certain she'd seen them before. Those piercing green eyes which looked upon her with kindness yesterday afternoon were definitely identical to the ones which stared at her with murderous hatred in the past, but how could it be? Were her head injuries driving her into madness?

As her room gradually brightened with the rising sun, Hortensia softly knocked at the door before entering with a cup of tea and a biscuit on a small plate.

"Good morning, mija," she said in a hushed tone. "Did you sleep well?"

"Not really," said Birdie. Noticing her mother's worried look, she added, "My head's still a bit sore, is all. I imagine I'll start feeling better once I have a headache powder."

Hortensia brightened as she offered Birdie the tea and biscuit. "All right, but have some breakfast first."

As Hortensia headed for the doorway, Birdie stopped her. Desperate for more information about Dr. Winston, Birdie had to find out what her mother knew about him.

"Ma, what did the doctor say to you yesterday after he examined me?"

Hortensia rubbed her chin as she recollected her conversation with the physician. "Well, he said that you were going to be aching for a couple of days and that he wants you to stay in bed and rest. He also said he was going to drop a note off to Miss Kinkade at the Montclair."

Birdie frowned. She already knew this much. She was hoping that her mother, a natural gossip, would have gleaned more personal details. She tried a different conversational tactic.

"Dr. Stokes has a strange accent, doesn't he?"

"Well of course he does," said Hortensia impatiently. "He's from Jamaica after all."

Jamaica, thought Birdie. Now we're getting somewhere. Aloud she remarked, "He obviously hasn't been in St. Augustine very long."

Luckily, that was all she needed to say before Hortensia's floodgates opened and all the information she acquired yesterday afternoon came pouring out.

"Actually, Dr. Stokes went to medical school in Virginia before returning back to Kingston where he set up his practice. Then, a couple of months ago, he sailed to Florida with his father, who is ailing and needs regular medical attention. While he's here, he is temporarily seeing Dr. Jennings' patients until a permanent replacement can be found."

"Oh, I see," murmured Birdie. The knot in her stomach started to relax. Perhaps he's no relation to Lonnie Stokes after all. Suddenly curious, she asked, "Did any other family come over with him from Jamaica?"

Hortensia raised her eyebrows as a gentle smirk crossed her lips. "If you're asking if he's married, my guess is no. Well, at least he didn't mention a wife or children. Besides, a man as busy as he seems to be probably never had time to start a family. He strikes me as one of those men who is married to his job." Pointing at the cup of tea that Birdie was still holding, she added, "Now you drink that up before it gets cold. I'll be right back with your headache powder."

"Yes, ma," said Birdie absently as she took a small sip. I need to stop letting my imagination run away with me, she admonished herself. Just because two folks have the same last name doesn't mean they always have to be related.

But those eyes still haunted her.

Lonnie Stokes wearily shuffled into Doheney's Saloon, Alice's voice still ringing in his ears. He and his wife had been trying to start a family for the past eleven years with no luck. She browbeat him about their childless state every chance she got. Tonight's fight was nothing unusual.

Lonnie had come home from a hard day of harvesting a disappointing crop of grapefruit. Exhausted, he slumped into his favorite chair and asked Alice to fetch the bottle of liniment to rub on his aching shoulders.

"You might as well get used to all that pain because unless you can produce a son, you'll be overseein' those groves all by yourself until you're an old man!" said Alice.

"Why the hell are you startin' this up now?" asked Lonnie, "I've had a tough day out there and all I want is a little peace and quiet. Is that too much to ask?"

"All I'm sayin'," replied Alice, "Is that you're gettin' a bit older now and will be needin' more help out there managin' the field hands and the production. We're obviously not meant to be blessed with a family and you're workin' yourself into an early grave. Why not sell your portion of the business to your brothers? They have plenty of sons who can help them. Then we can move up north into a nice, smaller place in the city."

"Here we go again!" cried Lonnie. "If you ain't bitchin' at me about havin' no kids, you're whinin' about wantin' to go back up north to dear ole Richmond. If you wanna go, I ain't gonna stop ya, but my ass is stayin' right here!"

"You don't think I'll go, do you?" goaded Alice. "Well I'll show you! I'm sick and tired of livin' with half a man. You're all tough as nails on the outside, but you'll never produce any children. The doc says there's nothin' wrong with me. It's your fault that we never started a family. Why didn't I stay in Richmond and marry Nathan Pierce?"

"You wanna marry Nathan Pierce? Go right ahead! Pack your bags and get your fat ass outta my house. I'm goin' out and don't wanna see you here when I get back!" With that, Lonnie put on his hat and coat and stormed out of the house, slamming the door behind him so violently that a framed photo of himself and Alice fell from its place on the parlor's front wall and shattered.

Doheny's was not as full as usual tonight. Lonnie guessed that Ralph Phillips' moonshining must be hurting the bar's trade. Although what he was doing was technically illegal, the Sheriff tended to turn a blind eye on it as it had significantly cut down on the number of fights that he had to break up every evening. Lonnie laughed to himself and shook his head. At least there was one Phillips male in that family that had a good head on his shoulders. His uncle Jeb was nothing more than a two-bit drunkard and that son of his was a nigra lovin' loser. The town was much better off without the pair of them.

As he took another sip of his bourbon, he spotted a gaunt old man sitting at the end of the bar. The stranger's eyes remained fixed on Lonnie as he sipped on a tall mug of beer. Although most of the man's face was covered with a thick grey beard, there was something disturbingly familiar about the sunken green eyes that stared intently at him.

"What the hell are you lookin' at?" growled Lonnie.

"Still got yer ma's temper I see," replied the stranger, punctuating his sentence with a rattling cough.

Immediately recognizing his father's voice, Lonnie slammed his glass on the bar and glared at him. "How dare you speak of my mother, God rest her soul! What the hell are you doin' here? I thought you moved down to some Caribbean island with your nigger woman and her half-breed pickaninny."

Marcus Stokes carried his mug over to the other side of the bar and sat beside his irate son. "I've been workin' in the sugar trade and manage a good size plantation in Jamaica. We just sent a huge shipment over to Jacksonville. Thought I'd go with it, take a quick train ride to St. Augustine and see how my sons turned out. I've already visited Tom and Nick. They seem to be doin' well with their juicin' factory and their families. You, on the other hand, look to be another story. I hear you have no children to speak of and that the family grove has been looking a bit sparse."

Still smoldering from Alice's earlier comments about his failure at becoming a father, Lonnie raged, "Who the hell are you to be coming back to town after all these years and start spoutin' off at the mouth about me? You were a pitiful excuse for a father – runnin' out on us like you did with your black concubine and bastard son. I've run folks outta town for doin' what you did. If them two were here with ya right now, I'd put a bullet in each one of ya."

"I can understand your anger at me," said Marcus, "but why kill Claudette and Winston? They've done nothin' to ya."

"Because they both exist," spat Lonnie. "As much as I hate niggers, I despise half breeds even more. They're like mongrel dogs. No race to call their own so they latch onto the white man and pollute our blood with theirs."

The old man's shoulders started to shake with laughter which slowly increased and got louder, rankling Lonnie even further. "What the hell's so funny?"

Marcus stopped laughing and stared levelly at Lonnie as he hissed, "You never did get it, did ya boy? You never noticed?"

Lonnie retorted, "What the hell are ya talkin' about?"

"I'm talkin' bout the texture of my hair, the slight wideness of my nose, that I hold a suntan a little too easily," said Marcus.

"So what? Is that supposed to mean somethin'?" asked Lonnie irritably.

"Listen here," began Marcus, "I never told your ma much about my family, but I think that now you ought to know. My pa, who you'd never met because he died young, was the son of a black man and a white woman."

Lonnie stopped breathing for a moment as his father's statement registered. "What the hell are ya talkin' about?"

After a brief coughing fit, Marcus continued, "Your great-grandfather was Lucas Stokes, a slave on a cotton plantation outside Savannah. He had a dalliance with Sally Burns, one of the plantation owner's daughters, which resulted in the birth of

Calvin Stokes, my pa. Lucas was lynched, Sally was sent to a convent and my pa was raised by a slave family. Being light skinned, he moved down to St. Augustine to start a new life and that's where he met my ma, Clarice. Because he was able to pass for a white man, he married my ma and they had five children."

"But," began Lonnie, "that makes you a......"

"I think the word you are looking for is 'quadroon.' Yes, my boy, that's what some would call me," replied Marcus.

Lonnie started to violently tremble as he whispered, "But then that would make me..."

Marcus venomously replied, "An octaroon!" His chuckle sounded more like a wheezy rattle in his chest. "So, you seen, my son, you never had any right judgin' and banishin' others for being niggers and nigra lovers because all this time you had that same black blood flowin' through your own veins!"

"No!" shouted Lonnie as he stood up, causing his bar stool to tumble. Several heads turned his way, including Jim Doheney's.

"Ya all right, Lon?" asked Jim.

Lonnie continued staring disgustedly at his father. He'd never noticed before but now he spotted the mullato-like features of the old man. The thick lips and slightly flattened bridge of the nose. This can't be true, he thought. All this time I was the very thing I hated!

"No, no! I'm a white man, goddamit. You're a lyin' sonofabitch." Lonnie snarled through gritted teeth.

"Whether you believe it or not is of no concern to me," said Marcus. "I know it's true and that's why I find your attitude towards folks like yourself so damn funny!" After downing the final swig of rum, Marcus slammed his glass on the bar as he delivered the final blow. "And by the way, your brother Marcus is now a full-fledged doctor. Yessir, that 'half-breed mongrel' turned out to be more of a success than you, my boy!!"

Marcus' hoarse, sickly chuckle followed Lonnie as he stumbled out of the bar.

There were only a few people walking about St. George Street on this warm and humid evening. Feeling dazed and desperate, Lonnie ran back to his house. Hopefully Alice was still there. He desperately needed to talk to someone.

He sprinted through the city's streets with a half-crazed look on his face, occasionally bumping into the odd passerby.

"Watch out bud. Where's the fire?"

When he finally got back home, the house was empty. As he ran into the bedroom, he saw that all of Alice's clothes were gone as well as her trunk. She must have taken him up on his dare and left. No doubt she was staying with one of her friends but which one? Dammit!

Going to the liquor cabinet and pulling out the glass decanter of scotch and a glass, Stokes sat down and poured himself a glass. He drank one after another for the next hour in a desperate pursuit of numbness. But he still felt the sting of his father's taunting laughter and the shame of hearing himself being called "an octaroon."

At 8:00 the next morning, Felix Garcia knocked at the door of the Stokes' home but was surprised to see that because it hadn't been shut properly, it swung open as soon as he touched it. "Señor Stokes! Señora Stokes! Estan aqui?" The grove's foreman had never arrived at work before his boss. Unsure as to what to do next, he stepped inside the front entry. Again, he shouted, "Jefe! Esta aqui?"

As he walked into the Stoke's front parlor, he discovered Lonnie Stokes' body lying on the carpet with a pistol in one hand and half of his head blown off.

Chapter 37

Hortensia watched the raindrops strike the kitchen window as she mechanically folded up the last of the laundry that would be returned to Della Compton's house later that afternoon. She'd just managed to get them off the line before the unexpected afternoon shower had hit. As she placed the final towel on top of the tall stack of fresh white linens and underthings in the wash basket, a shuffling sound from behind startled her.

She turned to discover Birdie had entered the kitchen, carrying the tray which Hortensia had brought to her daughter's bedroom an hour before. She had changed from her nightdress into her usual ivory blouse and fawn colored skirt which she wore when she was not working. Her hair was pulled back into a single thick braid.

"Birdie! You just about frightened the life out of me," exclaimed Hortensia. "What are you doing out of bed? The doctor should be here soon."

"I've been laying in that bed for almost two days now," Birdie peevishly replied as she took the dish and utensils off the tray and pumped water into the sink. "I needed to get up and get dressed so I could feel halfway human once again," she continued as she scrubbed the plate and cutlery "Besides, once Dr. Stokes sees that I'm already up and around, he'll have no choice but to approve my return to work."

"Just take it easy, mija," urged Hortensia. "Is your head still hurting?"

"No, I'm feeling much better today," replied Birdie as she finished the rinsing and drying. "In fact, I probably look a lot worse than I feel."

"You look quite nice, actually," said the older woman as a knowing smile played on her lips. "If I didn't know any better I'd say you were looking forward to the doctor's visit!"

“Oh, stop it, ma,” Birdie scolded as she picked up the morning’s newspaper from the kitchen counter and headed for the front parlor.

Hortensia looked smugly at her daughter. Birdie might deny any interest in Dr. Stokes but the fact that she not only bothered to get dressed but put on her best brooch said otherwise.

Birdie settled into her favorite rocking chair and perused the front page. The day’s headlines reflected the escalating war in Europe and the latest casualty statistics in the Battle of the Somme in France. Despite President Wilson’s policy of American neutrality, anti-German sentiment was beginning to spread like an infectious disease across the nation. Tales abounded of the burning of German books, the vandalism of German owned business and the arrest of German immigrants on charges of treason.

Finding the global news depressing, Birdie turned to the local section and the top headline made her freeze. “Local Citrus Businessman Alonzo Stokes Dead.” Blinking hard, Birdie stared at the article again. Lonnie Stokes was dead?

She quickly scanned through the story. Stokes was found with a severe gunshot wound to the head and gripping his own revolver. Suicide!

Long suppressed memories started to flood Birdie’s consciousness, threatening to thaw years of frozen grief. Birdie put the paper down, closed her eyes and took a deep breath. She had to keep her wits about her. For years, Birdie managed to avoid Stokes and keep his threats to her and her mother’s lives a secret from Hortensia. And as far as she was concerned, it would always remain that way.

A knock at the door brought Birdie to her feet. Hortensia came from the kitchen, smoothing her hair and her apron. “I’ll get it, mija.”

Both women went to the front door, which Hortensia opened. Winston Stokes, wearing a soaking wet overcoat, removed his raindrop stained hat and smiled at them warmly "Good afternoon, ladies."

"Come in, doctor," replied Hortensia, closing the door behind him. "It's pouring buckets out there, isn't it?

Winston chuckled as he entered. "Yes ma'am." Catching sight of Birdie standing a few feet away looking even lovelier and, thankfully, healthier than the last time he saw her, he remarked, "Miss Fairfax! I must say you're looking very well indeed!"

Birdie blushed. "Yes, doctor. I was just telling my mother that I'm feeling a lot better and ready to get back to the Montclair. But please, let's get you out of that wet coat."

As she helped the doctor off with the woolen overcoat, she saw the black arm band on the left sleeve of his tweed jacket.

Hortensia spotted it also. "Oh! Are you in mourning, doctor?"

Picking up his medical bag, Winston replied, "Yes, I'm afraid we had a death in the family yesterday."

Birdie, whose nerves were already shredded, felt weak. Not wishing to lose her composure, she tried to grab onto a nearby table to steady herself.

Hortensia, noticing her daughter's frail state, shouted, "Dr. Stokes, she's turning pale!"

Winston dropped the bag and rushed over to Birdie's side. Sliding a strong, steady arm around her waist, he helped her down the hallway while her mother anxiously trailed behind them.

Once they got to her bedroom, Winston gently helped Birdie back onto her bed. He was completely baffled as only moments ago she seemed in good humor and looked much healthier than she did during his previous visit. Her injuries were external, and she had initially shown no signs of concussion.

To be on the safe side, he performed a full examination as a concerned Hortensia hovered in the doorway. Birdie's pulse was a bit rapid bit otherwise her heart sounded fine. He checked her eyes and noticed a slight dilation of the pupils.

"Are you in any pain, Miss Fairfax?" he asked.

"No doctor," Birdie replied.

"Dizziness?"

"No sir."

"You seem to be trembling."

"I'm just a bit cold."

"I'll go make us all some tea," Hortensia offered as she headed for the kitchen.

Winston suspected that Miss Fairfax's symptoms were more psychological in nature but remained silent as he completed the physical exam. Storing the stethoscope back into his medical bag, he mentally went back over the earlier moments of his visit.

"Miss Fairfax," he began carefully, "Your physical health appears to be fine. However, you seem to be distressed about something."

He noticed that Birdie's eyes had briefly rested on his armband before she glanced downwards at her hands and softly replied, “Why no, doctor. I just had a funny turn, is all. Will you still allow me to return to work now?"

Winston absentmindedly stroked his close-cropped beard in bewilderment. The handsome spinster with the haunting amber eyes both puzzled and captivated him. Other than a few scrapes and bruises, there was nothing physically wrong with her, yet she definitely had some sort of spell when he arrived. Perhaps she was just one of those high-strung women who were prone to such occasional neurotic fits.

In any case, Winston felt almost reluctant to clear his patient for work as that would mean an end to his visits. There was something about Miss Fairfax which made him feel comfortable around her, something that didn’t happen very often for him.

"Yes, Miss Fairfax, you may return to work, but take care not to over exert yourself."

Hortensia soon returned from the kitchen carrying a small wooden tray which held two steaming cups of tea. She stifled the urge to grin as she noticed the unmistakable look of ardor in the doctor's eye. As she passed over the cups to Birdie and Winston, inspiration suddenly struck.

"Dr. Stokes, the Community Church is having an autumn festival in two weeks. We'd be honored if you could join us. There will be music, games and a lot of good food. You work so hard and even doctors need time to relax and enjoy life, do they not?"

Winston was pleasantly dumbstruck at the thought of seeing Birdie again in a non-medical setting. He quickly found his voice and replied, "I'd be delighted."

Birdie, still shocked by the possibility of this kind, wonderful man with the melodious Caribbean accent being related to a hateful scoundrel like Lonnie Stokes, glared over her teacup at Hortensia. What was she up to now?

Horst finished filling the last Windbeutel cream puff, carefully placed it with the others in the large wicker delivery basket and secured the lid. He then set the container next to three more filled with assorted strudels, rum cakes and stollen.

He looked at the clock by the empty display case which would soon be well stocked with fresh loaves of rye, wheat and pumpernickel that were currently in the ovens. It was almost 6:00. Frieda would soon be awake.

Horst breathed in the appetite-inducing aroma as he headed for the small utility room behind the kitchen. As usual, the smell of baking bread transported him back to his childhood when he would come home early from school to help his father in the family's busy bakery which was always teeming with customers.

His father Johann Metzger was a round, red faced jovial chap who actually came from a family of butchers. His choice of a career as a baker came less from a fondness of breads and pastries and more from a strong distaste of slaughtering animals. However, Johann's amiable and outgoing nature coupled with his creativity and keen aesthetic eye resulted in a successful business – one that he was eager to share with his sons.

Horst pulled the bucket out from under the sink and placed it under the pump. The water was ice cold this morning which didn't surprise him. There had been a nip in the air when he ventured outside an hour beforehand to bring in the empty baskets which were in the bed of the delivery wagon.

"Where is it?" Horst muttered to himself as he looked around for the vinegar. Once he found it on one of the wall shelves under a neatly folded kitchen towel, he grabbed the bottle, some rags and the heavy bucket of water and walked through the shop and out the front door.

A shiver ran down his spine. Frieda will no doubt insist he wear his coat today when he made his deliveries. Although she was the chronicly sick one of the pair, Frieda tended to fuss more about her husband bundling up against cold weather, the irony of which always made Horst chuckle.

He scrutinized the new sign in the corner of the window. "Official supplier of baked goods to the Montclair Hotel." It was crooked again. He'll straighten it up once he was back inside.

Horst sighed as he opened the bottle of vinegar and dipped one of the rags in the bucket. Both the sun and Frieda will be up soon and he had to work fast.

For the second time that week, Horst vigorously scrubbed at the words "Dirty Huns" which were scrawled across the shop's front display window.

Chapter 38

The day of the autumn festival started out drearily. An early morning shower had turned the church grounds muddy, transformed the outdoor paper decorations into mush and left puddles on the benches and tables which had been set up the night before.

As soon as the rain stopped, a brigade of volunteers including Hortensia, Birdie, Ophelia and a dozen others from the congregation headed over to the church armed with rags, mops, brooms and various odds and ends. The festival was to start at noon, so they only had a few hours to transform the sodden, pitiful scene before them into a place of celebration and merriment.

Hortensia and Ophelia spent the next hour wiping down all the tables and benches while the others policed the grounds picking up debris and laying straw down on the puddles. Meanwhile, Birdie was part of the group who took charge of redecorating the entrance of the church. While the rest were taking down the rain-soaked paper streamers, Birdie and a couple of others were furiously scouring the grounds for any flowers which were still in bloom.

One of the men returned with colorful branches of bright fuschia colored bougainvillea. Birdie found azaleas still in bloom on the south side of the property while two women returned with some sweet-smelling jasmine.

Together they managed to weave the flora into several decent boughs which were placed over the church's main entrance and wound through the front rails. The leftover flowers were placed in bottles and used as centerpieces on the newly dried tables outside.

What was left of the straw was bound into bales and, along with the pumpkins which were donated from Cy Boatwright's patch, were used to decorate the bandstand area on the side of the church.

After two and a half hours, everyone took a moment to rest and look around at the fruit of their labor before hurrying back to their homes to clean up and change into their finest clothing.

By the time the festival was in full swing, the grounds were abuzz with laughter, cheerful chatter, shouts, singing and dancing. Eddie Walker and his ragtime band were in full swing and several couples were hopping and twirling to the beat doing the one step, the cake walk and even the Turkey Trot. At one point, a cry of "It's a bear!" was heard as one of the couples suddenly broke into the Grizzly Bear dance to the delight of all the onlookers.

A group of boisterous youngsters were kicking a ball over the straw laden patch behind the church while a couple of small boys, including Ella's youngest son Charles, were attempting to climb one of the tall oaks.

Ella, sitting at a table with Ophelia, Betty and Hortensia, shouted, "Charles! Don't you dare tear them britches or I'll tan yo' hide!"

Betty, who held Ella's 4 month old baby Lilah on her lap, giggled. "Your husband was just as bad at that age! I declare, any time I wanted to find my Ronnie, all I had to do was look up into the nearest tree!"

"Now I know where to look next time he goes missin'!" said Ella as the others pealed with laughter.

Ronnie, who had been talking with a group of men near the refreshment table, returned to the table carrying several cups of lemonade. "Now what are you hens cacklin' about?"

"Never you mind!" retorted Ella as she took two of the cups from her husband, handing one to her mother and the other to Betty.

"Say," said Ronnie as he pointed towards the front of the church, "Who's that white man over there talkin' to Birdie?"

Hortensia glanced over at her daughter and smiled. “That’s Dr. Stokes, Lincolnville’s new temporary physician. And he’s actually a colored man from Jamaica.”

Ophelia craned her head to get a better look. “Well I’ll be! He’s the lightest colored man I’ve ever seen. He’s as white as Birdie.”

Betty glanced sharply at Ophelia. Hortensia, however, knew the comment was made in all innocence and merely smiled.

"Dr. Stokes, have you met Mrs. Barton?" Unsure as to whom Winston might have already encountered in the course of his practice, Birdie had made countless introductions that afternoon. When he first arrived, Winston was met with suspicious stares from some. Eventually word spread among the festival goers about his true identity and, as their initial reservations thawed, he was soon besieged with greetings.

"Why no, I don't believe I've had the pleasure," replied Winston as he courteously nodded to the elderly woman.

"So, you the new doctor I been hearin' about," Mamie Barton flashed a wide grin which was missing half its teeth. Despite her advanced age, the widow had a tendency to revert to a teenage coquette whenever she was in the company of young men. "Mah goodness, you sho do talk like a fine gentleman!"

Winston, who had heard this comment daily since his arrival in Florida, good naturedly laughed and replied, "You flatter me madam."

Casting a quick glance at Birdie, Mamie stealthily slid her arm through Winston's elbow. "Um, doctor? May I have a private word with you?" She lowered her voice to a whisper which caused Winston to stoop so he could hear her better. "I've got this...uh.....ladies' condition, ya see....."

Birdie quickly made her excuses. "I'll just go see how Bernie's doin' with the popcorn."

Winston cast Birdie an apologetic glance over Mamie's grey head. Birdie shot him a sympathetic grin before turning around and strolling over to the large ring of children which had formed on the church's front lawn. In the center of the young crowd was Bernie Talton, a gentle giant of a man who was tending a large black kettle over an open fire and would periodically shout, "Ya'll stay back, ya hear. I don't want no one gittin' burnt!"

Bernie slowly stirred the dried corn and oil around the bottom of the kettle until the first few kernels exploded into tiny white clouds, eliciting excited squeals from the younger children. Within minutes, the popping kernels gathered more momentum and soon the sound was deafening, only to be drowned out by the joyful screams of the exuberant onlookers.

"Now who wants some?" asked Bernie playfully. He was met with a loud chorus of, "Me! Me!"

Birdie smiled as she inhaled deeply. She loved the smell of fresh popcorn and enjoyed watching it pop as much as the youngsters.

Bernie caught her eye and tipped his hat. "Afternoon Sister Birdie!"

"Good afternoon, Brother Bernie. Need some help?" she offered, looking around for Bernie's wife.

"I'd be mighty obliged," he replied. "Evie had to go find a tablecloth fo' the cake booth but should be back directly."

Birdie made her way to the kettle and turned to the bustling children who were starting to push each other and quarrel about who would be first. She had to holler in order to be heard, "Ya'll need to quiet down! Now I want each of you to stand in line with the smaller children up front and the bigger ones at the end." This was met with moans of disappointment from the older youths but soon order was restored.

Once the popcorn was distributed and Evie Talton returned, Birdie took her leave. She looked around for Winston but he was nowhere to be seen so instead she joined Hortensia, Ella, and the others.

Her mother looked puzzled. "Where is Dr. Stokes?"

"Last I saw him, he had Mamie Barton on his arm," Birdie answered cheekily.

"Oh Lawd," exclaimed Ophelia. "That woman'll chew the poor doc's ear off 'bout all her miseries!"

Hortensia frowned as she scanned the crowd for the doctor but there seemed to be no sign of him. She wished her daughter had stayed by his side instead of letting him get waylaid by Mamie, a well-known hypochondriac.

The festival continued for a few more hours. Birdie divided her time between chatting with her friends and occasionally helping out at one of the food and game booths. She spotted Marcus a few times over the course of the afternoon. Although he was no longer in Mamie Barton's company, others were now clamoring for his attention.

As the sun started to drop in the sky, the crowd slowly dwindled until finally there was only Birdie, Hortensia, Ophelia and the rest of the church's ladies group left to clean up.

Hortensia was visibly annoyed as she furiously scrubbed the various food stains on the serving table. "Of all the nerve," she muttered to Birdie, who was nearby picking up crumpled popcorn bags, candy wrappings and fruit peels. "It's bad enough that we hardly saw hide or hair of Dr. Stokes all afternoon, but you'd think he'd at least have the good manners to tell you he was leaving instead of sneaking off like that!"

Birdie sighed. Although she too was puzzled at Winston's disappearance, she couldn't understand why her mother was so angry. "It's all right, ma. I'm sure he had a good reason. And besides, it's not like he and I are keepin' company." She shrugged and added, "I'm long past that stage of life, anyway."

The rag Hortensia was rubbing in quick circles immediately stopped as she cast her daughter a sharp glare. "Stop talking like an old woman! You still have time to get married and maybe have a family. I thought Dr. Stokes might have been a good prospect but now I'm not so sure." She shook her head as she carried on with her scrubbing.

"Ma, stop," said Birdie as she gently put a hand on Hortensia's arm. Once she saw that she had her mother's attention, she continued, "I'm 36 years old and in a few more years I'll be forty. I made peace with spinsterhood a long time ago and I ain't ashamed of it. Look at you. You done just fine by yourself all these years since pa died, and I know I can, too."

"But Birdie," protested Hortensia, "It was different for me. I was a widow. I already had the joy of loving a man and raising a child, and I had you here with me all these years since your father passed. Once I am gone, you'll have no one left." Wringing the rag in her hands, Hortensia looked around to make sure no one was nearby before she whispered, "Now I wish I'd let you keep your baby all those years ago. I suppose I could have passed her off as a distant relation and at least you'd have someone to look after you when I'm gone. But fear as well as my stubborn pride wouldn't allow it."

Hortensia's confession as well as the mention of Clara brought stinging tears to Birdie's eyes. She looked around to make sure none of the other women were within earshot. She put an arm around her mother as they both sat on the bench in front of the table.

"I know you were just trying to protect me, ma" Birdie said softly. "You only did what you thought was right back then. Sure, I was angry with you for a long time but now I know better because my girl went to a nice couple who've no doubt raised her right. And you can bet she's grown into a fine young lady."

"Mija, don't talk about betting while we're on church property," Hortensia chastised softly as she pulled a handkerchief from her sleeve to wipe a stray tear which was trailing down her nose.

Birdie chuckled. "Oh ma, it's just an expression, but I mean it. My Clara's had a ma and a pa who could give her everything that I couldn't."

"I know. You're right," replied her mother as she affectionately patted Birdie on the shoulder. Hortensia sighed as she picked up the rag. "I just don't want you to be left alone."

Birdie waved dismissively. "Don't ya worry about me, ma. Lord knows I've been through a lot and I'm still standin'. I'll be fine."

Buoyed by her daughter's reassurance, Hortensia flashed her a weak smile as she proceeded to another table.

Birdie looked pensively at Hortensia as she walked away. The thought had often crossed her mind over the years that eventually she would be on her own once her mother has passed but today was the first time they had openly discussed it. Despite the cheerful confidence she just displayed, Birdie still felt a twinge of fear inside – a deep terror of abandonment that she hadn't felt in a long time.

The bright three-quarter moon lit Winston's path as he strolled up to the front gate of the Fairfax home. He hoped the mint leaves he chewed on earlier would mask the smell of the alcohol. As he often did after a rough house call, Winston had settled his nerves with a couple shots of Jamaican rum earlier that evening.

After Mamie Barton had extracted him from Birdie's side earlier that day, he listened to her 45-minute-long litany of health complaints in the privacy of the reverend's small study in the rear of the church, giving her as much medical advice as he thought prudent and urging her to make an appointment.

Afterwards, Mamie introduced Winston to several curious festival goers including a distraught young woman named Yolanda Barnwell who had just run over to the church to seek out the Reverend. She wanted him to pray over her ailing father. However, when she learned Winston was a doctor, her eyes widened.

"Oh, thank the Lawd!" she had exclaimed. "Doctah, please come back to da house wid me and take a look at my pa. He's awful poorly and coughin' up blood. My ma's just beside herself!"

Even before he got to the house, Winston already knew what the diagnosis was. And once he saw the withered old man in the bed, feebly holding a blood-soaked handkerchief, he was sure. Consumption – the same illness which was slowly robbing his own father's life.

Winston squeezed his eyes shut as he tried to shake the memory of that afternoon from his mind. The decaying man with the death rattle cough, the sobbing wife, the frightened children in the next room. After a couple of hours, it was all over. Winston could still hear the screams of Yolanda and her mother as he closed the eyelids of Abraham Barnwell one last time.

Taking a deep breath, he strolled up the stone path leading to the front porch and gave the door a few sharp raps. Winston saw the lace curtains in the parlor window twitch and heard a couple of voices murmuring before the door opened. He was happy to gaze into the warm golden eyes of Birdie herself.

"Dr. Stokes, what a surprise!" cried Birdie as she opened the door further to let Winston inside. "Please come in."

Hortensia, who had been knitting in the parlor, stood up from her rocker. She stiffly but politely said, "Dr. Stokes. To what do we owe this pleasure?"

Winston took off his hat before he spoke. "I just wanted to apologize again for my disappearance. I'm afraid it's part and parcel of being a doctor."

"Apologize AGAIN?" asked Hortensia.

Winston was puzzled. "Why...yes. I had a medical emergency to tend to, so I sent one of the children to tell Miss Fairfax that I had to leave."

"So that's what happened," Birdie replied. "I'm afraid I never got the message."

"Oh no," Winston was instantly remorseful. "My apologies, ladies. You must think I'm a complete clod."

Hortensia, who had now softened her disposition, strongly retorted, "We think nothing of the kind! Please stay and take tea with us, Dr. Stokes."

Winston awkwardly fumbled with his hat. "Please don't go through the trouble, Mrs. Fairfax. Truth be told, I just wanted to speak to Miss Fairfax for a little while." Turning to Birdie, he asked. "Will it be okay if we sat on the porch?"

Birdie bashfully responded, "Certainly."

Hortensia beamed at the pair as they retreated outside and shut the front door behind them.

A wave of shyness washed over Birdie as she and the doctor sat on the wooden bench which overlooked the front yard and the street beyond. Even though dusk had fallen and no one was in sight, she still felt as though she was on display.

Winston, sensing Birdie's discomfort, made sure to keep a respectful distance between her and himself. He placed his hat on his knee as he nervously ran a hand through his coarse, wavy hair. Ever since staring death in the face earlier that day, all he wanted to do was spend some time in the delightful company of Miss Fairfax. But now that the opportunity was at hand, the words seemed to elude him.

Clearing his throat, Winston again apologized for leaving Birdie at the festival.

"Dr. Stokes, you don't need to apologize," she protested.

"And please, call me Winston," he replied.

"All right. Then you'll just have to call me Birdie."

"Birdie," Winston repeated thoughtfully. "I like it." He laughed as a childhood memory suddenly came to the forefront of his mind. "You know, back in Jamaica we had a song we used to sing when I was small."

Birdie was rapt with attention as Winston started to softly sing.

"Pretty little birdie
And her dulcet tweet
Awakens me each morning
With her song so sweet..

She sings
Tweedle-dee, dee
Tweedle, deedle doo

My sweet little Birdie
I love.......you..."

Abashed, Winston abruptly stopped as he fiddled with his hat as Birdie smiled timidly.

"That was lovely," she said. "You have a really nice singin' voice. I wish I did," she ruefully added. "For someone named Birdie, my tweets are anythin' but dulcet!"

Winston laughed and for the first time since his arrival, started to relax. He stared at Birdie for a moment, grateful for her putting him at ease. "Oh, I'm sure that's not true at all."

Birdie smiled. "I'm afraid it is. Now my friend Ella, she can sing. Takes after her mama. That's Ophelia Patterson, who you will no doubt meet soon."

"Do you have many friends here in Lincolnville?" Winston asked after a few thoughtful moments.

"Well, Ella is my only true friend. We grew up together," said Birdie. "She and her husband run a guest house for coloreds over on the island. Everyone else around here is kind enough, though." Looking down at her hands, she suddenly felt compelled to add, "But...I've... never truly felt like I belonged."

"I know," was all Winston said. Birdie, who was still surprised at herself for her utterance, slowly raised her eyes to meet Winston's and for the first time in her life, she knew she was with someone who completely understood. Someone who knew what it was like to be made up of different races but unable to be accepted by any of them. He really did know.

"I'm the illegitimate child of a man who once ran a large grove here in town but left it and his family for his Negro mistress – and for me."

Winston stared out over the darkened street as if he were gazing at something much further away. "To his credit, he did love my mother and wanted to give me a decent start in life, so we set sail for the Caribbean."

Birdie sat still as a statue as Winston revealed his past to her. She carefully studied his profile, illuminated by the silvery moon which was now prominent in the night sky, as he described the plantation he grew up on in vivid detail. The fair skin, green eyes and wavy thick hair which enabled him to pass for white at times were betrayed by his slightly thickened nose, full lips and West Indian accent. Overall, he was quite an attractive man, indeed.

Once the doctor was done telling Birdie his story, she asked, "How did they treat ya over there?"

Winston sighed deeply. "Well, I won't lie to you, Birdie. It wasn't that much different than it is here. The whites don't want me treating them while the Negroes look at me with suspicion. I saw a little of that today at the festival with some of your neighbors." He looked quizzically at Birdie and remarked, "It mustn't have been easy growing up around here for you."

Birdie again looked down at her hands and shook her head. "No, it wasn't."

Winston, who was well aware of the stories of his brother's involvement in the local Klan, remembered Birdie's initial reaction to him and her spell when she saw the mourning band that he wore for Lonnie's funeral. He finally asked the question that had been burning in his mind for the past several days. "Did you ever have any run-ins with my brother?"

The abrupt and unpredictable question stopped Birdie cold. A shiver ran up her spine as the short, fine hairs on her arms stood on end. Yet as thunderstruck as she was, when she looked into the kindly green eyes that were now gazing down expectantly at her, she felt safe enough to whisper the truth. “Yes, I did.”

And then it was Birdie’s turn to tell her own tale – slowly and haltingly. She kept her voice steady and low, so Hortensia wouldn’t hear. Winston’s face was stony as Birdie relayed to him the accounts of his brother’s threats along with the events of New Year’s Day, 1900.

Winston inwardly seethed. It was a good thing that Lonnie was already dead or else I would have gladly killed him himself, he thought. My oath to save lives be damned!

As Birdie finished speaking, a heavy silence hung between them for a couple of minutes as Winston took careful, deep breaths to calm himself. Once he was certain that he could trust himself to speak, he murmured, “Birdie, I can’t begin to tell you how sorry I am that someone I was related to caused you so much pain and suffering.” He gently reached for her right hand and gingerly held it between both of his own. “Please know that I am nothing like him. All we had in common was our father.”

“No!” exclaimed Birdie, “I wasn’t thinking that at all, Winston.” At the mention of his name, the doctor looked back over at Birdie. He loved how his name sounded when she said it in her soft Southern twang. “You’ve been nothin’ but kindness to me and I am so grateful.”

Overcome with a mixture of relief and affection, Winston brought Birdie’s hand to his lips and tenderly kissed it. The sensual delight of his warm breath and tickly mustache hairs on her skin caused her heart to pound and her face to flush.

After Winston took his leave, promising to return the next evening, Birdie felt like a giddy teenager again. However, remembering that she was now an older woman in her thirties, she immediately chastised herself.

But sliding into bed later that evening, Birdie couldn’t help smiling as she cradled her right hand close to her cheek.

Marcus Stokes sat up in his bed when he heard the key turn in the front door of the doctor's house where he and his son were taking up temporary residence while they were in town. Although he could have very easily checked into one of the lavish "whites only" resorts, he chose to stay with his son. This was not only out of family loyalty, but it was also medically necessary.

Holding a handkerchief to his mouth to stifle a brief coughing fit, Marcus hid the blood-stained cotton square under his pillow. It was getting harder to hide the extent of his illness from Winston, who was constantly badgering his father to submit to another physical exam. Marcus knew he was dying and as far as he was concerned, no damned doctor – not even his own son – was going to delay the inevitable.

He just needed to stay alive long enough to complete the business he had to do in St. Augustine before returning home to Jamaica and Claudette. His sons Tom and Nick were sending a man down to manage the Stokes family grove. But before he arrived, Marcus needed to make sure that the house was free of Lonnie's personal effects.

Marcus' heart felt like lead any time thoughts of Lonnie entered his mind. "Self-inflicted gunshot wound" was what the coroner's report had stated, but he knew otherwise. He was as guilty of his son's death same as if he'd fired that revolver himself. Why the hell did I have to run my mouth that night, he asked himself over and over again. As much as I despised his activities against folks of his own kind, I'd never wished him any harm. He was my son. My own blood for Christ's sake!

Before Marcus could ruminate any further, there was a soft knock at the bedroom door.

"Pop?" Winston asked hesitantly

"Come in, son," replied Marcus as he surreptitiously shoved the handkerchief further behind the pillow.

“You’re in bed already?” asked Marcus as he entered the room. “I thought you were playing cards tonight with Harry and Jake.”

“Yeah, I know, but I’ve got a lot to do tomorrow morning. I thought I’d better get some rest so I can get an early start,” lied Marcus. He had indeed intended to play cards but was too fatigued to make the trip across town. Plus, every joint in his body was aching which made movement next to impossible at the moment.

A worried look crossed Winston’s features as he glanced at his father. “You look a bit waxen. Are you sure you’re feeling all right? I wish you’d let me examine you.”

“Damnation!” exclaimed Marcus testily. “Stop fussin’ over me! I feel fine.” Seeing the look of shock on his son’s face at the unexpected tirade, Marcus immediately felt remorseful and decided it was time to change the subject. “So, where’ve you been?”

Winston sheepishly cleared his throat as he replied, “I was visiting with a patient.”

“Oh?” asked Marcus mischievously. From the time Winston learned to talk, his father always knew when he was skirting the truth. “Visiting a patient at this hour? Was he in a real bad state?”

Winston sighed as he gazed up at the ceiling. “The patient was a she, if you must know.”

“Oh, I see,” said Marcus, trying to suppress a smile. “And what is ailing this she?”

“Now Pop, you know I can’t talk about the folks I treat,” Winston feebly scolded.

“Well, isn’t that lucky for you,” remarked his father. “Just tell me this ain’t a white woman. I don’t need any trouble with the goddamned Klan. Just because Lonnie’s dead don’t mean there ain’t no more of them sonsabitches still prowlin’ around here.”

Winston was genuinely shocked. “Of course, she isn’t white! This is a Lincolnville doctor’s office for God’s sake!”

"All right, keep your britches on," said Marcus as he waved a palm towards his irate son. "Just make sure that any whorin' you do is discreet and stays 'round here. And don't forget..."

Winston knew what his father was about to say and immediately cut him off. "You can rest assured that no whoring of any kind is going on! As it happens the woman I saw this evening is of the highest moral character. And I haven't forgotten anything!"

Before Marcus could respond, his son stormed out of the room and slammed the door behind him. The older man sighed as he closed his eyes and reached behind him for his handkerchief. He felt another coughing spell coming on.

Chapter 39

For the next several weeks, Winston became a frequent guest at the Fairfax house. He often came in the evening when his office visits and house calls were completed and he knew that Birdie would be home from the Montclair. Hortensia always insisted that he had supper with them.

On Sundays, he would accompany both women to church. Afterwards, they would return to the Fairfax home for lunch which was followed by a stroll along the sea wall. They always invited Hortensia out of courtesy, but she always declined, wishing to give the pair their privacy.

One particular Sunday afternoon, they ambled along the top of the large, coquina fort just outside the town gate. Except for a couple of rambunctious young boys jumping off the lower wall to the east onto the grass below, the couple had the entire top floor of the fort to themselves.

"Watch your step, Birdie," cautioned Winston as he guided her by the elbow around a wide crack in the coquina floor near the corner sentry box.

"This fort's over two hundred years old," remarked Birdie. "I 'spose she's gonna have a few wrinkles here and there."

"I saw in yesterday's paper that the Department of War will be making repairs to it next year," said Winston.

"That's probably because things are getting' worse overseas and they wanna be ready," replied Birdie. "A lot of folks reckon we'll be at war soon, too."

They both grew silent as they gazed over the coquina walls at the Matanzas Bay below which reflected the slate grey early December sky above. A lone fishing boat was making its way over to the pier. The only sounds to be heard came from a distant automobile horn, a cathedral bell tolling the half hour and the faint shouts of the boys from the opposite end of the fort.

Although the sun was not due to set for another hour, the temperature was already dropping. Birdie shivered inside her woolen coat. Winston noticed her discomfort.

"Should we head back to your house?"

"Oh no, please let's stay," said Birdie. "After sweltering all summer, I'm loving this colder weather."

"All right, as you like," agreed Winston. "But I can't stand here and watch you shiver. Take my overcoat." As he started to slip out of his coat, Birdie placed her hand on his arm.

"No, I won't hear of it. You'll catch your death of cold, and then what good will you be to the rest of your patients?" she chided.

"Then there's only one other way to keep you warm," said Winston playfully as he slid an arm around Birdie's shoulders.

It was the first time in many years that Birdie had been held by a man. Up until now, while she was flattered and delighted by Winston's attentions, she never felt any true romantic feelings towards him. But now she found both his touch and his scent strangely intoxicating. It was almost as if she had been in a perpetual state of starvation and only just now realized how hungry she was. Something inside her was awakening.

"Is that better?" asked Winston.

"Yes, thank you," Birdie replied. Her tremoring only made Winston hold her tighter. She laughed nervously. "I'm surprised you're not the one shivering, coming from a tropical island."

Looking down into the amber eyes which had been haunting his dreams lately, Winston delicately cupped her chin and hoarsely whispered, "That's because I'm with you and nothing else matters right now."

Birdie was speechless. All she could do was raise her hand and place it over his, which tenderly stroked her face.

After quickly glancing around the immediate area to make sure they were still alone, Winston guided Birdie over to the nearby sentry box, a small cylindrical enclosure in the corner which extended over the bay. It was dark inside save for a narrow, wide peephole which looked onto the waters below.

Winston placed his lips over Birdie's, tentatively at first but when he felt her respond in kind, he started to probe her mouth with his tongue as he pressed himself firmly against her. Every nerve in Birdie's body was set ablaze as she wrapped both her arms tightly around his neck.

Eventually, Winston's lips worked their way from Birdie's mouth towards her bosom. As she let out a muffled gasp, he felt his warm breath on her earlobe.

"Birdie, I love you," he whispered. "Promise me you'll be mine."

Before Birdie could respond, the shouts of the boisterous young lads signaled their approach. Just as if a bucket of ice water was thrown on them, Birdie and Winston suddenly regained their senses and were once again aware of their surroundings. Winston straightened his cravat and Birdie patted her hair back into place before they emerged from the sentry box.

They walked side by side in companiable silence as they left the fort. Once outside by the sea wall, Winston was the first to speak.

"Please accept my apologies, Birdie. I didn't intend to take such liberties with you. I just lost my head."

"Well, I didn't exactly push you away," Birdie replied. "I think we both lost ourselves back there."

Winston stopped in his tracks and took both of Birdie's hands in his. "You know why? Because deep down we both know that we belong together. We're too much alike. You and I don't fit in anywhere else in this world except with each other."

Birdie gently squeezed his hands. "I must admit, you're the only man I've met who sees the world the same way that I do."

"That just proves I'm right," Winston replied excitedly. "We're made for each other. Oh Birdie, let's go away – far away. We could go up north. Or Canada. Or even Mexico. I don't care as long as we're together."

"But Winston, what about my ma? She's getting older now and I can't just up and leave her." Birdie protested.

"She can come with us. I like your mother. She's always been so kind to me."

"And what about your own pa?" asked Birdie.

"He'll be leaving for Jamaica soon anyway once he's finished with his affairs here. I'll give him a full exam before he leaves to make sure he's healthy enough to travel."

"And speakin' of Jamaica," began Birdie, "Don't you have a home there already? Why all this talk of goin' around the world?"

"Because we both could use a fresh start," Winston answered earnestly. Birdie had never seen him speak with such passion and conviction before. "It's time to liberate yourself from the South and its laws which were designed to keep people like us in subjugation for the rest of our lives just because we aren't 100 percent pure white. As for Jamaica, well...let's just say that I have my own ghosts there."

Birdie merely nodded. She had to admit that it all made perfect sense to her.

"Raise your side a few inches higher, Beulah," Hortensia called out to the widow McElroy, who along with Annie Evans were hanging a bough of greenery across the front of the sanctuary. "Yes, that's better."

The Altar Guild was busy decorating the church for its upcoming Christmas service the following week. Piles of assorted branches, vines twisted into wreaths and colorful paper chains made by the children of the congregation were strewn across the front pews, ready to adorn the walls, altar and main entryway.

Hortensia returned to the supply room where Ophelia was busily polishing up the candelabra that was to be placed on the altar. The strong smell of Brassy Brite overpowered the small enclosed space.

"Do you remember where we stored the altar cloth after last year's Christmas service, Ophelia?"

Ophelia paused and closed her eyes as she tried to jog her memory. Then, pointing towards the back of the room, she replied, "I think we put it in dat ole wooden chest over there so the moths wouldn't get at it."

Hortensia opened the chest and rummaged through a pile of choir robes before finding the familiar blue velvet cloth with the silver embroidered cross on it. As she lifted it out of the layers of vestments, she spotted the gaping hole in one of its corners.

"Oh no!" she wailed as she looked down the side of the chest. Sure enough, there was also a hole chewed through near the floor. "Well, the moths didn't get at this but the mice sure did!"

"Lawd, ain't nothin' sacred," muttered Ophelia.

Hortensia took another look at the damage. "At least it's just here in one corner. Birdie should be able to fix this for us. I'll take it home with me."

Ophelia giggled as she placed the lid back onto the can of brass polish. "Looks like yo' Birdie ain't had much time fo' anything else but Dr. Stokes lately."

"Ophelia! That's utter nonsense," chastised Hortensia. "Birdie would be more than happy to help out the church in any way she can."

"Oh, I ain't denyin' that, sista," said Ophelia. "But we all know where to find the doctah when he ain't at his office. We ain't gotta look no further than yo' front porch. I saw them two leavin' here earlier after service - side by side, their heads together and talkin' all quiet like so no one else will hear 'em. I'm sure he's up on yo' porch right now holdin' her hand and sayin' sweet things to her. If that ain't a couple in love, then I don't know what is."

Hortensia's shoulders sagged as she sighed. It was useless keeping up pretenses around her oldest and closest friend. Especially when Hortensia herself had silently made the same observations.

"Oh Ophelia, from your lips to the Lord's ear!" she cried. "I've been praying for years that my Birdie would find a suitor. I gave that up long ago. Who ever thought that she'd finally find someone now at this time in her life? And a DOCTOR, no less!"

"Mmm hmmm" agreed Ophelia. "Ya'll struck gold there. So, when do ya think he'll ask fo' her hand?"

"Soon, I hope," answered Hortensia. "But I'll just have to wait and let things unfold naturally, as the Lord wills it."

"Amen," replied Ophelia as she picked up the candelabra and headed for the sanctuary.

Birdie watched the retreating figure of Winston as he walked down Citrus Avenue and disappeared around the corner. As he often did lately on Sunday afternoons, he escorted Birdie and Hortensia to church and stayed for dinner afterwards. The past six weeks had certainly been an emotional and romantic whirlwind of evening strolls, long talks on the front porch, intense conversations, holding hands and stolen kisses.

It all still seemed unreal to Birdie. She would never have guessed that she would be courted by the brother of Lonnie Stokes, whose very name used to fill her with sheer terror. Even more unbelievable was that she finally found a suitor after years of being a confirmed spinster.

Birdie sat down on the bench just outside her front door. Leo, one of the more affectionate cats from Sugar's last litter before she passed away, jumped up onto her lap. As he often did when he wanted attention, he gently nudged Birdie's hand with his head.

As she absent-mindedly stroked Leo between the ears, Birdie's mind continued to ruminate. Despite her affection for Winston and the passion he aroused in her, something was amiss. While they were well suited for each other, Birdie wished she felt more certain about whether she wanted to spend the rest of her life with him.

It was times like this that she missed having Ella living nearby. Ella would know exactly what to say and what Birdie should do. But according to Ophelia, Ella and Ronnie had their hands full at the moment playing host to Ronnie's relations from Macon, Georgia who had come down to visit.

Birdie looked down at the calico cat who had now rolled over on his back in the hopes that his belly would be scratched. Running her fingers between his front paws, Birdie sighed. "Maybe it's time I finally grow up, take my life into my own hands and stop lookin' for excuses not to be happy."

As Winston open the front door of the doctor's residence, he noticed that an envelope with a Jamaican King George stamp had been shoved under the door. It was addressed in his mother's unmistakable handwriting. He placed it on the varnished wood shelf that hung over the parlor's fireplace, intending to read it once he made himself a cup of tea.

As he took off his jacket and hung it on the coat hook in the entryway, a knock at the front door startled him. Expecting it to be a neighbor with some sort of medical emergency, he opened the door and was surprised to see Dolly Vinson on his doorstep. For as long as anyone could remember, the elderly woman had done the cleaning and laundry for the doctor's surgery.

"Why Mrs. Vinson. What brings you out here on a Sunday evening? No one's sick, I hope," said Winston.

"Evenin' Dr. Stokes," replied Dolly. "I'm awful sorry to trouble you this late but when I was cleaning yesterday, I plum forgot to take the linens from yo' father's room. I just saw yo' pa headin' into town and reckoned I could come over and git the sheets from his room so I can git 'em done with the rest of my washin' tomorrow mornin'."

"Of course. Come in, Mrs. Vinson." Winston said as he ushered the older woman inside.

"Again, I'm mighty sorry, doctah. I declare – my mind must be on its way out," Dolly said cheerfully as she made her way to Marcus' bedroom.

Winston chuckled as he headed into the kitchen. "You're the sharpest person I know, Mrs. Vinson."

After several minutes, Dolly appeared in the kitchen doorway looking puzzled. "Dr. Stokes, what happened to the spare set of sheets that I stored in the armoire? They ain't there now."

Thinking that the elderly woman must have just forgotten where she put them, Winston followed her back into the bedroom to help her search for the misplaced linens.

"Fo' years I have kept the spare sheets down here," Dolly insisted as she pointed to the open armoire, which only held a few articles of his father's clothing and a spare pair of shoes.

Thinking that she might have accidentally stored them in the doctor's office, Winston said, "Mrs. Vinson, I might have accidentally put them in the exam room with the towels. Would you mind checking in there for me?"

"Now why on earth would you do something like that?" Dolly muttered as she shuffled down the hallway towards the office.

Winston cheerfully shook his head as he continued searching his father's room. He checked all the drawers in the bureau, the armoire once again and even under the bed. As his eyes glanced over the bed, he noticed that the mattress had a slight ridge in the center. Strange, he thought. That can't be comfortable to sleep on.

Lifting up the mattress, Winston found a large wad of balled up sheets crammed underneath. As he pulled them out, a chill ran down his spine when he saw the numerous dried up blood stains. His long-held suspicions were finally confirmed. The constant cough. The weakness. The sickly pallor. The fatigue, and now the profuse bleeding. His father was further along than he reckoned. It was time to return to Jamaica.

Birdie could barely keep her mind on her work the next day. Mavis had to remind her twice to get the menus from Rita. And when she was upstairs doing an evening gown fitting for Lottie Prescott, she had accidentally stuck her with a pin.

She had made up her mind and decided to say 'yes' to Winston the next time he popped the big question. Even though she was unable to do so yet, she reckoned she would eventually learn to love him and they would have a wonderful life together. And best of all, her mother would be able to live with them.

So, when Winston came to call later that evening, Birdie was bursting to tell him her news. However, she soon sensed that something was not right with him.

"Good evening, ladies," he said solemnly. He nodded courteously at Hortensia who was hovering in the background, holding a dish towel.

"Won't you join us for a slice of custard pie?" she asked.

"As much as I'd love to, Mrs. Fairfax, I need to talk to Birdie urgently," he replied.

Hortensia suppressed a smile. This is it, she thought. He's about to propose. Aloud, she replied, "Of course. Take all the time you need."

Once the couple settled on the porch, Winston took Birdie by the hand. His eyes were intense. Like her mother, Birdie also began to anticipate a proposal.

Instead, Winston said, "Birdie, I'm afraid I must go back home. My father's dying."

Feeling like the wind was knocked out of her lungs, Birdie whispered, "Oh Winston. I'm so sorry."

Squeezing his eyes shut, Winston brought both of Birdie's hand to his lips and kissed them both. "You can't be half as sorry as I am. Leaving you is going to be the hardest thing I've ever done."

Tears started to form in Birdie's eyes. Her voice broke as she asked, "Will you be back?"

Winston wrapped both arms around her and whispered in her ear, "Yes! I promise I'll be back. Will you wait for me, my love?"

Not trusting herself to speak, Birdie could only nod.

Winston sighed with relief. "Thank you, my sweet Birdie. Knowing that you'll be here waiting for me will help me through the tough time we'll have to spend apart."

Birdie suddenly remembered something. "I'll be right back," she said before disappearing into the house. A few moments later she re-emerged holding a small tissue paper parcel.

"This was the Christmas gift I was going to give you next week," she said as she handed it to him.

Now it was Winston's turn to keep a grip on his emotions. "Can I open it now?"

"Yes, of course you can."

Winston carefully opened the package and unfolded the white silk handkerchief inside. An ornate "W" was hand embroidered in the corner.

"Birdie, this is lovely."

"I made it myself. I wasn't sure what to get you, so I reckoned that most menfolk could always do with a handkerchief." Birdie said as she fingered the neatly hemmed edges of the silk.

"Then I'll treasure it all the more," Winston said as he placed it in the breast pocket of his jacket.

"So, when do you leave?" asked Birdie, with a heart heavy with dread.

"I'm going to the shipping office tomorrow to see what's going out this week and to send a wire back home to my mother. I hear there's a ship bound for Jamaica leaving on Thursday."

"Why that's only three days from now," remarked Birdie.

"That gives me three more days to be with you," said Winston as he leaned in for a kiss.

Winston stood at the railing as the R.M.S. Athena docked into Montego Bay. The ominously dark skies over the island which foretold of an oncoming storm reflected the doctor's somber mood. Since his last meeting with Birdie several days ago, he felt as if his heart had been ripped out of his chest.

He watched the scraps of his mother's letter floating aimlessly in the waters below. The letter which had arrived that fateful evening he discovered his father's ailing health had been forgotten about until earlier this morning when he discovered it in his doctor's bag, still unopened. After reading its contents, Winston knew his fate was sealed.

Marcus Stokes hobbled over with the aid of a newly acquired cane and stood beside his son. A crowd of people had formed on the dock. Many of them were eagerly waving to the arriving ship's passengers.

"Spotted them yet?" asked Marcus.

Winston just shook his head.

"What the hell's eatin' ya, boy? You've had the personality of a rattlesnake ever since we left."

"I'm all right, Pop," Winston replied irritably. Pointing towards the dock, he added, "Look. There they are."

Marcus squinted and after a few seconds, nodded his head and waved. "Yes! I see them."

At the edge of the crowd stood Winston's mother Claudette, dressed in her finest clothes and Sunday hat, and standing next to her was Winston's wife Eralia who was self-consciously hiding her swollen belly under a bright yellow wrap.

Just as his mother had said in her letter, his bride of six months was pregnant with their first child.

1917

Chapter 40

"That's too beautiful to eat, Mr. Metzger!" exclaimed Mavis as she, Rita, Birdie and the kitchen assistants stood gathered around the large four-tiered German chocolate cake which the baker had just delivered.

"How on earth did you make them roses?" asked Rita as she stared closely at the edible floral display which adorned the top layer.

"Those are actually chocolate curls. My wife Frieda makes those. She's got a steadier hand and a lot more patience than I," said Horst Metzger with pride. He loved to boast on his wife's creative talents whenever the opportunity presented itself.

"Mrs. Prescott'll love this," remarked Birdie as she admired the scallop shaped swirls of chocolate frosting which edged each tier. While the Montclair had always served ornately decorated cakes and pastries, she had never seen anything quite like this before.

Today was Lottie Prescott's birthday. Although she refused to reveal her age, word had it that this was a particularly special milestone. The Montclair employees quietly speculated about this with whispers and giggles in the staff dining room. The general consensus was that this was her 60th birthday but the lady herself remained silent on the subject. Only her husband knew the truth.

"I wish to thank you again for your continued patronage. It means so much to Frieda and to me," said Horst sincerely.

"We are happy to do it, Mr. Metzger," assured Mavis. "Your baked goods continue to bring delight to our guests, especially during these lean times. If you'll just follow me, I'll give you this month's payment."

"Poor man," remarked Rita after Horst and Mavis departed. "He and his missus have had a rough go of it lately, but bless their hearts, they continue to bring us their finest pastries – always on time and always top notch."

"And to think, we're pretty much the only customers he has left. I really feel bad for him. I wish there was more we could do," said Birdie.

"I know, I feel the same," said Rita. "But what else can we do? Money's tight for us, too with this hotel bein' half empty and all. All that fightin' over there in Europe has affected everyone in one way or another."

"Yeah, but the Metzgers have got it even worse," said Birdie gravely.

Since the United States entered the war in Europe, anti-German sentiment started to spring up all over the country, and Florida was no exception. Holding an anti-German attitude was the American way of showing patriotism to the United States war effort.

As a result, local schools and colleges were burning all books written in German or by German authors, German language classes were shut down, German speaking church services were banned, and musicians made sure not to perform polkas or any piece of music by German composers. Even the German measles became "liberty measles."

Street and town names which sounded German were Americanized. Therefore, Schultz Boulevard became Freedom Boulevard and the small town of Brattenburg reverted back to its original Indian name of Weekahumpka.

But the German business owners received the brunt of the public's resentment. Shop windows were smashed, stores were looted, profanities were painted on doors and in extreme cases like the Metzger bakery, the entire business would be burned down.

Three months ago, Horst and Frieda woke up in the wee hours of a Wednesday morning to the smell of smoke. Thinking he might have accidentally left an oven on, Horst ran downstairs and discovered that his entire bakery was ablaze. He tried in vain to put the fire out himself as his calls for help went unheeded. By daybreak, much of the entire first floor laid in ashes. As the Metzgers plodded through the wreckage, Frieda found a bottle with the remains of a kerosene-soaked rag inside.

This came as no surprise to Horst, who had spent the past couple of years cleaning the slurs off his windows each morning. But to Frieda, the world became a terrifying place overnight. Now she rarely ventured outdoors. With the Montclair as their only remaining client, the couple continued to fill the baking orders from their small kitchen upstairs.

In the head housekeeper's office, Mavis handed Horst a small manila envelope. "Here you go, Mr. Metzger. Has Rita given you her order for next week?"

Horst looked uncomfortable. "Yes, Miss Kinkade. But....eh...there is a chance I might be unable to fill it."

Mavis was puzzled. "Why is that, Mr. Metzger?"

Despite the pair of them being the only ones in the office, Horst looked around before speaking to make sure no one else was within earshot. "I received this letter yesterday." He pulled a folded piece of writing paper from his coat pocket and handed it over to Mavis.

We've burnt you goddamned huns out of your bakery.
Your house is next.

"Oh my goodness!" gasped Mavis. "Have you showed this to the sheriff?"

"Yes, but he said it was probably just a couple of jokers playing a prank that got out of hand," replied Horst. His brow was deeply furrowed with worry. "But they've still managed to completely destroy my bakery. What will become of us? We can't go back to Germany because of the fighting there and staying in this country is proving to be dangerous to us as well."

An idea came to Mavis. "Mr. Metzger, may I keep this note? I'll see what we can do."

Horst nodded his assent. "Thank you again, Miss. Kinkade. Let us pray that this is indeed just a one time incident and that I'll be back next week with your order."

"Oh, Johnathan!" cried Lottie Prescott. "You made sure they played my favorite song."

The small band, which was performing up in the music alcove, had just struck up the opening bars of "My Sweetie."

The Prescotts were celebrating Lottie's birthday that evening with a few friends at their private table which overlooked the entire Montclair dining room. Lottie was resplendent in her new gown of ivory and gold metallic brocade trimmed with embroidered netting and crystal beading. Her hair was a mass of grey streaked curls piled atop her head and crowned with a diamonelle princess tiara.

Despite the regal bearing that Lottie tried to exude, the two glasses of Dom Perignon had already gone straight to her head and she was singing at the top of her voice along with the band leader.

Wait till you see me with my sweetie
Showing her off to the crowd
Looking so dreamy at my sweetie
Feeling so terribly proud...

Lionel and Elizabeth Samuels shared a bemused look while Reverend Frederick Davis and his wife Beattie exchanged dubious glances. Johnathan, who had seen his wife in this state more times than he could remember, wearily stubbed out his cigar.

"Now dear. We're paying that gentleman up there to sing. Let's keep quiet so we can hear him."

"Say Prescott, your band's looking a bit long in the tooth," observed Lionel Samuels.

"Well, we're at war, aren't we?" Prescott tried hard to mask his irritation. "Half our band got drafted."

Looking around the dining, Beattie Davis remarked, "I suppose half of your wait staff is also in Europe? I've never seen so many old Negro waiters and women serving in a hotel dining room before."

Despite her inebriated state, Lottie realized that her husband's patience was being tested and that diplomacy was immediately called for. "Well, we try to make due as best we can. After all, we must all do our part for the war effort, mustn't we?"

"Here! Here! You're absolutely right," said Reverend Davis. "I applaud the sacrifices your resort has been making, and yet, you still manage to maintain a very high standard of excellence." Raising his champagne flute, he added, "To you, Mr. and Mrs. Prescott. And to the Montclair."

Lottie smiled gratefully at the Reverend and echoed, "To the Montclair." A clinking of glasses followed and was soon interrupted by the arrival of the birthday cake which elicited a chorus of "oohs" and "aahs."

"Oh! It's absolutely beautiful!" cried Lottie as she clapped her hands in delight.

"Indeed," Elizabeth Samuels chimed in. "Look at those flowers!"

"Impressive," remarked Prescott. Turning to his wife, he asked, "Is this from our kitchen or from our supplier?"

"Mavis told me it was made especially by our supplier," replied Lottie.

Beattie leaned in to take a closer look. "Is that coconut in the frosting? I don't think I've seen anything like this before. What kind of cake is it?"

"German chocolate," answered Lottie as she watched the waiter make the first cut into the bottom tier. Her mouth was already watering in anticipation. But her delightful reverie was immediately cut short by a gasp from Beattie and a "tut tut" from Lionel.

"German chocolate?" repeated Beattie. "Where on earth did this cake come from?"

"From a European baker in town who we've been using for the past couple of years," Lottie replied cautiously. Despite her slightly inebriated state, she sensed something was brewing.

"And by 'European', do you mean German?" asked Lionel.

Now it was Prescott's turn to intervene. "And so what if he IS German? He's here in St. Augustine baking bread, not over in Europe gunning down our boys."

"Now Johnathan, please keep your voice down," Lottie said soothingly as she patted her husband on the hand. "After all, this is meant to be a night of celebration and we don't want the mood ruined."

"Not to worry, my dear Mrs. Prescott," replied Lionel. "I for one am not about to make a scene. However, I will pass on the cake. I refuse to eat anything made by a German. You never know what he might have put in that."

"Utter nonsense!" Prescott snapped.

By now the waiter was passing around plates of the sliced cake. Only Reverend Davis, Lottie and Johnathan accepted. The rest politely declined, opting for the key lime mousse instead. The atmosphere at the table was now muted in contrast to the conviviality of the rest of the dining room.

Lottie only took two bites of her cake before putting her fork down. For the rest of the evening, she kept a polite and stoic façade which covered the rage she was feeling inside.

Two-year-old Lilah Simms squirmed as she sat on Birdie's lap and hid her face behind her small chubby hands. "Peekaboo!" The tot squealed with high pitched laughter.

Birdie couldn't help giggling herself. "You are one silly child!" she exclaimed as she proceeded to tickle Lilah under the chin, which only caused the small girl to laugh even harder.

The two sat on one of the several rockers which graced the front porch of the inn. Despite its proximity to town, Birdie rarely had a chance to go out and visit the Simms due to their constant stream of guests as well as her own workload at the Montclair. However, over the past several months, tourism had dwindled. At the moment, Birdie only had to work half days on Thursdays. So earlier that afternoon, she took the opportunity to ride the omnibus over the bridge to Anastasia Island.

The front door creaked open as Ella emerged carrying a tray of glasses and a pitcher of sun tea. Lilah pointed at the pitcher.

"I want! I want!"

"The only thing you want right now is a nap," said Ella as she picked the toddler up off Birdie's lap. "Say goodbye to Auntie Birdie."

But the child's attention was on the lemonade. "I want!"

"I'll be right back," said Ella as she took her daughter upstairs. The child's high-pitched screams could still be heard all the way from the second floor.

Birdie reclined, closed her eyes and breathed in the salt air. Even though the ocean was two blocks away, she could hear its roar just as loudly as if she were standing right in it.

A year and a half ago, any mention of the ocean had immediately brought with it thoughts of Winston. Birdie had received a letter from him six weeks after he left informing her that his father had finally passed away and that not a day went by when he didn't think about her. There was no return address on the letter except a postmark from Montego Bay. Birdie tried to send a letter to Winston via general delivery but several months later, it was returned to her unopened. She never heard from him again.

Looking back on it now, Birdie realized that she was more puzzled than heartbroken. Hortensia, however, was devastated when Birdie's letter was returned and took to her bed for a week.

She had pinned such high hopes on a betrothal between the doctor and her daughter. As far as Hortensia was concerned, the name of Winston Stokes was akin to a curse word and was never to be mentioned under her roof again.

The only one who was not surprised at the turn of events was Ella, who had always been suspicious and reticent when it came to the relationship between the doctor and her best friend.

"I just knew it!" she had said to Ronnie shortly after learning of the returned letter. "I just knew that man was up to no good from the first time I laid eyes on him at that church festival!"

Ronnie, who knew full well of his wife's thoughts on the matter, had only sighed and replied, "Yes, you sho' did."

"I knew there was somethin' fishy 'bout that man. No one that good lookin' stays single fo' that long. I'm tellin' ya, the only reason he ain't written to Birdie is because he got himself a wife already over there! After all, what else can you expect from the brother of that no good Lonnie Stokes. That high yaller doctor had the same evil blood runnin' through his veins."

"I reckon you're right, honey," Ronnie responded as he started to thumb through the guest ledger.

"The problem with Birdie is, she's too trustin' of people. And her ma wasn't makin' things any easier – pushin' that whole marriage nonsense," Ella continued.

"Well," said Ronnie as he turned over one of the ledger sheets, "Birdie's a grown woman. I reckon she can handle it."

Since then, Ella resolved to try to get over into town and see Birdie more often. Unfortunately, circumstances often prevented this from happening, so she was delighted when her best friend showed up on her doorstep today. Luckily their guest load was light that week and she was able to entertain Birdie properly.

Ella returned to the front porch and flopped into the rocker next to Birdie's. Lilah's initial howls had now subsided into occasional sobs. Soon she would exhaust herself into a deep slumber.

"I declare – between runnin' this inn and raisin' that child, I don't know which one wears me out most," Ella sighed. She poured out two glasses of the sun tea and offered one to Birdie.

"You're not foolin' me, Ella Simms," declared Birdie. "I know you too well. You might be exhausted, but you wouldn't have it any other way. You have a great life here and you wouldn't trade it for anything in the world."

Ella momentarily paused. "I guess I can't argue with that. Everythin's goin 'good fo' us right now. Well, almost everythin'."

Birdie patted Ella on the arm. Her brother Horace and his wife Kalise had a cross burned in front of their house a couple of weeks ago. The couple ran a successful general store in a historically black neighborhood just outside Jacksonville. The little shop took a significant portion of trade from a few neighboring white owned stores. Even though white customers were always shown preference and waited on first at these other establishments, the exodus of the Negro customers to Horace's shop was nonetheless felt economically.

Now Horace and his wife were in the Klan's crosshairs and were being pressured to shut down. With the KKK becoming more active than ever, similar stories were circulating around the Negro community more frequently these days.

"Just when you think things can't get no worse, they do," said Ella, shaking her head. "The whole world's gone plum crazy. Ronnie was readin' in the paper this mornin' 'bout white folks turnin' on other white folks and burnin' them outta their homes. I never thought I'd see the day when they start attackin' their own."

"That's different, though," said Birdie. "That's all about the war over there in Europe. Now it's the Germans here in town who are bein' targeted."

"Well, they can't be havin' it as bad as we do," opined Ella as she took a deep swig from her glass.

Birdie remained silent as she thought of the Metzgers.

Still a bit worse for wear after last night's festivities, the knock at Johnathan Prescott's office door sounded like someone was pounding on it with a hammer.

"Come in," he shouted as he rubbed his temples. When he saw Mavis enter, his tone became more cordial. "Ah, Miss Kinkade. Come in and have a seat."

Mavis shut the door and sat in one of the chairs which faced Prescott's desk.

"Actually, I'm glad you're here because I was going to come down and see you anyway," said Prescott. "We won't be requiring the services of that town baker you've been using. You'll either have to search for another one or we'll have to impose on our own cook to do more baking than she's already doing."

Stunned, Mavis asked, "May I ask why, Mr. Prescott? Was the birthday cake for Mrs. Prescott not to her taste? She's always seemed very pleased with the pastries and breads provided by Mr. Metzger."

"The cake was fine. It's the company that wasn't," grunted Prescott.

"I'm afraid I don't understand, sir," replied Mavis who was by now truly puzzled.

"Lottie and I have no problems whatsoever with the baker and his goods. That cake last night was one of the best I've ever tasted. But given what's been going on with the Germans lately....well, let's just say some of our guests would be less than understanding."

"Oh, I see," said Mavis. "Perhaps I should show you this." She handed over the note she'd been holding.

Prescott unfolded the sheet of paper, glanced down at it and, forgetting that he was in a lady's presence, exclaimed, "Damnation! What the hell is this?"

Mavis, used to ignoring her employer's rough language, replied, "Mr. Metzger received this two days ago. I'm afraid that the Montclair has been his sole means of financial support since the war began, and now it seems that he and his wife are in harm's way. Oh, Mr. Prescott. I know I have no right to ask you this, but is there any way we can retain his services for at least a little while? We can just order breads from him. Nothing with German sounding names, and I can always send Birdie to collect them so that he wouldn't be seen coming here."

Prescott smiled warmly at the housekeeper. "You have a heart of gold, Miss Kinkade." As he often did when dealing with a difficult matter, he walked over to the window overlooking the well-manicured grounds. After giving the matter some thought, he turned to Mavis.

"All right. We'll keep him on for right now and will do as you suggested. Just breads and send Miss Fairfax over for them. Let me know if he has any more trouble with these ruffians."

"Yes, sir! And thank you, Mr. Prescott."

The hotelier waved a dismissive hand to Mavis, a signal that their meeting was now over. As she headed for the door, his voice stopped her.

"Oh, Miss Kinkade..."

Mavis turned around. "Yes sir?"

"Not a word to Mrs. Prescott about any of this."

Chapter 41

As he strolled down St. George Street carrying two sacks of flour, Horst realized that he was whistling for the first time in months. It had been several weeks since he received the threatening note and nothing had happened since. Perhaps the police were right and it was just some youths letting off steam. However, he still remained vigilant, and Frieda continued to stay indoors and kept the curtains shut as often as she could. Horst rarely left the house unless he had to go for supplies, as he did this morning.

Eddie Hartsfield was the only grocer in town still willing to do business with the Metzgers despite the grief he got for it off the townspeople. For that very reason, Horst would always be as grateful to Eddie as he was to the Montclair staff. Without their support he wouldn't know how he and Frieda would survive.

As he approached the burnt out shell of his bakery, he noticed that the front door which led to the living quarters upstairs was ajar. Alarm immediately swept through his body because he always locked Frieda in the house every time he went out. He dropped both bags of flour, which split open when they hit the hot sandy street. Horst sprinted as fast as he could, leaving a small white cloud behind him.

When he got to the door, he noticed it had been pried open. He ran up the steps, two at a time, yelling, "Frieda! Frieda!" When he entered their small parlor, he stopped short. A strong smell of kerosene permeated the air. The furniture and rag rug under his feet were saturated in it. The small whatnot shelf in the corner was knocked down. Vases and knick knacks were shattered and strewn all over the floor.

"Frieda!" he yelled again as he peered into the kitchen, which was also doused in kerosene and littered with broken china and glass shards.

When Horst burst through the bedroom door, he heard a frightened moan coming from the other side of the room, which had also been ransacked. There on the floor in the narrow space between the bed and the window sat his wife, her hands and feet tied together, and a kerosene-soaked rag in her mouth. Her eyes were wide with terror. A large red welt colored her right cheek. Horst also noticed that the bodice of her dress was torn.

"Mein Gott!" shouted Horst as he pulled out the gag. His wife let out a loud, primal scream as he continued to untie her.

"I'm here now, meine Liebste," he said soothingly as he sat on the floor and held his sobbing wife for almost an hour until her cries eventually subsided.

"What happened? Who did this?"

Frieda shuddered as she recalled the event. "After you left, I was in the kitchen kneading the bread dough when I heard the door open downstairs. I thought you had forgotten something. And then three men......" She paused as she steadied her wavering voice. "Three men ran in and they started yelling. They called me a 'hun whore' and started breaking everything." Again, Frieda had to stop and gather her composure. Horst gently cradled her as she continued, "Two of the men were carrying big cans of kerosene and they spilled it everywhere. Then the third man..." Frieda collapsed into sobs.

"What did the third man do?" asked Horst, who dreaded the answer.

"The third man dragged me into the bedroom and threw me on the bed. He said he wanted to see what kind of 'hun whore' I really was and he started to rip my dress off. That was when I began to scream and I scratched at his eyes. He started to bleed badly and slapped me hard. The other men were shouting at him to leave me because they wanted to get out of here before someone heard the noise I was making. So he tied me up, put that cloth in my mouth and let one of the men spray me with the last of the kerosene. Before they left, they wrote that over there." Frieda pointed towards the opposite wall.

Horst looked over at the message scrawled in red grease pencil.

"We'll be back later with the matches."

Rita had just handed over the last of that evening's pans to the women in the scullery for scrubbing. Today had been a particularly trying day and all she wanted to do was go home and put her feet up.

As she often did before she left every evening, Rita walked around the kitchen a final time to make sure that everything was put away properly and that the stove was completely shut off. Only a few days prior she'd discovered that Estelle, her newest kitchen aide, had mistakenly left the oven on before she left for the day.

But tonight everything seemed to be in order. The stove and oven were both off, all the remaining pots and pans were being scrubbed by Eva and her crew, and Rita didn't spot anything else amiss until she turned her eyes to the meat preparation station in the corner where a jar of paprika still remained on the counter.

"Oh Estelle, will ya ever learn?" muttered Rita as she grabbed the jar and headed back to the pantry. That was when she heard the muffled but urgent knocks on the outside door which was normally used for deliveries.

"Now who in the world could this be?" she asked aloud as she went to open the door. She was shocked to see Horst Metzger and a small, frightened woman with a tear stained face huddled next to him. Rita was further perplexed by the unmistakable smell of kerosene which seemed to be wafting from them.

"Good evening, Mrs. Alvares. Is it possible to speak to you?" asked Horst as Frieda sniffled and wrapped her cloak around herself tightly.

"Certainly, Mr. Metzger. Come in. Both of you," offered Rita, stepping aside to let the couple in. As she shut the door, she added, "You caught me just in time. I was gettin' ready to leave."

Horst, feeling awkward, stuck his hands in his pockets. "I apologize for the inconvenience. We won't take up too much of your time. I was just wondering if Mrs. Kinkade may still be here. I really need to see her."

"I'm sorry, Mr. Metzger. She left a little while ago." Rita replied.

Frieda suddenly began to weep. Her bony shoulders shook violently under her wrap. Horst wrapped a protective arm around her as he remarked, "I'm afraid my wife is indisposed. We've had a very difficult day."

"Aw honey, come over here and sit down next to me," cooed Rita as she took the distressed woman by the hand and sat her down on a citrus crate. Rita sat next to her and motioned for Horst to have a seat on a nearby stepstool. As she held Frieda by the hand, she softly said, "Now ya'll tell me what's goin' on."

Slowly Horst relayed the events of the past several months, concluding with that morning's vandalism of their home and the personal attack on Frieda. By the time he got to the end of his story, Rita's mouth was agape.

"Oh. my Lord. Have you gone to the sheriff's office? You need to report this!" cried Rita.

"After I found Frieda, all I wanted to do was track down those men and kill them all," Horst viciously murmured. "But Frieda cried and begged me not to. She's afraid of me getting hurt...or worse. Plus, she didn't want to be left alone. I wanted to take her down to see the sheriff but she didn't want to go there, either. She's deathly afraid of being seen by anyone. So, we waited until it was dark and came straight here. I was hoping to speak to Mrs. Kinkade and get my payment a day early."

"What were you gonna do then?" asked Rita.

"We were hoping to catch a train and head out of town," said Horst.

"But do you have any idea where you'll go? From what I hear, things are bad for you folks all over the country right now," said Rita.

"Well, we hadn't thought that far yet. We just need to leave this town as soon as possible," said Horst wearily.

Rita thought the matter over for a moment and then made a decision. "Here's what we're gonna do. You'll sleep here in the pantry tonight." Seeing Frieda's eyes widen, Rita put an arm around her and continued, "Don't worry my dear, you'll be safe in here. I'll bring ya'll a basin and some soap so you can clean up, and I'll get some blankets to sleep on. I'll come back early tomorrow morning and will let Mavis know that you're here. Then we'll decide what to do next."

Frieda wrapped both her arms around the cook and squeezed her hard. "Thank you! Thank you so much!"

Horst sighed with relief. "Yes, we will be forever in your debt."

"Oh pshaw! It's the least I could do." Rita said flippantly as she stood up. "Now ya'll wait here. I'll be right back."

Horst joined Frieda on the crate and held her close as they both took in their surroundings. The hotel's pantry was bigger than their parlor. The shelves were stocked full of canned and jarred goods of every kind. A large ice box stood in the corner. Except for the delivery door, which was solid and had an industrial strength lock on it, there were no other windows or openings, which made the couple feel a bit more secure.

Soon Rita came back with the promised soap, water and blankets. She also brought with her an oil lamp, which she set up on the table next to the ice box. "The scullery maids will turn off all the electric lighting when they leave," she explained.

"I always lock the pantry from the outside, so they won't be able to come in. You'll be safe."

Before she left them, Rita opened the ice box and sliced off a couple pieces of ham, a wedge of cheddar, and a couple slices of bread. Placing it all on a plate, she handed it to Horst and said, "Here, you both look like you haven't eaten in ages. I'll see you first thing in the mornin'. Good night."

"Good night, Mrs. Alvares," the Metzgers replied in unison.

"And God bless you," added Frieda.

Johnathan Prescott returned the bottle of Pabst Extract tonic to his lower desk drawer. His digestive woes had gotten worse lately, often accompanied by a searing chest pain. The doctor he sent for last week diagnosed him with "chronic dyspepsia" and recommended this new elixir. It had just started to alleviate his complaints until last night during a blistering argument with Lottie.

Still vexed by the events which unfolded during her birthday dinner, she was mortified at the thought of their guests mistaking her and her husband for German sympathizers. She immediately demanded that all Bavarian crystal, wine, linens and anything else of German origin be expelled from the Montclair immediately and replaced with French and Italian goods.

While Prescott was as patriotic as the next man, he refused to believe that the average German trying to make a living and new life for himself in the U.S. was any sort of a threat to national security. However, Lottie would hear none of it. The only thing that scared her more than the Germans was the possibility of being shunned by her social circle.

Feeling his blood pressure rise, Prescott capitulated to his wife for the sake of his own health and peace of mind.

Unfortunately, the news which his head housekeeper just relayed to him further exacerbated his symptoms.

"Again, I apologize for you being put in this awkward position," said Mavis. "Mrs. Alvares was only doing what she thought best and, of course, I am willing to take responsibility for any repercussions."

Prescott slightly raised his hand as he shook his head. "Not necessary, Mrs. Kinkade. Truth be told, I probably would've done the same thing. Therefore let's not waste time on what's already happened and start thinking about what we will do from this point forward."

Mavis nodded in agreement. "Well, for right now, they're still in the pantry as we don't want any of the staff to see them. At the moment, the only ones who are aware of the Metzgers', presence are Mrs. Alvares, myself and you, sir."

"Very good," remarked Prescott as he rubbed the bridge of his nose, trying to think of a solution to the matter at hand. After a second, he abruptly stopped as an idea came to him. "I just read somewhere about these German settlements which are popping up over in Mexico. From what I understand, they've been there a while but have been growing by leaps and bounds since this war started. There must be a way I can get them on a westbound train to Texas and somehow get them across the border. I've got an acquaintance who runs a ranch out there in Laredo who owes me a favor. He might be able to help."

Banging on his desk like a judge who was about to give a final verdict, Prescott ordered, "Give me a few days to send out a couple of wires and get the train tickets. In the meantime, let's find a place here in the hotel besides our larder where we can keep these folks out of sight."

"Yes, Mr. Prescott," replied Mavis with relieved smile. "The entire third floor is currently unoccupied and sealed off. We can install the Metzgers in a room at the far end of the corridor and instruct them to stay inside. With your permission, sir, I'd like to assign Miss Fairfax to look after them during their stay here. After all, with all our other duties to attend to, both Mrs. Alvares and I would certainly draw suspicion if we were constantly running up to the third floor. And we both know that Miss Fairfax is the epitome of discretion."

Prescott nodded. "Yes, I quite agree. Do what you must, Mrs. Kinkade." Giving her his usual dismissive nod, he added, "I'll let you know when all the arrangements are ready. Good afternoon."

Although Birdie swore not to tell a soul about the Metzgers being harbored at the Montclair, she was forced to divulge the secret to her mother when Hortensia found her leafing through an old German primer from her school days.

"What on earth are you doing with that?" asked Hortensia. "You know full well that they're burning these German books left and right. Why are you suddenly interested in learning the language?"

"No reason. Just curious," replied Birdie, trying to sound casual.

"Don't you lie to me, Brigid Fairfax!" snapped Hortensia. "I know you're up to something no good. Is that hotel of yours harboring German spies?"

"What?" Birdie asked incredulously. "Ma! What makes you ask such an outlandish question?"

"I've heard a lot of talk out there about these foreign spies that are masquerading as aristocrats and staying at fancy resorts like the Montclair. They try to pump the other guests as well as the locals for information before sending it back to their homeland. And before we know it, they'll invade this country and murder us all!"

Birdie couldn't believe what she was hearing. "Ma, that's absolutely ridiculous! Who on earth is spreading such hogwash? I'd laugh if I wasn't so shocked right now."

"It's the God's honest truth, Birdie," protested Hortensia. "It's been in the Daily Express and everyone in town has been talking about it."

"Ma, the Daily Express is nothin' but yellow journalism," Birdie pointed out. "Don't ya remember that story last year about the woman who supposedly gave birth to a calf? We both giggled about it at the time."

"Well, be that as it may, this is not a time to trust anyone speaking German," Hortensia replied stubbornly. "And besides, you still haven't answered my first question."

Birdie finally had to relent and tell Hortensia the whole story of the Metzgers, which she herself had just learned from Mavis earlier that day. Hortensia's first reaction was one of mortification.

"Oh Birdie, Mr. Prescott is putting you and the others in a dangerous situation! To think, Germans being hidden at the Montclair!"

"The Metzgers are nice people, ma," Birdie spiritedly protested. "They're just a young couple who moved to Florida to start a new life for themselves. All Mr. Metzger ever wanted to do was bake bread and create beautiful cakes. And Mrs. Metzger is very frail and sickly. She was actually so scared of the townsfolk here that she had shut herself up in her house for months, never goin' outside. You oughtta be prayin' for them, not condemnin' them."

Hortensia paused for thought before replying, "Of course I'll pray for them, Birdie. I just hope you don't get caught up in anything that will eventually come back to haunt you."

The bells are ringing for me and my gal.
The birds are singing for me and my gal.

Lottie and Johnathan Prescott were both in good spirits that evening. This was the first time since Lottie's birthday that they had elected to have dinner in the main dining room instead of upstairs in their suite. To Mrs. Prescott in particular, being back in the public eye dressed to the nines and being able to hold her head high was all that was important to her.

The musicians were instructed to play mostly patriotic numbers such as Over There, Goodbye Broadway Hello France, When the Boys Come Home, and of course anything by John Philip Sousa. But Lottie also requested a few more romantic numbers such as the one they were now swaying to on the dance floor.

Prescott had to talk directly into his wife's ear so he could be heard over the music. "Everything looks marvelous tonight, my dear."

Lottie coquettishly replied, "Never mind the dining room. How do I look?"

"Of course, I meant you as well, Charlotte," said Prescott cheekily. "You almost made me take my eyes off that nice-looking roast there at our table!"

Both of them roared with laughter as they continued their revolution around the dance floor.

And sometimes I'm gonna build a little home
for two for three or four or more
In love land, for me and my gal.

After the number ended and the musicians went on a short break, the Prescotts settled into their places at the head table next to Beauregard and Candace Jessup.

"You cut a fine figure out there, Prescott," said Beau Jessup jovially. "I hope you'll let me have at least one dance with your fine lady at some point this evening."

Lottie giggled like a schoolgirl while her husband replied, "You are welcome to waltz Mrs. Prescott around the dance floor as much as you desire, Jessup. That will give me the opportunity to keep your missus company."

Candace Jessup shook her head and laughed. "Seems like we both married a pair of rascals, Lottie!"

A tall, solemn looking wine steward approached Johnathan Prescott. Holding a bottle wrapped in a napkin, he asked, "More of the Bordeaux, sir?"

"Yes, thank you Evans," said Prescott as he held out his glass. Looking around at the others, he asked, "Anyone else?"

The ladies politely declined but Beau Jessup pushed his glass forward and quipped, "Why it would be rude not to!"

The night continued merrily as both couples finished their meals and took several spins on the dance floor. This was the first time in Johnathan Prescott's recent memory that he was able to fully relax and enjoy his dinner companions.

Unfortunately, an innocent remark by Candace Jessup would precipitate a conversation which would eventually ruin his entire evening.

"Lottie, I just love that gown you're wearing. Who is your dressmaker?"

"Actually, our assistant housekeeper is an excellent seamstress who's made a lot of my dresses including this one," replied Lottie.

"It's exquisite," gushed Candace. "Say Lottie, do you think you can arrange for me to meet with your seamstress? I need to have a new tea gown made and I just had to let my previous dressmaker go. When my Beau here discovered that Helga's mother and father came from Frankfurt, he insisted that I dismiss her immediately."

"You're damned right I did," Beau said spiritedly. "We're about to send our boys over there to fight them sonsabitches and I'll be damned if I fill the pockets of any of them huns living here!"

Prescott lowered his glass as he fixed a firm gaze on Beau. "Steady on there, Jessup. There are ladies present. And besides, what possible harm could a seamstress do?"

To the women, Beau apologized. "Forgive my language, ladies." Turning to Prescott, he replied, "Woman or not, she's still a hun. It's the principle of the thing. Same goes for folks like that German baker. You know, the one who had his shop burnt down. Some folks were saying he wasn't much of a threat either. But he was still a hun and had to be made an example of as a message to the rest of them that we Americans will not be messed with."

Prescott's jaw tightened. Jessup's choice of words sounded almost incriminating, but Johnathan refused to believe that a friend of his would be involved in something so despicable. Not trusting himself to speak and desperately needing some sort of distraction, he reached into his pocket for a cigar and lit it.

Lottie, however, continued the conversation. "Oh, I quite agree, Mr. Jessup. Once the Germans are shown that we mean business, the war should come to a swift end."

"I hope so, Lottie," Candace chimed in. "The thought of us possibly having to send our Wesley to war in a few years when he is of military age sets my nerves on edge!"

The thought of the Metzgers hiding under his roof at that very moment also had Prescott's nerves on edge. He was awaiting an answer to the telegram he sent to Sam Peterson in Laredo that morning. In the meantime, it was of the utmost importance that the stowaways remained out of sight.

Chapter 42

Frieda awoke around daybreak the next morning. For a split second, she was completely disoriented in her new, unfamiliar surroundings, but Horst's warm, snoring presence next to her jogged her memory. Like a pampered house cat, she stretched her entire body as she wallowed in the large, soft bed of room 329. The luxurious sheets and feather pillows brought Frieda the best night's sleep she had in weeks.

She and Horst were smuggled up to the room by Birdie earlier that evening during the dinner hour while the Prescotts and all the other guests were in the main dining room. Frieda was awestruck at the opulent furnishings, masterful paintings, electric lights and thick carpets. She spent the first hour just taking it all in, committing every single detail to memory because she was certain they'd never again stay anywhere so palatial.

Frieda gingerly eased herself out of the bed so as not to wake her husband and tiptoed over to the window. She lifted up a corner of the heavy brocade curtain and looked out over the resort's well landscaped gardens. The sun wasn't completely out yet but Frieda could just make out the myriad of blooms which dotted the grounds below. She sighed heavily. She couldn't even remember the last time she walked through a garden, smelled the flowers and listened to the birds sing to each other.

"Are you all right, darling?" came a drowsy voice from the bed.

"I'm sorry, Horst. I didn't mean to wake you," whispered Frieda as she replaced the curtain.

"You forget, my dear, that I used to wake up around 4:00 every morning anyway," replied Horst as he sat up and stretched. As it was still semi-dark outside, they dared not turn on any of the lamps for fear of someone outside seeing the light in their window.

Frieda washed her hands and face before putting on the shapeless dress which Birdie had brought her yesterday. The Metzgers were given parts of unused uniforms to wear while Birdie took their own clothes home to Hortensia for laundering and mending. Frieda was wearing a pink maid's dress which was two sizes too large for her while Horst wore an old houseman's uniform without the vest.

After Horst rose and dressed, Frieda made the bed. They both then sat in silence in the small parlor area until they heard Birdie's now familiar knock about an hour later.

Birdie quickly entered and shut the door. Like the Metzgers, she also kept her voice low but cheerful. "Good mornin'. I hope you slept well last night. I'm sure it was at least a little better than the pantry."

Horst smiled. "Yes, we slept quite well. Thank you."

Birdie laid down the covered breakfast tray of biscuits and gravy along with two cups of hot tea. She carried a parcel under her arm which was wrapped with the previous day's newspaper. This she presented to Frieda.

"Here are your own clothes – all cleaned, pressed and mended. My ma even managed to fix that big tear in your dress," said Birdie. "But keep wearin' those uniforms while you're stayin' here. That way if you're accidentally spotted, folks will just think you're part of the staff."

Holding the parcel close to her chest, Frieda's eyes were watery. "Please send your mother my sincerest thanks."

"Miss Fairfax, have you heard anything from Mrs. Kinkade yet about where we go from here?" Horst asked anxiously.

"Mrs. Kinkade said she talked to Mr. Prescott yesterday and he's tryin' to get you on a train to Texas and then over the border into Mexico, where a lot of German folks are settlin'. So at least you'll be with your own kind."

Frieda gasped. Her eyes were as large and round as saucers. It took all her strength and resolve to leave her home a couple days ago and walk over to the Montclair. The thought of leaving the country was too much for her to fathom. A deep shiver ran up her spine.

"Mexico," echoed Horst. "But that's so far away. We hardly know anything about it except that it's a wild country full of bandits."

"But you'll be safer over there than you would be here or back home in Germany, and you'll have other German folks around ya. Except for the Spanish speakin' Mexicans and the cactus, you'll feel like you're back home!"

Horst shook his head. He wasn't so sure about that. "We had only just gotten used to living here in the United States. Now we have to start all over again."

Birdie saw that Frieda was shaking. She knew that the woman's nerves were frayed. She wished there was something she could do to help alleviate her apprehension. A thought instantly came to her.

"Today during my lunch break I'll head over to the Lincolnville Library and see if they have any books on Mexico. We can look through them at dinner later on."

Horst nodded and said, "That would be much appreciated. Thank you."

"That reminds me, I found my old German primer and was tryin' to learn some words so I could speak to ya in your own language. You just said, 'thank you' so I'll now say 'Bitte'. Did I say that right?"

Frieda and Horst were touched to see someone putting forth so much effort to make them feel comfortable.

"You said it perfectly," replied Horst.

"And now I'll teach you something new," said Frieda. "Du bist mein Freund. You are my friend."

Mavis softly cursed under her breath. Ever since she was a child, she hated arithmetic. She remembered being forced to stand up in front of the class and add up long columns of numbers in her head. She had often come home from school with severe headaches as a result. And now, as she gazed down at the housekeeping ledger, trying to figure out which of the figures was throwing her balance off, another migraine was looming. So fixated was her attention that she never heard the footsteps approach her office and the door quietly open.

"Mrs. Kinkade?" Lottie Prescott's voice startled Mavis, who immediately dropped her pencil and stood up behind her desk. The hotelier's wife rarely ventured downstairs to the staff area.

"Why Mrs. Prescott, what a pleasant surprise," said Mavis as she put on her usual professional façade. "Do you require some assistance?"

Lottie entered the office and carefully seated herself in a nearby chair. Harboring an intense dislike of being anywhere near the domestic nerve center of the Montclair, she also put on a false front and smiled brightly at Mavis and waved at her to sit down.

"Actually, Mrs. Kinkade, I'd like to borrow Miss Fairfax from you for a few days. My friend Candace Jessup desperately needs a gown for an upcoming garden party. She is currently without a dressmaker, so I recommended Miss Fairfax."

Mavis felt her pulse pounding in her temples. In addition to all her other duties, Birdie was meant to be keeping an eye on the Metzgers. Mavis desperately needed to talk to Mr. Prescott first but what on earth was she going to tell the woman seated in front of her who at that moment was staring at her and awaiting a response.

Taking a deep and steadying breath, Mavis replied, "I'm sorry, Mrs. Prescott, but Miss Fairfax is unavailable at the present. Perhaps in a few days' time..."

Lottie's brows arched as her steely blue eyes bulged. "I beg your pardon. What do you mean Miss Fairfax is 'unavailable?' Is she sick?"

"No, ma'am," Mavis heard her own voice quavering. "It's just that Miss Fairfax has a lot of important tasks to attend to at the moment. However..."

Lottie squinted and slowly rose. "Are you telling me that Miss Fairfax is too busy to attend to the wife of her employer?"

"I'm sure if I speak to Mr. Prescott, we can work this out," offered Mavis who also rose from behind her desk.

"Don't bother!" shouted Lottie. "I'll be speaking to him myself!" With a huff, she left the office and slammed the door behind her.

Mavis exhaled and flopped back down into her chair. At least Mrs. Prescott will save her the need to speak to Mr. Prescott. He'll know how to handle this.

Later that afternoon, Birdie brought the Metzgers some fresh fruit and petit fours left over from an afternoon tea held in the ladies' salon downstairs. She also brought a newspaper for Horst as well as the promised book about Mexico.

Looking at the map insert in the center of the book, Horst remarked, "It really is not as far away as I initially thought. After all, we had to travel much further when we left Germany and sailed to America."

Frieda thumbed through the book and marveled at the photographs. She was fascinated by the various pictures of the towns, vaqueros on horseback, women coming out of churches with lacy mantillas on their heads, and adorable grinning children. One photo in particular garnered her intense scrutiny. It was of a group of German settlers in a town called Soconusco, which boasted a very successful coffee cultivation industry.

"Horst, look at this!" she said excitedly as she pointed at the photo. Her husband came over for a closer look.

"Well, I hope it at least makes you feel a little less scared about goin' there," said Birdie as she gathered up the plates to sneak them back downstairs. "Oh, I almost forgot to give you this."

Reaching into her apron pocket, Birdie pulled out a small pink rosebud and gave it to Frieda. "I saw this in the garden and thought you might like it – eine Blume."

Frieda gasped as she picked up the stem and lovingly held it to her cheek. "Oh, thank you Fraulein Fairfax. It's been so long since I've held a flower. I was looking at the garden below this morning and wished I could just stand in the middle of it, breathing in all the sweet perfume of those beautiful roses.

Birdie walked over to the window and peeked through the curtains. Directly below was the rose garden in all its vibrant, full bloom glory. Remembering how happy she once was in that very spot on a special night long ago, Birdie instantly knew what she had to do.

"Mrs. Metzger, your wish will come true this evenin'," she declared.

Horst put down the newspaper and shot Birdie a curious look. "What do you mean? We can't go out there. Someone could see us!"

Frieda smiled and patted Birdie on the hand. "Thank you, Fraulein Fairfax. You are kind and have done so much for us, but I agree with my husband. It's too dangerous."

Birdie shook her head. "It doesn't have to be dangerous at all. What if I told you I could sneak you out there for a spell and back up here without a single soul seein' us?"

Horst still looked doubtful, but Frieda clapped her hands excitedly. "I would be over the moon!"

Look at his wife's animated face and realizing that this was the first time in months that he had seen her looking so cheerful, Horst capitulated and grudgingly said, "Very well, then."

"Wonderful!" replied Birdie. "I have a couple of things to do first, but I'll be back later."

"The nerve of that woman!" shouted Lottie, her face reddened with fury. "Refusing me the services of my own dressmaker!"

Like a caged tiger, she paced back and forth around the parlor of the family's private suite while Johnathan Prescott opened the liquor cabinet and pulled out a bottle of his favorite scotch.

"For Christ's sake, Lottie, she isn't your dressmaker!" he snapped back as he poured the gold fluid into a glass. "She's the assistant housekeeper and has a hell of a lot more things to do around here than sew up dresses for your goddamned friends!"

Lottie rounded on her husband, giving him a frosty glare. "First of all, don't you dare curse at me like that, and secondly, if Miss Fairfax is so vital to the running of this hotel, why on earth haven't I seen hide nor hair of her for the past several days? What exactly is she doing?"

Feeling the beginnings of the familiar pains starting to form in his upper abdomen, Prescott took a swig of the liquor. There was still no word from Peterson in Laredo and he wasn't sure how long he was going to be able to keep up this charade. "I apologize for my language, my dear. As for Miss Fairfax, I have seen her plenty this past week. And she's been doing what she's supposed to be doing – helping Mrs. Kinkade keep this hotel in order! Now please, let's hear the end of this nonsense."

"But what am I going to tell Candace?" wailed Lottie as Prescott grabbed his glass and headed off to his study.

"Tell her to kiss my ass," muttered Prescott under his breath.

"Okay, let's go," Birdie whispered as she looked down the corridor. As she expected, there was not a soul in sight. This was one of the few times that she was actually grateful for the hotel's low occupancy. It was a quarter til 7 and all the guests would be in the dining room and the chambermaids would be gone for the day. Birdie's only concern was being spotted by a houseman or stray guest, but at the moment, all was clear.

Frieda, frightened yet excited at the thought of being outside, quietly followed her husband out of the room as Birdie guided them down the staff stairwell and out the side exit door. The trash receptacle was on the right and about 10 yards ahead of them lay the path to the rose garden.

Earlier that afternoon, Birdie asked Felipe to place a couple of barriers on either side of the path to keep guests out of the garden. Assuming that Birdie was merely passing on an order from Mirs. Kinkade, Felipe placed the wooden barriers where Birdie had indicated. Upon each hung a sign saying "This area closed for maintenance. Please keep out."

The trio swiftly made their way into the round mazelike path in the center where they were hidden by tall trellises covered with thick rose shrubs. A heady sweet aroma hung in the air.

"Okay," Birdie whispered, "I'm gonna give ya some privacy and sit over here to keep an eye out. There are a couple paths back here which lead out to the arbor. When the cathedral chimes the half hour at 7:30, you need to head on back here, so we can get you into your room before dinner's over. Just remember to keep your voices low and make sure no one sees ya."

Birdie walked over to the stone bench by the main walkway and sat down. Twilight was descending upon the city as the sun, bright as a navel orange, sunk low in the sky and disappeared behind the cathedral steeple and tall buildings in the west. Except for the light traffic on the main road, the only other sounds were the chorus of crickets coming from the arbor and the ragtime music from the dining room.

The thought suddenly occurred to Birdie that she hadn't sat out here in the gardens for any length of time since New Year's Eve in 1899. For years she was afraid to go anywhere near this part of the hotel's property much less think about that night. But now she was finally able to look back on it without the old sinking feeling in the pit of her stomach and the heavy stone on her chest.

The sound of rhythmic shuffling made her turn around. She smiled as she caught a glimpse of the Metzgers embracing each other as they quietly danced to the faint music coming out of the Montclair. Feeling like she was intruding on their privacy, Birdie turned back around feeling slightly embarrassed.

As the clock chimed the half hour, the trio reconvened by the bench and quietly re-entered the hotel through the staff door. In the light of the dim lamp in the stairwell, Horst was pleased to see that his wife had color in her cheeks. She smiled up at him and squeezed his hand, looking for all the world like a teenager again.

As they entered onto the third-floor corridor, Birdie was the first one through the door. Seeing no one else in sight, she motioned for the Metzgers to come through. Frieda stifled a giggle as she rushed to the door of room 329 and ran inside. Horst turned around and shot a thankful glance at Birdie.

"I haven't seen her like this for a very long time. I'll never forget all you've done for us, Miss Fairfax," he whispered.

"The pleasure has been all mine," said Birdie who meant every word.

As they entered the room and shut the door behind them, swift footsteps could be heard at the opposite end of the hallway.

Chapter 43

Lottie tied her head scarf firmly under her chin as she and Candace Jessup sat in the back of the Prescotts' motor car, waiting for Cynthia Baxter to join them. They were on their way to call on Phoebe Ravensworth, one of St. Augustine's leading socialites.

Riding in the open automobiles could be a grimy affair and the well-to-do, especially the ladies, always made sure they were protected from road dust and insects with head coverings, goggles and riding coats. Cynthia finally emerged from the Montclair clad in a camel colored coat and a green and gold paisley head scarf.

"Good afternoon, ladies," Cynthia greeted the others cheerfully as Thomas, the Prescotts' driver, helped her up onto the back seat. "I declare I could just melt in this tropical heat. I don't know how you can stand living down here year-round, Lottie. You must have some cracker blood in you."

Ignoring the implied slight, Lottie shot a wide grin at Cynthia and merely replied, "I manage quite well, Cynthia dear. I do hope you're enjoying your stay at the Montclair."

"Oh, of course," gushed Cynthia. "The Ponce de Leon might be grander but to me, being around my friends is much more important. Wouldn't you agree, Mrs. Jessup?"

"I certainly do," said Candace, ready to defend her friend Lottie's social standing. "The Prescotts have always made us feel most welcome and are the epitome of southern hospitality."

After turning the crank on the front of the vehicle, Thomas jumped back inside and started the motor. As the car came to life, the ladies had to speak louder to be heard over the rumbling of the engine.

"I really enjoyed myself last night," remarked Cynthia. "Your chef does an exquisite coq au vin."

"Yes, she's the best there is in the city," said Lottie proudly.

“She? You mean you don’t have a male chef?” Cynthia asked incredulously. “My dear, everyone knows that the world’s best chefs are men. French men.”

“I’ll have you know, Mrs. Baxter, that our cook can make just about any entree that any of those foreigners could.” Lottie cried defensively.”

“Her roast leg of lamb is the best I’ve ever tasted,” remarked Candace.

“And she manages to do it all with a skeletal staff,” Lottie said. “In case you haven’t heard, we’re about to go to war and a lot of our young men are being drafted. Many of our past guests have not returned so we’ve had to let some of our people go.”

Feeling contrite, Cynthia replied, “My apologies, Lottie. I didn’t mean to rile you so. I really am enjoying my visit. The Montclair will always be our resort of choice when we visit Florida.”

Lottie’s mood started to brighten. “I’m glad to hear it. I do hope your room is to your satisfaction. As I said, we’re thin on staff right now but we made sure to hang on to our best cleaners.”

“Is it true you’ve shut down the entire third floor this season?” asked Candace.

“Yes,” replied Lottie. “Hopefully all of our guests will return next year, and the Montclair will once again be bursting at the seams!”

Cynthia frowned. “Did you say that the third floor had no guests staying there?”

The question startled Lottie. “Why, yes.”

“That’s strange,” said Cynthia. “Last night during dinner, I had to return to our room to replace an evening glove. The elevator was held up so I took the stairs. As I reached the third floor, I saw a woman and a man entering a room down the hall.”

“That’s impossible,” replied Lottie. “None of those rooms are occupied.”

"Are you sure it was the third floor, Mrs. Baxter?" asked Candace.

"I'm as sure as I'm sitting here," cried Cynthia. "I saw a couple enter one of those rooms. Oddly enough, the woman resembled one of your housekeepers. The mulatto one. I didn't get a good look at the man."

"Miss Fairfax?" Lottie murmured. Brigid Fairfax in a hotel room with a guest! No wonder she was unable to do any dressmaking at the moment. She was too busy having shameless trysts, and right under their roof. Lottie silently vowed to speak to Mavis Kinkade as soon as possible. But for now, she was once again forced to artfully change the subject.

Johnathan ripped open the Western Union envelope sitting on his desk when he returned from his budget meeting with Cyril Compton. After reading its contents, he sighed with relief. Peterson was going to help the Metzgers get to Mexico. Now Prescott's next step was to find out when the next Texas bound train was going out.

The newly installed intercom on his desk buzzed. As Prescott pressed the receiver button, the strained voice of Mavis Kinkade could be heard. "Mr. Prescott. Your presence is needed in my office immediately."

Having never heard that urgent tone in his head housekeeper's voice before, Prescott knew the matter at hand must be a pressing one. "I'll be right there!"

By the time he reached the staff corridor, he could hear his wife's raised voice coming from the Mavis Kinkade's office.

"I want her fired today! Do you understand?"

"What the hell's going on in here?" demanded Prescott as he burst into the office and slammed the door shut behind him. "I could hear your caterwauling all the way down the hall."

Lottie turned on her husband and shouted, "One of our guests spotted Brigid Fairfax entering a hotel room on the third floor with a strange man! Johnathan, she must be dismissed immediately. I won't stand for this kind of wanton behavior going on among our staff underneath this roof. This is a high-end resort, not a brothel!"

In an attempt to diffuse the tense situation, Prescott raised both palms towards his wife and spoke calmly. "Now Lottie, there's no need to shout at Mrs. Kinkade."

Laughing ruefully, Lottie retorted, "You're a fine one telling me not to shout. All you do is yell and curse. And now when something like this happens, you just stand there and tell me to calm down. Didn't you hear what I said? Your beloved assistant housekeeper has been going into empty rooms with who knows how many men. I want her fired!"

"That's enough, Lottie," Prescott replied firmly. "Miss Fairfax is one of our best employees and would never do anything to ruin the Montclair's reputation."

"I don't understand why you and Miss Kinkade continue to defend this woman," Lottie declared. "We already know that she's done this in the past. Aftert all, that's why our son is no longer living here."

"Now hold on," said Prescott. "That was an entirely different matter and you know that. She was not the one in the wrong."

"She's never in the wrong, isn't she?" Lottie firmly stood her ground. "Well if neither one of you are going to do it, I'll fire her myself!" Turning to Mavis, she asked, "Where is she now?"

Mavis looked helplessly at Prescott, who sighed and said, "No, Lottie. You won't do any such a thing."

"And why not?" Lottie asked coldly.

"Because..." Prescott raised his eyes heavenward as he mentally prepared for the rage that was about to be unleashed. "I know who's staying in room 329."

"What in the world are you talking about?" Lottie asked impatiently. The knowing looks being exchanged between her husband and the housekeeper were irritating her even more.

"There's a German couple hiding there," Johnathan finally confessed. "The baker and his wife. They were burnt out of their home and the wife was attacked. They've been staying here for the past few days. Miss Fairfax has been assigned to look after them and keep them out of sight until I can get them out of town."

"Germans!" Lottie was aghast. "Oh Johnathan, how could you? What will people say when they find out? Oh, it doesn't bear to think about!" She sat weakly down in the chair by Mavis' desk.

"People won't need to find out if we keep quiet about it," said Prescott. "I'm making arrangements to get them to Mexico. It will just be a few more days until I can get them on a train and out of town."

"Mexico? You're paying their fare to Mexico? After all the grief you've been giving me about spending money and now you turn around and waste it on a couple of strangers – Germans nonetheless! I swear, Johnathan. If word ever gets out about this, we'll be pariahs in this town, and I will never forgive you!"

With that, she got up and flounced out of the office.

Mavis immediately spoke up. "Mr. Prescott, I apologize for this. I don't know why Miss Fairfax let the Metzgers leave the room, but I will certainly be talking to her about it as soon as I can."

"Don't be too hard on her, Mrs. Kinkade," said Prescott. "Those folks had been cooped up in that room for days. They've got to be suffering from cabin fever by now. But from this point forward, let's keep a tighter watch on them."

"I'll personally see to it," promised Mavis.

Hortensia was both puzzled and concerned when Birdie came home that evening visibly upset. As she often did when her daughter was out of sorts, Hortensia left her alone for an hour or two until her temper settled down. Their dinner was eaten in silence. It wasn't until later in the evening when Birdie sat down in the parlor to work on an embroidered pillow case that Hortensia came in with a couple cups of tea.

"You know," she started, "A problem shared is a problem halved."

Birdie sighed and threw down the embroidery hoop. "Oh ma, you were right. I got myself in a real mess today."

"Did it have to do with the Metzgers?" Hortensia asked cautiously.

Birdie nodded. "Yes, but it was all my fault, ma. I tried to do somethin' nice for them but ended up getting Mr. Prescott, Mrs. Kinkade and myself in trouble."

Hortensia shook her head. She just knew that Birdie's involvement with the German couple was going to lead to no good. But at the moment, her daughter needed a listening ear above anything else. "I'm so sorry, Birdie. What exactly happened?"

After hearing the entire story about the rose garden, being spotted by a guest, the confrontation between the Prescotts, and the stern reprimand that Birdie received from Mavis that afternoon, Hortensia wrapped a loving arm around her daughter's shoulders.

"You did a nice thing for the Metzgers, Birdie. Even though it wasn't a very prudent idea, your heart was in the right place. It always is. And it's understandable that Mavis was upset. But like the clouds in the sky, this will all blow over. We both know that."

Birdie sighed as she realized this was true. "Yes, I know. Thanks, ma."

"How about some leftover blackberry crumble to go with this tea?" suggested Hortensia.

The Metzgers ate in complete silence the following morning after Mavis had dropped off the breakfast tray. Both were still in shock after the housekeeper's appearance at their door the previous afternoon informing them that Miss Fairfax would no longer be looking after them. When Horst asked why, Mrs. Kinkade merely said that it was due to Miss Fairfax being assigned to a dressmaking project for Mrs. Prescott. However, noticing the housekeeper's slightly brusque manner, Frieda was unconvinced.

"I just know it was because of us," she had said, wringing her hands in anguish. "Someone must have spotted us. We need to get out of here soon, Horst."

"Don't worry, Liebling," he had replied soothingly. "Mr. Prescott will find a way out for us any day now."

However, Mavis had brought more than dinner with her later on that day. She also relayed a message from Johnathan Prescott. While all was set in Laredo for their trip over the border, getting a train out that way was on hold at the moment. Torrential storms and floods had washed out a portion of the main railroad line heading west out of Florida. They would have to wait at least another week before normal operations resumed.

Soon the lavish hotel room with all its finery and trappings became an opulent prison cell which grew increasingly smaller. Each day started to look like the next. Waking up, the morning knock on the door, breakfast, sitting in the room until the evening knock on the door, dinner, and then bedtime. Frieda particularly grew more sullen and lachrymose as the days went by. Horst, who was initially sympathetic and understanding towards his wife's disposition, found his own temper growing progressively shorter.

It wasn't until the evening of the sixth day that the couple had their first full blown argument in all the years they've been together.

It started when Frieda went over to the window and cracked open the curtain to get a glimpse of the town at night. She liked looking at the lights of the other resorts, which twinkled like low lying stars in the city skyline.

"Frieda!" Horst said sharply. "Do you want to advertise our presence here to the world? Close that curtain!"

"Oh, don't be a fool," Frieda snapped. "We're facing the garden. No one is out there this time of night. Look." She spread open the drapes and waved frantically at the darkness outside.

Horst rushed over and drew the drapes shut. Clasping his wife firmly around the wrist, he roared, "What's gotten into you, woman? Are you trying to bring more trouble down on us?"

"Are you blaming all this on me?" Frieda asked incredulously. "It's all your fault that we're in this predicament. We should have just moved on that night we came here. But no, you agreed to trust this Mr. Prescott. And now look what happened. We're stuck here!"

"You certainly weren't complaining those first few days!" Horst vehemently retorted. "You seemed pretty damned happy, and don't blame me for us still being here. I have no influence over the weather!"

Before they knew it, both had reverted back to their native tongue as they continued sniping at each other in German.

"Albert? Do you hear that?" Estelle Blasek nudged her semi-conscious husband who laid with his back to her.

"Huh?" Albert grunted as he turned over. "I don't hear anything. Go back to sleep."

"But I hear shouting from the floor below," insisted Estelle.

"Maybe you were dreaming," muttered Albert. "Besides, I heard that whole floor down there is vacant. There's no one..." Before he could finish his sentence, the angry voice of a man could be heard coming from beneath them.

"You see," said Estelle smugly. "I knew I heard voices. What on earth is going on down there."

"Probably just some loud drunk," said Albert. He got up from the bed and took an empty glass tumbler from the nightstand. Placing it low on the wall, he listened to the magnified sounds coming from the floor below. The furious man was still speaking. The words were foreign, but the language sounded familiar. It took Albert another minute to identify it.

"Good Lord!" Albert cried. "That's German. They've got huns staying here!"

Cynthia Baxter swiftly made her way downstairs to the Ladies Salon where afternoon tea and pastries were being served. Groups of women were scattered about the room. One group was engrossed in a game of bridge, another had brought their needlework with them and the rest were engaged in animated discussions. A stocky woman with a mass of grey curls atop her head played a harp in the far corner of the room, giving the ethereal blue and cream-colored chamber even more of a heavenly atmosphere.

Spotting Candace Jessup on one of the settees between two elderly women, Cynthia discretely waved. Once she had Candace's attention, Cynthia beckoned her over. Excusing herself from her present company, Candace joined Cynthia near the entrance where they both had a perfect view of the entire room.

"Good afternoon, Mrs. Baxter," said Candace cordially. "I hear you are an excellent bridge player. Have you come to join the game?"

"I'm afraid I'm not here for recreation," Cynthia whispered. "I don't see Lottie in here. Have you seen her at all today, Mrs. Jessup?"

"Actually, I haven't," replied Candace. "I hope she's not indisposed." She noticed the note of urgency in Cynthia's tone. "Is something wrong?"

"I'm afraid so," Cynthia murmured. Leading Candace gently by the elbow, she guided her as far away from listening ears as possible before continuing. "Some mutual acquaintances of ours – the Blaseks – just checked out of the Montclair an hour ago. I was walking by the fountain up front and happened to see them both leaving the lobby with their luggage."

Candace, trying to figure out why this would be significant, stared back at the other woman blankly. "Is one of them ill?"

Cynthia shook her head vigorously. "That's what I initially thought as I approached them. But when I inquired as to the circumstances of their departure, they told me...." She lowered her voice to a whisper, causing Candace to lean in so she could hear. "...they heard Germans screaming in the room underneath theirs."

Candace gasped as she raised a hand to her mouth. "You don't say!"

"Mr. Blasek said the man sounded extremely angry. He also thought he heard the sound of something breaking. Estelle was afraid that maybe someone was being tortured in there"

"Oh my," exclaimed Candace. "Did they speak with the Prescotts about this?"

"That's the most curious thing of all," said Cynthia. "When they reported the incident to Mr. Prescott and insisted on calling the police, he told them that they must have misheard and that it was pointless to get the law involved. Mr. Blasek insisted that he knew German when he heard it and was deeply insulted, so he and his wife immediately checked out and moved down the road to the Ponce."

"That's so strange," said Candace. But as always, her loyalty to Lottie Prescott remained unswayed. "But I'm sure there is a logical explanation for it all."

"I can think of only one explanation and that is that the Prescotts are harboring Germans under this roof," Cynthia said resolutely. "And my husband Beau will definitely not stand for it. I suppose I better go upstairs and start packing my bags because we'll no doubt be joining the Blaseks across the road before the day is over."

Lottie felt like a pickaxe had been thrust into the top of her skull which was now crowned with the ice pack brought to her by Violet. Although she had kept her eyes closed, she was aware that her husband was still present in her bedroom where she had taken refuge.

"Oh Johnathan," she wailed. "I've never felt so ashamed in my life. The Blaseks looked at us like we were traitors or something! And I know it won't be long before Estelle Blasek starts running her mouth over there at the Ponce de Leon. I could just DIE!"

Prescott, who had been forced to listen to his wife's continuous tirade since their earlier confrontation with the Blaseks, puffed thoughtfully on a freshly lit cigar. "Now Lottie, your life is not in any kind of danger. All this falderal over a poor Bavarian breadmaker and his wife will blow over. I just got word that the railroad line up in the panhandle is finally clear, so I'll be able to get them on the next westbound train tomorrow."

Lottie sat upright on her bed and forcefully threw the ice bag across the room. "I don't give a damn where you send those people. They can go to hell as far as I am concerned. What you don't seem to understand is that we are already RUINED. Mark my words. We won't have heard the last of this!"

Prescott ran his hand through what was left of his hair. In all the years they'd been married, he had never heard his wife swear. Realizing that trying to placate her was going to be an exercise in futility at the moment, he quietly rose and left the room, shutting the door behind him. He'll wait until later to tell her that the Baxters and the Jessups had also checked out earlier that evening.

The next morning, Horst and Frieda were up early and dressed in their own clothes. Frieda had neatly folded the uniforms they'd been wearing over the past couple of weeks and made the bed a final time. Although things had been tense between them over the past week, now that their departure was finally imminent, they were once again the picture of marital harmony.

The eventual knock at the door caused them both to jump. Horst went to open the door. Mavis was just outside in the corridor, but this morning, she was not alone.

"Someone else wanted to say goodbye," she said with a smile. She stepped aside to reveal a balding, stout older man and Miss Fairfax, who Frieda was delighted to see.

"Mr. Prescott," Mavis addressed the well-dressed gentleman with the red face, "may I present Mr. and Mrs. Metzger?"

"Please to meet you, Metzger," said Prescott jovially as he shook the astonished baker's hand. Never in his wildest dreams did Horst ever think he'd be face to face with one of St. Augustine's distinguished hoteliers.

"The pleasure is all mine sir," Horst replied nervously. "This is my wife, Frieda."

Frieda, unaccustomed to being in such esteemed company, humbly nodded her head and offered a partial curtsy. "Pleased to meet you, sir."

"Despite the unusual circumstances, I hope you've been comfortable during your stay here," said Prescott.

"Sir, you've been most gracious with your hospitality," Horst replied with all sincerity. "I hope my wife and I have not been any kind of burden to you and your wonderful staff." He nodded towards Mavis and Birdie. "No matter where my wife and I eventually settle, we will never forget all you have done for us."

Prescott was touched by the modest man's genuine candor. "Oh, say no more about it. You're a good man, Metzger, and you bake a hell of a cake! We're going to miss those desserts around here. That's for sure. But I know that wherever you wind up, you'll land on your feet."

He reached into his jacket pocket and pulled out a pair of railroad tickets, a folded note and a small sealed envelope. "These tickets will get you to Laredo. Once you arrive, look up my friend Sam Peterson. His address is on that piece of paper. I already sent him a wire, so he'll be expecting you and will help you cross the border. As for the envelope, that is for you to open once you get on the train."

Horst was moved beyond words, so Frieda spoke up. "Thank you so very much, Mr. Prescott. Not only for the train tickets and everything, but also for giving me hope that there are still kindhearted people in the world."

Prescott was touched yet embarrassed by the woman's simple but heartfelt speech. "Well, I think it's time you headed downstairs. I have a car waiting to take you to the station. Try not to speak to anyone on the train if you can help it."

Both Prescott and Mavis said their goodbyes and departed, leaving Birdie to escort the Metzgers downstairs. Once again, they quietly exited the room, tiptoed down the service stairs and emerged from the hotel's west side door. Frieda gave the rose garden a final wistful glance as the trio walked over to the side street on the west side of the Montclair, where the promised car was discreetly parked.

Although it was still only 6AM and no one was in sight, Birdie didn't want to attract any more attention than necessary, so she gave Frieda a quick hug and said, "Auf Wedersehen, mein Freund."

Frieda erupted into tears as she responded, "Für immer Freunde." As the car pulled away, she looked back and continued to wave at Birdie until they rounded the corner.

Horst pulled the envelope from his pocket and opened it. Frieda gave him a disproving look. "Mr. Prescott told us not to open it until we were on the train."

But her voice wasn't registering. At first Horst thought his eyes were playing tricks on him, but the ten $10 bills in the envelope were very real indeed.

Chapter 44

Johnathan Prescott never noticed before how loud the clock on the mantle was. Each tic-tic-tic seem to reverberate throughout the room. Each passing second echoed thunderously in his ears.

Noticing that his glass once again required a refill, Prescott picked up the scotch bottle and shook it. Empty! He opened the liquor cabinet and searched its inventory. Looks like all the scotch was gone.

"I guess I'll be switching to gin," he slurred to himself as he opened a new bottle. His hands were a bit clumsier than usual thanks to his advanced inebriated state. Luckily, he was able to get most of the gin he was pouring into the glass.

As he walked back across the parlor to sit in his favorite chair, Prescott heard a paper crunch under his left foot. Looking down, he grimaced. It was that morning's edition of the Herald, still where it landed after Lottie had flung it at him in a murderous rage before she left.

Prescott picked up the periodical and turned it over. On the bottom half of the front page was a cartoon likeness of himself wearing a German war helmet and welcoming a line of Bavarian immigrants into the Montclair with his arms wide open. Underneath was a caption reading, "Guess which local hotel magnate is a hun-loving traitor!"

All that day, the front desk was overwhelmed with a sudden wave of unexpected check-outs, most of whom relocated to the Casa Monica and the Alcazar as the Ponce was filled to capacity.

An emergency staff meeting was called a few hours ago. With only 21 guests remaining in the hotel, the Montclair couldn't afford to remain open. So, it was decided to give the current occupants a week's notice to vacate and to temporarily lay off all the employees (except for a handful of maintenance personnel) indefinitely.

Prescott was hoping that the scandal would eventually blow over and the war in Europe would soon cease, putting an end to all this anti-German hysteria. In the meantime, he would pull himself up by the bootstraps and reclaim his solid reputation as an upstanding citizen of St. Augustine as well as a patriotic American.

He planned to contact Harry Ravensworth, his attorney, and file a libel suit against the Herald and that damned Lawrence Conrad. He will also gather together his senior staff and formulate a new marketing plan for the resort to not only repair the damage done to its reputation but to attract new guests. Personally, Prescott was tired of seeing the same old faces year after year. He knew he needed to appeal to a new demographic – younger couples and families.

But his first order of business was going up to Pittsburgh and convincing his wife to return home. When he had awoken that morning, he noticed that something was amiss. He usually could hear Lottie giving orders to Alma while Martine bustled about in the kitchen. However, there was nothing but deafening silence. Also, the daily morning aroma of brewing coffee was also noticeably absent.

After he rose and dressed, Prescott quietly knocked on Lottie's door. Getting no response, he opened it and poked his head inside. The room was empty, and the bed was made. Violet, Lottie's long-time ladies' maid and confidante, was nowhere to be found. He then headed down the hallway and peeked inside the dining room, but no breakfast was laid out. The adjoining kitchen was empty and in its usual pristine condition.

When he reached the front parlor, Prescott stopped short. There in his favorite chair sat Lottie, wearing her best travel clothes, her new grey hat, and an expressionless face. Stacked by the front door were a few of her travel trunks.

"What's the meaning of this?" Prescott asked as he waved a hand towards the baggage. "Going somewhere?"

Lottie shot her husband a steely glare. Her voice was cold. "I told you this was going to be the ruin of us."

"What's gotten into you, woman?"

Lottie wordlessly held up the morning's paper with the defamatory cartoon. Prescott, brow furrowed and eyes bulging, studied it for a moment as he comprehended the grim reality of the situation.

"Preposterous!" he exclaimed. "I'm not providing aid to the enemy here! I only gave a poor man and his wife a chance at a new life. Besides, that was a couple of weeks ago. Why am I being attacked now, for Christ's sake?"

Lottie crumpled the paper in her hand as she hissed, "It doesn't matter who they were or how long ago they left! All that matters now is that we're finished. Who on earth is going to stay here after seeing THIS?" She furiously waved the paper around.

Before Prescott could respond, a sharp knock sounded at the door. As he moved to answer it, Lottie cut him off sharply. "I'll get that. It will be for me."

Prescott was puzzled. "What in tarnation is going on here?"

Lottie opened the door to two housemen. Pointing towards the trunks, she instructed, "Take these downstairs where Thomas is waiting with the car."

"Yes ma'am." After the housemen departed with her baggage, Lottie spun back around to her husband.

"I'm leaving on the next northbound train back home to Pittsburgh. And don't you dare follow me!"

"Pittsburgh? Now see here Lottie," began Prescott. "You're always making a big deal out of nothing. Who the hell's going to take this seriously? Our guests have been nothing but loyal to us for years – even though they always had the option of staying at larger, finer hotels like the Ponce or the Alcazar. They won't be swayed by a stupid cartoon in a small-time rag."

Lottie fiercely threw the newspaper at her husband and, with clamped teeth, hissed, "Loyal, eh? That's got Beau Jessup's fingerprints all over it. You and I both know he's bosom buddies with that crooked editor Lawrence Conrad. And as for the others, you can bet they'll be checking out in droves later on today!"

As she opened the door, Prescott desperately cried, "Lottie, please! I can't do all this without you! You're the reason I got into the damned hotel business in the first place. Please stay and together, we'll muddle through until the dust settles."

For a moment, Lottie hesitated as if considering the matter. However, turning back to her husband with teary eyes, she murmured, "Don't you understand, Johnathan? I can't. I honestly can't. You more than anyone else should know how much I've strived to become a respected woman in this town. And now, the thing I've always dreaded the most has come true. We're both pariahs. You might be strong enough to face it but, unfortunately, I am not. I'm sorry, Johnathan." With that, she was gone.

Prescott's reminiscence of that morning was interrupted by the ringing of the telephone. Picking up the earpiece, he grunted "Yes!"

The voice of Myrna, the hotel's main switchboard operator, replied, "Mr. Prescott? There's a call to you from Mr. Edward Hastings of the Southeastern Savings and Loan in Jacksonville. Shall I put it through?"

Prescott pinched the bridge of his nose. Blast! Hastings was his major financial backer. Why the hell was he calling at this hour? This did not bode well at all. He must gotten wind of the recent goings on and is going to want an explanation.

"Shall I put the call through, sir?" Myrna repeated.

The pains that had been plaguing him earlier in the day were now returning in full force. Prescott winced as a heavy, sharp pain cut through the center of his chest. His left arm felt tingly. The telephone earpiece fell from his hand as his breathing became labored. He loudly groaned as the world faded to black.

"Mr. Prescott? Are you still on the line, sir?"

Birdie and Mavis walked down the corridor towards the housekeeping office, their arms loaded with spare dustcovers. Each footstep sounded like a thunderclap against the eerily noiseless backdrop of the vacant hotel.

Until now, Birdie had never experienced complete quiet. There was always someone nearby talking, laughing, shouting, dogs barking, cats squalling, crickets chirping, bells ringing, streetcars honking, plates clinking – at anytime, anywhere, there was always a sound to remind her that life was continuing. But now, with Montclair was as quiet as a tomb, Birdie found it very disturbing.

Mavis must have been of a similar mindset because when it came time to cover up the furnishings, she insisted that she and Birdie do it together, for which Birdie was grateful. The thought of having to go into each room on her own would have been more than she could handle.

With the exception of two of the landscapers to keep the grounds outside maintained and a general handyman, all the other employees had been dismissed yesterday with their full pay for the past week. Most promised they would be back when the hotel re-opened. Now Birdie and Mavis had just completed a final walk-through, making sure that every piece of furniture had been covered. Rita and Eva had both made sure the kitchen and scullery were left clean and in order.

It wasn't until they had stored away the dustcovers and were locking up their own office that Birdie started to feel emotional. As they silently gathered their belongings from the mudroom, she asked, "When do you think we'll be back?"

Mavis sighed as she buttoned up her coat. "I wish I knew, Birdie. At our last meeting, Mr. Prescott had assured us that we'd be back within a few months. But now that he's in the hospital, I'm afraid it's anybody's guess when we'll re-open or if Mr. Prescott would even come back."

Although she didn't want to mention it aloud, Mavis supposed that it was only a matter of time before Johnny Prescott Jr. will have to return and take up the reigns of the Montclair. And what would happen to Birdie then?

1918

Chapter 45

Emilia Phillips' hair stuck to her neck as she tried to sit up in her bed. Her night dress clung to her frail, sweaty frame. She was about to call for her daughters Susie and Maisie but then remembered that they both had married and moved away. Maisie now travelled around the Panhandle with her new itinerant preacher husband while Susie and her family settled in Alabama. "Newt," she whispered, "I need my boy. Where'd he go? I need to find him." She tried once more to sit up but, with less strength than a newborn kitten, her head never left her pillow.

She started to feel ill two days ago just after Ralph left with a wagonload of his brew. She'd grown used to Ralph's erratic comings and goings over the years. There were times when months would pass without a word from him until Emilia would awaken to find him out plowing the field or tending to the horses. This time he'd received a very large order which he had to deliver to Savannah. When he departed, he mentioned the possibility of heading further north to Charleston to see some distant relatives and take in the sights before heading back south to St. Augustine, so Emilia had figured she'd be alone for several weeks if not a month. Ralph offered to wire for one of his brothers to come help her out during his absence, but Emilia was adamant that she knew how to take care of her own farm and livestock. So as a compromise, Ralph left word with his friend Marvin Tucker to check on his aunt every once in a while.

When the fever, nausea and body aches started to set in, Emilia took to her bed. That was when the visions started coming. First, she thought she heard Susie and Maisie fighting out back. "You gals shut yo' mouths and stop actin' like savages," Emilia croaked. She had to get up and start making dinner because Newt would be home from work soon. The poor boy was always working from sunrise to sunset. There was a knock at the door. *That must be Newt now,* thought Emilia.

"Mrs. Phillips. Are ya in?" Marvin Tucker knocked again, this time a bit harder which in turn pushed open the unlocked door. Marvin stuck his head inside and shouted, "Mrs. Phillips?" He heard a faint cough coming from the next room. Walking slowly and uncertainly over to the door, he softly rapped and said, "It's me, Marvin, Mrs. Philllips. I've just come to see if you're all right."

He heard the sound of wheezing and gingerly opened the door. There in the bed was Mrs. Phillips looking worse for wear.

"You ill, Mrs. Phillips? Lemme get ya some water." Marvin grabbed a tin cup off a nearby table and jogged outside to the well to pump some fresh water. He brought it back to Emilia's bedside and helped her sit up to take a few sips. Noticing how feverish and sweaty she was, Marvin went to the kitchen, pulled a clean rag from the shelf above the stove and returned to the bedroom. Dousing the rag in the cup of water, he wrung it out and placed it over Emilia's forehead to help bring the temperature down.

"Mrs. Phillips, my ma and some women are helpin' deliver a baby over at the Temple place. I'll send one of 'em over to watch ya while I go back into town to find Doc Perkins."

Marvin dashed outside, climbed onto his wagon and rode out to Burt Temple's farm at top speed. He could hear Annie Temple's screams as he approached. Jumping down from the wagon, he entered the house without knocking and saw two colored women washing dishes and cleaning up the small front room. "Where's my ma?" he asked.

"She's in there gettin' ready fo' the baby comin'," Ophelia replied.

At that moment, the bedroom door swung open and Mrs. Tucker came out with her hair falling out of her usually neat bun and her sleeves rolled up. "Has that water boiled yet, Hortensia?"

Hortensia, who was at the stove, turned and said, "Almost, Mrs. Tucker."

"Ma!" said Marvin. "I need ya to come with me to see Miss Emilia. She's might poorly and her place is in shambles."

Juliet Tucker was startled to see her son standing by the front door. "Oh, Marvin. I didn't see you over there. You nearly gave me a fright. What's wrong with Emilia Phillips?"

"I don't know," said Marvin. "Her nephew had asked me to check on her while he was gone and when I went over this mornin', I saw that she'd taken to her bed, lookin' pretty pale and sickly."

"Oh dear," said Juliet. "Well, I can't leave Annie right now as the baby will be here soon. I should be able to manage on my own so go ahead and take Hortensia and Ophelia with you back to Emilia's place. Then go see if Doc Perkins is free. He's been mighty busy this week. Seems like almost everyone in town is sick."

Marvin brought Hortensia and Ophelia over to the Phillips homestead and dropped them off on the front porch of the dilapidated house before heading out to town.

Ophelia knocked softly on the door and said, "Hello," before pushing it open. "Oh my, look at this house," she whispered. There was debris everywhere - rusty cans, dusty furniture, dirty clothes, dishes encrusted with food, and even two chickens strutting freely about the kitchen.

Assuming that the sick woman was in the bedroom, Hortensia headed over to the door. "What was her name again?" she asked.

"I heard Mrs. Tucker say her name is Emilia Phillips," replied Ophelia. "You go tend to her while I clean up this mess and get these chickens outta here. Lemme know if ya need help."

Hortensia nodded as she turned the knob on the door. Phillips? Why did that name sound familiar?

As she entered Emilia's room, Hortensia glanced at the gaunt, sickly woman in the bed. Her strawberry blond hair, faded with age, was wet and tangled around her neck. The rag that Marvin had placed on her forehead had not moved.

"Oh, you poor dear," said Hortensia as she tiptoed inside while Ophelia peeked into the doorway. "We're sorry you're feeling poorly, Mrs. Phillips. My friend and I are here to help you. We're with the 'Ladies Society of Good Neighbors' from the Community Church. My name is Hortensia, and this is my friend Ophelia."

Emilia tried to focus her eyes and when she saw Hortensia and Ophelia, a sense of panic struck her. Why are these two Negro women in my house, she wondered. Is this one going to kill me? And why is that other one millin' around in my kitchen? Is she stealin' from me?

Gathering up what was left of her strength, Emilia managed to lift her head off her pillow and throw off her blanket. She wasn't going down without a fight. She tried to shout, "Get the hell outta my house, ya nigras," but her words came out as incoherent babble.

Hortensia, misreading Emilia's body language, mistook her for being hot. "With your fever you must feel like you're boiling in this summer heat. Let me tie up all that pretty hair for you." Glancing around the room, Hortensia found a frayed scrap of ribbon on the night table by the bed. She gathered Emilia's hair off her neck and managed to braid it, tying the ends with the ribbon. "There, that should feel better now. Let me bring you some more water to help bring down your temperature."

As Hortensia left to get the water, Emilia started to calm down when she realized that the women were there to help her and not hurt her. She felt better with her hair tied up.

As Hortensia passed through the kitchen on her way back from the well, Ophelia remarked, "This house isn't fit fo' pigs to live in. I wonder how long that po' woman's been sick in 'er bed."

"I don't know," replied Hortensia. "I can't understand a thing she's saying. She just sounds like a baby babbling."

"Well, at least I managed to get them chickens outside where they belong. Mista Tucker can put 'em back in their hen house when he returns with the doc," said Ophelia as she wiped her brow. "I'll get this house cleaned up if it's the last thing I do!"

Hortensia smiled as she returned to the bedroom. Helping Emilia sit up, she carefully tipped the mug to the sick woman's lips and made sure she took a few sips before gingerly laying her back down on the pillow. She wet the rag that had previously been on Emilia's forehead and put it back on her burning brow.

"The doctor should be here in a little while," she said soothingly. "In the meantime, I'll keep you company."

Emilia looked up into Hortensia's eyes and saw nothing but sincere kindness as the colored woman continued her amiable chatter.

"Do you have any family?" Hortensia was asking. "I don't see any signs of children or a man around this house so I'm guessing you're either a spinster or maybe a widow."

A tear trickled down Emilia's cheek. How she missed Jeb, Newt and the girls. This house, which was once full of family, was now an empty tomb of heartache and bittersweet memories.

"Oh honey, don't cry," cooed Hortensia as she took a handkerchief from her pocket and gently dabbed Emilia's tears. "I'm a widow myself so I know the pain of loneliness all too well. I've got a daughter, but my Birdie is so busy these days that I feel like I live all by myself."

Birdie! I remember that name. Could she be talking about the same Birdie who was responsible for my Newt going away? The memories of her son, bloodied and bruised that last night she saw him, flooded back and Emilia started to weep. She tried to utter, "I lost my son because of your goddamned daughter. He was run out of town and disappeared God knows where and it's all her fault," but all Hortensia could hear were disjointed grunts and incomprehensible gibberish.

Emilia was now violently thrashing about the bed in frustration at not being heard and understood. Hortensia softly stroked Emilia's feverish forehead and prayed to God for healing in the name of Jesus.

The deathly ill woman's agitation suddenly caused a violent coughing fit. Hortensia again reached for her handkerchief and placed it over Emilia's mouth, rubbing her back until the spell subsided. As she wadded up the handkerchief, she noticed some spots of pinkish mucus. She made a mental note to advise the doctor of this as soon as he arrived.

Emilia Phillips was dead two days later. With no next of kin to claim her body, she was buried in a mass grave next to four others who also perished from this deadly form of flu which was claiming hundreds of thousands of lives across the country and the world. A small generic marker with her name etched on it was the only proof left of her existence.

When they finally learned of how serious an epidemic this strain of flu actually was, the women of the Ladies Society of Good Neighbors started to wear masks and gloves when visiting the homes of the sick. Unfortunately, it was too late for Hortensia, who had already fallen ill three days after Emilia Phillips had passed away. When Doctor Perkins came by the house to see Hortensia, he immediately ordered for her to be taken to the colored hospital where a quarantine wing had been set up for advanced cases such as Hortensia's. Birdie and Ophelia were unable to visit her due to the highly contagious nature of the illness. Two days later, Birdie received a visit from a grim-faced nurse who informed her that Hortensia had died the night before.

In deep shock, Birdie heard the words that the nurse was saying but nothing seemed to register. It was only last week that Birdie, who noticed how tired Hortensia was looking, had told her mother, "You need to take a break from all this nursin' you been doin' lately. You're wearin' yourself out and you haven't been eatin' like you should."

Hortensia, who had been folding laundry, replied, "The only reason I look tired is because that cat of yours had been wailing outside all night and keeping me up. And I've been eating just fine, thank you. In fact, I had a piece of cherry pie over at Ophelia's earlier this afternoon."

"Just be careful out there, ma," said Birdie. "I'm not comfortable with you bein' around all those sick people. Who knows what kind of germs you've picked up."

"You better be careful, Birdie," warned Hortensia as she finished folding the clothes and picked up her wash basket. As she walked by her daughter, she said, "You're starting to sound just like me!"

Both Birdie and her mother had laughed at Hortensia's comment. Looking back at it now, Birdie sighed heavily. "If only you'd heeded my words, ma," she said.

Birdie slowly unwrapped the parcel of personal effects which the nurse had left behind. Inside was Hortensia's dress, shoes and her Bible. The dress still had Hortensia's rosewater scent on it. The familiar smell pierced Birdie's heart and suddenly the tears started to flow. Her mother was gone. The last person she had left in the world had been taken from her. Now she was truly alone. Curling up in a fetal position on the settee while clutching her mother's dress, Birdie cried bitterly for the rest of the day.

Chapter 46

Hortensia's funeral took place the following Saturday. Because both Uncle Epifonio and Aunt Esmeralda had passed away several years ago, Aunt Josie was too frail to travel, and the cousins moved further south to Miami, Birdie merely wrote a letter informing them of her mother's death and didn't forward any funeral information as she knew it was too far for them to travel.

However, her friends from the Montclair showed up in force to support her - Lito, Felipe, Mavis and Rita. Despite the hotel's closure last year after the newspaper fiasco and Johnathan Prescott's subsequent heart attack, they had all managed to survive doing odd jobs until Prescott recovered and the hotel eventually reopened. Lottie, upon learning of Johnathan falling ill, had long since returned and was instrumental in helping the Montclair reinvent itself.

Birdie was truly touched by their presence. Even some of Hortensia's laundry clients including Della Compton, who was loudly sobbing and sniffling, were also in attendance.

But it was the arrival of Ella, Ronnie, their four children as well as Betty Simms which produced the most emotional reaction in Birdie as she jumped to her feet and ran over to them in tears.

Clutching Ella like a lifeline, Birdie wept piteously. "Oh Ella, I can't believe she's gone! My ma's gone, and I got no one else left."

"Birdie, you ain't alone. You'll always have me as long as I'm drawin' breath. We're sistas, remember?"

Birdie nodded and clutched Ella a little longer before wiping her eyes and greeting Ronnie and the rest of the family. Once they were seated, the service started with six young men from the church bringing in Hortensia's casket. The sight of the wooden box making its way down the aisle had Birdie erupt into tears again. A few women also started to sob when they heard Birdie break down.

Reverend Bailey began the eulogy which included an overview of Hortensia's life, her love of her husband Patrick Fairfax, her pride in her daughter Birdie, and the Christian charity she showed to countless others who were needy, troubled, sick or dying. Birdie inwardly burned. It was her Christian charity that ended up killing her. What kind of a God allowed a poor woman to literally work herself to death in his name? And if God was all about love, how come he saw fit to take away almost every single person Birdie had ever loved?

As Birdie sat in a silent fury, the church choir – fronted by soloist Ophelia Patterson – sang Hortensia's favorite hymn, "The Old Rugged Cross." Ophelia, who prayed fervently before the service that she'd get through this song without breaking down, never thought she'd be performing this for her best friend's funeral.

With tears streaming down her cheeks, she began in a loud and clear alto:

To the old rugged cross I will ever be true;
Its shame and reproach gladly bear;
Then He'll call me someday to my home far away,
Where His glory forever I'll share.

The rest of the choir picked up the refrain:

So I'll cherish the old rugged cross,
Till my trophies at last I lay down;
I will cling to the old rugged cross,
And exchange it someday for a crown.

Ella put her arm around Birdie, who was visibly moved by the performance. She'd heard her mother humming the hymn around the house ever since she was a child.

Ophelia packed plenty of emotion in the final verse, which she sang with fervor:

To the old rugged cross I will ever be true;
Its shame and reproach gladly bear;
Then He'll call me someday to my home far away,
Where His glory forever I'll share.

After the service, Birdie, Ella and the rest of the Simms family were the first to follow the casket and the pallbearers out of the church. As she made her way down the aisle, all the other mourners were blurred. However, there was one lone person sitting in the last pew by the door. Birdie didn't get a good look but was sure she'd seen the face before.

As she walked behind the hearse wagon with Ella, Ronnie, the Pattersons and the Simms, Birdie secretly dreaded the moment when the funeral service and the reception afterwards finished and she would be left all alone in the house. She'd never been this lonely in her life and wondered how she was going to cope.

The graveside service was even more somber than the one in church. When Hortensia's casket was lowered into the ground and each of the mourners threw handfuls of soil onto it, Birdie couldn't do it. Throwing the dirt onto the coffin meant admitting that Hortensia was being planted in the ground and never coming back. Birdie wasn't ready or able to do it at that moment, so she dropped her arm and opened her hand, letting the earth drop back onto the ground.

Ella and the others standing around her patted her arm and embraced her to show their support and understanding.

After the interment, the mourners left to go back to Birdie's house for the reception. Birdie wanted to stay by the graveside for another couple of minutes to say goodbye to her mother. The Simms and the Pattersons stood a respectable distance away. As they waited for Birdie, Ella turned and noticed another lone figure standing nearby.

"Oh my Lawd," whispered Ella as she nudged Ronnie. "Look who's standin' over there."

Ronnie craned his neck to see who Ella was looking at. Narrowing his eyes, he glanced at the familiar face and asked, "That ain't Tangie, is it? How long has it been since we seen her?"

"Sixteen years and not long enough!" Ella murmured fiercely. "What the hell is she doin' here? She better not have come to cause trouble 'cause I ain't above stickin' my foot in her ass if I need to."

"Ella!" admonished Ophelia. "Why are you cursin' on sacred ground? My best friend has just been buried! Don't you dare start actin' up today!"

"I'm sorry, ma," said Ella. "But there's an uninvited guest over there and I'm gonna go see what she wants."

"No," said Ronnie. Ella looked at him with a mixture of astonishment and annoyance as he continued. "You ain't gonna do nothin' of the kind. I don't think Tangie is here to cause any grief. This funeral was for Birdie's ma and if anyone's gonna talk to Tangie and ask why she's here, it's gotta be Birdie."

Ella huffed and said, "All right. Here comes Birdie now. We'll see what she has to say about it."

Walking over to join Birdie, Ella put a comforting arm around her and asked, "Have you said your goodbyes to yo' ma?"

Birdie nodded. "Yes, I have. I told her that even though we had a lot of arguments and fights, I always loved her. And I told her to say 'hi' to my pa when she sees him."

"Yo' ma knew ya loved her, Birdie. Even when ya'll weren't speaking to each other." Birdie pulled a handkerchief from her pocket and dabbed her eyes. "Uh, Birdie. There's somethin' you need to know."

Birdie turned to look at Ella questioningly. "Is somethin' wrong?"

"Well, I ain't sure. All I know is that Tangie Foster is standin' over there, under that elm tree," Ella covertly pointed her head in the appropriate direction.

"Tangie Foster?" repeated Birdie as she turned to get a look. "I thought I saw her back in the church as we were leavin'. What is she doin' here, I wonder. We haven't seen her since '02."

"That's what I wanna know but Ronnie won't let me deal with her. I'll walk over with ya and if ya feel comfortable, I'll leave ya'll alone," said Ella.

Birdie nodded her assent, so the two girls walked across the graveyard to where Tangie stood against the trunk of the giant elm which shaded the graves of the colored section of the cemetery. Seeing the girls approaching her, Tangie straightened her spine and gathered up her courage to face the women she had hated and wronged in the past.

When the three of them were face to face, Birdie broke the ice, "Hello, Tangie. It's been a long time."

"Yes, it has," replied Tangie. Turning to attention to Ella, she said, "Nice to see ya, Ella. Hope all is well."

"Yes, it is," said Ella coldly. "And I'm tellin' ya right now that if you're here to upset Birdie in any way, you'll have me to answer to."

"No, Ella. Now is not the time and place. Tangie is obviously here for a reason and I think we should let her tell us why," Birdie said.

"Thank you Birdie," said Tangie. "Actually, I'm here to talk to you and to pay my respects to Mrs. Fairfax."

"Ella, I'll be fine. Why don't you, Ronnie and the others go on to my house. When ya get there, please tell everyone that I'll be around shortly."

"All right," said Ella with narrowed, suspicious eyes. "But if she says or does one thing out of line, you just let me know."

"Go on, we'll be okay," urged Birdie. Ella turned and re-joined her family who, together, headed back to Lincolnville.

Tangie sighed and half-smiled. “I ‘spose some folks will never change their opinion o’ me.”

“Oh, don’t take Ella’s comments to heart. We’re all very emotional today,” explained Birdie.

Tangie nodded and replied, "I can understand that."

"So, what brings you out here?" asked Birdie. "You never liked me, and you had never met my ma. I can’t even begin to imagine why you’ve shown up."

"But that’s where you're wrong, Birdie," said Tangie. "I met your ma years ago and had known her for a long time."

If the horse in the nearby field had suddenly started speaking, Birdie could not have been more surprised than she was at that moment. Tangie and Ma knew one another?

"How in the world did you know my mother?" asked Birdie.

"When I was in jail, she and her ladies group would come and visit us gals and try to save our souls, but your ma did much more than quote scripture and pray fo' me. She would talk to me like a human bein'. Now I suspected she was yo' ma because o' the last name so I made it a point not to mention I had worked at the Montclair. All she knew was that I was a thief. One day she asked me why I stole things and I told her 'bout my daddy dyin' and how there wasn't enough money comin' into the house because most of my brothas and sistas were too young to work and those who did weren't earnin' much mo' that me. After that, yo’ ma always went by my house to check on my family and would always bring them somethin' to eat or lend a helpin' hand with the chores. One o' the other ladies got jobs fo' two o' my brothas at Dr. Clemmons' orange grove. Mc and my family got a lot to thank yo' ma fo' and when I heard she'd passed...." Tangie started to tear up, "I just had to come and pay my respects."

Birdie could have been knocked over with a feather after this latest revelation. Hortensia had never said a word about visiting a woman in jail or helping out her family, but that was Hortensia all over. She was never one to boast about her good works, unlike Della Compton who had just made a big display of her grief inside the church earlier.

Looking at the woman who used to hold an inexplicable hatred towards her years ago, Birdie felt nothing but pity now. Taking Tangie by the hand, she said, "Come on with me to ma's grave so you can say goodbye properly. Then I'm takin' you over to my house for somethin' to eat."

After the burial, the mourners gathered at Birdie's house where Ophelia took over the hosting duties. Arriving there first, she opened the lonely little house and sadly looked over at the table where she and Hortensia had talked, laughed and commiserated over many plates of pie. She searched the kitchen and found Hortensia's favorite apron neatly folded in a drawer. With tears brimming her eyes, Ophelia hugged the apron to her chest before tying it around her waist. Trying to keep herself occupied so she wouldn't fall victim to another spell of sobbing, she got to work setting out the various covered dishes which had been coming to the house for the past couple of days.

Soon the guests started to pour in, with Reverend Baily and his wife Henrietta among them. The reverend's wife sported a feathery concoction on her head that resembled a prize Leghorn. If Hortensia were here, we would definitely have had a good laugh over it later on, thought Ophelia. Feeling another wave of sadness starting to descend upon her, she quickly set about pouring cups of coffee.

"Miss Fairfax, we offer you our deepest condolences on the loss of your mother. Mrs. Fairfax was a kind and very hardworking woman. She helped make our house a warm and inviting home any time we entertained guests." Although Cyril Compton rarely spoke because his wife often did it for him, when he was able to utter a few words like now, they were always well chosen and sincere.

"Thank you, Mr. Compton," Birdie replied warmly. "My ma really enjoyed working for you and Mrs. Compton."

Della Compton, who was sitting on the settee by her husband and sampling a slice of ham and some collards, said, "Yes, our gatherings won't be the same without your mother's friendly face there to greet everyone." Picking her handkerchief out of her reticule, she wiped away a tear that was traveling towards her double chin. "Say, Birdie. I know that you already work at the Montclair, but will you also be taking over your mother's laundry business? She had a good number of customers."

Cyril Compton quickly interrupted. "I don't believe that now is the time to have that discussion. Certainly Miss Fairfax has a lot on her mind."

Birdie smiled at Della and replied, "To be honest, I haven't had the time to think about it, but I promise that I will let you know as soon as I come to a decision."

As she walked away, Birdie's mind started to race. Mrs. Compton brought up a very good question, even if it was at a most inappropriate time. What will become of Hortensia's thriving laundry and part-time cleaning business? She did indeed have a decent sized clientele list. And she often heard her mother complain that Mrs. Compton alone took up much of her time during the week with the laundry, the three-day-a-week housecleaning and monthly dinner parties.

The group from the Montclair, headed by Mavis, approached Birdie. "I'm afraid we need to get back. Please know that you're in our prayers, Birdie, and if we can do anything for you, just ask."

Birdie was touched by their support. "Thank ya'll for coming. It really means a lot to me that you were here today. I'll be back next week."

"Now Birdie," said Mavis, "You take all the time you need to grieve. Your job will be waiting for you. Don't feel you have to rush back."

"Truth be told, I'd rather stay busy. Sure, I'll take two or three days off to take care of my ma's affairs and things, but then I'll be itchin' to get back to work. I mean, what else am I gonna do? Hang around this empty house all day?"

"All right, if that's what you want," Mavis relented. "But if you change your mind, you know it'll be fine with us."

One by one, they gave Birdie hugs and personal words of sympathy.

Rita lovingly pushed a stray strand of hair off Birdie's forehead. "Don't forget that you're a part of your ma so she will always be right here." She pointed to Birdie's heart.

Birdie hugged the cook and replied, "Thanks for bein' here, Rita. I'm glad I still got you and Ophelia to turn to when I need a motherly shoulder to cry on."

"You better believe it!" said Rita, who squeezed Birdie's hand as she departed.

Birdie was moved to see that the gardeners took time out of their busy day to pay their respects, especially Lito who after all these years still had not gotten over Isaiah's death and had a hard time getting himself to go to funerals. "God bless you, Birdie. She's in good place now," said Felipe in his broken English.

Birdie detected a light scent of alcohol about Lito when he gave her a hug and simply said, "Be strong, Birdie." Birdie watched sadly as Felipe helped him descend the porch steps.

As Birdie went back inside, she was waylaid every two steps by a well-wisher giving her a hug and words of condolence. By the time she finally reached the kitchen, she felt like she was being smothered and desperately needed to be alone. Making sure that no one was nearby, she quietly opened the back door and crept outside. Sitting on the top step, she exhaled deeply and closed her eyes.

Suddenly she felt something rubbing against her legs. Looking down, she discovered that her cat Snowball had escaped from her bedroom and, like Birdie, sought relief from the crowded house. Birdie picked up the purring feline and clutched her to her bosom.

"Looks like it's just you and me now," Birdie said sadly. "Please don't leave me like everyone else has."

Just then Birdie heard the back door softly open and close. Turning around, she was surprised to find Tangie who she last saw chatting with Ella and Ronnie on the front porch. Birdie had been pleased to see that they were at least trying to be civil to each other, even if it was just for her sake today.

"I'm sorry to disturb ya," said Tangie tentatively.

For some odd reason, Birdie felt Tangie's quiet presence comforting and replied, "No, you ain't disturbin' me at all. Please, sit down."

Tangie perched on the step just above Birdie and reached down to stroke Snowball, who was still in Birdie's arms. "Ain't it funny how you can feel all alone even when you're among lotsa folks?"

Birdie stopped petting Snowball as she digested what Tangie just said. "Why yes. That's exactly how I feel right now!"

"I used to feel that way all the time at the Montclair," confessed Tangie. "It was like I was livin' in a dark, cruel world while the rest of ya'll – you, Ella, Ronnie, Eva, Newt – were in another, laughin' and havin' a good time."

Birdie, who had been listening with rapt attention, cried, "Oh Tangie! Life wasn't all roses for us, either. And besides, you could have joined us any time you wanted to! We were all willin' to be friendly."

With a faraway look in her eye, Tangie shook her head. "But I couldn't. Ya see, I was always plagued by two sins – pride and ..." Looking Birdie squarely in the eye, she finished, "Jealousy."

"Jealousy?" Birdie was bewildered.

"Yes, I was so jealous of you back then, Birdie. I always thought you got all the breaks while I was always knocked down."

"Oh Tangie, that's just not true!" exclaimed Birdie. "I've..."

Tangie held up a palm and interrupted. "I know now that I was wrong. You've had your own struggles to overcome, and I just wanna tell ya how sorry I am fo' all the grief I gave ya."

Birdie affectionately patted the other woman's arm. "No need for apologies."

"Oh yes, there is," Tangie insisted. "I treated ya badly and I wasn't gonna rest until I made amends which is why I'm here today."

The two women sat in companionable silence for a few moments, each digesting what the other had said.

Releasing Snowball, who made a quick retreat under the stairs, Birdie had an idea. "Say Tangie, are you lookin' for work?"

"Always," came the eager reply. "Do ya know 'bout somethin?"

"I just might," replied Birdie. "One of my ma's biggest clients happens to be inside my house right now. She's gonna need someone to do her laundry and clean her house three mornin's a week. Plus, she likes to throw dinner parties every month and will need someone to help serve. If you're interested, I'll put in a good word for ya. I gotta confess, though, that the husband works for the Montclair so they'll already know about your time in prison, but I think I can still talk them into it."

"Oh, Birdie. I'd be forever obliged if ya could do that," said Tangie. "But I'll understand if they say no."

Birdie rose and dusted off her skirt. "Stay right there and let me talk to them first. I'll be right back."

Birdie sought out the Comptons who were conversing with Mrs. Simms. After she brought them into her bedroom for privacy, she told them that she already had someone in mind to provide them with the same services that Hortensia had given them. And best of all, this person had previously worked in a hotel.

Della Compton was excited about the prospect until Birdie eventually revealed the applicant's identity.

Cyril Compton raised instant opposition. "No. That is totally unacceptable, and I am disappointed that you would even propose anything of the sort. I'll chalk it up to grief which has made you temporarily devoid of rational thinking"

Offended and feeling her temper rising, Birdie took a deep breath and calmly said, "With all due respect, Mr. Compton, I am quite rational right now. I am rational enough to know that my ma was the only laundress in town willing to go anywhere near your house. I am rational enough to know that Mrs. Compton would be delighted to let her friends, church group and pastor know that she has reached out and given a social outcast another chance at making an honest living. And I am rational enough to know that the woman waiting outside is perfectly qualified for this position and will obviously be damned good at it."

"Now see here, Miss. Fairfax...." began Cyril Compton but his wife cut him off.

"Um, Birdie," said Della. "Is Tangie still here and may I speak to her?"

"Certainly, Mrs. Compton," said Birdie. She had a feeling that Della was already relishing the chance of being able to boast yet again about how charitable she was, despite any initial misgivings she and her husband might have.

Ophelia was the last one to leave. She wanted to make sure that everything was back in its proper place and tidy. She didn't want Birdie to have to lift a finger for the rest of the day.

"I hope ya don't mind me wearin' yo' ma's apron," said Ophelia gently as she ran he fingers over the ruffled trim. "I just needed to feel close to her today."

Birdie looked lovingly at the plump, old woman who was as much a part of her life as her own mother was. Taking both of Ophelia's hands into her own, she said, "Not only do I not mind, Ophelia, but I want ya to keep it."

Overcome with grief as well as gratitude, Ophelia sobbed. "Oh Birdie. Thank you. I'll treasure this always."

"But, that's not all," added Birdie. "I want you to come by tomorrow and help me sort through ma's things. There are some more trinkets that I know she'd want ya to have."

Ophelia gave the younger woman a warm, tight hug and said, "Honey, if ya ever need anything under the sun, just come on down and see us. We're yo' family now."

Too choked up to speak, Birdie just nodded as Ophelia departed.

Now she had the house completely to herself. It was too early to go to bed, so she sat in the rocker of the front parlor. The only noise in the house was the steady ticking of the clock on the mantel. She wished that there was at least some cleaning to do but Ophelia had already taken care of everything before she left.

Snowball slinked back inside after finding the house finally devoid of strangers. She jumped up onto Birdie's lap where she curled up into a purring ball and fell asleep.

Laying her head onto the back of the rocker, Birdie closed her eyes and thought of all her loved ones who were now gone – her ma, her pa, Clara, Newt and Sugar. Imagining that they were all surrounding her and feeling their loving energy, she eventually drifted into a deep sleep.

PART III

1921

Chapter 47

Birdie carefully maneuvered the large sewing basket she carried through the narrowed hedge-lined brick walkway which led from Dubois Street up to the front porch of the Ravensworth house.

The large white two storied colonial style home was trimmed with black shutters on each of its many windows. Tall white columns made it look more like a small version of the White House instead of the home of Harold Ravensworth, the town's most prominent lawyer. Birdie straightened her spine and patted down her hair as she wrapped the ornate brass knocker firmly against the large oak door.

This alterations job was an important one. After Johnathan Prescott passed away last year, his son moved back to St. Augustine with his family to take over management of the Montclair and one of his first orders of business was to fire Birdie. Since then, she was solely surviving on the earnings from the laundry business inherited from her mother as well as occasional sewing jobs such as this.

Birdie had been surprised to learn that Mrs. Phoebe Ravensworth had been referred to her by none other than Lottie Prescott before she left St. Augustine to return to Pittsburgh where she now resided with her sister Lavinia, who was also recently widowed.

The Ravenworths' daughter Nora, who was about to be married, had custom ordered her wedding dress from London. However, when she tried it on, she was dismayed to discover that the bodice was too large, and the skirt was a bit too long. The measurements had obviously been miscalculated.

The door was answered by an older Negro maid who ushered Birdie into a spacious parlor. "Mrs. Ravenscroft will be with you directly," she said as she retreated.

Birdie looked around at her surroundings. The rich golds and greens of the upholstery, the beautiful Middle Eastern carpet, the highly polished mahogany table with the inlaid pearl peacock design, and the floor to ceiling bookshelves gave the room just the right amount of luxury without being too gaudy. A large picture window overlooked a well-manicured rose garden which was in full bloom and colorfully bursting with fuscias, reds, pinks and yellows. Birdie was immediately transported back over twenty years ago to the rose garden at the Montclair where she sat with Newt Phillips on New Year's Eve. Feeling wistful, Birdie turned away from the window just as Phoebe Ravensworth entered.

Mrs. Ravensworth was a tall, angular woman with short, bobbed platinum hair and bright pink gums which were very prominent when she smiled.

"Miss Fairfax! So nice of you to come on such short notice. My Nora was absolutely devastated when she tried on her wedding dress. Lottie Prescott told me that you can work miracles with a needle. I'm hoping that my Nora won't be a lost cause!"

"That was mighty nice of Mrs. Prescott to recommend me. I'll certainly do my best, ma'am." Birdie replied.

"Splendid! Let's go up to Nora's room where she'll try it on. That way you can better see what needs to be taken in. Follow me," instructed Mrs. Ravensworth.

The household was a hive of activity. There seemed to be people in every room that they passed on their way to the staircase. As they started their ascent to the second floor, a couple of rambunctious young children were sprinting downward and nearly missed running into Birdie.

"Teddy! Sarah!" admonished Mrs. Ravensworth. "You know we don't run in this house. Apologize to Miss Fairfax immediately for almost knocking her down."

The boy, who was about five and wearing a small white sailor suit, took one look at Birdie and shyly shifted his focus to his shoes. "Sorry," he mumbled. The little girl, who looked to be a couple years younger, just stuck her thumb in her mouth and twisted her body away from the women in defiance. The huge white bow on the back of her head sat atop a mass of long brown banana curls.

"All right, you both WALK down the stairs, go into the kitchen and tell Miss Emmie that I said you could each have a cookie."

Birdie couldn't help but smile as both children's eyes lit up at the prospect of the unexpected treat. As the women slowly continued their ascent, she asked, "Those your kinfolk, Mrs. Ravensworth?"

"Yes," replied Phoebe. "They're my sister's grandchildren. She and her husband came into town from Georgia yesterday with her daughter and son-in-law, the parents of Teddy and Sarah, who you just met. They're all here for the wedding."

When they finally reached the top of the stairs, Phoebe knocked on a door located at the end of the hallway before opening it. They entered the bedroom which was almost as large as Birdie's house.

A huge bed with an ornate brass headboard dominated one end of the room. On the opposite side was a burgundy settee and a couple of chairs. Here is where a small group of women congregated, their highly animated conversation punctuated by giggles.

In the middle of the group sat a lovely young woman with shiny chestnut brown hair. She was wearing a blue silk dressing gown embellished with an intricate floral design. When she greeted Phoebe as "Mama," Birdie correctly ascertained that she was the bride.

"Not to worry, my dear. I have brought the cavalry!" Mrs. Ravensworth cried with good humor. "This is Miss Fairfax who is one of the town's best seamstresses. She needs to look at the dress. Be a good girl and put it on for her."

"Ooh yes, Nora. I'd love to get a look at it," said one of the girls.

"Me, too!" said another.

Nora smiled and said, "Sure! I'll just be a minute. Rose, you come and help me."

As a red headed girl stood up and disappeared with Nora into the adjoining changing room, Phoebe introduced the other girls. There was a petite brunette named Evangeline, a blonde girl with a porcelain complexion named Caroline and a soft-spoken young woman named Lilly.

Birdie looked at Lilly, who seemed vaguely familiar to her. She was tall, slender and had curly sandy colored hair and hazel eyes. She looked to be a few years older than the rest of the girls.

Phoebe explained, "Lilly is the mother of those two little hooligans downstairs."

Birdie nodded. That must be why Lilly seemed familiar. Her children bore a slight resemblance to her.

Lilly looked a bit anxious and apologetic as she said, "Oh dear. They weren't running again, were they? I'm sorry Aunt Phoebe"

"No need to apologize to me, my dear. It was Miss Fairfax who they almost knocked over," replied Phoebe.

"Oh my. Again, I am indeed sorry, Miss Fairfax, " said Lilly. The gentle tone of her voice sparked another feeling of familiarity in Birdie.

"Please, ma'am," she responded, "There was no harm done and they were both so adorable that anyone would've forgiven 'em anyway."

Lilly smiled at Birdie in relief. There was something about this young woman that Birdie liked which was strange because she was usually uncertain if not downright suspicious of strangers, especially white ones.

At that moment, Nora emerged from her dressing room resplendent in a white satin ¾ length dress trimmed with Irish lace and crystal beadwork on the front of the bodice. There was a collection of appreciative gasps, oohs and aahs from the women.

"Oh Nora, you look so beautiful!" cried Caroline.

"Bertie won't be able to take his eyes off you," said Evangeline.

"Bertie is the groom," explained Phoebe. Then she asked the question which she knew was foremost in her daughter's mind. "So, Miss Fairfax, what do you make of the dress?"

Birdie stepped up to take a closer look at the bodice which indeed hung loosely on Nora's slender frame. "Pardon me, Miss," she said to Nora before grasping the extra material and tightening up the bodice. Luckily the beading was closer to the front and wouldn't be affected, which made her job easier. Birdie then knelt down and looked at the hemline. It was edged with the Irish lace, so she'll have to be careful, but it wasn't anything she couldn't handle.

"When is the wedding?" asked Birdie.

"The week after next," replied Phoebe, "Saturday the 21st."

Everyone in the room was silent and stopped breathing as they waited for Birdie's decision. She looked at Nora and smiled. "You'll have it back in plenty of time!"

The girls all cheered while Mrs. Ravensworth put her hands together in thankful prayer.

"What's your given name, Miss Fairfax?" asked Nora.

"Brigid, Miss," replied a puzzled Birdie.

"Well, Augustine is no longer the only saint this town has. I present to you St. Brigid!" the bride exclaimed.

"Aw, go on with ya, Miss'" Birdie said laughingly. "Now I'm gonna need ya to hold still while I do some pinnin'. I don't wanna stick ya." She looked for her sewing basket which was sitting on the floor next to Lilly's feet.

Lilly, who also noticed the basket, bent to pick it up. As she passed it over, Birdie saw the back of Lilly's right hand for the first time and her blood ran cold. Just above her wrist was the same caramel colored moon shaped birthmark she'd last seen twenty-three years ago.

No, thought Birdie, it couldn't be her. Clara? Her pulse quickened and she felt light headed as the color drained from her face. She grabbed onto the arm of the settee for support.

"Miss Fairfax, are you all right?" asked Mrs. Ravensworth. "You've gone pale. Nora, bring me a glass of water for Miss Fairfax." To Birdie, she softly ordered, "Sit down, my dear. Just breathe slowly and deeply." Rose picked up a nearby fan and waved it slowly at Birdie's face to give her some air.

Lilly patted Birdie's hand. As Birdie gazed into the younger woman's concerned face, she wondered if this could in fact be her Clara. Her brow and her mouth favored Johnny Prescott however the nose was definitely from Birdie's side of the family. Oh my God, thought Birdie, after twenty-six years I'm once again staring into the face of my own daughter!

Nora brought over the glass of water and Birdie took a couple of slow sips.

Realizing that she had created a scene, Birdie rallied herself and with a false carefree front, replied, "I'm so sorry for causin' such a stir. I hadn't eaten this mornin' and I tend to get light headed if I skip meals. I'm okay now. Let's get this dress pinned, shall we?" She stood up again and picked up the pin cushion from her sewing basket.

"Are you sure you're okay?" asked Lilly doubtfully. She saw how white the woman's face got when she glanced down at her hand. Lilly self-consciously put her hands back in her lap, her left one covering the right one. She had always been embarrassed over the strange discolored marking and usually kept her gloves on as often as she politely could.

Although it took every ounce of her strength to keep her hands from shaking, Birdie managed to finish pinning up Nora's bodice. As she outwardly made polite chit chat, the wheels of her mind were furiously spinning. Didn't Phoebe mention that Lilly and her family were from Georgia?

As she knelt on the floor to start pinning under the hem, Birdie waited for a break in the general chatter before casually asking, "Miss Lilly? I believe Mrs. Ravensworth mentioned that you and your family were from Georgia. Whereabouts?"

"Well, my husband and I live in Tebeauville. But my childhood home was in St. Mary's," replied Lilly.

Hearing Lilly confirm that she was from St. Mary's caused Birdie to unintentionally jab a pin into her thumb and draw blood. She was in so much shock that the pain didn't register at first. Luckily no one else noticed as she stealthily retrieved a handkerchief from her basket and wrapped it around her wounded finger as she continued with the skirt.

Phoebe Ravensworth chimed in, "Oh yes, Blanche and Arnold have a lovely estate just north of the city. It's surrounded by towering oaks and a large stable out back. Arnold used to raise horses for racing. And some lucky girl used to have ponies of her own when she was little! Lilly looked so darling with her long frizzy golden hair trailing behind her in the wind when she rode. She was always stubborn about wearing her riding hat. Weren't you Lilly?"

"Oh, Aunt Phoebe! You're embarrassing me!" Lilly cheerfully scolded. Turning to Birdie, Lilly asked, "How about you, Miss Fairfax? Have you any family in Georgia?"

Birdie swallowed hard as she answered, "Yes, but we've lost touch."

Her heart couldn't take any more. Birdie stood up and, looking at the bride, said, "Okay Miss Nora. You can take the dress off now but be careful not to take out any of my pins, and don't stick yourself! Perhaps Miss Rose can help you again."

Rose and Nora retreated to the dressing room as the other girls, including Lilly, stood up. Evangeline and Caroline excused themselves to go back to their room.

"Aunt Phoebe," began Lilly, "I need to check on the children before joining Michael and the others out back. It was nice to meet you, Miss Fairfax. And please make sure you get something to eat. We can't have you fainting in the street!"

"Not to worry," said Phoebe Ravensworth, "She's not leaving this house until she takes some of Emmie's fried grouper and biscuits with her."

"That's wonderful. Good day, Miss Fairfax," said Lilly. Birdie watched her leave and softly said, "Bye, Miss Lilly."

After a few minutes, Nora came back out in her dressing gown and carrying a large box which contained the gown.

"We made sure not to touch any of the pins when we packed it up," promised Rose.

"Thank you," said Birdie as she took the box.

As they headed downstairs, Birdie furiously tried to think of a way to get one final piece of information she needed. "Mrs. Ravensworth," she began, "Will the other girls be Nora's bridesmaids?"

"Yes," replied Phoebe, "Except for Lilly, of course. She's already married. Besides, she's a bit older than the others."

Birdie's stomach started to churn. "Oh, she can't be that much older, can she? They all looked to be in their late teens."

"Oh no," said Phoebe, "Lilly's 23. In fact, she just had a birthday a couple of weeks ago."

Birdie didn't hear any more. What she had suspected all along had just been confirmed. She felt like she was in a walking trance.

Phoebe went in to the kitchen and brought back a covered plate for Birdie, which she carefully packed in the top portion of her basket.

"Thank you, Mrs. Ravensworth" Birdie heard herself saying, "I should have this done by next weekend. Then we can do a final fittin' and see if any more alterations are needed."

"Wonderful! Thank you, Miss Fairfax. I'll see you then!" Phoebe waved her off before shutting the door.

As Birdie carried the bridal gown box and the sewing basket down the front path, the sound of children shouting and laughing made her glance across the Ravensworth's wide front lawn where Teddy and Sarah were chasing after a small Golden Retriever puppy. Every time they got close enough to catch it, the little dog would dodge them and dash in the opposite direction as he playfully yapped and wagged his tail.

Birdie's initial smile at this joyful scene quickly faded as another revelation struck her. These are her grandchildren! Oh Lord, I'm a grandmother, she thought. Those beautiful young 'uns who I met on the stairs are my own kin! The tears she had been holding back started to form and made everything before her blurry. When she got back home, Birdie dropped the basket and the box and finally released the torrent of emotions she had been holding back.

The clock on the mantel struck 1:00. Birdie sat up in her bed as she listened to a chorus of crickets, cicadas and frogs drift in through her open window.

She was too wound up to sleep knowing that her daughter was staying only a mile away! Ella had been right all those years ago. A rich white couple did indeed adopt her baby and gave her the fabulous life that Birdie never could. Lilly had become such a lovely and kind young woman. Birdie wondered what Lilly's husband Michael did for a living and what his last name was. What was their house in Tebeauville like? Did they have any maids?

And she had two grandchildren! She wanted so much to run over and hug them both as she left the Ravensworth house but no doubt that would have frightened them. There was so much about that them Birdie was dying to know. What kind of toys did they have? Did they enjoy having stories told to them? What were their favorite foods? Did Lilly have trouble getting them to sleep at night?

Now that Birdie knew her daughter was in town, she was anxious to see her again. Perhaps she'd casually walk by the Ravensworth house tomorrow on the chance that she might catch a glimpse of Lilly or the children outside. Or maybe Lilly and Michael might take them over to see the lighthouse or the alligator farm on Anastasia Island.

Hopefully they'll be at the house next Saturday when Birdie was due to return with Nora's dress. She'll have another chance to actually speak to her daughter and maybe find out more about her.

Birdie laid back and closed her eyes. For the first time in over twenty years she fell asleep with a smile on her face.

Nora was panic-stricken as her mother desperately tried to fasten up the back of her altered wedding dress. But try as they might, the top portion of the dress was now too snug.

"I don't understand, Miss Fairfax," admonished Phoebe Ravensworth, "It was my understanding that you were one of the best seamstresses in town. I thought you had pinned the dress properly the last time you were here. I know for a fact that my daughter has not put on any weight over the last five days because she's been too nervous to eat. So therefore, the fault must lie with you!"

"I am so sorry, Mrs. Ravensworth," said Birdie. "I'll make everything right. You'll see! Give me a couple of days and this will fit Nora perfectly."

"May I remind you, Miss Fairfax," cried Phoebe, "that the wedding is next Saturday. You are cutting things awfully close!"

"I promise I'll fix everything and get the dress back to you in two days," said Birdie reassuringly. "And the alterations will be free of charge, of course, for all the trouble."

"All right. Two days!" agreed Mrs. Ravensworth as she and Nora went back to the changing room. Birdie breathed a sigh of relief. As much as she hated to do it, she had intentionally made the dress too tight for the purpose of having another excuse to come back to the Ravensworth house to see

Lilly. Even though she sacrificed both her pay and her professional reputation, it was worth it.

Lilly, who had been quietly standing in the corner and watching the dress drama unfold, came forward and put a consoling hand on Birdie's shoulder. "I'm sorry my aunt was so sharp with you, Miss Fairfax. She's in a real tizzy over this wedding."

Birdie's heart leapt with joy at her daughter's sympathetic gesture. "I understand, Miss Lilly. I'd be in a right state myself if I had a daughter who was about to get married."

"Do you have any children, Miss Fairfax?" Lilly asked.

A flash of sadness crossed Birdie's face as she was forced to answer, "No, I never married or had any young 'uns."

"I'm sorry. I had just assumed that the 'Miss' title was one of endearment. I didn't mean to be impertinent." said Lilly.

"No need to apologize, Miss Lilly." Birdie replied. Then she thought of another question. "What was your own wedding like? I imagine it was a very grand affair!"

Lilly smiled dreamily as she recalled her own special day six years ago. "Michael and I got married in the Episcopal Church in St. Mary's and my parents threw us a large formal reception at the family estate afterwards with over two hundred and fifty guests. My father had us driven to the church and back in a beautiful coach drawn by two of his best stallions. Being a horseman at heart, he refused to have us riding to church in what he calls 'a smoking tin can on wheels.' It was a beautiful affair but to be honest, the only thing I cared about was spending the rest of my life with Michael and becoming Mrs. Hastings."

Her name's Lilly Hastings, Birdie noted. *I bet she was a lovely bride.*

Phoebe and Nora emerged with the dress and handed it back to Birdie in its box. "We'll see you in two days, Miss Fairfax," said Phoebe dismissively.

"Yes, ma'am," said Birdie. Sensing that this was her cue to go, she picked up the box and her sewing basked and left the room, heading towards the stairs. To her delight, Lilly followed her.

"I'll see you out, Miss Fairfax," she said.

As they headed down, Birdie asked, "Where are your children today, Miss Lilly?"

"Their father took them into town for ice cream and a walk along the sea wall to look at the boats." Lilly replied. "Teddy adores boats. He says he wants to be a sea captain when he grows up. And Sarah just loves ice cream, especially if it's strawberry."

Now that Birdie knew what her grandchildren liked, she felt even closer to them.

When they got to the door, Birdie fought the motherly impulse to give Lilly a hug. Instead she smiled and said, "See ya in a couple days, Miss Lilly."

"Good afternoon, Miss Fairfax." Lilly waved as she shut the door.

Birdie was looking forward to going home and writing down everything she learned today about Lilly and the children, so she'll always remember it. Birdie only had one more day to talk to Lilly and then she'd more than likely never see her again. The thought of having to part with her daughter a second time was too much to bear. Tears streamed down her face as she walked back towards town. As she strolled past the new public park, she looked across the street at the waterfront and there she saw Michael, Teddy and Sarah sitting on the sea wall, eating their ice creams and pointing at a passing fishing boat.

Birdie's breath caught in her throat as she sat and watched them. Michael was a handsome, tall young man with dark hair and a mustache. He seemed to be patiently answering every question the children were asking him. Every now and then he would lovingly pat Teddy on the back or put a protective arm around Sarah.

After Birdie secretly watched them unseen for about ten minutes, Michael took both children by the hand and started back in the direction of the Ravensworth home. Teddy would stoop down every so often, pick up a shell and throw it as far as he could. Meanwhile Sarah's curls bobbed as she skipped to keep up with her father's long strides.

As Birdie was smiling after the departing trio, a male voice came up behind her. "Hey sister. You need to move on."

Birdie turned around and saw a middle aged white man in a Panama hat approach her. "Pardon?" she asked.

"I said you better move on," repeated the man as he pointed to the "Whites Only" sign which Birdie had not seen on the back of the bench.

"But I AM white!" Birdie retorted.

"Yeah, and I'm Chinese," said the man sarcastically. "Now git goin' before I have the Sheriff down here."

Birdie sighed as she rose from the bench, realizing that the social chasm between her and her daughter's family, who she could still see walking down the road, was very wide indeed.

On Monday afternoon, Birdie had once again arrived at the Ravensworth house with the dress box under her arm. This time she made sure to alter the dress to the correct measurements.

As she arrived at Nora's room, she noticed that Lilly was not among the small group of girls gathered there. Birdie panicked. Where was she?

Despite her inner turmoil, Birdie maintained a calm and cheery exterior. "Okay, Miss Nora. Try this on. Third time's a charm!" Nora and Rose looked at her oddly as they went back to the dressing room.

Trying to look and sound casual, Birdie asked, "Where's your charmin' niece today, Mrs. Ravensworth?"

"Michael surprised her and the children with a boat trip down the Matanzas," answered Phoebe. "Little Teddy is such a boat enthusiast that his father couldn't resist. Sometimes I think that man spoils those children!"

Birdie's heart sank. Today was her last chance to see Lilly and now that last bit of hope she had was gone.

Nora emerged from the dressing room looking radiant and lovely in her wedding dress which fitted her like a glove. "Miss Fairfax, thank you! It looks exactly the way I wanted it to! Mother, look! Isn't it gorgeous?"

Phoebe beamed at her daughter. "Yes, dear. It is lovely." Turning to Birdie, she said, "I apologize for my outburst the other day, Miss Fairfax. My nerves have been rubbed raw with all these wedding preparations and I didn't mean to take it out on you. Please let me pay you for your services because in the end, you certainly did come through for us."

"Thank you, Mrs. Ravensworth," was all Birdie could say. She didn't care about anything else at that moment besides Lilly. All she wanted was to see her one last time. Please God, she silently prayed, I know you and I don't have the best of relationships but if you are all about love, then please let me see my girl one more time.

"You've been a very gracious hostess, but I bet you'll be glad to have your house back to yourselves again when this is all over, Mrs. Ravenscroft," Nora's friend Caroline was saying.

Phoebe laughed and replied, "Oh, I'm afraid that won't be until Tuesday when Blanche and Arnold leave."

"Is Lilly and her family leaving with them?" asked Evangeline.

"No, Lilly doesn't live near them, so she is taking a different train that leaves Monday morning," answered Phoebe.

Birdie's ears pricked up. She'd just been given one last chance to see her daughter! Maybe God does listen to me sometimes, she thought.

Chapter 48

Birdie squirmed as she tried to make herself comfortable on the hard, wooden bench in the colored section of the train station.

She'd been there since 6:00 that morning so that she wouldn't miss seeing Lilly board. According to the schedule, the next Georgia bound train was due in at 8:30 so she still had a half hour to go. There were more people at the station now than when Birdie had first arrived. At least she could more easily blend into the crowd. Every so often she would glance over at the white section of the station to see if her daughter had arrived. About twenty minutes later, her wish was finally granted.

Lilly, Michael, the children, and an older couple emerged from a car. The driver unloaded two trunks and a satchel which were handed over to a porter. Birdie guessed that the older couple were Blanche and Arnold, Lilly's parents. Blanche looked sad as she hugged both her grandchildren and knelt down to talk to them. Birdie's heart tugged at her as she imagined herself over there, kneeling down and hugging Teddy and Sarah. Reminding them to be good for their mother and father. Promising them that she'll be sending them toys for Christmas.

Arnold was shaking Michael's hand and saying something to him. Probably to take good care of his daughter and grandchildren. Then Blanche hugged Michael while Arnold spoke briefly to Lilly before giving her a kiss on the cheek.

Finally, Blanche and Lilly embraced and Blanche kissed Lilly on the cheek. Birdie clutched her throat as she choked back the tears. That should be her hugging Lilly and kissing her cheek! Lilly was hers! Birdie needed to be near her. She started to shoulder her way through the crowd to get closer to the whites only end of the platform but stopped short when she caught sight of Lilly's face lovingly gazing at Blanche. That was when Birdie realized how selfish her own desires were.

For the past couple of weeks, she had been so fixated on her unrealistic dream of getting to know her daughter and grandchildren that she'd forgotten the most important thing - Lilly and the children already had a mother and grandmother in Blanche who obviously loved and doted on them. Plus, as far as Lilly knew, she came from white parentage which socially put her in a different world from Birdie, who was stranded over on the colored side of the station, unable to get any closer to her own child.

Birdie had no claims to her daughter. She gave those up the day she handed her baby over to the sisters of St. Mary's. To reveal herself to Lilly now would only upset the young woman and possibly ruin her marriage. The best thing to do for Lilly's sake, she realized, was to stay quiet and invisible. The weight of her decision was so great that Birdie had to grab onto a nearby column for support.

When train whistle tooted that it was boarding time, Blanche and Arnold departed. Michael picked up Sarah and Lilly took Teddy by the hand as they boarded the train. Birdie tried to keep sharp eye on them to see where they were seated but lost track of them. Soon after all the white passengers boarded, the colored passengers were allowed on. Birdie was now the only one left on the colored side of the platform.

As the train started to pull out, Birdie panicked. She couldn't help herself. She walked along beside the cars, looking for Lilly. When she finally saw her seated by a window, she burst into tears.

"Lilly!!!!!" The noise of the engine and the whistle drowned out Birdie's screams. "Lilly!!!!"

She started to run as the train picked up speed. "Lilly!!!"

It was just then that Lilly happened to look out the window and was shocked to see Miss Fairfax running beside the train. What in the world? She was yelling something that Lilly couldn't understand.

Lilly stared back at Birdie's desperate tearstained face and suddenly her world shifted as everything slowly started to fall into place – the conversations she used to overhear as a child, why she didn't resemble Blanche or Arnold and why her mother didn't have any stories about her birth. She also remembered Miss Fairfax's reaction the first time she saw Lilly's hand. She looked at the birthmark and back at the sweet, gentle mulatto seamstress who was now a tiny distant figure still running after the train. There always seemed to be something vaguely familiar about Miss Fairfax which Lilly couldn't figure out, until now. Her entire body started to involuntarily tremble.

Michael, who was sitting across the aisle with Teddy, broke into Lilly's anguished thoughts, "Lilly? Are you okay my dear? What are you looking at?

Lilly gazed back towards the direction of the station which was now almost a mile away. Tears stung at her eyes.

"My mother," she whispered.

1922

Chapter 49

Birdie shivered as she clasped her shawl around her shoulders. It was only mid-November and the wintery temperatures were already making their way into Northern Florida. As she unpegged the dried sheets and pillowcases from the clothesline, Birdie breathed in the heady aroma of burning firewood from a nearby chimney mixed with the sweet scent of orange blossoms from the citrus grove a few blocks away.

The afternoon sun was hidden by steely grey clouds which cast a somber pall over everything below. Birdie felt comfortable in weather like this because it reflected her current mood. She wasn't sad, but she didn't really feel joyful, either. Her body automatically guided her through all her daily routines, but her heart had long since left her.

Even though it had been over a year since she had seen Lilly ride out of her life on that northbound train, the heartache was still fresh each time she thought of her.

The bell on the Episcopal Church tolled four o'clock. Birdie quickly pulled the last blanket off the line. Mrs. Rafferty will be stopping by at 4:30 to pick up her linens. She was a very talkative woman who enjoyed sharing the latest tidbits of gossip over a cup of tea. Although Birdie did not make it a habit to provide refreshments for her laundry customers, she made an exception with Vera Rafferty who was a lonely widow needing a listening ear.

A few stray drops of rain hit Birdie's face as she scooped up the laundry basket and the canvas bag of clothes pegs. There had been sporadic rain showers all week which made hanging laundry a challenge, so she wasn't about to let this last load get wet.

As Birdie came through the kitchen, she heard a knock on the front door. She shouted, "Come on in, Mrs. Rafferty! I'll be right there."

The door slowly opened as Birdie was setting down the basket. As she turned back around to greet the elderly woman, she stopped short.

Framed in the doorway was not Mrs. Rafferty but a tall, wiry middle-aged man with a red and white patchy beard. He wore a brown overcoat and a weather-beaten hat over fading red hair which hung just past his shoulders. Anyone else who saw him might have easily mistaken him for one of the ranch hands who often came into town on the weekends. Ordinarily Birdie would have been frightened at a such a rough looking character on her doorstep. But there was something oddly recognizable about him which riveted her right where she stood.

Then he spoke in a halting, raspy voice full of long suppressed emotions. "Birdie?"

Her blood momentarily ceased flowing. The world was silenced. Even the clock on the mantel stopped ticking.

"My God! Birdie!"

Birdie's shawl slipped off her shoulders as the bag dropped from her limp hand. Clothes pegs clattered all over the floor. No, she told herself, this can't be real. I must be dead. Her heart started to beat wildly as reality slowly crept in. Dare she hope?

The man took a tentative step inside. His hand shook as he removed his hat. Years of working in the sun had creased his freckled skin. But even the beard could not hide the familiar wide grin that was slowly spreading across his face.

"Newt?" whispered Birdie. Before she realized it, she was in Newt's arms and sobbing uncontrollably. His voice also cracked as he kissed the top of her head and repeatedly murmured, "My Birdie. My sweet, sweet Birdie."

They stood locked in their embrace for a long time, holding on for dear life, each repeating the other's name over and over again.

There was so much to say and so many questions to ask but the only one Birdie was able to articulate at the moment was, "Where've you been, Newt? Your ma tole me ya got married. It just about tore me apart."

His lips still in Birdie's hair, Newt replied, "No, I never got married. I been livin' down near the Everglades. Oh Birdie, I missed ya somethin' awful. You still look as beautiful as when I last saw ya!"

"Oh, my Lord, I can't believe it's you!" Birdie looked up at Newt and ran her hands over his hair and beard. "I never thought I'd lay eyes on you again."

"I'd lost all hope after Maw sent word that you got married and were expectin' a young 'un. I just reckoned ya got hitched to Arthur Dickson." replied Newt. He bitterly added, "Looks like she hoodwinked us both."

Not wanting to speak ill of the dead, Birdie merely said, "No, I wasn't married either."

"Believe me, I never wanted to go," said Newt. "There were times when I wished Stokes had just killed me instead."

"No, please don't say that!"

For the first time, Birdie had a good look at Newt's eyes and noticed the haunted look about them. Even though he seemed pleased to see her, Birdie could also sense that he was struggling with some unseen demons. Although this left Birdie with an unsettled feeling, the sheer joy of being with him again outweighed anything else at the moment.

Birdie took his hand in hers, noticing all the calluses and scars on it. He had obviously been doing a lot of hard labor over the years. She brought his hand to her lips and gently kissed each fingertip and his palm, just as he had done to her so long ago.

Touched by the gesture, Newt tenderly lifted up her chin to get a proper close up look and drink her in. Her eyes were still the beautiful golden amber color he remembered. Her hair, now sporting a few stray greys, was plaited into a loose braid which hung down her back. Otherwise, she looked exactly as she did that last magical night they were together. The image of her in the moonlight wearing the floral crown he'd made for her was one he kept engraved on his heart throughout the long lonely years that had stretched between them.

Slowly leaning forward, Newt gingerly kissed Birdie's lips which tasted like nectar to him. She kissed him tenderly at first but slowly their passions were ignited, and they started to hungrily gnaw at each other. Their bodies were so tightly pressed together that Birdie could feel every one of Newt's muscles seeking out her own. She leaned back slowly as he kissed her neck and throat.

"Oh Newt, I love you so much. Please promise me that I'm not dreamin' and that you're really here."

"I've never stopped lovin' ya, Birdie. I been thinkin' and dreamin' 'bout ya for years, hopin' to see ya again. Sometimes that was the only thing that kept me from losin' my mind." Newt said hoarsely.

Realizing that the front door was still ajar, Birdie reluctantly tore herself away from Newt and went over to close it.

"I got a woman coming over in a few minutes," Birdie explained. She hated the thought of someone disturbing them at this very moment, especially Vera Rafferty who will have Birdie's business spread all over town before the sun had set.

"Do ya need me to go?" asked Newt tentatively.

"No!" Birdie answered more vehemently than she had intended. Her body started shaking at the thought of being apart from Newt. She put her arms around him and buried her face in his wet coat as she started to weep. "Please don't leave me. Don't ever leave me again."

Newt just nodded and held her tight. "You never have to worry 'bout that, Birdie. I ain't ever goin' anywhere without ya."

Birdie wiped her eyes. "Wait right here," she said to Newt. Running into the kitchen, she found a piece of scrap paper and quickly scribbled a note to Vera. Her hands shook so much that she could barely write. "Had to dash out. Will settle up payment with you next week." She left the note atop the basket of wash on her front porch where she reckoned it would stay dry. At this point, Birdie no longer cared about anything other than her true love who had walked back into her life and was standing in her parlor.

The years of separation, heartache, longing, and despair were instantly gone. All that mattered was now.

As she came back inside, Birdie remembered her manners. "I'm sorry, Newt. You must think I'm a terrible clod! Let me help you outta those wet things."

As she helped Newt off with his coat, she noticed that his hands were still tremoring. Thinking that he as probably just cold, she said, "I'll light a fire, and then I'll fix ya somethin' to eat. You must be starvin'."

Firmly grasping Birdie by the shoulders, Newt stared in the amber eyes he'd dreamt about for over twenty years and huskily said, "The only thing I'm hungry for right now is you."

"Yes, I know. I...I need you, too," she whispered.

Birdie locked the front door and shyly led Newt by the hand to her bedroom.

Their sexual reunion was quick, urgent and, for Birdie, frightening. Newt didn't even wait for them to remove all their clothes before he entered her with a series of violently desperate thrusts accentuated with unintelligible utterances which Birdie couldn't decipher. After a few minutes he climaxed, bursting into loud primal howls and collapsing into a sobbing and tremoring heap on top of her.

Although she was initially paralyzed with fear, Birdie realized that Newt was a broken man and not the boy she remembered. There was something seriously wrong and he needed her.

She tenderly kissed Newt's forehead and held him tightly until he settled into a peaceful slumber. As she softly stroked his beard, her eye caught a glimpse of something colorful. Birdie lifted up the beard and discovered that Newt was wearing what appeared to be some sort of an Indian choker. The multicolored beads were arranged in a diamond geometric pattern. Birdie guessed that it was probably the work of Seminole Indians. As she slightly lifted the up necklace to get a better look, she noticed a ring of red rashy skin encircled Newt's neck.

As Newt stirred and rolled over onto his side, Birdie froze in horror. His back was a mass of extensive scarring which resembled zebra stripes. It looked as if he had been flayed by a whip. Birdie reached over and once again lifted up the beaded necklace to inspect the markings around Newt's neck. Rope burns?

Birdie raised a hand to her mouth to stifle an overwhelming urge to cry out. What the hell happened to him down there?

Chapter 50

As Newt awoke the next morning from the best sleep he'd had in years, he was momentarily disoriented. Where was he? A steady stream of rain trickled behind the white eyelet curtains in the nearby window. He was in a strange but very comfortable bed with down-filled pillows and a thick patchwork quilt which was keeping him warm.

Then his memory returned and his first thought was of Birdie. Where was she? A sudden flash of panic struck him. Did something happen to her? Did the Klan get her like they promised? He couldn't bear losing her again.

He sat straight up and shouted, "Birdie!"

Within seconds Birdie appeared in the doorway carrying a plate of fried eggs and biscuits in one hand and a cup of tea in the other. Her expression was a combination of love and concern upon seeing Newt's anxious face. His eyes were full of fear and he was shaking.

"I'm here, my darlin'," she cooed as she set the cup and plate down on the nightstand. She held his hand as she added, "I've been makin' your breakfast and tendin' to your clothes."

Newt closed his eyes and tried to get his breathing back to normal. "Sorry, Birdie. I...ah...just got a bit confused there fer a minute."

"That's all right," Birdie soothingly replied as she handed the cup of tea to Newt. "You just need a nice hot meal in ya to start the day off right."

But Newt's hands shook so intensely that the tea almost spilled out of the ceramic cup and onto the quilt. Seeing his dilemma, Birdie quickly took the cup from him.

Newt looked sheepish. "I guess I still ain't too steady just yet."

Birdie kissed him on the top of his head and responded, "Aw, never mind. I'm here. Take a sip of this first." She held the tea cup to his lips as he took a gulp. The hot liquid felt good going down, warming him up and slowly alleviating his shakes.

As she helped Newt with his breakfast, he couldn't help but gaze lovingly at her. After years of eating whatever he could shoot, forage or make grow on his small patch of land, the simple breakfast of eggs and day-old biscuits tasted like heaven.

"Birdie, that was the best food I've had in ages. Not only am I gonna be the happiest man in the world but it's lookin' like I'll be the fattest one too!"

Delighted to see Newt enjoying her food, Birdie stooped, wrapped her arms around his neck and kissed his cheek before taking the plate away.

Newt closed his eyes for a second as he quietly thanked the good Lord above for giving him back his Birdie. Only a couple of months ago he'd never had believed he'd be laying in her bed, eating her food and feeling her arms around him again.

Just then there was a "meow" and the sound of scratching at the window, which was still being pummeled with rain.

"Oh, my goodness. I plum forgot about Snowball!" cried Birdie as she went to open the window. A large, waterlogged white cat leaped in looking like she'd just escaped drowning. Noticing the stranger in Birdie's bed, she darted behind Birdie and purred as she rubbed against her leg.

"Why who's this?" asked Newt amusedly.

"Do you remember the little white kitten named Sugar that you gave me years ago when I was depressed about missing my baby's first birthday?" asked Birdie.

"Sugar! Yes, I sure do remember 'cause that was when you said you loved me. How could I forget?" said Newt.

"Well, believe it or not, Snowball here is Sugar's granddaughter," replied Birdie with a smile.

"Yer kiddin'!" cried Newt. "Hey there, Snowball." The cat cautiously jumped up on the bed and slowly approached Newt, who reached down and scratched the feline behind her ears.

She purred once again, this time rubbing up against Newt. “I think ya got some competition here fer my affections, Birdie.”

Birdie spiritedly retorted, "Don't get too full of yourself, Newt Phillips. That cat loves everybody!" They both chuckled before Newt suddenly stopped and looked thoughtful.

Birdie noticed his quick change of mood and asked, "Anythin' wrong, Newt?"

"No, nothin's wrong," he answered as he continued rubbing Snowball's back. "I just realized that it's been a mighty long time since I laughed at anythin’."

Once again, Birdie's heart broke for the physically and emotionally wounded man who laid in her bed. There were so many questions to ask. She desperately wanted to know what he'd been up to over the past twenty years - especially regarding those scars on his back. But given his apparently fragile state, she didn't want to push him right now. He'll tell me when he's ready, she thought.

Instead, she cheerfully said, "Well, there's plenty of time for laughin' later. Right now, I need you to get up outta that bed. I brought the washtub into the kitchen and poured ya a nice hot bath. Keep that quilt around ya til ya get in there because even though I got a fire goin', it's still a bit chilly."

Newt dutifully did as he was told and immersed himself into the warm water. For the next half hour, he succumbed to Birdie's ministrations as she methodically ran the soapy cloth over his body. Self-conscious about his back, Newt realized that he was going to have to explain the scars eventually. He'd just been waiting for the opportunity, along with his courage, to present themselves. In the meantime, he was grateful that Birdie asked no questions. He closed his eyes and relaxed as she silently massaged his scalp and washed his hair.

Afterwards Newt sat in the rocker by the fireplace once again wrapped in the quilt. His freshly laundered clothes were hung nearby to dry. Birdie had combed back his hair and tied it neatly behind his neck. She also trimmed his beard, making him look less like a hobo. He almost resembled the Newt she remembered, except for the haunted eyes which followed her every move as she went about her household chores.

Over the next couple of days, Newt slowly regained strength and his hands shook a little less violently. He was able to help Birdie with a few chores such as bringing in logs for the fire, fixing a couple of the steps just outside the kitchen door, and helping her carry some of the heavier baskets of laundry out back to be hung on the clothesline.

Feeling protective of Newt in his current condition, Birdie took care not to let anyone else into the house. Instead she conducted her laundry transactions on the front porch, which puzzled longtime customers such as Vera Rafferty who was used to being invited in for a friendly chat.

Otherwise, Birdie and Newt spent those first two days in blissfully quiet, companionable isolation. It was during this time that they started to share their stories.

Birdie told Newt about Lilly, her grandchildren, the deaths of Isaiah and Jonathan Prescott, Sr., and the closure of the Montclair.

Newt was pleased to hear that Birdie had the chance to finally meet her long-lost daughter and marveled at the notion of her being a grandmother. He lamented the loss of the two men who he had very much respected and scowled at the mention of Johnny Prescott, Jr.

"I ain't surprised the hotel fell apart in the hands of that scoundrel!"

As Birdie shared more of her life stories, Newt slowly began to open up. He told her about his initial flight into Palatka after the severe beating by Stokes and company. "After I got word from my maw that you got married and were expectin' a child, I gave up and went south. I ended up just outside o' Miami. Wasn't much down there but swamp, Injuns and some colored families. Folks kept pretty much to themselves which suited me fine. I lived rough in the woods fer a while, takin' odd jobs in town til I saved up enough to put down on a small patch of land that had nothin' but a rickety shanty on it. Lived there fer the next fifteen years. Tell ya the truth, I was drunk most o' that time so I don't remember much else." Newt laughed uneasily. "I guess you could say I'd become my paw."

Birdie listened attentively, hoping to learn the truth behind the scars. But Newt seemed to close down, unwillingly to speak any more about his past, so she said nothing until later that evening when Newt awoke from a restless sleep shouting and sweating profusely.

Birdie wrapped both arms tightly around him and soothingly whispered, "It's all right, honey. I'm here with ya. You're just havin' a bad dream, is all."

"But it wasn't just a dream. It was a memory," said Newt through chattering teeth.

Birdie quietly held into him until his shakes subsided. Then she softly pried, "Newt, what's wrong? I know there's somethin' not quite right about ya. I knew it as soon as I laid eyes on ya. Please tell me."

"It was an accident. I didn't know...." Newt began in a tremulous whisper.

"What didn't you know?" Birdie gently prompted.

"The boy and his lil sister. I didn't know til I heard the screamin'." Newt screwed his eyes shut as if in pain and tightly clamped his fists over his ears, "I still can hear 'em!"

"What happened, Newt?" asked Birdie.

"The flames were everywhere. The whole thing went up in seconds like a tinderbox." Wide eyed and grabbing Birdie's hand, Newt's tone became persuasive. "I went back for 'em, Birdie. Honest! I tried to save 'em but it was too late. The door latch was jammed and then the roof collapsed. I got thrown back. Last thing I remembered hearin' were the screams." Newt started weeping again. "I tried to save 'em. God knows I tried."

"My poor darlin'," murmured Birdie. "Of course you tried to save them. That's the kind of man you are - good-hearted and always there to help others. That's was one of the things that made me fall in love with ya."

Newt vehemently shook his head and cried, "No! I ain't no good-hearted man. Don't ya see, Birdie? It was me who started the goddamned fire! It was ME!" In a small voice, he sobbed, "It's all my fault they died."

Birdie was stunned beyond all belief. "But...but surely it was an accident."

Newt grabbed onto Birdie as if her last sentence was a life line. "Yes! It was an accident. I didn't mean to start that fire. I didn't know them kids were in there!"

Eventually, the story slowly unfolded. Two children of a Negro sharecropper who lived nearby discovered the old chicken coop on Newt's property and, unbeknownst to him, used the little ramshackle structure as a playhouse. One day Newt, hung over after polishing off a bottle of hooch the night before, was on his way to the stable. He took the lit cigar from his mouth and carelessly tossed it away, unaware that the butt had struck the old coop where he stored bottles and jugs of moonshine. The entire coop went up in flames. Newt was paralyzed with shock until he heard the cries of the children trapped inside. He sprang into action and tried in vain to rescue them.

The sheriff was called out to investigate and deemed the fire as an accident, acquitting Newt of any wrongdoing. This did not set too well with the children's male relatives, who upon discovering Newt laying drunk by the side of the road one afternoon, tied him to a tree and tore open his back with a bull whip. They intended to kill him, but their plans were foiled when a couple of ranchers happened to ride by and scared them off. Newt was horrified to learn the next day that the children's father, two uncles and a cousin were caught and hung by local Klansmen. Their house was burned to the ground and the remaining family members fled town.

"If it hadn't been fer me, them children and all their menfolk would still be alive," whispered Newt. "You have no idea how many times I wished the good Lord had took me instead. Even tried to hang myself once but the damned rope snapped on me. All I got fer my trouble were scars on my neck. And to this day, I ain't comfortable 'round young 'uns."

Birdie, who had been silently weeping, gently kissed him on the cheek. "But Newt, none of it was your fault. You didn't know the children were in there. And you risked your life tryin' to save 'em. As for their kin, it was the Klan who killed 'em, not you. And you killin' yourself wouldn't have brought any of 'em back."

"No, but it would've ended the pain I gotta live with fer the rest of my life," muttered Newt. "Ya know, I even tried to volunteer to go fight durin' the war a few years back. Figured if I couldn't kill myself, maybe the Germans would do it fer me. But they laughed me right outta the recruitin' office. Said I was unfit fer duty. Called me a crazy ole man and told me to crawl back into the whiskey bottle that I came out of."

The thought of Newt volunteering for military duty just so he could die made Birdie shudder and cling to him even tighter. "Well, I for one am glad they didn't take ya. Then ya might not be here with me now."

"As luck would have it, last month I went into town and guess who I ran into! Eddie Hartsfield! I couldn't believe my eyes. He said he was in Miami on business and was then goin' on some sorta deep sea fishin' trip afterwards."

"Yeah," said Birdie as she thought back to her last visit to the dry goods store. "I remember him talkin' about that."

"Anyways, he told me about my maw dyin'. He also mentioned that you were still livin' here by yerself and was never married. That was when I decided then and there to sell up and come back fer ya. Of course, I had to dry up first. I was in a very bad way then. Eddie stuck around for a couple weeks and helped me out."

Birdie knew she would be forever grateful to Eddie Hartsfield. Wrapping her hand around Newt's, she said softly, "Please let me help ya get better."

Never having told his story to anyone before, even Eddie, Newt was already feeling a tremendous amount of cathartic relief. For the first time in ages, his hands weren't trembling.

"Believe it or not, Birdie, ya already have."

It was just before midnight and a full moon cast a silver beam across the bed. Birdie's head lay on Newt's shoulder as she played with the thin patch of gingery hair on his chest. Newt was gently stroking the Birdie's lower spine which made her insides tingle.

Softly kissing her on the nose, Newt asked Birdie the question which had been burning inside him since the moment he first saw her. "Birdie, will ya marry me? We'll have to get out of the south and go up to Pennsylvania where it's legal. I reckon I got enough money left to get us up there. Whattaya say?"

Birdie sat up and looked at Newt in the moonlight. She could see that he was eagerly awaiting her reply. She lightly stroked his beard and leaned over to kiss him. She did not have to think twice. In all her years, she had never been more certain of anything else. "Newt Phillips, I'd waited for ya long enough. Of course, I'll marry ya!"

Newt breathed easily. "I ain't never been so happy!" He softly kissed Birdie on the lips. "I know you been livin' here in your maw and paw's house all yer life and I hope ya won't be too homesick livin' up there."

Birdie stoutly replied, "Wherever you are, that's where my home is from now on."

Too overcome to speak, Newt rolled onto Birdie and kissed her deeply, his tongue intertwining with hers as his hands softly stroked her breasts. In response. Birdie parted her thighs and gently guided him inside her. There were no other sounds to be heard except for the crickets chirping outside and the rhythmic creaking of the bed as Birdie met each of Newt's urgent thrusts with one of her own. Newt waited for Birdie's back to arch before he released himself inside her and slowly pulled away, laying her back down and kissing her forehead.

Silently vowing never to let her go, he wrapped Birdie up in his arms where they both finally fell into a deep sleep just before dawn.

Chapter 51

Birdie visited Hortensia's and Patrick's graves to say goodbye and leave small bouquets of wildflowers by their tombstones. Newt refused to visit the plot where his mother was laid to rest so instead Birdie took him by the hand as they walked towards the opposite side of the cemetery.

They carefully searched each headstone until they found the one they were looking for. They both felt their eyes well up as Birdie placed a single white rose on Isaiah Jackson's grave.

"You were right, Isaiah," she murmured. "Newt came back for me after all."

Birdie looked around the house one last time. Each room and every corner was a treasure trove of bittersweet memories. Earlier in the week she met with Nelson Walker, one of the real estate brokers in town, and put her house on the market. She was selling it fully furnished. The only things she was taking with her were her clothes, Hortensia's bible and the small wooden bird that Isaiah had carved for her when she first started at the Montclair.

Snowball was given to Lilah who had been staying with Ophelia that week. The seven-year-old girl was overjoyed at the prospect of owning a cat and solemnly promised to take good care of her.

Birdie had given the Pattersons authorization to act on her behalf regarding the sale of the house and left a key with Ophelia so she could keep an eye on the place. Saying goodbye to her earlier that morning had been very emotional for them both.

"Leavin' ya is one of the hardest things I'll ever do," Birdie had said. "You were like a sister to my ma and another ma to me. Thank you for all you've done for us over the years. I love ya so much."

Ophelia burst into tears as the women embraced. To her, Birdie will always be the fair skinned, curly headed tot who used to love her peach cobbler. "I love ya too, chile. Please write me as soon as ya'll get settled."

"I will," promised Birdie.

Turning to Newt, Ophelia said, "Please take good care of my baby."

"You bet I will!" was his heartfelt reply.

Turning to Birdie, Newt playfully commanded her to close her eyes as he winked at Ophelia, who smiled knowingly.

Birdie's brow furrowed as she closed her eyes and let Newt guide her onto the front porch.

"Okay, you can look now."

Birdie opened her eyes and, seeing Ella and Ronnie standing in front of their new Model T, exclaimed, "Oh my Lord! I was prayin' I'd get to see ya'll before we left!" She made her way down the steps while Ella, whose face was tearstained, ran through the front gate and gave Birdie a bear hug.

"When Ronnie tole me that he saw Newt at the barber shop yesterday and that ya'll were gettin' married, I couldn't stop screamin'! I'm so happy for ya both!"

"It's true," said Ronnie good naturedly. "It took me the rest of the day to get her to hush and settle down. I didn't want all our guests thinkin' I was killin' her."

Birdie beamed at Newt, "This is the best surprise you could have given me!"

"Pure luck, actually," said Newt. "Wasn't it, Ronnie?"

"Yeah," agreed Ronnie. "I walked into the shop yesterday to get my monthly trim from Calvin and I was surprised to see he had a white man in his chair who looked like some kinda dangerous drifter. But even with that long hair and beard, I knew who it was and said 'Only one person in this world got hair that red! Welcome back, Newt!' And sure enough, it was him. That was when he told me that ya'll were leavin' to go up north and get hitched. I decided then and there that the wife and I would be here this mornin'."

Birdie knew how busy Ronnie and Ella were with the inn, which was always fully occupied. "That's mighty kind of ya'll to take the time to drive all the way out here to say goodbye. I hope you haven't gone to too much trouble."

"Oh, it's all right. We got our oldest boy Lawrence and his wife overseein' things until we get back," said Ella. "Besides, we didn't just come out here to say goodbye."

"That's right," Ronnie continued. "It would be our pleasure to drive ya'll down to the train station and see ya off."

"Oh! How nice! Thank you!" cried Birdie. "So this is why you wanted me to wear my Sunday dress and good shoes today. You knew we wouldn't be walkin' to the station!"

Newt shot her a mischievous grin. "Nothin' but the best for my gal."

Ronnie took the satchel and placed it in the car. Then opening the door, he held out his hand to Birdie and haughtily said, "Madam?" as he helped her into the back seat. He gave Newt, who climbed in next to Birdie, an over-exaggerated bow. "Sir!"

Remembering that day Newt drove them all to the beach in his wagon, Ella started to sing:

When you hear dem a bells go ding, ling ling,
All join 'round and sweetly you must sing
And when the verse am through, in the chorus all join in,
There'll be a hot time in the old town tonight.

The others joined in and sang the rest of the way to the train station. Birdie was thankful for the musical interlude which helped distract her from the inevitable sadness of parting.

Once they arrived at the depot, Ronnie went with Newt to the ticket window while Ella and Birdie waited on the "colored" section of the platform.

Ella clasped Birdie's hand and said, "Ya must've dropped dead in yo' tracks when ya first saw Newt!"

"I sure did," agreed Birdie. "Ya know, Ella. Even though it's been two weeks, I still can't believe he's here. I still keep waitin' to wake up and find out that this is all just a dream."

"Miss Birdie," began Ella. "I'm here to tell ya that ya ain't dreamin'. You been apart far too long. You're allowed to be happy now!"

Smiling gratefully, Birdie replied, "You're right, Ella, but it feels kinda strange bein' happy. I reckon we both just gotta get used to it. Especially Newt. He had it rough these past twenty years." Even though Newt's physical and emotional state had vastly improved over the past week, he was still prone to periodic tremors and night terrors.

"I'm sure he did, but don't forget that the past couple o' decades haven't been all roses for you either," Ella pointed out. "It's high time that ya both get the happy life ya'll deserve and don't let anyone tear ya apart again."

"No chance of that as long as either of us are livin' and breathin'!" said Birdie spiritedly.

Ella had a thoughtful look in her eyes as she cocked her head sideways. Birdie smiled quizzically and asked, "Why are ya lookin' at me like that?"

"I was just thinkin' how different ya are now from that sad and scared lil gal I went to school with."

"You were my best friend and champion back then. Always ready to fight my battles for me," Birdie said wistfully.

"But all these years of dealin' with trials and tribulations have made ya stronger. Plus, ya got Newt to love and protect ya now. You don't need me anymore."

A stray tear streamed down Birdie's cheek as she patted Ella's arm. "That's not true. I'll always need ya. You're my sister, remember? I'll write ya every month and will come back to visit. And, of course, we want you and Ronnie to come up and see us in Pennsylvania."

"I'd like that!" Ella was crying now. "Oh, I'm gonna miss ya so much, Birdie. Even though we didn't get to see each other that often lately, at least I always knew that you were still just over the bridge. Now you'll be way up north!" Both women were hugging as Newt and Ronnie returned from the ticket window.

"Train's boardin', Birdie," Newt said gently.

"Bye, Ella," Birdie managed to say as she embraced her one last time.

Ronnie and Newt shook hands. "Bye Ronnie, and thanks again fer comin' out this mornin'. If yer ever up our way, ya got a place to stay!"

"We'll definitely be takin' ya'll up on that! Safe travels, my friend."

As Birdie bade Ronnie farewell, Ella repeated her mother's earlier plea to Newt. "Please take care o' my sister."

"You'll never have to worry about that because I ain't ever gonna leave her side," Newt replied.

As he took Birdie's arm and her satchel, he headed for the front cars where the white passengers sat. Birdie looked back uncertainly at Ella. They were both puzzled as they assumed that Newt would be travelling in the colored car with Birdie.

"What's he doin'?" Ella hissed to her husband.

Ronnie shrugged and responded, "He got tickets for the white car. So what? Birdie's got that white blood in 'er and should be able to pass, especially now since she's with Newt."

Having seen Birdie involved in too many racial confrontations during their childhood, Ella was fearful for her friend. She held her breath as the couple approached the conductor, who resembled a fat, red walrus with thinning blond hair.

As Newt held out the tickets, the sweaty man took a cold look at Birdie, who instinctively glanced down at her feet. "Say bub. You can come aboard but the gal will need to ride in the colored car. Whites only up here."

Glaring at the conductor, Newt's jaw tightened as he growled, "But she IS white."

Staring hard back at Newt, the man retorted, "She may be light skinned, but she ain't foolin' nobody. She's obviously a mulatto and needs to ride in the back car!"

Getting up into the conductor's face, Newt shouted, "She also happens to be white and has every right to ride up here!"

Ella and Ronnie, who were still standing on the colored side of the platform, witnessed the heated exchange. Ella's temper started to flare. "Dammit, I knew this would happen! Poor Birdie's lookin' scared. I gotta get to her."

Ronnie firmly clasped Ella's arm. "Hang on there, woman. Newt's handlin' this."

Ella looked on helplessly as Newt and the conductor carried on their argument as Birdie continued looking down at her tightly clasped, gloved hands.

"Look, she either rides in the colored car or neither one of ya'll gets on this train!"

"All right then," Newt shot back. "I'll ride with her in the colored car!"

"You can't do that!" the conductor cried. "We got segregation laws here. Ever heard of Jim Crow?"

"Jim Crow my ass!" Newt yelled. By now, curious faces were peeking out of both the white and colored cars. "Why the hell can't I ride in the colored car? I done paid more fer a white car ticket so what does it matter?"

"Look, if ya'll don't get outta here right now, I'm callin' the law on ya!" the conductor threatened.

"Go right ahead. You'll only delay yer train from departin' on time and I'm sure all them white folks at yer next stop'll be mighty sore."

The conductor muttered an obscenity under his breath as he checked his pocket watch. "Get in the colored car, then. But once ya get to where you're goin', I don't ever wanna see either of ya on this train again!"

Newt grabbed Birdie by the hand and, noticing that she was still looking downward, gently lifted up her chin. "Hold yer head high, Mrs. Phillips."

Ella breathed more easily as she saw them boarding the colored car. She knew that Birdie was now in good hands.

Ronnie cheered loudly and shouted, "That a boy, Newt! You told 'im!"

Newt waved back at them as he and Birdie boarded the rear passenger car. The conductor scowled at Ronnie and yelled, "That's enough outta you, boy. Move on!"

Several of the colored passengers who had witnessed the confrontation smiled at Newt. An older man moved up a row so that the couple could sit together.

Newt gave Birdie a wink as he slid in the seat next to her. Even though she was still shaken, and her legs felt like jelly, Birdie's heart was swelling with pride. The old Newt was definitely back.

Christmas Eve 1923

The sun was low on the horizon and twilight was about to set in. Birdie reached up into the evergreen, cut one more branch and placed it in the basket on her arm. She had enough greenery now to twist into a wreath for the front door.

Birdie headed back to the little two-story house that was nestled in the woods on their small patch of land. Shortly after they'd arrived in Pennsylvania and got married last year, they bought a second-hand car and put a sizeable deposit on their home with the funds that Newt had left from the sale of his Miami property as well as the proceeds from the eventual sale of Birdie's house on Citrus Avenue.

They had settled in a sparsely populated area between York and Lancaster, not too far from the Sussquehana River. Their nearest neighbors were German speaking Pennsylvania Dutch, hardworking plain folks who dressed in old fashioned clothing. Best of all, they kept to themselves for which Birdie and Newt were grateful.

Newt had found work as a gardener at an estate house just outside York. Although there was not much work for him during the winter months, he used that time to tend to his own land and do odd jobs in town.

Even before she reached the door, Birdie could smell the goose that was roasting in the oven. She also heard Newt's soft drawl coming from inside.

"When what to my wondering eyes should appear..."

Birdie stepped inside and was immediately grateful for the warmth of the fire which gave the room a soft, golden glow. Beribboned boughs of holly adorned the mantel and in the far corner of the parlor stood a small fir tree festooned with strings of popcorn and pretty glass ornaments which Birdie bought from a shop in town. Underneath the tree were several colorfully wrapped presents.

Newt sat in the rocker by the hearth. He had a burgundy leather-bound book open on one knee and five-month-old Patrick Isaiah Phillips on the other. The baby gurgled as he reached out for the book.

Newt looked up and grinned at Birdie before he continued reading. "But a min....mini..... Hey Birdie, what's this next word?"

Birdie walked over and glanced at the word Newt was pointing at. "Miniature." Having left school when he was eleven, Newt occasionally had trouble deciphering long or unfamiliar words. But he was determined that he was going to read to little Patrick every night.

"But a miniature sleigh and eight tiny reindeer..."

As she smiled adoringly at Newt and their son, Birdie realized that it was almost a year ago when she discovered she was pregnant. At the time, she was 42 years old and reckoned that she was going through the change of life which she often heard the older women whispering about. So Bird was flabbergasted when she discovered that she was actually with child.

Having given up on the notion of being a father many years ago, Newt had wept with joy when Birdie told him the good news. From the first moment he held his son in his arms, his discomfort around children finally vanished. His tremors were all but gone and he rarely had the nightmares any more.

As soon as Ella learned that Birdie was pregnant, she had insisted that she be there for the birth. So once Birdie reached the end of her eighth month, Ella came up on the train from St. Augustine by herself. Ronnie had to stay behind as the inn was fully booked with guests in town for the Independence Day celebrations.

For Birdie, having Ella there was a godsend. She not only needed help with the household chores, but despite having had a baby before, Birdie was frightened at the prospect of having to endure childbirth at her age. As always, Ella was a tower of strength when the time came. She held Birdie's hand, wiped the sweat off her brow, assisted the midwife and periodically went to check on Newt, who had been pacing the parlor in nervous anticipation.

"A bundle of toys he had flung on his back, and he looked like a peddler just opening his pack..." Patrick cheerfully babbled incoherently as he reached up and patted his father on the cheek.

Birdie started twisting together the greens and formed a large ring. Using some twine, she attached the oversized plaid bow she had made for it. Hmm, not bad, she thought.

As she carried it over to the door, she passed by the small mirror that hung near the front door. Birdie habitually peered into it before going outside and tonight was no exception. As she gazed at her reflection, she realized that for the first time in her life she liked the woman who was looking back at her.

After hanging the wreath on the front door, Birdie took a second to admire it before going back inside and enjoying the rest of the evening with those she loved most.

"But I heard him exclaim, ere he drove out of sight, HAPPY CHRISTMAS TO ALL, AND TO ALL A GOOD-NIGHT!"

AUTHOR LINDA M. WHITE was born in Ft. Dix, New Jersey but has lived in Central Florida for most of her life. A retired graphic designer, she enjoys yoga, cooking, crafts, volunteering and exploring Florida's historic sites and nature trails. She lives in Davenport, Florida with her husband Stuart and son Hayden.

"Yella Gal: Queen of the Montclair" is Linda's very first novel which is set in her favorite Florida city of St. Augustine and explores the complex subject of racial identity.

Printed in Poland
by Amazon Fulfillment
Poland Sp. z o.o., Wrocław